Sister Secrets

by Breggie James

Library of Congress Catalog Number: 97-94202

ISBN: 0-9659042-0-2

BeeJay Publishing
P.O. Box 1373
Alpharetta, GA 30009

This book is a work of fiction. Names, characters, places and incidents are either the product of the author's imagination or are used fictiously. Any resemblance of actual events or locales or persons, living or dead, is coincidental.

Acknowledgements

Many thanks to my family and close friends who supported this project.
To my sister Shirley, thanks for staying up all night to read it.
To my niece Monique, your undying support to see it
from beginning to end will never be forgotten.
To Alecia Carelock and Debra Lake, thanks for taking the time and
energy to make Sister Secrets a reality.
To Allyn Leftridge, your prayers helped me
through the tough times.

To the one who wanted to read more:
Had it not been for you, there would be no Sister Secrets.
I owe all gratitude to you, Nishani Frazier.

Dedication

In remembrance of those who have passed on:
Steven Micko, Nicole Jones, Pauline Frazier and
Arvell Joyner

Prologue
March 1964

"**B**arbara, recording secretary is just another step to the presidency. The sorority hasn't changed. It's the same politics. You just don't have us around for support. Remember, you must be patient," said the soft voice.

The other voice continued to complain but stopped suddenly, "Are you sure this is what you want to do?"

"Lies have consumed our lives for years. It's time for all of us to heal," she said. She paused before continuing. "Barbara, I need money. I can't seem to catch up with what I'm making on this teacher's salary."

"I got another job from a very rich white lady. I know I will make a profit this time. Remember, you get twenty-five percent of what I make. We are going to be business
women," Barbara said. There was silence.

"Catherine, I'm sorry. I thought Ed's business would have picked up by now. Most of his patients are poor. As soon as I get the money, I'll pay you back," Barbara said.

"I understand." More silence.

"How is my goddaughter?" Barbara asked.

Catherine watched the child mimic her older sister, trying to do everything and constantly following her around. Her baby wasn't retarded, she reminded herself. She was just quiet and a little clumsy. The angels must be guarding her. They always protected the very innocent.

"She's fine! She's much better than the last time you saw her. It takes awhile for premature babies to develop completely," Catherine said.

"I know she's beautiful. JoAnn and Susan send their love and I hear that Marilyn is pregnant again."

There was silence again. "Is she still the sorority's chaplain?"

"Yes. Have you heard from Debra?"

Catherine chuckled and then laughed. "Debra and I had a nice long talk recently. She wants us to become active with the chapter in St. Louis."

"Just like old times. You two should have never been enemies. You worked well together."

"Debra can do this one solo. I have no desire to impress people anymore. I have to think about my daughters. It's time to leave the past behind."

"Are you two friends again?"

More laughter rang from her voice, almost uncontrollably. "Debra is friends with no one, but our talk was needed. We are on the same side now. Besides, we both came out losers. I'll tell you about it later."

A man entered the room reeking of alcohol and frowning. An older woman followed. She was frowning too.

"Let's go, Catherine. The rain is getting worse. There's a traffic jam near the airport," the man said irritably, slurring his words. The older woman stared at her daughter with an opened mouth. The glow that the old folks talked about was surrounding her daughter.

"I have to go now. I'll talk to you when I come back. You won't believe what I have to tell you," Catherine said and hung up the phone. She put a sweater on the small child. The larger child started to whine, "Mommy, I want to go too."

"No sweetie, you have to stay here with your grandmother. I will bring you back some ice cream. Okay?" Catherine leaned forward and gently kissed the pouting child on the forehead. Then she looked at her mother who was shaking her head sadly. Catherine ignored the old woman's silent suggestion and left with the child in her arms.

The rain was coming down harder. Carleton tried to concentrate on the road. The alcohol blurred his vision and Stevie Wonder's "Fingertips" blasted the air waves, occupying his attention. He heard her say, "Hurry. His flight will be leaving in thirty minutes."

He tried driving faster and safely. In his rearview mirror, he saw the child sitting patiently, smiling and clapping. She did not say nor do much. She just smiled a lot. Everyone thought she was retarded but her mother knew differently.

Carleton looked at Catherine out of the corner of his eye. For the first time in years, she was optimistic. He only hoped her little plan would work. His gut feelings told him it was hopeless. She had suffered quietly for so long, losing a part of her that he admired, her endurance.

Carleton's attention came back to the road. The rain was gone. Flames engulfed the road. Was it just his imagination? He rubbed his eyes with the hand that was on the steering wheel. The figure in the road looked real. Its eyes were on fire and it reached into the car. Carleton tried avoiding the figure, but the car swerved sharply off the road. It skidded sideways into a tree. The glass from Catherine's door splattered. The side of the car crashed in, crushing her. She screamed.

Carleton didn't know what to do because the rain came again. It drenched her, washing the blood down her face onto the rose-colored dress. She asked about the child. He looked at the back seat. The little girl was thrown to the floor. He reached over the car seat to pick her up. She was limp.

Catherine gasped. Blood was coming from her mouth. She felt herself drifting away. The pain left when she saw the figure put his hands to his face, protecting himself from the light. He went away.

The pain was back. It was unbearable, causing Catherine to lose consciousness. She looked at the child in her brother's arms. The little girl slowly opened her eyes and looked at her mother. She was beaming. Catherine stared knowingly at the beam around the child. "Promise me you will take care of her. Don't let anything...happen...to...her," she said and closed her eyes. The child did too.

It had been two years since the accident. Death slowly haunted Miss Mattie but she could not bring herself to tell the truth. Her mother always said, "The truth will set you free. Lies keep bad spirits unrested." She believed in spirits. She felt them all of the time. But since the day Joe died, she felt haunted.

Miss Mattie stirred up a bowl of icing and spread it on the cake. It would be the last birthday she would celebrate with her remaining grandchild. Six candles were on the cake. Before they were lit, a knock sounded on the door. She paused, taking her time to look out the window. She sighed and opened the door. She stared directly into the face of the bold, young woman.

"I have to work tonight. I was hoping you could watch her for me."

Miss Mattie looked tenderly at the beautiful child who was a physical replica of her mother. Miss Mattie didn't mind babysitting, even if the young woman thought she did. It felt good having children around the house again. She knew her other grandbaby would come home again. It just wasn't time.

"Come in baby. You can celebrate Angel's birthday."

Before the young woman turned to leave, she gave the child a kiss on the cheek, trying to erase the guilty feeling. It would be days before she would come to get the little girl. The young woman could not stand to look the older woman in the face. Miss Mattie often told her they were just alike, survivors.

"Thank you," the young woman said with her head half turned. She left. The little visitor rushed inside and immediately began playing with her friend. They hardly ever talked. Occasionally, they giggled aloud. Miss Mattie smiled at the two girls, as she lit the candles.

"Look! Angel look like one of the candles," the little visitor shouted, pointing to her friend. The woman smiled but it faded. It was the same glow. This time, it pulsated. The child did not belong to her or anybody else.

Someone knocked on the door again. Miss Mattie walked slowly to the door, not looking out of the window as usual. The door creaked open. He stood straight, not wanting to look at her. He was clean, very neat. He looked in control of himself. She invited him in but he declined. She went to get the child who was sitting at the table smiling. She picked up the suitcase and walked the child by the hand to the door.

"I'd agree, she needs to be with you but she still needs a mother. You can't hide the truth forever. She will find out. I'd hope you're ready when she does," Miss Mattie said and gave him the suitcase. The child peeked through the doorway and waved good-bye to her friend. She left smiling.

"Miss Mattie, where Angel going?"

The woman said nothing.

"Why do she sparkle like that?"
"Because she's an angel."
"Ain't that her name?"
"Yes, but she's an angel too."
"What's uh angel?"
"They are spirits that God sends to help us."
"What are spirits?"
"They are what you think and what you feel."
The child looked perplexed. "Is Angel coming back?"
"Yes, but she has work to do. Let's eat some cake."

Chapter 1
October 1988

Jennifer looked at her alarm clock. It was 1:00 a.m. Four hours to go before she had to get up to prepare for the trip to Chicago. This was the second time she would drive five hours alone. She had been restless for the last three nights, contemplating the trip. The forecast of thunderstorms in St. Louis and Chicago made the thought of driving alone increasingly uncomfortable. She continued to wrestle with the idea of calling instead of visiting, but there was no way of getting around what she must do in person. The investment of a five-hour drive to Chicago, she thought, would end all the hurt she was feeling.

She remembered the caustic statements he made to her, belittling her potential. He told her that she did not have what it takes to be successful. His words dripped with sarcasm and ice. She tried convincing herself that he was wrong. The first time she talked to him, she did not say much, so how could he pass judgment? He was not a compassionate man, and seeing him again was not inviting.

At 3:00 a.m., she got up and went to the living room. She stared at the boxes that shared the story she lived for the last month. The apartment would be vacated in thirty days, and a new life would begin in Atlanta, Georgia. If only she could talk to Kyle, it would ease the anxiety and fears. She had not heard from him in two weeks, which was unusual. They usually talked once a week long distance. Since their trip to Chicago, the last telephone encounter was so abrupt that it bordered on rudeness. She could not believe how he talked to her. Her eyes filled with tears as she thought about the conversation. Never in ten years of friendship had he ever treated her so badly.

Kyle's friend in Chicago was suppose to help her find a job, or so she thought. The man seemed to despise her. He knew nothing about her, only information Kyle shared with him. What did he tell him?

Kyle met her in Chicago on the Fourth of July weekend to meet his friend William Smith. William was an older gentleman. His presence was intimidating. He was well over six feet and moved gracefully. He was fairly attractive and spoke three other languages fluently. His wife, Jean, on the other hand, was an average looking woman. There was nothing physically striking about her. She spoke very well and appeared quite intelligent. The two were mismatched physically, but intellectually they were quite stunning.

During the Fourth of July weekend, William invited Jennifer to come back and visit with them to work on her resume and interviewing techniques. What should have been a mentoring period turned out to be sessions of gratuitous remarks, leading to insults. At first, Jennifer was impressed with William. His professional track record was impeccable. He took a declining division of a large manufacturer and made it a money-making venture. Of course he had to make drastic cuts in expenses that included large layoffs, but he did the job. Kyle practically worshiped William. Many statements and clichés made by William were also said by Kyle.

At 4:00 a.m., Jennifer heard the rain. She decided to start an hour early. As she showered, the memories of William filled her with anxiety again. He gave her a mock interview. Instead of going through the entire process, he interrupted and criticized her unjustly. She thought his comments were spurious. The sound of the rain increased the anxiety.

As the water from the shower touched her dark, brown body, it felt like needles. She hurried out of the shower and dressed slowly, debating whether to wear her long, thick hair up or down. She picked out a navy blue suit which was perfect for a professional look and for the weather, which was cool this time of year in St. Louis and Chicago. Jennifer removed the rollers from her hair and quickly inserted hair pins to keep the curls from falling. She took one last look in the mirror and decided to put on lipstick once she arrived in Chicago. Who was she trying to impress while being cooped up in a 1985 Corolla for five hours?

She picked up her briefcase and keys. She took five seconds debating whether to call her father and tell him that she would be out of town for one day. With the thunderstorms in the forecast, she knew he would speak against such a trip and she did not need anything that could change her mind.

Jennifer cursed silently about the umbrella left in the car. She searched her kitchen for a plastic grocery bag to put on her head. She went to the utility closet where she kept them. They were not there. She knew she had plenty because cashiers never ask if you wanted plastic or paper anymore; they always gave plastic.

Jennifer breathed heavily as she raced to her bedroom. She sat her briefcase down and paced the bedroom floor. This was a sign for her to stay home. She believed in signs.

Just last month she was en route to the Amoco gas station on Kingshighway. Two blocks before she arrived, she realized she had no money and went home. Later that evening, her friend Lisa called and told her about the woman who was abducted at gunpoint at the same Amoco gas station. It happened about fifteen minutes after she turned around to go home. Now that was a sign, and signs were real. This was a sign for her to stay home and call William from St. Louis.

Jennifer stopped pacing and her breathing became normal again. She sat on the bed and sighed. She would call William and tell him that she could not make it. She wondered how to begin the conversation. She smiled, remembering the discussion she had with William about keeping your word. She found the discussion humorous. He thought he had enlightened her on a subject that ruled as principle in her rearing. The idea of not keeping your word was just ridiculous.

It was important to her that people did what they said they would do. She thought about Kyle, how he would go to great lengths to keep his word. But that was in college. In the past year, he hardly called when he said he would. He would forget or say he was busy. Sometimes, he wouldn't say anything.

Kyle Thomas was six feet tall and barely tipped the scale at one hundred and forty-five pounds. He weighed less in college. He was caramel brown with big, brown, inquisitive eyes and full lips hiding short, even, white teeth. No one noticed but Jennifer. She looked beyond the very thick wire frames and saw adorable eyes. She looked beyond an average mouth and saw sexy lips. She looked beyond what others deemed as "goofy" and saw a bashful, intelligent, attractive man.

Kyle was different from the other guys in college. People thought because he grew up around white people he was different, but Jennifer thought he was just different. She remembered how Lisa almost died laughing the night when she shared her feelings about Kyle. Lisa kept asking, "Kyle who? Kyle Thomas? You must be kidding."

Jennifer and Lisa had been friends since their freshman year in college. Lisa was light brown, short, and slim. She had an oval face with almond-shaped eyes. Her lips were on the thin side. They exaggerated the beauty mark on top. She was street smart and could read people better than a polygraph. She was smart enough to graduate summa cum laude with a double major in economics and finance. She was a junior economist at the Federal Reserve Bank of St. Louis.

Lisa once told Jennifer that Kyle sought approval. She did not use those words, but that is what she meant. She said something like "primping in other folks mirrors." She got the expression from their friend, Rochelle, who was also smart, but people didn't know it.

Jennifer stretched out on the bed and stared at the ceiling. She was so tired of thinking about Chicago. She decided to take off her suit and call William. She would use the thunderstorm forecast as an excuse for staying. She got up, took off her suit jacket, and opened the closet door. She reached for a hanger and stared at the floor. She was paralyzed for a moment. How could she forget that she was using the plastic grocery bags to wrap her shoes for storage? Now, she had to go.

There was the umbrella, which Lisa gave her for a birthday present, lying on the floor. How could she forget that gift? Lisa bought it from SAKS Fifth Avenue. Jennifer had not seen one like it. The sign was clear for her to leave immediately. She put back on her jacket and grabbed the umbrella and briefcase. She left quickly.

"Rain will continue throughout the day. Thunderstorms in Illinois are moving west and are expected to reach St. Louis by noon. High today sixty-three degrees."

Damn weatherman! Today he will probably be right! She was traveling north on Interstate 55, which stretched to Chicago. One highway, one visit, one day, no problem. Wrong. The rain was coming down harder. She cursed the windshield wipers for not moving the water fast enough from the window. As long as she maintained 50 mph, she could make it to Chicago by 10:30 a.m. It would take an additional thirty minutes to meet William. She told him she would arrive in Chicago by nine-thirty and meet him at ten o'clock. She could see the look on his face when she arrived an hour late.

The rain became worse. Jennifer could barely see the road. She thought about pulling over to sit for awhile but abandoned the idea because of time. She slowed down to 40 mph and put in a cassette tape of her favorite songs. She thought about Kyle. He had to know it was difficult for her to be out of work. She thought about the job she left. Working sixty hours a week without a vacation in a year had made her ill. The doctor told her to rest for at least three days, but taking time off was not acceptable for an assistant controller.

She had relapsed with the flu twice in February and had only taken one day off each time. Her supervisor called her at home asking silly questions which he could have solved. It was later rumored that she had taken the time to participate in black history events around the city.

She was promised another employee, but it never came. She could not continue the pace, so she quit. On the day she resigned, the supervisor had the audacity to tell her that she didn't work hard enough. How dare the bastard! She was good because her reviews showed excellent in all areas and an eight percent raise, the highest allowed. If she wasn't good, she would not have been given additional responsibilities; she would have been terminated instead. The other assistant controller they hired after her did get the additional staff but quit within five months.

She became angrier thinking about her old job and no job. William commented that she was foolish to quit and her actions were unprofessional. He was probably right, she thought, but it felt good to be alive and not a half-dead professional employee. He also said her chances of finding another job were slim. She never worked for a big name company nor did she graduate from a top ten university. She would have to start at the bottom and work her way up to the top again because she just didn't have it. Hopeless, that is how he made her feel. Tears filled her eyes.

Suddenly, a car in front of her lost control and, within seconds, she was off the road. She wasn't hurt nor was the car damaged. She was upset. What point was she proving by going to see William in person? She really did not know what to say to him. She told him she had an interview in Chicago and she wanted to stop by to say "hello."

The driver in the spun-out car came to see if she was alright. She quickly pulled herself together and took off. She took the next exit to get gas and to call William. His voice mail picked up and she left a message. She felt relieved.

She was five miles away from International Foods, and still clueless as to what to say. She went to the receptionist desk and asked for William Smith. She sat patiently. Within five minutes, he appeared. "Hello Jennifer."

She stood up and extended her hand. "Hello William. Thanks for seeing me."

"So you have an interview?"

"Uh, yes. I tried calling Jean, but they said she was interviewing someone."

"Let's go to the cafeteria. Are you hungry?"

"No, I'm okay. So how do you like your new RV?"

"It's okay," William smiled and sat at one of the empty tables. Jennifer sat down across from him. She made eye contact and then looked away. The cafeteria was empty. Her finger tips tingled.

Finally Jennifer spoke, "My last visit was a disaster. I know you were trying to help, but I wasn't ready. I just don't want any bad feelings."

"There are no bad feelings," William said, feeling guilty. He had difficulty facing her as well. It was his fault that things happened the way they did. He continued to look at her, wondering why she had appeared again.

"I don't want this to reflect on Kyle because I know your friendship is important to him. I don't want anything to stand in the way."

William looked at her and nodded slowly. "Where is your interview?"

"Downtown. I better get moving. I'll assume we'll both keep our word that my trip today and before has never happened."

William nodded again. He walked her to the door and extended his hand. "Give them hell, slugger."

Jennifer noticed William's behavior was more accepting. She could not figure out why but she smiled and said, "Sure." She shook his hand and walked away.

"Jennifer," he called out. She turned around. "Let me know how it turns out," William said seriously.

Jennifer stared at him oddly and said softly, "Okay." As she walked to her car, the sun was shining. It was exceptionally bright. It brought a smile to her face.

It had been two weeks since her trip to Chicago and she still had not heard from Kyle. She started the chore of packing. She pondered over what purpose did the trip serve. She drove five hours to tell William there were no hard feelings and primarily apologized for ever meeting him. She knew she had a problem with confrontations.

Her father had an enormous impact on her development. He made it clear in her early years that there would be no lying, no smoking, no drugs, no sex, no anything he opposed. He never gave a reason but maintained a "do as you are told" approach to raising her. It often hindered her from initiating many things.

After college, she took charge of her life. When the first disagreement surfaced between him and her, she was out of control. She accused him of not allowing her the freedom to experience life. She also questioned his responses to her inquiries about her mother's death. She was never satisfied with the "hemorrhaging story."

A great amount of internalized anger exploded when he disapproved of her staying out late with Kyle. Although they did nothing wrong, her father insinuated the intentions were disgraceful. The argument escalated into him slapping her. Jennifer gathered the courage to move out. She continued to talk to him and her stepmother, but the fight changed the course of their relationship.

The telephone rang. She had to move two boxes before reaching it. The anticipation of the caller made her skin tingled. "Hello," she said in a rush.

"Hello stranger. Why haven't you called?"

"I didn't feel like it. What's up?"

"Nothing. You've got two weeks before you head out. Need some help packing or is this a solo venture like the trip to Chicago?"

"Oh Lisa, stop it!"

"What's the matter, Jen?"

"Did you call me Jen?"

"I said, What's the matter, Jen?"

"Stop calling me Jen."

"I know you're under a lot of pressure but damn! Has Kyle called?"

"No."

"Are you closing the chapter on this story?"

"Everything is fine. We're just friends."

"Why don't you call him?"

"I'm not calling him and what's up with this Jen crap? You've never called me, Jen. You've never liked Kyle calling me that either. "

Lisa paused for a moment. "I have nothing to do. I can bug you on the phone or in person," Lisa said.

"Come over and help me," Jennifer said and hung up in a huff. The guilty feeling of snapping at Lisa nagged her. Lisa was a real friend. Even if Jennifer got mad for no reason, Lisa understood. Kyle was the only person that called her Jen. Why did Lisa say that? Jennifer knew it was a sign and maybe a good one.

Jennifer was marking boxes when a knock sounded at the door. She wasn't expecting anyone but Lisa. They had just hung up. Jennifer walked softly to the little peep hole. She was stunned. She almost tore the handle off the door trying to open it fast. It finally opened and she screamed. The two women in the doorway were smiling brightly.

"Are you going to invite us in?" one asked.

"Come in and have a seat on the floor," Jennifer said laughing. "What are you two doing in St. Louis?"

"Looks like you're moving. Where are you going?"

"Atlanta," Jennifer said, focusing her attention on one of the women.

"What did papa Peterson say about you moving?"

"Our relationship is a little different now. I'm twenty-eight years old so what can he say? You haven't answered my question. What are you doing in St. Louis?"

"I found my grandmother. She's alive!"

"Oh Angel, that's great! How did you find her? You have been looking for a long time."

Jennifer looked embarrassed as her other guest stood smiling. "I'm sorry Gina, I got caught up in the excitement of seeing Angel. How are you? I haven't seen you since Linda's wedding."

"I'm married and have a twenty-month-old son."

Jennifer and Angel said in unison, "Ooooo."

"I'm a market analyst with International Foods."

"Ooooo," they said once again.

"You two need to stop. So Jennifer, how have you been since school?" Gina asked.

Jennifer became embarrassed. She wanted to jump in a deep hole and hide. She was very happy to see Angel because they were very close in college. She knew Gina, but not that well. Gina had always been focused on goal-setting and the thought of telling her she had quit her job without having another one filled her with shame. How could she say the word *failure*? Now the words of William Smith came back to haunt her.

Jennifer smiled and looked at Gina. "I am not married."

Angel and Gina said in unison, "Ooooo."

"I don't have any children."

The two women repeated, "Ooooo."

"And I don't have a job."

The two women looked surprised. "You are not working?" Gina asked, almost gasping.

"I quit my last job. I was the assistant controller for a non-profit organization. I couldn't handle the pressure so I quit."

"Without having another job?" Gina asked, shaking her head.

"That's correct," Jennifer responded with as much pride as possible. There was silence for awhile. The two women saw that Jennifer was embarrassed.

"I know a few people in Atlanta," Gina said and pulled out an electronic telephone book. She began searching for names. Jennifer couldn't take it any longer. She turned her back   and cried softly.

"Sweetie, is everything okay?" Angel asked. No response. Angel walked over to Jennifer. "Everything is going to be fine," Angel said.

Gina walked over to the others and they all embraced.

"How can we help you?" Gina asked. Jennifer could not talk. The tears choked every word in her throat.

"I told you I will always be here for you. Can I help?" Angel asked.

Jennifer just shook her head. The person she had always admired had to see her spirit broken. It seemed as if she could never get to the same level. Had she not opened the door, she wouldn't have been reminded of the pain that she had to accept. She was searching for a way out.

"I'm sorry for getting teary-eyed. Is anyone hungry? I can fix some hors d'oeuvres."

The two women declined. Jennifer thought they were feeling sorry for her. She looked around the apartment and decided to continue packing as if they were not present. She went busily around the two women wrapping items and placing them neatly in boxes. The two women looked at each other before Angel spoke. "We can leave if you feel uncomfortable with us being here," she said.

"I'm not uncomfortable with you two being here, but it seems as if you feel uncomfortable with me being unemployed."

"I don't remember anyone saying anything about you being unemployed. I don't see anything wrong," Gina said.

"We are your friends, Jennifer," Angel said.

"Whoa, I didn't know we were friends. Usually, friends pick up the telephone and call one another. Friends would probably respond to a birthday card or a letter saying 'Please call me.' Friends don't fall off the face of the earth and show up when it's convenient, especially for them," Jennifer said in anger. She continued to pack, walking around the two women.

"I had always thought we were friends regardless of how many telephone calls or birthday cards. You know I love you," Angel said.

"Did you ever notice I was the only one doing the writing and the calling? Or did you remember saying that you would always be there when I needed you? You knew I needed you," Jennifer continued fiercely.

"I'm sorry if I have disappointed you. You seemed to be satisfied with your career. You've never complained, so I assumed everything was okay. Are you going to tell me what's going on?" Angel asked softly.

"Angel, I can leave so that you two can have privacy," Gina said.

There was a knock on the door. Jennifer knew it was Lisa and that meant trouble. Lisa and Angel had become cordial since college. They had not been more than fifty feet of each other since Gina's wedding.

"That's Lisa," Jennifer said, searching Angel's face for approval.

"Good. I haven't seen her in years. It would be good to see her now," Angel said with excitement.

Jennifer walked slowly to the door. Lisa knocked harder. "Coming," Jennifer called out. She opened the door to a smiling Lisa with arms outstretched.

"Did anyone call a packer?" Lisa said happily.

"Come in," Jennifer said slowly. Immediately Lisa sensed something was wrong. She walked inside Jennifer's apartment and stopped.

"Hello Lisa," Angel said.

"Hello Lisa," Gina said.

Lisa said nothing. She looked at the two women. "Look Jennifer, it seems like it's a full house so, I'll check you later," Lisa said saluting and starting toward the door.

Now Jennifer was confused. Lisa was never one to back away from anyone, especially not Angel. Gina had always been her idol and she was not happy to see her either. Jennifer wondered about her friend's behavior. Ever since Lisa's long hospital stay, her behavior was unpredictable.

"You haven't changed much," Gina said while making an intense eye contact with Lisa. "Look, I tried but...I'm here," Gina said half choking with a smile. Lisa walked to Gina and hugged her.

Jennifer's face became blank. She had no idea what was happening. She thought this was another sign, but she wasn't sure if it was good.

Chapter 2
March 1980

Jennifer held the invitation close to her chest with both hands like a winning ticket to an expensive door prize. She stammered through all the questions the three young women asked. All wearing black dresses, pearl necklaces and pearl earrings. Their makeup was barely visible. Jennifer noticed their shoes were polished, something she never did.

One young woman pounded her with questions about her family. Jennifer shifted as she responded without confidence. One intensely scrutinized her appearance from head to toe. The other just stared, almost to the point of contempt.

Jennifer's eye contact was poor. She couldn't retrieve the confidence she had before the three young women accosted her. She knew it was going to be tough when one asked how her mother died. All she could say was, "from hemorrhaging." She did not want to lie. It became hopeless when she silently compared her father, the hard-working postal worker, to the doctors, lawyers and engineers whose daughters were in full attendance.

Her appearance alone was conspicuous. Only a few who wore the black dresses were as dark as she, and fewer had been invited. Everyone else looked the same. Her white cotton blouse, grey wool skirt and black shoes were no match for the silk blouses and dresses that were invited. She closed her eyes and counted to three slowly, praying for the spirit that Lisa's grandmother believed in. She felt a tingling sensation travel up her spine, causing her to stand straight. She felt a rush, sending her shoulders erect. Her chin lifted slowly. She smiled at the three black dresses.

"Excuse me. I know I have taken up a great deal of your time. I'll circulate the room now. It was nice meeting you," Jennifer said politely and walked away slowly.

The one who stared the most spoke first, "Can you believe it? She comes to *our* Tea looking like an orphan and has the audacity to tell us she wants to circulate the room. I don't care whose roommate she is, I'm not voting for her."

"Oh, come on Annette. You know some of your questions were, shall we say, inappropriate. Besides, she's pretty. I like her. We can do more with her looks than her father's income."

"You, of all people, who wants to see a check stub before a date, are not interested in her father's income?"

"I heard she was voted to represent the Beta Swans at the Barons' Ball. I also heard some other things, too. I want her to pledge. It will be good for us."

"What do you have up your sleeve? You know we rarely accept girls like her."

"Miss Melanie Smith is pushing for her and it is going to be tough convincing twenty-two hypnotized women to go against her."

"Your roommate is a little weak, too. Do you think she will make it?"

"She had better! Her father is an engineer and her mother is a teacher. What more can you say? It beats that mailman and his wife, the secretary." The three black dresses laughed softly.

Jennifer walked around the room and spotted Lisa's friend standing alone. One of the black dresses had just left. Jennifer decided to speak. "Hi Rochelle. How is the cross examination going?"

Rochelle tried to whisper but her voice carried slightly, "These women are a *trip*! That last heffa asked me if I attended the last art exhibit at the museum. The hussy before her asked me about some Mozart or Chopin shit. I told her the last good music I heard was from the Kool Jazz Festival."

Jennifer never understood why Rochelle wanted to be a Kappa. She and Lisa were friends with similar personalities. Lisa said the Kappas were too stiff and stuffy for her. It appeared the same held true for Rochelle. "I never thought you wanted to be a Kappa," Jennifer said innocently, not knowing she hurt Rochelle's feelings.

Jennifer saw Rochelle's opened mouth and rebounded quickly. "What I mean is they tend to act stiff. I just thought that didn't interest you," Jennifer explained.

"My mother, sister and cousin are Kappas," Rochelle mumbled. She looked around the room to end the conversation.

"If they are anything like you, I know they made it lively. I can't wait until we pledge, uh, if we get accepted to pledge. We are going to loosen up the sorority and bring it down to earth," Jennifer said smiling.

Four black dresses were standing off talking amongst themselves. They studied the crowd as they spoke. One said nothing while the other three acted as cameras.

"What can we expect from this group?" the quiet one finally asked.

"They are fairly nice and humble girls. We have many from strong financial backgrounds. We have one ghetto crawler in the bunch. One seems mousy, almost invisible. We got one who talks too much, a socialite. Overall, they will probably work out fine, at least most of them."

"What about Jennifer?"

The one who was talking fell silent. The one who asked the question looked at her. "Well?" she asked.

"When I talked to her, she was quite comfortable, but I have already heard comments about how invisible she is. She might have trouble if it continues throughout the evening."

"I overheard them asking about her dead mother. They kept pressing her for information and she became nervous. They asked her to describe her stepmother in detail. It became silly when they asked about her wardrobe. That was when she really became nervous."

The tallest one folded her arms. "Which one is their prize choice?" she asked, articulating every word.

"The one in the maroon blouse and skirt set; the socialite who talks too much."

"Hmm, let me pay her a visit. I was never introduced to her," the tall one said and sashayed to the innocent victim of sorority war. She brushed passed the girl who was holding a cup of punch which almost spilled. The tall one turned and looked with question mark eyes at the girl.

"Oh, I'm sorry," the girl said with an embarrassing grin.

"It's okay. My, my. I have seen you around campus but you never speak. What is your name, dear?"

The girl was very embarrassed. She had often seen the tall black dress but every time she tried to speak, the tall, young woman turned her head every time, avoiding her. "My name is Alexis Michels," she said, trying not to stammer.

"Umm. Miss Michels, isn't this tea lovely?"

The girl nodded, feeling uncomfortable. The tall one looked at her fingernails and smiled as usual when sharpening her claws. "I think back to my first Kappa Tea," she said. "I didn't have the nerve to wear the sorority colors until I was initiated. In other words, when I earned them. Although it was only two years ago, I see times have really changed. Young women tend to be bolder, less caring of etiquette."

One of the black dresses, who had talked to Jennifer earlier, approached the girl.

"I see you have met Miss Michels," she said proudly to the tall black dress.

"Oh, yes I have. I find her quite charming," the tall one said.

"So what do you think?" one mean black dress whispered.

The tall one turned to the girl and extended her claws. "Chaus?"

"Chaus?" the girl asked, not understanding.

"Your garment, is it Chaus?"

"Yes it is!" the girl exclaimed.

"I know. I bought the same garment for Mina, our housekeeper, for Christmas. I didn't have to buy it on sale. I find Chaus a real reasonable label."

The other black dress looked at the tall one with discontent. "Well, I must meet some of the other girls. Good-bye Miss Michels. I guess we will be chatting again soon. Ta-ta," the tall dress said and sashayed away.

Lisa looked around the room at all the blue suits in attendance. Most had already talked to her. She had to fight for answers the entire evening.

She was ill prepared. When asked, "Who was the most influential black female that touched her life," Lisa was silent. She never gave thought to the most influential black female that touched her life. She knew if she had said "Gina," they would have thought she was sucking up. She thought of an answer, "My grandmother."

"Oh really, why?" asked a rehearsed, smooth voice.

"Because she raised me."

"She reared you?" the voice said, correcting Lisa. She looked at the blue suit as if she had a hearing problem.

"What does your grandmother do?"

"She used to be a maid," Lisa said bluntly.

"Oh, a retired domestic employee?" the blue suit responded. Lisa looked at the person strangely, wondering if she were not speaking loudly enough.

"So Lisa, tell me about your mother. What does she do?"

Lisa panted slightly. How could she answer the question without being embarrassed. "She's dead," Lisa said out loud, hoping the blue suit heard her. The blue suit jumped and gasped slightly.

"I'm sorry. What did she die of?"

"Heart problems," Lisa lied quickly.

"Cardiac arrest?" the blue suit asked. Lisa looked at her as if she had a comprehension problem. "What about your father?" the blue suit continued.

"He's dead, too, a car accident," Lisa said louder before the young woman could ask. Lisa looked over the crowd to keep from becoming more nervous. She wanted the questions to end. The young woman looked perplexed. She figured Lisa was finished talking.

"It was nice talking to you, Lisa."

"Same here."

The blue suit walked to a taller suit. "Is that the one?" she asked slightly piqued. The taller suit nodded. "What is she, some kind of product of a juvenile detention rehabilitation program? I tried talking to her, but she only gives one word responses, no explanation or conversation. What is she hiding? Anyway, she needs work, a lot of work," the young woman said and walked away.

The taller suit blinked her eyes and turned to the other two. "How does it look?" she asked.

"We got one who has a chip on her shoulder. One whose clothes are too tight. One who acts as if this is a beauty pageant. One who jumps at everything and one who has on enough makeup to cover a two-inch facial mole. It's the usual spread."

"Is there anyone who stands out?"

"Yeah, the one in the blue dress. She just happens to be the tallest person in this room. They are all a little nervous, even Lisa."

"Oh really? Jessica just said she wasn't impressed with her."

"That doesn't surprise me. She is pushing for the one over there in the dress that's riding her butt."

"What's her name?"

"Phyllis O'Neil."

"Hmm. Let me chat with Miss O'Neil. Maybe I was wrong. I'll see you later." The taller suit took off toward the girl in the red dress who was the target of disagreement.

"Hello. Phyllis O'Neil? I'm Gina Smith, chapter president. Nice to meet you," she said, extending her hand. The girl became nervous and left Gina's hand dangling. She quickly put her hands behind her back and began to talk to the girl.

The taller suit spent ten minutes talking and then excused herself. She walked back to the small group of blue suits who were waiting for her analysis. She stood beside the one who was her roommate and whispered, "All oxygen, no brains."

Her roommate nodded. "That's what I've been hearing, too. She's trying to build a case against Lisa. We need to be extra careful during the pledge period. You know how Lisa is. It might give ammunition to convince some of the others. They only need one-third for approval."

"I know."

"Ladies, welcome to our 1980 Kappa Tea. Each of you were personally invited by one of our sisters who was impressed with you at our informal rush. As you know, we extend only one invitation per member, so each of you must be very special. Let's start with our guests introducing themselves and sharing who extended the invitation."

Jennifer put her hand over her mouth in disbelief after hearing the announcement. The idea of one invitation per member was just too selective. She looked at the name on her invitation over and over. The introductions were getting closer and she was becoming nervous again. She closed her eyes and felt the tingling sensation again. She opened her eyes slowly.

"Hello, my name is Alexis Michels. I was invited by Miss Annette Spencer," said a cheerful voice.

"Uh, hi. Uh, my name is Rochelle Overton and I um, was invited by Cathy Marks."

It was Jennifer's turn. She took a deep breath and stood up slowly. She smiled as she spoke. "Hello ladies. My name is Jennifer Peterson. I was personally invited by Miss Linda Stevens," Jennifer said and sat down with a straight back.

Jennifer sat attentively listening to the president give the sorority history and information on the very few public service programs the sorority sponsored. Her attention was focused on the twenty girls who were invited. She knew most of them. Some lived in the same dorm and others were in her classes. She counted twenty-five black dresses and only twenty girls in attendance. She quickly calculated five no-show invitations from Angel, Maria and three others. She wondered who would personally turn down an invitation from Angel or Maria. She also wondered why Linda, instead of Angel, invited her? Linda barely spoke to her. Jennifer felt Linda did not like her.

Jennifer continued to focus her attention around the room. She looked at the ones she believed would be selected. They were dressed nicely and looked as if they had just gotten their hair done. Jennifer continued her analysis. She immediately eliminated three girls: Rochelle, who seemed out of place; Michelle, who had one of the worst reputations on campus; and Julia, who may not have the GPA.

"As you know, Phi Kappa Psi only accepts the highest quality women on campus. We believe the success of our sorority lies in the high standards of acceptance. A Kappa woman is a well-rounded individual; versatile in many respects. She puts forth every effort in looking her best, as well as being her best at all times. Our pledge period is designed to cultivate those attributes to make one fine-tuned. After all, our symbol is the diamond, one of the world's most precious and elegant jewels. It takes a great deal to wear eleven of them."

Jennifer's heart pounded after hearing the requirements: a transcript reflecting a minimum of twenty-four hours and a cumulative grade point average of 2.85 or above; a biographical sketch of her parents' background; an essay on Why I Want to be a Kappa Lady; and three character references, one being from the member who extended the invitation. Jennifer didn't have the nerve to ask Linda for a reference.

"Those of you who are interested for consideration into our sorority, please submit these items to our Chapter room by six o'clock Wednesday."

The girls gave a low gasp. It gave them less than a week to complete all the requirements. The president continued, "After you have successfully met the requirements, you will be invited to interview with a select group of our members. Our interview committee will make recommendations to the sorority on your acceptance for membership. You will be notified on whether or not you were selected. Ladies, are there any questions?"

Three girls raised their hands slowly. The speaker pointed to Rochelle. "Yeah, like-uh, how long should the essay be and about how much does it cost to pledge?"

There were looks circulating among the black dresses. There were some looks from the invites, too. Jennifer looked at the faces of the black dresses. She did not understand the problem. The question seemed legitimate.

"Is it Miss Overton?... Your essay can be as long as you deem necessary to answer the question. We do not discuss the cost of our pledge program at this time. We believe the cost should be insignificant, especially *at* this time. You will be given an application form once you have been accepted. That information is on the form. Uh yes, Miss Washington?"

"Is it possible to discuss the pledge program at this time?"

"Yes it is, but let me answer questions regarding the requirements. Are there any more questions concerning the requirements.... Okay, I know you ladies are anxious to hear about the pledge program so let me introduce Miss Denise Henderson."

"Our pledge program matches one of you with one of us. We expect you to develop a special relationship with your Kappa mentor. You will be told specifics once you have been accepted for membership."

"Thank you Miss Henderson. We ask that you stay awhile and talk one-on-one with us. Thank you for coming and good evening ladies," the president said and stood back. The rest of the black dresses stood back as well.

Jennifer noticed how girls gathered quickly around black dresses. There was no one she had felt an urge to talk to. They all had approached her earlier. She noticed Alexis around five black dresses and the one named Candice around three. Jennifer decided to thank Linda for the invitation and leave.

Jennifer walked slowly to Linda, who was standing with Angel and two other black dresses. They stopped talking when she came close. Jennifer cleared her throat and smiled, "Hello ladies. I had a very nice time. Miss Stevens, I would like to thank you for inviting me this evening. I don't know how I could ever repay you," said a humble and sincere Jennifer.

Linda smiled. "Miss Stevens? Um, I like that! Honey, you don't owe me a thing," Linda said, throwing a quick glance at Angel.

"Jennifer, make sure you thank everyone this evening." Angel said gently.

Jennifer nodded and smiled, "Good night ladies and thank you." She walked away.

"She's very sweet and very pretty. I see why she is on the Beta's court," one black dress said.

"I heard a few of the who's who among fraternity men have their eyes on her," said another.

"She seems very earnest and sincere. We have to dress her up in order to pull it off," said the first black dress.

"She must be very special for you to go through so much trouble," another said.

"She is," the quiet black dress said emotionless.

Jennifer went around the room thanking everyone. Most were naturally pleasant, but others were just polite. She walked toward the door where Rochelle was headed.

"These women are so fake," Rochelle mumbled under her breath.

"Are you going to turn in the information?" Jennifer asked.

"Yeah."

"We would like to welcome everyone to our Soiree this evening. We are happy to see so many who have met the initial requirements. You must have impressed at least one of our sorors to be invited to our formal rush. We would like each of you to stand and introduce yourself. Tell us who invited you this evening. Let's start with the young lady to my left."

Lisa looked at the very frightened girl. She knew her. They tried out for the gymnastics team last year. The girl was short and very petite. She stood and looked at one of the members the entire time.

"HH...um.... Hi, my name is Tina Richardson. I am a sophomore majoring in sociology. I was invited by Sheila Temple and Diane Cole," said the tiny voice.

Lisa looked at Gina who seemed unmoved by the girl's nervousness. Lisa counted the hopefuls, twenty-eight. There were at least fifty girls at the informal rush two weeks ago. It only took one member to invite one of the fifty.

Lisa heard some of the girls announce receiving invitations by two members. She shook her head. She personally received four invitations. She knew most of the girls present and was only friends with a few of them. She wondered who would make line. Her calculation came up to ten, including herself.

"Hello, my name is Alicia Sims. I am a sophomore majoring in elementary education. I was invited by Cheryl Hicks and Rita Wyatt," said a smooth, alto, nervous voice.

It was Lisa's turn. She caught a glance from the one who last talked to her, correcting her as she spoke. She also noticed a couple of others who excused themselves in the middle of her sentences. No way was she going to be scared like Tina or nervous like Alicia. She almost shot up out of her chair. She looked around the room and made eye contact with all the blue suits. She saw the corners of Gina's mouth spread into a grin.

They wanted to know a little about her so she smiled and spoke loud and clear, "Good evening ladies! My name is Lisa Arvell. I am from St. Louis, Missouri, a graduate from Hillside Preparatory Academy."

A gasp came from the crowd. Hillside was a private black college preparatory school whose students tended to be Merit scholarship winners. Some had the highest scores on the SAT test in the state of Missouri. Lisa's adrenaline continued to flow. "I am a sophomore whose majors are economics and finance. I was invited by Miss Gina Smith, Miss Carla Merriweather, Miss Marsha Lewis and Miss Rita Wyatt." Lisa sat down smiling, looking around the room, especially at the one named Jessica.

The girl next to Lisa stood but the president interrupted with slight sarcasm, "Thank you Miss Arvell. We don't want to take the thunder from Miss O'Neil." Gina stood back and whispered to her roommate. The two young women smiled.

After the introductions, the president spoke. "We have some impressive young women here tonight and that is what we are looking for. An Alpha woman is influential, educated, powerful and above all, altruistic. She must be able to make a difference. We want the best; highly respectable young women; leaders. Those qualities are exemplified in the standards we set. We will distribute application forms this evening, listing the necessary information needed for consideration."

Lisa relaxed after hearing the requirements: an official transcript with a minimum of twenty-four hours and a cumulative grade point average of 2.85 or above; three character references, one from an Alpha and another from a professor; a three-page paper, typed and double-spaced on "Women Leaders: Past and Present; and a one-page biographical sketch.

"All items must be completed and submitted to our chapter room by March 1, that's next Thursday. It will give us a week to review all the material and determine who will be interviewed. The interviews will begin the following week, March 5. We anticipate an induction date of March 12. Everything you do from this point on is a reflection on you, so I suggest you put your best foot forward. I would like to take this time to field questions.... Miss Jefferson?"

"How much does it cost to pledge?"

"All cost information is on the application.... Miss Brown?"

"What about the pledge period? What should we expect?"

"There will be no physical, verbal or emotional abuse during your pledge period. This will be a period to help develop character. If a pledgee has been hazed in any form or fashion, you must report it immediately. This goes for all pledgees as well as sorority members. The details of the pledge period will be given at the time of induction. I'll take one more question before we allow our sorors the opportunity to a one-on-one interview with you.... Yes, Miss Richardson?"

"Do we have to get a reference from a professor?"

"Yes ma'am, that is our requirement. Any more questions?.... Okay ladies, we ask that you stay around for any questions we might have. Thank you for coming."

Lisa was bombarded with questions about Hillside. She did not respond as she did earlier. She answered the questions intelligently and in detail. Several blue suits asked about her majors. She elaborated on her interest in economics. She felt fortunate that no questions were asked about her parents. The blue suits that talked to her later did not seem to care.

She was constantly asked why she was not politically active on campus. She found it difficult to say she had no interest. To the blue suits, it was important. Finally the blue suits left and Lisa rushed to the door.

As she walked down the hall of the Student Union, she saw Jennifer and Rochelle walking in the opposite direction. To Lisa, they didn't look happy. Rochelle looked as if she had been given one month to live. The three girls stopped when they made it to the top of the stairs.

"How did it go?" Lisa asked.

"Those women are a trip!" Rochelle responded.

"How was it Lisa?" Jennifer asked.

"I'm tired. Let's get something to drink."

Jennifer saw the familiar sight of students playing Bid Wist in one of the lounges in the Student Union. One of the boys yelled out for Rochelle to take his hand while he used the restroom. She waved him off. The three girls walked inside the cafeteria in dresses and heels. Boys whistled as they walked by. Lisa and Rochelle walked ahead, ignoring the catcalls, whereas Jennifer looked around to see who was talking.

They got sodas and sat down. Jennifer bought a bag of potato chips too. Lisa and Rochelle talked while Jennifer stared out the door at the Kappa hopefuls. They laughed and talked to one another while leaving the Student Union.

Jennifer's concentration was broken when a brown figure leaned close. It startled her, making her spill the potato chips.

"I'm sorry. Let me buy you another bag," he said.

"That's okay. It was my fault. Hi Michael."

"I heard you made the Beta's court, congratulations!"

"Thanks."

"Hello, Michael," Rochelle and Lisa said together with their eyes shooting fire from being ignored.

"Hello, ladies. I see everyone has been to somebody's rush. I know Jennifer is pledging Kappa, are you two pledging Alpha?"

"I went to the Kappas' rush," Rochelle said pleasantly.

"Come again? *You* are pledging Kappa?"

"Hell yeah! And what is that suppose to mean!" Rochelle said loudly.

"Calm down Roach, he's just kidding. How come you haven't been to march practice lately? Aren't you stepping next Friday?" Lisa asked.

"Uh, no, but I'm quite sure the show is going to be *bad*! You ladies take care and good luck next Saturday, Jennifer." The young man left the area.

"He thinks he is so fine. The only thing fine about him is his body," Rochelle said.

"I think he has a nice face too!"Jennifer said. The two girls looked at Jennifer hard.

"He does!" Jennifer said in defense.

More boys came into the cafeteria. Lisa and Rochelle became excited.

"Look at the rump roast on Kevin. I heard he's pledging Epsilon," Rochelle whispered.

"I thought he wanted to be a Lambda," Lisa said.

"Un-Un. Word is out that the Lambdas don't want him, so he's jumping ship and connecting with Epsilon. They are going to kick his ass," Rochelle said.

"Excuse me but I'm going back to the dorm. I'll see y'all later," Jennifer said. The two girls barely heard her as she left the table. Jennifer saw Margo by herself. The two walked out together.

Seven black dresses were left in the room sitting with legs crossed.

"Angel, you have to be careful. My sources tell me that it is going to be difficult for Jennifer."

"Can you reveal your sources?" asked a calm Angel.

The younger black dress shook her head sadly, "I just can't afford for them to know I told."

"It's okay sweetie. You still have another year left and I don't want to make it uncomfortable for you. I'll be alright."

"I'm sorry Angel. If they ever found out that I told…"

"We will talk later, okay?"

The younger black dress nodded and kissed Angel on the cheek. She waved to the rest and left the room.

"Do you trust her?" one whispered.

"Not with information."

"She's a nice girl, but I don't respect people who have a difficult time choosing sides. Straddling the middle has never been comfortable."

"It is not worth my energy to get upset about it. What have you all heard about Jennifer?"

"I know a few were going to vote against her, but it seems like they have changed their minds for some reason."

"They think I'm angry at her. They will probably vote her on line just to spite me, which is good. The whole key is for her to make it," Angel said softly and took a sip of punch. "This is too sweet."

"So you are not mad at her?"

"Why should I be? Jennifer is one of the most loyal and sweetest people I know. She hasn't done anything wrong," Angel said.

"So how are we going to keep any of them from casting a 'no' vote?" the tallest dress asked. "They were shocked that you want her as a member. She doesn't have the background or the popularity. Why, Angel?" the tallest dress continued.

The quiet dress ignored the question. Jennifer was more than a roommate to her. It was difficult to explain to the other black dresses what Jennifer meant to her.

Angel swallowed slowly and spoke, "When she interviews, she must score high. They are taking a chance on the other candidates who fall after her. Jennifer will probably interview very well but I don't want to take any chances, if you know what I mean."

The tallest dress gave a mischievous grin. "I'm really going to miss these girlie conversations when we graduate. It was a pleasure doing business with you ladies," she said.

"A good relationship doesn't have to end, even if he is married. Isn't that what your mother told you?" a black dress asked the tall one. The group chuckled, except the quiet dress.

"She must be very special, Angel. You have just about called a sorority war on this," one said.

"I didn't like how that other girl was treated just because she didn't fit the bill. I was the one who invited her and it was an embarrassment when she dropped line without us doing anything about it. She could have gotten the chapter pulled, but she chose not to say a word like I did. It won't happen to Jennifer because I'm prepared to do something about it this time. Matter of fact, I want them to try. It's time to even the score," Angel said.

The tallest black dress handed Angel two envelopes. "Here are her references."

Angel was surprised to see the cream laid paper with the gold sorority seal. She looked at the tall black dress. "You didn't have to."

"My pleasure. I think this is going to be fun. At least we will leave with a bang. What is your next move?"

"I need to keep my enemies close, very close."

"So she graduated from Hillside Academy, how impressive," one blue suit said.

"She's a leader. She just needs a little polishing. Besides, I have never heard of Hillside Academy," said the taller one.

"That's because you live in Kansas City. You have to test high to get in Hillside. Money alone can't get you in. Her parents must have a bankroll, or is it her grandmother?"

"I never thought she came from money. She is here on a scholarship. I'm praying that she can afford to pledge."

"If she attended Hillside, she can afford to pledge. I'll see you at the meeting for the interview team."

"Okay, Sheila." Gina looked at the three blue suits left in the room. They didn't look convinced.

"I think she may have pissed off a few already. Some are calling her arrogant," one said.

"They are just jealous. Lisa is pretty common," Gina said.

"Yes, too common. I heard her mouth can be matched with the boys' locker room and she would win."

"Let's put it to the test. I believe I have an open mind. We will sit down and chat with her to get an idea about who we are nominating. I want it to be a non-threatening atmosphere; casual; a kick off your shoes and talk session. If she's too rough, then we will choose someone else. I can't afford to go soft on this. We have worked too hard," Gina said.

"Who shall we invite?"

"It doesn't matter. Anyone who wants to be convinced. Anyone besides Jessica."

"We don't need a large audience. It can be just us and a couple others."

"How about next Friday night after the step-show?"

"Sounds good to me. How about it Gina?"

"Any time or any place. I doubt if she disappoints me."

Chapter 3

Jennifer knocked on the bathroom door and shouted, "ANGEL! ANGEL! WHERE IS MY STARCH?"

"I DON'T HAVE YOUR STARCH!"

"This is ridiculous," Jennifer mumbled.

"When she comes out the bathroom, talk to her about your shit. You are always complaining about your things being taken without your permission. I say approach the heffa and nip it in the bud," Lisa said as she relaxed in an inclined position on Jennifer's bed. "You need to tell her to go to hell."

"I don't like trouble. Angel is a nice person, a little spoiled but nice. She shares sometimes."

"You act like she's some kind of queen. She doesn't share. She knows your size eleven hips can't fit in her size five jeans. I don't understand why you let her use your shit anyway. She's got money," Lisa said and sat up. "I've seen you check brothers when they step out of line, but you seem to have a hard time with Angel. She is so selfish with you."

Jennifer thought the pot was calling the kettle black. Angel and Lisa were so much alike. Both had egos larger than life and looked similar.

Angel, Melanie Smith, was a senior. She and Jennifer had been roommates for two years. Angel was very calm and spoke softly. She never argued. Although she would get irritated at times, she never lost control. She maintained a very small circle of friends, mainly her sorority sisters.

Angel bonded quickly with Jennifer. They spent a lot of time together. Jennifer mainly enjoyed the nights, staying up and talking about boys, parents, school, or just anything. Angel was patient with Jennifer because she was naive. She trusted Angel and vice versa. Angel embraced Jennifer as a little sister.

Lisa Arvell was a sophomore. She graduated from high school with honors. Her behavior didn't reflect her grades. It was rumored that her SAT scores were high enough to earn a scholarship at any of the major universities around the country, but she chose Missouri State University. She and Jennifer met trying to get a room on their first day at Missouri State.

"I think you're jealous," Jennifer said teasingly.

Lisa laughed. She walked over to the mirror and began to play with her shoulder- length hair. "I know I'm fine. Even my name is cute, 'Lee-Sa.' I know I look good and so does Angel. I guess you can say we are similar. We both wear the same size, but my waistline is an inch smaller. Our hair is about the same length, but mine is about a half inch longer. She has those big, brown eyes, but men tend to like my almond-shaped, hazel ones better. Our noses are the same too." Lisa frowned and then puckered her lips. "She has a beauty mark on her cheek but my sexy one above the lip is cuter."

"I have to say, you pay attention to the finest details," Jennifer said.

"All I'm saying is when Angel and I look in the mirror, we like what we see. But you, on the other hand; How do I look?; Does this look right?; or Should I wear red or blue? You use other people for your mirror."

Jennifer tried walking away, but Lisa grabbed her arm and pulled her back. She unbraided one of Jennifer's french braids. "You have all of this beautiful, black, thick hair that hangs half way down your back but you wear two french braids like a sixteen-year-old. Lord knows if He gave me your hair, we wouldn't be friends because you couldn't talk to me. You have high cheek bones and smooth, brown skin. You got that muscular build, the kind brothers call healthy. You won't wear shorts, skirts, or anything that shows your shape."

Jennifer went to her closet and took out her iron and ironing board. Jennifer took a skirt and blouse out of her closet and turned to Lisa to ask for her opinion. She hesitated and began ironing the blouse. The bathroom door open. Angel stepped out wrapped in a red towel. Her nose twitched. "Hi Lisa," she said.

"Hi, Angel," Lisa said in a southern accent.

Angel ignored her. "I let Carol borrow your starch a couple of days ago. She might still have it. Jennifer, do you mind pressing my slacks and blouse? I need to go down the hall and call Steve to see what time he's meeting me at the House tonight."

Jennifer was stunned. Angel loaned her starch to Carol who might still have it and did not bother to get it back. Now Angel wanted her to iron a pair of slacks and a blouse while she chatted with her boyfriend. Jennifer could not believe what she heard.

"I'm sorry Angel, I need to take a shower and get dressed just like you. I don't have time to iron your clothes," Jennifer sputtered.

"Fine," Angel said and grabbed a robe. She left the room.

Missouri State University was located in a small town named Harrisburg, Missouri, population one hundred thousand, not counting the students at the University. The university's population was ten thousand students, two thousand being minority. The black student body represented fifteen hundred. Mostly Asians and Africans made up the balance. The black students formed a few organizations to unify the black student body, but the primary source of socialization for black students was the Greek organizations. Others formed the International Students Organization.

Many students were going to the House, a small building where all the black sororities and fraternities gave dances. Beta Gamma Delta, one of the most popular black fraternities on campus, was having their annual scholarship weekend. It was usually the biggest event for black college students at Missouri State. Friday night was the dance at the House, Saturday was the Barons' Ball (the crowning of Miss Beta), and Sunday afternoon was the informal dinner by invitation only.

The Betas, Barons and Swans were all performing a "step-show" at the Friday night dance. The Barons were young men interested in joining the Beta fraternity. The Swans was the little sister interest group to the Beta fraternity. The groups had rehearsed for weeks on songs, chants, and movements to impress the alumni and visiting college students.

Angel decided to participate for the first time in two years. She choreographed the show for the Swans and Barons. She selected the uniforms for both groups too. This was a very big night for the Betas and everything had to be perfect. The new president asked her to come out of retirement and do him a favor. He wanted it to be a big show.

Jennifer could not get over Angel's attitude. She had been behaving strangely for the last few weeks. Lisa thought Angel might have had a twinge of jealousy because Jennifer, an unknown sophomore, was selected from a group of fifty girls to represent the Swans at the Barons' Ball. She would compete against very popular girls from sororities and other fraternities' female interest groups.

One person was picked from each sorority and interest group. Two other girls with no Greek affiliation were also selected. When Jennifer received her formal invitation, Lisa was shocked because she figured herself a better choice. She was outgoing, smart, and much better looking than most of the girls on court. But since it was Jennifer representing the Swans, she released the jealousy.

Jennifer showered slowly. She thought about how she would wear her hair for the evening and how she would wear it the next night. She continued to practice, in her mind, the curtsey to the reigning Miss Beta. Over and over, she practiced the movements; step out to the side; step back; and go down slowly leading with the chest. Once the chest touches the knee, drop the head for three seconds. Remember to use the escort's hand to come up slowly. Pause and wait for the escort to lead her to the chair. She didn't know who would be her escort. She figured Tim Rylander, one of the Neophytes.

Jennifer stepped out of the shower and dried off slowly. She had to start taking things slower. Her second year in college and already she was selected to be on a fraternity's court, a very popular one at that. She did not know her chances of winning and didn't care.

The interview Wednesday night appeared humorous to the Betas. They chuckled lightly at a couple of her responses and laughed loudly at others. She arrived early, waiting in a small room in the Student Union. Either the girl before her came late or the Betas were slow.

Finally the door across the hall opened and Linda Stevens, a member of Phi Kappa Psi sorority, came out. She wore a red dress showing every curve imaginable with a wide, black belt that emphasized her small waistline. She had the shape for the dress and wearing the fraternity's colors didn't hurt either.

Jennifer became jittery. She was wearing a blue, pleated skirt and a white blouse. It was her church usher board uniform. She didn't have many clothes, especially in the way of dresses. She had on a little lipstick and a little blush. Angel was supposed to style her hair, but she never came back to the roomso Lisa hot curled her hair and pulled the top part back with a large barrette and fluffed the back. She told Jennifer it didn't make sense to style her hair sexy when she looked like a church lady.

The Betas asked Jennifer if she could change one thing about Beta Gamma Delta, what would it be and why. Her response was to get rid of the Swans or change the group's purpose. She commented that the need for a female group to serve the mission of the Beta organization had become personal. She thought it was a nice way of saying fraternities shouldn't use interest groups to get girlfriends. The group chuckled and the president, Lionel Johnson, stared at Jennifer.

One of the most cocky members, Marvin Coleman, asked her if she had her choice of escorts who would she pick and why. She told him she would choose the fraternity's national president because if she had a choice, she wanted the best. They laughed louder, which confused Jennifer because she was being honest. The finale was she asked to leave before being excused. She told them she realized they started late but she had someone to tutor at 8:30 and it was already 8:15. She flashed her biggest smile and left.

Jennifer came out of the bathroom and saw Angel lying down. There was a moment of silence. "Are you going to fix my hair tonight?" Jennifer asked low.

"How do you want to wear it?" Angel asked.

"What do you think, up or down?"

"How do you want to wear it?" Angel asked again, but firmly.

"Uh...down. I think it would look...nice with my...red blouse."

There was a knock on the door. Angel went to the bathroom to plug in the curling iron and Jennifer went to the door.

"You don't have much starch left. Why aren't you ready? You don't have your hair fixed or anything. I brought Dee Dee's black riding boots to go with your black kick-pleat skirt. She's not performing tonight."

Jennifer said nothing which was unusual. Angel came out of the bathroom and brushed by Jennifer.

"What's wrong with y'all?" Lisa asked.

"Thanks Lisa" Jennifer said and took the boots from Lisa. "Angel is getting ready to fix my hair now."

"Angel, how are you going to fix it? Give it the Farrah Fawcett look. Girl, you are going to be hot!" Lisa said and bumped hips with Jennifer.

"Come on, Jennifer so, I can get started," Angel said impatiently.

"What's your problem Angel?" Lisa asked, staring at Angel in the bathroom.

"I'm ready Jennifer!" Angel demanded. Jennifer proceeded to the bathroom. Lisa pulled her back and walked in the bathroom instead. "Why are you trippin'?"

"Get out of here, Lisa."

"Naw, I asked why are you trippin'?"

Jennifer saw something for the first time; Angel getting angry.

"You still haven't congratulated Jennifer for making court," Lisa said, exposing one of the secrets. Angel said nothing. Lisa became angry and moved in closer, pointing her finger in Angel's face. "You got your nerve asking somebody to iron your clothes like you're some damn queen. And another thing, you need to leave her shit alone."

"Look little girl, GET...OUT...OF...MY...FACE!"

"Lisa, stop! Just stop!" Jennifer yelled.

Lisa looked at her friend in disbelief. Jennifer chose sides against her when she was right. She stormed out the room and slammed the door. Although Lisa was rambunctious, Jennifer had never seen her ready to fight. Something was wrong. The feud between those two was getting worse. And she was in the middle.

"Are you going to fix my hair," Jennifer asked with teary eyes. Angel said nothing and went back to bed. Jennifer pulled back her hair in the comfortable french braids. Angel got up and walked toward Jennifer.

"Don't do that," Angel said softly. Jennifer continued to braid.

Angel stepped behind Jennifer and stopped her hands. Angel could not control herself. She had no one else to tell. "He doesn't want to see me anymore. He said that I was trying to trap him. He told me the guys on campus warned him about me. Kappas only come to school to find husbands, he said."

Angel's focus went to the ceiling. "He gave me three hundred dollars and told me to go away. I haven't told him I started my period. I'll just let him wonder," she said, without thinking. Her face was solemn.

Jennifer was shaking. The tears flowed. "Please Angel, fix my hair."

"I can't sweetie."

"Aren't you coming tonight?"

Angel was silent.

"I'm scared. Everyone will be staring and comparing me to the other girls. I don't know if they will clap when they introduce me. Please come, I need you to be there," Jennifer begged.

"I'll always be there when you need me, but you don't need me tonight."

Jennifer started to speak. "Shhh," Angel said. She unplugged the curling iron and placed the handle in Jennifer's hand. "Talk to Lisa. She knows how to mask fears. She's good at it. She does it all the time." Angel walked to her desk and began writing. Jennifer opened the door and closed it quietly. As she walked down the hall, she heard the door open. She stopped and turned around.

"Congratulations Jennifer."

Lisa was quiet when making Jennifer over. She styled Jennifer's hair like Farrah Fawcett, arched her eyebrows, and applied little make-up, more like blush and lipstick. She was quiet when making Jennifer over. Jennifer apologized, but it did not seem to help.

The walked to the dance in silence. Out of nowhere a voice called out, "Hey Jen, wait up."

"Oh Lord, here comes old goofy Kyle. What brother calls a black Jennifer, Jen? Where is he from anyway?" Lisa complained.

"He said he grew up in St. Paul, Minnesota," Jennifer said happily because Lisa finally said something.

"How many black people live in the state of Minnesota? Probably just his family," Lisa commented.

Jennifer laughed. "He's okay. He's just a little different."

"Different? You mean weird."

"Hey Jen," a voice said happily. "Boy don't you look attractive tonight."

"Thanks Kyle. Will you be at the Barons' Ball tomorrow?"

"Of course I will. I want to see them crown you Miss Delta!"

"It's Miss Beta," Lisa said smartly.

"Thanks for correcting me Lisa, and might I say you look charming as always. But of course, you are well aware of that."

Lisa tossed her head back and said, "Kyle, brothers don't give sisters white nicknames."

"What's a white nickname? And which of my sisters are you referring to?" Kyle said smartly.

Lisa was about to shoot back until Jennifer shouted, "Boy it's a bunch of niggas here tonight!" The group looked at the building. The music at the House was loud and the crowd was huge. Cars were parked everywhere. People were standing around the building and on the empty lot adjacent to the building. This was bigger than Jennifer ever imagined. Lisa was excited.

Two girls approached the three students. They were wearing heavy jackets and the same attire as Lisa. One was singing aloud and the other yelled out loud, "Hey Lisa, what's up?" Kyle looked at the girl and turned up his nose. She looked at him and then at Lisa. When the two made eye contact, they burst into laughter. "You ready to throw down?" the girl continued.

"Hey Roach, what's up!" Lisa said.

"Hi Lisa."

"What's up Anita? Sounds like you're tuning up the voice box."

"I'm practicing, just in case Angel doesn't sing. She called and told me to practice her song."

Lisa put her hands on her hips. "Angel's not coming?" Anita hunched her shoulders. Lisa shook her head. "She trips too much! She called herself going off on me. I felt like putting my foot up her butt."

"What happened?" Rochelle asked. Lisa looked at Jennifer, who looked away. "I don't want to talk about it," Lisa said.

"You look hot, Jennifer. I ain't never seen your hair down. Damn it's long!" Rochelle exclaimed.

"I fixed her hair, thank you," Lisa responded.

Rochelle began dancing to the music but stopped when three girls approached the group. "My goodness. Here comes old loud mouth Alicia and her deputy dogs," Rochelle whispered.

"She's always been cool with me," Lisa said.

"For some reason, she gets on my nerves," Rochelle said. The three girls got closer and Lisa's posture straightened. Jennifer stepped closer to Kyle who put his hands in his pockets.

"What's up everybody?" Alicia said coolly. She was a dark girl. She talked slowly and hardly smiled. She stood five feet and five inches. She had a long waistline and narrow hips. She wore a curl that came to her shoulders. She and her friends wore jeans and Lambda Dove sweatshirts under heavy jackets.

"I see y'all are ready to throw down in those cowboy hats," Alicia said and flipped Rochelle's hat.

"Tonight, y'all are going to see a real show. It ain't going to be like that shit y'all came up with last month," Rochelle bragged. She was light brown and the same height as Lisa. She wore a curl that hung in a shag close to her shoulders. She wore two sets of dolphin earrings. She had big, light, brown eyes and a diamond-shaped face. Her full lips were always smiling.

Rochelle walked to the other girls. "What's up? Y'all talking this evening?" Before they could respond, a group of four young women almost walked pass them. They all had on leather jackets.

"Hello Gina, Marsha, Cheryl and Donna," Lisa interrupted quickly. She stood at attention and so did Alicia and her two friends, who also spoke.

The four young women looked at the girls for a quick moment. They said a quick, "Hello" and kept walking.

"Woo! I feel sorry for y'all if they accept y'all on line. I heard Gina kick ass," Rochelle said.

"I heard Annette and Denise ain't nothing to play with either. So if you get accepted on line, you will remove those earrings," Lisa said.

As the five girls talked, a group of five boys were chanting loudly as they came from the other direction. "Girl look! Here comes some Barons. Brad and Tony have got to be the finest men on campus," Rochelle said under her breath.

"They look alright," Alicia said.

"Honey, those brothers are fine. Even nerdy Cameron Johnson looks good," Rochelle said.

As the boys came closer, Rochelle yelled out, "I know y'all are going to wish your sisters good luck tonight."

The boys smiled as they approached the group. "Hello ladies," one said cheerfully.

"Hi Brad," the group of girls said, almost in unison.

"Hello Jennifer."

"HHH...uh.... Hi Brad."

"You look very nice tonight," he said. The girls turned to look at Jennifer as if noticing her for the first time.

"Hello Lisa."

Lisa took her attention off the other boys and looked at the medium tall one who flashed the brightest smile. "Hey Cameron, what's up? Why didn't you come to class Thursday?" she asked as if he had interrupted something important.

"I had to study for a test. I got a hundred on the quiz Tuesday so I figured Dr. Ganton was still covering derivatives Thursday."

"Just because you got a hundred on the quiz doesn't mean you're going to ace the class. You are still black and that white professor wants you there everyday, regardless. You need to come off that white boy's attitude," Lisa said and turned her attention to the one name Tony. "Where are y'all going? The show will be starting in an hour."

"We're going to get something to drink for the after-party little woman. Are you ladies coming?" Tony asked, looking around the group.

"I'm assuming it's a private party unless you're inviting all of us," Alicia said.

"I'm sorry. It's private," Tony said, grinning at Alicia.

"Let me get to steppin'. I'll see y'all at the House," Alicia said and walked away, followed by her two friends.

"Man! That babe got a body on her that will melt ice and an attitude that will freeze mercury. No wonder she's pledging Alpha," Brad said, looking in lust after Alicia.

"And what is that suppose to mean?" Lisa asked quickly.

"Nothing," Brad said.

The one named Cameron walked over to Jennifer and Kyle. He shook hands with Kyle. "Hey man, what's happening! Hello Jennifer, you look very nice," Cameron said.

"Thanks Cameron," said a very shy Jennifer.

"The Betas have *got* to pick you for queen," Tony said. Jennifer blushed from the compliment.

"Wouldn't it be nice if one of our Swans took the title instead of a stuck up Kappa?" Brad said, without thinking again.

"And what does that suppose to mean?" Rochelle asked loudly with her head cocked to the side.

"Uh...nothing! Hey baby, if they put you on line, I know you are going to change all of that," Brad answered with a grin.

"Come on man before you stick your arm down your throat, too. Lisa are you coming to the after-dance?" Cameron asked.

Lisa's attention was on the dance. The crowd was getting larger. "I don't know. It depends on the pickings," she said without looking his way.

The other boys looked at Cameron as he raised his eyebrows and rubbed the back of his head. He forced a smile. "We'll see you ladies later. Good luck, Jennifer," Cameron said.

"Yeah, baby, good luck!" Brad said. All of the boys kissed Jennifer on the cheek and left. Kyle looked on in jealousy and so did the other girls.

"Why did you play Cameron off? He's got a thang for you. The brother is fi-eene," Rochelle said.

Lisa frowned. "He acts so white. I like brothers who understand their identity," she said, throwing a look at Kyle.

"I don't care how white he acts, his ass is fine and nice too. Let's go so we can practice," Rochelle said.

"This is the first time it has ever been this crowded, I bet. There are men to meet and I want to meet as many as I can," Lisa said. She looked at Jennifer. "See y'all later," she said. The three girls took off walking fast.

Kyle and Jennifer were standing alone. He would steal glances at her as she stared at the crowd. She was beautiful. Her rich, brown skin was the true essence of her beauty. She was nothing like the girls he dated in high school, primarily white.

He watched as she slightly frowned, looking at the crowd. Her eyebrows where thin, arching high above deep set eyes which wore no colors. She had long lashes that curled slightly. Molly McDey had green powder that caked in the middle, he reminisced. Jennifer's small nose that rounded at the tip was much different than Molly's or Susan's sharp ones. He stared at the small mouth with the two puffy lips that hid the whitest teeth he had ever seen.

He remembered asking if she had ever worn braces. She responded almost as if he had insulted her by saying, "Black people can't afford braces. They can barely afford the dentist." He knew that wasn't true because both of his sisters had worn braces. The final analysis was the hair. This was the first time he had ever seen Jennifer's hair curled. It was black and thick. The other boys talked about Jennifer's hair when she interviewed with the Betas, but they were wrong. It was beyond "bad," it was gorgeous.

He remembered asking if she was part Indian and, once again, she was insulted. The other boys said she must be mixed with Indian to have long, thick hair. He saw no harm in asking. Susan Windsor's family was from England and she was proud of it. He felt awkward at times when he was around Jennifer. It took her forever to get used to the nickname "Jen." She said it sounded white. At times she would answer his questions without hesitating but then there were those times when she would treat him as if he were stupid. He liked her anyway.

She caught him staring at her. "What's the matter?"

"Nothing, I was just looking to see if I could spot Tommy, Gerald, or Malcolm."

"I thought they were boycotting the Betas?"

"Well, since you're on court, how could they? You know we're your fan club."

And what a fan club, Jennifer thought. Malcolm Reed was so short that he looked like a midget. Tommy Jefferson wore black-rimmed glasses with a big wad of white tape in the middle. Then there was Gerald Shaw who spoke with a lisp. They were all friends and good friends at that. But she had a special closeness with Kyle. She felt as if she were educating him on black culture. They would have dozens of arguments about being black and they both agreed that all black people did not think the same.

Jennifer met Kyle at the first dance given on campus for all freshmen students. The disc jockey played pop, rock, and R&B music. She noticed a very thin black boy dancing with a white girl. It appeared that he had rehearsed a routine. He would kick-shuffle twice, spin around, slide into a split changing sides from left to right. He slid up, spinned around, crossed one foot over the other and threw out his hands as to say "ta-da," as if waiting for an applause. He would do this three times before doing the "Robot" until the song was finished.

All the moves were very old but the white girls seemed to enjoy it. The other black boys were doing a dance called the "Gigolo." When Kyle asked the black girls to dance, they would turn him down before he could get the words out. They preferred being entertained by his performance instead. There were times when they laughed so loud, the crowd would look at them.

He danced every record with the same routine. Once, he threw out his hands after doing his splits and Jennifer applauded and so did the other girls. He noticed what she had done. When the next R&B song began to play, he walked to her. The other girls squealed, telling her to run because "James Brown was coming to town." Jennifer stood still. Normally, she would have been nervous. Not with him. He extended his hand, asking her to dance, as if to get even. She told him, "Sure, as long as you don't do any James Brown splits or the robot. Those dances are older than Kunta Kinte." They danced together. She taught him the latest dances. A special friendship started after the dance.

"I better get moving before they start the court presentation without me," Jennifer said.

"Hey wait!" Kyle said and tugged her hair. *Yes*, he thought. It was soft like he imagined.

"Ouch! That hurts!" Jennifer complained.

"I had to do something drastic. You were moving too fast," Kyle lied.

They walked to the dance. When they arrived at the lot where the students had illegally parked, Jennifer noticed the infamous navy blue Delta 88 with its trunk opened. A boy they called "Blue," was handing a small bundle to another student who gave him some money. Blue looked around suspiciously and quickly closed his trunk.

Jennifer saw members of the other fraternities standing outside trying to sneak in free. She saw other contestants talking to some of the Betas. Jennifer felt her confidence weaken. She couldn't strike up a conversation with the Barons, so the idea of talking to a Beta was unthinkable. She wished she were like Lisa. It was clear to Jennifer that Cameron asked Lisa to the after-party. She courageously told him, in so many words, that she was scouting around for the best offer.

Jennifer jumped when a young man tapped her on the shoulders. He wore a sweater cap over a very long outdated afro. He had on wire frame glasses. He was a member of the Gamma Zeta Tau fraternity. He said in a very cool voice, "Check it out! Dutch would like to tell the fine lady in the black skirt that she is soothing to the eyes." He was holding a cup and swayed as he talked.

"Hello Dutch."

"Dutch would like to wish the fine lady in the black skirt good luck tomorrow."

"Thanks."

"When will the fine lady in the black skirt hook up with Dutch?" the young man asked and took a drink from his cup. He was about to fall.

"Good-bye Dutch," Jennifer said and stared the young man down.

"Dutch says good-bye. And to the fine lady in the black skirt, Dutch says don't be so cold." He staggered away. Jennifer closed her eyes and blew air.

A deep voice sounded in Jennifer's direction, "Excuse me, Jennifer, could you come over here, please. I would like for you to meet some people."

Jennifer turned her attention to Lionel Johnson. He was standing with three young men. She looked back at Kyle and said, "I'll see you later." She walked to Lionel.

"Gentlemen, I would like for you to meet Miss Jennifer Peterson. She's representing our Beta Swans," Lionel said, introducing her to each of the out-of-town fraternity members. One was president of the Betas at a small college in Kansas City.

Jennifer thought, *Gentlemen? No way! They looked like animals; more like wolves*. It was their eyes, hungry eyes, eyes that pierced her skin. They looked rough, the kind that were not nice to girls. One of them took her hand and kissed it. Before he let it go, he stroked the palm of her hand with one of his fingers and pressed the tip into her palm. She yanked her hand away and frowned at him. Lionel quickly notice her expression.

"Well brothers, I need to take our contestant inside. Let's go Jennifer," Lionel said and took Jennifer's hand. They left, leaving the wolves on the lot. Jennifer did not realize she was holding hands with Lionel. He walked her to Steve Ross, the president of the Barons.

Steve, a defensive lineman on the football team, stood six feet and three inches tall, weighing two hundred pounds. He had sandy brown hair, light brown eyes, and deep dimples. His broad smile was his trademark, which drove all the girls wild. He approached Jennifer, "Hey lady, don't you look fine. It would be a pleasure escorting you tonight." He bowed in front of her.

"No Steve, the pleasure is all mine," Jennifer said sarcastically. She looked at him bent over and thought, *What a bastard*. He abandoned Angel because he thought she was pregnant and now he was pretending as if nothing happened. Steve was always pleasant and never mean to anyone. It wasn't like him to be cruel and shuck responsibilities.

Lionel excused himself and left Jennifer with Steve. She turned her attention to a small group of sorority girls wearing maroon blazers. The tallest one with a creamy, coffee-colored complexion used her hands delicately as she spoke. Her facial expressions were quite expressive. The other two seemed to make the same facial expressions as they spoke, too. The tallest one saw Jennifer staring and stopped talking. Jennifer became nervous when the other two turned to look at her. She tried looking away, but it was too late. The tallest one said something to the other two and they approached her. Jennifer shook in her boots.

The three young women stood two feet away forming a semicircle. One had a very pleasant, friendly smile and the other was expressionless. All were very thin with shoulder length hair. They wore pearl earrings. They looked out of place from the jeans, sweatshirts and casual slacks that filled the dance. The tallest had a mischievous grin. "You ladies remember Miss Peterson from the Tea? She's Melanie's roommate," she said, enunciating every word while extending her hand to Jennifer.

Jennifer reached deep to pull enough courage to speak to the three young women without her voice shaking. "Hello Linda, Joni and Maria," she said with a smile. She knew them all. The tallest one visited Angel frequently and the other two came by the room often when they pledged last year.

The one who was expressionless smiled a little. "Miss Peterson, I see you are an accounting major," she said. Her eye contact with Jennifer was sharp.

"Are you an accounting major, too?"

"I am double majoring in accounting and finance. If you ever need help, don't hesitate to ask."

"Thanks Maria."

The tallest one looked at and through Jennifer. She looked at Jennifer's shoes and then her face. Jennifer was very uncomfortable. She looked in the direction of the five Barons who had left to get something to drink. They were gathering their escorts. The one named Brad strutted to the group. He made a macho stance in front of the tallest young woman and announced proudly, "Miss Stevens, I will be your escort this evening!"

The three young women looked at Brad as if he were an intruder. The tallest one looked at the young man from feet to head and glared into his eyes. "Oh boy, am I lucky tonight!" she said, almost frowning. She took off with Brad trailing. The other two said good-bye to Jennifer and went inside the House.

Jennifer watched the three young women with admiration before she heard a pleasant voice say, "Miss Peterson, are you ready to go inside?" Jennifer smiled as she took Steve's arm.

Lionel started the court presentation. The girls were lined up with their escorts. The sorority girls were introduced first. Jennifer heard screams and yells with sorority calls as they entered the opening with their escorts. Jennifer's legs wobbled. People hardly knew her and the embarrassment of no one clapping or cheering filled her with anxiety.

Finally, her name was called and she had to walk in on the arm of the Barons' president. She was so nervous that she practiced the curtsey in her mind. She quickly remembered it was for the next night's event. Then she heard it, the cheering, clapping and boys whistling. It was loud. She heard girls say, "Git it girl." She spotted Lisa, who was smiling, yelling and motioning to her to smile. Jennifer did and it was big.

After the court was introduced, the step-show started. The Beta Swans performed first. They wore black pants pushed down inside black riding boots, black bolero vests, red tie blouses, and black cowboy hats. The Swans stood at attention. Someone shouted military commands like "about face" and "forward march." The Swans walked seductively to the middle of the floor forming a triangle. The rhythm of feet with hand claps started the show, followed by dance movements and chants about how Beta Gamma Delta was the best fraternity on earth. The crowd enjoyed it. They clapped and shouted compliments.

A soft voice begin singing a song to the tune of "America the Beautiful" but substituted "Beta the Beautiful." It was Angel, she came. When she finished, someone yelled out, "Let's play ball!" The audience cheered with Jennifer cheering the loudest.

The Barons were next. They wore blue jeans; black, V-neck, cable- knit sweaters; and red shirts with black GQ ties. They started stomping and dancing saying things like how they wanted to be Beta men and how Beta Gamma Delta was the best fraternity in the whole goddamn world. They stopped abruptly. One shouted that he was hot and the rest said they were hot too. They removed their V-neck sweaters and the girls screamed. They unbuttoned their shirts and loosened their ties, exposing sweaty chests. The girls went wild.

The Baron named Cameron Johnson stood front and center. He slowly opened his shirt wider, showing off a smooth, brown, muscle-toned chest. The other Barons stomped their feet, making a rhythm pattern as the muscles in Cameron's chest pulsated with each beat. The girls screamed louder. The seriousness on his face added to the intensity.

The one named Brad walked forward and made a side stance. He yanked open his shirt. Buttons flew everywhere. Girls went after the buttons as if they were money. He pulled his shirt down over his muscular shoulders, exposing a hairy chest and a tight stomach. The girls walked forward as they screamed.

The one named Tony stood at the other side of Cameron. He allowed his hand to travel sensuously down his chest to his belt buckle. He flipped it out of the loop and so did the others. Girls screamed at the top of their lungs, grabbing at Barons, pleading with them to take it off.

The Betas performed last. The crowd was still going crazy from the Barons' show. It took awhile before everyone settled down. The Betas did some of their old routines and then the show was over.

Steve and Jennifer danced together slow and fast; then the dance was over. Steve invited Jennifer to the Barons' after-party, but she declined.

She spotted Lisa talking to one of the leather jackets who passed them earlier. Lisa nodded and the young woman left. Jennifer walked over to Lisa and asked, "Are you going back to the dorm?"

"Yeah, I guess. Boy did some ugly brothers come here tonight. This cat daddy with a big, gold tooth and brown, polyester pants with a matching 'Super Fly' shirt insulted me," Lisa complained.

"What did he say?" Jennifer asked.

"Girl, he asked me to dance!" Lisa said, looking outdone.

"What's wrong with him asking you to dance?"

"I don't need a reputation like you, a friend to the friendless. How come you're not going to the after-party? You need to be there since you're on court," Lisa said.

"I'm tired. The only thing they're going to do is drink and smoke weed. I refuse to wash my hair again, trying to get that smell out." Jennifer wanted to get back to see if Angel was okay. "Yeah Lisa, y'all threw down tonight. Angel laid the show out, didn't she?"

"I have to give it to the girl; she can put a show together. You know, I think you have a good chance at winning."

Jennifer was startled. She had a good chance at winning? Impossible. Linda Stevens was sure to win. She was very pretty and all the boys seemed to like her. If not Linda then Audrey Cole would take first place on her personality.

"I don't think I'm going to win Miss Beta, Miss Gamma or Miss Delta. I think it's going to be Linda or Audrey."

"Linda is a has-been and Audrey is too ugly. Betas like personality, but they are men first. Seriously, you've got an excellent chance at winning. You should have seen how the Betas were looking at you when you came into the room. I don't think you are aware of how you strutted in on Steve's arm." Lisa began to strut playfully. "Mark my word, it will be either you or Monica."

"But Monica doesn't belong to any organizations."

"She doesn't need to because she has enough confidence to stand alone. Monica has confidence, Jennifer. You better get it together before someone takes advantage of your innocence!" Lisa yelled.

They walked through the dorm doors. Some members from the Sigma Phi Pi sorority were in the lobby. The Sigmas were jealous of every sorority. Some of their members started off nice, but after awhile, they cliqued with the others and developed bad attitudes. Some had tried pledging the other two popular sororities, but were rejected or dropped line. They looked at Lisa and Jennifer and turned their heads. The whispered amongst themselves then one burst into laughter.

Jennifer looked at the floor as she walked towards the hallway. Lisa yelled out, "Thank God the Betas are forced to pick a girl from each sorority because some sororities would never be invited." Jennifer and Lisa hurried up the steps to avoid the name callings and comments.

They were on the second floor where the Phi Kappa Psi members lived. They were the most stuck up girls on campus, which made them unpopular with some of the girls and liked by a lot of the boys on campus. They conducted themselves formally. They appeared to be distant. They barely supported any other organizations' functions, except the Alpha Theta Lambda sorority. The Kappas had a reputation of being "easy," but it was reputation only because they stayed to themselves. A lot of them came from well-to-do families. Angel was one of the few Kappas who was outgoing and that wasn't saying much.

The Alphas were known as "sisters with an attitude," which made them popular with the girls on campus and unpopular with some of the boys. They were lively girls who attended a lot of the parties on campus. Most of them were business majors, which became evident in how they conducted sorority business. Some organizations allowed people to attend their activities for free after a certain time had elapse, but not the Alphas. They charged up to the last minute. They were given the nickname the "money making heffas" by the other sororities.

Jennifer took off toward her room. Lisa pulled her arm, "Let's go to Gina's room." Jennifer was uncomfortable around Gina because she was opinionated. Lisa really liked Gina because she had an "I don't give a damn" attitude.

"I don't think I want to go upstairs with all of those Alphas. They're always talking about somebody."

"At least they say it in front of their faces instead of behind their backs like the Kappas. Come on, let's go," Lisa prodded. She needed support because she had to put forth her best effort. Jennifer went reluctantly. As they approached the third floor, they could hear a lot of laughing and "honey, please."

Lisa took a deep breath and knocked on the door. One of the girls inside opened the door slowly. "Come in. Hey Lisa, it was a good show tonight," the girl said.

"What's up y'all?" Lisa said happily. "Y'all like the show?"

"It was *bad*, Lees. Y'all threw down," one of the girls said and giggled.

"Those Barons are fine. Tell them the next time they unbutton their shirts, I'm taking them off. They got their nerve teasing somebody," said another.

"Damn, Lisa. Why did the Betas put on that old ass show when everybody else was jamming? That shit was old," said the girl who opened the door. Gina's flesh crawled after hearing her sorority sister curse. She wondered what was up.

"Angel put together our show and the Betas put together their show. That should explain it. Y'all got something to drink?" Lisa asked.

"There's a cup on the dresser and some Alpha punch in the jug," said Gina. There were five girls in the room. They were lively and friendly.

"You're looking good, Jennifer. What are you trying to do, steal Angel's man?" one of the girls teased. They all began to tease Jennifer.

"Did you see how Steve was walking with her? He acted like she was his woman," one said.

"I know it, girl. They were dancing together. Looking all cozy. I better keep my man away from you because if you don't have a problem taking your roommate's man, I know you won't have one taking mine." They all laughed, except Jennifer. She had not made herself comfortable.

"Did Marsha go to the after-party?" Lisa asked.

"Um-hum. She's trying to make a last ditch effort to win," Gina said and they all laughed including Jennifer.

"Jennifer, why didn't you go?" one of the girls asked.

"I didn't feel like it," Jennifer said, slightly irritated.

"What's your problem? You should be there dancing and prancing, skinning and grinning. I know I would," said one of the girls.

"Did you see the chest on Cameron Johnson? I thought I was going to die! That brother is *bad*," said one of the girls.

Lisa got a cup of punch and sat down. She felt comfortable but something told her to keep her mouth shut. Jennifer was still standing. "You can sit down, Jennifer. We won't bite," said the girl who opened the door. "We had our rabies shot last week," said another girl and they all laughed loudly. Jennifer sat down.

"Did y'all see that 'fuck me' dress Linda had on?" one of the girls asked. They all laughed again, except Jennifer and Gina.

"What's up with tired looking Audrey? Was she the best choice from the Sigmas?" one asked.

"Maybe she'll let Stevie Wonder do her hair tomorrow, at least she will have an excuse," another said and the laughter got louder.

"You looked hot tonight, Jennifer. I think you're going to walk away with the crown this year," said Gina, slightly annoyed with the attitudes of the others in the room.

Jennifer looked at Gina with surprise. "You really think so?"

"It's either going to be you or Monica, but I say it will be you."

"Maybe she'll believe you, Gina, because I told her the same thing," said Lisa.

"But there's a twist. If Linda Stevens doesn't place and you win, you are fried once you pledge Kappa. The same thing happened to your roommate when she won the crown of Miss Lambda," Gina said, trying to scare Jennifer.

"I remembered that," said one of the girls. "She and Lori Bass were real tight. Lori's hot butt thought she was going to win but, huh, the Lambdas showed her what time it was. Angel was queen and Lori was honorable mention. The honorable thing to do was to mention her," the girl said and everyone laughed.

"When Angel pledged Kappa, they kicked her ass," one added.

"I remembered the time when Lori called Angel to her room for a pajama party. Angel had to stand up all night long and watch Lori sleep. She had to be a 'guardian Angel.' If it were me, I would have smothered her ass," the first girl said.

"I would have dropped line. But Angel wanted to keep alive the legacy of her dead mother," Gina said.

Jennifer became fascinated with the discussion. Angel told Jennifer a little about her mother. She died when Angel was six years old. Her father took her from her grandmother shortly after the accident. He didn't remarry until Angel was twelve years old. Jennifer wanted to know more about the one person she admired most.

"Gina, what kind of person is Angel?" Jennifer asked.

"Angel is sharp and smart. The sister just has a lot on her mind. She's trying to live with the death of her mother and little sister."

"Little sister? I didn't know Angel had a little sister," Jennifer said.

"The little sister was supposed to have died in the car accident with her mother, but Angel never remembered the body ever being buried. Angel said she remembered crying when her mother didn't take her along. Her mother promised to buy her some ice cream, but she never came home. She told me that she wished they all would have died together," Gina said in a soft voice.

"That's deep. She doesn't seem like she wants to die. She act as if she's royalty," Lisa said.

"It's just an act. She doesn't like to get too close to people. A lot of girls were jealous of her in high school as well as in college. She doesn't have to do anything but exist and sisters get excited," Gina said.

"Well, I can't stand her," Lisa said, getting too comfortable. Everyone fell silent. Lisa continued, "She trips too much. The girl is a bitch." All eyes fell upon Lisa. "Hey I call 'em like I see 'em. She's a bitch. Why y'all looking all crazy?"

Gina looked insulted. "When is your interview?"

"Wednesday at six thirty," Lisa said.

Gina's tone changed from soft and explaining to stern. "Why do you want to pledge Alpha?"

"Y'all are the most together group on campus. Y'all are down to earth and about business," Lisa said.

"Let me give you a tip young lady. When you come to our interview, you come in speaking like you have a high school education. I don't want to hear "y'all so cool" or "y'all down to earth". You are definitely correct when you said we are about business because the sorority business takes precedence."

Although Lisa was tough and could take punches, Gina was her idol and hearing this from her was painful. Lisa mustered up enough strength to speak, "Under no circumstances did I ever consider disrespecting your sorority. I find your innuendos inane." Lisa stood. "You ladies must excuse me, I have to go. Thanks for the punch." She and Jennifer walked to the door. The room was silent.

Before Lisa walked out the door Gina said, "I know Angel is a bitch but that bitch happens to be my cousin. I take family business just as seriously as sorority business. See you Wednesday at six thirty?"

"I'll be there," Lisa said without looking back.

"To be on time is to be late," one of the girls said.

"I'm never late," Lisa said and closed the door.

The Alphas looked at Gina for a response. She said nothing. "What do you think now? You got her worked up," said one of the girls.

"She'll work out. She only talked about Angel. It's personal," Gina said unflinching.

"We can't afford having her call other sorority members bitches. We have always been even kilt with the Kappas and everyone else for that matter," another said.

"She's too lax Gina. If I had heard her say 'y'all' one more time, I was going to scream," one said.

"We know she can use words with more than one syllable. 'I find your innuendos inane.' That's impressive," another said.

"You ladies didn't help much by cursing like sailors. I said make the atmosphere comfortable, not uncouth. What was this, a set up or sabotage? And you with 'It was *bad*, Lees.' Where in the hell did you get that from?" Gina said in anger.

"I heard some Epsilon Sweethearts call her Lees!" the young woman said in defense.

"Anyway, Angel was impressed with the way she handled the Swans and Doves situation. It could have been a fraternity war. Her own friend started the confusion and she was able to convince the Doves to give a bake sale with the Swans in a show of unity. I like that!"

Gina Smith was a senior and seriously preparing herself for the workforce. She was very smart and a hard worker. She worked during the school year as well as during the summer. She took pride in her appearance. She wore very nice clothes and was one of the few girls who paid to have her short hair styled while others relied on their roommates.

Gina was fairly tall and slightly hippy. She was coffee brown with small eyes that went well with her small face. It was her decision to look serious so no one could see her pretty wide smile. Her personality was dominating, but the other girls did not seem to mind. She wasn't glamorous, but her attitude convinced everyone that she was.

Jennifer and Lisa walked down the hall in silence until Jennifer said, "What time are you going to the ball tomorrow? I thought we could walk over together."

"They are going to have someone pick you up. You won't be walking in a ball gown." They were at Lisa's room. "See you tomorrow," Lisa said and opened the door.

"Lisa, don't let Gina upset you."

"I'm not upset," Lisa said angrily.

"Yes you are. Let's talk about it."

"Talk about what? Talk about how everybody likes you? Or would you like to talk about how people don't give a shit about me even when I don't do anything to piss them off. What do you want to talk about because I don't feel like talking!" Lisa shouted.

"I didn't know Gina and Angel were cousins either."

"Who cares! Good night, I'm going to bed." Before Lisa closed the door,

Jennifer snuck in behind. She didn't know what to say to Lisa. She could not leave her alone.

Lisa began undressing but stopped. She sat on the bed and put her head in her hands. Jennifer sat beside her and put her arms around Lisa.

"I hate this damn school," Lisa mumbled.

"Me too. It's so boring. There's nothing to do but pledge these damn sororities," Jennifer said.

Lisa's head shot up. "You don't sound right cussing. It's not you."

"It's not you either," Jennifer said in defense. "You're not all that tough. You have feelings like everyone else. You try so hard to hang with the fast crowd. You're just as green as I am so admit it."

"You don't know what I've gone through."

"You don't know what I've gone through either. Just because I don't act tough or curse doesn't mean I've lived a sheltered life."

Lisa went to the dresser and pulled out a big shirt. She opened her closet and took out a pillow. She tossed the two to Jennifer.

"Lisa, why did you come to Missouri State?"

"To meet you."

"Get serious. Everyone says you could have gone almost anywhere."

"Since you are listening to everyone else, ask them why. You can sleep at the foot of the bed."

"Why is it when I try to get serious, you play me off? I tell you my innermost secrets."

"I don't recall you telling me anything sacred," Lisa said, trying to snuggle under the covers in the small bed.

"I told you that I had a crush on Brad Morris," Jennifer said while shifting on her side, adjusting the covers.

"Yeah, right, some secret. Not only do you have a crush on Brad, but half the damn school does too," Lisa said while relaxing under the covers.

"I told you that I hate it when Angel uses my things," Jennifer said, shifting to the other side, still trying to get comfortable.

"Secrets are things you wouldn't tell anybody. What's up with this sweet sixteen bull?"

"You're the only one I've told this sweet sixteen bull to. Forget it. I don't care why you came here."

Lisa sighed. She had never told anyone why she chose Missouri State. Harvard University offered her a minority scholarship and so did Stanford. She was afraid to tell people, but she trusted Jennifer because she was sensitive and polite. She would never insult her the way other people have done in the past.

"My grandmother chose Missouri State," Lisa said irritated.

"Why?" Jennifer asked perplexed.

"She said I would find what I am looking for."

"What are you looking for?"

"Answers," said a trembling Lisa. She was looking for answers to the past, but she couldn't tell anybody.

"Could you have found them at another university?"

"No."

Jennifer's forehead creased. She was relieved knowing Lisa could not see her expression. "Why not?" Jennifer asked.

"My grandmother believes in spiritual forces that are here to guide us. She prayed and asked God to give her a sign about my education. He did. Missouri State."

"What was the sign?"

"A phone call. Good night, Jennifer," Lisa said and relaxed.

Jennifer did not want the conversation to end. "What did your grandmother say about spiritual forces and signs?"

"My grandmother said you must first believe in a power greater than yourself. Once you believe in that force, then you must believe that you are here for a purpose. You are given signs to help you through this existence. If you second-guess yourself, then you don't believe in spiritual guidance. If you are wrong on your first impulse, the spirit is helping to fine-tune your analytical reasoning or your sixth sense."

"That's deep. She said all that?" asked an inquisitive Jennifer.

"Not in those words, but in my research, I equate Miss Mattie's philosophy to what I've told you. Bon soir Mademoiselle," said a tired Lisa.

"How long has it taken you to get to the point of believing," continued a fired up Jennifer.

"Who said I've arrived?" said an annoyed Lisa.

"It seems like you know where you're going."

"Sometimes looks are deceiving. Good night, Jennifer," Lisa said.

"How come you call your grandmother Miss Mattie?"

"Everybody calls her Miss Mattie. She's not my real grandmother. She raised me after my mother died. I call her Grandma Mattie, too. She's really a special person, a little different, but special. Good night," Lisa said conclusively.

Jennifer knew better than to press her luck. "Good night, Lisa and thanks!"

"For what?"

"For being my friend and a good one at that."

"Oh please! Get some rest so that your eyes won't be too puffy in the morning."

They both chuckled and Lisa turned off the lamp.

Chapter 4

All the dorms were buzzing with excitement surrounding the night's event. Rooms were busy with girls running in and out. The Barons' Ball was a sell out and students were still trying to get tickets for fear they may miss something spectacular. Angel slowly began participating in the main event. She was making sure Jennifer's debut would be flawless. Angel made the cleaners press Jennifer's gown to the point that it stood by itself. Angel did inventory on the gloves, slip, panty hose, makeup, perfume and money. Jennifer didn't understand why she might need money, but Angel told her she should never go anywhere without cabfare.

Jennifer rehearsed the curtsey until she became exhausted. She practiced her entrance and smiling. She practiced how she would react if she were to win. Angel assured Jennifer that the practice was necessary to run on automatic without thinking. Angel was rehearsing and grooming her to what she entitled "a very important time in her life."

Angel had Jennifer take a nap around two o'clock. When she awoke, someone had brought her a hamburger with two glasses of water. Jennifer practiced eating slowly. Angel wanted Jennifer half full so that she wouldn't eat very much later.

As Jennifer showered, she hummed, letting the hot water hit her back and legs. She concentrated on the water hitting her body. It rolled off her shoulders and down her chest. It felt good. For the first time in her life, she felt special. People were making a fuss over her, waiting on her hand and foot, pampering her. Now she knew why Angel carried herself with royalty. People treated her the way she acted.

"Jennifer, hurry up. It's almost five o'clock!" Lisa shouted as she banged on the door. Jennifer ignored the demand and continued to enjoy the shower. The door opened and Jennifer heard a familiar soft voice, "Jennifer, please hurry, you will be late."

Jennifer perked up. "Okay, I'm almost ready." The door closed. Jennifer turned off the water and stepped out of the tub. The mirror was steamed from the moisture. She took a towel and wiped it.

She saw herself, but this time she looked hard. The vision of an African princess came to mind. The yellow towel wrapped around her head posed as a royal headdress. She looked at her well-shaped arms and how her collarbone jutted from her chest. Angel said the rhinestone necklace was going to look great around her neck. She looked at the roundness of her breasts. Her brown skin glistened from the water. As she wiped the water with her hands, she noticed the softness of her skin. Someone knocked on the door before she could finish exploring. "Okay, I'm coming," she said.

She dried off quickly and wrapped the towel around her body like she had seen Angel do so often. She made her entrance into the room. Angel motioned her to sit on a chair in front of the dresser that had a mirror so Jennifer could see the transformation.

Lisa applied a mud mask while Dee Dee filed Jennifer's nails. "Angel, what color should I polish her nails?" Dee Dee asked.

"Give them the French look," Lisa responded. She looked at Angel apologetically.

"French sounds good," Angel said smiling.

"I don't know how to give a French manicure," Dee Dee whined.

"I have a French manicure kit in my closet. Use the white chalk pencil under her nails instead of the white polish. Will someone plug in my curling irons?" Angel ordered. Lisa rushed to the demand. She went into the bathroom and ran hot water on a hand towel. She removed the excess water and hastily placed it on Jennifer's face. She shrieked.

"I'm sorry. I didn't want to ruin the mask," Lisa explained.

Angel removed the towel from around Jennifer's head and took the rollers out of her hair. She parted Jennifer's hair from ear to ear, across the middle and swarmed the top portion into a very short beehive. She brushed around the edges to smooth the appearance. A rat tail comb came next to loosened the curls at the bottom half, letting them fall down her back.

Jennifer looked at herself in the mirror. The hairstyle made her eyes slant and her neck appear longer. Lisa applied moisturizer to Jennifer's face, followed by press powder to remove the shine. While Lisa dusted Jennifer's face with powder, she tried opening her eyes. "Keep your eyes shut," Lisa complained. Someone knocked on the door. Angel rushed to open it. More girls came into the room.

"We came to see Jennifer's dress," one said.

"Yeah, I heard it is *bad*," said another one.

The rumor of Jennifer's dress had spread like wildfire. Angel designed the dress and had it made. She worked at Linda's mother's boutique during the summers. Angel's designs were on the line of formal wear from old movies, which she loved. Jennifer's gown was a black and white, strapless, taffeta gown with a black, wide sash forming a big bow at the side. The bottom ballooned under the sash. The dress sparkled when the light hit it at various angles. Angel bought black onyx rhinestone earrings; long, black evening gloves; and silver shoes with a small silver evening bag to match.

The intercom sounded a visitor signal for student B. It was for Jennifer. The girls gasped. "They are here already?" Angel asked nervously.

"They can wait fifteen minutes. Here put this on," Lisa said anxiously and handed Jennifer a tube of plum-colored lipstick and rushed out of the room.

"Do you think they will get mad if they have to wait long?" Jennifer asked Angel.

"Honey, please! Men like waiting on women. It gives them something to complain about. If we were always on time, they wouldn't have anything to be mad about. So it's our duty to keep them fussing," one girl said.

"I heard that!" one said. Dee Dee held her hand up for five. The girl who made the comment jumped up and hit Dee Dee's hand. All the girls laughed.

Angel took the jewelry out of the boxes and gave the earrings to Jennifer to put on. Angel took the necklace and placed it around Jennifer's neck. The sparkles from the jewelry caught her attention in the mirror. The colors almost hypnotized her. Lisa walked in looking disgusted. Jennifer looked nervous. "Did you tell them I'll be ready in a few minutes?"

"It was Kyle," said an angry Lisa.

"What did he want?"

"He came to take you to the ball, Cinderella. I sent his ass away," Lisa said sarcastically and continued with the makeup.

"That is one strange brother," Dee Dee said.

"What's wrong with a strange man?" asked the girl who made the earlier comment. "I like strange men. Like I've always said, the stranger the better. I bet Kyle is a freak. Brothers like him that keep their heads in them damn books gits all kinds of ideas running through their minds. Yeah, give me a strange man any day. Especially a *freak*...ahhh freak out; Let's freak; C'ést chic; Freak out...." Vernise sang and moved her hips provocatively. Angel frowned and Jennifer turned her head.

"Vernise, you are so wild. Anyway, I bet Kyle is a virgin and the only thing he has had is a book. He probably doesn't know what to do with it," one said.

"Well, he better learn because you know what they say about skinny men with big feet," Vernise said.

Lisa turned around and asked, "What do they say about skinny men with big feet?"

"They say that shit be hangin' long like ten inches soft, so imagine what it's like hard. Let me hook up with Kyle," Vernise said and continued to dance.

"The way you act, Vernise, you will probably scare poor Kyle," one said.

"I'm telling you the nigga is a *freak*," Vernise said but she stopped dancing and singing. She tilted her head to the side and dropped her bottom lip. She eyed Jennifer suspiciously. "Why would Kyle come to take to you to the ball? Y'all ain't messin' around, are you? I don't want to be steppin' on somebody's toes," Vernise said, rolling her eyes.

"Jennifer ain't got nothing going on with Kyle. He's just crazy," Lisa said in defense.

Jennifer tried to ignore them by asking, "So Kyle is coming to the ball?"

"Yes, but it didn't look like it," Lisa said while finishing her art work.

"What do you mean?" Jennifer asked.

"He had on a short-sleeve, yellow shirt," Lisa said with her eyes closed.

"Girl stop! No he didn't," one of the girls said in shock. "You have gotsta be kidding."

"He had on a wide, brown tie that looked like a bib, with a pair of beige

Poly and Ester pants that flared at the bottom. Brother was committing fashion violations all over the place," Lisa said. She threw her hands up in disgust.

"Like I said, y'all are going to be lined up once y'all find out how much Kyle is slangin' in them damn Poly and Ester pants," said Vernise and the other girls giggled.

Angel removed the gown from the cleaner's bag. Vernise shouted, "Damn, that dress is *bad*! Did you really design it, Angel?"

"Why don't you ladies go downstairs and wait in the lobby? You will be able to get a better view of everyone. It is too crowded in this room. Jennifer needs some air before she begins to perspire," Angel said gently.

"Oh sure. We'll see y'all later," Vernise said apologetically and beckoned the others to leave.

"It's almost six o'clock. Step into your slip and we will lower the dress over your head," Angel said nervously to Jennifer. She stretched her arms over her head as the three girls carefully lowered the dress. Angel zipped the dress at the side and snapped the bow in place. She smoothed over Jennifer's hair and stepped back. All the girls stared in amazement at their creation.

"How do I look?" Jennifer asked. Lisa turned her to face the mirror. Jennifer looked at herself. "I look so...different," she said.

"Please say it Jennifer. Just say it once," Lisa pleaded.

"I look beautiful tonight," Jennifer said with a little smile. The girls clapped.

"Tonight and every night, sweetie," Angel said.

The intercom signalled a visitor for student 'B. Jennifer looked at them as if she were to never see them again. "It's show time," she said with courage. Each girl hugged her.

"Remember Jennifer, when you drink, place the glass on the inside of your lower lip to keep from ruining your lipstick. Do not talk a lot and do not laugh at everything. Smile constantly and make sure you compliment each contestant. Whoever escorts you does not own you. Under no circumstances do you go home with anyone and I mean anyone," Angel preached. Jennifer nodded after each statement.

Angel handed Jennifer the cape. She was about to put it on before Angel stopped her. "Let your escort help you with it. Make sure he takes it off, too. Lisa, will you and Dee Dee walk Jennifer to the lobby? Wait a minute," Angel said. She carefully rubbed glittered perfume lotion on Jennifer's shoulders, chest and neck. Angel sighed, "Okay, I'm finished." The three girls looked wide eyed at Angel. She was a nervous wreck.

Lisa turned to Jennifer. "Mademoiselle, are you ready?"

Jennifer smiled and they walked down the hall. As they passed the other girls who were rushing to get ready, Jennifer received compliments and girls wishing her well. Someone took her picture.

Steve was waiting in the lobby in a black, double-breasted suit. He turned around when he heard the girls in the lobby get excited. He looked at Jennifer and smiled his biggest smile. He took her cape and placed it around her shoulders. They left the dorm and walked to Steve's car. Another girl was sitting in the back seat. Another Baron was sitting in the front. Steve opened the back door and helped Jennifer inside.

A friendly voice said, "Hello Jennifer."

"Hello Monica, you look very nice."

"Thank you and so do you."

"Thank you."

Steve drove carefully to the Betas' house. Everyone was talking and soft music was playing in the background. Thomas Parker greeted Monica as her evening escort and walked her into the living room where all the other guests were relaxing. Meanwhile, Jennifer and Steve waited patiently in the foyer for her escort.

"Hello, beautiful. I will be your escort this evening," he said while bowing.

Jennifer spoke softly, "Hello Lionel." She could not believe Lionel Johnson was escorting her. She thought Tim Rylander would be the one.

Lionel, like all the other Betas, was wearing a tuxedo. The ones escorting girls wore tails with red bow ties and red cummerbunds. His hair was cut low and his mustache trimmed. To her, he was handsome, but the tuxedo made him look elegant. He was tall and slim like most Betas at Missouri State. Their members were usually athletes. He had a soft golden brown complexion with naturally wavy hair. His face was squared. His eyebrows were thin over deep set dark eyes. He had full lips that emphasized his always present smile. His misfit baritone voice completed the picture.

Lionel was particular about whom he dated. No one had seen him with a steady. The ones he was seen with were usually sophisticated, but not necessarily pretty. They weren't too aggressive either. He had noticed Jennifer while participating in various fraternity events. She appeared invisible. She didn't care to be the center of attention, but it seemed as if she yearned for it. He had become attracted to her merely by being in her presence.

Lionel removed Jennifer's cape. His eyes could not leave her bare shoulders. She was a class act and he wanted to show her off. His staring made her squirm. He robbed her space by standing very close. When he talked, it was low and behind her, forcing her turn to hear. He was able to get a good look at his evening prize. "I'm sorry, the Beta's National President was not available this evening. I hope that I will make good company," he said charmingly.

"I asked for the best. I must say 'well done' to Beta Gamma Delta," Jennifer responded. Her confidence was beginning to cement. Surprisingly, the comment not only knocked Lionel off balance but it caught his interest. She never made advances toward him like the other girls. She treated him as if he were an ordinary person. He remembered the first time he called her cute. She said "thank you" and kept walking without missing a beat. Now, the other girls would throw themselves at him in hopes of getting a date. Some had offered to go to bed with him, just to be with him.

"Can we join the others?" Jennifer asked.

"Do you care for some wine or champagne?"

"I don't drink."

"Can I make a suggestion for a beginner?"

"Only if you are a connoisseur."

"I was thinking in terms of a gingerale punch with papaya and lemon juice. Can I get you some?"

"Sounds great...uh, yes. Thank you."

Lionel chuckled. "I don't drink either." He disappeared and came back with punch in a wine glass. He watched as Jennifer sipped the punch. Her chest expanded noticeably when she took a breath after each drink. Her brown skin sparkled. Her lips were very sexy to him, but something gnawed him in the stomach as he sized her up.

"What time are we leaving?" she asked.

Lionel looked at his watch. "Any minute now. Are you excited?"

"Yes I am," she said with the biggest smile.

He saw how her eyes danced when she spoke. "Let's go in the other room," he said. They joined the others. All the contestants were filled with anticipation, except one. She sat relaxed as she talked to the Betas. She was accustomed to the court scene.

Thomas, who was president before Lionel, walked over to the pair. "Jennifer, you look extremely nice tonight. Will you save me a dance?"

"It would be my pleasure," she said smiling.

"Only after I'm tired," Lionel added.

Both Thomas and Lionel were seniors preparing to go away to law school in the fall. They had been good friends since their sophomore year when they pledged together. Their attention went to a young woman who sashayed toward them. She wore a red, halter- back dress with a diamond cut front. This dress, like most of her dresses, was form fitting. It was straight with a split in the back. She stepped in front of Jennifer. "Hello Lionel. I don't remember you speaking to me," she said.

Before Lionel could speak, a meek voice behind her said, "Hello Linda. You look very nice tonight."

Linda half turned with a half smile. "Hello Jennifer and how are you tonight?"

"Fine, thank you."

"Linda, may I say you look extraordinary," Lionel flirted.

"I hope you will save me a dance," she said, brushing her fingers down his collar.

"Oh, I will," he said and smiled.

"Ta-Ta," Linda said and walked away, ignoring Jennifer.

Thomas leaned close and whispered to Lionel, "Looks like you won't have to work so hard for a date afterwards."

"Yes, I see," Lionel whispered back with suspicion.

It was time to go. Two Barons rode in front while a Beta and a contestant rode in the back. Ten cars were in a line with two Barons standing at each open door. Jennifer felt like Cinderella. This was a good sign. The evening was going to be the best time of her life.

She and Lionel rode in the first car. Once they arrived at the Student

Union, the show began. It was a mini version of the academy awards. Who was escorting whom would be the topic.

A Baron jumped out and opened the door for Lionel. Steve, the other Baron, opened the door for Jennifer. Lionel walked around and extended his hand through the open door. Jennifer appeared. The crowd went wild with cheers. Jennifer was performing on automatic. She rehearsed the scene repeatedly. She smiled and waved at friends. Lionel nodded, acknowledging compliments. He stopped Jennifer and they posed for pictures. Jennifer's heart raced in the ambience of royalty.

Jennifer surveyed the crowd for Angel and Lisa, but they were nowhere in sight. For the first time, Jennifer saw jealousy and envy. As she smiled at girls, they would turn their heads. Some smiled back or just stared. As she and Lionel led the parade through the Student Union, another crowd formed. When Lionel approached a large group of young men from other fraternities, he stopped Jennifer and removed her cape, exposing her bare shoulders. They roared with comments.

Jennifer gave him a confused look. He whispered, "It is called revenge." She still could not make the connection. She figured it was a male thing. She looked to her right and there stood Gina, Lisa and Angel. All three had witnessed the performance of the male ego. They smiled as she walked by, except Angel.

Jennifer spotted Kyle standing alone near the restrooms. She smiled and waved. He smiled back and nodded his head. She stopped running on automatic and beckoned for him, but he shook his head, declining the offer. He looked like a fish out of water. She looked at him a little longer before turning her head.

"Did you see that?" Lisa said with surprise. "The heffa beckoned to Kyle and waved us off like ghetto crawlers. She's trippin'."

"Let her have this evening. You will have your chance next year," Gina told Lisa. She kept quiet until she sat for dinner.

Most girls dreamed of being on the Beta's court because the Beta's went all out to make a success of their biggest event of the year. They raised enough money to award a five-hundred-dollar scholarship to an incoming male freshman. Although the Lambda fraternity gave larger scholarships, their efforts were minuscule in comparison to the Betas.

Jennifer was ready to take a bite into her dinner. For some reason, she wasn't hungry. She heard students complaining about the food. Some called it dog meat and taunted the student servers. She and Lionel talked and danced the entire evening. Although Angel warned her about talking too much, she could not keep quiet. Lionel wanted to know her opinion on politics, business and personal relationships. She felt comfortable discussing the first two but pleaded the fifth on the last. She told him that discussing something as intimate as relationships was too personal, especially to a stranger.

"Oh, I'm a stranger?" Lionel teased.

Jennifer laughed. "Let me explain," she pleaded while laughing. She was too embarrassed to tell him that she never had a boyfriend so she could not speak on the subject with authority. *Thank God he played it off*, she thought.

"That's quite all right. I'll put my candy away, little girl," he said, trying to recoup. He realized he might be moving too fast because she seemed uneasy. Other girls freely discussed dating, marriage and children.

Lionel enjoyed the debate they had when she challenged him on his career choice. She told him that the courtroom was filled with black criminal lawyers and that he should try corporate law. She also told him that she did not see him as a lawyer. He would make a better business man. No other girl told him anything different from what they thought he wanted to hear, except Angel.

"So what kind of business man do you think I should be?" he asked curiously. He chose law because of Thomas' constant prodding.

Jennifer looked into his eyes and said, "Maybe something in marketing. You like to show off. You don't mind being the center of attention or letting someone else get the attention as long as you are connected in some form or fashion. Your presence attracts people."

"Are you calling me conceited?" asked a concerned Lionel in a very low voice.

Jennifer shook her head wildly. "Of course not! You are quite comfortable with your appearance. Conceited people are insecure," she said, hoping she hadn't insulted him.

He smiled as she tried desperately to express herself. He knew she didn't mean to insult him. He was concerned about her impression of him. He had hoped she didn't find him conceited because so many girls accused him of being stuck up. "So marketing people are secure individuals who can draw an audience? It sounds more like a politician," he said pleasantly.

Jennifer grinned. "Lawyers can make excellent politicians, only if they're clean," she said and looked around the room thinking of a way to salvage the conversation.

Lionel looked at the beautiful woman sitting beside him. She was prettier than he had imagined. She looked so honest and sincere. As he reached to touch her, something stood in the way. He pulled his hand back.

"I see you as a tax preparer or an IRS auditor. You will call me into your office, 'Mr. Johnson, there is a problem with your return. You owe back taxes'," he said in a high-pitched voice. "Then I, on the other hand, will try to charm you into going easy on me," he teased and covered her hand with his. It made him shiver so he eased it away.

Jennifer looked at him and blinked her eyes. "You sound like Barry White."

Lionel chuckled and then laughed out loud. "Hey Thomas, she called me Barry White," he teased.

"Wait a minute, I said you *sound* like Barry White," she chuckled.

Thomas turned around and joined the discussion. He helped Lionel tease Jennifer. She was having a great time while Monica sat still and smiled the entire time.

The Barons summoned the girls outside the room. They were ready to make the presentation of the new Miss Beta. Jennifer was so relaxed that she began to tease Lionel again. "You're not going to leave me on the floor when I curtsey, are you?"

"You don't want to be with a stranger, do you?" he teased back.

"I see you are not going to let me forget what I said."

"I will give you an opportunity to redeem yourself."

A baron excused himself and asked Lionel and Jennifer to take the seventh spot by standing behind Tim Rylander and Linda Stevens. As they began discussing the impact of Ronald Reagan winning the presidency, Linda turned around and tapped Lionel on the shoulder. "Have you forgotten about our dance?" she asked.

"Why of course not, Miss Stevens. You seemed preoccupied with the other suitors. I hope I'm forgiven," he said with a smile.

"I will give you an opportunity to redeem yourself," she said with a catty grin and turned around. The comment didn't bother Jennifer because she was flying high on excitement.

"We are number seven, Jennifer. It has always been my lucky number," Lionel said. Jennifer remembered another conversation she and Lisa had about "signs." This had to be one she concluded.

A hush came over the crowd when the announcer spoke. Jennifer looked at her competition. No one was prettier than anyone. No one had bad skin or crooked teeth or any physical deformities. She thought earlier that Linda was the winner. She realized that her earlier observation was wrong. Even Lionel felt that Linda was a nuisance. Jennifer's attention came back to the Ball when she heard the sorority call of the Kappas. She would be next to enter the room. She went back on automatic.

"Next we have representing the Beta Swans..." the audience cheered. "Miss Jennifer Peterson." Lionel extended his arm and smile.

Cameras flashed as Jennifer and Lionel passed by. He walked her to the spot to curtsey the reigning Miss Beta. Jennifer performed it like clock work; step out to the side; step back; go down slowly leading with the chest. Once the chest touches the knee, bow the head for three seconds.

Jennifer went all the way down to the floor, a full curtsey to the reigning Miss Beta. Jennifer's head was down with her arms extended out. The audience cheered louder. No one did a curtsey to the floor. They all bended at the waist, nodding their heads.

Lionel, being a showman, stood back so the audience could view the performance. He let Jennifer gather the applause and helped her up. They walked to her chair and Lionel took his place behind it.

After announcing the last contestant, the Master of Ceremonies allowed the audience to take pictures for ten minutes. There were whispers and low chatter.

"This is the moment you all have been waiting for. In third place with the title of Miss Delta, representing Alpha Theta Lambda Sorority, Incorporated is Miss Marsha Lewis."

The Alphas shrilled with delight. Marsha took her place at the left of the reigning Miss Beta. "In second place with the title of Miss Gamma, representing the Beta Swans, is Miss Jennifer Peterson."

A camera caught Jennifer's mouth opened. It was like a dream come true. As far as she was concerned, she had won. Lionel escorted her to the chair at the right of the reigning Miss Beta. Jennifer was given roses, a trophy and a gift-wrapped box. She was no longer on automatic. Although she had rehearsed this moment, she did not believe it while practicing.

The audience applauded as Thomas escorted Monica to the queen's chair. The reigning Miss Beta crowned Monica. She cried and so did Jennifer. The two hugged one another while cameras continued flashing. After ten minutes, the crowd of picture takers sat and Thomas escorted Monica to the floor for the court dance. The others followed.

Lionel saw the joy in Jennifer's face mixed with tears. You would have thought she had won the title. He was the one who nominated her to represent the Beta Swans. She beat Thomas' nominee, Lisa, by three votes. Jennifer and Monica tied for queen. Lionel had to determine who would represent the fraternity as Miss Beta Gamma Delta. He selected Monica. He figured Jennifer would have other opportunities to win queen for other fraternities and since it was Monica's senior year, she deserved to be a queen. She was extremely pleasant, articulate and politically active on campus.

Lionel held Jennifer close. He then kissed her softly on the forehead. The grinding feeling came back as he reminisced on the conversation with Thomas earlier...

"Hey Lionel, do you think you'll get a chance to bust that tender ass tonight?" Thomas asked.

"She's more like a child than a woman. What makes you think I want to screw everything that's interested in me?" Lionel responded.

"Well you got a point. She's got taboo written all over her. You might end up paying again."

Lionel held Jennifer close until the song was over. Students quickly crowded the court giving congratulations. Jennifer saw Lisa dancing with Cameron, talking a mile a minute. He did not seem to mind. In fact, he looked as if he enjoyed her rambling.

The Ball was over. Lionel could not wait any longer. He whispered in Jennifer's ear, "Let's go for a ride." She looked at him and smiled in agreement. She rushed through the crowd to Lisa.

"Excuse me," Jennifer said, pulling Lisa away from Cameron. "Will you take my things back to the dorm?" Jennifer asked while placing the gifts in Lisa's arms. Jennifer rushed around students, trying to get to Lionel but Lisa was on her heels.

"Where are you going?" Lisa asked, struggling with the items.

"Uh, Lionel is taking me to the after-party," Jennifer lied.

"There's no after-party," Lisa said and stopped. "Are you going home with Lionel?"

"I'm going for a ride, that's all," Jennifer said, trying to convince Lisa.

"Look Jennifer, you don't have to go anywhere with anyone. You don't owe anybody anything. You won on your own merits. What you need to do..." Lisa was cut off.

"It's just a ride. I'm not going to have sex with him. I'm getting a little tired of people telling me what to do," Jennifer snapped.

Lisa nodded. "No problem. See you in the morning," Lisa said and whisked the items away.

Jennifer felt a little guilty for snapping at Lisa but she wanted to go with Lionel. The evening had gone so well and nothing was going to stop the momentum. She saw Lionel in the hall waiting for her. She rushed to him. Before she could say anything, he kissed her on the lips openly. It took her breath away. It was warm and hungry. It wasn't like the kiss he gave her on the dance floor, which was friendly and gentle.

He took her hand and walked her to the back of the building and down the steps. Jennifer was lost. She had practiced what to do during the ball, but not after the ball. Angel told her not to go home with anyone, but she was going for a ride. He pressed his weight against her while kissing and stroking her neck. He ran his fingers through her curls. His hands gently swept over her shoulders and down her back. He pulled her closer, but again, the nagging feeling gripped his stomach which caused him to press harder, trying to ignore it.

At last she felt the hardness that so many girls gossiped about. It didn't make her feel good; it made her jittery. He made all efforts in forcing his tongue into her mouth. She began to breathe hard. Her body was running on automatic but her mind was at war. He continued with small kisses on her face and whispered, "Do you want to be with me?"

"I thought...we were going for a ride. I really don't want to do this."

He looked into her eyes. They weren't playing tricks nor were they lying. She really didn't want him that way. He smiled and said, "Taboo." He straighten his jacket and said, "Let me take you back to the dorm."

"You are not taking her anywhere. Let's go Jennifer," said an angry Angel. She and Gina witnessed the scene from up top.

"Hello, ladies. I didn't know you were watching," Lionel said and straightened his jacket again. Jennifer hung her head low. She felt ashamed and angry at herself. She could not face Angel or Lionel. He too was embarrassed. Never had anyone felt ashamed or embarrassed to be with him.

The scene paralyzed Jennifer. She could not move. Lionel reached for her arm to escort her up the stairs.

"Leave her alone," yelled Angel.

"Let's go Jennifer," Lionel said as he took her arm and walked her up the steps.

Angel moved in on Lionel, pushing his hand away. "You keep your goddamn hands off of her."

"Did the precious little Angel curse?" Lionel mocked. "You ladies have a nice evening." He tried walking away but he could not get around an angry Angel. She stood in his path.

"So what were you going to do, add her to the list?" Angel asked between clenched teeth.

"Let's not get into this, okay?"

"Why not? Don't you want her?"

"When I told you I was interested in her, it wasn't meant as a slap in your face. This doesn't need to be discuss..."

"You are not slapping *me* in the face, and if you want to date her, then fine."

Jennifer perked up. Lionel wanted to date her and Angel was angry about.

"Let's go, Jennifer," Gina said, trying to walk Jennifer away from the ugly scene, but Jennifer would not budge.

"Don't you have Steve to parade you around like a trophy? You don't need me," Lionel said, trying to maintain self control.

"You said you didn't want a serious relationship. You even went after my own cousin," Angel said.

"I said I didn't want to get married and further more, I didn't go after Gina. I took her out twice," Lionel said in defense.

Gina interrupted, "Wait a minute. I didn't know you two were seeing each other. Look Angel, don't bring me in this. I don't have anything to do with what you are talking about. Come on, Jennifer, let's go." Gina tried pulling Jennifer away from the soon to be uglier scene.

"You liked her dress didn't you? What about the jewelry and oh, don't forget the shoes," Angel said and lifted Jennifer's dress to show the shoes. "It's you, isn't it?" Angel said.

"No baby, that's you. That's your dress, your jewelry and your shoes. You wanted me to think about you while I was with her, didn't you?" Lionel said with a grin.

Swiftly, Angel slapped him hard across the face. He frowned and then grinned. "You know all of this," he pointed to Jennifer, "is you. You remind me of those sisters who are out to bait a man, and I'm not biting."

Angel tried slapping Lionel again, but he caught her arm and held it tight. He turned to Jennifer. "If I said or did anything to disrespect you in any way, I'm sorry." He gripped Angel's arm tighter and clenched his teeth. "This discussion wasn't meant for public hearing. I tried for two years to keep our relationship under wraps. I'm going to be with someone who wants me for who I am and not if I go well with their outfit," said an exhausted Lionel. He slowly let Angel's arm go.

"Well I hope you do like her outfit because you paid for it," said an egotistical Angel almost in tears. But she held them tight.

"If you needed money, all you had to do was ask," Lionel paused and looked at Jennifer. "You know, I do like your ensemble. It really looks elegant. Melanie, you did a good job in selecting everything I would have wanted to see you wear. I say the money was well spent," said a hurt Lionel. He took off down the back stairs.

When he made it to the bottom, he saw a bashful figure in the corner. "Are you part of the rescue team, too?" The figure remained silent. "So, you like her. Like I've always told you, if you snooze you lose. When you're trying to impress someone, my brother, wear a suit. Sisters like it when you put your best foot forward."

Lionel rushed through the door. He took a deep breath as he leaned against the wall. The last thing he wanted to do was hurt Jennifer. She was so innocent. He could still see her leaning against the wall with her head hung low. He could still see the fire and water in Angel's eyes. He couldn't blame her. He was very mean when he practically threw the money at her and told her to go away. It wasn't his personality to behave that way. Thomas had coached him through the whole incident. He wished Thomas wasn't in the house at the time Angel came to get the money. It would have gone smoother.

He was weak, easily influenced by his friends and Angel too. He remembered when she called him "emotionally malnourished." It hurt his feelings but he liked her anyway. Thomas almost hated her. Thomas accused Angel of controlling Lionel without him knowing it. Lionel figured some of Thomas' accusations could have been true.

A car pulled close to him. The face was a very familiar one. She played the background for two years and now she figured the time was right.

"You need a ride?" the sweet voice asked.

Lionel looked at the young woman who was preying on his weakness. She, like so many others, threw themselves at him, except Angel. He was strong enough to not fall for everyone, but this one could read him well.

"I guess I could use a ride," he said pleasantly.

She smiled as he got into the car. "Is it finally over between you and her, or is it going to be Jennifer now?" she asked.

"Does it matter?" he snapped. He wanted the games to stop, but he wasn't strong enough to get out of the car.

"I guess not," she smiled slyly.

He looked at her curiously. She chased him for so long. She liked playing the other woman for some obscure reason.

"Where to?" she asked, stroking his hair with her manicured finger-nails.

"The house," he said without looking at her. He remembered the times she was with him. She was one of the few who had no problem with fellatio. He hoped she did it again. If not, he had a condom in his pocket. He could not afford another mistake, especially not with her. He felt her fingers stroke between his legs, which caused a rush from his groin to his stomach. He let out a sigh. It had been a long time.

"Will this time be as good as the other ones?" he asked with a devilish grin.

She chuckled, "Of course. You've never been disappointed with me. I can't say that about some people."

He knew she was referring to Angel. Some way, she convinced him to tell her about Angel's bedside manners.

"Okay Miss Dark and Lovely, I say we get moving. My room is clean this time," he said in a very low tone. She narrowed her eyes.

"Dark and Lovely, I like that. It must be my special name because I doubt if you are talking about anyone else," she said and drove off with a smile on her face.

Jennifer looked at Angel in disbelief. Angel took off walking down the hall with Gina and Jennifer following. Jennifer was back on automatic, smiling at people as she made her way through the small crowd. She spotted Steve talking to some friends. She boldly approached him and asked him to take her home. He was a little stunned by her behavior but complied. As he excused himself from the group, Jennifer took off walking fast with Steve and Angel almost running, trying to keep up.

When Steve opened the front door of the car, Jennifer hopped in. The evening still belonged to her. She dared anyone to take it from her. Angel sat quietly in the back. Steve tried stirring up conversation, but no one was talking. When he arrived at the dorm, Jennifer remained seated until he opened the door and escorted her out.

"Good night Steve," Jennifer said and walked away.

"Uh.... Good night Jennifer," Steve said and looked at Angel. "What's the matter with her? She was fine a few minutes ago," Steve said in the mix of confusion.

"I will talk to you about it tomorrow. Good night, sweetie," she said and kissed Steve on the cheek.

Jennifer was in the room rushing to remove the dress. She tossed all the clothing on the bed and left the shoes in the middle of the floor. She put on jeans and a sweatshirt. She passed Angel on the way to Lisa's room. The two did not speak.

Jennifer knocked hard on Lisa's door. Lisa rushed to answer. She looked at Jennifer with suspicion. Jennifer walked in quickly. "You decided not to go for a ride?" Lisa tiptoed.

"I'm not pledging Kappa," Jennifer said, unaware of the question. "Where did you get the wine coolers? Can I have one?"

"Grab one. Some of us chipped in and Rick bought them. So did hotsy totsy Linda say something to you this evening?"

"It's not Linda I'm concerned about, more like Angel," Jennifer said and sipped the wine cooler.

Lisa broke into a grin, "Angel? Oh please, that's your girl."

Jennifer shook her head and sipped the wine cooler. "You wouldn't believe what happened tonight. Did you know Angel and Lionel had been seeing each other?"

"Yes."

"I didn't, and neither did Gina. He was supposed to have asked Gina out along with a stretch of other women, I guess," Jennifer said.

Lisa didn't respond. She let Jennifer talk for fear of saying anything that would upset her. "She and Gina saw me and Lionel kissing on the steps in the Union," Jennifer said.

"You kissed Lionel? You barely know him. Why would...I'm sorry Jennifer. I'm sorry. I'm just surprised that you would kiss him so soon," Lisa said, waving her hand apologetically.

Jennifer gave her an angry look to shut up. "It was more like he kissed me. I told him that I didn't want to be with him that way so he said 'let me take you back to the dorm' and that is when Angel started hollering at him. It was ugly," Jennifer said and sipped the wine cooler.

"Angel hollered? She was mad," Lisa said.

"I found out that Lionel was interested in seeing me. Angel..."

"Lionel is interested in you?"

Jennifer gave Lisa another angry look. "If you don't shut up, I won't finish the story," Jennifer snapped.

"I'm sorry. Damn, this is unbelievable! Not the part that Lionel is interested in you, but Angel creating a scene," Lisa said, hungrily drinking the cooler.

"I can't believe she would embarrass me to get back at Lionel," said a somber Jennifer. She put the half drank wine cooler down. "This is nasty."

"Angel is like that Jennifer. She likes getting her way. You know, Lionel was seeing me for a little while earlier this year. The next thing I know, he's seeing Angel. About two and a half months ago, Steve was coming around. Now he and Angel are dating. I can't stand her."

The conflict between Lisa and Angel was clear to Jennifer. It was more like Lisa having a conflict, not Angel. Lisa was insecure when it came to dating because it never seemed to last long. She would date some of the most attractive and popular boys, but she had a problem with longevity. She often blamed them for wanting to have sex when she wasn't ready.

"Angel knew that Lionel and Steve liked me but she made it her business to interfere," Lisa complained.

"Well, they had to go willingly. She can't force them to like her."

"There you go again, taking up for her. That's why she embarrassed you this evening."

"If a man wants to be with you, he will! Just because I don't agree with you doesn't mean I'm against you," Jennifer defended.

Lisa lowered her voice and replied, "I am not accusing you of taking sides. It seems like you don't have a problem expressing yourself to me, but you won't jump bad with Angel."

Jennifer knew it was true about the differences in how she treated both friends. She had put Angel up on a pedestal and always feared disapproval. Angel was formal, most of the time, and almost outside her reach. Lisa was down to earth. If she wanted to, she could behave the same way as Angel, but she chose not to. Lisa had a common background. Her grandmother could not afford the luxuries like Angel's parents.

Jennifer remembered a statement made by Lisa, "People respect things they valued." Jennifer hoped that she wasn't placing less value on Lisa's friendship. She never wanted Lisa out of her life. Jennifer sat on the bed next to Lisa.

"I'm sorry. I'm just mad. The first time in my life, I feel important, and someone has to come and spray graffiti on me. You don't have anything to worry about because it seems like all the fellas like you," Jennifer said while struggling to keep from becoming emotional.

"Lionel just told you that he was interested in you and you act like it was nothing. He's not small potatoes, you know. All the men, and I say all of them, commented on how fine you looked this evening. You act as if nothing has happened. I just don't understand you. I've tried being your cheerleader, but I'm going to stop," Lisa paused a minute. "You choose to run with the nerd herd, whereas, you can run with some nice brothers that look better than Kyle, Tommy, Malcolm or Gerald. You choose to be with the worst. Why?"

Jennifer walked to the door, but Lisa stopped her. "Naw, you tell me why. You are always asking me about my grandmother and her signs when you know I don't want to talk about her, so fess up colored girl."

The request caught Jennifer off guard because Lisa was usually a little gentle with her. Lisa knew things about her without saying a word so why did she need to bare her soul?

"People have teased me so long about being dark that sometimes I almost equate dark with ugly. Kids used to call me Blackie or Charcoal Girl, like something is wrong with being dark. Someone had the audacity to tell me never cut my hair because that was my God given beauty. So, I try to place less emphasis on looks and try to see people from the heart," Jennifer said. Her head was bowed as she shared her heart.

"Now, that's what I call innermost secrets, not that crush on Brad Morris junk. Anybody who had eyes could tell you had a crush on Brad. You wore those tight-ass Gloria Vanderbilts on the day you had to do a skit with him at the ABC drama night. Shoot, I remember how kids would call my momma a welfare cipient. When we had to bring food for class parties, they would tell me not to bring that government cheese. They would also tease me by asking if we mailed our letters with food stamps. That's why I don't take shit off of nobody now," Lisa said trying to make a joke of it.

Both girls were quiet, never expecting to share the pain they hid for so long. Lisa pulled out the same pillow and shirt from the night before and handed them to Jennifer.

"I don't feel like going to the dinner tomorrow, and I'm still not pledging Kappa," Jennifer said and put on the night shirt.

"You're Miss Gamma. You have to be there. You can't run and hide when problems arise. Put your pride away and face Angel and Lionel because they are definitely going to be there. And believe me, they are going to act as if nothing happened. Sometimes you must go out of your way to show a person there are no hard feelings so they can respect you."

Lisa jumped under the covers. "You shouldn't worry about Angel hazing you when you pledge Kappa. That's not her nature. She's a manipulator, not a true troublemaker. Friendship means a lot to people like her because they don't have many. She likes you too much."

Jennifer listened to her friend's lecture. A thought came across and she smirked.

"What's up?" Lisa asked. Then Jennifer chuckled. "What are you laughing about?" Lisa demanded.

"I felt Lionel's...uh...you know... I felt his...thing," Jennifer said with a high school flare.

"Was it long like Vernise said?" Lisa asked excited.

Jennifer had to think. She could only remember a hard knot pressing against her stomach. "Yeah, it was long." They laughed.

"Did you know that Kyle and Lionel went to the same high school?" Lisa asked.

"Really?"

"Cameron told me. We danced and talked all evening long. He's a nerd but he's cool."

"Kyle never told me that he grew up with Lionel and Cameron."

"I told Cameron that Kyle has the biggest crush on you. He said that he was glad to see him interested in a black girl. When they were in high school, Cameron and Lionel tried dating all the black girls. They dated white ones, too, but Kyle only liked the white ones. One black girl had a crush on Kyle, if you can believe that, and she told him so. He really didn't like the sister because he was chasing some Molly chick. When he told the sister he wasn't interested, she went completely off."

"Well, it doesn't surprise me," Jennifer said, trying to remove the makeup. "Oooo God, I can't wear this crap on my face everyday."

"You better get use to it."

Jennifer took her place at the foot of the bed. Lisa turned off the overhead light and left the lamp on. "Why do you treat poor Cameron as if he doesn't exist? You know he likes you."

"He acts like a white boy."

"He wasn't that white at the step show last night. He shocked me."

"You and me, too! Can you believe that shit? I called him on that. He just laughed and said there were a lot of things I didn't know about him. I said nigga pleez."

"A lot of girls are talking about him, so you better stop playing him off!"

"Let them have him. I'm not fighting over a man," Lisa said and turned off the lamp. She struggled to get comfortable and kicked Jennifer's leg in the process.

"Where is Dee Dee?" Jennifer asked trying not to fall out of the bed.

"Probably with Johnny Evans. That girl is crazy about that brother. He told her he didn't want her performing in the step-show last night because he's going to pledge Gamma. He doesn't want his woman performing in a Beta show. Can you believe that? Of course, Dee Dee, with her whiny butt, just said, 'Okay', like a damn baby. I just shook my head."

"Does Dee Dee jumps every time he says so?"

"Hell Yeah! That shit makes me sick. He knows I can't stand him. Oh well, if she wants to play a fool then throw the dice for me, too."

"I heard Michael is going to pledge Lambda. It shocked me because he was a Baron for two years. I can't believe the Lambdas are accepting him."

"Michael knows that Jimmy East was going to beat him to the ground for trying to pull game on Charise. She didn't want Jimmy anyway. Michael is a 'ho' so if the Lambdas tag his ass for switching, no better for him. They have gotten desperate these days. They would have never taken someone who switched interest groups."

"I heard Damon Marberry is pledging Epsilon. Maybe he figures it won't be much competition to be their president. You know he had too much comp with the Lambdas."

"He will probably be the president of Epsilon and I bet J.D. is going to be president of the Gammas after he pledges. He told me that tonight. He's really sharp."

"You better be careful. I think he's going with Vicki. You know Vicki, who wears a lot of makeup? She wants to pledge Alpha."

"I don't like him! I don't care about who he goes with. Good night!"

"Lisa, can I ask you a personal question?" Jennifer asked, trying to get comfortable.

"What?" Lisa asked while relaxing under the covers.

"Are you a virgin?" Jennifer asked with no shame.

"Why are you asking me that?" Lisa asked, pulling at the covers.

"I want to know," Jennifer said sincerely.

"Yes, I am," Lisa said and jerked the covers.

"I am too," Jennifer said while snuggling under the covers. Lisa rolled her eyes. "Did you ever have any play mommas or play cousins when you were growing up?" Jennifer continued.

"You won't believe this, but I had a play sister, more like a make believe friend named Angel." They laughed.

"I had two make believe friends named Mamie and Meese." They laughed again.

"What are you going to wear to the dinner tomorrow?"

"I thought my black pants with a gold sweater would look nice."

"The Betas are going to accuse you of trying to be on the Lambdas court next."

"Yeah, especially Lionel. Do you think he will speak tomorrow?"

"Yeah, him and Angel. Good night, Jennifer."

"Good night, Lisa."

Chapter 5

The room was bright and colorful. Plants were on the window sill and on tables around the room. There was a large plant in the corner near the window absorbing the sunlight. The color scheme was wine and gold. Dry floral arrangements decorated the room in colors of orange, red, rust and green. Plaques and pictures of black women covered the wall. A very large acrylic crest occupied the center. It was in the shape of a diamond with a dark red background. A gold torch was in the middle with a red flame, outlined in gold, shooting at the top. Greek writing was at the bottom in black print, encased in a gold background.

An anxious Jennifer stood in the center of the room encircled by a group of ten onlookers who represented the interviewing committee. They were seated on hardback chairs, wearing wine-colored skirts and vests with white-tie blouses, tied in nice, neat, large bows. Their legs were crossed, displaying the Aigner "A" on wine-colored pumps. They were all well manicured, sitting patiently with yellow note pads on their laps and pens at attention. They were all smiling, mainly forced ones, waiting to ask a nervous Jennifer questions. She could feel the scrutinizing stares as she waited to give answers. As she answered questions about sisterhood and her goals, she saw the forced smiles eased up. She relaxed as she turned to the person asking the question.

The floor lamp focused on one chair in front of a large mahogany wood desk with four leather chairs strategically placed behind it. Six hardback chairs were positioned behind it. There was a tall bookcase on one wall with a short one adjacent; both filled with books. The wall was covered with plaques and photos of black women and a huge wooden crest in the middle. The crest had the head of an Egyptian queen with a high headpiece on the top in bronze. It had a navy blue background with a bronze cross dividing it in fourths. The room looked more like an executive office than a sorority Chapter room.

Lisa sat rigidly in the chair. Ten interviewers entered the room wearing navy blue blazers and gold skirts. They sported gold blouses with navy blue pumps. They carried small black notebooks and a serious look. The room had just been polished and so were the girls. The process was ready to begin.

The young women wrote copious notes as Lisa elaborated on her definition of sisterhood and what she perceived as the goals for the sorority. Occasionally, she threw in economic information to impress her interrogators.

Within thirty minutes the interviews were over. Before the candidates were escorted out of the room, they were told that what goes on behind the Chapter room doors must remain a secret. Any violations of those secrets would cause immediate disqualification from the selection process. Both girls took a deep breath and exhaled. Jennifer was on the second floor and Lisa was on the third floor.

When Jennifer left the room, a friendly voice approached her, "Next time honey, try not to have a run in your pantyhose, okay?"

"Oh, yes," Jennifer said, slightly embarrassed while looking at her legs. "I didn't notice." The girl smiled and walked back into the room.

The next candidate, Margo Washington was waiting timidly outside the door. Jennifer smiled at her. "Hi Margo," Jennifer said.

"Hi Jennifer. How did it go?"

Jennifer looked up at the ceiling and said, "Tough. Good luck."

"Thanks and the same to you."

A warm voice called out to Lisa, "To communicate well, people must be able to understand you. Try not to talk over a person's head. I would like to hear more on the 'trickle down' theory."

"I have a paper you can read," Lisa said, slightly embarrassed. The young woman nodded and went back inside the room. Alicia Sims was waiting outside the door. Usually she was calm but not this evening. "How did it go?" she asked Lisa.

"It went well, quite well," Lisa said, trying to maintain confidence. "Good luck."

"Yeah, thanks."

Jennifer could not wait to see Lisa. Jennifer rushed down the steps and Lisa rushed up the steps. Both girls almost collided in the stairway. They looked at each other and laughed. Their hearts were racing as fast as their legs. Both wanted to share the secret thirty minute session but was forbidden. They kept laughing, seeing who would break the silence first.

"How did it go?"

"Okay, I guess." Still more silence.

"I felt interrogated."

"I felt scrutinized."

The awkward chuckles continued for several more seconds. For the first time since they became friends in their freshmen year, secrets developed between the two. Lisa knew that Jennifer felt Lionel's erect penis and Jennifer knew that Lisa let Clifton Taylor kiss her without dating him.

"Well I'm glad that's over. Let's go to the Union and split one of those nasty cheeseburgers and fries. We might as well enjoy it before we pledge," said a thrilled Lisa.

"Let me take off these heels," said an edgy Jennifer.

"No, let's stay dressed up so that everybody can see."

"Okay, lets go!"

They walked happily to the Student Union. The March air was cold and breezy. Jennifer snuggled closer in her coat, trying to avoid the wind. She focused on the door ahead that led to the Student Union. Before she could open it, someone had rushed ahead and held it wide open.

"Hello ladies. How were your interviews?"

They rushed inside. Jennifer's teeth chattered. She rubbed her hands together and put them on her face. "Hi Cameron. Everything was okay, I guess. When do you interview with the Betas?"

"Tomorrow at seven. Hello Lisa, how was your interview?" Cameron asked, trailing behind them. Lisa did not bother to look back at him.

"It's cold outside! I'll be glad when Spring kicks in," Lisa complained. She stopped abruptly and looked at Cameron. It caught him off guard. "So what's the story now? You skipped class again. I guess you think your good manners are going to get you an 'A.' When you pledge, you won't be able to keep up the Mr. White Boy attitude. You ain't that smart," Lisa fussed.

"I didn't know someone was checking on me," Cameron said grinning.

"Don't say nothing if you get a 'C.' You won't get into Rolla," she continued.

"I think you meant to say 'don't say anything.' With those double negatives, that means…"

Lisa pursed her lips and gave him a contemptuous look. Jennifer walked inside the cafeteria quickly, leaving Lisa to fight alone. Lisa took her slim finger and poked hard into the young man's strong chest. "Let me tell you something, I don't play that!" she chewed at him.

Cameron looked apologetic and said, "Can I buy you something to eat?"

"*No!*" Lisa snapped and marched off, leaving Cameron standing alone.

Brad stood next to him and whispered, "Hang it up man! She's a tough one to get to know."

Cameron turned around and slapped five. "What's up man?"

"I say try for the other one. Oh, I forgot, that's your brother's lady."

"There's nothing going on between Jennifer and Lionel. I just need to get Lisa in a compromising position. Maybe I'll take her to a scary movie," Cameron bragged.

"Say what? Man I heard Cliff took her to see a scary movie about a dude killing prostitutes. When one of the prostitutes ended up killing the dude, Cliff said Lisa complained about the woman not killing the dude bad enough. She wanted the dude's heart on a plate. The babe is dangerous!"

"She's not that bad. You just have to know how to handle women like her. You don't take them to see movies about prostitutes. Maybe drug dealers, but not prostitutes." The two roared with laughter.

"Okay Shaft!"

Jennifer split the cheeseburger in half. She divvied up the french fries and trimmed her portions. She gorged the burger with mayo and mustard and plotted a glob of ketchup over the fries. Lisa looked at how happily her friend dressed her dinner. Jennifer looked up before biting the burger.

"What's the matter?" Jennifer asked.

Lisa shook her head. "Nothing."

Just before Jennifer took a bite, a brown figure stood beside her. She quickly put the burger down. "Hi Michael."

"Hi Jennifer. Are you ready to give up your freedom?"

"Hey Michael, I heard you chose Lambda. Why?" Lisa asked.

"I changed my mind," he growled.

"What's up with the attitude? You have been a Baron for as long as we have been Swans. You know Betas and Lambdas don't get along," Lisa said, slightly offended.

Michael felt bad insulting Lisa. She was one of the few Swans that wanted his friendship and nothing else. He remembered how she made him accept her free tutoring for college algebra. She cared about his grades. She liked his company, nothing more.

"Don't worry, little lady. Me and a few others are going to change all of that. We are going to be so close to the Betas that we might combine the Doves and the Swans and call them Dawns," he teased.

Lisa rolled her eyes. "Hum, I don't want to be close to the Doves. They got attitudes!"

"That's what they say about the Swans. Anyway, me and the boys are going to always be cool. I can't cut Tony, Brad, Cameron and Cliff loose. I see you ladies later. Get ready for a tough pledge period," he said and left. Jennifer watched as he walked out of sight. She quickly picked up her burger and began to eat hungrily.

"Slow down, it ain't going to run away," Lisa chastised like always. Jennifer ate slower.

"I think he's pledging Lambda because of the competition with Tony and Brad. He was always overlooked. The competition won't be that easy with the Lambdas because a few fine ones are pledging too. They are going to kick his ass, I just know it," Lisa said and took a bite of her burger.

"Now ladies, let's vote on our list of candidates. The interview committee has submitted a list of recommendations. I hope that everyone was able to talk to the candidates one-on-one at our Tea, so let us be honest and sincere as we discuss each person. If you disapprove of any candidate, please do so by raising your hand and state your reasons as tastefully as possible. It will be brought to the floor for discussion and another vote. As I call a name and there are no comments, the candidate will be accepted based on the committee's recommendation. Are there any questions? Good, let us begin the process with the top scores. First we have Candice Stewart, next is Alexis Michels, next is Jennifer Peterson.... I see three hands. The floor is open for discussion on Miss Peterson."

"Madame President, I think Miss Peterson should wait before joining our sorority. She is lacking in many areas, including social grace. I think it would be better for her to wait another year."

"After all, soror, Miss Peterson did have the third highest score. I am quite sure social grace can be taught. Could you be more specific when you say that she lacks in many areas? The young lady would have scored higher had it not been for the run in her pantyhose." A small group of Kappas chuckled.

"What I mean is she lacks character and confidence. She seems to stammer when she speaks. We need women who are sure of themselves."

"Lacks confidence? She seemed to have handled herself quite well at the Beta's Ball. She had Lionel Johnson eating out of her hands. She was able to keep him away from me and a few others that evening. She must have something and I want to know what it is," the arrogant young woman said and maliciously gave a quick glance at another before the small group chuckled again.

"Let's get serious ladies. She did not stammer when she interviewed. She might have been a little nervous meeting us one-on-one. We cannot hold that against her."

"My only concern is I do not think she has the money to pledge."

"She signed the application form which gave an approximation of the cost, so she is aware that it might be expensive."

"She told me that she worked this summer to earn the money to pledge. I think she is covered," one said.

"I see low self-esteem written all over. She cannot wear these eleven diamonds with confidence," said the young woman as she brushed her sorority pin. "If she cared about herself, she would try to lose some weight." A small chuckle went through the group.

"How did you see low self-esteem?"

"She did not make eye contact when I was talking with her. She reacted like a scary cat."

"What is the real problem, Annette? Is she too dark for you?" A hush went over the room. All eyes turned to the speaker. "Let's face it. I'm hearing this juvenile shit which has nothing to do with whether Miss Peterson will make a good Kappa. The young lady has damn good grades, a humble spirit and a drive to succeed. She can lose weight and we can teach her how to eat with a twenty-piece serving while looking people in the eyes."

"First of all, I am not prejudiced. I am not that much lighter than her."

"Only by five shades." The group chuckled again.

"Sisters, my only concern is, her background is not stable. She said her mother died, but she really does not know how the poor woman died. Her father does not seem to be an important figure either. We really need to take all of this into consideration."

"Yes, I know what you mean. I am not from a stable background either. My parents had to work for a living, too." Now the group laughed.

"Okay ladies that is enough. We need to move this along. There are twelve more candidates to discuss. Miss Peterson was the only one who received a character reference from a National Official," Angel said. She looked at the three before speaking. "Let us vote on Miss Peterson again. I take it that you three will join the rest in accepting Miss Peterson as a member?" The young women looked at one another to see who would speak up. Angel looked at the three very hard before speaking again. "With a show of hands, all those disapproving of Miss Peterson becoming a member of Phi Kappa Psi Sorority Incorporated.... Good, let us move on."

"Sorors, we must vote on the recommendations by the interviewing team. As I call out each candidate, please acknowledge any nays by standing. All nays must be discussed in detail, leaving personal feelings in the background. Sorors, we must remember that each candidate must be accepted by everyone, so let's be serious with our votes. I hope that everyone was able to talk to each of the candidates at the Soiree. The candidates are listed in alphabetical order. First on the list is Lisa Arvell." The speaker saw a few standing.

"Soror President, I really don't have a problem with Lisa, but she seems extremely arrogant."

"It's a show of confidence. Most straight-A students tend to be arrogant. Isn't that right Sheila?" A small group of Alphas laughed.

"Her language is unbecoming. She curses like a sailor."

"We can help correct it. She who has not cursed cast the first stone; everyone except you, Angela." The group laughed again.

"She is confrontational and hot tempered. I don't want to get involved in any fights with other sororities because of her. We finally got rid of Fist Fighting Freida and we don't need another one."

"She seems like she's from the streets, a ghetto sister. We don't need sorors speaking dialect better than English."

"She is a straight A-student. We know she can speak English properly. We can channel that energy into something positive. I will see to it myself." The group became quiet before the president spoke again. "Can we put this to a vote? I ask again are there any nays on Miss Arvell.... Good, next is Crystal Brown."

"Soror President, Crystal is okay but how can we get her out of those jeans?"

"I don't see that as a problem, soror, I just wonder if she owns a dress? We don't need a reputation as a haven for lesbians."

"She is not a lesbian. She is just extremely casual. She does have good grades and is very pleasant. She does lack confidence, but we can work on that, too. If you can accept Crystal, Jessica, I will have no problem accepting Phyllis when her name is called."

"Okay, it's a deal."

"Okay ladies, we are down to our last three candidates. I know it is getting late but we must finish. Next we have Margo Washington."

"Madame President, that girl is a mouse. She is practically invisible so why does she want to pledge *our* sorority? I mean give me a break!"

"Yes, you have a point but we can help her. She has impressive grades, a gentle spirit and integrity. For her to apply for membership to *our* sorority should say something about her. Her interview was a little weak, but I took it as being nervous."

"What is this? Are we accepting every handicap case?"

"No, but we have to go beyond some of the weaknesses to get to the true person. We do not need any more whores, sluts, or lazy people. So ladies, what is it going to be?"

"Look Cathy, I held off on Anita, the potential happy hooker, so I do not think it will kill you to accept Margo."

"Fine. I concede."

"Next is Rochelle Overton." Several hands shot up. "The floor is opened for discussion."

"Madame President, I do believe this is a joke. She has an attitude that we do not need. Let her pledge Alpha, they seem to coalesce well with those types."

"Her language is too rough. She curses and uses slang and...oh, I just do not see her as a Kappa," the young woman said in exasperation.

"She is a little rough around the edges, but I want her as my Special. I want to see if I can do the *My Fair Lady* routine. If she does not smooth out by the third week, we can force her to drop line. Agreed?"

"We do not want to get the sorority in trouble again. I do understand your concerns but I think it can work, after all, she is Cora Reed's cousin and her mother is the treasurer of the St. Louis Alumnae Chapter, if you can believe that. Let us vote ladies. Are there any disapprovals?.... Good. Our last candidate is Michelle Locks." Several hands were raised.

"The girl has the worst reputation on campus. How did the interview committee select her? Let us get real here."

"I am not cutting a deal with anyone on this one. She needs to pledge Sigma; they take our rejects."

"I am not budging on my 'no' vote either."

"Miss Locks has been rejected. The interview committee will telephone each accepted candidate and personally invite her to the induction ceremony. Let the record show that five candidates were rejected and they will be notified by campus mail. Some of you are well aware that there are some candidates who were accepted without a strong consensus. I do not want this to reflect in their pledge period. We want to not only develop sisterhood among ten strangers but sisterhood among us all. I hope I have made myself clear as to favoritism and abuse. Will someone make a motion to close the meeting of Phi Kappa Psi Sorority Incorporated, Zeta Chi Chapter?"

"Sorors, we are down to our last two candidates, please be patient. Next is Alicia Sims.... Okay let's open the floor for discussion."

"She is about as bad as Lisa. Can you imagine those two on line? It will be Muhammad Ali versus Joe Frazier."

"She is going to be bad news if she gets in. I say if she is accepted, I'm not having any mercy."

"Okay, we can make her your pledge daughter. Anybody else has anything to say on Alicia…. Good. Our last one is Shawna White. Let's…"

"No, no, no. They call her Christmas Cheer!"

"Why?"

"Ho, ho, ho! She's a slut and a bad one at that."

"I can't cut anyone a deal on this one. We don't need any whores. Let her pledge Kappa, they tend to have a heart of gold."

"Let the record show that Shawna White has been rejected by the group," Gina said quickly without pursuing discussion. "Letters will be mailed to all candidates. Those who have been accepted will be given specific instructions on the induction ceremony. These letters will be mailed tomorrow by the interview team. Sorors, I want to remind you that some of our candidates were accepted by means of negotiations. I do not want anyone abusing a pledgee that was not your choice. Nor do not want any particular pledgee to be treated more favorably than the others. Remember, we are to develop sisterhood and sisterhood shows no favorites or rejects. Will someone make a motion to close this meeting?"

The Dean of Pledges from the four largest black Greek organizations met for dinner. They were discussing pledge practices old and new. It gave them an opportunity to reminisce on old days and complain about the new prospects. The purpose of their meeting was to try to develop a united coalition because the organizations had been heavily criticized by some black students. They felt the need for such organizations did not serve a positive purpose for the black students at Missouri State. The black Greek organizations were also criticized for their humiliating pledge process. Although the black Greeks many times defend their purpose by explaining how they offered free tutoring and scholarships, many students saw them as social cliques with little to offer.

Marsha Lewis, a member of Alpha Theta Lambda ,and Denise Henderson, a member of Phi Kappa Psi, were meeting Thomas Parker, a member of Beta Gamma Delta, and Carlos Simmons, a member of Lambda Phi Chi. These organizations worked the hardest in trying to maintain harmony because they were the biggest rivals of their genders.

"This is going to be the biggest line ever, sixteen pledgees. I really don't know how we're going to encourage brotherhood with so many brothers. I really didn't want it but I was outvoted. You know how it is," Thomas said.

"It seems like we are experiencing an attrition in quality candidates too. We had brothers ranging from the 'You know what I mean' to ones that had police records. I wouldn't hold anything against a young brother who pulled pranks at an early age, but we had ones who have serious problems," said a more disgusted Carlos. "I couldn't help wondering why they wanted to pledge us. We were able to select eight strong brothers."

The four students stood in line to order their food. "Since this is the start of the eighties and the Women's Lib movement has made progress, are you ladies treating?" Thomas teased.

"We have our own money, thank you," Marsha replied.

"But if we offered to pay, you wouldn't turn it down," Carlos added.

"If you offered, we would take it as a gesture of kindness and allow you the opportunity to express goodwill," Denise said sharply.

"But would you offer to pay?" Thomas asked.

"Maybe," Denise said flirtatiously. The young men laughed.

"At least you can mold eight brothers, Carlos. Who can shape sixteen different personalities with only twenty prophytes?" Thomas asked.

"You know most of them because they were Barons right?" Carlos asked.

"You have to be a Baron before you pledge," answered Thomas.

"You should know the good ones from the bad ones. I say assign a frat brother to a group and make sure they do the job on them," Carlos said laughing.

"That is why your chapter was almost suspended. You don't have to beat those guys in order for them to behave," Denise said.

"We are talking about men, Denise, not women," Thomas said trying to defend Carlos. "I guess hazing doesn't go on with you precious ladies of Kappa."

"You guys are going to have to find a better way of pledging people. Our Nationals told us that lawsuits are increasing, so it doesn't take much for us to lose our pearls," Marsha said, trying to defend Denise. They were at the cashier.

"Does anybody feel like spreading goodwill?" Carlos teased.

"Separate checks, please," Marsha said.

"I know you haven't forgotten how you had those pledgees running two laps on the track in high heel shoes," Thomas told Marsha. She tried to ignore Thomas' accusation. They took their food to the table.

"It seems like you ladies had a good crop this year," said Thomas.

"Don't get me lying. We had our share of egos, sluts and slicksters. One sister had the nerve to tell Gina at the interview that she wanted to be an Alpha because her initial are A-T-L. Now you know how that sat with Gina," said Marsha.

"I remember getting in trouble for dancing with her when we were pledging. Boy, oh, boy did I pay for it. I should have known that girl was trouble from the beginning," Carlos said smiling. The group chuckled. "My big brothers would tell me, 'See how a fine woman can get you in trouble'." Carlos kept smiling.

"I want to know why André Jackson, the shortest man in America, danced with me all the time? I had never danced with him before because he was too short. I couldn't reject him because I would get in trouble with my big sisters. He would dance, not one, but several dances at every dance," Marsha said, looking at Thomas for an answer. All four had pledged their organizations at the same time.

"Marsha, honey, you were such a strong-willed person that our big brothers kind of used you to help build André's self-confidence. They made him dance with you at least ten times at the first party. He was on his own at the other parties," Thomas said, trying to keep from laughing.

"I had to slow dance with big Dorothy Banks at least five times at every party because my big brothers said I was an arrogant son-of-a-bitch. They made me slow dance with the biggest girl on campus. I could barely put my arms around her. I had to sing in her ear, too. The big brothers would stand next to me, making sure I did it. But come to think of it, I would ask her to dance every so often after I pledged," confessed Thomas.

"I don't ever think I turned André down for a dance afterwards either," added Marsha.

"My big sisters said that since I was so stuck up that it would be better for me to watch the common folks dance. I had to stand up all night long just watching people dance."

"Oh, so that's why you turned me down," Carlos said and slapped five with Thomas. "I thought you were just being stuck up, even on line," Carlos continued. They all laughed, including Denise.

"The music was good and I was itching to dance but I couldn't. Once I finished pledging, I threw myself at the first opportunity," Denise said.

"When you look back on those times, they were fun, but they sure weren't the hell fun then," Carlos admitted.

Marsha, like most Alphas was ready to get down to business. She cleared her throat. "We are going to have twelve Genies pledging this year. They will speak to all the Greeks, including their pledge lines. We will continue to support everyone's functions," Marsha said with authority. "How does that sound?"

"Sounds good to me. Our ten Cherubs will do the same," added Denise.

"We will make sure that our Aristocrats dance with your pledgees so they can get their books filled," Thomas said.

"Our Pharaohs will be pleased to do the same and make your girls paddles if needed," Carlos said with pride.

"We appreciate that fellas. If you guys are going to make those poor, pitiful pledgees cook again, we can have a joint dinner so the Genies can help," said Marsha.

"We can do the same thing, too," said Denise.

"Why don't the other organizations join us in this unity effort. We all know that the Kappas and the Alphas don't get along," Thomas joked.

"Who said that? We love each other," said Denise while hugging Marsha.

"Most of us started off as friends. Sometimes that helps," Marsha added.

The group continued to eat and discuss memories. Jennifer and Lisa entered the cafeteria with some other girls who had been accepted by sororities. They were laughing and talking.

"It looks like they may be able to keep the unity going," Thomas said.

"I think we all tried picking the best," responded Denise as she watched the interaction between Jennifer and Lisa.

"What's this I hear about Lionel trying to, you know, get some action with Jennifer on the steps after the Ball?" Carlos asked.

"I heard that Angel and Jennifer got into it over Lionel. He was supposed to be seeing both of them at the same time," Marsha said while avoiding Denise.

Thomas was shaking his head in disbelief. "Where did y'all get that garbage from? Lionel told me that he was walking Jennifer home when

Angel and Gina stopped him. Angel thought his intentions were dishonorable. My man had to explain to the overly zealous women that he was just taking her home. They were probably outside the dorm by then. Isn't that right Denise?" Thomas said laughing. Denise closed her eyes.

Marsha looked unbelieving at Thomas. They finished their meals and left the Union cafeteria.

Sunday had finally come and Jennifer's excitement had escalated to the point that she could hardly sleep. She and Angel were on moderate speaking terms. They had not discussed the incident from the Ball. Since Angel knew that Jennifer had a difficult time with confrontations, she took advantage of her and kept silent on explaining or apologizing.

The two had discussed the pledge period months earlier. Angel advised Jennifer to move in with another pledge sister to avoid any problems with pledging. That way, she would get to know her pledge sisters better. Jennifer moved in with Margo who lived in another dorm and shared a room with Denise Henderson. Jennifer was even more excited because she would be suitemates with Lisa and her line sister, Janet.

Jennifer came back to the room to gather the rest of her personal belongings. Angel was in the room with her new roommate. "Hello Jennifer, how do you like your temporary home?" Denise asked casually.

"I love it," Jennifer answered with enthusiasm.

"You will like Margo. She is really sweet," said Denise.

"We were up half the night talking," said Jennifer.

"I know I am going to enjoy living here because I do not have to share a bathroom with three other women," Denise said with relief.

Jennifer went busily around the room gathering the items. Angel was quiet the entire time. Jennifer felt the urge to apologize, as she had done so many times before. This time, she did not want to.

"I guess I have all of my things. Thanks for switching rooms with me, Denise. I will see both of you tonight," Jennifer said.

Angel went to the dresser and opened one of the drawers. She removed a small, black velvet box and handed it to Jennifer.

"You are going to need this," Angel said.

Jennifer opened the box. Her mouth dropped open. It was a pearl necklace. She looked at Angel with a big smile and wet eyes.

"My mother was a Kappa. She wore that necklace. I was hoping all of my life to find my little sister so that she could wear mom's pearls. They are going to look nice around your neck," said Angel. Jennifer hugged Angel. Jennifer knew this was one of those "signs" again. She started to apologize, but Angel stopped her. They embraced a few seconds more.

"The ceremony starts in five minutes, so under no circumstances are you to be late," Angel preached. Jennifer laughed.

"Yes mother," she replied and left.

"Please Dee Dee, don't start whining. I will only be gone for six weeks," said a rushing Lisa. It was tough leaving Dee Dee. They had been roommates since freshmen year. Dee Dee wanted to pledge Alpha, too, but she didn't have enough money. Dee Dee moped around since Lisa's interview. Dee Dee became upset with Lisa because she could not discuss her interview. She was angrier when Lisa went to dinner without her to celebrate with other girls, who were pledging sororities.

"Things are never going to be the same, Lees," Dee Dee whined.

"We are always going to be cool," Lisa tried to say reassuringly. "Help me take these things to Janet's room." Dee Dee acquiesced.

As they walked to the lobby, they saw a happy Jennifer. Lisa called out to her. They laughed and talked with excitement leaving Dee Dee out of the conversation. She knew she was losing her closest friends. She remained quiet as Lisa and Jennifer chattered happily.

"Oh my God, it's almost seven thirty. Let's hurry," said a frightened Margo. Jennifer was carefully taking her time to prepare for tonight's ceremony. She wanted to make sure her makeup was perfect and there were no runs in her pantyhose. The Kappa inductees had to wear white dresses, white pumps, pearl earrings and bring a pair of pantyhose to the induction ceremony. Jennifer took one last look in the mirror and was pleased with her appearance.

Lisa and Janet were instructed to wear lipstick only, navy blue skirts, navy blue pumps, white blouses with navy blue and white scarves. Those with long hair had to pull it back into a bun. Both Lisa and Janet had their hair gelled down and pulled back. The two girls walked through the bathroom to say good-bye to Margo and Jennifer. They walked into Margo's room. Jennifer looked at the dark blue skirts. It gave a more serious aura, like business women. Lisa looked at the white dresses and pearl earrings. It gave an elegant appearance.

Lisa looked at Jennifer and Janet looked at Margo. Silence fell upon the four girls. The idea of separating really never dawned on them until now.

"You look very pretty Jennifer," Lisa said.

Jennifer looked at her friend and smiled. She was beginning to choke.

"You two really look sharp," Jennifer finally said.

"I guess we can walk to Morrison Hall together for the last time," Lisa joked.

The girls left the room. A friend of Janet came out with a camera and took pictures of them. Jennifer and Lisa stood very close together as the girl snapped the camera.

The excitement that was exploited earlier that day was gone. The girls were quiet and subdued. They arrived in the lobby at 7:45 p.m. Each unconsciously split in different directions. All the white dresses were sitting on one side of the room and the blue skirts on the other.

Lisa occasionally made glances at Jennifer to see if she was nervous, but there were no outward signs. Marsha Lewis entered the lobby. The blue skirts stood, except Lisa, whose focus was on Jennifer. At that time she realized their friendship may not be the same. The two would be transformed into sorority girls. She hoped they would continue to be friends because Jennifer was her best friend. Lisa defended Jennifer when people were mean or would try to take advantage of her. Who was going to protect her from the Kappa bitches? Lisa was getting cold feet.

Lisa remembered how they talked for hours about their likes and dislikes. Jennifer was able to bring out that special side in her, whereas, no one else could. Lisa told Jennifer that she would pledge Kappa but decided not to because she feared the girls who had money and parents. It reminded her of the past, which made her feel inferior and sad.

Lisa looked at the other eleven blue skirts. None understood her like Jennifer, she thought. She knew none would ask her about the grandmother who believed in "signs" because she wasn't going to tell them. These girls didn't know how smart she was nor did they care about what she thought. She was convincing herself not to like the other blue skirts.

"Ladies, let us go upstairs and prepare ourselves for the induction," Marsha said. The blue skirts followed Marsha, except Lisa.

"Miss Arvell, are you coming?"

Lisa quickly fell in line. She waved good-bye to Jennifer and left.

Jennifer watched her friend leave with a group of strangers, leaving her behind with strangers. Lisa was her best friend who always defended her when she was afraid to speak up. No one had ever taken an aggressive approach in being her friend, except Lisa. She was strong and confident, which Jennifer was not. Lisa liked change; Jennifer feared it. She thought about pledging Alpha but was afraid of the very aggressive and open women that made her feel weak.

Jennifer thought about how Lisa would get angry and she would have to help her to control her temper. She would tell Lisa that people liked her when it was evident that they didn't. She wondered how the Alphas would treat her friend, especially Gina. She did not want them taunting or picking at her, making her feel inferior.

Jennifer was getting shaky. She worked hard at not getting emotional tonight. She was not sure if pledging Kappa was what she really wanted to do. She admired Angel. She wanted to be closer to Angel, like sisters.

"Ladies, we must prepare ourselves to be inducted into the Kappa pledge class," said Denise. It startled Jennifer. She could hear nothing, but she saw the white dresses follow Denise and she did the same.

Denise walked them into the room adjacent to the sorority's Chapter room. "There must be silence throughout the ceremony. Speak only when given permission," said Denise. She picked up a box of candles. "Take a candle from the box and pass it down. I want you to line up by height. Take your pantyhose and place this cloth in the middle of one leg," Denise continued as she handed wine-colored cloth pieces to each girl. They lined up quietly by height. Jennifer was number three. Denise took each girl's pantyhose and tied it across the eyes as a blindfold.

Jennifer heard chanting in the other room. One person would say something and the others repeated the words. Denise whispered to the girls to hold hands. She guided the line of shaking girls into the other room. The leader quoted something about angels being on earth, assisting people as they go through life. Jennifer was getting antsy with the nylon stocking around her eyes. She could feel heat in the room, which was making her head light. Her body felt heated. Something was consuming her. A minute later, the girls were instructed to remove the blindfold.

Jennifer rushed to remove the stocking. The room was bright with candles. The Kappas were wearing black dresses, black pumps, pearl necklaces, pearl earrings and a sorority pin on the left with diamonds in the middle symbol. They each held a lit candle. A large candle was burning brightly in the middle of a desk with items placed around it.

Each girl was called forward and given a pin in the shape of wings. The leader ask them to extinguish their flames and the ceremony was over.

Jennifer did not know what to expect on her first night of pledging. Although she had discussed it many times with Angel, she was unaware of what to do. The line of white dresses stood in front of the black dresses.

Angel walked forward and strolled up and down the line of white dresses. She began her inventory. She spoke softly as she walked back and forth. "Kappa women have character, which is not only evident in their achievement, but appearance as well." She stopped in front of Anita Houston and took a quick glance. "Hair shall be clean and well managed at all times. Wild, untamed hairstyles are not considered an element of a Kappa woman." The girl slowly reached for her hair. "What is done is done, Miss Houston. I do not think we need to remind you again."

Angel stopped at Patrice Weathers and looked at her shoes. "Kappa women are polished and so should your shoes. They tell a lot about you, where you have been and where you are going. Some of you have been in a lot of fights." The group of black dresses chuckled lightly.

Angel paced again. "Dresses are to be worn Monday through Thursday and slacks on Friday." Angel stopped in front of Rosalyn Bright. Angel asked her to turn around. "A Kappa woman's presence should attract attention, not her paraphernalia. Clothing should fit properly, never too tight. You are as comfortable as you feel." Rosalyn tugged at her dress. "Miss Bright, pulling at your garment will not loosen any seams." Rosalyn looked down the line of girls who dared not look back.

Angel stopped her stroll at Allyn Arrington, who was standing next to Jennifer. Angel asked to see Allyn's hands. "Nails must be clean and manicured at all times, just like a Kappa woman. If you cannot afford to pay to have them done, teach each other."

Jennifer felt a knot in her stomach when Angel passed her and stood next to Natalie Lake. "Kappa women blend well in society and so should your makeup. Ladies, makeup is not an option, it is mandatory. It should be invisible. Large rouge circles and powdery eyelids are not considered distinguished traits of the Kappa woman."

Angel walked to the first person in line, Margo Washington, who was shaking in her shoes. She dropped her head. Angel gently lifted Margo's chin. "Only your makeup should be invisible, not you. Kappa women are not mousy. Miss Washington, never let me see you drop your head again. Is that understood?" Angel demanded, bearing down on the girl's fragile self-esteem. Margo nodded. "Miss Washington, I don't understand..." Angel said while nodding her head.

"Yes Ma'am," Margo whispered, ready to cry.

"I cannot hear you, Miss Washington," Angel said firmly.

"Yes Ma'am," Margo said much louder.

"Please save the tears, sweetie."

A grin came across Angel's face as she walked down the line in the other direction, passing Jennifer who was shifting nervously. Angel walked to Rochelle who was slouching a little; looking from side to side. "Proper posture is required during your pledge period, Miss Overton." Rochelle slowly stood straight.

"Kappa and class are synonymous. Adorning jewelry is not considered appropriate. Pearl earrings are to be worn Sunday through Friday from 8 a.m. to 6 p.m. Very trendy hairstyles and fashions are not considered characteristics of the Kappa woman." Rochelle rolled her eyes to the ceiling. "Is something wrong, Miss Overton?"

"Naw," Rochelle answered sluggishly with eyes sparing with Angel's.

"Kappa women communicate well, without an attitude. Proper English is *our* primary language. Clear diction and distinct articulation is expected. No slang, swearing, nor contractions are to be spoken during your pledge period."

Angel stood face to face with Rochelle and said firmly without raising her voice, "We understand if our way of doing things may not fit your past lifestyle. You have been given the opportunity to join our sorority, so you have the option to stay or leave. If you stay, you will answer with 'no Ma'am' or 'no Miss Smith.' Now let me ask this difficult question again. Is there something wrong, Miss Overton?"

Rochelle looked at the large, brown, authoritative eyes that challenged her spirit. "No, Miss Smith," Rochelle answered defeated. Angel stepped back. Her eyebrows raised in victory. She walked two girls down to Candice.

"Quality is important. It goes hand-in-hand with Phi Kappa Psi. I realize pantyhoses are expensive but you do yourself an injustice when you choose a color different than that of your own. Some of us may have fair complexions but we are still black women. Choosing a cheaper brand of pantyhose cheapens the total effect of your appearance."

Angel finally approached Jennifer, whose chest was expanding with every breath. She had never witnessed Angel in a dictatorial role. Jennifer wondered what would be the open analysis. She shifted in her shoes, daring not to look at Angel.

"Like I told Miss Overton, proper posture is required, Miss Peterson. Shifting in ones shoes is a display of low self-esteem and lack of confidence. Stuttering and stammering confirms the two. If everything is in order, there is nothing to be afraid of. If one's personal appearance is well managed, polished, and manicured, and ones intellectual abilities are confirmed by high grades, then shall we say one is complete?" Angel looked into Jennifer's eyes which looked back in agreement.

Angel did her final stretch. She walked slowly up and down the line of girls. "Now, one may have everything in order and still not be complete. Pledging Phi Kappa Psi is not a popularity contest, although some of you may think so." Angel stopped at the tallest girl at the end, Alexis Michels.

"The mark of good character is standing for what you believe whether it is popular or not. No one respects a straddler, one who stands where it's comfortable. Kappa women are strong, not in attitude but endurance. It is time that we remove the nickname 'airheads' from our sorority's character and adopt a new one like, 'smart'." Angel walked away.

The room was still. Every president had to give an analysis and final approval of the pledge class. No one expected anything less from Melanie Smith. Her smooth way of giving the girls a quick analysis of their character was always respected by the Kappas. She quickly saw characteristics that took others awhile to notice.

"Miss Denise Henderson will give you details on your pledge program. It was nice meeting all of you personally and have a pleasant pledge period," Angel said without looking at the girls. "Good night ladies," Angel said to the Kappas with a shrewd smile. She and Maria left the room.

The Kappas talked amongst themselves, ignoring the line of girls. One complained about her feet being tired. "Cherub number seven, give me a foot massage," she said. Rochelle looked at Denise, who motioned her to comply.

"We sure have a bunch of Chubby Cherubs this time," said one, looking at Jennifer.

"I know and they look real pitiful too. I want my shoulders massaged Cherub number five." Candice rushed to massage the girl's shoulders.

"Look at those hair-dos."

"Hair-dos? They look more like hair-don'ts."

"Cherub number ten, my nails can sure use some polish. You want your big sister to look pretty tomorrow, don't you?"

"Yes big sister," Alexis said pleasantly and hurried to polish the waiting girl's nails.

"Who applied your makeup, number four. My goodness, it looks like war paint. Come and give me a foot massage." Natalie went quickly to satisfy the girl's demand.

Annette walked over to Jennifer, who was still waiting in line to service someone. "Is this a run in your pantyhose?"

Jennifer looked at her legs. She didn't see any runs. "No big sister, there are no runs in my pantyhose."

"Did you say *my*? You are not pledging by yourself. You are to speak in plural. Do you understand me?" Annette yelled.

"Yes, big sister. We do not have any runs in our pantyhose," replied a shaken Jennifer.

"Are you calling me a liar?" Annette asked, walking closer to Jennifer's face.

"No, big sister," said a frighten Jennifer.

Annette bent down and Jennifer felt the opening of a run travel up her leg. "Now look again Cherub, are there any runs in your pantyhose?"

"YYYesss, bbbig sister," stuttered Jennifer.

"Cherubs listen up. Your line sister has a run in her pantyhose. Take them off," snapped Annette. The white dresses stopped what they were doing and took off their pantyhoses.

"My legs are tired and I can use a footstool. How about it Cherub number one?" Annette said loudly. Margo looked around the room for a footstool.

"I, uh, we don't see…"

"You are not to speak in contractions. Is that what our darling president just preached about?" Annette snapped. Margo nodded. "What in the hell does this mean?" Annette yelled while nodding.

"We understand big sister. We do not see a footstool."

"Well, you will have to do," Annette said and raised her legs. A timid Margo got on hands and knees, mocking a foot stool.

"Oh, Annette, lay off. It's their first night. You don't want to scare them away," Linda said, letting out a sigh.

The Cherubs were asked to give foot massages, comb hair, and perform skits. If the Kappas didn't like them, they booed loudly and threw nerf balls at the performers. All the Cherubs took turns acting as a footstool for Annette, except Jennifer. Annette refused her request.

The Dean of Pledges motioned the Cherubs to form a line. She explained the purpose of the Pledge Special. She would be that special person who would help prepare the girls for initiation. Jennifer pondered over who would be hers. Angel and Maria had both left. She trusted no other person, except Joni or Glenda. She closed her eyes and prayed that it would not be Annette or Linda.

Jennifer heard Margo's name matched with Joni's. The two sat in a corner of the room talking. Next was Allyn. She was matched with Danielle; another nice one, Jennifer thought. She was next and her heart pounded hard. Denise said it and Jennifer almost passed out. She looked at Linda, who sat on the sofa with arms and legs crossed. Jennifer had to force herself to walk to her, but Linda stopped her.

"We will do this bonding thing another time, dear. I'll see you Wednesday at six o'clock sharp," Linda said and left the room.

Jennifer could not believe what was happening to her that evening. She would have to spend her whole pledge period trying to bond with someone who hated her guts. She wept inside. Soon it was over and the Kappas left the room, leaving the girls with the Dean of Pledges.

"Ladies, take a candle from this box and line up in alphabetical order by last name. There shall be no talking or laughing from this point on. After you are in line, remove the scarves from around your neck," Marsha said with authority. The blue skirts moved swiftly, taking candles and lining up. Lisa was number one in line. Marsha took each girl's scarf and tied a blindfold around the eyes.

Lisa's right hand was holding Marsha's left and her left hand held Crystal's right hand. Marsha led the line of nervous blue skirts into the room. As they walked into the room, someone was reading about the power of magic. The blue skirts were asked to remove the blindfold. Lisa looked around the room. The Alphas had on white robes with books in their hands. One very large candle on the mahogany desk was lit with twelve other unlit candles lying around it.

Twelve Alphas took a candle off the desk and lit it from the large one. They stood in front of the line of blue skirts. They repeated words before lighting the girl's candles. The blue skirts were told to repeat a vow of community service and development for the betterment of mankind. Everyone blew out their candles.

Marsha stood in front of the line of girls. She made eye contact with each of them before speaking, "From now until you are initiated, you will be addressed as Genies." Marsha stepped close to Lisa and look hard at her. "You are considered representatives of the most influential sisterhood in the world. With that in mind, there are rules you must follow to ensure the integrity of our organization is maintained."

Marsha stepped back and continued her glare at Lisa. "Rule number one: You are not Greek; that is what you must earn. You will address all Greeks as Miss or Mister upon entering their presence." Marsha walked to Crystal whose head was slightly lowered. Marsha waited until Crystal lifted her head.

"Rule number two: You will look your best at *all* times. Clothes will be clean and pressed. Hair will be neat, well managed. Makeup shall be extremely light. Your posture is to be straight with head held high."

Crystal head's straighten but her focus was at Marsha's feet. Marsha stood in front of her until she made eye contact. Marsha put her hands behind her back as she walked down the line to Alicia. Marsha stepped so close to Alicia that it forced her to step back. Marsha spoke two inches away from Alicia's face.

"Rule number three: You must exemplify a pleasant persona. All chips on the shoulders must be removed. We have been nicknamed 'Sisters With Attitudes.' We say, so what! That doesn't bother us because we do have attitudes and they are not bad ones."

Marsha walked down to Evelyn and stepped on her foot. Evelyn looked at Marsha with an obvious attitude. Marsha's head tilted slightly and she stared. Evelyn made eye contact at Gina, who also stared at her. "Rule number four: Your language is to be clear of profanity, slang, contractions and violence. To be influential, you must be able to persuade by using the English language correctly," Marsha said without losing eye contact.

"Is there a problem Genie?" Gina asked. Evelyn looked around the room at the other Alphas and they stared, too. Evelyn shook her head.

"I'm sorry. What did you tell Ms. Smith, Genie?" Marsha asked.

"There are no problems, Ms. Smith," Evelyn said.

Marsha stepped back and looked at the line. "Rule number five: There will be no talking to individuals outside the Alpha family, no dating, no smoking, no drinking and no use of illegal drugs.

"Rule number six: You are expected to perform two student service projects. You will be reviewed by a team of our peers and rated on your performance.

"Rule number sever: You are one so whatever you do as individuals will reflect on the entire group. You must speak in plural at all times. If you are caught by yourself, you run the risk of being kidnapped.

"There will be no verbal or physical abuse to any Genie. If ever you experience any mistreatment, report it immediately to myself or Gina Smith. Also, we respect privacy. The basis of sisterhood depends on trust. What goes on behind closed doors is your business. You will be tested during your pledge period so it is in your best interest to be prepared at all times. If for any reason a Genie is not performing her share of the assigned tasks, you may vote her off line with two-thirds majority.

"I hope that I have made your pledge period expectations clear. And yes, you must wear this attire every Tuesday and dresses or skirts on Mondays and Thursdays. Blue slacks and your gold Genie T-shirts must be worn on Wednesday. Friday and Saturday are optional. You will attend church every Sunday.

"You will be matched with a soror who will serve as your pledge mother. Her responsibility is to prepare you for the vows you will soon make. Like all mothers, she works in your best interest. Your responsibility is to act upon that guidance for your benefit. If at any time you believe your pledge mother is not fulfilling her obligations, then another one will be assigned. Ladies, the journey to Alpha land should be an enlightening experience. Remember, you are one. All for one and one for all."

Marsha called off names of Alphas, matching them to Genies. Lisa saw how friendly the pledge mothers were when meeting their Genies. She only hoped Jessica wasn't hers.

Marsha called three names of Alphas and then Lisa's. She became excited. She had three pledge mothers: Gina, Rita and Carla. They walked to her, but not close. None offered a smile, no hugs, no welcomes, nothing like the others. Lisa became tense.

"I need you to give me a schedule of the days and times you can meet with me. Since I'm in graduate school, I don't have time to waste so be prepared when we meet," the older one said. "Looking forward to seeing you," she said and extended her hand. Lisa gave it a firm shake. Gina and Rita continued to look at her, not smiling.

"Good-bye ladies," the older one said. Everyone stopped and said good-bye. She walked swiftly out the door.

Lisa became increasingly uncomfortable with Gina and Rita. They said nothing. "Y'all want me to give a schedule of meeting times too?" Lisa asked earnestly. Gina glared into Lisa's innocent eyes and Rita sucked in her lips.

"I guess you didn't hear what your Dean of Pledges said," Gina said low, trying not to be heard. Lisa was fed up with the feeling of uncertainty. She was tired of feeling on guard.

"Gina, I just asked a question!" Lisa said, getting excited.

Gina walked behind her and stood very close. She leaned in to whisper. "First, I want you to lose that attitude. Second, I want you to stand up straight and stop slouching like a street corner hooker." Lisa stood straight and pouted. Gina continued, "My name is Big Sister Hail to the Chief or Ma'am. My soror said you are one so *me* is not appropriate and *y'all* ain't eitha'! You have a 4.0 grade point average. It's about time you sound and act like it. My soror also said you are representing Alpha Theta Lambda, so I suggest you tuck that lip in before I do it for you."

Gina walked in front of Lisa and smiled. Gina chatted with other Alphas like nothing happened. Lisa could not believe what had just happened. The very one who talked against hazing had just threatened her.

"I'm hungry. Is anyone hungry?" one Alpha shouted.

"Yeah, I am," answered another.

"Hey Genie with the afro hair-do, get me some chips out of the machine," one of the Alphas said. No one moved. "If I have to show you which one has the afro hair-do, you are *not* going to like it." Evelyn rushed over to get money from the girl.

"Boy, I tell you. I feel sorry for that skirt on Genie number nine. Sister is definitely imposing on some seams," one Alpha said. Some Alphas laughed including a few the Genies.

Evelyn was about to go out the door by herself when Lisa shouted, "Take somebody with you." The Alphas were taken by surprise. Janet rushed to the door before Evelyn walked out.

"Let me see your scarves," Pat said. She walked down the line scrutinizing scarves. "Oh looky here sorors, somebody wore makeup to the ceremony. Didn't we give you specific instructions on what to wear Genie?" Vicki nodded. "Do you think I'm a deaf mute? Speak up," Pat snapped.

"Yes, big sister."

"How can we teach Miss Fashion Fair about following directions?"

"I know, sit-ups. Lord knows they can use them," one Alpha responded.

"You with the too-tight skirt, get on the floor and do some sit ups for your sister who couldn't follow directions," Pat demanded. Trish got on the floor and Lisa rushed down to hold her feet. "What's up with you? Your little butt is all over the place. Get back in line and let that lazy one over there help Miss Piggy," Pat said and pointed to Alicia.

Other Alphas had the girls run errands, getting things out of their rooms and delivering messages to their boyfriends. Lisa had to do sit-ups, push-ups and jog in place for knowing too much. Soon it was over and the Alphas left the line of girls with the Dean of Pledges.

Chapter 6

"**L**adies, there are complaints about some of our behavior. These girls are pledging to learn the meaning of sisterhood and discipline. They are not here as our personal servants. The floor is open for discussion."

"Madame President, I have not seen my Special since she was inducted. I want to know, why are some of us imposing on the Special's time? I barely remembered how this girl looks. I want these errands to stop."

"My Special has been doing everything from cleaning rooms to setting hair. I ask now, does anyone have a beef with me? If I don't hear any complaints today, I will assume my Special will be visiting me this week."

The room was quiet. Although Linda did not hold any office, she did carry a lot of political weight in the organization. Her mother was one of the chapter founders. She was also one of the sorority's national officials. Mrs. Stevens was the owner of a boutique that specialized in women formal wear. Linda's father was a surgeon. Her parents wanted her to attend a much better university, but Linda wanted to be with her high school friends, Angel and Gina.

"The Lambdas have asked if our Cherubs can assist the Pharaohs at their annual dinner party, and of course, we are invited," Denise reported.

"Will Craig be there without a date?" one asked.

"Probably. This year's Pledge Jamboree will be April 27, so mark your calendars," Denise concluded.

"Thank you, Miss Henderson. Does anyone care to share news or information about the relationship with their Special. Also, are there any concerns about any particular Cherub that need addressing?"

"I want to let everyone know that Cherub Ghetto Girl is coming along fine. She is becoming conscientious about how she reacts and interacts with people. Our next step is to teach her how to use makeup." Some Kappas giggled. "I mean honestly, this girl really wants to be charming so I know I will collect on those bets made back in March."

"Believe it or not, Cherub Don King has finally gotten her hair under control."

"I guess I can give an update on Cherub Fuss Box. She is calming down tremendously. She doesn't seem to complain as much or maybe I'm getting use to her. In either case, thank God!" The group laughed.

"Cherub Helen Keller is becoming a little more attentive and observant. She doesn't seem to be as nervous, but we still have a long way to go."

"There is just no hope for Cherub Miss America. She is too rehearsed. It will be difficult trying to change a lifestyle that was embedded at birth. She is making me sick. Does anyone want her?" Quite a few laughed, except Annette and some others.

"Unfortunately, Cherub Could Care Less may be a potential problem. We might have to meet with her to see if she really wants to be a member. I do not want her creating problems on line or in the sorority."

"Is it that bad soror?" one of the girls asked.

"I think she is only pledging because of Cherub Weight Watchers. Madame President, if we do not nip it in the bud now, we are going to have a problem later."

"The interview committee will meet to discuss the future of Miss Bright. We will act upon the committee's recommendations. Sorors, it is important that we meet with these girls. There are only six updates and that means four Cherubs are going unnoticed. Does anyone have any questions or concerns?" Angel looked around the room and saw no hands. The meeting was adjourned.

Jennifer and Margo were busy cleaning, working off demerits that Annette had given them for being disobedient, just because they existed. Jennifer and Margo did not know what they had done wrong. They were scheduled to visit their Specials but Annette had them running errands that evening. Jennifer was too afraid to tell Annette she needed to leave and Margo would not dream of leaving without permission.

Jennifer wasn't sure if she was using the errands as an excuse to avoid Linda or if she was really afraid of Annette. Linda called Jennifer earlier that day to make sure she visit at six o'clock. It was already seven o'clock and Jennifer was trying to get Annette to approve her work.

Annette was complaining about the dusting and the windows not being cleaned when someone knocked on the door. Jennifer rushed to open it. In the hallway stood Linda, Joni, Angel and Denise. Jennifer's heart almost dropped. Linda frowned after seeing Jennifer with a ragged tied around her head.

"Hello Cherub Queen For A Day. I haven't seen you since you've been inducted. Looks like you got a lot of housework to do. Well, well, well. Here is Cherub Hypo-Allergenic. I guess you two run in pairs," Linda said and strutted into the room followed by Angel, Joni and Denise.

"We are sorry, Big Sister Sparkle. We are working off demerits and cannot leave until Big Sister Sweet Sensation give us permission," said a timid Margo to Joni.

"Well, now, I just know Big Sister Sweet Sensation doesn't mind if you two leave to be with your Specials. And I'm quite sure those demerits can be worked off another time. Just run along and we will meet you two in the lobby, okay?" Linda said with a smile. She looked at her fingernails. They were growing.

Jennifer and Margo looked at Annette and said a quick good-bye. They stepped outside the door and leaned against the wall. They let out a big sigh. The door flew open a few seconds later. Jennifer looked in horror at Linda.

"Honey, does this hallway look like the lobby? I asked that you meet me in the lobby. You do know where it is, don't you?"

"Yes, Miss Stevens," Jennifer said quickly and walked down the hall with Margo trailing.

Linda looked around the room and sniffed. She swiped one of her fingers across the dresser and then she looked at Annette. "Do we have a problem? It seems as if you have a gripe with me or Jennifer. I say that we settle it now, if it's okay with you because she will be initiated." Annette looked at Linda and then at Angel.

"Margo will not be coming here to work off anymore demerits. I realized you didn't want her to pledge, but this is ridiculous," Joni added.

"What are you trying to do, keep all of the brown beauties out of the organization?" Linda asked while looking in the mirror. She put on some lipstick.

"Don't you ever come in my room talking shit to me you stuck up bitch," Annette said to Linda. "You got your nerve calling somebody class conscious. You definitely have a problem with fair skinned women. Every light skinned woman is color struck according to you."

Linda remained calm. "I have a problem with people who insult or humiliate someone because they don't fit into their nice little package. You and your little entourage forced that one little girl to drop line because, what was it 'she lacked social grace?'"

"We cannot afford for another Cherub to drop, Annette, so ease up," Denise added. But Annette was fired up. She narrowed her eyes at Joni.

"Don't you ever tell me what to do," Annette said, pointing her finger in Joni's face. Joni jumped back.

Linda walked next to Annette and whispered, "All of this is about Thomas, isn't it?" Linda looked at Annette for an answer, but received none. Linda shook her head and stood next to Angel.

"Sisterhood is built on respect. We do not want these girls despising you after they pledge. If you cannot follow the pledge rules, we will disallow any Cherub from interacting with you and anyone else that steps across the line," said a firm Angel.

Linda turned to face the mirror. "It's time for a new breed of Kappa women," she said while playing with her hair. Annette got off the bed and pushed Linda.

"Bitch, get out of my room!" Annette snarled. Before she could strike Linda again, Angel jumped in between them and said, "If you ever hit another soror or pledgee again, you will give up those diamonds."

Linda and Joni left the room leaving a frustrated Denise and Angel holding an angry Annette.

"I hope this isn't about Thomas. I tried to tell you about him but you wouldn't listen. You should have never sent Linda to talk to him. She can be very abrasive."

"He likes you."

"I doubt it. He's too arrogant. You deserve better."

"I deserve better? Like Lionel?"

"Just let it go."

Gina, Marsha and Donna were busy collecting Lisa's belongings. She was upset, but continued to pack her things. She was ordered to move out because she and Jennifer were caught talking. They would meet in the bathroom around midnight and update each other on the latest. Janet informed her pledge mother that she could hear Lisa and Jennifer talking at night. Of course, her pledge mother told the Dean of Pledges and Lisa was told to switch rooms with Alicia. Lisa was stunned that Janet told on her. It was suppose to be all for one.

"Do we have everything Genie Motor Mouth?"

"Yes ma'am." Lisa looked at the three women who had her things. "Big Sister Hail to the Chief, may we have permission to speak with you?" Lisa asked.

Gina motioned the other two to leave the room. She looked at Lisa impatiently, waiting for her to begin. Gina was the one who silenced Lisa after the first week of pledging. She felt Lisa talked without thinking. She needed to concentrate on listening. "What is it Lisa?"

"We do not understand why we cannot be friends with Jennifer. We do not want to lose her friendship because we are pledging a different sorority." Lisa was trying not to become upset.

Gina grinned. "No one told you that you couldn't be friends with her. You were told that you couldn't talk to her. As I told you before, you have to use your head to think around situations. You are smart enough to understand what I am saying without me telling you."

"Why can we not talk to anyone. How is this helping us?"

"How well do you know your line sisters?" Gina asked.

Lisa took breaths and looked around the room. She didn't say anything because she didn't know anything about them and she didn't want to know anything about them. "Do you want me to repeat the question a little louder?" Gina demanded. Lisa admitted not knowing anything about the girls.

"Didn't I tell you that you will be tested on how well you know them?" Lisa nodded. "Don't nod your head Lisa."

"Yes ma'am."

"If you continue to spend your time talking to other people, you will not take the time to know the people who you will be working with. If you don't know them at the time of the test, you are going to put the line in trouble."

"Why do we have to live with Genie Green Bay Packer?" Lisa continued stubbornly.

"Who cares who you live with! I don't want anybody to use ammunition against you. Let's go!" Gina snapped. Lisa didn't know what Gina meant and she didn't care. She gathered the last of her things and left.

Jennifer waited twenty minutes in the bathroom. Lisa was never late.

Jennifer cracked open the door to Lisa's room.

"What the hell do you want?" a voice shouted. Jennifer eased the door close and went to her room. She could not make out the voice in the room. She knew it wasn't Lisa's. Something was wrong. Jennifer wanted desperately to tell Lisa about her first visit with Linda. She wasn't a bad person after all. They shared many things in common. They were only children. They both liked Earth, Wind & Fire and collecting teddy bears.

Jennifer became worried. She wanted to know who was behind the voice in the room and what happened to Lisa. She hoped that Lisa didn't quit. Before Jennifer crawled into bed, she heard a soft knock on the door. She went to the door. Lisa shoved a note in her hand and waved good-bye as she rushed down the hall. Jennifer looked curiously at the piece of paper before opening it. She went into the bathroom to read it:

Hi *Jennifer,*

We were sold out by you know who. We are staying in Clark Hall until the pledge period is over. We heard that Michael has the hots for you. He wants to date you after pledging is over. Cameron told me that at the dance Friday night. We got a "B" on our Monetary Analysis test and we are mad. We cannot afford to lose this scholarship so we will be studying now. Did you ever meet with Big Sister Tight Dress? She might not be so bad so stop dodging her. We will communicate like this until the pledging is over so write back. Oh, by the way,, we are beginning to like Shaft a whole lot now. He is so fine so stop eyeing him (joke). Keep in touch!
Yours Truly,
Cleopatra Jones

Jennifer took a deep breath and folded the note. A big load was off of her mind. Now she could rest easy.

Lisa and Gina were meeting for the fifth time. The first three visits were tough for Lisa because Gina had silenced her. Lisa barely said anything. On the fourth visit, Gina insisted that Lisa do all the talking. They talked about classes, careers, boys and pledging. They talked about all of this for more than three hours on a Saturday afternoon.

"Big Sister, do you ever want to get married?" Lisa asked.

"Yes, but I've got time. I have to make sure my career is up and going before I settle down. My mother told me that a woman needs her own money and a future independent of a man."

"Are you and your mother close?"

"We became closer a couple of years after she married Angel's uncle. He was her long lost sweetheart from college. They attended Lincoln University. My mother and Angel's mother became good friends when they pledged Kappa. Angel's mother married my stepfather's brother right after she graduated."

Lisa remembered her mother attended Lincoln University too, but she dared not discuss her. "Did your father die?" Lisa asked.

Gina was always surprised when people asked if her father was deceased. She was a little embarrassed to tell them that he left her mother for another woman.

"My father is alive. He just left. It was difficult being a good daughter when I blamed my father's disappearance on my mother. It took time, more like years, to stop blaming her. My mother is a nurse. She worked a lot of long hours. I was a little rebellious until my mother met up with Paul. It became worse. Paul spent a lot of time with me and my brothers while momma worked. He not only had his own business but rental property too so what he did with us was extra special."

"Sounds like you got a good set of parents."

"It wasn't roses in the beginning. My mother and Paul argued a lot about discipline before they got married. She got a little pissed when he put me on punishment."

"What did you do?"

"I talked back to her and Paul decided that I would work for him, without pay, on the weekends until I got my act together. I had to mow lawns, rake grass, paint and help him lay carpet. My mother got a little mad about it. Paul told her that if they were going to continue to see each other, he wasn't going to tolerate any bad children so momma let him have his way. After awhile, I start liking Paul because my real father didn't come around nor did he do a damn thing to help my mother with us."

Lisa was engrossed with the story. She wanted to hear more about the fairy tale family. "How old were you when your mother married Paul?"

"I was a little over twelve when she met up with him and about fourteen when she married him. My brothers started acting out when they reached their teen years because Paul's business was picking up and he couldn't afford to spend time with them. He nipped it in the bud. You have to give it to a man who adopts another man's three children."

Lisa looked at Gina while she told her story. She seemed so relaxed and at peace with herself. Even though her father was a bastard, it didn't bother her to call him one.

"What about your parents, Lisa?"

Lisa became agitated and looked at the floor. She never told the entire truth about her background, only very little to Jennifer. "My mother died when I was twelve years old. I don't have a clue about my father. I was given several names, but none have panned out."

"What did she die of?"

Lisa took a deep breath, "Drugs and alcohol." Then Lisa tried to make a joke, "She wasn't much of a mother or a woman if I've got four names as possible fathers."

Gina gave a sympathetic look that Lisa knew too well. She didn't want Gina's sympathy, only her respect.

"Hey, she never came home. She ran the streets constantly and fooled around with as many men as she could so I say good-bye and good riddance."

Gina didn't know what to make of Lisa's attitude. "Sometimes people don't make good parents, even the nicest of folks. Whoever takes the time to raise you deserves the honors; even if it's someone that's not blood."

"You got that right! Mattie June Clairmont will always be mother to me and as for as Debra Arvell, she can go to ..." Lisa paused. "Big Sister, may we go now?"

The name Debra Arvell rang a bell with Gina and a clear one too. She didn't want Lisa to leave angry. Gina searched her mind for something upbeat to talk about. Then it came to her. "You can get Cameron in trouble by dancing with him all the time," Gina teased.

Lisa blushed.

"Why are you looking so surprised? Just because we haven't said anything doesn't mean we haven't noticed. Remember, the fraternities are much tougher on their pledgees than the sororities when it comes to that sort of thing. You may want to take that into consideration when he asks you to dance for the hundredth time. Carlos got in trouble all the time because he hung so close to me. This is nothing new," Gina said.

Lisa continued blushing. She really couldn't say anything because it was true. Cameron hung so close to her at the dances that she hardly danced with anyone else. He whispered jokes in her ear, making her giggle. She had warned him, but he didn't seem to mind. They were the ones who developed code names to communicate with each other while pledging. The other pledgees caught on and now everyone does it, except for some of the guys. "We are just friends," Lisa said. Her face was beet red.

"It's good to start as friends, that means it will last a long time. I think Cameron is smart, extremely handsome and courageous. He is going to make some lucky woman a good catch one day."

Lisa knew this to be true as well. She and Cameron had taken Calculus and Quantitative Methods together. She realized that he was just as good at math as she was. There was no doubt about how attractive he was. He was an inch shorter than Lionel and a little larger. Lionel had a soft look, whereas Cameron had a more rugged exterior. He was bashful and socialized just a little. Because he was a bookworm, none of the girls paid him any attention until the night the Barons performed and took off their shirts. Lisa would hear his name mentioned in numerous conversations.

Lisa smiled upon remembering the conversation with him about his performance. She teased him, calling him a closet stud puppy. "We are going to have a lot of competition after he finish pledging because every girl and her momma are talking about him."

"You don't have to compete for him because there is no competition. A man either likes you or he doesn't. My mother did every thing she could to hold on to my father, but he wanted someone else. I don't understand sisters who confront another woman over a man. My mother said maintaining your self-control is power. Under no circumstances am I losing my dignity over a man. If Cameron starts falling into the 'big head' scene after he pledges, let him have his fun without you because he knows where home is when the party is over."

Lisa listened attentively. Their conversations were getting much better.

"It looks like you have dropped some weight. What's going on?" Gina asked. Lisa weighed one-hundred-ten pounds before the pledging began and now she was at one-hundred-five pounds.

"We are just doing a lot of running around trying to get ready for the Jamboree," Lisa answered.

"Is everyone pulling their weight?"

"Yes Ma'am," Lisa lied without blinking. Alicia, Janet and Evelyn had been goofing off since the pledging had started. They knew Lisa would make sure everything was done because she was something of a perfectionist. The line voted Alicia, Captain and Lisa, Co-Captain. Alicia was loud and intimidating and usually Lisa ignored her, but the other girls fell victims. Lisa would never tell on the three lazy girls because it was all for one.

"Let me ask again," Gina said softly as to convince Lisa to tell.

"Everything is fine, really," Lisa responded before hearing the question.

"Okay," Gina said hesitantly.

Lisa excused herself for the evening. She had to meet with Carla, Big Sister Let My People Go, a graduate student who was the chapter president before Gina. Lisa knew it was going to be an hour of social and political discussions, but this time, she was ready. A Sigma pledgee slipped her a note. She waited until she was outside before opening it.

hey, hEy, hEY, HEY Swiss Mocha Almond Fudge!

Yeah Hot Chocolate, me and the fellas are planning on kicking butts at the Jamboree, so you girls better be ready to tho' down! We have been practicing our slang lately. We hoped that you are impressed. (smile) See you Friday and remember Pi ain't square...theys round.... ha.Ha.HA!
SHAFT

Lisa had teased Cameron about sounding like a white boy for so long that he would use slang to get back at her. It was his way of asking if slang is considered Black. Before she entered the student apartments, another girl slipped her a note. She noticed the handwriting was Jennifer's.

What's Happening Cleo,

Big Sister Tight Dress is visiting us tonight. Yes, her highness is coming to our room. We received a note from Big Bank Hank today, inviting me to personally assist him at the Lambdas' dinner party this Sunday. Of course I had to turn him down because Super Fly asked first. Are things getting better with Big Sister Hitler? Let me give you the lowdown. The Kappas approached Big Sister Charles Manson and told her to stop the abuse. She has been keeping a low profile. Ask us do we care!
Hang tough,
Christy Luv

"Oh honey, why did you buy four of the same blouse in different colors? And who is Marjorie Williams? I've never heard of her," Linda asked while browsing through Jennifer's closet. "Thank God! Gloria Vanderbilt. Honey, where do you shop?"

"J.C. Penneys," Jennifer said almost in a whisper.

"Look sweetie, you are going to have to learn how to buy quality and put a little spice in your wardrobe. Everything in here is either blue or dark." Linda closed the closet door in disgust. "I need to touch up my nails. Do you have any soft pink nail polish?" she asked.

"No, Big Sister. We just have the red color that is required."

"Good Lord Queenie! What am I going to do with you?" Linda continued to survey the room. She looked at the dresser. "Where is your makeup?"

Jennifer went to the dresser and opened a drawer. She pulled out a small square compact and a tube of lipstick. She handed both to Linda, who looked in horror after opening the square compact revealing green and blue squares of eye shadow at one end and pink blush at the other.

"Is this a freebie? Where in the world did you get this?" Linda gasped.

"From a friend."

"Who was she, some white girl? Black women don't wear these colors, especially one of your complexion. This lipstick doesn't look like Fashion Fair or Flori Roberts. What is it?"

"It is called Crazy Colors. Everyone wears it. We usually put lipstick on our cheeks and around our eyes for the right color because it matches and it does not cost..." Jennifer had not finished when Linda began waving her hands wildly to silence her.

"I've heard enough. Let's go. Since you've lost forty pounds, you can wear some of my old clothes now," Linda said and walked out the door.

"We have lost only fifteen pounds, Big Sister," Jennifer said and locked the door.

"Oh!"

The Genies were in position to rehearse their Jamboree show for a few Alphas. Lisa knew that it was going to be a disaster. Half the Genies barely knew the steps because they hardly attended practices. The choreography was boring and the singing was horrible. Alicia and Janet had made up the routine and they barely came to rehearsal themselves.

Lisa looked at the excitement on the Alphas faces and felt badly. The Alphas were excited because they had a new breed of performers joining the organization. Some had dance training, a few could do gymnastics, a couple played musical instruments and a few could sing. In the last two years, the Genies usually came up short against the Cherubs because Angel choreographed all the shows.

"This is the year the Genies are going to show up those damn Cherubs!" one Alpha shouted with excitement.

"Wait until I see the look on Angel's face," Marsha said. They all laughed. Marsha was excited. "Come on ladies, we don't have all night."

Alicia gave the signal. They came out singing "We Are Family" in a straight line doing hand motions. Half the girls did one set of motions while the other half did their own thing. The singing was off key. Some had stopped singing while the others continued.

They formed a circle rapping to "Funk You Up" by Sequence. Some girls forgot their lines and some said rap that did not rhyme. They did pivot steps and change ups, which made the show a total mess. It was obvious to the Alphas who had skipped practice. Marsha stood up and waved her hand for them to stop.

"I know this is not what's going on stage at the Jamboree next Saturday," she said angrily.

Cheryl walked over to Alicia and said, "So, you couldn't visit because you had practice. Whatever practicing you have been doing hasn't been for the Jamboree. We have only met twice. Just because I'm nice doesn't mean I'm stupid. I don't appreciate anyone taking advantage of me like this," she said and gave Alicia a push with her finger.

"I don't care how long it takes, I better see a damn good show next Thursday night or else there will be no representation from the Genies this year. This is an embarrassment to the sorority. If you can't put forth an effort in working together now, I doubt if you will when you become sorors," Marsha said and walked out. The other Alphas followed.

Before the Alphas were down the hall good, they heard Lisa and Alicia arguing.

"Should we break it up?" one asked.

"No, it's been long overdue," Marsha answered.

Dear Christy Luv,

The show bombed and the Big Sisters threw a fit! We had an argument with Genie Psycho Path and the group voted me the show choreographer. We think the show is going to go off well but we could sure use your Big Sister Switchy Bitchy's help. By the way, we got busted by Big Sister Napoleon. She knows about us (or is it we, who cares!) and Shaft. Oh well, see you at the dance Friday. Remember, if a train leaves out at 6:30 going west at 50 mph and one leaves at 7:00 in the same direction at 65 mph, we say find a seat and go home.

Later,

Cleopatra Jones (Hey, somebody stole my rabbit fur coat......smile)

Jennifer felt Lisa's frustration all too well. It was good that Angel was putting together their show because it would be a mess like the Genies. The Cherubs were experiencing difficulties with Rosalyn and Patrice. They hardly met at the Cherubs' sisterhood meetings. They were usually sneaking around with their boyfriends.

As Jennifer dressed for the dance, she stole looks in the mirror. She could not believe Linda parted with so many clothes. All Linda told Jennifer was, "I'll buy some more when I go home."

Since the Cherubs were wearing skirts to the dance, Jennifer decided on a black, midi-skirt with a split in the front and a red, puffed-sleeve blouse. The outfit looked exceptionally neat on her. Linda harassed her about eating junk food. When she stopped, the weight peeled off quickly.

She went from a size eleven to a size seven.

The music at The House was loud as usual and the crowd was primarily sororities and fraternities with their pledge lines. The line of Cherubs walked in and immediately began dancing. Jennifer looked for Lisa, but the Genies hadn't arrived. Cameron asked Jennifer to dance. Her friend Stephanie took pictures of them dancing. Then Jennifer danced with Michael.

The Genies filed in. Lisa looked angry. She had taken the time to curl her hair all over which was rare. Cameron slowly approached her and took her hand. Usually, with a big smile, he would ask, "May we have this dance" but he didn't. He pulled her very close as they slow danced.

Lisa sensed something was wrong. Cameron had never held her so tight as if she would run away. She had to say something because he had yet to tell her she looked nice. When she looked up at his face, she gasped. "What happened?" she asked, trying to keep her voice down.

"You look very nice tonight," he said as if she had said nothing.

It was a stupid question. She knew what happened. Somebody hit him in the face. His bottom lip was busted and his right jaw was swollen. She sucked in her bottom lip, trying to keep her anger under control.

"Maybe we should not dance together so much," Lisa whispered.

"Next Saturday is showtime and the following week is Hell Week and then its over," Cameron said with a sigh.

"You should not hold us so close. You might get in trouble."

"Your hair smells nice and the perfume is driving me wild."

"Cameron, listen…"

"Feels like you lost more weight."

Lisa was not getting anywhere with him. He rubbed his hands on her back. It made her shiver. He had such a gentle touch. His roaming hands moved slowly up and down her back, making her relax. She had forgotten about the pledge rules. She let her head rest on his chest. He took the other hand and playfully curled her hair. She smiled as he explored. She felt someone standing next to them. It was Marsha.

"We have to go now, Genie," Marsha said. It startled Lisa to the point that she almost stepped on Marsha foot trying to pry herself from Cameron.

"Where are your three sisters?" Marsha asked the line.

Since Lisa was co-captain, she had to answer. "We do not know Big Sister Good Witch of the North." Lisa knew that they were not suppose to come to the dance without the whole group. Lisa was tired of waiting on the three girls. They were always late. This time she decided to leave without them. Lisa thought it was time to teach them a lesson, but it might not have been such a good idea after all.

"The party is over ladies. Let's find your sisters." Marsha took off with the line of girls following. "Why didn't you tell me your sisters weren't with you? You start partying as if everything was okay," Marsha fussed.

"We are always getting demerits because of them. It is not fair for the line to continue to be punished because of three people," Lisa said.

"You are still getting demerits. You should have told me what was going on. I need to make some calls." Marsha went inside the Student Union.

One Genie told Lisa where the three were and why they were not coming to the dance. Lisa let out a huff. They were still mad about her being selected as choreographer for the show. Crystal tried to convince Lisa to tell Marsha so they would not get in trouble, but Lisa refused. She could not stand a tattle teller.

Marsha came out of the Student Union steaming. They walked to Morrison Hall. She made the Genies wait in the lobby. In fifteen minutes, twelve Alphas had walked through the lobby. Marsha had come back with two Alphas all swinging car keys. Everyone piled in three cars and drove across town.

They arrived at a house three miles away. They all got out of the cars and walked to the front door. Marsha knocked on the door and a young man cracked it open. Marsha pushed it wide open. There was Alicia, Janet and Evelyn laughing and drinking wine coolers. When the three saw them, they tried to hide their activities.

"Let's go Genies," Marsha ordered. Evelyn and Janet jumped quickly from their chairs and joined the others. Alicia took her time. Marsha stopped Alicia with an open palm. "You don't have to come Alicia. I just want the girls who want to pledge." Alicia walked around Marsha and got in line.

"I'm sorry if I disrespected your home, Danny. I thought the brothers of Epsilon would at least respect our pledge rules," Marsha said and left. The ride back to the dorm was quiet. The Genies knew that it was serious.

Jennifer saw Kyle dancing wildly with a girl having a good time. She had not seen much of him since the night of the Ball. He had danced most of the evening with the girl. Jennifer was becoming a little jealous because he had not looked her way that evening. She decided to ask him to dance. When she approached him, he half turned his back. He seemed reluctant. Jennifer suspected the girl was his girlfriend but she asked anyway because they were friends. As they danced to a fast song, Kyle hardly looked at her.

"So, what has been happening?" Jennifer asked.

"Not much. I thought you couldn't talk to anyone?"

"We are not suppose to, but who cares."

"So what's up with the war paint on your face?"

Jennifer looked at Kyle strangely. She knew her makeup was on nicely. His comment was rude. "You don't need to wear makeup. Why are you so dressed up? You look better in jeans and sweatshirts," Kyle said.

"We look nice in makeup and skirts too. There is nothing wrong with the way we look."

"What's up with this 'we' stuff? I guess it's some more of that Kappa crap," Kyle said and turned his back to her.

Jennifer was angry. She thought about leaving him on the dance floor. He had never been rude to her. When the song was over, he rushed back to the other girl without turning around. Jennifer thought to herself that she would never ask him to dance again.

Denise rushed to Jennifer. "Where is Rosalyn and Patrice?"

Jennifer looked around the room. There were no signs of either girl. "They were here a minute ago," Jennifer said.

Denise bit down on her bottom lip. She had told Alexis, the line captain, it was an unsupervised evening. Denise had given specific instructions to stay at the dance until 1:00 a.m. and then they were on their own to spend a night with their Specials or with other Cherub sisters. Denise came back to the dance at midnight to give Alexis the key to clean the Chapter room the next day.

Denise gathered the girls and took off walking. They went back to Morrison Hall. Denise motioned the Cherubs to stay put. She rushed up the stairs. Within minutes, she came back with Angel and Maria.

"Hello ladies," said a tired Angel.

"Hello Big Sister Bon Ami. Hello Big Sister Mariaaaa.... We have just met a girl name Mariaaaa," the Cherubs sang to Maria with arms extended.

"You ladies wait for us in the Chapter room," Angel said as she, Maria and Denise left the dorm. The Cherubs knew it was serious. Angel and Maria hardly became involved in the pledge projects or the meetings. Neither one had Specials and none of the Cherubs had ever visited either one.

Angel drove to the boy's dorms. The three women snuck passed the night host and up the stairs to room 217. Angel could hear noises in the room. She knocked on the door and the noise stopped but no one answered. She knocked again and still no reply. She looked down at the knob and turned it. The door was unlocked and the three women walked in. In their haste, Patrice and her boyfriend forgot to lock the door. Maria turned on the lights and Patrice was in bed, pulling a sheet to her chest. Angel grabbed a chair, sat down and crossed her legs as if she lived there.

"What's up with this shit?" the young man asked angrily.

"Shut up," snapped Angel. "How would you like if I told your Big Brother Sadistic Rho Psi that not only did you not speak to a Greek but you cursed them as well. I don't think he is going to like it." The young man spoke and apologized to the young women.

"Are you pledging tonight Patrice or do you want to continue to fuck?" asked a calm Denise. Patrice rushed to grab her clothes.

"Stop right there. You take a quick shower. You are not getting in my car smelling like a five dollar hooker," Angel said coolly.

Patrice rushed into the bathroom to take a shower. The three women looked at the young man, daring him to say something. He sat quietly with a sheet wrapped around his nude body. They could hear the water running. Finally, Patrice came out of the bathroom fully dressed. They walked out the door. Maria turned off the lights and closed the door. Denise spun around to Patrice. She jumped. "Where is Rosalyn?" Denise asked.

"She's at, uh, I mean, uh, we mean she is at a party at the Beta's house," Patrice said and began to cry. The three women looked at her without sympathy. The last thing Angel wanted to do was create a scene at the Beta's house. They walked down the back stairway and exited the emergency door. The bell sounded as they walked swiftly to Angel's car.

Angel pulled her car in front of the house where Lionel and Thomas lived. Usually, the president and the vice president and two other members of the Beta fraternity occupied the house. The lights were off and there was no sign of a party. Angel asked Maria and Denise to see if Rosalyn was still inside. The two walked toward the house while Angel stood next to the car waiting with Patrice. Before the two women got to the door, a car pulled up behind Angel. Thomas and Lionel got out looking worried.

"Hello ladies, what's going on?" Thomas asked. Lionel looked at Angel for an answer. It was unusual to see Angel, Maria and Denise out on the streets late.

"One of our pledgees is in there at your party," Denise said with sarcasm.

"We're not having a party," Lionel said while rushing to the front door.

The women looked at Patrice and then at Thomas. He hunched his shoulders indicating he did not know what was going on. It took awhile for Lionel to come out with Rosalyn and an Aristocrat walking behind him. Lionel was steaming. When the two delinquents made it to Angel's car, Patrice cried again. Rosalyn looked at her in anger.

"First, young brother, I want you to apologize to this Cherub for seducing her into breaking her pledge rules. Next, I want you to apologize to these women for disrespecting their sorority," Lionel said, trying to hold his temper. The young man sputtered an apology to Rosalyn and the Kappas.

The Kappas were so embarrassed that they stammered as they thanked Lionel. He, Thomas and the Aristocrat went inside the house. Angel swung around to the two girls. Patrice was crying harder. "It's people like you who give sororities a bad name." Angel looked at Patrice. "You didn't have the decency to be discreet." The girl was so ashamed. She apologized profusely.

Angel stared at Rosalyn hard. "You decided to fuck an Aristocrat in the Beta's house? I got something for you Miss Bright. It is time we settled the score with you." Angel got into her car and the others squeezed in.

The Cherubs were sitting in the Chapter room waiting for Denise. They were tense and angry. Rosalyn was calm. One of the girls stood up and pointed her finger in Rosalyn's face. "We have busted our asses for you two and this is how we end up? We should say not."

"We are not going to sit quietly and let this one go by. What are you going to do about it, Alexis?" Jennifer asked angrily.

"She's not going to do a damn thing about it, you jet black bitch!" Rosalyn snapped. Before she knew it, Jennifer leaped up, grabbed Rosalyn by the shirt and swung her to the floor. Before Jennifer could punch her, Alexis, Rochelle and Anita pulled her back. Candice took off for the door. Jennifer's instincts kicked in. "Where are you going?" Jennifer yelled. "You better not tell or I will give you something to tell about." The girls became quiet.

Rochelle continued holding Jennifer, looking around the room. Her line sisters were quiet as mice. "We do not know about the rest of y'all but if we get demerits from that crazy ass Annette because of these dummies, we are kickin' ass. We do not care if you are jet black, pecan tan, high yella or polka dot," Rochelle said, looking at Patrice and Rosalyn. "Alexis, we are sick of this shit! We know that they are your girls, but not tonight. Either we are your girls or you can fry with them."

Margo and Patrice began to cry. "Oh shut up!" one of the Cherubs yelled.

"Let us calm down and talk," Alexis said, trying to maintain order.

"Talk? Dammit, what is there to talk about?" Rochelle snapped. Everyone knew she was telling the truth even if she had a peculiar way of saying it.

Alexis helped Rosalyn up. "Do you two want to continue pledging with us? It is not fair for the line to get in trouble because of your behavior," Alexis said. Patrice nodded and Rosalyn looked away. "Come on Rosalyn, are you with us?"

"Hell, don't beg her, let her walk!" Rochelle yelled.

The door opened. It startled the girls. They were trying to straighten up quickly. Angel walked in with Maria and Denise. The Cherubs were getting ready to speak but Angel silenced them. She walked over to the sofa and sat down, tucking her legs underneath. She had an envelop in her hand. In her soft voice, she said, "Miss Bright, could you please come over here?" Rosalyn walked slowly to the sofa, but maintained an air of confidence.

Angel did not bother to look at Rochelle. "Miss Bright, I cannot see your face." Rosalyn knelt in front of Angel. "What surprises me is your attitude. How can you come into my sorority acting like a, uh…tramp?" Angel opened the envelope and handed the girl a check. Rosalyn looked befuddled. It was her parents' check for the sorority fees. It was never deposited. She looked at Angel like an injured animal.

"I sensed that you may not work out, so I took the liberty in helping you with that decision. I have done this before, it is nothing new. You see this woman in the picture?" Angel asked, as she took the picture off the wall and handed it to Rosalyn.

"That is my mother, Catherine Peterson Smith, a founder of this chapter. It would break her heart to know tramps, like yourself, are trying to destroy her hard work. I will not let that happen. You can call our national headquarters and complain, but of course, we will deny all charges and so will your line sisters. Isn't that right ladies?" Angel asked shrewdly. The girls looked at one another.

"Yes Big Sister," Alexis said, looking at Angel who looked at Maria.

"Ladies, all of you did not answer Big Sister Bon Ami," Maria said firmly. The rest of the girls answered, except Jennifer.

"Excuse us Big Sister. Can Cherub Could Care Less do something to continue with the rest of us?" Jennifer asked earnestly.

"What are you suggesting?" Angel asked cunningly.

"Can her Special suggest something?" Jennifer asked.

"Her Special has failed. Don't you think so?" Angel continued to play.

"Maybe you can be her Special," Jennifer said innocently.

Angel pretended to think to herself. "Um, that's a thought. Do you want me to be your Special, Miss Bright?"

"Yes ma'am," Rosalyn said low.

"You don't sound thrilled!" Angel said with a chuckle.

"Yes ma'am," Rosalyn said louder and looked at the check.

"Okay, Big Sister Bon Ami will be Miss Bright's Special. As my Special, you must wake me at six thirty every morning for breakfast. If I do not want to go to breakfast, you will have to get if for me. You will make my bed, too. Because you are such a pretty girl, I want to see your face before I close my eyes to slumber and when I open them in the morning. I have plenty of washing and ironing that needs to be done. My room needs cleaning as well. You will perform these tasks with a smile. That is just for starters, do you understand Miss Bright?"

"Yes ma'am"

"Miss Weathers, if you want to continue pledging this sorority, meet Maria in her room at seven thirty tomorrow morning. Miss Bright if you are still interested in pledging, bring that check to my room at 6:30 a.m. Good night ladies." Angel and Maria left the room. As they walked down the hall, Maria smiled at Angel.

"Can we deposit all the checks Monday? We need to pay for their pins and fees," Maria asked.

"Sure."

Rochelle sat smiling. "Damn, Angel is bad! We like her."

"We heard she used to be worse," Allyn said, trying not to look at Jennifer.

"We feel sorry for you, Rosalyn. She is going to wear you out!" Rochelle taunted.

"Angel will help you before she will hurt you," Jennifer said.

"That ain't what we heard," Rochelle said.

Marsha ushered the Genies into the Chapter room. They did not know what to expect. They had barely talked among themselves in the lobby. Marsha had them sitting on the floor while she lectured.

"Tonight was very embarrassing for the sorority. There was an intentional disregard for the pledge rules and a violation of law. What is even more disturbing is your lack of respect for our sorority rules. You three have made your line look sloppy and unorganized. Tonight, it will be up to the line to decide your fate because the women of Alpha Theta Lambda Sorority don't want women who have no respect for authority or themselves. Ladies, I give you permission to vote these girls in or out. When you have made your decision, let me know seven o'clock tomorrow morning."

Marsha left the room and stood outside the door. She could hear the Genies fuss and argue. The surprise was Crystal, who had always been quiet during the pledge period.

"We have cleaned rooms, washed and ironed clothes because of you three," said a once quiet Crystal. "We worked extra hard in our classes to get the GPA to pledge. You three are trying to ruin it for us. We are sick and tired of you, so we are voting off line."

"We are sick of you three, too, especially you Genie Talkin' Loud. We think we can be sisters with Back Stabber and Five Fingers Discount but not you. You got an attitude that we do not like," Phyllis said.

"Forget you, Phyllis! I don't like you either!" Alicia shouted.

"Listen to you! You do not talk like the rest of us. We are to call each other by our Genie name, not speak in contractions or as individuals. You do not want to be an Alpha, so why are you pledging? We vote off line, too," Vicki said.

"We vote off line on all three of you. You act as if you have no manners Genie Talkin Loud. Where did you grow up?" asked a snobbish Anne.

Alicia was steaming after hearing the last two Genies talk. They called one, Genie Fashion Fair and the other, Genie Flori Roberts. Alicia was jealous of the two. She usually felt insecure in their presence. They came from middle class backgrounds. Their parents paid cash for their education, whereas Alicia was attending with the assistance of grants.

"Who in the hell do you think you are?" Alicia shouted, as she moved toward Anne. Trish, who was rather large, jumped up.

"We are not going to have any fighting," Trish said in a high-pitched voice, which belied her frame.

"We are not afraid of you either," a very tiny voice said. Alicia turned quickly at the small person and walked toward her. Lisa rushed to stop Alicia who was on the verge of a fight.

"We are not going to let you fight anybody. If you want to throw down, then all of us will tag your ass. You did not have to go to Big Danny's tonight. We are sick of all three of your shit, but we are not voting y'all off line," Lisa said.

Marsha was at the door, trying to keep from laughing out loud. She had to catch herself. She didn't want to be heard.

Lisa was still for a moment. "We are going to do laundry for all the Big Sisters in a show of apology for you three," Lisa said loudly.

"Who said anything about us doing laundry?" April asked.

"We should come up with our own punishment to save face. Nobody is going to be voted off line. We started together and we will finish together. If you, Genie Talkin Loud, want to drop line, that is a personal decision," Lisa continued loudly. The Genies looked at her strangely.

"If you three want to be our sisters, then fall in place. If any of you fuck up again and we get demerits, we are going to tag your ass real good. Can I get an Amen!" Lisa said loudly. The girls laughed and cheered, except Alicia.

"We are trying to earn our symbols and you three are creating problems so what is it going to be?" Lisa asked out loud. The group looked at the three girls.

"I'm sorry," Evelyn said.

"It is not 'I,' Genie Five Fingers Discount, it is 'we'," said a pleasant Anne.

Lisa clapped and the others did, too. "What is going to be Genie Back Stabber?"

"We are sorry, too," said a humble Janet. The girls cheered again.

"Okay, Miss St. Louie, Miss Gateway Capitol, what about you?" said a fired up Lisa. Alicia looked at Lisa. They both came from the same side of the tracks and she was defending that reputation. She knew who had the captainship now.

"We are sorry," Alicia mumbled.

Lisa shook her head. *"No, No, No!* Say it loud Genie, that is your name!"

"We said we are sorry!" Alicia shouted with an attitude.

Lisa stood closer to the door and talked even louder. "We are going to show Big Sister Good Witch of the Got-Damn North, Big Sister Big Ass Barbie Doll, Big Sister I'm too Damn Cute Tender Loving Care and all the other damn big sisters that we are for real! Can I get an Amen!" Lisa said. The girls cheered.

After hearing that, Marsha decided to leave. Lisa beckoned for Alicia, Phyllis and Crystal. Lisa opened the door slowly. The girls peeped their heads out, watching Marsha go to her room. They closed the door.

"We felt someone was outside the door. Listen up everybody, we have got to work together. Big Sister to Hell with the Chief is expecting us to give a good show at the Jamboree. We will deal with anybody that steps out of line in our own way. And by the way, we are not doing laundry or cleaning anybody's room."

An exhausted Marsha looked at Gina and closed her eyes. She shook her head. "These girls are driving me crazy," she finally said. There were fifteen senior Alphas in Gina and Marsha's room.

"What's up?" one Alpha asked.

"Genie Talkin' Loud Ain't Sayin' Nothin' has lost. Her sidekicks, Genie Back Stabber and Genie Five Finger Discount have abandoned ship. It looks like it's going to be okay. Lisa is smarter than I thought."

"Oh really! Are they ready for the test?"

"Everyone except for those three. I know they will flunk it big time."

"Make sure they take it tomorrow morning."

"Soror President, what are we going to do about Genie Talkin Loud. Rumor has it that she drinks heavily at parties. Initiation is just two weeks ahead. How are we going to correct her behavior?"

"She is more like a brazen hussy, if you ask me."

"You are both right, but there is little to do at this point. She has gotten over on us but Plan B might work. Is our nominee holding strong Marsha?"

"She is doing fine, but she might be too much for Rita. She has a much different personality than what we thought."

"Good or bad?" Gina asked concerned.

"Oh, it's good but I don't know how the other sorors are going to take her as Vice President."

"We'll discuss it later. Whoever are the pledge mothers of those three delinquents, I want you to tie up their time every day until the Night of Solitude. Make sure they practice for the Jamboree. I want them to kick ass Saturday night."

Some looked at one another. They did not have the heart to tell Gina the rehearsal was horrible. She would die if she had seen their show. This line of girls was important to her. She bet Linda that the Genies would walk away with the trophy this year. Betting was something Gina didn't do.

The Genies had rehearsed long hours every day. Lisa met with various groups of girls to perfect the dance steps and movements. The most exciting part was when they found out that Crystal and Alicia could sing very well. Since the night Alicia got caught, she and Lisa worked together closely. It was difficult for Alicia to appreciate Lisa going the extra mile. Lisa was the only one who defended her when the line voted her to quit. She had to give up her captainship.

During one rehearsal, Lisa found out that Alicia had two brothers and one sister. They all had different fathers. She, like Lisa, had no idea who he was. They spent time together bashing their fathers unmercifully. It gave them a sense of connection and relief.

The Genies were rehearsing in the television room at Morrison Hall. Lisa got a chance to see Dee Dee as she walked by. They both smiled and waved. As they practiced on spins and turns, Lisa felt dizzy. She stopped, trying to catch her bearings. The room was spinning. She reached out, grabbed Alicia's shirt, and collapsed to the floor. One of the girls gasped. They all gathered around her.

Alicia tried to get Lisa to open her eyes, but she wouldn't. The girls became scared. Alicia sent someone to get Gina. Some Genies began to cry. Alicia tried to quiet them, but they wouldn't stop. Lisa finally opened her eyes and then closed them again. Some Genies panicked.

Gina rushed in the room. Immediately, she checked Lisa for a pulse and for breathing. Lisa was breathing. The girls helped Gina lift Lisa onto the sofa. It didn't take much because she was so light. Gina unbuttoned her blouse. She had a Genie remove Lisa's T-shirt and switched it with her blouse. Gina stared at Lisa's frail chest. It looked like she hadn't eaten in weeks. Gina turned Lisa's shirt inside out and squeezed into it.

Lisa opened her eyes and mumbled something. She tried to get up but failed. She moved around listlessly. She saw Gina and called her "momma."

The girls talked at once. One said they heard Lisa mumble how tired she was. Crystal said she didn't understand how Lisa had lasted as long as she had, running nonstop doing homework, special projects and trying to make a success of the show.

"What special projects?" Gina asked. The girls looked at one another wondering who would tell. Gina looked at them and they dropped their eyes one by one.

"Let me ask again, and I better get an answer. What special projects?"

Crystal broke the silence. She told how Lisa had been running errands and working hard to remove demerits from Big Sister Barbie Doll. Another girl told how Big Sister Barbie Doll had her working hard too. Other girls told about how they had been running errands and how it interfered with their studies. Gina tried to maintain her cool. She tried to quiet them, but they kept going. Some cried and some yelled.

Gina asked if they had told the Dean of Pledges and they all said, "No." Tina begged Gina to keep it a secret and not to tell Big Sister Natural Woman. Gina looked into the fear-filled eyes of the girl and said, "It's going to be okay." She smiled and hurried everyone away, except Alicia. Gina had her turn her shirt inside before getting the house mother.

Gina explained what had happened to the house mother, who explained it to the paramedics. They strapped Lisa onto the bed and took her away. Gina and Marsha hurried to the hospital to admit Lisa. It took two hours before Lisa was assigned a room.

As Lisa slept, Gina took a good look at her. Lisa was pale. There were dark circles around her eyes and her hair was dry. Gina began to pace. She considered herself an observant person and for her not to have noticed Lisa's condition was unacceptable. They met weekly and sometimes more. She couldn't understand why she had not notice Lisa's declining condition.

"Gina, I'm sorry. I didn't know they were running themselves ragged. They never said anything," Marsha said.

"It looks like Jessica is trying to undermine me again, but I will put an end to it," Gina said.

Marsha gave her friend a questionable look. Donna came into the room with Cheryl, Rita, Carla and Marie. They walked to Lisa's bed and looked at her. Donna shook her head.

"We need to do something, Gina. This is not good politically," Rita said.

Gina paced the floor trying to plan her next move.

Chapter 7

The Genies talked with Lisa, trying to keep up her spirits. She had received several get well cards and many visitors throughout the day. She was surprised to know how many people liked or cared about her.

It was easy for her to listen to the chatter in the room since she had been silenced for so long. Crystal talked more. Janet had become extremely quiet. She didn't have an added comment to make on everything Alicia said. Alicia still talked "big" but the others didn't seem to care as much. Evelyn continued to socialize but it was with Anne and Vicki and they were not wild girls. Tina was still timid. She hung close to Lisa like a little sister more so than an equal. The big surprise was Phyllis. She was arrogant now. She used to talk and laugh loud. Now she sat quietly with her nose turned up. It was understood to be because she had the most arrogant pledge mother, Jessica.

Lisa wanted to get some sleep because she had been up all day talking to people. She wanted to ask everyone to leave. She thought about how she used to say the first thing that came to her mind, regardless if it was rude or not. Now she considered other people's feelings before speaking.

"Genie Motor Mouth, we are going to put on a good show tonight for Big Sister Good Witch of the North," Tina whispered to Lisa in her tiny voice.

"We heard that, Genie Munchkin," Lisa whispered back.

Tina looked jumpy. Lisa wondered what was up. Tina slipped Lisa a note trying not to look guilty which made her look guiltier. She turned her head from side to side to see if anyone was watching as she passed the note. Lisa closed her eyes in a huff and grabbed the note. She slid it under her leg.

"We need to go Genies. Tell Lisa good-bye," Marsha said. They all lined up and kissed Lisa on the cheek. They left Lisa in the room with Gina, Carla, Rita, Cheryl and Marie. Lisa looked at the five women and wondered why they were staying? She didn't know what to say to them so she just stared at them. They didn't say anything. They began whispering amongst themselves. There was a knock on the door.

"Come in," Rita said. The door opened and Lisa almost lost consciousness when she saw Cameron, Brad, Tony and Evans, four Aristocrats and Michael and Kevin, two Pharaohs, entered the room, unescorted by their Big Brothers. The five women turned around and stared at the young men suspiciously. They became tense, including Lisa, under the glare of the Alphas.

"Our Big Brothers told us to deliver these cards in case they could not visit Miss Arvell," Cameron announced. The women continued to look unconvinced.

"Miss Arvell, this card is from the brotherhood of Beta Gamma Delta Fraternity Incorporated, Alpha Psi Chapter," Cameron continued in announcer-style voice and handed the card to Lisa.

"Miss Arvell," Michael bellowed, "this card is from the men of Lambda Phi Chi Fraternity Incorporated, Phi Nu Chapter." He handed the card to Lisa.

The boys looked around the room. They looked at the women and the women looked at them. This went on for five minutes.

This was a tough audience, Cameron thought. He discreetly tugged Brad's jacket. He followed Cameron to the foot of Lisa's bed, blocking the Alphas' view of Lisa.

Cameron apologized for not greeting them upon entering the room. While he rambled on, Michael slipped a card and a note under Lisa's sheet, which caused her to jump. He cleared his throat and Cameron stopped talking in mid-sentence. He joined the rest of his partners in crime and said, "We must be leaving now. Miss Arvell, get well soon. And ladies, have a nice evening." The young men left.

The Alphas turned their attention to Lisa. She held the two cards tightly. Before anyone could say anything, someone knocked on the door.

"Come in," Rita said.

When the door opened, Lisa mouth dropped opened. It was Kyle carrying a plant and a card. "Hello ladies," he said, looking daringly at the women. "And how are you doing Lisa?" he asked and handed her the card. He put the plant on the table next to her bed.

"We are fine Kyle. Thank you," Lisa said.

"Are you really doing fine, Lisa?" Kyle asked suspiciously. He looked over at the women and then at Lisa.

"Yes we are."

"What happened to you?" he asked accusingly, looking back at the women.

"We are suffering from exhaustion. We are also malnourished and have low iron," Lisa said, trying not to get irritated. She figured if she got in trouble, it wouldn't be because of Cameron but because of this nut.

Kyle continued his interrogation. "How did that happen?"

"We did not get proper rest nor did we eat properly. That is all," Lisa said, trying to bring an end to Kyle's questions.

"But why?"

"Kyle please! We are okay. How did you do on your COBOL assignment?"

"I got forty out of forty. Oh, by the way," Kyle said, pulling a folded paper from his back pocket, "here is the homework assignment for the next speech." He handed it to Lisa.

"Thank you," Lisa sighed with relief.

The women watched as Kyle bent over toward Lisa's ear and whispered, "Look little woman, Jennifer sent me over here with that plant to see what happened to you and to make sure everything was okay. So if you are going to get huffy with someone, get huffy with her."

This was too much, Lisa thought. She looked at Kyle and he was serious. He really wanted to find out what had happened.

"Lisa, you are here for an education. All of this pledge stuff must be put in perspective," Kyle said and shot an angry look at the five women. Gina pursed her lips. Rita's mouth opened. Marie crossed her arms. Donna just stared and Carla fought to keep from laughing.

"Get well soon and see you in class Monday. Good evening ladies," Kyle said with his head high and left. The Alphas were flabbergasted. They looked at Lisa. Carla finally laughed.

"Where in the hell did he come from?" Rita asked.

"Who is he?" Donna asked and they all looked at Lisa.

"He is Kyle Thomas. He is in our Speech class," Lisa answered. Before anyone could continue, there was another knock on the door.

"Come in," Gina said angrily. Linda, Angel and Denise walked in.

"I don't know whether to come in or to stay out! Who is behind the angry voice?" Linda asked.

"Look what the wind has blown in," Gina said.

"I should have known," said Linda. She walked over to Lisa's bed. "Honey, how are you feeling?"

"We are fine, Miss Stevens."

"Hello Lisa, are you feeling better?"

"Yes, Miss Smith."

Angel, Linda and Denise over to the others and began to talk low. Linda turned around and looked at Lisa, "Sweetness, you don't mind us girls being rude for a few minutes do you?"

"No, Miss Stevens."

Linda watched Lisa grip the cards in her hands. "Looks like you've gotten a couple of cards, how nice."

"Girl you won't believe this," Marie said trying to control herself from laughing.

"What's up?" Angel asked while prodding her.

"Four Aristocrats and two Pharaohs delivered those cards to Miss Arvell for their Big Brothers," Marie said, trying to sound like Cameron.

"Without their Big Brothers?" Denise asked.

"Honey yes. That fine ass Cameron Johnson gave some spiel about their Big Brothers being unable to visit Miss Arvell," Rita added. They all gave Lisa surprised looks. She blushed.

"Just think, ladies. Wouldn't it have been nice to have had a man put his life on the line when we were pledging? What I wouldn't have done to have had Craig slip me a note every once and awhile. I would give almost anything to see your cards, Lisa," Linda said slyly.

"It would be nice to read what the Betas and the Lambdas wrote to our poor little sick Genie. Are you going to read your cards, Lisa?" Rita asked.

Lisa had no choice. She hoped that Cameron and the Forty Thieves were careful with the cards. She read the cards with the sayings next to the signatures. Linda looked at Gina. They couldn't imagine the Betas or Lambdas sending any personal greetings.

"Can I see your cards?" Gina asked smiling. Lisa extended her arm. Gina took the cards and opened them. Her expression immediately went blank.

"Some Howdy Doody brother came in here, accusing us of beating Lisa," Cheryl said, ignoring the expression on Gina's face.

Lisa opened the card Kyle delivered, thinking it might be from Jennifer. Too her surprise, it was from him.

"Oh, let me see, Gina," Marie said, taking the cards. She looked down and said nothing as well. They passed the cards around. All the women noticed that the signatures were forged. Half the Betas names were written in a left hand slant. Carlos' name was spelled with a "K." Someone left an "n" out of Kenneth's name.

"Not only are they cute and courageous but they are illiterate as well," Linda said with spite. The women laughed. Another knock sounded.

"Come in," Rita said in a huff. Lisa was tired and sleepy. She didn't want to see another visitor. Carlos and Thomas entered the room. They spoke to everyone and handed Lisa a card. Gina quickly put the Aristocrats' cards in her purse.

"This reunion reminds me of freshmen year," said a happy Carlos.

"Hello ladies," Thomas said, exasperated.

"What's wrong with you?" Denise asked Thomas.

"Four of our Aristocrats have been missing for awhile. How long have you ladies been here?" asked a weary Thomas.

"We have been here most of the evening," Gina answered.

"We've just arrived," Angel said.

"Good, maybe they have changed their minds about coming," Thomas said trying to convince himself. "These brothers are driving me crazy. I will be so glad when all of this is over. We got some devilish ones pledging this time."

The women smiled. Thomas just assumed they would inform him of any delinquent acts. They figured if he didn't ask specifics, they weren't going to volunteer any information.

Lisa felt herself drifting. She didn't care if it was rude but she was going to sleep. She made sure the notes were secured under her legs. As she drifted, she heard them talk low. She thought back to the dance when Cameron caressed her back and made her body tingle. The idea alone made her relax more. She began to dream.

An older woman was pleading with a younger woman about staying home with her child. She preached about how smart the child was and how she was no trouble. The older woman told the younger one that she was wasting her time thinking he would come for her and the child but the woman wouldn't hear it. The older woman continued to preach about how the younger woman was smart enough to get a job and stop living off men. The younger one came to borrow money. She waved off the older one. She was upset. She just wanted some money.

The child asked the younger woman if she would get a chance to go home soon. The woman told the child if she can borrow the money, she can put it down on a new apartment, big enough for both of them. The child would have her own bedroom and go to a new school. The child asked when, and the woman said soon. She kissed the child on her forehead and looked at the older woman. The older woman let out a deep sigh and went to her bedroom. She came back and handed the woman something. The younger woman dropped her eyes and left. The child never saw her again.

Lisa sat around pouting. She re-read the card that the Forty Thieves had given her. She chuckled after reading their notes. The names some of them had were outrageous such as: Superfly, Big Bank Hank, Agent 007, Bingo Long, The Mack, Superman, Batman, The Green Hornet, James Brown, Rev. Ike and, of course, Shaft. She read Cameron's note over and over:

Hi Pumpkin,

It will be tough getting this note to you but you are worth every minute of the struggle. We have received the awaited for letter from Rolla. We will start their engineering program this coming fall. Now we have to make sure the money will be there in August. We think you need to reconsider what we've discussed.
SHAFT in Africa

Everything was perfect until now. She had hoped Cameron would not get accepted. His grades were too good. He asked her to join him in Rolla but she needed to stay at Missouri State to receive the answer she awaited for so long. What if her grandmother was wrong? Miss Mattie felt something strong spiritually. It was going to work out, Lisa kept telling herself. She just needed to be patient. If Cameron was meant for her, then she would have him. She had been alone all of her life so why should it change?

Another thorn in Lisa's side was Gina's refusal to allow her to perform at the Jamboree. This was the first time in years the Genies were a threat in the overall competition and she had to miss it. She was allowed to attend the Jamboree, but not to participate.

There was a knock on the door. Crystal opened it and greeted Carla and Gina.

"Well little lady, you look much, much better now," Gina said.

"We are well enough to perform tonight, Big Sister," Lisa said in a rush.

"Let's not continue this discussion," Gina said.

"Big Sister, we know you do not want to discuss it any more, but hear us out. We will not be doing any strenuous movements that will wear us down. We can't, uh, cannot sit on the sideline like a cheerleader while our sisters perform. We have worked too hard for this night. Oh please, Big

Sister, you got to let us do this," Lisa pleaded.

"Okay Lisa, you can perform tonight," Carla said with a sigh. Lisa looked at Carla with a frown. Who was she to give permission? "Big Sister Hail to the Chief said we could not," Lisa explained.

"*I* said you can perform," Carla emphasized. Lisa looked at Gina for a sign to indicate Carla's blessing was an override. Carla continued, "Make sure you don't over exert yourself. Just do your best." Carla smiled at Lisa and Crystal.

"Big Sister Let My People Go, are you coming tonight?" Lisa asked.

"I've pledged enough lines, mothered enough Genies, and attended enough Jamborees. I'll just wait to hear the results," Carla said.

Lisa liked seeing Carla smile. She reminded her of the super model Beverly Johnson. She was tall and graceful like Beverly. She wore her hair in a ponytail like the pictures she had seen of the supermodel.

Lisa never heard Carla raise her voice. She might emphasize something but she never snapped at her like Gina. Since Lisa's visits with Carla, she learned a great deal about Black History. Carla gave Lisa information that she had never learned in school. Lisa learned about the black woman's role in slavery, the Women's Suffrage Movement, the Civil Rights Movement, as well as the Black Power Movement. Lisa was fascinated by Carla. The visits were only one hour long and Lisa always hungered for more.

"Big Sister Let My People Go, can we spend a night with you?" Lisa asked without thinking.

"Can we spend a night too?" Crystal asked. The two requests stunned Carla. It was the first free weekend in weeks and the last thing she wanted was two eager beavers ruining it. Her boyfriend Dennis was in town and she only had one more night to share his company. These two girls were so excited that she really had to think about it.

"Forgive us Big Sister Hail to the Chief, we spoke without thinking. We are supposed to spend a night with you. We are very sorry," Lisa apologized.

"Please forgive us too. We are supposed to spend a night with Big Sister Elusive Lady," Crystal added.

"Who is Big Sister Elusive Lady?" Carla inquired.

"Diane," Gina answered.

"How appropriate," Carla mumbled to Gina.

"Okay ladies, come directly to my apartment after the Jamboree. Gina, don't let anyone tie up their time. I don't won't them coming over too late," ordered Carla.

Lisa and Crystal bumped hips. "Can other Genies come, too? They will get a kick out of your research on the black woman's role in the Black Panther Party as well as the Nation of Islam," Lisa begged.

"Look Lisa, your Big Sister will have enough on her hands with..." Carla silenced Gina in the middle of her speech.

"Whoever wants to come are welcome. Gina, make sure their pledge mothers don't hassle them about it. I need to go before I commit myself to something else," Carla said and turned the knob on the door.

"We won't let you down, Big Sisters," cheered an excited Lisa. Carla and

Gina nodded and smiled. When they closed the door, they could hear Lisa and Crystal scream. The women shook their heads. Gina looked at Carla with surprise.

"You know you didn't have to do that," Gina said.

"I know. It will give you and the ladies time to work on your plan."

"What about Dennis?"

"He will get mad, throw a tantrum and the rest, but I'll make it up to him."

Lisa was still jumping up and down. "Did you hear that? Carla said I can perform," Lisa said, emphasizing Carla's name. She sat on her bed with eyebrows raised. No one had ever gone against Gina openly; this was the first. "Let's go to the television room. I need to brush up," Lisa said.

There were plants on the window sill. The room was very neat with a scent of peach potpourri in the air. The two beds were dressed in floral comforters with matching pillow shams and bed skirts. Two teddy bears sat on each bed, resting on a pillow. There were posters of Earth, Wind & Fire, Prince and Teddy Pendergrass on the waslls.

"You can hang your things in the second closet."

Jennifer walked over to the closet and hung up her clothes. She was spending the whole day with Linda. Usually, she enjoyed meeting with Linda but today was different. She saw Rosalyn carrying her things to Angel's room to spend the day.

Linda was trying to read Jennifer's expression. "Queenie, why are you moping? You don't want to spend the day with me?"

"Oh no, oh, we mean, yes we do. We have been thinking about some things lately and it has us a little down," said a solemn Jennifer.

"What's the matter?"

"We are wondering about our relationship with Big Sister Bon Amie. We have not talked to her since we have been pledging. We really miss her."

"What did you want to talk to her about?"

"We just want to apologize for our behavior at the Beta's Ball."

"What did you do?"

"It is a long story. We just want to tell her that we do not like Mr. Johnson and he does not like us." Jennifer wondered if telling Linda about Lionel was risky. Linda seemed to know about everything anyway. She might know about Angel and Lionel.

"Oh Queenie, she knows. She is allowing you to grow during this period. She has had a lot of influence on you for two years. She just wants you to spread your wings. It's time for someone else to corrupt you," Linda said teasingly. Jennifer chuckled too.

"She doesn't spend a lot a time with any Cherub," Linda said.

"It seems like she is spending a lot of time with Cherub Could Care Less. I just saw her go to my, uh, our old room with clothes in her hands."

Linda saw that Jennifer was jealous. "Rosalyn is in a heap of trouble, Jennifer. Any time when the President and the Vice President become involved, it means trouble. Let's hope your sisters will learn from their mistakes," Linda said.

"Miss Smith of Alpha Theta Lambda is Genie Arvell's, Special. We do not think she is in trouble," Jennifer complained.

"That's Alpha Theta Lambda. We do things differently in Phi Kappa Psi."

"We just do not want her to think that we like Mr. Johnson. Did you know that he kissed me, uh, us? He told us at the dinner, the next day, that he was sorry and it was not the right thing to do. He told us that he wanted to be our friend. We agreed."

"Believe me, Angel knows everything. She and Lionel are still very good friends."

"What about Steve? We thought they were dating. She just dumped him like that?" Jennifer asked and snapped her fingers.

"Steve and Angel are very good friends. Steve came around a lot more when Angel and Lionel were fighting. Angel has quite a few male friends."

"Miss Stevens, do you mind me asking why you were flirting with Mr. Johnson at the Ball?"

Linda looked playfully at Jennifer. Linda picked up a teddy bear and began to laugh. "I'm what you call a buffer. Angel thought you might be a little vulnerable that night, so she asked me for a favor."

Jennifer was off balance after Linda's explanation.

"I'm not a whore," Linda continued. "Although people might say that I am. They can't find one man on this dreadful campus that I've had sex with. I like to flirt and my friends know that I do. If they want to know if their man will cheat, they send me. I flirt and if they jump at the bait, I stop the stallion in his tracks and tell my friends. I know it's juvenile but some women are."

Jennifer kept staring at Linda in disbelief. "Why do you do that?"

"Because my friends are insecure. It also helps me to understand the male ego. They are so vulnerable when it comes to sex. I find it hilarious. Lionel caught on to me because he has known me as long as he's known Angel. He informed me that he had no intentions of taking advantage of you, so later in the evening, I stopped. Angel still wasn't satisfied so she had to see for herself. The kiss didn't help matters."

"If they like each other so much, why are they keeping everything a secret?"

"It's really Angel that's keeping it a secret. When her daddy met Lionel, Mr. Smith took one look at him and immediately disliked him. If you knew Bill Smith the way I do, he doesn't hold his tongue for nothing. My dear friend is paranoid so she won't bring him around to the family get-togethers. She was trying to keep it a secret from her close friends, just in case we slip up or something."

"Why does he not like Lionel...Mr. Johnson?"

"That's what Angel and Lionel both want to know. Lionel, with his temper, got pissed and said a few things to Angel's daddy. Well, the rest is history."

Jennifer got an earful on this visit. Angel's father doesn't like Lionel, but she wants to keep seeing him and keep it a secret. How crazy!

"Lionel reminds me of Angel's father, Bill, and Cameron reminds me of

Gina's stepfather, Paul. Bill was the type that liked the Creole look, fair skin and beautiful hair. He liked them sophisticated and glamorous. To my understanding, that was how Angel's mother looked. My mother said he wanted a Mercedes but only had enough money to buy a Volkswagen. But Paul Smith, Gina's stepfather, wanted a woman that would tend to the children."

"We are not glamorous or sophisticated, so why would Mr. Johnson be interested in us if it were not for sex?"

"You have that look if you groom it. Fair skin doesn't make you pretty nor does long hair. You can learn how to behave the right way. You are very innocent and men like Lionel know that if they catch you before some sister with an attitude comes along and digs in her claws, they can mold you to be pretty much whatever they want you to be," Linda said in a scary way.

"Thank God for buffers," Jennifer said with relief.

"Let's fix your hair. I hear you are going to be in the spotlight this evening," Linda said and plugged in the curling irons.

Jennifer grinned. "We have a little something to do in the show."

Linda smiled and then it faded as she combed Jennifer's hair. It was much thicker and longer than she expected. It was so black that it shined. "You don't have a relaxer, do you?" Linda asked and plugged in the electric hot comb that Jennifer brought. Jennifer shook her head. "Maybe you need to give it a thought. You either need a relaxer or cut it," Linda said and parted Jennifer's hair in sections.

"Miss Stevens, do you believe in God?" Jennifer asked with her head tilted forward, waiting for Linda to began pressing.

"Most of the times."

"Do you believe in *signs*?"

Linda's forehead creased. "What are *signs*?"

"Something that happens, giving indication of whether something good or bad is about to happen."

Linda continued frowning, mainly because of Jennifer's hair. "I guess I do. I don't put much stock in it. I believe that whatever is going to happen will happen. You have to be smart enough to rebound if it's not good."

Linda's frown lessen as she pressed Jennifer's hair. She was enjoying helping her Special get ready for the Jamboree. She had bought the ribbon that would go in Jennifer's hair. What impressed Linda about Jennifer was the fact that she appreciated the small things. Any and everything Linda did for Jennifer, she appreciated with such adulation. Jennifer impressed Linda most when she nursed Linda through a cold one weekend. She made sure Linda had plenty of orange juice and aspirins. She cleaned Linda's room without her having to be asked. No one had ever done that before because Linda never asked for anything.

"Miss Stevens, who was your Special when you pledged?"

"Someone by the name of Estelle Oliver. She was a bitch!"

"Why?"

"Because she's crazy."

"Was Big Sister Bon Amie a good Cherub? Was her Special a bitch too?" Jennifer paused. She turned and looked at Linda. "We are sorry, we did not mean to say that."

"Let's just say she was a very clever Cherub. She had the biggest bitch as her Special, Lori Bass." Jennifer jerked her head up and turned around quickly. Linda almost burned her. They both jumped. "Queenie, if you want me to do a good job, you must keep still," Linda said shaking. Jennifer nodded and tilted her head forward again.

"What were some of the clever things Big Sister did?"

Linda gave a devilish grin. "Now, your big sister never confessed to anything. Most of us knew she was behind the scenes. She has a very innocent way of staying, uh...clean. We joined forces with the Genies, Aristocrats and Pharaohs to get through the tough times. The men helped us more than we helped them. Sometimes I wished we would have done more to help them. Anyway, for some reason, those two bitches I mentioned and a couple of others couldn't make it to our birthing."

"What is the birthing?"

Linda realized she didn't mean to discuss the birthing. "I can only tell you it's a trying ceremony. Those women claimed that some fraternity pledges, all wearing black, kidnapped them. They were kidnapped one by one. We waited for them, but they never showed. The other big sisters had to go on with the birthing without them because my mother and the other chapter founders were coming for the initiation."

"Did they make the initiation?"

"Oh yes! A note was left on the Chapter room door telling where they were. We went and got them out of the Chapel's basement. They were mad." Linda laughed. "My mother asked what was going on and they said nothing. I learned to respect those ladies afterward because they didn't retaliate. They had been beaten by one of the best and they made sure she became president. They respected intelligence, which we found out later. Those four women are still good friends today. They remind me of my mother and her entourage. Life is a game to them. They have a knack that I love, mystery. That is why I like Angel so much, there is a lot of mystery behind those big brown eyes."

Linda finished pressing Jennifer's hair. She took smaller sections of hair and began curling. After she curled several small sections, she rolled them with the few large rollers that Jennifer had brought.

"Miss Stevens, is Big Sister Sweet Sensation like those other big sisters?" Jennifer asked, tiptoeing.

Linda had to smile at Jennifer's gentle attempt at calling Annette a bitch. "No, Annette is a little different."

"Why does she hate us?"

"She hates what you can become."

"And what is that?"

"Competition!"

"Competition?"

Linda let out a low sigh and pulled a chair next to Jennifer. She sat relaxed with arms and legs crossed, toes pointed down. "My mother told me that fear causes people to behave irrationally. You can't be afraid to become something different. What I'm telling you is to play the hand that God gave you. If the game is fair complexion, don't play because you will lose. If the game is rich parents, walk away from the table. If the game is beautiful women, tell the dealer to deal you in. Men are into long hair so play it up. Men like slim shapely bodies so be conscientious about what you eat. Men like perfect features so flaunt them."

"Men like intelligence too, Miss Stevens."

"Queenie, I don't care how smart you are but if you are not easy on the eyes, you can forget it! Men don't see personality. We do. Physical attraction is first and mystery is second. Smart women make men look dumb, but mystery intrigues them. The number one thing to remember is, if you don't act beautiful, then you will never be beautiful. It's all about perception."

Jennifer looked at herself in the mirror. The large rollers looked like antennas shooting from her head. She laughed. "I look like a moon monster."

Linda stood behind her and smiled. "This moon monster will get five minutes in the spotlight. How well you play your hand tonight will determine if you can play with the big girls. The idea of me failing as a Pledge Special is unthinkable."

"We won't fail you, Miss Stevens."

Chapter 8

All the sororities' and fraternities' pledgees were at the Student Union. Uniforms ranged from Egyptian attire to army fatigues. Students were excited about the night's show. For those who wanted to pledge the next year, it gave them indication as to who would be the powerhouses on campus.

The Jamboree was a fundraiser to help pay for whatever necessary to complete the pledge period. The total take would be divided by eight organizations equally. In the past, not all organizations participated in the Jamboree. They soon found out that this was a good marketing tool to get potential interested candidates.

The pledge lines were in the upstairs meeting rooms working on last minute moves. The line captains had to pull the number for of order appearance in the show. The Pharaohs of Lambda Phi Chi Fraternity were first followed by the Squires of Gamma Zeta Tau Fraternity. The Cherubs of Phi Kappa Psi Sorority held the number three spot followed by the Unicorns of Epsilon Eta Rho Fraternity. The Pearls of Sigma Phi Pi Sorority would perform fifth and Lisa pulled the number six spot for the Genies. Steve pulled number seven for the Aristocrats and the Kittens of Upsilon Psi Xi Sorority would perform last.

Lisa felt good about performing sixth. The way Cameron had talked, the Aristocrats were sure to win. Lisa did not want the Genies to get nervous performing before the Aristocrats. The Genies were wearing navy tams on their heads, navy slacks with gold belts, and dark gold, wide-sleeve poet blouses.

The Cherubs wore white dropped-crotch, baggy pants shoved into black riding boots. They had on white, puff-sleeve blouses with ruffles around the collars and cuffs. They wore wine colored vests which belonged to the Kappas skirt-and-vest uniform. Jennifer's hair was pulled back into a long, curly ponytail with a wine colored ribbon tied in a large bow.

The Ballroom at the Student Union was large. It could seat over a thousand students in folding chairs. The judges were at the front of the room. One was a city councilman, one was a teacher from the university, one was a teacher from the high school, one was an owner of a small business and another was a member of the PTA. Three judges were women and two were men.

The performers sat in chairs at the front over to the right. The Pharaohs were positioned to begin the show. Girls screamed at the sight of them. They had oiled their chests and wore white kilts and Egyptian headpieces. They stood with legs apart, barefoot with fists on hips, like Yul Brenner in "The King and I."

Jennifer couldn't help but notice Michael's chest. No wonder the girls were screaming. He looked irresistible. He was five-foot-eleven with a clean-cut look. Jennifer stared at his broad shoulders and sleek physique. She could physically feel the excitement that the others verbally expressed.

The Pharaohs marched out singing a song that no one could hear. They were in desperate need of a microphone. They told the history of the Pharaohs, but they did not talk loudly enough. Even the performers could not hear themselves. Students yelled from the audience, telling them to speak up and stop sounding like girls. They performed a play, more so than a traditional Jamboree show. The audience became bored. They saw the Pharaohs walking off the floor. Someone yelled, "It's about time!" The audience laughed.

The Squires were next in their black jeans and black T-Shirts with "SQUIRES" printed on the front in white. They came out yelling, "We are the squires." They yelled it several times, over and over until someone yelled, "Hell, we know," and the audience laughed again. Some Squires performed one set of motions and the others did another. They stomped and yelled about being the best. They performed their entire show walking around in a circle. Finally it was over and the audience barely clapped.

The Cherubs were next. A lot of boys whistled as they lined up. Angel and two other Kappas positioned three microphone stands in front of the audience. Anita walked to the center microphone and began to sing.

Anita finished her prelude. The Cherubs came out singing "Sophisticated Cherubs" to the tune of Natalie Cole's "Sophisticated Lady." The audience clapped as the Cherubs sang. As Anita sang, the Cherubs struck Playboy Bunny poses. After Anita finished, the girls stomped and clapped out a rhythm. Jennifer walked and grabbed the microphone to the left of Anita and started strutting around. The audience yelled. She took the mic and began rapping. Rapping had just started to gain popularity on the airwaves and the Cherubs were on the cutting edge.

A boy behind the girls played the bongos and the girls shook their shoulders and danced. Jennifer was still in front. She snatched the ribbon from her hair and, with one motion, she removed the ponytail holder and let her hair drop. The audience clapped louder. She turned sideways to the audience, teasing them by doing hip rolls. She ran her fingers through the length of her long hair and the boys barked.

They sang another song and performed some more dance routines. After they finished their show, Lisa sat stunned. She could not believe Jennifer running her fingers through her hair. She hated wearing her hair down. The thought of Jennifer being the center of attention was also surprising. As the audience clapped louder, the Genies looked uptight.

Lisa signaled them to go outside the room.

The Unicorns were performing in army fatigues and black army boots while the Genies were outside getting themselves together. Lisa thought that she would have to give a pep talk, but it wasn't necessary. Some were stretching and some were practicing harmonizing. She saw Alicia singing to herself doing hand motions.

While the Unicorns were finishing their show, Linda turned around in her seat and asked, "Do you want to pull out now or wait till after the little darlings perform?"

Gina responded, "A bet is a bet Linda. Don't tell me you are getting nervous?"

Linda smiled and said, "So it's not over until the fat lady sings."

"You're right and she's about to sing soon," Gina said playfully.

"You do have a couple of fat ones on line. Toodaloo," Linda said maliciously, waving her fingers. She turned around.

The ten Pearls performed next. They wore purple jumpsuits with pink blouses. They sang very softly. They sang that they were cute and pretty. They didn't have much in the way of movements. They walked around, telling the audience to check them out. Someone let out a loud yawn and the audience laughed. Soon the show was over.

Alicia, Crystal and Janet placed the three microphones in front again. Alicia gave a three-snap signal. All three began to rap. They motioned the audience to stand. Three Genies walked out with iron folding chairs. They opened them and staggered them behind the three rappers. They gave the rappers a clap, stomp signal. Lisa, Tina and Vicki ran out, leaped on top of the chairs and did back flips off the top in unison. They did two additional back hand springs after they landed. Instead of the audience cheering, they gasped.

The other girls stopped the rhythm and the three acrobats pointed to the audience and sang "We Are Family" with Alicia singing the lead. The last three Genies ran out and jumped on top of the chairs stomping.

The audience clapped and danced. The Genies stunned the crowd with their acrobatics and stunts. It was time for Crystal to shine. She sang Cheryl Lynn's "Got To Be Real." The Genies were so fired up that they harmonized loudly. Their show was over and the audience roared. Gina tapped Linda on the shoulder and whispered in her ear, "What do you think of the fat ladies now?"

The audience was still cheering when the Aristocrats came out in red Karate gear with black sashes as belts and black army boots. It took awhile until the audience settled down. They stood with legs apart, fists out in a Karate stance. Finally, the audience settled down. Someone sang out, "Kung Fu Fighting." The audience laughed. The Aristocrats were unmoved. They waited for the signal from the leader. Steve walked down the line of boys, punching them in the stomachs. As he passed them, they fell forward in pushup formation.

Steve blew a whistle. They jumped to attention and chanted something about being mad as hell and not taking it anymore. They did a rhythm with their army boots that no one had ever heard before. The audience started clapping. The line of boys slid out in staggered formation doing movements and slid back in a perfect straight line.

Cameron, Brad, Steve and Tony jumped up and down while the rest of the boys continued to stomp. They jumped forward chanting, "We're too hot to handle," grabbing their crotches. They rotated their hips. Girls were beyond excited. Next, the top of the Karate gear came off. Girls screamed again. The Aristocrats stopped and leaned back. They paused and Steve yelled. They fell forward in pushup formation, stretching out face down. The audience saw the boys' hips moving up and down. The Aristocrats chanted, "Yes! Yes! Yes!" Girls raced to the front.

Lisa blushed. She could not believe Cameron or Steve would do such a dirty act. They got up and did more stomps and a couple of combinations. Their show was over.

The last group was the Kittens. They usually had a good show but this year was going to be tough. For them to come right behind the Aristocrats and they behind the Genies was going to be tough keeping the audience's attention. There were six of them. They had on dark green smock tops and gold pants. They came out singing a song to the tune of "Groove Line" by Heatwave. They did good moves and combinations. They had two girls that could sing well but the audience was ready to hear a verdict. They did some rhythm patterns with their hands and feet which concluded their show.

Lisa realized that the Kittens performed well like always. The audience clapped loudly, but there was no loud cheering or screaming. Lisa felt as if the Kittens were overshadowed by sex.

The Master of Ceremonies came to the microphone. A hush fell over the audience. The M.C. introduced the judges to the crowd, but nobody cared. They wanted to know who had won.

Third place went to the Kittens of Upsilon Psi Xi Sorority. The girls ran to receive their trophy. Lisa did quick calculations. If the Kittens won third, that left only two spots for the three top performers. She wondered who would lose out. She figured with the dirty little act in the Aristocrats show, maybe they were disqualified.

Aristocrats took second place. The boys shouted as they went to receive their trophy. Lisa's heart raced. It was between the Genies and the Cherubs for first place. The Cherubs were too good to lose out to the last two groups.

Lisa's concentration was on the speaker's next announcement. She was able to block out the audience noises just to hear who won. She heard him speak, "In first place, the winners of Jamboree 1980, the Cherubs of Phi Kappa Psi..." Lisa's head dropped. She had blocked out everything after hearing Cherubs. She could not believe the Genies didn't place. All she heard were girls screaming. She had her head down, not believing the Cherubs beat them. Tina rushed over to her and told her to come. Lisa looked at the excited petite person and asked, "Why?"

"We won. We tied with the Cherubs," Tina said.

Lisa looked at the tiny person as if she had told one of the biggest lies.

She saw her Genie sisters at the front of the stage jumping up and down. She walked to the stage with Tina. The judges' decided to give the trophy to the Genies and have another made for the Cherubs the following week. Lisa saw Angel walking away from the judges table looking happy. Lisa found out later that Angel had insisted that the Genies take the trophy and the Cherubs would wait.

Tons of students congratulated the performers. Jennifer blushed as people called her "hot stuff." Angel realized, during practice, that Jennifer yearned to shine in the show, so she thought of something that would give her the opportunity. Jennifer looked at the Pharaohs. She could see on Michael's face that trouble was ahead for getting beat out by three groups of girls. The Aristocrats might be facing trouble as well because Steve didn't look happy either.

Lisa saw the Aristocrats form a straight line and walk to the lounge where no one was around. She quietly followed to witness the scene. Three Betas passed by and walked to the line of boys. Lisa let out a sound when one of the Betas slapped only Cameron upside the head.

"He has been catching hell from the beginning,"Alicia said.

Lisa jumped. "I thought he and Lionel were friends," Lisa said eagerly.

"Lionel only has a few friends and he is not one of them. Come on before we get in trouble for looking at some boys," Alicia said and walked away.

Lisa could not stop watching as the other Betas shoved Cameron. He kept his head high, not weakening. She decided she had seen enough. Before she walked back, her attention went to Jennifer, who was talking happily with Candice and Alexis. She flipped her hair as she talked. Lisa saw how she made the Kappas' famous facial expressions-she closed her eyes and turned up her nose as she spoke; she threw out her hands and hunched her shoulders in a look of surprise. Lisa figured she had seen enough when Jennifer tossed her head in an act of exasperation.

Lisa also noticed a change in Rochelle, too. She was talking happily with Rosalyn and Patrice. Rochelle was different. Usually, she waved her hands wildly when laughing. Now, she put them to her mouth as if she were controlling herself. She did not move as much when she talked anymore. Her posture was straight. She wore her hair smoothed back in a bun. She wore makeup which she had never done before. Lisa noticed how the makeup and pearl earrings gave Rochelle a sense of sophistication. Her close friends were changing and she wasn't.

When she passed the Cherubs, she caught Jennifer's eye. Jennifer smiled and gave a sneaky wave. Lisa forced a smile and gave a quick nod.

As Gina talked to the Genies, Kenneth Carnes, her boyfriend, the President of Lambda Phi Chi Fraternity, whispered in her ear. She nodded.

"We are going to get our things and spend a night with Big Sister Let My People Go. Genie Motor Mouth said we could go," said an excited Tina.

"Who all are going to spend a night with Carla?" asked a worried Gina. All but two Genies raised their hands. Gina closed her eyes. "It's quite a few of you visiting your Big Sister tonight so don't keep her up with all kinds of questions," Gina said.

The girls gave their promises and hugged Gina. Lisa and Alicia turned their heads. Gina sent them off and joined Kenneth. He was talking to Jessica. Gina approached the two smiling. Jessica smiled back and casually said, "Good-bye Ken." He waved. Gina's eyebrows raised as she watched Jessica walk off like a beauty queen.

"Hey baby, I won't be able to hook up with you tonight. The brothers are pretty pissed about the Pharaohs not placing so I need to keep peace," Kenneth said.

"Dennis Williams is in town if you need help. He's over at Carla's," Gina said.

"What is he doing here?" asked a surprised Kenneth.

"I said he's visiting Carla."

"I didn't know they were still together."

"Is he screwing around on her?" Gina asked sharply.

"Look baby, Carla and Dennis are not up for discussion. I'm not implying or insinuating anything. I just made a comment so let's drop it," Kenneth said angrily.

Gina was embarrassed. She looked around to see if anyone was watching. Kenneth walked closer to Gina. She turned her head to the side. He put his arms around her and said, "I don't want to argue or fight tonight, okay?"

"Sure," Gina said nonchalantly with her head turned. He walked her to the back stairs of the Student Union. He took a step back.

"It seems like we are always arguing about something. Maybe we need to mellow out for awhile. I don't want us to ever start hating each other," Kenneth said softly. Gina tried to make eye contact but Kenneth avoided her.

"Are you trying to call it quits?" Gina asked, trying to control herself. She searched his eyes for an answer, but he kept turning his head away.

"Maybe we should just be friends for awhile," he finally said.

"At one time our fighting was healthy conversation, as you once put it. Now you want to go from making love to shaking hands. If that's the way you want it then fine," Gina said, fighting for control. Kenneth remained silent. She knew then that he was seeing someone. "Are you seeing someone?" she asked bluntly.

"It's time for us to see other people," he said with his voice cracking.

"No honey, it's about time for you to see other people. I'm not going to hold on to someone who wants to be free," Gina said angrily. She realized she was losing control but she could not stop herself. She looked around the area and at the steps. It was the same spot that Angel lost it with Lionel. The place had bad spirits.

Kenneth wasn't what the girls called good looking but his status as president of one of the most popular fraternities always drew a flock of women. He and Gina became friends in freshmen year. She was the one that made advances toward him by way of notes while they were pledging. He was happy when she made the approach because he never had the courage to say anything but "hi." She helped him to become what he was today, outgoing and president of Lambda Phi Chi.

As Kenneth gained more popularity in his senior year, girls became more aggressive in their advances. Some even flirted in Gina's presence. Their arguments were mainly about how he handled the obnoxious women.

"I don't want to lose your friendship. We just need space until we decide if we really want to continue seeing each other."

"If you want out then say so," Gina said in her demanding voice. "Don't piss me off with this *we* shit." Gina was devastated. She had to know who was the other person. "Are you seeing Jessica?" she asked directly. Kenneth did not respond. He was searching desperately for a way out.

"People have seen you two together so am I the last to know?" she continued, hoping that he would bite the bait.

"We have been seeing each other platonically for two months," he finally confessed.

"What about intimately?"

Kenneth said nothing.

"You were having sex with her while you were with me?" Gina asked, almost losing her breath. "My own sorority sister, you son-of-a-bitch! How would you like it if I screwed every Lambda that made a pass at me?" Her fight for control was gone. She was so enraged that she pushed him hard.

"Look Gina, that's enough," he said.

She pushed him again. Before he could grab her, she punched him in the chest several times. He caught her fists and held her tight. She was kicking and fighting trying to release his hold.

"Gina, stop it!" he shouted.

She elbowed him in the stomach and it broke his hold. She thought about how she trusted him and he didn't have the decency to end the relationship before jumping in bed with someone.

She wanted to say something but the words would not come out. The more she tried to talk, the tears fell. Kenneth walked to her. She put out the palm of her hand to stop him. She quickly wiped her eyes.

"Baby, I'm sorry. I'm really sorry. I didn't mean to hurt you. Let's talk…"

"Talk? Remember, you need to keep peace," she said in a shaky voice and stormed off.

"Gina, wait!" Kenneth shouted as Gina turned the corner but she was not going to look back.

"He wants his freedom, he can have it," she mumbled.

Carla heard a knock on the door. "They're here!" she announced.

"Why tonight Carla? We have hardly spent time together since January," Dennis complained, putting on his jacket as he trailed her to the door.

"I'll be home at the end of the month. You are coming to my graduation, aren't you?" she asked with raised eyebrows.

"Of course I am. I want to see…" The knocks became louder.

"Okay, I'm coming!" Carla shouted. She opened the door and her mouth flew open.

"Big Sister Let My People Go, we won!" the girls shouted, holding up the trophy. Carla didn't care. She wasn't expecting to see so many Genies.

Lisa looked at Dennis suspiciously. She knew the scene all too well. The Genies were imposing. "Big Sister, we do not have to spend the night tonight," Lisa said while looking at Dennis. Dennis smiled at Lisa.

"Now her, I like," Dennis said jokingly.

Carla nudged him with her elbow. "Dennis, these are my Jamboree winning Genies. Say hello to Mr. Williams." The girls shouted their greetings with happy faces, except Lisa.

"Don't tell me you ladies won," Dennis said as if he were disappointed.

The Genies walked through the door carrying bags of clothes, personal items, pillows, blankets and food. Carla thought they were moving in for good.

"We tied for first place with the Cherubs," Anne confessed.

"What about the Pharaohs?" Dennis asked.

The girls gave thumbs down and Carla laughed.

"I'll leave you ladies to your victory party," Dennis said. He took Carla by the hand and walked her out the door. He hugged her tight. "So you really are baby sitting tonight. I thought you were trying to rush that other guy in here," he said, planting soft kisses on her face.

"I'll make it up to you," she whispered between kisses.

"I know you will," he said and kissed her long. He gave her two quick ones on the lips. "I'll give you a call once I make it back to Kansas City."

"You're driving back tonight? I thought you were going to stay at the frat house?" she said slightly worried.

"If the Pharaohs did as badly as your girls indicated, I don't want to be around for the action," he said.

"You can keep it from getting out of control, Dennis," Carla said, somewhat complaining. Dennis looked at her. She looked so beautiful in her jeans and the big Snoopy sweatshirt with her hair pulled back neatly in a ponytail.

"I'll make sure nothing gets wild. I'll give you a call when I make it to K.C." He took off down the stairs and waved to her.

Carla went inside her apartment. The Genies were busting at the seams, dying to give her all the details, no matter how long it took. They talked at once. Carla wondered if it was a mistake. It was the liveliest and the most affectionate line of girls she had ever seen pledged. The telephone rang. She had to squeeze through several girls to reach the phone. "Hello."

"Hello, Carla?"

"You have to speak up."

"Carla, this is Gina. I need to talk to you."

"Hi Gina. Excuse me for yelling. As you can see, we're celebrating the victory. What's up?" There was a long pause. "Gina, are you still there?" Carla shouted.

"It looks like you got your hands full. I'll talk to you tomorrow."

"Gina, what's the matter?"

Gina took a deep breath. "Nothing. I'll talk to you tomorrow. Good-bye." Gina hung up.

Carla heard the dial tone. She stared at the phone and put it down.

Lisa was standing in the doorway. "What's wrong with Big Sister Hail to the Chief?" she asked.

"Let's join the others."

"Miss Stevens, are you going to marry Keith after you graduate," Jennifer inquired as she prepared for bed. Linda knew she was in for a long night. Jennifer had asked four questions already and she seemed to be running on full. Angel had warned her that Jennifer was long-winded.

"Once he has been in practice for a couple of years and has had no major law suits, I'll marry him. Right now, he's doing his residency so I've got time to play," Linda said while putting on a satin night shirt. Jennifer had on a big post office shirt with two noticeable buttons missing and a large hole where the pockets were sewn.

"Queenie, you can't sleep in that. It will give you nightmares," said a disgusted Linda.

"We are just going to bed. We won't see anybody but you." Jennifer hoped that Linda wouldn't key in on her using contractions. Jennifer did it a lot when she visited Linda.

"I'm nobody?"

"We did not mean it that way!" Jennifer exclaimed. Linda walked to her dresser and pulled out a short, soft pink, silk night gown with spaghetti straps. She handed the garment to Jennifer.

"Take this with my blessings," Linda said, letting out a deep breath. It was a Valentine's Day present Keith gave Linda. She wore it once and, to her, it was enough.

Jennifer looked at the gown as if it were the most precious thing on earth. She rubbed it lightly with her palms. Jennifer quickly pulled off the old shirt and slipped on the silk gown. It felt cool against her body. She took her time to pull back the floral comforter and slipped into bed.

"Thank you," Jennifer finally said.

"When you dress pretty for bed, well, you have pretty dreams," Linda said smiling.

"Miss Stevens, why don't you date any of the boys at school?"

"First and most important is, they don't have any money and second most important is most of them are boring. They have never traveled anywhere. Some don't know what it's like to eat at a restaurant other than McDonald's or Wendy's. I cannot be bothered." Linda finished rolling her hair and looked at Jennifer. "I went through all that trouble curling your hair and you are going to lay on it? I should say not! Get up and roll it," Linda demanded.

Jennifer was a little perturbed. She never did a good job rolling her hair, that's the reason why she never did. She grabbed a slug of hair and wrapped it around the roller. Linda watched Jennifer struggle.

"Queenie, you have to learn to be gentle to yourself. Take your time and part the hair. Your hair should be just as pretty and neat as your night gown," Linda said patiently. She took Jennifer's comb and parted her hair in sections. No one, not even Angel had helped Jennifer roll her hair.

Linda helped Jennifer take the time to place the tip of her hair around the roller and round it up to the snap. It took only fifteen minutes to put twelve large rollers around twelve large sections of hair. Linda gave Jennifer a pink scarf to wrap around her head.

"When you get married, you will probably sleep many nights without that head gear and gown, but until then, it's required." They both slipped under the comforters.

"Miss Stevens, are you a virgin?" The question took Linda by surprise. She could not answer Jennifer right away.

"Why are you asking me something so personal?"

"We just wanted to know."

"Are you one?" Linda knew Jennifer's answer but it was part of the bonding process. Jennifer nodded with her focus on one of the teddy bears.

"You act as if you are ashamed of being one," Linda said as gently as she could manage. Jennifer was awkward. She looked slightly embarrassed.

"We're not ashamed. We just don't know much about it." There she finally said it. She couldn't talk to Angel. Lisa confessed that she was one as well. She had nobody to tell her about sex but possibly Linda.

"Don't you have these discussions with your mother or stepmother?" Linda asked concerned. Jennifer shook her head slowly.

"If you approach her about it, she would probably be happy to talk to you. Sometimes it's difficult discussing something like sex. How did she handle the talk about your menstruation?"

"We never talked about it," Jennifer said.

"When did your father marry her?"

"When I was nine."

Linda was amazed. How could Jennifer's stepmother not discuss something as important as a period? Linda thought maybe Jennifer was an early starter.

"When did you start your cycle?"

"When I was thirteen."

Now Linda was beyond surprised. Jennifer's father was married four years and the stepmother never took the time to discuss the change in a girl's life.

"How did you know what to do? I mean, how did you learn about feminine products?"

"I would hear girls talk about what their mothers told them and I would ask questions. Then one day, we had a segment on it in sex education. I started my period in my last class of that day. My teacher was a woman so she took me to the bathroom and shared some information. She took me home too. When I made it home, I told my stepmother about it. She just asked did I take care of it and I said yes. That was the end of it."

Linda sat up in her bed. No wonder Jennifer asked so many questions.

She didn't have anybody to talk to her about important things. "Jennifer, you do know that if you have sex with a man during a certain time of the month, you can get pregnant," asked a worried Linda.

Jennifer smiled at her, "Yes, I know that. I just wanted to know how does it feel to have sex. All the girls in Morrison says it feels good."

Linda shook her head. "The first time you have sex may not feel so good. It may hurt badly because your hymen is being torn. After a few more times, it may feel good, only if your partner knows what he's doing," Linda lectured.

"Does Keith knows what he's doing," Jennifer asked in her most innocent voice.

Linda had to be patient with the extremely naive person. "You don't ask those types of questions. Women will try your man to see how good he really is, so keep all comments to yourself. Besides, if you love someone, you don't want to tell anybody how good or how bad he is."

Linda was feeling sorry for Jennifer because she had no one to help her through these tough times, especially when she was considering exploring her sexuality.

"Are you thinking about having sex with someone?" Linda asked.

"I'm not dating anyone now, but you never know."

"Who are you interested in?"

"Michael."

"Why?"

Jennifer hunched her shoulders like a kid.

"Sex doesn't have many rules, Jennifer. Sometimes it just happens, even if you are not dating someone. You might have an orgasm; you might get pregnant; or you might catch a disease. It goes beyond a man inserting his penis. If you like Michael and he likes you, then talk to him about having sex. Get it out of the way." Linda knew her Special was becoming very special to her.

Jennifer was so embarrassed that she had to force a smile on her face. She got under the covers and adjusted her pillows. Linda knew their talk was over.

"If at any time you want to discuss something or just plain ole talk, you can always ask me, even after you pledge," Linda said with a smile.

Jennifer smiled back and nodded. Jennifer believed that Linda thought she was probably the dumbest nineteen-year-old that she had ever knew.

"Good night Miss Stevens."

"Good night Queenie."

Chapter 9

Linda felt a gentle tap on her shoulder. She struggled to sit up. She cracked her eyes to find Jennifer standing beside her bed with hair combed and fully dressed.

"What time is it?" asked a groggy Linda.

"Seven o'clock. Would you care to join us for breakfast?" asked a pleasant Jennifer.

"Do you normally get up this early on the weekends?" Linda asked trying to focus.

"Yes we do. Usually, Big Sister Bon Amie will go with us," Jennifer said with clear eyes. Linda could not imagine Angel up at 6:30 in the morning, eating breakfast.

Linda continued to focus on a fresh, neat and crisp Jennifer in Calvin Klein jeans and a blue cotton shirt she had given her. Jennifer must have used a whole can of starch on the jeans and shirt because they hadn't been that crisp since Linda first bought them.

"Sweetie, why don't you go on to breakfast and we can lunch together, okay?" Linda pleaded.

"Sure," Jennifer said. She grabbed her bookbag and took everything out. She threw it over her shoulder and walked toward the door. Linda was curious. "What's up with the empty bookbag?"

"We will bring you something back. When Big Sister Bon Amie cannot make it to breakfast, we usually bring her something to eat," Jennifer responded, standing with the door opened. Just like Angel to have somebody serving her, Linda thought. Students weren't suppose to take food out of the cafeteria. If they got caught, they risked losing their meal ticket.

"Oh honey, that's okay. I usually don't eat this early. I'm trying to maintain my high school figure," Linda joked. She saw a look of disappointment on Jennifer's face. "But if you really don't mind, bring me a slice of toast without butter and a tea bag," she said and snuggled back under the covers.

When Jennifer walked through the cafeteria, she saw Rosalyn sitting with Angel and Denise. A twinge of jealousy nagged her but she shook it off immediately. Under no circumstances was she to be jealous or envious of any of her Cherub sisters.

She went through the food line, selecting fruit, a tea bag, one slice of bread and corn flakes. She had learned to eat her cereal with skim milk and without sugar. After she got her meal ticket punched, she and Angel almost collided. "Ooops, excuse me Big Sister Bon Amie," she said.

"Hi, sweetie. Why don't you join us at that table by the window?" Angel said pleasantly. Jennifer rushed to the table and sat down grinning from ear to ear.

"Why are you so happy Cherub Queen For A Day?" Rosalyn asked. She was a little edgy with Jennifer since the fight.

"If everything goes well, this could be our last week pledging, right Big Sister?" Jennifer asked. Denise nodded.

Angel came back to the table with an apple. She looked at Jennifer's tray. It was nothing like the way she used to eat. For breakfast, she would have meat, eggs, hash browns and two donuts with whole milk.

"You have a smart breakfast there, Jennifer. Now I see how you lost weight. I was beginning to think Linda was starving you skinny," Angel said.

It was starving in the beginning. Annette purposely had her skipping meals doing things to work off demerits. Some days, Jennifer only had crackers to eat and other days she had nothing. When Linda rescued her, she banned sugar from all of Jennifer's meals. Linda, did not eat sweets. She once told Jennifer that she was too vain to eat junk food or to gorge out on food. She would always keep her stomach flat because she believed in having choices with whom she wanted to date.

Angel looked at Jennifer closely. Her whole presence was different. She smiled more and her mannerisms displayed more confidence. She sat upright and crossed her legs like Linda. Her clothes were pressed with starch. She didn't rush through her meals. She maintained eye contact when she talked. Her face was leaner, which made her eyes a little wider. They were deep set with high arching eyebrows. It was something about them that made Angel stare. Jennifer's eyes were so familiar. Angel could not think when and where she had seen them.

Jennifer excused herself from the table and went to the toaster. When she came back, she wrapped the toast neatly in napkins, trying not to get caught.

"Are you sneaking out food?" Angel asked astonished.

Jennifer found it odd because she snuck food for Angel many times.

"This is for Miss Stevens. She could not make it to breakfast," Jennifer answered. She carefully tucked the food in her bookbag and excused herself from the table. Angel watched as the proud thief walked by the cafeteria worker smiling.

The Genies talked until three o'clock in the morning. Carla went to bed and let the Genies talk. They talked about Betty Shabazz and Coretta Scott King. Carla talked about the women in the Black Panther Party. She talked about the burning of Watts. She talked about welfare and how it was destroying the black family.

Most of the girls weren't familiar with Betty Shabazz. They thought Malcolm X's wife name was Mrs. X. It was so much they did not know and Carla could not teach it all in one night.

When Carla woke up, some Genies were still talking as if they had never slept. She smelled food cooking in the kitchen. She got out of bed, stepping over Genies. Lisa and some others were cooking breakfast for everyone. Carla hoped they had not cooked all of her food. She looked at the smiling faces. How could they be so cheerful with so little sleep? Maybe she was getting old she thought.

"Good morning, ladies," Carla said yawning, dragging herself into the kitchen.

There was a plate of bacon, eggs, toast, fried tomatoes and a glass of orange juice waiting for her. Her eyes narrowed at the plate. She had never eaten fried tomatoes. They looked delicious, but how would they taste? She never trusted anything pledges cooked. For some reason, she trusted these girls. She dug in. The fried tomatoes were good. "Who made these?" she asked with a full mouth.

Lisa blushed. "Our mother taught us how to make them before she died. She was from the South."

The other girls fixed their plates. They immediately started with the questions. The telephone rang. Thank God, Carla thought. "Hello?"

"Hi sweetheart, I'm home."

"Were there any problems last night?"

"Surprisingly, no. I was up most of the night consoling a confused Kenneth. It seems as if he and Gina have broken up. He and Carlos talked me to sleep. I guess you may say it was a bad night for the Lambdas."

So that's why Gina called, Carla remembered. "I think he and Gina will work it out," Carla said.

"I don't know, sweets. Gina has a reputation of being hard on men," Dennis said.

"If we can do it, I know they can too," Carla said.

"You are much more understanding when it comes to second chances. Baby, I'll see you at your graduation, okay? Love you," Dennis said to end the discussion.

"Love you too. See you soon," she smacked a kiss over the phone and hung up. As soon as she turned around, some Genies were looking at her. They didn't say a word. Damn, Carla thought. "Let's finish with the questions," she said.

The Alphas were preparing for the Week of Solitude induction ceremony. News about the break-up between Gina and Kenneth had already hit the sorority. No one knew what to expect from Gina. She was never involved in personal conflicts. She was highly respected by her sorority sisters and other students as well. People admired her ability to maintain self-control.

Everyone waited anxiously on Gina to start the ceremony. It was unusual for her to be late. The Genies were in the room adjacent to the Chapter room blindfolded. The tension among the Alphas was thick. Hardly anyone spoke. How the sorority reacts to the break-up rested in Gina's attitude once she arrived. Everyone sat still. Jessica was whispering to an Alpha who was sitting next to her. She giggled. The door opened, in walked Gina. All the women stood in respect to the President's entrance. Gina rushed to the mahogany desk to start the ceremony.

"Sorry I'm late. Let us proceed with the Week of Solitude ceremony," Gina said quickly, avoiding eye contact as her gavel made contact with the wooden block. The women recited passages. Gina kept stumbling and mispronouncing words. She repeated sentences at times.

The Genies were ushered in. The women continued with the passages. It came to the part where Gina had to read the meaning of sisterhood. She read slowly, thinking back to the time when she stood where Lisa was standing. The young woman was going to have a huge amount of responsibility. She thought how Jessica's captainship was stripped just like Alicia's and Gina was voted line captain in the first week of pledging. Jessica came late to all of the meetings and the Big Sisters made the line vote for a new captain. The Big Sisters, back then, were much more observant than the ones now. They settled problems without blinking an eye, not waiting for someone to get themselves together.

Gina read on. Next was Marsha's turn to read about the virtues of love and respect. Gina found it hard to focus on the ceremony with so many emotions rushing through her head. The thought of Jessica having sex with Kenneth was a little too much to forget. It was the first time the sisterhood had been challenged in that manner. She made up her mind that she wasn't going to let the break-up with Kenneth destroy the sisterhood. It was already embarrassing. If she didn't handle it well, it could get out of hand.

"Soror President...Soror President," Marsha said, trying to get Gina's attention. She quickly looked at Marsha. Gina had the girls remove the blindfolds. She gave instructions on the week's activities. They were to live together the entire week. They had to visit their pledge mother every day for at least one hour. After Gina gave the instructions, she dismissed them.

The line of Genies rushed out of the room wearing blue skirts and gold blouses. Gina recited the closing passage of the ceremony and gathered her things to leave.

"Excuse me, Soror President, maybe we need to have a sisterhood meeting," Rita said. Gina looked at Rita with piercing eyes. She did not want to discuss what happened.

"I don't think this is the time or place so let's drop it," Gina said as she gathered her things.

"This is not a sorority problem, Rita. It's personal," said one of Jessica's supporters.

"When one soror hurts another one, it becomes a sorority problem," Rita said, trying to keep from losing her temper. She knew it was going to be a heated discussion.

"Shit, y'all act like this is everybody's business," another Jessica supporter shouted. Several of them turned to look at her. Gina put her things down and stood in front of the young woman blazing with anger.

"Don't you ever curse in the Chapter room again. You faked being sick during your entire pledge period, allowing your sisters to take up the slack. And if you don't like what I'm saying, you can walk like you should have done last year," Gina said, eyeing the young woman until she turned her head.

"I don't want to talk about this!" Gina shouted. She picked up her things. The tears were starting to block her view. She wanted to leave before she exposed her weakness. Marsha stood in front of her, blocking her from leaving. Gina was face to face with her line sister, Genie number seven, the ship's navigator. Gina eyes were filled with tears but she refused to let them fall.

"If you walk out that door without resolving this, I can't let you be pledge mother to Lisa. This is not the example she needs to follow, running away. I won't let you leave hurting," Marsha said with tears trying to make its way down her face. She knew how Gina worked extra hard for the sorority. Marsha hugged Gina and chuckled through the tears.

"Remember the time when Marie washed your blue pants and dried them for two hours? They shrank up to the middle of your legs. You walked around in floods for a whole day until Carla made you sew blue material at the bottom. Remember how we had to wear those pants everyday during the Week of Solitude?" Marsha blabbered.

Gina remembered how she wanted to choked the life out of Marie. She washed some of the Genies clothes. The students learned how to rig the washers and dryers without paying. Marie put too many "clicks" on the dryer and forgot about the clothes. Because the pants were polyester, they shrunk and Gina didn't have time to do anything about it. The Genies teased her, calling her Genie Split-Level Bell Bottoms. Gina laughed, still fighting to hold back the tears.

"I can't talk about it. Gail's right. If he wanted me...there would be no other person," Gina whispered to Marsha. Gina cleared her throat. "I have to go now. *I,*" Gina emphasized, "won't let a man come between this sisterhood," Gina said as strongly as she could. She gave Marsha another look. The tears fell. She picked up her things slowly. Marie walked up and embraced both Marsha and Gina. Cheryl got up and joined the group, followed by the rest of Gina's line sisters except for Jessica.

The girls sang the pledge song, "All For One." The tears came freely as the women sang. The Neophytes witness, for the first time ever, Gina, their Big Sister All In All, become emotional. Most of them cried as they sat watching the scene. Gina and her line sisters sniffed and hugged tighter, reminiscing about the pledge period. Gina gently broke away. She looked at Jessica who was looking out the window. She walked up behind her. Gina had to break the ice.

"Everybody wants to know if everything is okay. Kenneth is a nice person. He doesn't deserve to be hurt. If you really want him, I say congratulations, and if you are trying to hurt me, I say congratulations," Gina said without the tears. Jessica turned around. Gina extended her arms to embrace.

Jessica couldn't refuse the offer. She would be outlawed. Gina came out shining again, Jessica thought. She didn't want Kenneth. She walked up to Gina coldly and the two embraced. The women clapped. Before Gina released Jessica, she whispered, "We both know now that he isn't that great. And if you put another hand on Lisa again, I will put my foot up your ass."

Gina stepped back looking at Jessica with a fake smile. Jessica was fuming. She felt like a fool.

"Good-bye Sorors," Gina said and walked out the door. She felt better and for some strange reason. She walked down to Angel's room. Gina figured that by lunchtime Monday, the whole campus would know that she got played. She knocked hard on Angel's door. When it opened, Angel gave Gina an uneasy look. She walked in uninvited. She saw Linda sitting on Denise's bed, polishing her nails. She glanced up at Gina and continued to polish. Gina knew that the two knew what had happened. Gina wondered how to break the silence to explain?

"So I hear the Alphas are having a little girl trouble," Linda said nonchalantly and blew her nails. Gina sat next to her.

"No more than what you Kappas are having," Gina said.

"We're use to that kind of thing. I say chalk it up to experience and let the chips fall where they may. Your bleeding heart line sisters will take care of her," Linda said as she blew her nails dry.

"How did you find out?" Gina asked out of curiosity.

"The question is, who doesn't know. I didn't think you Alphas had *one*. I couldn't imagine Jessica being so desperate. It seems so beneath her," said a sarcastic Linda. Gina tried to stay calm. Neither one did things intentionally to hurt one another. They did battle in conversations.

Because their mothers pledged together and lived in the same city, Linda and Gina knew each other from the crib. When Gina's mother married Paul Smith, they moved into the same school district where Linda's parents lived. Paul helped his brother Bill Smith, Angel's father, network to find a job as a manager for one of the airlines in Kansas City. He moved his daughter and second wife from St. Louis to Kansas City. They moved to the same school district as his brother.

"You know I've never tried to run your life, even when I saw you skate down skid row with Kenneth," Linda said.

"What do you mean?" Gina asked.

"You helped him become president of ABC. You were the one everybody wanted. You and the Alphas campaigned for him more than his own frat brothers. Then you had to help him run the damn organization. Next you helped position him for the Lambda's presidency. You have done more for that country bastard than his own, so-called, friends. I say, the only person you should work that hard for is yourself. If he's broke when you find him, stop shopping at the Goodwill," Linda preached.

Gina looked angrily at Linda who continued unconcerned with her nails. "How did you know they were messing around?" Gina asked. She was numb. Linda did not look at her.

"I saw them at the Teddy Pendergrass show in Kansas City," Linda said, engrossed in her polishing.

"And you said nothing?"

Linda stopped polishing. "We have been friends for a long time. I didn't want you to choose between the sorority you would give your life for and a friend who remembers when you had your first kiss. I knew you were smart enough to know Kenneth was screwing around. You just didn't expect one of your sweet Alpha sorors," Linda said.

"Talk to your mother about it," Linda continued. "Talk to my mother about it. Talk to Angel about it. This shit happens. I say, you can't trust a man until he's dead," Linda said and fanned her toes. "And besides, I heard he wasn't that good anyway. Something like he wasn't a full size man. I heard his nickname is Embryo, but every man is considered small to Denise if he isn't hanging a foot long," Linda said.

Gina was beyond devastated. "Denise was screwing around with Kenneth too? You heffa, why didn't you say something?" Gina said and shot an angry look at Angel.

"As far as I know, it was hearsay," Angel said defensively. "I thought you and Kenneth were seeing other people for awhile anyway. It was at that time I heard the rumors about Denise. Why are you mad about who he slept with at that time?" asked a somewhat unconcerned Angel.

Gina suspected that Angel had a different agenda. It wasn't going to be the conversation she had hoped for. Angel was probably mad about Lionel asking her out. Gina knew the game Linda played, but Angel was another story. Gina never really knew where she stood with Angel. Her method of keeping people off balance with her silence was always a ploy to keep her on top. Gina thought that Angel figured she did something underhanded. Gina decided to leave.

"You're right. Why should I be mad? He wasn't that good. Let me go upstairs to my room," Gina said without looking at anyone.

"Ta-ta," Linda said smiling. The door closed. Linda looked at Angel. "Now dear, you could have been a little nicer. After all, she is your cousin," Linda said.

"She could have let Lionel do the asking. She's no different than the others. She just has too much dignity to lay down," Angel said.

"So are you saying that she consciously went after Lionel?" Linda probed.

"I don't know yet," said a pondering Angel.

"I know now that it's really over between her and Kenneth. Gina would never admit if he was good or bad in bed," Linda said.

There was a knock on the door. Angel got up and opened it. She was surprised to see Gina again.

"Can I come in?"

"Sure."

"Well, look who's back!"

"Angel, if you got something on your chest, I want to hear it," Gina said firmly.

"As in...?" asked a strategizing Angel.

"You know what I'm talking about," Gina continued.

"If you can be a little more specific, maybe I can answer your question," Angel continued slowly, acting as if she was clueless to Gina's inquiry.

Gina was irritated with Angel. Gina looked angrily at Linda who was enjoying the play. Linda liked Angel's style, calculating. Gina knew that Angel would play the game forever, especially if she didn't want to show her hand. Gina knew if she wanted to get a straight answer from Angel, then she would have to come straight with the question.

"The night at the Beta's Ball, you said Lionel went after me. Are you under the impression that I was seeing Lionel?" Gina asked, forcing Angel in a position to show her hand. Those were Angel's words, not hers. Now Angel could lose respect and insult her by playing confused or save face and play fair, Gina thought.

"I thought you knew," said a shy Angel. Gina was wondering if it were an act.

"You never told me so how could I know," Gina said, getting frustrated with Angel who took advantage of Gina's deficiency. To be calm was natural for Angel but Gina worked hard at it.

"I'm sorry," Angel said softly.

"I'm sorry? I'm sorry? Did you know about her and Lionel?" Gina asked Linda.

"Of course! Who couldn't help but notice Angel sneaking out with an overnight bag. Lionel was constantly in her face. He did everything but squeezed her ass in public," Linda said trying to sound convincing. Gina knew then that Angel had told Linda and not her.

Last year, Gina saw Angel and Lionel together. It wasn't the way Linda tried to make it sound. After Gina had the few personal conversations with Lionel, he had too much of an ego to sneak.

"I'm a little surprised at you Gina. You really are slipping. You don't notice half the things that are going on, especially when it involves you. If you are getting strung out on love or sisterhood, you are going to get burnt down the road," Linda said.

Gina was hurt. They had left her out again. She was no longer part of the group. There was a time when Angel told her almost everything. Gina remembered introducing Linda to her cousin, Angel. Linda immediately disliked Angel. It wasn't until all three began hanging out together that Linda began to like Angel. Sometimes they would exclude Gina in some of the activities, innocently. Gina was more of a tomboy and the other two were prissy. Although Gina would never tell Linda how she felt, feeling inferior when it came to attracting boys, Angel had a special magic that made her feel pretty.

"Angel, I had no idea that you were seeing Lionel. He called me and asked if I would have dinner with him. We met two more times and that was it. No kissing, no hugging, *No nothing*! He had no interest in me," Gina said. She looked at Angel breathing heavily. It had been an upsetting night for her.

"Lionel and I had been seeing each other for two years. When dad met him, he didn't like him and I don't know why. I wanted to keep it a secret because dad was ranting and raving about pulling me out of school. Lionel didn't want it that way so he pretty much gave me an ultimatum. Like I said, I thought you knew," Angel said as meekly as she could. Gina noticed how Angel chose her words.

"Didn't you ask him out, Gina?" Linda asked.

"No. He called me," Gina said calmly. Linda looked at Angel. Gina knew something was wrong.

"Angel, I wouldn't do anything to hurt you. I know we're not blood but we're still family," Gina said. "If I can't trust you and you can't trust me, then who can we trust?" Gina threw a glance at Linda and playfully said, "Well maybe we can trust her." All three laughed.

"I have to go ladies. This mushy stuff is boring me. Gina, if you ever call me a heffa again, I will slash all the tires on that Flintstone mobile of yours," Linda said in a dainty way, letting Gina know that name-calling was unacceptable.

Linda was at the door. "By the way Gigi, why don't you bring that little street urchin pledge daughter of yours to have dinner with me and my little Special vagabond this Wednesday. We all need to do a little bonding," Linda said and left.

Angel felt a little awkward being with Gina by herself. They had never argued about boys nor accused each other of anything. Angel knew that Gina was the most loyal person she knew. To have her on your side was a friend to death.

"You don't know how embarrassed I am about all of this. You and Linda are so close now. I guess if I had pledged Kappa, we would still be close," Gina said, trying not to get emotional.

"We are still close. You and Linda are different. Sometimes it's easier to tell her things than it is telling you. You have such high standards and you are so strong. I always feel stupid if I do things like second chances or sneaking around. You will probably be over Kenneth before we graduate next Saturday. It's hard for me to get over Lionel," Angel said softly.

"Men don't flock to me like they do to you and Linda. You can throw Lionel away and get a much better one. It's not that easy for me," said a vulnerable Gina.

"Don't ever say anything. I'm tired of you comparing looks. You look great!" Angel said.

Gina smiled. "Thanks, Angel, I've got some business to take care of," Gina said proudly.

"So do I. Now, don't forget to meet Linda for dinner," Angel said as she walked Gina to the door.

"I see you girls made your choice. I think she will work out fine," Gina said.

Chapter 10

Dear Nadia Comeneci,

We want to personally congratulate you on the choreography that stole the show. We are beginning to see another side of you, a creative one, and we like it. We are asking you for a date on May 5, yes, the Greek picnic. Please don't turn us down. We hate rejections.
SHAFT Big Score?

Lisa folded the note and sighed. It felt good to have quiet time because the Genies were visiting their pledge mothers, except Vicki; she was asleep. The Genies occupied two suites in Garrison Hall. It was stressful living with so many girls.

During the week, Lisa listened to the Genies fuss and argue about pantyhose, laundry and time in the bathroom. She noticed Phyllis, Evelyn and Vicki were lazy and selfish; April complained a lot; Anne freely took what she wanted; Janet never volunteered to help; Tina didn't want anyone sitting on her bed; Alicia was extra clean; Crystal was a morning person; Trish was nocturnal; and Paula was pleasant all the time.

Before Lisa began studying for the final exams, she started a quick note to Jennifer. In Lisa's heart, she believed things would never be the same between the two because Jennifer was different. She was becoming a true Kappa girl. Lisa concluded that she did everything possible to keep the friendship alive.

Hello Flaming Mamie,

There have been rumors flying around about Big Sister Hitler stealing Big Sister's Napoleon's boyfriend. The Big Sisters have been real cool with us. Just think, in a few days, we will be sorority girls. Let's make plans for a slumber party. We miss you and your one thousand questions.
Best of Friends,
Olga Korbut

Lisa sealed the note with tape and went to Rochelle's room. She knocked on the door and handed Rochelle the note. "You got a few minutes?" Rochelle asked, looking down the hall. Lisa walked in and sat down at the corner of a bed. The Cherubs were living together as well. Rochelle's room looked like an atomic bomb had hit it.

"You need to pull your friend's coattail. Some Kappas are planning on giving her a hard time Thursday night. They are also going to try and turn her back Friday night," Rochelle said as she sipped a wine cooler. She handed one to Lisa, who was steaming. She had a feeling Jennifer would be in trouble soon. Things were going too well and that wasn't a good sign.

"Why can't you tell her, Roach. It will be suicide for me to talk to her," Lisa said in a rush.

"You know sisterhood won't let me tell on those crazy heffas. I didn't know Jennifer that well before pledging, but she is really cool," Rochelle said and giggled. "Girl, let me tell you. One night, Jennifer almost beat the shit out of Rosalyn," Rochelle said grinning. Lisa's mouth opened wide.

"Jennifer got into a fight? Why?" Lisa asked.

"Rosalyn called her a jet black bitch and Jennifer slam dunked her to the floor. We had to grab her before she tagged her ass again. I was ready to let them fight, but you know, sisterhood don't allow it," Rochelle said, turning up the bottle.

"That's wild. I didn't think she had it in her," Lisa said, sipping on the wine cooler.

"One more thing, Rosalyn has been eyeing Michael. I've already helped deliver two notes. Instead of taping hers like everyone else, her lazy butt just fold them so I read them. She already got caught with Fred at the Beta's House and now it's Michael. I tell you, the girl is a loose boody," Rochelle said as she finished her cooler.

"I think Jennifer might have more enemies than she can handle. I think Michael might resist Rosalyn. I'm quite sure he doesn't want what Fred had," Lisa said.

Rochelle looked at Lisa questionably. "Honey please! What have you been drinking besides that cooler? What man turns down a free piece of ass besides Cameron?" Rochelle said with a wink.

Lisa stood quickly. "Who's been after Cameron?" she asked loudly.

"Calm down Sugar Ray. The funny part is, Cameron wrote Alexis a note and said no thank you," Rochelle said. She took Lisa's empty bottle and wrapped them in newspapers and paperbags before throwing them away.

"So how are things moving between you and Carl?" Lisa asked.

"I don't know. I'm thinking he's interested but the word on the street is your Genie sister Phyllis is interested too. So we will see," Rochelle said with her hands out.

"After we finish pledging, you, me, Jennifer and Alicia need to get together," Lisa said standing and stretching. Rochelle stepped back.

"I thought you and Alicia were on the outs," Rochelle said. She continued in a low voice, "Didn't you take her captainship?"

"Hell naw! I didn't take anything. The Big Sisters caught her at Big Danny's drinking. The line took her captainship, not me. Matter of fact, we're closer now than ever before," Lisa said in defense to the accusation.

"I knew it wasn't like you to undermine anybody," Rochelle said and walked Lisa to the door. "Pledging has been an eye opening experience for me. I didn't know Angel was so smooth," Rochelle said smiling.

"She's not all that smooth," Lisa replied.

"I know you don't like her, but the girl is smooth. I think you would like her once you got to know her. She's just like Gina but more feminine," Rochelle said.

"What has she done that is so smooth?" Lisa pushed.

"All I can say is, she is pretty sharp. I like her," Rochelle said and looked at Lisa for an answer.

"Well good for you," Lisa said in a huff.

"Hey, loosen up! Big Sister Switchy Bitchy will be my soror soon. I can't have you talking about her," Rochelle said jokingly.

"Don't worry, I won't talk about your soror," Lisa said defensively. The two girls were silent for a few seconds.

"Now don't forget to talk to Jennifer so she can tell Linda," Rochelle finally said.

"What can Linda do?" Lisa asked sarcastically.

"We're talking money and power. Her mother and Gina's mother are founders of Zeta Chi chapter," Rochelle said.

Lisa looked at Rochelle to continue. "Now Linda is something else! That hussy won't open the door when we come to visit her. She talks to us inside her room. When we had to get her signature, we would slide our books under her door and wait for her to slide them back. Sometimes she would make us wait an hour. She said she doesn't want to be bothered with us until we become her sorors," Rochelle complained.

"I thought she and Jennifer got along fine," Lisa said.

"They do and that is one of the reasons why some Kappas are gunning for her. It seems like Linda threw down on a few of them last year on the last night of pledging. They said she slept all day and dealt with them all night," Rochelle said.

"Do you think she will turn on Jennifer?" Lisa asked.

"Honey please! That's her girl! Linda won't let nothing happen to Jennifer. Sometimes, Jennifer would take our books to get Linda's signature so we wouldn't have to wait until she 'felt like it.' I think heffa is crazy," Rochelle concluded.

"We have been catching hell from Cheryl, Jessica and Marsha. They have really been riding Alicia's back for the last two weeks," Lisa shared.

"Wait a minute! I thought Marsha was the Dean of Pledges. Why is she acting all ugly? I know Alicia has an attitude, but why are they being so mean?" Rochelle asked slightly angry.

"I don't know. I make sure at least three of us go with Alicia every time they want to see her. I try to make sure I'm with her most of the times," Lisa said.

"I heard that Gina was something else too," Rochelle said.

"She's not that bad. She has to keep Marsha in check because she doesn't cut us any slack. She was a mean Dean of Pledges. Well, let me get going. Oh, by the way Cherub Ghetto Girl," Lisa said in a high pitched soft voice, mocking the Kappas.

"Yes, Genie Big Mouth?"

"It's Motor Mouth, dear."

"Oh, sorry."

"You need to clean up your vocabulary. Shit, damn and hell is considered inappropriate language. Do I make myself clear?" Lisa finished role playing. Both girls laughed. "Your mouth has really gotten bad since freshman year. You have hung out with Estrilita too long. Do they know your father is superintendent of a school district?" Lisa asked.

"No and don't you go telling. They said I was a ghetto girl because I don't talk the correct way. They are just jealous," Rochelle said, tossing her head back before she opened the door. Lisa looked at her out of the corner of her eyes. Rochelle turned her nose up.

"Girl, you are crazy," Lisa said, still laughing.

Rochelle looked down the hall.

"The coast is clear. Good luck Friday night Lees."

"Good luck to you too."

Lisa hurried to the room to start studying before the other Genies came back. When she opened the door, Crystal and Tina were standing in the middle of the room crying.

"What's going on?" Lisa asked.

"We...we were visiting Big Sister Most High and Noble Greek. She made us cry," Crystal said through tears.

"Alicia is dropping line," Tina added.

"What? Where is she?" Lisa asked. The two girls pointed to the bathroom. Lisa's heart beat fast. She knew something bad had happened for Alicia to drop. Lisa pounded on the door.

Alicia yelled out, "What do you want?"

"We need to talk." Lisa waited before pleading again.

Paula and Evelyn walked in the room, asking questions. Lisa kept pounding on the door. Finally, Alicia came out. She looked as if she had been crying. Her Genie shirt was stained very badly with a dark substance. It had a large rip up the back.

The girls were silent as Alicia walked around Lisa. Alicia took her shirt off and threw it on the floor. Anne and Trish came from the other suite to witness the scene. They looked at everyone. Alicia stared at Lisa for a few seconds. Lisa saw hurt in Alicia's eyes for the first time ever.

"I'm tired of taking shit off of them. If they don't want me as an Alpha, then I say to hell with them. Y'all can have this shit," Alicia said slowly, in a low husky voice.

"Crystal, you and Trish get Dee Dee to buy another shirt from the Union. Tina, get the rest of the iron-on felt and cut some more letters. Come on y'all, hurry up," Lisa ordered.

The girls rushed to start their duties, but Alicia shook her head.

"I am not a Genie anymore so don't go through all this trouble for me. I'm supposed to have eternal love for those heffas? After today, I don't have nothing for them," Alicia said firmly.

"Look Alicia, we are in this together. You can't drop. Whatever went down between you and Cheryl is over," Lisa said.

Alicia walked close to Lisa. "They are purposely giving me hell. You choose to catch it. They want you. Gina, Rita and Carla treat you like some damn queen," Alicia said, bearing down on Lisa.

"That's not true. They ride my back like everyone else," Lisa said.

"That's not true Lisa. They hardly ever give you trouble in sessions. They are constantly hassling Alicia," Trish said low.

"That's because she was caught drinking. How do you think they felt about a pledgee bold enough to openly break the rules. They had to live that down with the Kappas and Sigmas. They have only been hassling her for two weeks, we've been pledging for eight," Lisa said defensively.

"Janet and Evelyn were drinking too. They don't do half the stuff as Alicia. They really don't bother you, Lisa. You do choose to take it with us," Anne said.

Lisa was becoming excited. Her line sisters were turning on her. They felt she had an easy ride. She looked at all of them in disbelief. "Y'all see them whispering in my ears don't you?" Lisa asked, trying not to become upset. She looked around the room for a response. Only Crystal and Tina nodded.

"They tell me if I don't fall in place with everyone else, they are going to take care of business when I see them alone," Lisa confessed, but no one believed her. She put her hands on her small hips. "So it's like this, huh? I didn't hear any complaints when Jessica pushed me down the steps. I guess I was getting off easy when she made me eat that garbage for all of y'all and I had to vomit in my shirt to keep from ruining her floor," Lisa said with almost wet eyes. She looked at her line sisters again. Tina slowly walked to her.

"Why didn't you eat that garbage Alicia? You were captain? You let me do it by myself. The doctor said it was food poisoning," Lisa said. The tears almost came. She had to pause for a second. "They want you to respect the sorority after you cross so take it like a woman, I did," Lisa said. Alicia lowered her head slightly.

"I have taken shit all my life from people who think they are better than me. I'm tired of people looking down on me," Alicia confessed. She kicked at her Genie shirt on the floor.

"Gina told me that the only way a person can look down on you is when you are looking up at them. You have a 3.25 GPA and I have a 4.0. We sound like uneducated girls. Maybe if we start acting our grades, people won't look down on us. They told us that if we disobeyed the pledge rules then we would have to pay the piper. Cheryl is blowing the horn loudly so suck it up and get through it," Lisa said, looking at the other girls. Some were wiping their eyes.

"We have to get Genie Talkin' Loud another shirt. The sooner we get it done, the better our chances are for not getting caught," Lisa said and looked at Alicia. "You need to lay low. After you meet with Cheryl on

Thursday, we will do everything as a line. It's all for one and one for all. Anyone who doesn't want to be an Alpha, leave the room now because we are at the stretch," Lisa said looking at Alicia who walked to the dresser. She took out a sweatshirt and put it on. She sat on Tina's bed.

"Get off of my bed!" Tina complained. Alicia looked at the tiny person and rolled her eyes. She got up and went into the bathroom door.

"I do not want to wait an hour to get into the bathroom tomorrow morning, Anne, and if Phyllis doesn't clean out the tub tomorrow, all hell is going to break loose," Alicia said and slammed the door.

Carla hoped that Gina's visit wouldn't last long. She had to finish practicing the presentation of her thesis. "Gina, you are still dwelling on what has happened instead of why it happened. First of all, you don't trust him so how can you forgive him?" said a slightly irritated Carla. She and Gina rarely had these types of conversations. Gina hardly ever got upset over men.

"How did you handle the situation with Dennis?" asked Gina.

"When Dennis decided he wanted space, I gave him the galaxy. He thought just because he was two years older, I was stupid. I wasn't going to hold on or wait for him to realize he really wanted or needed me. I went out with other men just like he dated other women."

"It was different with Dennis. He didn't go after your soror. Matter of fact, I think she went after him."

"There is no difference. He wanted another woman. You have to handle Kenneth differently than the soror. If you think he's worth the effort in trying again, then reconcile. Once I forgave Dennis, I didn't bring it up anymore. Put the pride aside if you want this man," Carla said.

"People know he has shortcomings," Gina mumbled.

Carla's eyes slowly narrowed. "What shortcomings?"

"How he makes love is a joke. I'm finding out a whole crew has slept with him. Jessica has already broke it off with him," Gina said with her head down. "Can you imagine what they are wondering? Especially if I reconcile."

Carla sat upright. The gentleness in her voice was gone. Gina was a tough young woman and she couldn't afford for her to lose sight of the plan for Friday night. "I heard you handled yourself well at the induction ceremony. We can't afford to have you crying over a man with shortcomings, especially one who can't keep his pants up. You can find another man who doesn't need as much work. Men with sexual problems have low self-esteem," Carla preached. She went to the kitchen and got some juice. She handed Gina a glass.

"I see Jessica has played this one very well. She wanted to embarrass you and she did. You don't need to think about reconciling anything. What people want to know is if Gina is desperate. The sorority can't afford any squabbles over a man. We have to make sure there is no political turmoil when the election takes place. Are there any more problems?" Carla asked with an end of discussion attitude. Gina shook her head.

"Dennis is giving me a graduation dinner next Sunday. His younger brother Arthur will be there. He will have recently graduated from Mizzou with a degree in Information Systems. I want you to be my guest." Gina nodded and walked to the door. "I think you will like him. He's quiet. He likes women who are intelligent and don't play games," Carla said smiling.

"What if he doesn't like me?" Gina asked softly.

"You will always have a choice," Carla said with a big smile. "Before you leave, go over your plan again. I want to make sure everything is covered."

Linda and Jennifer were waiting inside the Student Union cafeteria for Gina and Lisa. Jennifer looked very elegant in a navy blue, sleeveless dress with a matching navy blue sweater. Her hair was curled. She sat patiently, smiling as if she were posing for pictures.

Kyle walked into the cafeteria. He spotted Jennifer looking his way and headed for her table. Jennifer took a deep breath when he stood beside her.

"Hello Ma'am. Hello Jennifer. You look very nice tonight," said a very polite Kyle. Since the scene at the dance, Kyle had become a little more cautious as to how he treated her. She wrote him a note, chewing him out badly about his attitude at the dance. She also told him that if he ever treated her that way again, she would never speak to him again.

Kyle extended his hand to Linda. "I'm Kyle Thomas, a very good friend of Jennifer."

"Oh, how nice," Linda said with a forced smile and shook Kyle's hand.

"Uh, Kyle, this is our Special, Miss Stevens," Jennifer said, trying to make the scene a little more comfortable.

"I don't know what that means but I'm quite sure it must be good," Kyle said trying not to be sarcastic. "Are you going to be finished pledging this Saturday?" he asked Jennifer.

"Kyle, we do not want to keep you from your dinner," Jennifer said as she narrowed her eyes and pursed her lips.

"Fine. I'll leave. It will be great to talk to Jennifer again," he said and walked away disappointed. Jennifer sat frowning.

"Oh honey, don't frown. It gives you wrinkles early," Linda said. Jennifer stopped frowning immediately.

"But I do admire his courage. Men like him can be pretty interesting if you can stand to look at them," Linda said without realizing she had insulted Jennifer.

Gina and Lisa walked into the cafeteria. They spotted Linda and Jennifer and walked to the table. "Hello ladies," Gina said.

"Hello Miss Smith."

"Hello Miss Stevens."

"Hello Lisa. You look very nice," Linda said as she surveyed Lisa's slightly too big dress. "Make sure you gain that weight back. I've always thought you had such a cute little shape. Gina, it's good to see you at last," Linda said as she acknowledged the time by pointing at her watch.

"Are you ready to eat?" Gina asked, ignoring the comment. They walked ahead of Lisa and Jennifer. The two girls looked at each other, not knowing what to expect. As they walked through the line, Lisa playfully pushed Jennifer and she in turn gave Lisa a soft tap.

"Gina, that grilled ham and cheese is going to add dents to your thighs," Linda said, reaching for the cottage cheese and fruit cup. "You know big butts and thunder thighs run in your family. Just look at your Aunt Beulah." Linda poured unsweetened tea in a small styrofoam cup.

"You are practically starving yourself trying to stay thin. You are too tall to wear a size five. By the way, her name is Aunt Bernice and she's not fat," Gina said, grabbing a bag of chips.

"No, but she's about two chocolate chip cookies away from being fat," Linda said low. She walked back to Jennifer and handed her three dollars. "That should take care of some tuna salad and a fruit cup," she said smiling. "Oh, you can get some tea too."

Jennifer took the money and put the items on her tray. Lisa got a grilled ham and cheese with fries and a coke. They took their trays back to the table.

"Gina, do you want to give the two darlings some space?" Linda asked, pulling out a chair at another table that was twenty feet away. Everyone sat down to eat. Lisa cut her sandwich at a diagonal and took a bite. Jennifer took her time spreading tuna on the few crackers she had.

"Yuck! How can you eat that? You should have gotten some fries or something," Lisa said turning up her nose.

"It is not so bad, I am use to it. Do you know why we are meeting?" Jennifer asked as she slowly ate her crackers.

"I asked Gina and she said we were going to do some girl talk. Gina ain't hardly into girl talk so I have no idea. It doesn't matter. I need to give you the lowdown," Lisa said as she leaned close toward Jennifer, eyeing Gina's table suspiciously. "I heard you might be in for some trouble tomorrow and Friday night. Some Kappas are going to try and turn you back," Lisa said.

Jennifer's expression dropped. Lisa was saddened at her friend's disappointed look. "Why? I thought they did that to people they don't like. What are they going to do?" Jennifer whispered.

"Maybe it's just a rumor," Lisa said, trying to ease the pain.

"Who told you?"

"A Genie overheard some Kappas talking. Don't get scared. Just don't get caught without Linda tomorrow night. As far as Friday, make sure you are always with at least two Cherubs," Lisa schemed.

Jennifer played with her food. Even if she had ordered a sandwich with fries, she wouldn't have wanted it. It was a bad sign she thought. As soon as she was beginning to feel good about herself, someone pulled the rug from under her feet. She thought about the night of the Ball. "I guess I chose the wrong sorority," she said with tears in her eyes.

Lisa shook her head wildly. "It's just some bad people in the sorority. You seem to look pretty happy. Every time I see you, you're dressed up and your hair is always curled. Something must be going right," Lisa said, trying to be cheerful. "My Grandma Mattie always told me if you want something bad enough, you have to work long enough and fight hard enough for it. You've come this far, don't let a few people piss on your parade," Lisa said, hoping to convince Jennifer not to get discouraged.

Jennifer forced a smile. She enjoyed Lisa's grandmother's sayings. She wiped the tears away.

"And don't start crying. They will think you're weak. If they hit you, hit 'em back, just like you did..." Lisa stopped. Jennifer nodded and wiped the tears away. It had been such a long time since she and Lisa talked. She hadn't realized how much she missed their conversations until now. Like always, Lisa was her cheerleader.

"What I found out about pledging is most of the time, someone has problems with your pledge mother or they may be jealous of you," Lisa said.

"I can see why they might have problems with Miss Stevens, but who could be jealous of me?" Jennifer asked unconcerned. Lisa looked at the once shy, invisible, timid girl who was becoming an elegant, talk of the campus woman.

"You would be surprised," Lisa confessed.

"I'm beginning to wonder about you, Gina. You have a tough time picking men," Linda said.

"Are you talking about Kenneth?" Gina asked without looking up.

"In our freshmen year, you dated that junior named Stewart Jinks. You helped him become president of ABC. When he went off chasing other women, you hitched up with Marvin Coleman, who was a nobody, and still is if you ask me. You made him shine as well. He didn't have the decency to tell you it was over. He just helped himself to every woman who gave him a play. Now it's Kenneth. Gina, it's a pattern, just like your mother," Linda concluded.

"Don't you ever say that again," Gina said in a heavy whisper, pointing her finger at Linda. Gina never imagined Linda throwing those embarrassing times in her face, especially knowing how it affected her.

"Oh calm down. At least she found a caring man in Uncle Paul. Aunt Marilyn doesn't have a problem talking about it, so why should you? When are you going to invest your time in Mr. Right?" Linda continued. Gina was ready to get up and walk.

"I guess Keith is perfect?" Gina asked, trying to keep her voice low.

"No, but as long as I remember he is a choice, I'll always have another choice if he screws up. I don't go looking for someone to fix up. Stop trying to wear the skirt and the pants," said a slightly angry Linda.

"I'm sorry, Linda. I'm just not the prissy type," Gina said sneering.

"You don't have to be the prissy type to let a man be a man. You are afraid to deal with a man who doesn't need you," Linda said and took a breath.

"Why are we talking about this?"

"Because I care and Carlos does too. He wants to know how you are handling the breakup. So what shall I tell him?" Linda asked smiling. Gina looked at Linda for a moment. A little smile came across her face. Gina knew that Carlos liked her at one time but she wasn't sure about now. He had always considered her as a woman whose bark was worse than her bite.

"So is Carlos seeing anyone?"

"He's a tough man to handle. You of all people should know."

"I don't know about dating fraternity brothers. It doesn't seem right."

"You are a free woman. We will be graduating soon so who cares? You don't have to worry about any political bull."

"I guess you are right. I could have sworn he was seeing Shelly."

"Soror Shelly wasn't his type. He likes them strong and aggressive. You know, the kind that don't mind asking for sex," Linda said, whispering the last part. "Besides, Carlos looks so much better than that bumpkin with a curl. I don't see how you put up with that gook in his hair."

Gina finished the last of her potato chips. She wiped her fingers on a napkin. "I don't chase men anymore. Tell Carlos if he is interested, give me a call."

"My pleasure."

Linda and Jennifer walked back to the dorm in silence. Jennifer desperately wanted to talk about the rumor. Lisa warned her about snitching. Grandma Mattie's theory was "people will only respect you if you can stand your ground." Jennifer thought how different her life would be if she had a Grandma Mattie.

"You have been very quiet, Queenie. Is anything wrong?"

"No, Miss Stevens. Thank you for dinner."

"It was only three dollars."

Jennifer knew that was Linda's way of saying "you're welcome." Jennifer noticed that Linda had a difficult time with compliments and affection. She squirmed if Jennifer hugged her or sat too close.

When they reached Morrison Hall, Jennifer muscled enough strength to smile. "Good night Miss Stevens."

"Good night Queenie. Now don't forget, tomorrow I need to give you a passage for Friday night's ritual. I should have done it today but we can do it tomorrow. I have a meeting at six but I should be back around seven."

"Okay," Jennifer said and walked to Garrison Hall. She thought it had to be a good sign. Linda meeting her will keep away danger.

Linda rushed Angel to drive faster. Jennifer was waiting on her and the last thing Linda wanted was Jennifer to be kidnapped because of her tardiness. It was already 7:30 p.m. Linda had a gut feeling that something was wrong. She suspected that some sorors might try to pull a pledge session before initiation.

Angel parked the car and Linda hopped out quickly. She rushed down the hall and saw no Queenie. *Maybe she got someone to let her into the room*, Linda thought wildly. She rushed to open the door. "Damn," she cursed loudly. She knew Jennifer was in trouble. Linda rushed out of the room. Angel was rushing down the hall.

"What's going on?" Angel asked, trailing Linda down the hall. Before Linda could answer, they saw Maria walking down the hall with Rosalyn, Patrice and Candice.

Maria was angry. "They left Jennifer with a few misguided sorors who saw her standing outside your door. They kidnapped her," Maria said.

"Where is she?" Linda demanded of the girls.

"She left with Big Sister Sweet Sensation, Big Sister Cutie Pie and Big Sister Dark and Lovely," Candice said. "We did not know she was in trouble, especially being with Big Sister Dark and Lovely. She was the one who told us to leave."

"You were told not to leave your sisters alone!" Linda yelled and Angel jumped. She had never witnessed Linda outraged and neither had Maria. "Where did they take her?" Linda continued yelling.

"We do not know," the three girls sang, almost in tears.

Angel knew Linda considered it a personal attack. No one had ever challenged her in any manner. Jennifer was under her care and they went against her.

Linda and the three Cherubs hopped in Angel's car. They drove around town. Something told Angel that she would find Jennifer and to keep driving. It was the strangest feeling. She felt guided.

A figured darted across the street and ran into some bushes. Angel drove up faster, almost hitting an oncoming car. It was them, Jennifer's nightmare. The car kept going. Angel pulled over. Linda got out and rushed to the bushes. Jennifer sprinted off like a rabbit. Angel called out to her and she stopped.

Linda and Angel walked closer to Jennifer and saw the humiliation. Her checks had large red circles from lipstick. An eyeliner pencil shaded her entire face. Flour, broken eggs and syrup were in her hair and running down her face, causing her eyes to glue shut. Her blouse was ripped badly. Linda walked away, but Angel took Jennifer in her arms and walked her to the car. The other three Cherubs looked on in horror.

Finally, Jennifer spoke in a toneless voice, "Miss Stevens, we told them that we had to wait for you. Big Sister Dark and Lovely said she would bring us back. We never saw her again. They said our blouse was cheap like us."

Linda looked viciously at the three terrified girls who left Jennifer. They were stupid. Linda paced in front of the shaking girls.

"I will be at session tomorrow night," Linda said and got in the car.

The ride to the dorm was quiet. Angel parked the car. "You three clean her up and bring her to my room," Linda said.

"Make sure the water pressure is low when you wash her hair," Angel added. One girl placed a jacket over Jennifer's head. The Cherubs rushed through the dorm.

Angel was quiet for a few seconds. "Linda, this is not about you, it's about me."

"She's my Special so I say it's about me."

Angel paused for a moment. "It may not be about either of us. Whatever you do, play it cool."

Linda laughed out loud. "Queenie is one of the few people I like."

Angel snickered a little. "You are not going to believe this, but she has been lying to the sorors about why she could not meet with them. Miss Stevens wanted her to run some errands."

Linda looked surprised. Angel continued, "Did you know she was diabetic?" Linda shook her head. "I didn't either, but I had to laugh when I heard she told Brookes she couldn't eat Kappa food because she was diabetic. She had to eat a proper meal three times a day or else she would fall-out." Linda laughed.

"How many demerits did you give the Cherubs this pledge period?" Angel asked.

"None. I gave Jennifer demerits to keep her free from the witches. It was her excuse to leave when they were being unreasonable. I haven't seen the Cherubs since the second week of pledging. I don't want to be bothered with them."

"That's what I figured. It was her excuse and the whole line's excuse for leaving. They used you to get out of visiting the witches. You must have given her several sheets of demerits because all of them had to work off demerits for Miss Stevens," Angel said, trying not to burst into laughter.

"She used me! The little devil used me!" Linda said grinning.

"The Neophytes are a little pissed about it. They won't go against you, but our line sisters will. They figured out that you hadn't seen the girls this pledge period, so they were trying to get to the source. I don't like the idea of them singling her out."

"I agree. I don't like it either."

"It took a long time before they caught on to her. And another thing, Annette's, Debbie's and Courtney's batteries were taken out of their cars and placed on their front seats. Do you have any idea who was behind it?" Angel asked and looked at Linda with a smile.

"It doesn't have the same flare. I have to give it an 'A' for effort. Unfortunately, they don't respect intelligence like Lori and Estelle."

"She will be okay."

"I want to see how smart she really is. It won't be like last year. Let's go to the Union and get something to drink."

Angel stopped smiling. "I don't have any money. Since I paid Lionel back, I can't ask dad for any more money."

"Let's see if our charm still has the same magic. Maybe some fellas are just waiting to buy us something to drink."

They walked to the Student Union and talked about Jennifer the entire time. When they entered the cafeteria, a table of young men stopped talking and stared at them. They were all familiar stares. Angel's and Linda's presence in the Student Union's cafeteria was an unfamiliar sight. Angel became internally nervous and Linda smiled and waved.

"Good evening ladies, how about joining us this evening."

The two young women walked to the table of jogging suits and baseball caps with fraternity symbols displayed on the front. The caps were the same except for one. They stood when Angel and Linda arrived at the table. Linda took a seat next to the one who spoke and Angel sat next to the different baseball cap.

"Can I get you ladies something to drink?"

"How nice! I would like..."

"An ice tea for Miss Stevens and a punch with a dash of Sprite for Miss Smith."

"Oh, you remembered?" Linda said. The different baseball cap left to get the drinks while the group talked.

"So what have you fellas been doing this evening?"

"Relaxing. Shooting the breeze. We were just beaten badly by Lionel and his crew, but our Pharaohs beat the Aristocrats. What brings you two outside your castle?"

"Must we continue to be insulting, Carlos? Within days, we will be separated for life so can we act civilized?"

"I'm sorry, Miss Stevens. It's always good seeing you. You seem quite happy this evening."

"I am. I'm getting ready for initiation tomorrow. It should be exciting."

"Knowing you, Linda, excitement equates to abuse or danger. I remember how we kidnapped those Kappas for you ladies. Had it not been for Lionel knowing how to pop a car hood and removing spark plugs, our big brothers would have killed us. Those brothers were more worried about their rides than us."

"Lionel knows about cars?"

"The brother is a grease monkey!"

"I think the term is *shade tree mechanic*," the baritone voice said. He set the drinks in front of the two women. He pulled a chair very close to Angel and turned it around backward, facing the side of her face.

"Is something wrong with your car?" he asked smiling. Angel shook her head. "They were talking about how you helped them kidnap Lori and the girls two years ago."

"We did all that work and you never responded to any of my advances. Why?" the young man sitting next to Linda asked of her.

"Well Craig, you expected me to stand in line and wait my turn. You should know me better than that. Besides, you gentlemen enjoyed that little rendezvous. That was probably the only time you were ever able to get that close to a Diamond Lady," Linda said. The group laughed softly.

"It seems like my man Lionel doesn't have a problem," one said as the group watched Lionel lean close to Angel. He whispered in her ear, "Thanks for making me a respectable son again." He kissed her lightly on the ear. She took a sip from her cup and looked at Linda who was grinning with the rest of the group.

"Lionel, where is the rest of your entourage? I heard the Betas taught the Lambdas a little lesson in basketball."

Lionel flashed a very bright smile. "These brothers are weak. Most of our team was sick."

"Is a virus going around campus?" Angel asked.

Lionel sucked his bottom lip. "Our Aristocrats delivered a couple dozen of chocolate chip cookies to their big brothers, claiming it was from the sisterhood of Phi Kappa Psi. It had a note from what appeared to be your handwriting Linda."

Linda put her hand over her mouth and let out a low gasp, then she smiled, shaking her head.

"We believed it was laden with Ex-Lax. The brothers have been running off for two days. I guess you can call it poetic justice."

The other baseball caps roared with laughter.

"So you didn't eat any?" Linda asked.

"I don't eat sweets. I take it that you didn't write the note."

"I wrote the note but I didn't send it. Don't laugh too loud fellas, your turn could be next," Linda said to the other baseball caps.

"Excuse me for interrupting, Miss Steven. Did you get an answer to my request?"

"Yes Carlos. It's a go. Angel, I think we better let the boys continue their bonding." Linda said.

"We are going to play ball again. Why don't you ladies come out and be our cheerleaders? Maybe it's time to get on the winning team with BGD," Lionel bragged.

"The Diamond Ladies only have eyes for a Lambda, isn't that right Miss Stevens?"

"You had your chance but you chose Denise. Maybe in the next life," Linda said and removed the baseball cap off the head of the one named Craig. She placed a gentle kiss on his forehead. He looked sheepishly at her. "That's for good luck if I can't make it to cheer for you. Lionel, go easy on these guys next time. Good night fellas," Linda said. She and Angel left the cafeteria. The young men stared in awe as they walked away.

Chapter 11

It was Friday night. Jennifer was in Linda's room receiving the last ritual. Someone knocked on the door. Before Jennifer could open it, Linda shouted, "Come in!" In walked four older women wearing wine colored blazers with the Kappa's crest on the left pocket and cream color skirts. Two were very tall and slender. One was medium height and a little hippy and the other was petite. They were carrying heavy garment bags and brief cases. All looked as if they had stepped out of the beauty salon and were ready to go shopping. Jennifer stared at the diamond rings on the tallest one, who looked very familiar.

"Malinda honey, what have I told you about yelling? It is so tacky," said a smooth affluent voice.

"Hello Aunt Marilyn. Hello Aunt Susan. Hello Aunt JoAnn."

"Am I going to get a greeting?"

"You didn't give me a chance. Hello mother."

The tallest one looked at Linda as if she were lying. She went to one of Linda's closets to hang up the garment bag. Her facial expression dropped when she opened the door. "Sweetie, where are all of your clothes?"

"I lost a lot of weight so I gave some of them away."

"Some of them? It looks like you gave away all of them. I will be so glad when you get a job and buy your own clothes. I don't know why your father keeps catering to you. I'm not buying you another thing."

Linda smiled at the other women, while the tall complained as she hung the garment bags in the closet.

"Aunt Susan, how is Andrea?" Linda asked.

"She's doing fine. I will be attending her graduation at Spelman next week. She will be going away to graduate school at the University of Chicago."

"Tell her I said congratulations."

"Malinda, have you thought about what you are going to do after graduation?" the tallest one asked as she relaxed in a chair with her legs crossed, toes pointed down, while the others stood.

"Mother, can we talk about this later? I would like everyone to meet Jennifer." All eyes focused on Jennifer. The tallest one stared the most.

There was something familiar about the girl.

"What is your mother's name, sweetie?" the woman asked gently.

"Michelle Peterson," said a meek Jennifer, looking around the room. She tried not to look into the woman's glare.

"Who is your father?"

"Carleton Peterson."

The woman beckoned for Jennifer to come closer. She wanted to get a good look. It was her. "Nice to meet you, Miss Peterson," she finally said.

"Barbara, I'm going upstairs to see if Gina is in her room. I should be back in fifteen minutes," the hippy one said and left.

"Oh darn! I broke a nail. Malinda, give me a file," the tallest one said, frowning at the chipped nail. Linda handed the woman an emery board. She jumped as if a rattle snake was thrown in her lap. "I asked for a nail file not sand paper. Where is the file I gave you?" she asked.

"I think I lost it," Linda said uncaring.

"You lost a twenty-dollar diamond chip nail file?" the woman asked in disbelief.

Linda threw her hands out and hunched her shoulders. Linda had given the nail file to Jennifer after receiving the same emery board to file her nails.

"This girl is going to make me kill her," the woman said as she rambled through her purse and finally pulled out what she wanted. Someone knocked on the door.

Linda yelled, "Come in!"

The tallest one frowned at Linda. Her yelling came as a surprise to Jennifer as well. As long as she had been around Linda, she seemed so relaxed and unmoved, but now, these women unnerved her.

Angel walked in. She greeted the women with "Aunt" and hugged them each. The tallest one smiled broadly as Angel hugged her.

"I sold three of your designs, sweetie. Have you thought about what you are going to do after graduation?" she asked pleasantly.

"I'm going away to graduate school at the University of Minnesota," Angel said proudly. The woman's hands went to her mouth. "Neither Bill nor Dora mentioned anything about you going to Minnesota. When did you decide this, dear?" she asked.

"I got my acceptance letter about a month ago. Now it's a matter of money," Angel said brightly.

"Why Minnesota?"

"It's an excellent school for psychology," Angel said, avoiding eye contact with the woman.

"Before you leave for school, make sure we talk," the tall one insisted.

Linda was slightly annoyed at her mother. She behaved as if Angel were her daughter. When Angel and her father moved to Kansas City, Barbara Stevens went out of her way to ensure that Angel assimilated well. Catherine Smith, Angel's mother, was Barbara's best friend in college. When Barbara found out that Angel had a talent for designing clothes, they became closer because they shared something in common.

Linda often found herself competing for her mother's attention, but she didn't let it interfere with Angel's friendship. Angel had a knack for smoothing out misunderstandings. As long as Linda's father catered to her desires, it helped ease the unpleasant relationship between her and her mother.

"Mother brought the uniforms. They are in the closet," Linda said to Angel.

"That's all that is in there. Princess Ann gave away all of her clothes," Barbara threw in.

"Now what is going on, Malinda. You said that Betty's daughter is stirring up trouble that will cause the chapter a probable suspension?" Barbara asked in attorney fashion.

Angel asked Jennifer to leave the room.

Linda and Angel told the three remaining women what took place at the voting and throughout Jennifer's pledge period. Linda gave graphic details about how Jennifer looked last night and how she ran for her life. She painted a picture of monsters brutalizing a child. The three women listen closely. She explained how the jealousy and arrogance had escalated to the point of hazing and Zeta Chi Chapter will eventually be suspended.

Barbara knew they were blowing some things out of proportion to get her to respond, but she knew it had to be bad if her daughter asked for help. She didn't ask for her help the last time the same girls misbehaved. Angel called Aunt Barbara.

Barbara raised her hand to silence Linda and Angel. "Sorors, don't you think it is time for these ladies to meet the founders of this chapter? I say we need to make an impromptu appearance, do you all agree?" Barbara asked the others with an impish smile.

Several Kappas were in the Chapter room waiting for the Cherubs to arrive. There was a knock on the door. They yelled. Some cursed. In walked four women, followed by Angel and Linda. The National Official identifier under the crest on the wine colored blazers made the girls squirm. A hush went over the group. The girls recognized the four faces as they appeared on the large picture next to the sorority crest. Embarrassment filled their faces as they did not expect to see four of the chapter founders walk through the door.

Barbara Stevens eyed each one. Heads dropped and eyes lowered. She twisted the very large diamond ring as she so often did when delivering a speech. She cleared her throat and lifted her head high. As she spoke, she articulated each sound in every word.

"I was beginning to think I had just walked in on a group of Alphas until I saw the picture of Susan, Marilyn, JoAnn and myself. I'm having a difficult time figuring out which one of us is the stupid bitch. It's quite disturbing, knowing that the sorority has succumbed to vile language and insults to potential members whom we identify as the Cherubs, the basis of the organization," Barbara said in an authoritative tone. She motioned a younger Kappa out of a chair and sat down.

Barbara examined the room. She crossed her arms over her chest and spoke in an extremely arrogant persona. "Those drapes need cleaning. When were you girls planning on cleaning the upholstery on the furniture my husband and I donated? Maybe I'm asking for too much, since I am a stupid bitch." Barbara crossed her legs, toes pointed down. She turned facing all of the young women, including Angel and Linda.

"Let's just say we are here on a little sorority business and I doubt if we will stay long since we really don't feel welcomed," Barbara said with a little laugh. It sounded like a hiss. Linda watched her mother put into play that which she had seen her do so well, humiliation. Marilyn Smith took notes.

"Girls, we have received one of the most disturbing phone calls from a concerned mother who says her daughter was not only humiliated but physically abused. Does anyone know what I'm talking about?" Barbara asked in a slightly high-pitched voice. No one uttered a sound.

"Well that's okay, I do have a few names. Since you girls are going to bond together, and after hearing what I just heard, I'm asking for all of your sorority pins in acknowledgement of termination of membership," Barbara said without blinking. The young women gasped. They looked at one another, shaking their heads in disagreement.

"That also includes the President and the Dean of Pledges as well, for not reporting the activities," Barbara added in a slow and serious tone. Angel's mouth dropped. Her heart pounded.

"Excuse me, Mrs. Stevens. I was not a participant in what happened to Jennifer Peterson. I just heard about it and..." one girl confessed and one of the women looked at her in amazement.

"Who said anything about a Jennifer Peterson? Was she abused too?" Susan asked.

Barbara looked surprised. "You mean to tell me that more than one girl has been abused? This is outrageous! It looks like the chapter will have to be suspended," Barbara concluded. The young women cried. Linda felt her mother laid it on a little too thick, especially upsetting Angel.

"I would like the President to continue with the initiation ceremony and the rest of you ladies, meet me at the Ramada Inn to discuss the termination process. If you feel this is unjust, I need your response in writing tonight by nine o'clock. Girls, I'm tired. I do need my beauty rest. Ta-ta!" Barbara said and walked out the door. The other founders followed. The distraught young women watched the four women take the only thing that mattered to them away in a matter of minutes.

"Barbara, do we have to be bothered with these girls tonight, I'm tired? It's time we stopped rescuing the chapter. Maybe it needs to be suspended until respectable women decide to become members," Marilyn complained.

Barbara reclined on her bed and stretched. "We've worked too hard to get where we are. Friendships were lost, trying to get this chapter started. Maybe this will be the last of the brutal women if we play this thing right," Barbara said.

Marilyn understood her friend's concern. Barbara worked hard to get them to the National level, but it wasn't enough for Barbara. She wanted more. She was the one who had a score to settle with Thelma and the rest. There could be no embarrassment or scars left on her work or Catherine's work for that matter. It was Catherine and Debra who worked hard to help get the chapter started. It was Barbara who worked harder to keep the friendships together, but it didn't matter. She was dealing with women who sought power like men.

"Did you notice something familiar about that child?" Barbara asked as she sat up.

"Which one?"

"The Jennifer Peterson girl. She said her mother's name was Michelle Peterson. Those eyes and that beauty mark on her face gave me the impression of Catherine," Barbara said as she unpacked her suitcase.

"Guess who I saw?" Marilyn said.

"Who?"

"Debra Arvell's daughter."

Barbara stopped unpacking. "You are kidding me!" she said, almost shouting.

"I wish I was. She's Gina's pledge daughter. She was in Gina's room when I went upstairs. She is the spitting image of Debra," said a slightly depressed Marilyn, but Barbara was excited.

"I want to see her. Debra Arvell's daughter at the same university with our daughters and Catherine's daughter too? How could this have happened? Are you sure she is Debra's daughter?" Barbara asked.

"Lisa Arvell is her name," Marilyn said.

A knock sounded at the door. The two women looked at each other. Marilyn closed her eyes and turned her head and Barbara smiled as she walked to the door.

"Come in ladies."

The Cherubs sat in a circle at Patricia Tate's house, a graduate student.

"Jennifer, how do you feel about your pledge period and your Pledge Special?"

A huge smile came across Jennifer's face. It had appeared in the past that no one was interested in what she thought or how she felt, except Lionel.

As Jennifer babbled on about her relationship with Linda, the door opened. In walked Angel followed by Linda and Maria. The Cherubs scrambled to stand in order to greet them. The Kappas became quiet. Eyes were fixed on Linda.

Angel paced in front of the girls the way she did the first night of pledging. She did her inspection of the line slowly. Finally, she nodded, indicating her approval, but the Cherubs were unaware. The Kappas smiled.

Linda stepped forward and walked up and down the line of girls with a bowl. She rubbed the tips of her fingernails. "My, my, my. A full line of Cherubs. Guess what I have girls? Ta-da, Kappa food! Cherub Miss America, why don't you take a big spoonful of Miss Stevens' special gourmet dish and pass it down the line," Linda said and handed Alexis a bowl.

The Cherubs were filled with fear, knowing of Linda's reputation. They all looked at Alexis who looked at the chili and spaghetti mixture. She hesitated. Linda stepped very close to Alexis and looked harder. Alexis took a big spoonful and shoved the mixture into her mouth and swallowed quickly. She frowned as the mushy meal slipped down her throat.

Linda shook her head. "No dear, I want you to chew it. You are missing the flavor. Try another spoonful," Linda said forcefully.

Alexis panted. She took another spoonful and chewed. She frowned as the flavor of brown sugar, tomato paste and syrup clung to her teeth.

"What's the matter, you don't like Miss Stevens' gourmet dish?"

"It is excellent, Miss Stevens, we like it."

"Good, take another big heaping spoonful - no take two spoonfuls and pass the bowl down. I want your sisters to enjoy it too."

Alexis slowly took two more spoonfuls and quickly passed the bowl down. Linda watched as the bowl got closer to Jennifer. When it was her turn, Linda grabbed the bowl. "None for you, Queenie. Remember, you're diabetic," Linda said smiling, handing the bowl to Allyn.

Jennifer was a little stunned. "Miss Stevens, we must take a spoonful like everyone else."

"Oh no, Queenie. We don't want you falling out," Linda said. Jennifer pouted. "Well, if you insist," Linda said and took the bowl from Allyn. Before she gave it to Jennifer, she poured tabasco sauce on top and stirred it in well. Jennifer's eyes became wide.

"Here you go Queenie, finish it."

Jennifer stared at the bowl and slowly took it out of Linda's hands. She ate slowly. The tabasco sauce made it almost impossible to swallow. She gagged.

"Don't you just love it? It has that Mexican flavor," Linda said, smiling at Jennifer. Linda turned her attention to the other Cherubs. "Guess what ladies? I've got dessert, Chocolate Chip cookies! Miss America, take a cookie and pass the rest down the line. They are *loaded* with chips."

Alexis was breathing heavily. Linda pushed the bag at her. Jennifer stopped eating. "Cherub Miss America, we cannot eat sweets. Miss Stevens banned sugar from our diet until we are initiated," Jennifer said, coughing with watery eyes.

Linda looked surprised. "That's right, I did. What's the matter Queenie, is Kappa food too hot?"

Jennifer shook her head until she saw Linda take out the bottle of tabasco sauce again. "It's much too hot!" Jennifer shouted.

"Maria, Kappa food is too hot for Jennifer. Could you cool her down?" Linda asked with her hands on her face. Maria took out a water gun and squirted water on Jennifer. All the Kappas took water guns and squirted the girls until they squealed with laughter.

Linda's eyes jumped with delight as she saw Jennifer scream with laughter. Linda cut Angel a look. She cleared her throat. "Ladies, can I see your books please? I promise to give them back," Angel said. She flipped through the books until she found what she was looking for. "Oh my goodness. Linda, most of these girls still have demerits from you. By all means, they cannot be initiated until all these demerits are removed."

Linda walked over to Angel and gasped. "I had almost forgotten that I had given Cherub Ashy Dashy two thousand demerits. Matter of fact, none of them have worked off my demerits. I'm hurt," Linda said pouting. "Soror Neophytes, the Cherubs have my permission to work off my demerits according to your wishes. Oh looky here! Queenie has one million demerits," Linda said as she wrote them in Jennifer's book. "Maria, I want you to personally make sure Miss Peterson has a clean slate before initiation. I'm going to take a nap ladies so ta-ta," Linda said and sashayed out the door.

Angel looked at the fired up Neophytes who were fooled the entire pledge period. They were ready for action. Angel saw Jennifer breathing steam. "Remember ladies, you must think through all responses and actions. Cherubs are smart heavenly beings," Angel said and left the room.

Jennifer looked at all the angry stares. She wondered how would she get out of the messy situation? The Kappas ordered them around as personal servants.

After the Cherubs had worked like slaves, the Kappas had them performing skits which broke the tension. The Cherubs sang songs and did stand-up comedy. The Kappas threw nerf balls at them if they were bad. Later that evening, the girls sat around and laughed at themselves.

Jennifer didn't see the Kappas who gave her a hard time Thursday night. Rosalyn and Patrice were missing too. "Big Sisters, where are our other Cherub sisters?" Jennifer asked. The Kappas looked at each other, trying not to show any signs of information.

"Are we your sisters' keepers? No we're not! That's your responsibility. Maybe they dropped line," one responded. The Cherubs gasped.

"Dropped line! Why?" Margo asked trying to keep still.

"What do you ladies care? You let them go out by themselves. You sit here and have a good time. What has happened to them is probably the same thing that happened to Jennifer on Thursday night. We are getting ready to start the Renaissance Ritual. You performed this part of the ritual without them so I say let's get the show on the road," Joni said.

The Kappas began singing a song, sounding ritual in nature. The Cherubs were scared, not knowing what to do, especially without a Dean of Pledges.

Jennifer whispered to Alexis, "We have got to find them. We cannot be birthed without them. Let's keep asking until we wear them down. Maybe they will tell us." The word spread quickly among the line of girls. They asked the Kappas continuously on the whereabouts of their sisters but were ignored. The Cherubs whined, but no information was given. Jennifer motioned Alexis to leave to find the girls. The Cherubs ran out of the house as if it were haunted.

Angel, Linda and a few other Kappas were in the Chapter room where Rosalyn and Patrice were held as hostages. "You two have been screwing up from the beginning and now I'm getting ready to kick your ass," Linda growled. Patrice cried, begging for mercy. Rosalyn was afraid but she was a tough one to make cry.

"You set up my Pledge Special because you were jealous of her," Linda said and pushed Rosalyn hard.

"No Big Sister, we had nothing to do with..." Rosalyn was interrupted when Linda stepped close to her face. She grabbed Rosalyn by the collar.

"You know where Big Sister Dark and Lovely is? She is with four national officials, deciding whether or not you two sorry sluts are going to be members. I say to vote you two out," Linda said in a low voice.

"It's bad enough to disrespect my sorority but to have no respect for yourself is even worse. My mother is one of those officials. I will make sure that she and her friends know about everything you have done so she can tell your cheap ass to take a hike. If I kicked your ass right now, nothing will happen to me. I've done this before," Linda said.

Rosalyn shook with fear. Her mind scrambled for a way out. She closed her eyes, thinking Linda was going to hit her. Linda looked over at the other Kappas with a smile and then she looked at Patrice. "I just need a letter from you, begging forgiveness." Patrice sat down and wrote quickly.

"Big Sister..." Rosalyn begged.

"My name is Miss Stevens."

"Miss Stevens, can we write a letter too?" asked a humble Rosalyn.

Linda laughed hard and so did the other women in the room. "I want you to kiss the picture of the founders and apologize for your behavior."

Rosalyn complied quickly. Tears ran down her face. She faced the Kappas in the room with a tear streaked face.

"What have you and I discussed this week, Rosalyn?" Angel asked firmly.

"We are sorry Big Sisters of Phi Kappa Psi Sorority. We did not mean to disrespect the sorority," Rosalyn cried. She panted, trying to catch her breath. "So much has happened in our life and we just can't help ourselves. We have..."

Angel interrupted, "That's enough Rosalyn. That's enough." There was a knock at the door.

Linda yelled, "Who is it?"

"We are the Cherubs. May we come in?"

"NO!" all the Kappas in the room shouted.

The Cherubs could hear Rosalyn in the room crying. All Jennifer could think about was the night she was left alone.

"Miss Stevens, are you in there?" Jennifer asked politely. Linda looked at the Kappas and chuckled. She whispered something to Maria.

"Yes she is, Jennifer, but she's busy right now. Have you finished your dinner?" Maria asked.

Jennifer heard laughter in the room. She had to think quickly. "Miss Stevens, may we have our sisters back? We cannot be initiated without them."

The Cherubs pleaded for the return of their sisters. Maria went outside the room to silence them. It was 2:00 a.m. They were making too much noise. The girls were breathing hard not only from running but out of fear and frustration. Jennifer walked to the door.

"Please, Miss Stevens," Jennifer begged.

"I'm doing this for you, Queenie. Remember how these two bums left you to die. Too bad I didn't get my hands on that big eye Cherub that left you. She would be in here too. They set you up, Jennifer, so it's payback!" Linda shouted, trying to keep from laughing. She looked at the other Kappas in the room. They too had to turn their heads to keep from laughing.

"Miss Stevens, you said if we ever needed anything to just ask. We need our sisters back. Please, Miss Stevens, you promised," Jennifer said in tears, remembering the horrible night. The Kappas looked at Linda with frowns on their faces. She threw her hands out and hunched her shoulders.

"A promise is a promise. I'll give you back your sisters, Queenie," Linda said, trying to act disappointed. She opened the door and the Cherubs rushed in. Patrice was still writing her letter. The girls all hugged Rosalyn and each other.

It was time to crawl through the birth canal into Kappa Land. The girls were blindfolded wearing shower caps in underwear. They were led to a Kappa who would recite a passage and performed a ritual.

Jennifer was first. When she arrived at the birth canal, she was given a balloon to burst. She felt water splash in her face and run down her leg. She had to stoop to crawl through what felt like a very large duffle bag, filled with slimy substances. She was shaking as she made the trip. A voice came to her in the sack that told her to calm down and not be afraid. She continued to crawl quickly, trying not to touch what she thought were worms. As she emerged from the sack, she heard cheering. She was helped from the floor. Her body shook off the foreign objects that clung to her bare skin. A sheet was placed around her. It was finally over.

"Soror, what shall you name her?"

"Queen of the Nile," Linda said proudly and removed the blindfold. Jennifer wept like a baby. All the hard work was over.

"Honey, you have to leave the room while we birth your sisters," Linda said with a smile.

Angel put her arms around Jennifer to lead her away. Angel told Jennifer that she must wear the pearl necklace with a black dress for the initiation ceremony.

Jennifer faced Angel, "Now...we are...really sisters," she said gasping through tears.

"Yes we are sweetie," Angel said with a smile and placed a gentle kiss on Jennifer's forehead.

The Genies sang the pledge song over and over as they walked to Carla's apartment. They were dressed in navy blue sweatshirts, navy blue baseball caps, jeans and bright white tennis shoes. They had their wooden paddles swinging in unison to the rhythm of the pledge song "All for One and One for All."

Lisa let the words of wisdom from Gina roll over in her mind, "Everything you touch must be of gold and if ever you are in trouble, remember the pledge song." They had arrived at Carla's apartment. Lisa knocked on the door and chanted the beginning ritual passage. An unfamiliar face opened the door.

There were many new faces in the room. Lisa examined the room. It was filled with talkative women that looked older than Carla. She approached Lisa with an unfamiliar woman. The room became quiet when Carla spoke, "Clarisse, I want you to meet your pledge granddaughter, Lisa," she said cheerfully.

"Hello Lisa. What is your pledge name?" Clarisse asked pleasantly.

Lisa looked strangely at the very round woman who sported a very short afro. "We are Genie Motor Mouth," Lisa said proudly. Most of the women in the room roared with laughter.

One asked aloud, "Wasn't that your pledge name Carla?"

"No, it was Genie Talk Too Much," Carla said slightly embarrassed. The women laughed again.

"I remembered silencing her in the first week of pledging. She had an answer to everything," Clarisse said laughing.

Another one asked out loud, "Clarisse, what was your pledge name?" Clarisse narrowed her eyes. The woman continued, "Don't be shamed, tell us!" Clarisse remained silent. A medium height, medium built, very brown woman stood up. She walked to Lisa. She reminded Lisa of Jennifer with the long hair and arched eyebrows, but her eyes were like Lisa's.

"She was Genie Diarrhea Mouth, Always Running," she said and everyone laughed including some of the Genies. "It runs in the family," the woman added and everyone laughed again. "I'm your great grand pledge mother Angela Base, Genie China Doll," the woman said in a friendly voice.

It was customary for the line captain to be introduced to any pledge mothers that were present before the others met theirs. All the other grands and great grands introduced themselves to the rest of the Genies.

The Rite of Passage ritual began. Lisa was summoned into the living room first. They called this point The Time of Judgement. The Genies were told to be honest and sincere as they spoke to the Big Sisters.

"You were caught talking, disobeying pledge rules. What is your reason?"

Lisa slowly told of her relationship with Jennifer and how she didn't want to lose her friendship. Lisa looked for a sympathetic eye, but there were none.

"You were silenced by your pledge mother. Why?"

Lisa still got no friendly eye contact. She didn't think being silenced was a big deal. "Our pledge mother said we talked too much," she said nonchalantly. She looked around the room, no smiles, not even from the woman named Angela.

"You wanted to remain friends with a Cherub who will become a Kappa soon and you talk too much. What kind of loyalty can we expect from you? After all, this is a sisterhood. We can't afford sorority business all around campus," a very unfriendly voice said.

Lisa looked around the room at the different women. Some were tall and some were short. There were dark ones, light ones. Some had long straight hair, some had short afros, and there were some with curls. Some women were very thin and some were heavy. They seemed to have different personalities too.

Lisa cleared her throat, "Under no circumstances do I intend to divulge sorority business. When we look at our big sisters, we see all types of women. It is not like other sororities whose members all look alike. An Alpha is not threatened by differences. The Genies know that not only can we be an Alpha but an individual as well."

Someone cleared her throat aloud, "Hum, I guess she told us."

"Why did you accept the invitation to pledge Alpha Theta Lambda?"

Lisa mumbled when she spoke. "When we came to school in our freshmen year, we had to catch the bus because we did not have a car nor did we have parents to take us. As we walked toward campus, Big Sister Hail to the Chief and Big Sister Good Witch of the North stopped and offered us a ride. They told us if ever we needed anything to just ask. No one had ever been that nice to us before. They were wearing the Greek symbols of Alpha Theta Lambda. They told us that they were sorority sisters, so from that time on, we wanted to be sorority sisters with them."

Something about the way Lisa told her story was moving. She saw a few smiles in the room even from Gina. She remembered seeing Lisa struggle with a very large, old suitcase and a bookbag thrown over her shoulder. She and Marsha stopped to give her a ride because campus was three miles away and she was having a difficult time carrying all of her things. They practically had to force her into the car by asking her questions, trying to make her feel comfortable.

After the Alphas finished with the Time of Judgement, emotions swept the women. Some of the Genies had come from broken homes and wanted a relationship with women who they could call sisters. Several were legacy. Some were treated kindly by Alphas who never knew they touched them in that capacity. Like Gina had said, the line was special.

The Genies were sent on a scavenger hunt to find all the letters of *Alpha*. They were scheduled to return in two hours. It was time to get down to sorority business.

"Sorors, we have a process that has worked very well over the years, identifying potential leaders and grooming them for that purpose. I open the floor for discussion," Clarisse said.

The older women were hearing complaints about how the sorority had turned into a clique and how some sorors called all the shots, not letting it be democratic anymore.

"Never air dirty laundry in the streets. What has me concerned is that some of you have the audacity to undermine the authority that was voted in. Unfortunately, this is not the government. It is a sisterhood," one of the grand pledge mothers said.

Another woman stood up. "Jessica, you tell Gina right now what is the problem so you two can work it out," said Jessica's grand pledge mother.

Jessica remained silent. "Are you saying there are no problems?" she asked Jessica. She shook her head.

"I heard that some of you are plotting mutiny. Let's hear your complaints so that we can get this thing settled," said one great grand pledge mother. No one spoke.

Angela stood and spoke. Her voice was calm. She smiled the entire time as she spoke, "Sorors, this is not about man stealing, it's about respect. The problem is some of us neglected our extended roles as pledge mothers. We graduated, left and never returned to see if our daughters were okay. Sorors who are grand as well as great great grand, we have a responsibility to these women. This is the first time I have ever seen so many of us at an initiation night. The Genies are saying how they want to be like us and we don't like us."

Angela walked to Gina and took her by the hand. She led her to Jessica. The two faced each other. "Don't ever let a man come between the sisterhood or friendship. Do you two understand?" Angela asked.

Both said, "Yes."

"Sorors, we have heard the two pledge sisterhood as well as friendship. I don't think there will be any more problems," Angela said. Everyone clapped.

Jessica hugged Gina hard and whispered, "I'm sorry."

"I need to know does anyone have a problem with the process of leadership?" Clarisse demanded.

One Neophyte's hand crept up. "Sometimes people are picked because they are liked. Leadership talents in other people are ignored. How does the process address that?" she asked.

"Does anyone else feel the same way?" Clarisse asked. Two other girls raised their hands. "I'm truly sorry that you are having a difficult time with the process sorors. Are there any more problems?" Clarisse asked. There was a look of shock on the three young women's faces as they watched all of the grand and great grand pledge mothers talk amongst themselves.

The Genies came back at midnight, filled with excitement. They found all the letters of *Alpha* in an hour-and-a-half. Lisa handed over the large white letters. No one took them. The women frowned. Lisa wondered what was wrong. They found the letters in less time than allowed.

"Big Sisters, we found *Alpha*," Lisa said.

"Our *Alpha* is gold," Angela said as she frowned.

It dawned on Lisa that everything must be gold. She was in a situation that she now regretted. What kind of captain was she?

"We should have known. These girls are not as smart as we thought," one older Alpha said. "I don't like Genie number four anyway. She has an attitude," she said making reference to Alicia.

"I bet she was the one who told them to pick out the white *Alpha*, trying to sabotage the line. We know Carla's grand pledge would never do that," another Alpha said.

Lisa was beyond embarrassed. Now they were picking on Alicia. "Big

Sisters, it was our fault," Lisa said.

"Look at the big husky one down the line rolling her eyes, I bet she had something to do with it too," one said, making reference to Evelyn.

"Well, I know it's three that we don't want. They don't deserve the Last Rite. They have embarrassed the sorority with misconduct. When I call your name, step forward," one announced. She called out Alicia, Evelyn and Janet. The three girls looked at the other Genies and stepped forward and so did Lisa slowly followed by the other Genies.

"I ask for three Genies. I want them to step forward if they are not cowards," the woman said firmly. The three girls stepped forward and so did Lisa followed reluctantly by the rest of the Genies.

One woman bumped Alicia. Another did the same to Janet. One stood behind Alicia and whispered in her ear. Lisa saw Alicia's head snap forward. Someone pushed Janet out of line. One wrestled with Evelyn for her paddle. Lisa immediately shouted commands to form a circle around Alicia, Evelyn and Janet. As the women tried to push the girls, they stood very close, strong, interlocking arms.

One of the great great great grands, the oldest Alpha in the room, stood in front of Lisa. "You seem to have a problem following directions. I asked for three Genies," the woman said again.

"We are one," Lisa answered nervously, trying not to make eye contact with the woman who was smiling at her the entire time.

"So you want to go down with these three lazy girls?" the woman asked with a cocky grin.

Lisa looked her in the eye and said, "All for one and one for all."

The woman stepped back. "Genie number four, I understand you are majoring in Elementary Education. Young lady, heavy drinking is not the example we need to set for our black children and that example starts with you. You will have the greatest amount of influence on our children. Is that understood?"

"Yes, Big Sister!" the Genies shouted.

The older one looked at Alicia, "I want to hear it from you."

"Yes, Big Sister," Alicia said, trying not to let the tears fall.

"I want to know why?" she demanded of Alicia.

"We do not know," Alicia answered, fighting hard to control the tears. She shook as she looked in the eyes of the woman.

"If you are initiated, I will give you my phone number. Whenever you don't know, you call to get an answer," the older woman said, looking hard at Alicia who couldn't look at her.

"Yes Ma'am," Alicia whispered with her head down.

"Hold your head up and look at me. You have nothing to be ashamed of," the woman said firmly with a stone face. Alicia slowly lifted her head and turned her sights on the woman. She let the stone face soften.

"Okay, here is the first clue to the first 'A,'" she said, handing Lisa a note.

Lisa looked at the note. They had to go near Big Danny's house to get the first gold 'A. It was three miles away.

"You will receive clues at each station. You have five hours to get all the letters before the time of the Genie expires. Little lady, I hope you don't disappoint me because I'm Angela Base's pledge mother and we don't want any failures in the family," the head matriarch said. The Genies rushed out the door.

"Sorors, get in place quickly. These girls may beat the five hour mark so we must be ready to greet them at the specified stations to give the passage," Clarisse said.

"Sorors, we are proud of you for picking a line of strong young women with integrity and dedication. We believe they will uphold the honor and loyalty of our beloved sisterhood. Gina, it is time for you to take your place with the ruling body. Rita, you must prepare yourself for the Ritual of Wisdom," said the head matriarch. She went to the three Neophytes who were in disagreement.

"Sometimes, we may not like everything that happens but we must learn to work with and within the system. I heard you ladies were very lazy when they were scouting these girls. You need to work closely with Rita, so the next leader will have the qualities that are required and needed," she said and extended her arms. "Are you with us?" The three walked to her slowly, each kissing her on the cheek in acknowledgement of acceptance from the highest level of wisdom.

The Genies had been waiting for twenty minutes for an Alpha to give them a clue to find the last letter. They had the golden "H" but no clue for the "A." It was 4:45 a.m. and the magic of the Genie would expire at 6:00 a.m. The girls were tired and dirty from going through ditches and small ponds of water. There were no Alphas there to give them the last clue for the final letter.

The girls were three miles from the dorms. They were getting restless waiting for someone to come. Frustration escalated as they sat clueless in an open field. Tina screamed at Evelyn, claiming it was her fault. As some continued to argue, Alicia approached Lisa. "I was told the secret was in the pledge song," Alicia said.

"Let's go back to Big Sister's Let My People Go," Lisa said to the exhausted girls. She started the line on a slow pace jog. They sang songs from the Jamboree Show to get their minds off of the long jog back.

It was 5:15 a.m. and they were less than two miles from Carla's apartment. They rested a few minutes and then continued their journey with a fast pace walk. It was 5:45 a.m. when they arrived at Carla's apartment. Lisa hoped that the last clue would not take more than five minutes, given the other clues ranged from thirty minutes to an hour to find. When the door opened, Jessica was there, holding the last "A." The girls jumped with excitement. Some rushed and hugged her. Lisa and Alicia stood back.

Jessica told the Genies to go back to their rooms and clean up. They were to meet at the Chapel wearing blue skirts, gold blouses, blue shoes and makeup. Their hair was to be done nicely. They were to perform these tasks in total silence, even to each other.

"An Alpha never walks alone. She has the love and comfort of her sisters in times of need. An Alpha never walks alone. She has the united strength of her sisters, committed to the purpose of cause. I pledge loyalty to the purpose of the sorority and the bond of sisterhood." Lisa's heart beat fast as she repeated the words out loud to her pledge mothers, grands, great grands and great great grand. For the first time, Lisa felt she had a family. There was a connection.

Lisa and her line sisters formed a semicircle and listened to the President.

"If ever you believe you can no longer devote love, loyalty and respect to the sisterhood, you must relinquish your pearls, the ones that sit proudly over your heart. I now pronounce you members of Alpha Theta Lambda Sorority, Incorporated."

The new members jumped up and down. They cheered. The old members clapped. The girls rushed to hug and kiss them. Lisa grabbed Carla and squeezed her hard. Tears fell.

"Are you crying? The tough little Genie?" Carla asked as she hugged Lisa.

Lisa wiped her eyes and shook her head. Gina approached Lisa and Carla. Lisa caught Gina off guard with a hug too. They embraced for a few seconds. The new members hugged one another, crying unashamed. It was all over. Alicia caught Lisa's eyes. Without words, they spoke, forgiving one another and thanking the other.

"We have pastries and orange juice in the Chapter room ladies. Let's celebrate," Marsha announced.

The new members looked at each other and yelled, "Yes Big Sisters!"

Chapter 12

Barbara flipped through the pictures in her wallet. She looked hard at the only picture of her godchild. She was so beautiful now. She remembered when Catherine asked her to be the godmother. Catherine knew she understood. Barbara closed her wallet and put it in her purse. Marilyn came out of the bathroom.

"I didn't think we were staying for initiation, Barbara. I thought we had accomplished our goal with the little talk to those girls."

"It would be good to initiate these girls. We have to! After all, we are the Chapter's founders. Why are you rushing to get back?"

"Paul and I are going out to dinner tonight. I want to get some rest before we go."

Barbara looked at her friend suspiciously. Something else was bothering her. "What's the matter, Marilyn?"

"I'm thinking about going inactive. The sorority is taking a lot of my time."

"You only travel four times a year which, includes conferences and conventions. What's the real problem?"

"Ronnie is becoming a little difficult to handle and Paul thinks I need to stay closer to home."

Barbara released a low chuckled. "When did you start listening to a man?" Marilyn remained silent.

"Well dear, I will not dissuade you into anything different. What is Ronald doing?"

"Just being a teenager. We are going to Florida for a week in June and then we are going to take a few weekend trips to go camping and fishing." Marilyn looked nonchalant as she spoke.

Barbara was curious. "Is camping and fishing something you want to do at your age?"

Marilyn let out a huff. "What do you mean at my age?"

"Nothing dear. I know you two did the outdoors adventure in the earlier years of your marriage, but why now? Are you trying to put a little spark back into the marriage?"

"Oh Barbara, please! Let's initiate these girls."

The four women wore white robes. They chanted a passage and one hit the chime. The ceremony was long, but Jennifer listened closely. She was still filled with excitement. Four National Officials presiding over an initiation was an honor.

An hour-and-a-half passed. Candles flickered brightly in the sanctuary of Mount Nebo Baptist Church. The very tall one asked the initiates to stand and repeat several sentences. They did and sat again. The four robes continued with the ceremony. The old members placed little white caps on the girls' heads and quoted a passage. The very tall one hit the chimes. Next came the very large white collars that were fastened around the girls' necks.

Three hours passed. The tall robe stood facing Jennifer. She could not concentrate on the voice as it talked about the most precious jewel on earth, the diamond. Her focus was on the elegant woman who stood in front of her.

Innocently, Jennifer looked at the woman's face. It was pleasant. The only thing that revealed her age were the few crinkles around the eyes. Her hair was brown. Jennifer could not tell if it was natural or dyed. The makeup was very light, just a hint of blush on the cheekbones and reddish brown lipstick. Her eyes were filled with mystery. When she smiled at Jennifer, she knew the truth.

"I vow to uphold the integrity and excellence of Phi Kappa Psi Sorority, Incorporated. I also vow everlasting services to my community and mankind," was the last thing Jennifer said before Barbara Stevens placed the brightly shining diamonds on her chest. Next came the pin guard underneath. Jennifer glanced at the pin. The colors from the diamonds put her in a trance.

"Welcome ladies. Welcome to our beloved sisterhood," the hippy robe said.

Clapping broke Jennifer's trance. "Thank you, Mrs. Stevens," Jennifer said.

"My pleasure, Miss Peterson. I had to meet the person for whom I wrote the character reference," Barbara Stevens said.

Jennifer was startled. She remembered submitting a character reference from her English professor but not from Mrs. Stevens. Jennifer continued to smile as Linda taught her when she was unsure of what to say.

Barbara noticed the girl's hands. The nails were freshly manicured, french. The cuticles were neatly trimmed and the nails were filed nice and round, no points.

"Your nails look nice. Did you do them yourself?" Barbara asked, knowing the girl couldn't possibly have given herself a french manicure.

"Actually, one of my Cherub sisters did all of our nails," Jennifer replied.

"Oh? You must be very special. My daughter usually does not attach well with women. I hope to see you in Nationals one day." The tall elegant woman walked away. Alexis quickly approached her and soon she was swarmed by many Kappas. Barbara Stevens enjoyed the attention.

"So now you have met the Head Honcho, Miss Zeta Chi herself. What do you think?"

"She is a little bossy but quite appealing."

"Yes, she does have a very strong self image."

They were just alike, Jennifer thought. "It was really nice of her to pin me. I thought you would do it."

"Miss Phi Kappa Psi wanted the honors. You must have done something to impress her. She doesn't take to women quickly."

Jennifer hesitated before speaking. "You two are so much alike." She braced herself to see if Linda was offended.

"Not really. I mind my own business." Linda smiled a little as she looked at her mother talking happily to her newly formed fan club.

"I never thanked you for being my Special."

"You turned out fine. I need to get my beauty rest. I'll see you at the Neophyte Dance. Ta-ta!"

Jennifer watched the younger version of Barbara Stevens leave the room with head held high and shoulders back. She walked as if waiting on an applause.

Lisa and several others were waiting outside of the Beta's house. She and some others were displaying newly acquired Greek symbols on T-shirts. The front door opened and the crowd cheered. Steve was the first to step out, chanting something about Beta Gamma Delta. Girls rushed to hug him. The Beta's Neophytes stepped out of the house one by one, some taking longer than others.

Lisa saw eight boys step out, but no Cameron. Her excitement was growing. She didn't know how to react once he stepped through the door. They were just friends before the pledge period began. Now it was different.

The door opened again and brother number twelve walked out. As he chanted, the crowd screamed from the sounds of women. Lisa felt a rush when Cameron spotted her standing in the crowd. She still did not know if she should hug or kiss him. They were a couple through pledge notes only. No one asked the other if they were dating. All she knew was that he had asked her to the picnic on Sunday.

As the girls crowded around Cameron, Lisa felt herself move on instinct to claim what belonged to her. As she moved in close, girls moved out of the way. She was standing face to face with Cameron. His right eye was a little puffy which made her mad. She stood quietly, trying not to ask the obvious. Cameron extended his arms.

"Ahhh shuck it now. Girl, if you don't grab that man, I will," one girl yelled and the crowd laughed. Lisa walked to Cameron and he hugged her.

"Did you think I had cooties or something?" He hugged tighter. Lisa didn't say a word. It felt like the first time, warm and gentle.

Jennifer and Margo waited outside the Lambda's house for the initiates. Jennifer saw Rosalyn and some other Kappa Neophytes get out of a car. Jennifer waved happily at her new sisters who gave a courtesy wave in return. Margo waited on Peter whom she had gotten to know while pledging.

Jennifer waited on Michael.

As she remembered some of the notes Michael sent her, she blushed. Some were borderline obscene, asking if she was a virgin, and if so, could he be the first. She ignored his sexual advances and continued writing nice, clean, friendly notes. He wrote and told her to meet him after initiation so they could spend time together before the Neophyte Dance.

The line of new Lambdas walked out of the house. The crowd cheered as they sang their fraternity song. Jennifer started toward Michael, but stopped in her tracks when Rosalyn ran up to kiss him. Jennifer was stunned because he ignored her. She was so close to him that it became embarrassing. She didn't know how to exit without looking stupid. Michael gave her a friendly wave and walked away with Rosalyn. Jennifer was distracted, watching all the girls hug and kiss the new members. She wanted to get away quickly.

"Hello Jennifer," said a kind voice. It brought her back to reality.

"Oh, hi Sean," she said. She looked at him closely. He had the biggest smile on his face. Usually, he hardly had anything to say to anybody. Everyone called him the most stuck-up boy on campus. He was medium height with heavy eyebrows. He wore nice clothes and kept his hair trim. His personality took away from his looks.

Jennifer remembered him dancing continuously with a girl named Mimi during the pledge period. She was dark and wore obviously fake straight ponytail wigs. She had baby hair glued around the side of her face. That type of girl was the least of his interest.

Sean struck up a friendly conversation with her. As he talked, it helped take her mind off the most embarrassing moment in her life. "See you at the dance tonight," Sean said.

Jennifer smiled and nodded. She had to say something before he left. She didn't want to appear rude since he did most of the talking.

"Congratulations, Sean. See you tonight," Jennifer struggled to say. He smiled and walked away.

His conversation surprised her. Everyone said he was color struck and never dated a girl darker than Lisa. Maybe he changed, Jennifer thought. Michael had.

The D.J. played the music loudly and the crowd tried to talk even louder. The Neophyte Dance was held in the Game Room at the Student Union. Only four Greek organizations were sharing the night's event. Most students came to see who gave and received the best gifts.

Lionel, the president of the Black Greek Council, started the presentation. Twelve chairs were placed in front for the new members of Alpha Theta Lambda. The new members walked to the front in dark gold jackets that flared at the waist and navy blue skirts that were two inches below the knees.

Jennifer waited anxiously for Lionel to call the Kappas so they could present the new Alphas with navy blue pillows, with gold Greek symbols in the middle and gold tassels at each end. When the Kappas were called to make their presentation, Jennifer rushed to Lisa with her gift. Lisa stood and hugged Jennifer tightly. After Jennifer congratulated everyone, she took off first, going back to where Angel and Linda were standing.

Jennifer sashayed in the form fitting maroon jacket that tied at the side with a white and maroon scarf as an ascot. It was completed with a white calf-length skirt with a twelve inch split up the front. Someone whistled out loud. She almost tripped from the attention and other boys whistled too. She scooted off quickly, looking embarrassed. Some of the boys laughed.

Linda whispered to Jennifer, "That was good. The innocent, *Don't look at me*. I like that." Jennifer's eyes squinted as she looked at Linda.

The Betas were the next to make their presentation. The Neophytes approached the girls wearing black leather pants, red shirts and black GQ ties. Girls commented as they walked to the front. They sang a sweetheart song to the girls, bowed down, took their hands, and kissed them. They presented them with yellow silk roses and champagne glassed with a decal of the sorority symbols in the middle.

The Lambdas Neophytes were next, wearing black suits and gold shirts with black bow ties. They presented the girls with wooden paddles with a decal of the sorority's crest in the center.

When it was time for personal gifts, Kyle walked to Lisa with a gift in his hands. He dropped it in her lap and rushed back quickly before she could thank him.

It was time for the Alphas to make their presentation to their new sorors. The grands, great grands and great great grands presented their daughters' daughter and her daughter gifts. Usually Lisa felt awkward when women showed any affection toward her, but tonight she was at peace. The beautiful women of all shapes, complexions and heights presented the entire line with gifts and kissed them all.

Ten chairs were waiting for the new members of Phi Kappa Psi Sorority. Lisa jumped with excitement, holding the maroon sun visor with the sorority's symbols at the top. It was the gift the Alphas were giving to all new members of all organizations. Linda and Angel stood behind Jennifer's chair to thank the presenters as they gave. The other girls' Specials stood behind their chairs too.

Linda whispered to Angel, "Look at those ugly sun visors the Alphas are giving. *Cheap!*" Angel nodded in agreement and smiled at the audience, so did Linda. When the Alphas were called, Lisa rushed to Jennifer. They hugged again.

"Thank you, Lisa. This is really nice," Jennifer said as she clutched the visor.

Linda whispered to Angel, "Maybe we should have called her Helen Keller." Angel continued to smile, trying not to laugh out loud.

The Betas came with red silk roses and champagne glasses. They did their sweetheart song and kissed the girls' hands. Next were the Lambdas. Michael headed to Rosalyn with the wooden paddle and Sean went to Jennifer. He congratulated her and kissed her on the cheek. As the groups gave gifts, the girls handed them to their Specials. Jennifer smiled as she handed the wooden paddle to Linda who took it with her pointer finger and thumb, as if it were dirty. All the Lambdas congratulated Jennifer with the exception of Michael.

"It seems like your little friend turned out to be a dog, but the new one seems rather nice," Linda whispered into Jennifer's ear. Jennifer never paid much attention to Sean, especially after hearing the rumors about how he was color struck.

Lionel called for personal gifts. Jennifer saw her fan club, Malcolm, Tommy, Gerald and Kyle bearing gifts. "Who are these re-tards?" Linda asked loud enough for Jennifer to hear. Angel elbowed Linda and pointed to Jennifer. Linda rolled her eyes to the ceiling.

Kyle watched the other three give Jennifer gifts and kiss her on the cheek. He wondered if she would mind if he kissed her too. As he got closer, he became tense. She really looked pretty in makeup with her hair curled. He saw many boys kiss her and she smiled after each one. They were far more attractive than he and the idea of her frowning to a kiss from him made him even more nervous. He was next in line. He scratched the back of his neck and pushed up his glasses.

Jennifer beamed at Kyle. He gave her the gift and stood still. He rocked on the back of his heels. "Thank you Kyle. Whatever it is, I know I will enjoy it," she said. He looked at her without making a sound, examining her beauty up close.

"C'mon brother, move it. The rest us gotsta git our turn!" someone yelled.

Jennifer's smiled dropped when Kyle stumbled away looking awkward. She looked forward and Lionel was standing in front of her with a snow white teddy about two feet tall with a wide maroon ribbon tied around its neck. Jennifer clapped with excitement. Lionel had the biggest grin.

"Calm down. This is for Margo," he teased. Jennifer looked dumbfounded. "Psych!" he said and kissed her on the forehead. When Kyle saw how Jennifer jumped with excitement over Lionel's gift, he decided to leave the dance.

The sorors of Kappa made their presentation. Everyone waited in anticipation to see what the Neophytes would get. The Kappas usually gave their new members very nice gifts. As the women approached the girls with personal gifts, the audience gasped at the jackets, sweaters, large stuffed animals and roses.

The Betas were next to receive gifts. The young men could not keep still in their chairs. The Alphas came forward with the sun visors. Lisa rushed to Cameron's chair. She gave him the visor. He pulled her close for a kiss. She was taken by surprise and so was the audience. She blushed, not knowing how to recover.

The line of young men began to tease, "Hey Lisa, do we get the special treatment? We're all brothers?" She smiled at them, pulling back the curls from her face. Cameron pulled her forward again. He pulled back her curls and kissed her again. The line of young men clapped.

"Hey, Ron man, you took my kiss," Steve joked. Lisa walked back to the crowd dark red.

The Lambdas were preparing the front for their Neophytes. Jennifer decided to give her gift to Sean since he had given her the Lambda's gift. As the Kappas approached the new Lambdas, Rosalyn took off quickly toward Michael, waving the baseball cap. She kissed him long after she placed the cap on his head. Jennifer pretended not to see. She gave Sean his cap and congratulated everyone including Michael. He appeared troubled when she spoke. Jennifer tossed her head back and walked away.

A girl who had flirted with many fraternities' Neophytes walked by Jennifer, Angel and Linda. She pleasantly spoke, smiling at Angel and Linda. Jennifer was the only one who returned the greeting, whereas Angel and Linda nodded. As the girl walked away, Linda looked at Jennifer and said, "Make sure she doesn't pledge." Jennifer asked no questions and nodded.

The dance was over. Lionel approached Angel, Linda and Jennifer. "The brothers of Beta Gamma Delta are giving a Neophyte afterset. We would like to see you ladies tonight. Everything will be provided."

"Oh goody! We don't have to spend any money. Ooo wee!" Linda said.

Lionel was a little flustered. "I hope to see you ladies later," he said walked away.

Jennifer looked at Angel beaming. "Are we going?"

"*You* really should go, Jennifer," Linda emphasized.

"Of course we are going! I'll take your flowers and teddy bear. Can you handle the box?" Angel pointed to the box of gifts near the front.

"Sure," Jennifer said and took off.

"*We* are going to a Neophyte afterset?" Linda asked irritated.

"Most of the sorors are going to the Lambdas' set. We need to balance our socializing. A couple of Betas have their eyes on her."

"If they do, she won't notice."

"Are you sure? She has fooled us once, don't let that innocent look fool you again," Angel said.

They watched Jennifer pull back her hair and blush while talking to one of the Beta's Neophytes. "She has become a little vain," Linda said.

Angel shook her head, "Vain is too insecure. Confident sounds better."

Cameron offered to take Lisa back to the dorm with her gifts. She invited Jennifer and Alicia to come along. When Cameron turned around, he saw the three happy girls struggling with large boxes filled with gifts. He wanted to be alone with Lisa but smiled and helped them pack the things away in Lionel's car. The ride to the dorms was jubilant. They laughed and talked until Cameron dropped Alicia off first. He walked her to the door, carrying the box of gifts.

"Cameron wants me to go with him tonight," Lisa said looking at Jennifer for approval.

"Where?" Jennifer was concerned. Lisa hunched her shoulders, indicating she didn't know. She was glowing. Jennifer started to say something but stopped when Cameron came back to the car.

"Next stop is Morrison Hall," Cameron yelled liked a conductor. He helped Jennifer with her things and started toward the dorm. Jennifer ran back to the car. Jennifer looked at Lisa's glowing almond eyes.

"Be careful, you hear?" Jennifer said sincerely, breathing heavily.

"We will, I mean, I will," Lisa said smiling.

"I want to see you two at the afterset, okay?"

Lisa nodded. Jennifer kept turning around to look at Lisa as she walked to the dorm. Cameron helped Jennifer inside the dorm with the box and rushed back to the car. Lisa sat smiling.

"Where are we going?" she asked pleasantly, but a little nervous.

Cameron flashed the award winning smile. "To my favorite hang out. You are going to like it. Did I tell you that you look nice this evening?" he asked. Lisa shook her head.

"Well, you look nice my dear." Cameron drove off.

The doorbell rang. One of the Neophytes opened the door. He stared at the five women. They were smiling. The young man continued to stare.

"Can we come in? We were invited."

"I'm sorry. Come in."

Jennifer walked in first followed by Angel, then Linda. Maria was next and Joni was last. They stood in the foyer and looked around the house as if it was unfamiliar. The house was crowded and lively. People were sitting everywhere but stopped talking when the five came inside. Rochelle and Anita were talking to Alicia but stopped when they saw the five. They walked quickly to them smiling. They did the traditional kiss on the cheek to the President and left.

Jennifer surveyed the set. A good mixture of Greeks were in attendance. The majority of the Alpha's Neophytes were there with several old members. She scouted the room for Lisa but she wasn't there.

Thomas nudged Lionel and pointed to the new guests. They were wearing maroon jackets and white skirts, except Angel. She wore all white. Lionel liked seeing her in all white. He noticed her split was higher than everyone else's.

"This is a first. They've hardly ever participated in anything we've done. Why tonight?" Thomas asked.

Lionel shook his head. He narrowed his eyes and noticed how the four hung back and allowed Jennifer to be the center of attention.

The doorbell rang again. This time, three more Kappas entered, Denise, Annette and Alexis. They all kissed Angel on the cheek. "We decided to stop here first before going to the Lambdas house. Where are the hosts?" Denise asked.

They all looked in the kitchen where Lionel, Thomas and three Neophytes were standing in amazement. "Oh boy, they have spotted us. You are in trouble now," Thomas laughed and took a drink of champagne.

"Why are the top dogs here tonight?" one Neophyte asked, looking at Lionel for an answer.

"Brothers, let us greet our guests," Lionel said without confidence. They walked to the foyer.

"Hello ladies. I'm happy you could join us. Can I offer anyone something to drink?"

"Perrier?"

Lionel cleared his throat. "Miss Stevens, would you like some champagne?"

"Is it cheap?"

"What about punch?"

"A tea bag and hot water would be nice." Linda looked at the Neophyte named Brad. "You do know how to boil water, don't you?" she asked.

The young man looked around and realized she was talking to him. "Yes ma'am," he said and gave a salute.

"Lionel, could you please get me some punch?"

"Of course, Denise. Anyone else? How about you, Melanie?" She shook her head.

"I would like some," Jennifer said. Lionel disappeared.

"Hello ladies."

"Hello Thomas," all said together. Alexis excused herself and left to socialize. So did Joni and Maria.

"Are you ladies ready for graduation?" Thomas asked.

"I heard you and Lionel were accepted at the University of North Carolina's law school. Congratulations!"

"Thank you, Annette, but I will be doing this solo. Lionel is attending the University of Minnesota's graduate school of business."

"Oh really?" Linda said, looking at Angel. "The University of Minnesota?"

Lionel came back with the punch. Denise stood very close to him. "So you are not going to law school?"

"I had a change in plans," Lionel said. Angel excused herself to the kitchen and Jennifer went to the living room. Thomas laughed a little.

"Maybe we should have some sort of graduation celebration since quite a few of us live in Kansas City," Thomas said.

"What about those who live in Chicago or Minnesota?" Denise asked. She brushed her shoulder against Lionel.

"We can think of something," Thomas said with a devious grin. He turned to Linda, "So Linda, I hear you and Gina received offers from World Airlines."

Brad announced to Linda that the water was ready. "Excuse me," she said and left the group. Thomas looked at her in spite. He and Annette struck up a conversation and walked away from Denise and Lionel.

"What are you doing after the set?" Denise asked Lionel.

Lionel tried to remain comfortable. "Denise, let's put an end to this. Why are you doing this to her?" He said cowardly, blaming her for his weakness. He refused to look at her.

"Are you telling me that you and Melanie are dating?"

"You know the situation well. You know how she feels about me and how I feel about her," he said low.

Denise looked at Jennifer who was talking but stealing glances at them.

"What about Jennifer? Is she in the chase too?"

"I have plans with Melanie tonight," Lionel lied nervously.

She read through it. For some strange reason, he had no desires for her this evening. He didn't need consoling.

"I don't believe you. Are you being a coward?"

He became angry at her comment. "There is nothing between us so why are you doing this?"

"I never said there was anything between us. I thought we were having fun. It seems there isn't anything between you and Melanie either. I know you don't think she is waiting for the next romp in the sack. No one does."

Now he knew he wasn't taking advantage of her. She was using him too. He caught a glimpse of Angel in the kitchen. She had watched the interplay, then turned her head. She stood, preparing to leave.

"You are a very smart woman, Denise. I think I am going to take your advice." He walked to the kitchen. Angel was in the doorway. He stood very close to her, forcing her to walk backward to her chair.

"Where are you going? You just got here. It's not often you visit me." Lionel was smiling. Angel's face was flushed.

"I really have to go. We planned to visit briefly. We have to get by the Lambda's set," Angel said, trying not to look at him.

Lionel knew she was inviting him this evening. He loved her in white. The split in her skirt was four inches above the knees. She looked elegant. He did not want her to go.

"Cameron hasn't come back with my car. Do you mind driving?" The question completely threw Angel off balance. He was never aggressive. It intrigued her.

"I have to take Linda and Jennifer back to the dorm," she said.

"*You* are going to the University of Minnesota? How interesting. Angel, we can ride back with Maria. Besides, I'm having a wonderful time talking to Tommy and Brach" Linda said and took a sip of tea.

"It's, uh, Tony."

"And Brad is the name, but I like Brach better."

"You are so cute," Linda said to Brad. He blushed.

Angel had no choice. He wasn't hiding behind his smile. He challenged her openly. "Are we leaving now?" she asked. Steve walked into the kitchen. He smiled, showing the deepest dimples.

"Well, if it isn't my favorite lady. You've never congratulated me," he said. Angel hugged him and kissed him on the cheek. "Miss Peterson is quite thirsty. I'm getting her something to drink," he said.

Lionel took Angel by the hand. "Let's leave Miss Stevens alone with Terrance and Bob. Make sure you treat our guests appropriately."

"Even if they call us by the wrong name?" Brad whined, eyeing Linda.

"If Miss Stevens says anything to you, consider yourself honored. Good night."

Lionel left the kitchen holding Angel's hand. He walked to the living room and motioned for Thomas. "When Cameron gets back with my car, could you tell him to leave the keys in my top dresser drawer?" Thomas nodded. Jennifer looked at the pair and smiled.

Lionel held Angel's hand tightly as they walked to the door. Before he opened it, he extended his hand. "Keys please. You have a lead foot." Angel was flabbergasted. She slowly placed the keys in his hand. Denise walked into the living room.

Lionel escorted Angel to the passenger side. Before she got in, she looked at him questionably. His behavior was way out of character. "Where are we going?" she asked.

"To one of our favorite places. I need to check on someone."

Cameron and Lisa drove to the next little town which was eleven miles away. There was an air force base nearby. Cameron parked the car in an open field where the moon shone brightly. It was deserted and it looked as if it would stay that way until he came again.

"Let's sit in the back seat," he said. Lisa moved slowly. She felt if they were going to do "it," she did not want her first experience to be in the back seat of a car. She slowly moved to the back seat. She looked into Cameron's eyes. They were dancing with excitement as if he were about to share a well- kept secret. She knew then that they weren't going to do "it." *Whew*, she thought. Cameron cuddled her in his arms.

"I wanted to be an astronaut when I was little. I would look at the stars every night, wondering what it would feel to be close to them. When I noticed there were no black astronauts, I changed my mind. My father told me that I could be whatever I wanted to be if I was willing to work hard at it."

"What kind of person is your father?"

"A listener. People say Lionel looks just like him when he was younger. Some say I have a touch of his personality. I'm much closer to my mother."

"What kind of person is your mother?"

"Now she's a talker. Sometimes she drives my father nuts, but he just listens. At one time, she hardly said anything. I watched her get so angry at my father for nothing. When I was little, I would spend a lot of time with her because she seemed so sad, but she has pretty much gotten it together. She taught me how to cook. Maybe one day, I'll cook you a meal," Cameron said proudly. Lisa snuggled closer to him. He rubbed her shoulders and kissed her on the forehead.

"Do you and Lionel get along?"

"He's my Rock of Gibraltar. He tries to act bossy but I ignore him most of the time. I have a younger brother named Jason. He's an athlete like Lionel. When me and Lionel come home from school, all of us go to the gym and play ball. We wrestle at times until somebody gets hurt which is usually me. I guess you can say I'm just a nerd," he said with twinkling eyes.

"You're not a nerd, you're real cool. If you haven't noticed, a lot of girls are interested in you. Your little performance at the Jamboree was quite surprising, even to me," Lisa said, rolling her eyes. He threw out his hands, showing his innocence.

"Who me?"

"Yes, you!"

He cuddled her closer. "The only girl I'm interested in is Lisa Willet Arvell. Tell me about your parents?"

Lisa knew it would surface. She pulled away slightly. He pulled her back. She pulled away again and he pulled her back. "You're not going to tell me?" he asked gently. She shook her head. She seemed a little impatient.

"I don't deserve to know about my little Lisa?" he asked softly.

"They're dead," she said. She wouldn't look at him.

Cameron was shocked. "What did they die of?" he asked softly.

"I was young when it happened. They said my mother died from...a car accident," she said without looking at him. The answer just popped into her head. She was too embarrassed to tell the truth.

"It had to be hard coping with death when you're young. Attending a parent's funeral had to have been difficult."

"I didn't go. They said I was too young."

Cameron paused for a few seconds. "Who are *they*?"

She was really becoming uncomfortable. She hoped that he would not be turned off by her response. "The Angels," she said with an attitude implying that he should know. He looked confused and she laughed. She believed in angels and hoped he would find it humorous.

Cameron chuckled a little but became serious. "You know you can always count on me if you ever need anything, okay?" he said, turning Lisa's face toward him. She was the prettiest girl he had ever dated and he wanted nothing more than to be with her.

He kissed her tenderly. He caressed her shoulders, rubbing her back gently. He looked at her legs as they extended across the seat. For a person her size, she had very nice legs. He envisioned her in a bikini on the beach with her hair curled all over. He thought about her having three boys like his mother. He thought about not allowing her to go to bed angry for something he did or didn't do. Lisa was the person he wanted. She reminded him of his mother.

They sat relaxing for several minutes, forgetting about the afterset. Cameron kissed Lisa on the top of her head. He rubbed his chin through her hair. He slowly caressed her shoulder with one hand and let it drop to her waist. He rubbed it slowly. His eyes stared down at her once nicely developed breasts. She had lost a lot of weight for a person her height. They weren't the same size as before. He used to stare at them in class, trying to guest her bra size.

His hand dropped into her lap. He couldn't control himself. He rubbed her thigh. She stiffened. She was about to say something but he stopped. Headlights were coming their way. They sat up quickly. The car drove slowly toward them. They had no idea who it was. Finally, the car drove beside them. The window came down. Cameron was embarrassed.

"Cameron, I was wondering if you remembered that an afterset was going on. You two need to be there."

Lisa unconsciously fluffed out her hair and Cameron nodded. They sat in the back seat stiff, looking guilty.

"Are you going to be leaving soon?"

They got out of the back seat and sat in the front. Cameron drove off.

Angel laughed. "I cannot believe you did that. I have never seen this side of you."

"When I get tired of being pushed around, you would not believe what I will do."

"We don't have to go inside. Larry will understand if I don't come. Hell, he better!" Marsha said.

"I promised. I hope it's not too boring. The Lambdas are so stiff," Gina said.

"Everyone except for Larry and Carlos. They're pretty loose."

"Is that suppose to make me feel better?"

"He has always liked you. Why don't you give Mr. Black Power a chance?"

"I'm not working hard to fix up a man. If he's broke, I'm leaving him at the repair shop."

"No one ever thought anything different. We all know you don't take shit off of a man. Carlos knows too."

"He better. I'm not desperate for no one." Gina stopped trying to convince herself for a moment and looked at the cars. "Looks like a large Kappa turnout. I guess most of us are at the Betas' set."

"Are you stalling?"

"I just don't want him to make a scene."

"We know you've got it together. Screw him. Oops, wrong word. Ignore him. Talk to Carlos and see where he's coming from."

Gina took a deep breath. It was easy with Kenneth. It didn't take much to impress him, but Carlos was different. He carried his six-foot, one-hundred-seventy pound frame with confidence. He was bronze brown with a slightly squared face. His eyebrows were thick and his eyes seemed to pierce. His nose was a little broad and his lips were nice and full. He had a strong jawline which made his features appear carved.

Everyone called Carlos the Militant Lambda. He was majoring in history but his primary interest was black studies. Missouri State didn't have a strong black interest curriculum, but Carlos did a lot of outside studying. Sometimes he got into heated debates with Greeks about their role in the black community. The only reason he pledged Lambda was because he received one of their scholarships as a freshmen student. Dennis Williams was another factor. He helped Carlos acclimate to the majority white school. He also helped Carlos find a grant for history majors to help fund his education.

Gina took a deep breath. "What are we waiting for? Let's go in."

The Lambdas afterset was mellow. Mostly older members of Greek organizations were in attendance. There was a table in the middle of the living room with a very nice spread of tuna salad, dip, chips, cheese, crackers and chicken wings. Champagne bottles and a bowl of punch were at the other end of the table. Gina and Marsha walked in and spoke to most everyone. They began filling a plate with food.

"Hello Marsha. Hello Gina."

"Hi Carlos," Marsha said. A few seconds went by. She looked at Gina who pretended not to hear. She continued to fix a plate.

"Hello Gina," Carlos said louder.

"Hello Carlos," Gina finally said. She looked nervously at the strong attractive man who was wearing a black suit and black shirt, different than that of his fraternity brothers. It made him look stronger. She was starting off wrong. Weak.

"I'm glad you came. I keep forgetting how you are about food," Carlos said, trying to make a joke. He could not stop the words. He knew no other way of getting her attention. She looked nice in her two-piece ensemble. Real nice. She always looked nice in suits. Medium tall, slightly hippy, strong legs and a courageous, beautiful, brown face were her attributes. Her calling was a business woman. She was always direct. He never understood what she saw in Kenneth. The brother was wishy-washy, never could make a decision. It seemed he would bore her. But he was starting off wrong. Pushy, ready to pick a fight.

"Where is Larry?" Marsha intervened before Gina said something to ruin Carlos' chances. Maybe it would give her time to cool off.

"Check out the kitchen. He was on ice duty ten minutes ago," Carlos said with a smile. Marsha grinned and left.

Gina's plate was full. She pondered over what to say. She did not want to start one of their infamous arguments. She also did not want to immediately invite him into her life. What could she offer him? The few girls he dated on campus were very pretty. Much prettier than she. Not only were they pretty but smart too. It seemed like the relationships never lasted longer than a year. What did he want from her?

"Are you ready for graduation?" she asked.

"Uh, yes. I heard World Airlines made you an offer. Congratulations," Carlos said. He hoped she would not ask if he had a job offer. It would be embarrassing telling her he was waiting for Dennis to hook him up with a contact at the Boys' Club. There was no money with the job. She was probably going to the airline with a much higher salary. She was always a step ahead of him. Still, he was no match.

"I'm a little nervous about the job. I will be assisting in market demographics. What about you?" She figured he would go on to graduate school and later into politics. He probably wanted someone elegant and charming or at least someone who thought she was. That is what he dated.

"Dennis has gotten me a contact at the Boys' Club. It should do while I'm in graduate school."

"I've always figured you would go to graduate school and later dive into politics. It sounds like you."

He moved in closer, invading her space. "Oh really? What else have you figured?" He wanted to know. She was smart and ambitious. She could help him make a decision on what to do. He wasn't so sure anymore.

Gina blushed. Carlos saw it for the first time. When he danced with her while they were pledging, he felt as if he got on her nerves. Later, they fussed playfully and teaseed each other about everything. She always kept him at arms length.

"Tell me what else you have figured? I want to know." Carlos was smiling with his hands in his pockets. Gina avoided eye contact throughout their conversation. The closer he stood, the more jittery she became.

"Why? So you can tell me I think I know it all?" she said defensively.

"No. I want to know. Although you may *think* you know it all, I still respect your opinion. Why are you blushing? Do I have that kind of affect?" he asked genuinely.

She stepped back a little and immediately put up the defenses, "No."

"I thought I knew you well."

"I guess you don't."

Carlos saw his chances slipping. When they talked, their conversations were always good until he made her mad. He told himself he would not argue with her. He was trying hard to be sensitive. "I would like to get to know you better. Like I said, I respect your opinion even if it might be wrong."

Gina giggled. "Oh really? So Carlos wants to know Gina. Do I stand in line or…"

"Wait!" Carlos said, holding up his hand. "You know me better than that. I don't play those games. I like you and you know it. I had hoped we could go out sometime and get to know each other a little better. Maybe you can tell me what else you've figured." Carlos was serious. He wasn't grinning nor was he shifting. He had hoped she would come around. The last thing he wanted was a reputation as a womanizer.

"The Wiz is coming to Kansas City in three weeks. Are you into Broadway musicals or plays?" Gina asked, expecting his answer to be the usual, *Not really but I'll try anything once.*

"Sophisticated Ladies is coming, starting, uh, June…June 27 and Dream Girls is coming the middle of July. Does that answer your question?"

Gina looked Carlos in the eyes for the first time that evening. "Yes," she muttered. They took a few seconds looking at one another until Gina turned her head. Carlos wanted to touch her face. He knew she had been hurt. He gave a pleasant smile. She smiled too.

"Hello Gina."

The familiar voice did not move her. She had gathered enough strength to respond without feeling embarrassed. She looked at Carlos as she spoke, "Excuse me, Carlos. I need to check on the ice patrol. Hello, Kenneth," Gina said and walked away without looking at Kenneth.

That's my girl, Carlos said to himself.

Chapter 13

It was the Tuesday before graduation, election time. The Alphas were sitting in the Chapter room discussing the Greek picnic when Gina walked in with Rita. They all stood. Gina hit the gavel on the wood block to start the meeting. She started the nominations. They moved smoothly through the election.

For the office of First Vice President, Lisa was nominated by Rita and Phyllis nominated Gail. When the voting took place, everyone including Gail with the exception of a couple of Neophytes voted for Lisa. She was stunned.

After the requirements of President were read, only Rita qualified. She had to receive a quorum of two-thirds majority. Everyone voted "yes" without any discussions.

"Sorors, let us prepare for the ceremony to install our newly elected officers," Gina said.

After the installation, the older sorors sat down and explained the selection process to the Neophytes. The new members had to take an oath to abide by the selection of officers and not allow personal feelings to disrupt the order.

Lisa figured out why she was the only one with three pledge mothers. They were all presidents and she was expected to fill the role because next year. Now this was her sign to stay at Missouri State University. Under no circumstances was she to follow Cameron.

"Ladies, we must now vote on the Second Vice President. She will be the assistant to the Dean of Pledges. This person must be loyal, patient, dedicated and friendly. She will be our Goodwill Ambassador at the Greek Council meeting, accompanying the President. The floor is opened for nominations."

"Madame President, I nominate Candice Stewart," Denise said.

"Madame President, I nominate Alexis Michels" Annette included.

"Madame President, I nominate Jennifer Peterson."

Jennifer was stunned to hear Linda call her name.

"Are there any more nominations? Good, write down your choice and the Sergeant of Arms will collect them."

The girls wrote busily. Jennifer debated if she should vote for someone else, but she decided to cast the vote for herself. After the names were collected, Angel and another Kappa called out the votes. Jennifer and Alexis tied as it came down to the last vote. Jennifer's heart raced. She heard it in a distance, "Ladies, our new Second Vice President is Miss Jennifer Peterson." Jennifer felt as if she had won the presidency.

It was Wednesday and Lisa had no one to accompany her to Wal-Mart. She needed time alone since Dee Dee told her she was pregnant and would not return next year. As Lisa walked, a car pulled up beside her. A boy yelled out the window, "Say baby, can I go?" She turned around. It was Cameron hanging out the window with his arms outstretched. She laughed and waved him off.

"Get in. We'll take you where you need to go," Cameron said. Lisa jumped in the front seat, sandwiched between Kyle and Cameron. "Where are you going?" Cameron asked.

"To Wal-Mart."

"What are you buying?" Kyle asked.

"I just need to pick up some things before I go home."

Kyle turned onto the lot at Wal-Mart. All three hopped out of the car. Lisa walked around the store slowly. She did not want Cameron and Kyle following her. She tried sending them away.

"You haven't gotten anything. What are you looking for, maybe we can help?" Kyle asked.

"Why don't you two go and price some blue material. I'll meet you at the checkout line. Take your time," Lisa said.

"What kind of material, polyester, cotton or linen?" Kyle asked.

Lisa was about to lose her temper. "Price all of them," she said.

Kyle and Cameron looked at each other and took off walking. Lisa rushed to the aisle of the feminine products. She picked up a box of maxi pads. Before she could throw them into the basket and take off, Cameron and Kyle were standing beside her.

"What are you doing here?" Lisa asked anxiously.

"We didn't know what time you wanted to leave," Cameron said nervously.

"You finally bought something," Kyle said and picked up the box of pads. Lisa snatched them out of his hands.

"What's the matter? My sisters wear these kind," Kyle said and picked up another brand.

Cameron scouted the aisles. "Hey Lisa, you get forty eight for the same price if you buy these," Cameron said, holding high the generic bag of pads. Lisa walked over to him and snatched the pads out of his hands and Kyles hands too. She threw them back on the shelf.

"Will you go and price the material like I asked you to," she said with clenched teeth and a frown. Cameron and Kyle walked away backwards.

"What's wrong with her?" Cameron whispered to Kyle.

"They get like this around that time of month. My sisters are like that,"

Kyle said.

The two boys looked at the fabric to kill time. Lisa's anger concerned Cameron. She had been edgy since the last discussion about Rolla University. He wanted her to go but she was unsure. He was still waiting on her answer. Cameron watched as Kyle became interested in the fabric.

"Man, put that down. She doesn't want us around her monthly products. She's embarrassed," Cameron said.

"I don't know why. It's just an act of nature. Jennifer is the same way. I tried helping with her laundry. She went nuts when I began putting her clothes in the washing machine. She start hitting me saying I was touching her underwear. So I stopped. Then she made me turn my head while she put them in the washer. Babes are crazy at times, especially around their period."

Cameron listened as Kyle talked about Jennifer as if she were his girlfriend. "You really like Jennifer don't you?" Cameron taunted.

Kyle pushed up his glasses. "We're friends, good friends." He picked up another bolt of fabric.

"Why don't you ask her out?" Cameron asked.

He did but she invited four of her friends to go along. She treated him like one of the girls. "We go out sometimes but our relationship is different than yours and Lisa's. We will always be friends." He looked like a nerd and behaved like one too; at least that is what the black girls said.

"A lot of brothers got their eyes on her, but she isn't giving up any play. They're trying but the babe ain't biting. She's a nice girl; your type. Lisa and I were friends first and look what happened."

Kyle realized that Cameron really thought he had a chance with Jennifer. Cameron saw him as equal to the other boys. But Cameron was naive, Kyle thought. Girls found Cameron attractive because he was. The girls around campus were throwing themselves at him. He pretended not to notice.

In high school, all the girls, black and white, wanted Cameron and Lionel. Only the white ones would date him. None of the black girls had any interest, not the ones he liked. They practically laughed in his face.

"I got my eyes on somebody," Kyle lied.

Cameron perked up. "Yeah? Who?"

Kyle didn't know what to say. He could not think of one girl on campus that would go out with him without Cameron knowing he was lying. "I don't know her name yet. I'll show her to you later," Kyle said.

As the two boys talked, two girls approached them. "Hello Cameron. Don't tell me you know how to sew?" one asked pleasantly.

Cameron smiled at the person who sent him notes during the pledge period. She asked him out. He thought it was unusual for someone like her to be aggressive. Women like her waited on men to ask.

"Oh, you didn't know? I am making some evening gowns for the Alphas. I have been hired as their fashion consultant. You can call me Jean-Claude Cam-Rone," he joked.

Alexis was tickled to death. He was so cute when he played. "Bonjour

Monsieur Cam-Rone. Comment va tu?"

Alexis and Cameron began a friendly conversation in french.

Kyle saw Lisa look in their direction and then walk away. He elbowed Cameron so hard that he winced. "We have to go Cameron, *Lisa's* ready!" Kyle said.

"You ladies have a nice evening. Au revoir!" Cameron said smiling. Alexis waved and walked away giggling. Cameron's eyes narrowed as he watched Alexis and Rosalyn leave.

"What's wrong with you? Didn't you see Lisa looking?" Kyle asked, punching Cameron again.

"What are you talking about? You act as if I'm guilty," Cameron complained.

"You are!" Kyle said and stormed off. He knew his friend was aware of his behavior. Cameron watched Kyle hurry to the front. He still did nothing wrong, he told himself.

"What time will you and mom make it to Harrisburg?" Lionel asked.

"It is going to be tough but we will be there. How was the interview with Dalton's Manufacturing?"

Lionel paused. It didn't go well because he didn't go. His father's friend assured him he would wear a suit and tie but that wasn't what he wanted. "Dad, I think I'm going to graduate school." There was silence.

The voice became firm. "That's fine son, but you need to work too. Did you talk to Robert at Dalton's?"

"I'm going to graduate school at home."

"First it was law school, now it's graduate school. You can't keep wavering over you future. Your mother and I allowed you to pick Missouri State and we paid for it. We can't pay for your graduate education too."

"I'm not asking you to!"

"Have you been accepted in graduate school?"

There was silence.

"Where did you plan on working? Have you set up any interviews?"

More silence.

"When you get home, I want you to talk to my friend Dave at the telephone company. They have a management trainee program for college graduates. I'll set it up for you. Your mother and I will see you Saturday morning."

Lionel held the phone until he heard the dial tone. His father was angry at him as usual. All he wanted to do was go to graduate school. He did not want a job where he had to meet with people all day and wear a suit and tie. He liked working with his hands.

Thomas was angry when he changed his mind about law school. Everyone thought he was crazy, except Angel. She understood. He didn't know why. She wanted him to work on an MBA.

His mind went back to the night at the air force base. She gently broke it off, telling him he needed to find himself and stop allowing people to run his life. She told him she wasn't going away to Minneapolis. She was accepting a job offer in Kansas City.

She said he desperately needed to make his own decisions. She had. How could she say that? She was the one who convinced him to pledge Beta. He had charm, which was supposed to be characteristic of the Beta man. He had charisma too. His personality attracted followers. He was easy to talk to, a good listener with a good sense of humor. He hardly became angry, never a participant of conflict. His pleasant smile helped diffuse tension. He was all of that, but she didn't want him anymore. She was probably still angry about the way he treated her when she told him that she thought she was pregnant.

He didn't understand why the fraternity wanted him as president. He remembered how the crowd went wild when the Betas wore tuxedos for the first time at last year's Barons' Ball. The Betas got so much attention that they put him on a pedestal for his idea, Angel's idea. From that point on, the fraternity worshipped him, electing him president in almost a landslide. He thought Thomas would win again, but the brothers wanted him. He didn't understand.

Everyone thought he had good ideas, except his father who was always pushing him to do things he had no interest in. His father picked at him constantly for not showing more initiative like Cameron. Angel didn't treat him that way and she felt the same way.

He wanted company. It would make him feel better, at least for awhile. He picked up the phone and dialed a familiar number. He waited patiently. He figured she would be angry with him because of his behavior at the afterset, but she never stayed mad long. Finally she answered.

"Hello Miss Dark and Lovely. What are you doing tonight?"

"What are the plans for Saturday?"

"If you and Paul arrive by nine, we can attend the service at the chapel. It will be about an hour long. It would be better if you two come up Friday evening. That way, we can have dinner and go to the pre-graduation ceremony later."

"I can't afford to take off work Friday. I need to get a report completed before Monday. Since the service at the chapel is an hour, I don't think we will miss much. I just want to get there in enough time to get good seats before the ceremony begins."

Gina paused and listened to the forever busy woman, always on a schedule. "Okay, momma. Don't let me interrupt your busy schedule. Maybe you should stay at home."

"Look here young lady, don't get smart with me! You know darn well Paul and I worked hard to give you a good education. I don't..."

"Momma, I worked hard too! I have always worked. You and Paul helped but y'all didn't do it all."

"Stop saying y'all! When you start working at World Airlines, those white people expect you to speak English, not dialect. I'm not arguing with you this evening. What time is the ceremony over?"

Gina paused again. "Two o'clock."

"The boys and Paul should be there Saturday before eight to move your things. I'll be arriving at ten."

"Ask Paul if he wants to come up Friday night," Gina said, almost in tears. There was silence.

"You can ask Paul to come up Friday."

"Bye momma." Gina hung up the phone without giving the woman a chance to respond. She took deep breaths. No one ever had time anymore, not even Paul.

Gina thought back to the Neophyte afterset. She ignored Kenneth. It didn't seem to bother him. He chatted with other girls that evening. She wondered if she was too hard on him. He tried apologizing but she had to keep a level head. Everyone expected her to. When they spent time together, the date lasted the entire day. She didn't understand what went wrong.

Kenneth began slacking in his visits, offering lame excuses. He complained they spent too much time together, whereas, she felt it wasn't enough. He was the only boy who told her that she was pretty. He said her small eyes were cute and her large lips were sexy. He complimented her on her hair all the time. She felt attractive with him. She missed him.

She thought about Carlos. As long as she had known him, it was always an argument, except at the afterset. The whole evening was uncomfortable. He was way out of character. He agreed with her on most issues, wanting her to talk. He stared constantly, standing too close. He also told her she looked nice but not pretty. It was different, much different.

It was almost six o'clock. Carlos was coming soon. She rushed to get dressed but stopped. She wasn't going to be on time. If he wanted to go out with her, he would have to wait. If he liked her, he would have to prove it. No longer was she going to be anxious to go out with someone. No more.

"Why didn't you tell me you received an offer from World Airlines?" There was silence. The woman was becoming angry. "Malinda, you hear me talking to you! What is your position?"

"Account executive." Linda could hear the woman release a deep breath.

"When was the last time you talked to Keith?"

"Last week." More silence.

"Are you two discussing marriage?"

"Mother, he has to finish his residency. Why should I discuss marriage with someone who is still working on his career? I have to work on my career too."

"What career? A job at World Airlines as an account executive? Do you want someone else to grab him? Stop acting spoiled. When he finishes, he is going to make a great deal of money as an obstetrician gynecologist."

She didn't respond. She maintained her silence.

"You could have attended any of the top ten schools, but you chose that dump in Harrisburg. Gloria's daughter is graduating from Ohio State with a job offer from the *Wall Street Journal*. She didn't have half the grooming as you and Melanie. You two picked one of the tackiest schools to attend."

"Mother, *Wall Street Journal* is a name. What will she be doing? Editor? No, I don't think so. She has a job just like everyone else."

"It's useless talking to you. Your father will be there Saturday morning at eight to move your things. I'm coming with Marilyn. We should arrive by ten. Tell Melanie to give me a call. I need to know if she wants to work in the shop. She probably accepted an offer from Burger King, knowing you two."

Linda let out a huff. "Sure mother. Good-bye." She slammed down the phone. She knew she could not move back home. She needed her own apartment. Angel would have to hurry and make a decision as to whether she wanted to share an apartment.

Linda stretched out on the bed. She had no intentions of marrying Keith. She did not care if he was a doctor or a trash collector. It wasn't that she didn't like him. Although he looked like Mickey Mouse, he was nice, very pleasant. One of her mother's friends' sons.

They dated two years. Keith really liked her. He called her exciting and interesting. He was the opposite: quiet and predictable, just like her father. She could not understand why her mother wanted her to marry someone like her father. She knew her mother had an affair or two. Her father never found out, or at least he never said anything. She knew her mother married for money but she wasn't following in the same footsteps.

Do not embarrass me, young lady! were her mother's favorite words. She said them constantly. It was crazy. Her mother took her everywhere, always wanting her present. The woman got on her nerves. When Angel moved to the city, her mother dragged her along too.

There was a soft knock on the door. She was puzzled. She hardly ever got visitors. She walked to the door and opened it quickly. She returned the friendly smile.

"I thought I would visit before graduation. I know you are going to be busy with your parents on Saturday."

"What a pleasant surprise! You know I will make time for you. I want you to meet Keith. He's nothing to brag about but you will get a kick out of him."

"The ceremony won't be long, maybe two hours at the max. You can leave immediately afterward. It only takes an hour to drive back to Kansas City. You will have plenty of time before your business dinner. Dad, I'm graduating magna cum laude. You have to be there," Angel begged.

He knew his daughter didn't whine unless she wanted her way. He hated when she whined. The business dinner was too important. It would probably determine if he would be a serious candidate for the position of Regional Vice President. This was tough. "Honey, this dinner is going to decide my future. I know you understand what it means to me. It is not going to be easy trying to do both."

"Dad, this is important to me. How can you not come to my graduation?"

He knew his daughter was pouting, something her mother did all the time. His daughter constantly came in the way of his career. He believed he was passed over the first time the Regional Director's position was available because he came late to the Christmas reception. He was attending her induction into the high school honor society. It wasn't going to happen this time.

"Sweetheart, I want to be there but a lot is riding on this dinner. I can move your things Sunday and..."

"Dad, please! Can't you stay an hour?"

He took a deep breath. "Okay, Dora and I will come for an hour. I will come back Sunday to move your things."

She knew it was going to be the best deal he would offer. The whole idea was to get him to come. She would get him to stay longer. "Okay, dad. I love you. See you Saturday."

"Good-bye kitten."

She hung up the phone feeling a small victory. No one had to beg their parents to come to their college graduation. Linda's mother was angry when she didn't tell her the graduation date.

Her father gave large sums of money every time he couldn't make it to any of her events. Sometimes she made up events to make him feel guilty. He would sent checks in the mail, telling her to buy something nice.

She pulled out the letter from the Youth Development Center, offering her a position as Program Director. The interview went well. She impressed the group with her problem-solving responses to a list of hypothetical situations. They told her she was ahead of her years.

A hard knock sounded at the door. When she opened it, she got a surprise.

"Is Jennifer here?"

"She will be back any minute. You can wait if you like."

Lisa thought back to what Gina said, "Everything you do reflects on the sorority. Pride must take a back seat at times." Lisa nodded and walked in. Phi Kappa Psi was displayed everywhere. She sat down at one of the desks.

"I hear you are First Vice President. Congratulations."

"Thanks," Lisa said shyly. She didn't know what to say. She had always been in conflict with Angel since she had known her. She didn't know why.

"I hope you will work with Maria, Joni and Jennifer next year. They want a closer relationship with the Alphas." Lisa nodded. Angel decided to break the ice, "I see Cameron finally got the courage to ask you out."

Lisa shifted in her chair. "We weren't doing anything but talking."

Angel chuckled. "I know. He has always liked you. He used to hound Jennifer constantly about you."

Lisa perked up, "He did?"

"Um, hum. He's a nice boy."

"He may not stay nice for long. A lot of girls want him." Lisa stopped herself. She had never shared intimate feelings with Angel.

"He seems fairly strong. If he chooses to play games, you have other choices. No one is worth a hassle, not even Cameron. Besides, a lot of boys like you."

Lisa blushed. Angel was relaxed when she spoke. Her face was calm, not uptight like Gina. Angel had a lot of confidence when it came to fooling people. Lisa had always felt that Angel was a little insecure, but it never showed, so people never knew.

"He's going to Rolla next year. He might meet somebody else," Lisa confided.

"That's true but he may not. You might meet someone else too. Cameron is trying to handle his new popularity. He really doesn't know why girls are going crazy over him."

"He knows. I'm quite sure Lionel knows too."

Angel hesitated before speaking. "Cameron is a little different. He's yearning for attention like anyone else who has lived in someone's shadow."

Lisa had to think before speaking. The last thing she wanted was Angel thinking she had man problems. "Who cares, I'm too young to get serious about anyone anyway."

"Now you're talking. By the way, you may want to get to know Maria a little better. You will like her. She's just like you."

Lisa didn't know how to take the last statement. "What do you mean by that?" she asked calmly.

"Once you talk to her, you will know what I mean."

Jennifer walked happily into the room. She gave Angel a quick glance.

"Lisa and I were having a nice little discussion. Is Linda in her room?" Angel asked.

Jennifer nodded.

"I'll leave you two alone. Nice talking to you Lisa." Angel walked out the room, head high, half smiling.

Saturday was warm. Graduates, along with their parents, were standing around the auditorium and on the parking lot. Angel and Lionel were talking inside the front entrance. A very brown, tall, older gentleman approached Lionel and Angel gracefully. He wore a heavily starched white shirt, a colorful blue, silk tie and dark blue slacks with his jacket over his arm. He had a touch of grey around a hairline of naturally wavy hair. His eyebrows arched high over deep set eyes. His beard and mustache were trimmed neatly.

"Dad, I want you to meet Melanie. We call her Angel," Lionel said. The man was taken by the young woman's beauty. She had large brown eyes and a beautiful smile.

"I see why they call you Angel and that you are. Nice to meet you Melanie," he said in a soothing baritone voice, smiling the entire time as he spoke. He took Angel's hand ever so gently and shook it. He couldn't believe it. It was her. He thought he would never see her face again.

"Nice to meet you Mr. Johnson," Angel said softly, blushing from the gaze of the older gentleman. He watched how her eyes twinkled when she smiled. He nodded in agreement.

Gina approached the group of adults waving her diploma with Lisa on her heels. Everyone congratulated Gina. Lisa stepped around Gina. Everyone stared at her. Gina quickly introduced Lisa to the group, identifying each parent. Lisa extended her hand, shaking Paul Smith's first. He said nothing. Gina's mother tried desperately to look pleasant and Linda's mother grinned from ear to ear. Bill Smith looked at Lisa in almost disgust, forcing himself to shake her hand. Lisa never felt so unwelcomed before in her life.

"Excuse me, I need to get going," Bill said, anxiously trying to leave.

"Where are you going Bill?" Barbara asked.

"I've got a business dinner tonight. I have to finde Melanie," said a very tall, elegant Bill Smith. He left the group, walking in the opposite direction of Angel.

"What did you say your name was, dear?" Barbara asked Lisa.

Lisa looked around suspiciously. "Lisa Arvell," she finally said.

"You look very familiar. What is your mother's name?" Barbara continued.

"Debra Arvell."

"Nice meeting you, Miss Arvell," Barbara said.

Before Lisa could leave, Angel, Lionel and his father were approaching the group. Barbara's eyes lit up as she recognized the older gentleman. "Charles Johnson? I can't believe it's you," she said, bubbling with excitement. The man walked up to Barbara and kissed her on the cheeks.

"Hello Barbara, Paul and Marilyn. What a pleasant surprise," he said with such grace. Marilyn was just as happy to see him as Barbara. Paul shook his hand.

"Let me introduce you to my husband, Dr. Edward Stevens," Barbara boasted. Charles shook Edward's hand. He seemed accustomed to his wife's behavior.

"Don't tell me. This handsome young man has to be your son. He looks exactly like you when we were in college," Barbara said with enthusiasm looking at Lionel.

Charles proudly introduced Lionel to the group. He, like his father, was very graceful and polite.

"Where is your wife, Charles? Didn't you marry Elaine Carter?" Barbara asked for the sake of conversation rather than being interested. She already knew.

"No, I married someone else. She's with my other son, Cameron. They are packing his things. I see you have someone graduating too," Charles said to change the topic.

"Yes, my daughter Malinda. Everyone calls her Linda. You know my daughter, don't you Lionel?" Barbara stated than asked.

"Yes ma'am," Lionel answered politely.

"It looks like me, Marilyn, Catherine and Debra had the girls and you had all the boys," Barbara said happily.

Angel and Gina looked puzzled at one another. They had no idea their parents went to school with Lionel's parents. Lisa looked at Barbara Stevens with deeper suspicion. How did she know her mother? Why would she ask her mother's name when she already knew? Her grandmother was right. She would find the answer she had been waiting for. Lisa tried excusing herself when Bill Smith walked up looking irritated. He took a look at the new member of the group and stood still. He was almost face to face with Lionel's father.

Charles Johnson extended his hand. "How have you been Bill? I just met your daughter," he said pleasantly. Bill shook his hand reluctantly.

"I was looking for Melanie. We need to go," Bill said in a rush to Angel.

"What are you doing now?" Charles continued, trying to break the ice.

"I am Regional Director of Operations with Farmington Supplies. How about you?" Bill said, slightly boasting. Farmington was one of the largest outfits in office supplies.

"I am a sales representative with Magna Electronics in Minneapolis. I'm helping them break ground in the computer industry," Charles said with extreme confidence. Magna Electronics was the largest manufacturer of electronics in the country.

Bill knew it was time to go. Once again, he was outshined by Charles Johnson. "It sounds like you are doing well, Charles. Good luck in the computer field. It is the growing industry," Bill said politely.

"You're not doing badly yourself. I hear Farmington is ready to buy a paper factory on the east coast," Charles said.

"Yes we are. It should give us a stronger position in the industry. Matter of fact, I have to go home for a business dinner. I will probably have some heavy travel over the next four months," Bill said, feeling better. The two men felt equal now or at least Bill did.

"We must be going. It was nice seeing you again, Charles," Bill said.

"If ever you need anything, give me a call. I have several contacts in manufacturing," Charles said and handed Bill a business card. He looked pleased. He enjoyed talking about business. He and Charles would probably be friends again had it not been for Catherine. Bill left with his wife and Angel.

Lionel looked at his father in shock. "You know Melanie's father? Man, he hates my guts!" he whispered.

Charles nodded, "And mine, too." Charles said good-bye to everyone. Barbara tried to get him to stay around. She wanted him to meet Linda who was with Jennifer and Keith. Charles apologized and left with Lionel.

"Dad, can Uncle Paul take me back to Kansas City tomorrow? He brought his van. What doesn't fit in the van, I can put in my car," Angel whined as she left the auditorium.

Bill hesitated. The last thing he wanted was his brother being responsible for moving his daughter. Paul always called him irresponsible. Bill had borrowed so much money from Paul in the past that it created a chasm between the two. He couldn't think about the relationship between him and Paul. He had to think about the dinner. It was too important.

"Sure honey. Make sure you trail them back," he said, giving in to the whims of his daughter like always. She was his little girl. He worshipped the ground she walked on. He knew he had spoiled her after the death of his wife, but he couldn't help it. Angel kissed him and rushed off.

"There you go, giving in to her again."

"Dora, let's not start this. I have to concentrate on my meeting tonight. I want you quiet until we get back to Kansas City."

Dora stopped. "Melanie is the child, not me. I don't want you to ever talk to me like that again. What's wrong with you anyway?"

"Let's go. I can't be late for the dinner."

"Why, aren't you bringing me along?"

"This is about business, not a social party."

"Everyone is bringing their wives except you. Why?"

"I'm not going to fight with you about a business dinner. Everyone's wives understand when they can't attend except you. It has to be an argument."

"Wives play an important role in their husband's career. You don't want me around your peers, even when they tell you to bring me. This has gone on long enough."

"End of discussion, Dora." Bill opened the car door.

Dora didn't understand her husband anymore. Bill made it clear that he wanted a wife who supported his career. Dora had done it very well. Now he didn't want her around his career anymore. It was time to put an end to the madness. It was time to take her life back and move on. "I guess I need to give you what you've been wanting," she said.

"What's that?"

"A divorce."

Lisa was busy packing her things in the large, brown suitcase. Cameron and Kyle were coming at 2:30 p.m. to take her to the bus station. It was 11:30 and everyone in the dorm was practically gone.

Lisa wanted to take a relaxing bath and a quick nap before getting on the bus for the six-hour trip to St. Louis. She was glad that her suitemates were gone. She had the bathroom to herself. She had taken off her clothes when someone knocked on the door.

"Who is it?" Lisa yelled.

"Cameron."

She cursed to herself hunting for a robe in the suitcase. She had to unpack a few things to get to it. "Just a minute," she yelled. She slipped on a short, light green, terry cloth robe and tied the belt around her waist. She opened the door. Cameron was smiling. The first thing he noticed were her legs.

"I wasn't expecting you until two-thirty. I was getting ready to take a bath," she said, hoping he would leave.

"I thought I would come by and keep you company," he said, not catching the hint.

The formation of her breast under the robe tickled his stomach. Her hair was pulled up and back in a ponytail. She looked sixteen. He continued to look at her shapely legs. She had nice calves. Lisa saw him examining her closely. She moved around the room. It broke his concentration.

"You can take a bath. I'll keep myself busy until you're finished," he said trying not to look at her. They both were quiet, looking around the room.

They began talking at the same time. "You go first," he said.

"No, no. I wasn't going to say anything," she said smiling.

"Lisa, I don't want to lose you. It would be better if you attended Rolla with me. I know if we're not at the same school it won't be the same. You are probably going to end up dating Drew Scott," he teased, knowing she had no interest in his chubby line brother.

Lisa sat next to him on the bed and nudged him with her elbow. "If we write each other, it will be the same," she said, knowing that she felt the same way too.

Cameron shook his head. He looked at her lips. He had always thought she had the sexiest lips on campus. A beauty mark occupied a space above her small lips. Her hazel almond-shaped eyes accentuated her face. He liked her the first time he saw her but she was too social for him. When he found out that she was smart, he let his feelings date her from a distance.

He lifted her in his arms and sat her on his lap. She was light as a feather. She probably weighed one-hundred-five pounds. He placed little kisses on her face. He saw it in a movie. He kissed her on the lips and nibbled on them. He place his hands under her robe, searching for what he stared at for so long.

When Lisa felt his hands touch her breast, she jumped. He caressed her back, which he did so well. She was less tense but stiff. He stretched her out on the bed and disrobed her, looking at her fully nude. She shook, not knowing what to expect. She had thought of this moment but never dreamed of it. The idea of losing her virginity in a dorm room wasn't it. She thought it would be on an island surrounded by blue water or in the desert of Egypt, not a dorm room.

Before she knew it, Cameron had positioned his well shaped body above her. She wasn't sure if she wanted to go through with it or get up and take a bath. He kissed her nipples and sucked them gently. The sensation made her hands tingle. He kissed her navel, the way they did in the movies. She shivered under his touch.

A few seconds went by before she felt the large object between her legs, pushing its way in. It was painful. It continued to push, trying to get in further. Finally, it pushed so hard that she felt the pain slash her insides. It was the most painful thing she ever experienced. She screamed. She felt it move in and out several times. She cried out.

He looked down and saw the tears streaming down her face. It scared him. He stopped and stood up quickly. He saw the blood. It was on him and her. She continued to cry with blood staining her legs and the sheet. All he saw was blood and tears. He went towards her, but she turned her back crying, "Oh God." He wanted to put her in his arms but she wouldn't let him. His breathing became heavy.

The other two girls who said they were virgins didn't bleed. One yelled at him, saying that he was putting it in the wrong place and the other said he went too fast. He figured he did something wrong. "Lisa, are you okay? Let me clean you up," he said, trying to come close.

"Get away," she screamed. He jumped back.

The last thing he wanted was to hurt her. She was the type that never cried so he had to have done something wrong. He looked at her crying and asked shakened, "Lisa, did I rape you?" She didn't answer but continued to cry.

He rushed to the bathroom to clean up. He had to get out. All he wanted to do was touch her. Now, he had made a mess. He rushed to put on his clothes. "Lisa, I'll be back," he said leaving her crying on the bed. He ran down the hall to the telephones.

His fingers trembled as he punched the numbers. "Hey Kyle, it's me. Look, we have to delay our trip home. We need to take Lisa to St. Louis," Cameron demanded. Kyle complained.

"Look man, this is serious. She's hurt."

Kyle asked more questions.

"Hey, I don't know what's really wrong, I know she's hurt. Are you going to do me a favor? You will get a chance to see Jennifer," Cameron threw in quickly. Kyle perked up. Cameron continued, "I'll see you in thirty minutes."

He placed the receiver on the hook. He felt his dream turn into a nightmare. He picked up the phone again and made a collect call to Minneapolis. Lionel answered. Cameron's heart was beating fast.

"Hey Lionel, where is Mom?" he asked anxiously.

"She's at work," Lionel said sarcastically. He could hear Cameron breathing hard. "What's up Ron?" Cameron would not answer. "When are you and Kyle coming home?" Lionel continued. Cameron could not answer, he was on the verge of tears. Lionel could hear his brother breathing heavily. "Cameron, what's wrong?" Lionel yelled through the phone.

"She won't stop crying. I can't get her to stop crying," he managed to say without crying. Lionel knew that Cameron was very sensitive and if he wanted him to talk, he had to be patient.

"Who's crying?" Lionel tried to ask gently.

"Lisa is crying. We made love and she started screaming. She's bleeding all over the place. I don't know what went wrong," Cameron said in a shaky voice.

"Nothing went wrong. She was a virgin. Did you hear me? She was a virgin. Virgins cry and bleed. She's okay," Lionel said, trying to act comforting, but he was impatient. He knew his nineteen-year-old brother was inexperienced but he didn't know it was to this degree. Lionel was more concerned about Cameron getting Lisa pregnant.

"The other two were virgins and this didn't happen," Cameron said.

"Those two had been around the block and up the alley. They were not virgins. Lisa was a virgin," Lionel said. Cameron became preoccupied with the idea of the two girls he dated in high school lying to him. It was hard to believe.

"Did you use a rubber?" Lionel asked.

"What rubber?" asked a naive Cameron. He could hear Lionel blow out air over the phone. Cameron didn't think to use a condom.

"When are you and Kyle coming home?" asked an exasperated Lionel.

"We are taking Lisa to St. Louis first, then we will probably leave there early Saturday morning," Cameron said.

"St. Louis is eleven hours from Minneapolis. Do you have money to do that?" Lionel asked paternally.

Cameron had not given it any thought. All he wanted to do was to get Lisa home safely, and the only way he could was to take her himself. He figured Kyle had money. He never bought anything. He usually had money when they were in high school so he must have some now.

"Yes, we have money," Cameron finally said. "Tell Mom I'll be home late Saturday night."

Cameron hung up the phone and let his head rest against the wall. He didn't want to go back to the room but he had too. He took a deep breath and walked slowly to Lisa's room. He knew she hated him and he didn't blame her. He knocked on the door. There was no answer. He rushed in. He saw the bloodstained sheets first. He called out to her. She answered him from the bathroom. She was sitting in the tub of water with her head down and arms wrapped around her legs.

"Kyle and I are going to take you to St. Louis," he said softly, sitting on the floor beside the tub.

"I've already bought my ticket," she answered in a whisper, keeping her focus on the water.

"I'm sure they will give you a refund," he said. He looked painfully at his once good friend. "Lisa, I'm sorry. I would give my right arm if I knew we could be friends again. I didn't mean to hurt you," he said.

It took awhile before she looked at him. "I didn't think it would be like that. Everyone said it feels good but they also said it hurts on your first time," she said.

Cameron eyes were watering as Lisa spoke. She took her hands, dripping with water, and rubbed his face. She leaned forward and kissed him. He smiled.

As Lisa rested in the back seat in Kyle's car, lying in Cameron's arms, she thought about that younger woman again, how upset she was because the man she loved hurt her. The conversation with the older woman was vivid:

"Sweetie, the Bible said vengeance is the Lord. He will repay. You can't make that man pay for anything." The younger woman didn't want to hear it. All she knew was he lied and he had to pay. All those years and she had reaped nothing. She and her daughter had to be taken care of. If it wasn't going to be her, then it would be her daughter. The younger woman looked at the older, tired woman and said, "If it takes me the rest of my life to get what's due me, then that is what I'm going to do. That bastard is going to pay and I won't stop at nothing until he does."

Chapter 14
August 1981

It was their junior year. Jennifer walked swiftly with Kyle and Malcolm trailing her. As she walked, she flipped the large curls that occasionally fell into her face. She looked fresh and crisp in her blue cotton oxford shirt and jeans. All three students were carrying an arm full of flyers. Kyle decided to chair the ABC's Black Freshmen Orientation committee. He asked Jennifer and Malcolm to help distribute the materials to the new students. They started at the girl's dorms.

As the three moved closer to Kingston-Hillard Hall, the sight became very familiar to Jennifer, fraternity members in Greek T-shirts. The dorm primarily housed freshmen girls. The fraternities usually hoped to talk them into pledging their little sister interest groups. The boys generally hung around King-Hill for a few weeks to check out the new crew of girls. It gave them time to determine if they would break up with their girlfriends and try for a freshman. If the thrill left early, they had plenty of time to go back to the old flames.

Parents and new students alike carried boxes, suitcases and footlockers to the new home away from home. Jennifer thought back to her first day at college. What she remembered was a frightening moment. She had received a letter assigning her to Kingston-Hillard Hall but when she got there, her room and board arrangements were mishandled by the school. There were a few rooms available in Morrison Hall. Jennifer had to receive permission from the Kappas for her to move into their section. That was when she met Angel. When Angel came to greet Jennifer, she immediately took a liking to her but Jennifer was terrified. Angel spent the entire day consoling her. Angel's original roommate decided not to return to school, therefore, the two became roommates.

Jennifer remembered she and Lisa standing in the lobby looking for rooms. She cried and Lisa pouted. Gina and Marsha were with her and found a room with a junior, a white girl. The two got along fine until the day Lisa pressed her hair. The white girl complained terribly, claiming the smell was disgusting. She didn't want Lisa pressing her hair in the room anymore. The house mother agreed, claiming it was a fire hazard. Lisa went to the Dean of Women, requesting a black roommate who understood hair pressing. The school moved slowly on Lisa's request.

The tension between Lisa and her roommate became intolerable. Lisa befriended Rochelle and a few others. They cooked up a scheme to rid Lisa of the problem roommate. They came to the room at midnight one Wednesday, wanting to play Backgammon. The girls made so much noise that the white girl complained loudly and called them niggers. Rochelle plopped herself on the girl's bed almost sitting on her head. By Saturday, Lisa was rooming with Dee Dee and she and Rochelle have been friends ever since.

Jennifer passed out flyers and talked to new students and their parents. A tall boy approached her. At one time, she would get jumpy but she welcomed the visitor.

"What's up Jennifer? How was your summer?"

"Hi Brad. It was nice, how about yours?" Jennifer flipped her hair.

"What can I say about K.C.? I worked and worked and worked. I'm happy to be back in school. Is the rumor true?" Brad smiled and Jennifer got an attitude.

"What rumor?" Jennifer asked.

"That you and Sean got a little thang going on."

"We don't have a thang going on. We are seeing each other, if that's what you're asking," Jennifer said with one hand on her hip.

Brad looked her up and down. He cleared his throat. "What's up with the attitude? You sound like your girl Lisa."

Jennifer's hand dropped from her hips. Kappas were not known for attitudes. She softened her voice and smiled. "I don't have an attitude. When you said the word rumor, it made me mad."

"Alright foxy lady. So Sean is the lucky dude. I guess none of your brothers could measure up to a Lambda, huh?" Brad said with a smile.

"None of my brothers asked. My brothers are off chasing Alphas, like Vicki or is it Anne?" Jennifer asked, looking at Brad for an answer.

He shook his head wildly. "No ma'am. I'm a free dude." Jennifer giggled a little and shook her head.

"Naw! What are you laughing about?" he asked, showing off one dimple.

Jennifer continued to giggle at the brown, attractive person. Brad had the dreamiest large eyes and a clean face. He smiled a lot showing one dimple in the right cheek. His attitude was always pleasant. "Sure you're free. I think Vicki had your time before we left school in May. Don't tell me you two aren't together?"

"Me and Vicki had a little thang happening, but I mean, we're still cool, you know. So you dumped Michael for Sean?"

"Oh please, don't insult me! I never had anything going on with Michael."

"Yeah, I know, but the brother ain't got nothing going on with your sister Rosalyn, either. I don't see what she sees in him. All you women think the Lambdas got so much money. Honey, git you a Lambda!" Brad teased, talking like a girl and throwing his hand out with a bent wrist.

Another tall figure approached Jennifer and Brad. He was a shade lighter than Brad. His features were broad. His eyes looked gray at times and his eyebrows went straight across the top of his eyes. His lips were full. He wore shorts, showing off well built thighs and legs. "Hey man, what's up?" he said and grabbed Brad's hand. They did the fraternity's secret handshake.

"What's up bro?" Brad said.

"Hey Jennifer, what's happening?" Tony asked, sizing her up.

"Hi Tony."

"Yeah man, what's going on?" Tony asked.

"I'm just talking, shooting the breeze. You're ready to play some ball." The new member nodded. "How are the prospects?" he asked.

"Hey, some are looking real fine. We should have a nice line of Swans."

Kyle came toward Jennifer looking happy. "Jen, I think we are going to have a nice turnout Friday."

"Jen?" the two tall boys said in unison.

"Uh, let me leave. I have to finish handing out these flyers," Jennifer said, excusing herself from the group.

"What's it for?" they asked.

"ABC is having a Black Freshmen Orientation in the Little Theater Friday morning at ten. Are you two coming?"

"A Black Freshmen Orientation? We never had one. ABC is really coming along. Yeah, I'm coming. It should be a lot of babes there. We can get a better look," Tony said. The two tall boys slapped five.

Jennifer closed her eyes and shook her head. "Let me leave you two on your Babe Alert. Good-bye," she said.

"Ah baby, don't leave with an attitude. Your brothers still love you, even if you are hooked up with a Lambda," Brad teased.

"Who?" Tony asked almost out of breath.

"Sean. Man, can you believe she overlooked us for Sean?"

"Good-bye fellas. I still love you," Jennifer said and walked away with Kyle looking lost. She handed a flyer to a new student.

"Hey Jen. Who is Sean?" asked a humble Kyle.

She stopped abruptly, scaring him. "A friend!" she snapped.

Jennifer observed the meeting. It was nothing like the ones Angel presided over. Maria constantly had to remind people about staying on the topic. Some commented on their parents, some about boys and others talked badly about other sororities.

"To our new members, you need to write your Specials, the ones who have graduated, and tell them how you are adjusting to the sorority. It is mandatory. I hope you ladies have good things to say," Maria said. Laughter went throughout the room. Jennifer noticed how well Alexis, Patrice and Candice blended with the others. Rochelle seemed to have a difficult time acclimating and Anita appeared awkward at times too.

"The floor is opened for new business. Oh, before I forget, I would like to announce that Miss Peterson has been voted Outstanding Collegiate for the month of October. She has helped the Association of Black Collegiates develop a tutoring program. Her picture will be featured in the University's newspaper and the sorority will be mentioned, of course."

The group clapped and cheered.

"Madame President, are we doing a Thanksgiving project?" Margo murmured.

"We do a Christmas project, Miss Washington."

"The Alphas are doing a Thanksgiving project."

"Miss Overton, we do not compare ourselves to the ladies of Alpha Theta Lambda. We have...."

"Ladies? You are being much too kind, Maria." The group burst into laughter again.

"Ladies, please. Like I was saying, we have our own agenda," Maria said. The girls began whispering comments among themselves.

"Madame President, I would like to extend an offer to the sorority to become tutors for ABC. We are in need of English, College Algebra and Speech tutors. I know some of us have strong backgrounds in these areas."

"You are right, Miss Peterson. Some of us are very strong in these areas. Those of you who are interested, please see Miss Peterson. If there is no new business, this meeting is adjourned."

Lisa tried to be patient until the meeting was over. The sorority's executive council was discussing the Thanksgiving service project. The meeting had turned into a complaint session about boyfriends and the lack thereof. Lisa's thoughts shifted to the B she made on her Economics test. She was in danger of losing her 4.0 GPA. She thought about how she had not heard from Cameron. She had sent him seven letters since school began and had only received two. She knew it was going to happen.

She became irritated after hearing Rita complain about Tim Rylander not calling her as promised. Lisa wanted the meeting to end. They were talking about no good men again. Lisa expected more from the executive council.

"Soror President, I would like to volunteer to chair the Thanksgiving project, if it's okay?" All the Prophytes looked at Lisa unbelieving.

"Soror, usually Neophytes wait their turn before chairing any committee."

"Soror President, I nominate Soror Arvell to chair the Thanksgiving project. We need to break some of these traditions. I think she will do a good job. Besides, she is Gina's protégée." The group laughed lightly. "Does anyone object to Soror Arvell, a Neophyte, chairing the Thanksgiving project."

Lisa looked around the room. No one said anything. "Well soror, it's all yours. Have fun!" Rita said.

"Thank you. Soror President, is it okay if I leave early? I have a test tomorrow."

Everyone looked at Lisa again in shock. She shifted in her chair.

"I have to leave, too, Soror President," Vicki said.

"Me too," Crystal said.

The four Prophyte officers looked displeased at the three antsy Neophytes who looked for approval to leave. Donna made a motion to close the meeting, Chandra seconded it. The three Neophytes left the room in a hurry. Lisa let out a deep breath.

"They still think we are pledging. Why do we have to wear skirts to a sorority meeting anyway? They didn't do this last year," Crystal, the sorority Chaplain, complained as she looked back at the door continuously while walking down the hall.

"Because of *you*! Don't you realize you're in a sorority now? Why don't you dress like it," Vicki snapped. Crystal's feelings were hurt. Many Alphas complained about her very casual appearance. The executive council, meaning the six Prophytes, voted that either skirts or dresses were to be worn to sorority meetings at all times.

"Ease up Vicki. Crystal is right. They do treat us like we're still pledging. I'm sick of it too," Lisa complained.

"We have to earn their respect. Raggly jeans and sweat pants just don't do it," Vicki said while frowning at Crystal who was wearing a peasant skirt and blouse.

"What are you planning for the Thanksgiving project? I'll help," Crystal said, hiding next to Lisa, trying to ignore Vicki's frown.

"I don't know. I'll think of something."

Lisa was concentrating on her presentation. She had to sell the idea of cooking and serving a pre-Thanksgiving dinner to the elderly at Mount Nebo Baptist Church. She couldn't think of any other project to do. She had already committed the sorority. The pastor was happy to hear about the project. He told the Seniors' Club. Everyone was excited he said.

Lisa's mind drifted to Cameron. She had written him again, asking if he was still interested in the relationship. No answer. It had been two weeks since she mailed the letter. She had assumed he had found someone else.

"Next we will hear from Soror Arvell on the Thanksgiving project."

Lisa jumped back to reality when she heard her name. She began her spiel about cooking and serving the elderly on Saturday before Thanksgiving. She heard a few negative comments. Some cursed about cooking. Rita had to remind them they were in the Chapter room and to watch their language.

Lisa had to think quickly. She started a story of an elderly woman she met at the church whose family had left Harrisburg. Lisa continued with how the woman's family was not able to visit and the old woman was going to be all alone on Thanksgiving. Lisa told how she adopted the older woman for that day, to be her family. The woman was excited and told Lisa of other elderly people who had no family because their families had left Harrisburg. Lisa talked about adopting a grandparent for one day as their project. She continued to stress one day.

The magic of the story touched some of the girls. They softened quickly. "I'm sure the sorority will be more than happy to be adopted granddaughters to those in need. What do we need to do, soror? As you heard, a lot of us know nothing about cooking."

"The committee will meet tomorrow and develop a strategy. The Seniors' Club will be more than happy to teach us how to cook a turkey, dressing, sweet potato pies and all of that. The church will supply everything we need. All we have to do is show up to work. Someone at the church is on the Harrisburg Sentinel newspaper. They are going to do a story on this project. I also got a photographer with the school's newspaper to photograph the event. He promised it will be in the next edition of the school's newspaper."

A smile came across Rita's face. "Good work, soror. The sorority will look good being in not only the school's newspaper but the community's newspaper too. We can probably enter our project to Nationals and receive the undergraduate public services award. Let's move on to new business."

Lisa let out another deep breath. She thought it was going to be tougher trying to convince the sorors than it was the Seniors' Club. The old women complained about how young folks don't know nothin' 'bout cookin' no Thanksgiven dinner. She had to sell the idea to the Seniors as performing a community service project to neglected sorority girls from broken homes. She had to share a portion of her life story to get the Seniors interested in wanting to help. She figured at least six Alphas fit closely to the description she gave the old women. It was a small lie. She chuckled to herself as she thought about teaming Alicia up with the one who complained about young gals not using sage no mo'. It was too easy Lisa thought.

As the girls scampered around the church kitchen, tempers began to flare. The old women complained and shouted commands. Alicia was ready to curse out her adopted grandmother. The woman complained because she didn't understand what a "taste of sage" was. Gail sat one woman down to talk to her because she didn't feel comfortable yelling at her. The poor woman couldn't hear too well. Lisa knew it was falling apart when one woman told Evelyn to sit down and let her make the pie crust. All anger focused on Lisa.

"These old heffas act like they are doing us a favor. What's up with them, Lisa?" Alicia asked, blowing off steam.

"No wonder their families don't want to be bothered with them, I don't either," Evelyn said. She was getting ready to leave.

"Did you hear that old one with the stockings falling down go off on me?" Paula asked.

Lisa had to do something quick. She found Miss Lucille, the president of the Seniors' Club. "Miss Lucille, we need to talk. It seems like the Seniors want to cook everything themselves. Y'all are suppose to teach us," Lisa stressed.

"Baby, we can't serve dem people food da way y'all cookin' it. Folks needs to eat good on Thanksgiven. Some of y'all ain't never cooked befo'."

"I know, Miss Lucille, but we need to learn. Some of us have never had anybody to teach us." Lisa tried to look humble. "All we need is for the Seniors to be patient with us."

Miss Lucille let out a deep breath. She watched Edna and Gladys go to town on the pies. Dorthea was basting the turkey. Miss Lucille let out a deep sigh and looked in the young woman's innocent eyes. "How about if we do this together, okay?" Miss Lucille smiled.

Lisa smiled back. "Okay," she said. She rushed to tell the girls the new plan. She was happy no one left. Tina was the only one who had not been offended. Her grandmother had her in the kitchen picking greens, telling her about how the arthritis had "set in." Tina seemed to enjoy the old woman's company.

"I got a taste for some chitlins," one old woman yelled out. Alicia and Gail looked angrily at Lisa who tried looking away.

"I'm not cleaning chitlins for this grandmomma or any other one," Alicia said and went back into the kitchen.

It was February. Jennifer was reading one of the two letters Angel had written since graduation last year. The letter was fairly upbeat so Jennifer decided to pull it out and read it again.

Dear Jennifer,

I'm sorry I haven't written you more often. I have been very busy with the Spring Dance Concert. I have received a grant to help inner city youths. I decided to teach dance since everyone has gone crazy over the movie Fame from two years ago. I have some very talented students and I extend to you an invitation to see our first public performance. I also have a line of evening wear in Linda's mother's boutique that is doing fairly well. Aunt Barbara is pushing me for more designs but I just can't concentrate on anything new with this job at the Youth Development Center.

Linda told me to tell you "hi" and nothing else. She doesn't want me to spread her business, so I'll let her tell you what is happening with her. She wants you to call her collect because she hates writing.

Also, I talked to Lionel recently. He is working on an MBA in marketing at the University of Minnesota. Thomas is still hanging tough in law school.

I know you have always said that Lionel and I looked good together but sometimes looks are deceiving. He and I have gone our separate ways, trying to find what makes us both happy. Don't get too discouraged with the sorority. You have a very important position. It will be up to you and Joni to decide the pledge process. Just make sure it's fair. I hope you like the dress. If you need me, call! Remaining

Yours truly,
Angel

Jennifer folded the letter and filed it with the other one. She was happy but yet a little sad after reading the letter. It wasn't that Angel and Lionel looked well together, there was a certain chemistry between the two. Jennifer always felt responsible for the break-up. Somehow, she thought, she would be responsible for them getting back together.

She had to get ready for the Lambda's Ball. She remembered how she had helped getting ready for the Beta's Ball last year. The Lambda's Ball did not have the same excitement like the Beta's Ball, which was the following month. Students on campus decided to stay in for the evening. It was too cold to go anywhere, they claimed.

Jennifer was representing the Kappas and Rita was representing the Alphas. Lots of students picked Rita to win over her. It did not matter to Jennifer who won. There was no excitement in attending the Ball.

Jennifer looked at the dress Angel sent her. It was a simple, red, straight gown that fastened at the left shoulder with a rhinestone clip. The right shoulder was bare. The dress had a split in the back. It was made out of soft polyester, causing it to cling to her body as she walked. She practiced a curtsey kneeling because the dress did not allow one that went to the floor. She decided to style her hair first before applying makeup. She combed it up into a large ball at the top leaving small sections of hair in the back for kiss-curls.

As she dressed, her mind flashed back to the big argument with Lisa that caused them not to speak since Thanksgiving, and it was already the first of February. Lisa decided to tell her that Sean was seeing Phyllis. The rumor was that Jennifer was the daytime friend and Phyllis was the nighttime lover. It wasn't so bad until Lisa told her how some people on campus were calling her a "stuck up bitch." Lisa told Jennifer how she changed from the sweet innocent darling to a "you are beneath me" witch.

Jennifer accused Lisa of being jealous since she had now developed confidence and no longer tried to please people. She also told Lisa that she had changed as well. Lisa behaved as if the sun rose and set on Alpha Theta Lambda. Nothing but the sorority mattered anymore. Lisa told Jennifer if the Kappas had as much sisterhood as the Alphas, she would feel the same way.

The argument escalated until Lisa called Jennifer a stuck up Kappa and Jennifer called Lisa an angry, manless Alpha. The comment hurt Lisa because she had not heard from Cameron since the first of September and Jennifer was the only one who knew. The anger created silence between the two girls.

Jennifer knew there were problems between her and Sean. What was supposed to be a boyfriend-girlfriend relationship was merely an agreement to escort each other to various parties. Jennifer felt that Sean was pretentious. He hardly ever had anything to talk about. He felt uncomfortable with the two of them alone just talking. It was difficult for him to relax. When they were out together, he practically ignored her until it was time to go. He tried on numerous occasions to get her into bed. She flat out told him that she was waiting for the right time with the right person.

She really did not care if Sean was seeing someone else because she really didn't like him. She hated the way he touched her and how he kissed her. He was forceful. She recently began hanging out with her fan club again, everyone except Kyle. He had a girlfriend.

Jennifer finished with her hair and makeup. She took her time slipping on the dress. She didn't have the audience like before. Not even her roommate or suitemates were around. No one seemed to care about how she looked as she went to what the students called The Stuck Up Bitches Ball.

The door opened. Margo came in, happily carrying a dress. She was surprised to see Jennifer ready to go. It was only six o'clock. "You look so pretty. I can't wait until they crown you Miss Lambda," Margo said happily.

"Thanks, Margo, but there are nine other strong contenders," Jennifer said.

"Rita and Pam are the only strong contenders, and they are not going to beat the girl who is what's happening on campus," Margo said.

Margo's comment had Jennifer thinking. According to Lisa, people did not think she was "what's happening." Jennifer always felt that the argument between her and Lisa was more personal than anything. There were some girls who treated her differently but on the whole, lots had complimented her. The key was not to be too popular, Jennifer believed.

Margo put on a robe and stepped into the shower. Jennifer thought about how happy Margo was dating Peter. He was pleasant and very polite, especially being an only child. He seemed to enjoy Margo's company when they were out together.

Peter was a short, average looking guy. He had a lot of self-confidence for one so short. He mixed well with Margo's friends. Jennifer wished she could date someone like Peter. She kept reminding herself to be patient and Mr. Right would come along.

Margo came out of the bathroom with a big red towel wrapped around her. She was shaking because the room was cool. The heat wasn't working well in Morrison Hall. The girls were sleeping in long johns and gloves to keep warm.

"Will you arch my eyebrows, Jennifer?" Margo asked.

"Sure," Jennifer said. She went into the bathroom to get the razor. She could hear Alexis and Patrice in the next room. She knocked on the door to say "hi." They looked at her with surprise.

"You really look nice, Jennifer. You got your nerve wearing a red dress to the Lambda's Ball! Who did your makeup?" Alexis asked.

"I did," Jennifer said with a smile.

"Well, you did a good job. What time are you leaving?" Alexis asked.

"I'm supposed to be there at seven. I guess I'll leave when Sean gets here," she said blandly.

"Good, that gives me plenty of time to get ready and take pictures. Knock on the door before you leave, okay?" Alexis asked.

"I will," Jennifer said and left the room.

Patrice let out a loud huff. They had just seen Sean in the car with Phyllis. Alexis shook her head. "She doesn't deserve to be treated like this. She's too nice for him," she said.

"The idiot doesn't care who sees him. I wish she would find somebody else," Patrice added.

Jennifer was busy arching Margo's eyebrows. They small-talked for awhile. Jennifer helped Margo with the makeup. She watched how Margo smiled when she finished. Margo hardly wore makeup but she liked when other people applied it.

Jennifer looked at her watch. It was almost seven-thirty. Patrice and Alexis came into Jennifer's room. They were ready to leave.

"Jennifer, do you want to ride with us to the Student Union? It's after seven," Alexis said, looking worried.

"Sean will be here any minute," Jennifer said with a forced smile. Patrice and Alexis looked at each other, trying not to look suspicious.

"Are you sure?" Patrice asked. Jennifer nodded.

Alexis and Patrice left. Jennifer was wondering what was keeping Sean. He knew she was supposed to have been there at seven o'clock. It was not unusual for him to be late. Sometimes he wouldn't show at all without any explanation. The first time he came late, Jennifer threw a fit and he did not care.

The buzzer sounded a visitor for student "A," which was Margo. She gathered her purse and coat. "It's getting late, Jennifer. Sean should have been here by now," Margo said.

"Do you think Peter will mind if I come along?" Jennifer asked as she gathered her coat, gloves and purse.

"Of course not. He has the biggest crush on you. He would probably tell me to wait for Sean and take you," Margo teased.

As Jennifer, Margo and Peter walked to the car in the snow, Sean drove up looking aggravated. He blew his horn for Jennifer, but she kept walking with Peter and Margo. Peter looked at Jennifer, wondering if she saw Sean, but she hopped into the back seat of Peter's car, forcing a smile. It did not matter if Sean was angry and never spoke to her again. She had decided to call it quits after the Ball.

The crowd was sparse at the Student Union. There were a few onlookers who came to see who had on what. Dinner was in progress and Jennifer had to rush to get to the reserve table for the court. She sat next to Rita and her date Tim Rylander.

"Hi Jennifer, I was wondering if you had gotten cold feet and decided not to come," said a cheerful Rita.

"I've got cold feet alright, but it's from the snow," Jennifer joked.

Jennifer surveyed the room. Most of her sorority sisters were in attendance. The Kappas were big supporters of the Lambdas. The sorority made large contributions to the Lambda's scholarship fund. The Alphas' participation was less than usual. Jennifer saw Lisa sitting at a table close to the court's entrance. She was sitting with Tina, Alicia, Rochelle and Crystal. They seemed to be having a good time. Jennifer saw Michael sitting at a table with a different girl. She was giggling and cuddling next to him. Sean finally arrived and sat at the table with Michael.

"Why did I let y'all talk me into this shit. I want my money back," Rochelle complained and the girls laughed. People turned around to see who was making noise.

"Girl, I hear you. Lisa thinks Jennifer is going to win," Alicia said out loud.

"I thought you and Jennifer weren't speaking?" Rochelle asked.

Lisa looked unconcerned. "I don't have a problem with her," she said.

"What happened?" Tina asked low.

"She's trippin', that's all," Lisa said with an end of discussion attitude. The girls looked around the room. Phyllis walked by their table and waved.

"Will one of y'all please talk to Soror Big Butt. Sistah needs to know that if panty lines are showing, it means the dress is too small," Rochelle said and Crystal burst into laughter.

"You ought to quit! Look at Jennifer in that spring and summer get-up," Alicia shot.

The girls' table was receiving a lot of traffic because the court was lining up.

"Check out Cathy with the Jheri curl juice running down her back," Alicia said.

"Oops, excuse me. I thought that was part of the pattern in her dress," Rochelle said, covering her mouth.

"Look at that Sunday-go-to-meeting dress Marcia got on," Alicia said.

"Naw, that ain't the one. Veda needs a new bra. That shit needs to be lifted and separated," Rochelle added.

Tina and Crystal laughed at all of the comments.

"Lord knows Sharon needs a girdle on," Alicia said.

"Why is it that the Lambdas look like deacons of somebody's church?" Rochelle asked frowning.

"Y'all need to stop talking about people," Lisa finally said.

All the girls looked at her with surprise.

"Honey, please! What's your problem?" Rochelle said loud enough for people to hear.

"Leave her alone, Roachy. She has to act nice in public. She's just practicing for her seat on death row," Alicia said, pointing to the table where all of the presidents from the different Greek organizations were sitting.

The court was in line, ready to walk forward as they were called. As each girl's name was called, the crowd clapped softly except when they called Jennifer's name. Her line sisters yelled with joy. She looked out of the corner of her eye and saw Lisa clapping softly. When they called Rita's name, everyone at Lisa's table, except Rochelle, stood up and yelled. They were the only ones making noise.

Jennifer sat patiently, waiting for the event to be over. People took pictures. Jennifer forgot to smile on most of them. Even Lisa took a picture of Jennifer. The feeling of being on court wasn't in Jennifer's spirit. She just wanted to go home.

Suddenly, Jennifer saw Pam in tears, being escorted to a chair next to Joni, the reigning Miss Lambda. Jennifer felt sorry for her because she was crying. Then she saw Rita get up and walk to the other chair but she was happy. Jennifer just shook her head. She looked at her watch. It was nine o'clock. She couldn't believe she had been there for less than an hour. It felt like all day.

Darryl James tapped Jennifer on the shoulder. He smiled at her. She smiled back. He helped her out of her seat. Joni walked to her with a big smile and tears in her eyes. She took the crown off her head and placed it on top of Jennifer's. Someone handed her a scepter. Jennifer realized she had won.

When the court danced, Jennifer's heart sank after seeing Lisa, Tina, Alicia and Crystal leave. The idea of Lisa not staying around to extend congratulations made her even unhappier. Jennifer talked to people as they congratulated her. All of the Kappas surrounded her, giving her hugs and kisses. Sean approached her with a smile. He gave her a hug in front of everyone. He whispered in her ear, "Let's go."

She waved good-bye and got her coat, gloves and purse. She followed Sean out the door. The expression on his face changed. He turned around quickly and looked at her with a frown. "What's up with you embarrassing me in front of my frat brother?" he snapped, almost biting off her nose. She stepped back and looked back at the Union Ballroom. Hardly anyone was around.

"We need to talk," she managed to say.

"Let's get out of here," he yelled.

Jennifer was still wearing the crown with the scepter in her hand. She followed him to the car. Something told her to walk to the dorm, it was only ten minutes away, but she followed him. He didn't open her car door as usual. She sat down in the passenger seat. She figured they would talk on the way back to the dorm. He pulled off, turning a corner away from the dorm.

"Where are we going?" she asked.

Sean continued driving, ignoring her worried expression. She knew they were going to the trailer park where he and his roommate lived. Jennifer felt uneasy. "I thought we were going to talk?" Jennifer said trying to keep from becoming nervous.

"Did you think we were going to talk in this damn car where it's almost zero degrees outside?" he yelled. The drive to his trailer was dark. There were no street lights. It was one-and-a-half miles from Morrison Hall. He pulled onto the lot near his trailer. He got out of the car and slammed the door. Jennifer continued to sit, looking straight ahead. She had no money and the evening shoes she had borrowed from Candice were becoming uncomfortable.

Sean walked back to the car and opened her door. "Are you coming in?" he asked irritatedly.

"I want to go back to the dorm," she said stubbornly.

"After we talk, then you can go back to the dorm," he said.

Jennifer felt her eyes swell with tears. She got out of the car grudgingly and walked to the trailer. It was warm inside but she refused to remove her coat. Sean took off his coat and got comfortable on the couch.

"What's the matter with you? I'm not a stranger. Come on and sit down so we can talk," he said, looking like a snake. She continued standing, holding the scepter tighter. "Oh, so I have to beg like Michael did," he said with a smirk on his face. "How do you think you won that crown on your head?" he continued.

"What do you mean?" she asked angrily.

"Don't try to play innocent with me. Michael said he got some when he was pledging, he just had to beg. Why are you playing me?" he asked with a sneer.

Jennifer was stunned. Not only was Michael a dog, but a lying one. She also knew she won the crown on her own merits. She buttoned her coat and walked to the door. Sean jumped up and pulled her back.

"So you don't think I can measure up to Michael?" he asked while gripping her arm tighter. She tried pulling away. He pushed her onto the couch, causing the scepter to fall out of her arms. When she stood up, he backed her into his bedroom. He pushed her onto the bed and fell on top of her. She tried pushing him off but could not manage.

He yanked at her coat, causing four buttons to pop off. She felt his hand travel under her dress. He pulled at her panties. She could feel the rubber break around the legs of her underwear. She kicked which gave him an opening to put his hand between her legs. She was terrified and screamed. He yelled for her to shut up. He pushed his forearm at her neck. The pressure from his arm hurt her throat. She stopped screaming.

She could feel his finger make its way inside. She squeezed her legs tighter, trying to stop him. She pleaded with him to stop but he kept going. She felt his finger move in and out. She started crying, begging him to stop. He put all of his weight on top of her and took his finger out. He pressed one of his knees between her legs. She screamed again but no one listened.

Finally, his knee freed a place for him to position himself on top of her. She screamed louder and swung wildly. It could not be happening, she thought. She hit him in the chest but it did nothing.

He ripped the front of her dress down, exposing her breast. He sucked wildly, thinking it would quiet her and maybe she would soon enjoy it. Jennifer fought harder but he pinned her arms down above her head with one hand.

She heard his zipper. She figured the worst was about to happen. She only heard about it but never did she ever imagine it to happen to her. She felt it on her legs. He released her arms and straddled her legs wide and high. She could feel it move closer toward the opening.

With every ounce of strength, she kicked hard causing the heel of her shoe to catch him at the side of his face. It stunned him. Blood streamed down the side of his face. He slapped her hard across the face. She kicked again, catching him in the groin which almost paralyzed him. She scampered off the bed but he recovered quickly.

Jennifer felt pain explode in her face. The taste of blood filled her mouth. When he punched her in the face again, she felt the pain go from her jaw to her eyes. He punched her in the mouth. She felt her teeth dig into her bottom lip. She fell against the dresser. She tried to scoot pass him but he pushed her so hard that she fell against the dry wall, causing it to crack.

Jennifer hit the floor and crawled quickly pass him and into the kitchen. She got up and opened the drawer. She pulled out a knife. He looked at her with fire in his eyes. Blood was running down the side of his face. Blood was splattered all over Jennifer's face. Her eyes and jaw hurt badly but she held the knife in front, ready to strike. He picked up his car keys and left.

Jennifer was hysterical. She cried loudly. She was unaware that the crown was still on her head and her torn dress exposed her breast. She ran into his bedroom. She took the knife and slashed his comforter, going deep into the mattress. She pulled clothes from the closet and tossed them onto the bed. She ran to the kitchen and opened the cabinets until she found a huge jug of bleach. She poured it over his clothes. She looked in the refrigerator and removed ketchup and grape juice and dumped them on top too. She screamed the entire time as she vandalized his belongings.

She picked up the knife and ran back to the dorm, trying to keep her balance as she waddled through the snow in the thin evening shoes. Her feet were wet and cold. They were going numb. She held the knife out in front, ready to kill the first thing that came within an inch of her. She used the snow as light to guide her back to the dorm. As the wind blew, she pulled the coat tighter to keep warm. Only two of the six buttons were left on the coat. She tried to stay out of sight as she walked closer to Morrison Hall.

The familiar sight of dorm lights were in view. She ran faster on numb feet. She arrived at the front door panting. The night hostess took her time to open the door. Jennifer cursed the old, white woman loudly. When the woman saw Jennifer, a look of horror came across her face. Jennifer thought the woman had the nerve frowning at her when she looked like the Bride of Frankenstein herself. Jennifer flashed her identification card and walked pass the woman to a chair in the lobby. She rushed to take off the wet shoes to massage her feet. They tingled under her soothing touch.

"Honey, what happened?" the woman said almost breathless as she saw the knife next to Jennifer's foot. Jennifer ignored the night hostess until life was in her feet again. The woman rushed to the switchboard. Jennifer left with the knife and shoes in her hands.

She walked up the stairs absentmindedly to the third floor. She knocked on the fifth door to her right. She heard unfamiliar noises in the room. She waited for someone to answer. Lisa opened the door wide and gasped out loud. What she saw made her speechless.

Jennifer looked at the girls in Lisa's room, especially the small one who was lying at the foot of Lisa's bed. Her spot. She always slept there. Jennifer looked at the girls as they stared at her in shock. She walked away backward from the door. Lisa called Jennifer but she took off running to the room that was familiar.

She knocked on the door continuously. Maria finally opened it. Jennifer looked at the strange person. Maria's mouth dropped opened.

"Where's Angel?" Jennifer mumbled with the large knife in her hand.

"What happened?" Maria asked. Joni came to the door. She immediately put her hand over her mouth when she saw Jennifer.

"*Where is Angel*?" Jennifer asked louder with deep breaths. When she spoke, blood spilled from her mouth down her neck and onto her chest. The girls became frightened, not knowing what had happened or what to expect because Jennifer gripped the knife tighter.

"Where is Miss Stevens?" Jennifer asked as tears mixed with blood on her face. Joni turned sideways and wiped her eyes.

"Come inside and wait for them. You have to put the knife down, okay?" Maria said slowly and carefully. Jennifer slowly handed the knife to Maria. "What happened, sweetie?" Maria asked softly. Now that sounded familiar.

Jennifer looked at Maria and said, "I screamed but no one listened."

"Who did this to you?" Maria asked.

"He said we were going to talk, but he really wanted sex."

"Was it Sean?" Joni asked.

"I feel ugly. I feel really, really ugly."

There was a loud bang on the door. Joni opened it. Lisa was leaning against the wall with Tina and Crystal standing behind her. "What happened to her?" Lisa asked in short pants. Joni stepped outside the door and closed it behind her.

"She's okay. Maria is with her now," Joni said smiling.

"She's not okay. She's hurt badly," Lisa barked, trying to go inside.

"I know, Lisa, but she's with her sisters. Why don't you come back in the morning?" Joni said pleasantly, blocking Lisa's view.

"But I'm her friend!" Lisa said out loud. "I need to see her. I need to talk to her."

Joni tried to be pleasant, but she had to be firm, "Lisa, she is going to be fine. She's with us now. We are going to take her to the hospital."

Lisa was still panting. She didn't understand what Joni meant by Jennifer being with her sisters. She was her friend since freshmen year. Lisa felt her chest tightening. It was hard to breathe. Something was squeezing the life out of her.

"Come on, Lisa. You will be able to see her in the morning. She's going to be okay," Tina said trying to convince Lisa to leave. Crystal pulled Lisa's arm. The two girls struggled with Lisa. It was as if she couldn't move. Her body stiffened. She could feel the pain in her face. She had to pause to catch her breath. Her friend was wounded beyond the flesh. Lisa walked away reluctantly.

Six young women sat obediently, keeping their focus on the head chair. The young woman maintained her composure as all eyes waited for her directions.

"Madame President, what do you suggest?"

"First we give back the crown. This guy is not one of the top dogs and they have the audacity to cover for him."

"They said she vandalized his trailer."

"So?"

"It will be costly for him to replace everything."

"Soror, you can replace clothes, but you cannot replace your virginity."

"He said they didn't have sex."

"I don't care if they did or didn't. She was beaten badly."

"Madame President, what are you suggesting? Shall we bust out his windshield or slash his tires?"

"Oh no, no, no, no, NO! The fraternity sees no wrong in a no name Neophyte beating up one of our Angels, so I say we pull out from the Lambdas."

"I agree!"

"Me too!"

"I do too!"

"They hardly made any money from the Ball. They are counting on our contribution."

"That is not our problem."

"Soror, whose side are you on?"

"I'm for the sorority, but..."

"We understand your feelings for Derrick but let's not lose our head."

"She was next in line, soror. We cannot afford to have the sorority humiliated."

"I say we team up with the Betas. They can use a little financial help."

"We might have a problem with the Alphas. They seem to have a healthy relationship with the Betas."

"A little competition never hurt anybody and besides, we just want to get our point across."

"Madame President, they might say this is, shall we say, personal?"

"It is."

"Do you think the rest of the sorority will approve?"

"Of course. When has anyone gone against the executive committee. Brooke, arrange for me and Joni to have dinner with Rita and Donna. After that embarrassment with Kenneth, I think we are on one accord."

Chapter 15

Jennifer concentrated on getting to her marketing class. No longer did she smile or make eye contact. Rumors from her getting raped to her stabbing someone hit the campus like war. Students sympathized with her, especially the women. She missed the sorority's rush because she did not want anyone to see the black eye. It took her two weeks to go back to class. Kyle was so excited to see her in class that the instructor called him twice for talking.

Kyle reacted almost violently when he saw Jennifer two days after the incident. He brought her homework. She refused to see anyone but he just walked into the room and became shocked seeing her swollen face and partially destroyed lips. She struggled to see with one eye barely opened and the other shut.

Kyle winced out loud. He pounded his fist in his hand and stormed out of the room, bumping into Lisa, almost knocking her down. He was ready to fight. As Lisa sat and talked to Kyle, tears fell. His emotions made her vow to not let the incident fall through the cracks.

When Jennifer arrived at the top of the stairs, she made eye contact with Lisa. It was the first time since that night they had seen one another. Both felt clumsy.

"I heard you made the Beta's court. Congratulations!" Jennifer said smiling as she looked away.

"I know I'm not going to win, but what the heck," Lisa said.

"You sound like me last year. I think you got a real good chance at the crown," Jennifer said, looking down.

"You sound like me," Lisa said with a smile. The two stood a few seconds in silence. Jennifer looked down the stairway. Lisa watched as Jennifer crawled slowly into the shell she worked so hard to crawl out of.

"Are you going to the Lambdas' Casino Night?" Lisa asked by accident.

"I'm going to the International Students' potluck with Kyle."

Lisa felt stupid. How could she say something so ignorant. The Kappas were boycotting the Casino Night along with the Alphas and most of the Betas weren't participating either.

"Let me get to class. I'll see you around," Jennifer said bashfully.

"I'm sorry, Jennifer. I didn't mean..." Lisa said before Jennifer stopped her.

"Don't worry about it. I hate this place. I hate this school," Jennifer sniffed and ran up the stairs. Lisa watched helplessly as Jennifer attacked the stairs. She wasn't a stuck up bitch. She was a person, trying to gain self-confidence, something they had talked about constantly over two years. She was almost at that point until someone pulled the rug from under her feet and that someone was a person she trusted.

Lisa was very nervous as Vicki and Anne, the two glamour queens of the sorority, assisted her in preparing for the Barons' Ball. Lisa wore one of Vicki's dresses, a black, halter-back dress with a choker collar. The girls tried desperately to pin the slightly too big dress on Lisa.

The buzzer sounded for student "B," Lisa. She hurriedly picked up the purse, gloves and cape she borrowed from Jennifer. Lisa became more nervous when she arrived at the Beta's house. She walked slowly up the stairs, in fear of tripping. Lisa wondered who would be her escort, as she looked around the room. People were already in pairs. She wasn't good at these types of events. She did not have a person like Angel to coach her through the evening. She was relying on gut instincts.

"Hello Miss Arvell. I will be your escort this evening," said an all too familiar voice. Lisa jerked around and stood face to face with a clean shaven Cameron.

Lisa just gawked. She had not heard from him in six months. What should she say? He just appeared out of nowhere. She wanted to hug him, but her pride would not allow it. "Hello stranger, this is definitely a surprise," she said and tugged her dress. She looked off to the side.

"You look very nice," Cameron said. He knew she was angry. How could he tell her that his engineering courses were more important than writing letters?

There he goes again with those damn compliments, Lisa thought. "Thank you," she said.

"I need to say it so let me get it out the way. I'm sorry for not writing. I've been so busy with my studies that I didn't make the time. I'm sorry. Will you forgive me?" he asked, looking at her face for an answer.

"So, how is school?" Lisa asked, turning her head away.

Cameron took his hand and turned her head around. Her eyes told him that she knew he was lying. She was used to disappointments, like him. Any other girl would have cursed him severely for ignoring her, especially around the holidays, but she became silent, like his mother. He wondered if it was fair to come back to Missouri State to see her when he was seeing someone else. It wasn't fair to Lisa or to his new girlfriend for him to pretend as if nothing happened.

"School is tough. I spend most of my time studying," Cameron said.

Lisa looked hard into his eyes. They weren't tired from studying for tough examinations. His eyes looked happy, not from driving over two hundred miles to see her, but they were just happy.

"I see you grew a beard and you're wearing your hair low. It brings out your eyes. You look nice," Lisa added for small talk.

"Thank you," Cameron said with the famous Johnson smile.

A Baron announced that it was time to leave. The couples teamed up in cars. It wasn't as many cars as last year. Lisa and Cameron rode with Maria and Steve, who came back for the event too. Steve and Cameron did most of the talking on the way to the Student Union. They talked about the fraternity and more about the fraternity. Lisa and Maria looked at each other as if to say, *Shut up!*

Soon they arrived at the Student Union. There was a mob of students outside, lined up to see the court and their escorts. Maria got out first, lifting her Gone With The Wind red ball gown with a big bow in the front which Angel designed. An after-five, black, quilted jacket with a large rhinestone button at the top completed Maria's ensemble.

Lisa was next. As soon as the girls saw Cameron, they screamed. He waved at people and shook hands. Tons of cameras flashed in Lisa's face, catching her off guard. She and Cameron posed for pictures. A very familiar sight approached Lisa. It was Jennifer with her hair pulled back in a ponytail, looking very plain. She wore a skirt and a blouse with very little makeup. She and Kyle were standing side by side, looking like nerds. Jennifer smiled at Lisa and took a picture. Jennifer quickly stood behind Kyle, her bodyguard. Cameron shook hands with Kyle and gave Jennifer a kiss on the cheek which caused her to jump.

Students called this year's court The Executive Girls. Every president from all the sororities, except the Alphas and various black organizations were represented. The competition was tough. Some contestants had been awarded outstanding achievement. There were no sophomores represented this time.

Lisa knew her chances of winning were slim, but she decided to make the best of the evening. She began a long conversation with Maria while Cameron was catching up on school news. Lisa was intrigued by Maria. Her analytical and methodical approach to life interested Lisa. According to Maria's mother, everything was an investment, from the food one ate to the men one dated. Maria talked and Lisa listened.

Maria was honey-brown and slim with shoulder length hair. Her eyes were nowhere near innocent. She seemed to be observing people as she talked. When Lisa talked, Maria looked directly into Lisa's eyes until she finished. It didn't bother Lisa because she did the same.

"Has Jennifer talked about that night?" Maria asked as she observed Jennifer sitting happily at the table with her nerdy friends.

"No."

"Aren't you two close?"

"We don't talk like we used to."

"Is it because of the different sororities?"

"We had a big disagreement," Lisa said and played with her food.

Maria was a little surprised. She could not think of anything that would make them separate.

Maria liked Lisa's feisty spirit. They were both alike, a fighter and a survivor. Maria was the one who extended the invitation to Lisa to attend the Kappa's rush, but she chose to pledge Alpha Theta Lambda.

"I hope your falling out was worth it because I never let anything stand in the way of friendship. It's too important. My mother says it's hard finding people you can trust. We all have our good days and bad days. Nobody's perfect. I think Jennifer could really use your friendship now," Maria said.

Lisa took a deep breath and sighed as she watched Cameron talking happily with his fraternity brothers.

"It's good seeing Cameron again. He is so sweet," Maria said smiling.

Sweet my ass, Lisa thought. She knew he had a girlfriend. "If you say so," Lisa sighed.

"I thought you two were a couple? No man would drive from Rolla if he wasn't in love," Maria said with a grin.

"I think he came the distance to see his frat brothers," Lisa said.

"Maybe not. While he's here, enjoy his company," Maria said.

"He ain't got nothing coming here!" Lisa jumped to say.

"I'm not talking about sex. My mother says never let a man know he's gotten the best of you. Play crazy like he does. Life is a game. You can enjoy it if you understand the rules."

"What are the rules?"

"Self, self and more self. How can I benefit? should always be the question." Maria took a drink of water as if it were business as usual. Lisa was amazed. She never took Maria as selfish. She seemed nice, but her thoughts were hardened. Lisa could not think of being selfish and enjoying it. There were many times when she gave, despite the circumstances, especially for the sorority.

"I don't consider myself selfish, Maria."

"What I meant to convey is being a survivor. Whatever you do should benefit you some kind of way. Nothing is free. My mother feels that women give too much and receive too little in return."

Lisa listened to Maria carefully. She was serious about everything she said. Her expression never changed. "Then why are you in a sorority? Didn't you vow public service? That's giving without receiving," Lisa said, challenging Maria's philosophy.

Maria laughed a little. "There are ways of benefiting. You wouldn't believe the amount of contacts you make from being in a sorority. Doing a little public service is nothing compared to the possibilities of meeting people who can help you. I've met more doctors, lawyers and engineers just by being a Kappa. I couldn't have met them if I just walked the campus."

Lisa thought back to Angel's comment about her and Maria being just alike. Lisa didn't know if it was a compliment or an insult. What Maria said did not fit the description of what she believed the president of a sorority would say openly. Lisa respected Maria's honesty. All in all, Maria was smart, Lisa concluded.

The contestants lined up for the court presentation. The atmosphere was filled with excitement. When Lisa's name was announced, a lot of girls screamed. Lisa didn't know if it was for her or Cameron. As she approached the point to curtsey, she saw Jennifer and her fan club standing and clapping. Lisa walked quickly to position herself for the curtsey that stunned the crowd. With body control, she slowly sat in a yoga style position, allowing the upper half of her body to bend forward to the floor, bowing to Monica. The audience gasped.

When Lisa's name was announced for third place, Miss Delta, she was so nervous, she forgot to hug the reigning queen. The president of College Students for Christ took second place, and Maria walked away with the crown.

The court went back to the Beta's house for an afterset. They sat around talking and eating pizza. Lisa left the living room. She wanted to talk to Cameron. He was busy talking to a few of the Forty Thieves. She turned around to go back to the living room when Cameron spotted her and excused himself from the group. He caught up with her. They walked to the foyer and sat on the stairs.

Both stumbled at an attempt to break the ice. At one time, they talked constantly. Now it seemed as if they had nothing to say. Lisa knew she had to say something because Cameron would continue to ignore the problem.

"Who is she?" Lisa finally asked.

The question took Cameron by surprise. He smiled and looked at her as if he had no idea of what she was talking about.

"Is she a girlfriend or someone you want to be your girlfriend?" Lisa asked looking directly in Cameron's face. He had to tell the truth.

"I came to see you," he said quietly.

Anger churned in her stomach. "You used to call long distance on my birthday, Thanksgiving and Christmas. We were just friends then. I didn't hear from you on any of those days last year," Lisa said, clenching her teeth.

"I called on Christmas. Your grandmother said that you were out. I forgot to call back," he said, trying to prolong the inevitable.

"It's not your personality to forget, Cameron. If you really came to see me, we would have talked long before now. You've been talking to your frat brothers all evening," Lisa said, feeling the anger grab her chest.

"I came to see you. I just got carried away with the brothers. I..." Cameron said before Lisa walked in front of him, pointing her finger in his face.

"Don't avoid the question and don't treat me like I'm stupid. If you don't answer, I'm leaving," she said, gripping her bottom lip with her teeth.

"I'm seeing someone at Rolla," he said hesitantly.

"When were you planning on telling me or did you want me to disappear?" she asked, trying not to yell.

Cameron shook his head, avoiding eye contact. "I don't know. I just, I don't know," he said dejected.

Lisa's eyes narrowed as she looked at him with his head hung low. How dare he toss her to the side without saying anything. She felt the anger at her ears. They felt heated. Her head felt light. She wanted to punch him in the face. "What the hell do you mean you don't know?" she asked and looked around cautiously. She was getting louder.

He remained silent, no longer looking for a way out. "Let me make this easy for you, since you don't know. I don't want to see you nor do I want to talk to you anymore. I have given you the perfect excuse to call it quits. Now you can tell your friends I called it off. Let me get up out of this mothafucka. I really don't want to see your sorry ass," Lisa said and stormed to the closet to get her cape.

She found Tim Rylander and asked him to take her home. Before she could get out of the door, Cameron ran to her and told Tim that he was taking her home. "I don't want you to do a mothafuckin' thing for me so get out of my way," she puffed, trying to keep her voice down so that the others wouldn't hear. Cameron jumped back, staring at the angry woman. Not only did it shock him but it hurt him as well. He never thought Lisa would talk to him that way or hate to see the sight of him again. He closed the door behind them slowly.

"Soror President, what should we do? Since the Kappas gave a contribution to the Beta's scholarship fund, I hear they want them to co-sponsor the Sickle Cell Anemia Drive instead of us, and they asked us first."

"There is nothing we can do. I don't appreciate any underhanded tricks, especially when they came to us for help."

"This doesn't sound like Maria. She would never use her feminine wiles to go to war. Maybe we need to rethink the Beta's motives. They seem to jump at the first good thing that comes along."

"Soror, you did say it was rumored. Has any Beta confirmed this rumor?"

"Who cares if they want us or the Kappas. I'm tired of making plans around these fraternities. Forget them!"

"Let's do something that will be beneficial in improving students' lifestyles, not whether a fraternity wants to work with us."

"You have a good point, soror, but we get better participation if we work in conjunction with fraternities."

"We think we get better participation working with fraternities. We need to know how to market our events. Maybe we can do something on rape awareness? It seems to be the hot topic now. If we talk seriously to the white sororities, as well as to the black sororities, we can come out shining. We can use Jennifer's incident to show that we are really serious. Because she is not an Alpha, people will think we are for real."

"The Kappas will have to participate since it's one of their sorors. It's about thirty of them and thirty-five of us. One hundred women at a rape awareness seminar would give us leverage on campus. I doubt if Maria will support a boycott on a rape seminar."

"It seems like you are sold on the idea, Soror President."

"Aren't you?"

"I know I am. If the Betas want to jump ship, I know the men of Gamma Zeta Tau would love to do an event with us. For them to participate in a Rape Awareness Seminar would show their sensitive side or some shit like that. We can help build them just like we did the Lambdas."

"You mean like Gina did. She single-handedly helped build them until the Kappas came to town. Now they're after the Betas."

"Well let them go with the Kappas. You see what happened to the Lambdas. I heard their alumni has to help with the scholarship this year."

"I'm getting tired of sharing everything we earn with these sorry ass fraternities. We do most of the work, so why not keep all the profits?"

"Sorors, let's be mindful of our language. Soror Arvell, since this rape awareness is your idea, plan a short seminar. Make sure it's during the pledge period. With our fourteen Genies and the Kappas fifteen Cherubs, that's an additional thirty people. This is going to be big. We will discuss it at the sorority meeting. Meeting's adjourned."

As the two women looked at the snapshots, they became ill. One tossed them on the table and looked disgusted at the four young women who had been summoned into the room. "Why are we just finding out about this, sorors? Had Cameron not told his brother, we would have never known this had happened to one of our Angels."

"We did not want to bother you. We took the pictures and had them developed immediately, just in case she wanted to press charges."

"It was Miss Peterson's suggestion that we select another Second Vice President. She is having a difficult time dealing with the incident."

"Who is she suggesting?"

"Alexis Michels."

"Miss Peterson was not present at the interviews of the pledge class, nor does she participates in any of the pledge meetings. I must say she did attend the voting of the pledge class."

"Has anyone tried to help her through this crisis?"

"We are all trying. It's been tough on all of us. She refuses to talk to anyone."

"The Alphas are sponsoring a Rape Awareness Seminar next Saturday. We will make sure Miss Peterson is in attendance."

"Why are the Alphas sponsoring a Rape Awareness Seminar when one of our Angels has been raped? Shouldn't it be us who sponsors such an event or at least co-sponsor with the Alphas?"

"They came up with the idea first."

"That's bullshit. Who's participating?"

"Two large white sororities and all the black sororities. We hear that the men of Gamma Zeta Tau are helping too."

"Who pissed off who?"

"Madame President, are there any conflicts with the Alphas?"

"I had a long talk with Rita. There seemed to have been a misunderstanding about the sorority's relationship with the Betas?"

"What relationship with the Betas? We don't have a relationship with the Betas."

"It's a long story. Maybe we should talk about it later."

"Madame President, we have never turned a personal problem into a

Greek war. This incident should have been handled through the court system. Sean should be serving time, not walking around ready to rape another girl. I told you that men stick together on issues like this. Not only has Miss Peterson been humiliated by your error but the sorority has too. Do you understand what I'm saying?"

"Yes, Miss Smith."

"Make sure when Alexis is voted Second Vice President, everyone is aware, especially Miss Michels, that it was Miss Peterson's recommendation. If she gets better, make sure she becomes Dean of Pledges or something."

"Yes, Miss Stevens."

Jennifer got up slowly to answer the knock on the door. Her mouth flew opened when she saw the two women standing in the hall. She screamed with delight. "Hi, Sweetie. I came to see how you were doing," Angel said and gave Jennifer a hug. Jennifer wouldn't let go. She began to cry again. She mumbled words about hating Sean.

Angel looked down the hall to see if anyone was watching. She rushed Jennifer inside quickly. Jennifer sat on the bed and rocked in place. She looked at the two women. Linda would not look at her. Jennifer was embarrassed about being fat again. She had regained all but five pounds of the weight she lost last year. She could not wear any of the clothes Linda had given her. As she rocked, tears flowed.

"I heard there is going to be a Rape Awareness Seminar next Saturday. Are you going?" Angel asked in her usual soft voice. She took her hands and wiped away Jennifer's tears.

"I made sure that girl didn't pledge, Miss Stevens. I had a tough time but she's not a Cherub," Jennifer said, looking for approval. She wanted Linda to say something.

"That's my girl. We don't need any more troublemakers. Did you hear what Angel said, honey?" Linda asked gently, barely looking at Jennifer.

"I don't want to go. I'm fat," Jennifer said stubbornly.

Angel thought back to the time when she won the title Miss Lambda as a sophomore. Her escort took her back to his apartment, thinking she would have sex with him. Before he knew it, she took off running without any money and scantily dressed. Lionel happened to be driving by as she was running. He stopped the car and ran behind her. He finally got her to calm down and took her back to the dorm.

"You are not the first person this has happened to. We accept that it happened and we continue to live," Angel said.

"It happened to you?" Jennifer asked between tears.

"No Sweetie, but it happened to one of your line sisters and it almost happened to another one. I know having your first sexual experience to be a rape has to be horrifying," Angel continued.

Jennifer shook her head. "He didn't rape me. He just stuck his finger in and out," she said in disgust.

"Sweetie, it's still rape. Whether it's a finger or a penis, it is still rape," Angel said firmly.

"He was my boyfriend. I chose to go back to his apartment," Jennifer added.

"Jennifer, rape is any unwanted sexual act. It's called date rape when it is with someone like Sean. Honey, go to the seminar. Do you want me to go with you?" Angel asked, trying not to cry.

Jennifer's attention was on Linda who was looking out the window. Jennifer tried to smile, "I'm going to lose some weight and get back in those clothes."

Linda knew Jennifer was trying to get her attention but she couldn't look at her. She wasn't like Angel. She couldn't touch her. All she could think about was her Queenie in those pictures. Good thing it happened after she graduated. The Lambdas would have paid dearly. "Oh tsk, those clothes are old. When you lose weight, I'll have a slew of new ones to give you," Linda said as a matter of fact.

Jennifer kept thinking about how her first mind told her to go back to the dorm and how she didn't listen. Lisa told her about following her gut feelings, instincts, the signs. The terrible incident would have never happened to Lisa. She was just too smart. Jennifer became angry at herself.

"Are you two going to spend a night?" Jennifer begged.

Angel found it tough to answer. "Linda and I have to go to work tomorrow. I'll come and spend Sunday with you, okay?" Jennifer nodded. "It's not your fault, Jennifer. You didn't deserve any of it."

Hearing those words made Jennifer cry again. She looked horrible. How could she kiss another boy? Her bottom lip would never be the same.

"Now the game is courage. You have to show everyone you can get through this. You must be brave. You can prosecute him, if you want," Linda said. Jennifer shook her head frantically. She never entertained the idea of prosecuting Sean.

"Think about it, okay?" Linda said.

Jennifer felt good hearing Linda's voice. She missed the girl talks they had during the pledge period. "I miss our talks, Miss Stevens," she said.

"So do I, Queenie." Linda looked at Jennifer's distraught face. It was very lonely. Linda quickly looked away. "Well Queenie, I will be back Sunday. I don't know who is doing your hair, but those split ends must go. I hate split ends," Linda said, turning up her nose.

Jennifer stood and walked Linda and Angel out the door. They walked to the lobby. "We'll see you Sunday," Angel said and kissed Jennifer on the cheek. The line of Cherubs rushed pass them. Jennifer stopped and looked back.

"Excuse me ladies," she said loudly. "Are you going to speak?"

The fifteen girls looked back. They were mumbling something among themselves. Some said "Hello Big Sister;" a couple said "Hello Jennifer;" a few said "Hello Miss Peterson"; and some said nothing. Jennifer put her hands on her hips. "My name is Big Sister Angel of Positive Punishment and I'm not the only Kappa standing here."

The girls looked at Angel and Linda as if they were strangers. "Big Sister Angel of Positive Punishment, we are going to be late for our pledge meeting," one of the Cherubs said.

Jennifer blew out air. "Before you go anywhere ladies, you will speak to Miss Smith and Miss Stevens. I want you to apologize for your ignorance."

The Cherubs spoke and apologized to Angel and Linda.

"Another thing, ladies, you will write Miss Smith and Miss Stevens every week to update them on your pledge program. Is that clear?" The girls said, "Yes." Jennifer paced up and down the line complaining about the Cherubs' appearance. The girls looked fearful. Angel and Linda slowly turned their heads to one another, watching the little tyrant at work. Jennifer continued to fuss.

"Miss Smith and Miss Stevens, I must apologize for the sloppiness you have witnessed this evening. I assure you the next time you see them, they will be much better. Isn't that right, ladies?" Jennifer said with her arms folded.

"Yes Big Sister Angel of Positive Punishment," the Cherubs said in unison.

"I'll see you two Sunday along with our sharp Cherubs. You girls better be ready," Jennifer said, looking at them with a frown.

Angel's eyebrow raised. "Uh, thank you, soror," she said.

"Say good-bye to Miss Smith and Miss Stevens," Jennifer commanded. The Cherubs said good-bye. "Let's go!" Jennifer snapped. She and the Cherubs disappeared, leaving Angel and Linda bewildered.

Lisa was busy making sure everything was in place for the seminar. She got a speaker from the Harrisburg police department, the Rape Crisis Hotline and the Women's Self-Help Group in Kansas City. Kyle was busy setting up the microphones on stage. Jonathan Davis, a member of Gamma Zeta Tau fraternity, was talking to Lisa. The two looked as if they were having a very cozy conversation. Kyle left the stage and joined them.

"Hello, I'm Kyle Thomas," he said extending his hand to Jonathan.

"I'm Jonathan Davis, everyone calls me J.D.," he said, shaking Kyle's hand. Lisa looked at Kyle, wondering what was up.

"I'm finished with the microphones, Lisa. What else needs to be done? Maybe J.D. and I can pull forces and finish the rest," Kyle said.

"You've done everything Kyle. We can sit back and wait for the students to arrive," Lisa said with a smile. All three students stood quietly. Lisa wondered what Kyle wanted.

J.D. broke the silence, "I'm going to see if they need help at the door. Lisa, the frat is having a party tonight. You ladies are invited. Nice meeting you, Kyle."

J.D. left Lisa standing, looking awkward. She looked around the auditorium, ignoring Kyle's presence. Everything was in place and the event was going to be a success. The plans for next year were going to be even better. The Alphas were going to be a powerhouse, especially in the way of large scale events. Lisa smiled to herself. "Do you know what time Jennifer is coming?" she asked happily.

"No I don't! Are you seeing other guys?" Kyle asked angrily.

"What?"

"Cameron really liked you and you dumped him."

"Oh really? Cameron has a girlfriend, but her name isn't Lisa Arvell."

"Like I said, Cameron really liked you."

"You need to mind your own damn business. I don't give a damn about what he likes," Lisa snapped.

"You're right, I do need to mind my business, but you really need to clean up your mouth. It cheapens everything about you," Kyle said.

Before Lisa could respond, he walked away. Several Alphas entered the auditorium with the line of Genies. Several white students filed in behind them. Lisa left the auditorium. She caught a few angry looks from the Beta representatives. She decided to speak. "Hello fellas," she said with a smile.

"Hello Lisa. We see that you ladies decided to go with the Gammas on this affair," Tim said slowly.

"The Gammas volunteered to help, they are not co-sponsors. This is all A-T-L," Lisa said proudly.

"I heard there was a little misunderstanding about the Sickle Cell Anemia Drive. I hope it doesn't mean we can't work together," Tim said softly.

"We can use some help now. The audio needs to be checked. There are microphones on stage and I don't know if they are working. Could you check them for me?" Lisa asked innocently. The three young men agreed and walked away.

Lisa saw Maria talking to Joni. She decided to speak. "Hello Maria. Hello Joni," Lisa said pleasantly.

"Hello Lisa. It looks like you are going to have a large turnout," Maria said, unimpressed.

"Yes we are. Is Jennifer coming?" Lisa asked tiptoeing.

"Of course. After all, she is the guest of honor," Maria said with a forced smile.

Lisa cleared her throat. "Our Genies could use some help with the programs," Lisa said, fighting for a way out.

"Candice, could you tell the Cherubs to help the Genies with the programs please?" Maria asked politely.

"Thanks a bunch, Maria. Let me know if we can be of any assistance," Lisa said with a big smile.

Maria smiled back. "Oh, I will," she said. Lisa went inside the auditorium.

"She is going to be unstoppable next year," Joni whispered to Maria.

"I like her much better than Gina," Maria said as she gently rubbed the side of her face.

"I heard the Alphas are positioning themselves to run the Black Greek Council and the Association of Black Collegiates. It seems like it would be a risk to control both organizations. They won't be well liked," Joni said.

"They probably won't run it visibly but they will have a great deal of input. I want to know who is going to be the front person, that's if they're smart. Now I see what Angel meant. Jennifer would have been the perfect president to help balance Lisa's behavior. Angel says that Jennifer is Lisa's alter ego," Maria said while looking at Alexis. Joni looked too.

"What can we expect from her?" Joni asked, watching Alexis laugh and talk with friends.

"Just what you're seeing, socializing. If Lisa smooths her rough edges and classes up her act, she can pull the girls with the strong financial backgrounds. We can't afford that to happen," Maria said looking concerned. But Lisa's actions excited her. Maria wished Lisa was president of the Alphas. They could probably work much closer at achieving the things they both desired.

"Hello Maria. Hi Joni," said a pleasant voice. The young women turned around to see a smiling Jennifer. She had taken the time to put on makeup and curl her hair.

"Hi Sweetie, you look very nice. How are you?" Maria asked.

"I'm fine. I see it is going to be a large turnout," Jennifer said.

"If you don't feel like staying, we understand," Maria said.

"The sorority has committed itself to this event and I need to support it too. I've been a little lax lately, but I'm ready to be a member again," Jennifer said with a smile. "I'm going inside to see if Lisa needs help," she said and left.

"Do you think we can get the sorority to vote her Dean of Pledges?" Joni asked.

"I don't want her as Dean of Pledges. Something tells me she's not as fragile as some people think. I have an excellent idea. I can't wait to talk to Angel. Maybe she will stop her bitching," Maria said and rolled her eyes. The two went inside the auditorium.

Jennifer sat still and listened to a petite, white woman from the Rape Crisis Hotline tell her story about how she was sexually assaulted six years ago at the age of twenty-four. The woman was calm as she described the details of her attack. Jennifer watched the expression on the woman's face. She wasn't crying nor was she pitiful. She told how she triumphed over the most traumatic experience in her life. She married three years later and gave birth to two children.

Next was the black woman from the Women's Self-Help Group. She too was a victim of rape. She wasn't as gentle as the other woman. She was direct and forceful as she discussed how rape was an act of violence and not sex. The sentence stunned Jennifer. She had always thought that men raped women because they wanted sex.

The woman spoke about how women are embarrassed and too frightened to press charges. She went on about how frequently date rape happens on college campuses. Jennifer sat in agreement. The woman discussed the healing process: denial, anger and acceptance. Jennifer realized she had already experienced denial and anger. She was beginning to feel better.

Kyle found Jennifer and sat beside her. She ignored him. She looked to her right and saw Rosalyn wipe her eyes with her head hung low. Kyle looked at Jennifer as she looked around the room. Her eyes were no longer optimistic as he had always described them. She looked as if the world had betrayed her. He wanted to hold her hand and tell her it would be okay, but he was afraid. He could still see where they stitched her lip. There was a dark patch under her right eye that would probably never go away. Despite it all, she was still a gorgeous girl, even if she had gained weight. He liked her the way she was.

The police officer was last to speak. He talked about convicting a rapist and how to protect yourself from an attack. He talked and Jennifer continued to look around the room, identifying the ones who had experienced the terrible ordeal. To her surprise, several girls looked as if something so horrible as being sexually violated had happened to them.

Carl Williams from Gamma Zeta Tau fraternity was on stage announcing the start of a self-defense class for women. He had a black belt in Tai Chi. All the students called him Kung Fu. Jennifer saw Rosalyn get up and leave. Jennifer decided to follow. She had to run to catch up with Rosalyn.

"Are you going to the self-defense class?" Jennifer asked out of breath. Rosalyn didn't respond.

"If you go, I'll go," Jennifer said and pulled Rosalyn by the arm.

"I don't need a self-defense class," Rosalyn said and rushed off. Jennifer looked in grief as Rosalyn broke into a run toward the dorms.

Several Alphas were walking to J.D.'s apartment for the party. They were complaining about the pledge program.

"The Genies don't come to visit me and Donna doesn't make them either. What kind of Dean of Pledges is she?"

"I gave one fifty demerits and she hasn't worked them off. Marsha would have had a fit if we had demerits over a week old."

"I had to threaten one. This is pissing me off. Something has to be done about it."

Lisa was in agreement but her experience with the Genies was different. They visited and worked off demerits. She didn't have the same problems as her other sisters but Alicia was right, something had to be done. They were outside the apartment building.

"I don't hear any music. What's up Lisa?" Alicia asked.

"Let's find out," she answered.

"These niggas are slow. Everybody else got a frat house except them. They got a frat apartment," Evelyn complained.

"It takes time to get a frat house. They're pretty cool. We're so hung up on the Betas and Lambdas that we have overlooked the Gammas," Lisa said.

"Something about them is boring. Calvin looks good but something is missing," Alicia commented.

"If he was running a game, I guess you would like him," Crystal said.

"A man doesn't have to treat me bad for me to like him," Alicia said.

"One group that is giving the Betas a run for their money is Epsilon. Did y'all see their show last Friday night? It was laid out," April said.

"Yeah, but the brothers are ugly, tore down ugly," Evelyn said.

"Did y'all hear about Sean slapping Phyllis a couple of days ago?" Tina snuck in. The girls looked at Tina as if she lied. "Someone saw them fighting in his car. They said he hit her and she hit him back. They said she got him pretty good," Tina said. The girls let out a sigh of relief.

"Phyllis tries to act uppity, but I've seen her fight in junior high. I know she dusted his ass off. That's what Jennifer should have done. I heard he beat her up bad. You know how she is anyway, always flipping that damn hair." All the girls became quiet as Evelyn talked about Jennifer.

"She's cool like Rochelle. She's just not wild. You're just jealous because she has that damn hair to flip. I'm getting this curl taken out of my hair so I can flip my hair too," Alicia joked.

"Did y'all hear Kung Fu on stage talking about starting a self-defense class for women? That ain't nothing but a way for him to get dates with his Superfly hairdo. I wonder if he's going to be here tonight," Evelyn said.

"Let's go in so we can leave early if it's dead. I'd rather watch 'Saturday Night Live' anyway," Alicia said and the group followed behind.

The girls went inside the building and up the stairs. They could hear music but it was low. They frowned. Alicia knocked on the door. J.D. opened it with a big smile. He invited them in.

"Alright, we got some women to party with," one Gamma yelled.

"What do you have to drink?" Alicia asked unconcerned, still checking out the scene.

"We got beer, wine and soda in the kitchen," J.D. answered.

"Anything to munch on?" Evelyn asked. J.D. nodded and pointed to the kitchen. The Alphas were getting angry looks from some members of the Upsilon sorority. Lisa decided to speak.

"Y'all got some Curtis Blow? Put him on so we can party!" Evelyn yelled.

One of the Gammas smiled and quickly changed the music. Evelyn yelled to pump up the volume and he did. J.D. looked a little nervous because the music was too loud. He didn't know how to keep from becoming embarrassed because he could not play loud music in his apartment. He eased his way to the stereo and turned it down a little. He went back again and turned down the volume.

Lisa saw one of the Gammas turn his back and spray something into his mouth. One sniffed under his arms. The Alphas were pulling men onto the floor to dance. They were having a good time. Lisa watched the expressions on the faces of the Upsilons turn sour.

The music was slow. J.D. pulled Lisa onto the floor to do the Kansas City Two-Step. It had been a long time since she Two-Stepped with anyone. J.D. was one of the best in school. He was a smooth dancer. He turned her with ease. He would spin and then she would spin. She did things she never did before. She thought about how Cameron would only slow dance and he couldn't do that very well.

The room got quiet when they heard a loud crash. Apparently, Calvin was talking to Alicia near the bathroom. When he became comfortable and leaned on the door, he fell inside while Crystal was using the bathroom.

After everyone recuperated from Calvin's incident, they sat on the floor to play cards and Backgammon. Evelyn tried to get Alicia to leave but she teamed up with Lisa to play Spades against J.D. and Calvin. Evelyn became angry and left with some of the Upsilons.

The group talked and played games until 3:00 a.m. Lisa made a move to leave. All the others followed. The young men walked the girls to their dorms. Everyone was in a good mood. The girls giggled as they walked pass the night hostess, flashing identification cards. She gave them angry looks. They made mean comments out loud.

They all piled in Lisa's and Crystal's room. Tina took her place at the foot of Lisa's bed. Alicia jumped on Crystal's bed. Crystal complained so Alicia got up and made a pallet on the floor.

"Looks like Cameron is old news," Alicia said giggling.

"History," Lisa said, putting on a night shirt.

"I had a good time," Alicia said, trying to get comfortable on the floor.

"So Calvin isn't so bad after all," Lisa said, looking down at Alicia.

"I told you so. He comes from a nice home and has a sweet disposition," Crystal added.

"Girl, shut up. I'm not trying to marry anybody. It just felt good not hearing somebody trying to run a game or trying to get some action."

"I know what you mean. The Betas and Lambdas are always trying to get somebody in bed," Crystal commented, pulling the covers to her chest.

Alicia sat up to look at Crystal. "Who tried to get you in bed?" Alicia asked.

Crystal was a little bothered by Alicia's implication. "You would be surprised," Crystal answered.

Alicia's mouth twitched and her nose turned up. She looked at Lisa who tried to keep from laughing. "So Lees, are you going to give the Fancy Dancer a try?" Alicia asked.

Lisa hunched her shoulders. "What about you and the Tidy Bowl Man?"

Alicia laughed. "That was funny, wasn't it?"

Maria picked up a newspaper clipping of the Alphas at the Thanksgiving dinner for the elderly. There was a picture of Alicia smiling as she mixed something in a bowl while looking at a fussy old woman. There was a picture of Rita putting a plate in front of an old man who had obviously forgotten his dentures. Regardless of the humor Maria saw in the pictures, the Alphas received a lot of coverage on their Adopt a Grandparent for Thanksgiving project. Maria put the article to the side.

She looked at the small article written about the Kappas giving a Christmas party for a nursery school. The Alphas went to the same nursery school and performed Christmas carol skits. The article described the jubilant reaction from the children on the skit "The Twelve Days of Christmas." And then there was the big article on the Rape Awareness Seminar. The clipping stressed the unity among white and black students, coming together in an effort to combat a colorless crime. There was a picture of Lisa shaking hands with the president of one of the white sororities.

A knock on the door made Maria put the newspaper clippings down. It was time to greet her guest. Lisa was surprised to see Maria's very casual appearance. She was wearing oversized sweat pants and shirt. Lisa took the time to iron her blouse and slacks.

Lisa looked around the room. One side was frilly and the other was posters and books. The dresser was covered with makeup. Lisa saw the unmade bed and decided to stand. Maria laughed. "I forgot how messy Joni is, I guess I'm used to it. Have a seat," Maria said and pulled a chair next to her bed. She sat on the bed Indian style.

"Thanks for coming. I thought we could have a little talk. I see the Rape Awareness Seminar was a success," Maria said.

"We would like to thank the Kappas for participating. It helped made it a success," Lisa said.

"It wasn't the Kappas, it was Jennifer's incident that made it a success. You girls used her story to sell a successful event. I don't have a problem with it as long as she reaps some of the rewards," Maria said smiling.

"What do you mean?" Lisa asked carefully.

"We know the Alphas are pushing to control the Black Greek Council and ABC next year. Too much popularity can make one unpopular. I don't know if you want to take the risk," Maria said casually. She had her plan in order.

"We also realize these fraternities are mainly working with us so they can skate on the profits. We would like to work with you ladies on one event, to show unity, of course." Maria paused and looked Lisa in the eyes. "We would like for one of our members to become President of ABC. How does that sound?" Maria asked coolly.

Lisa was quiet. It was a lot to digest. The Alphas had their own plan. They were ready to strike. No other sorority had taken the effort to become active in the political organizations on campus. Maria was doing the same thing she accused the fraternities of orchestrating. Lisa knew a Kappa president of the Association of Black Collegiates meant high visibility.

"You are asking *us* to help one of your members to become president of ABC?" Lisa asked, waiting impatiently for Maria to respond.

"You did say let you know if the Alphas could assist us in any way. I took you as a woman of your word," Maria said with a devious smile. Lisa felt cornered. The sorority would die if she cut the deal that Maria was suggesting.

"Who are you suggesting?"

"Miss Peterson has gotten better from the unfortunate incident and since she has become the topic of discussion these days, I'm sure the women of Alpha Theta Lambda Sorority will see to it that she excels as president," Maria said, playing to win.

"What do we get out of it?"

"What do the Alphas get out of it? The Black Greek Council! You can have lots of pictures in the newspaper. It would mean more Alpha Theta Lambda."

"So what do we get out of it?"

"Well, *you* get a chance at restoration. You see, when Gina had her little run in with Soror Jessica, we didn't do a seminar on sisterhood. We wouldn't think about embarrassing a member of another sorority to get our picture in the papers. If you ladies had asked us to co-sponsor, it would have been at least decent. You took our soror, your friend, and exploited a very personal and traumatic experience."

Lisa listened intensely. She couldn't tell if Maria was serious about the Alphas exploiting Jennifer to gain attention. "Do we have an agreement?" Maria asked.

Lisa had to think quickly. She knew Maria was going to win, but the victory was going to be shared. "I think Jennifer is an excellent choice for president of ABC. Since Sean and Titus will be her opposition, she will probably win with flying colors."

"Do we have an agreement?"

"It sounds great, a Kappa President and an Alpha Vice President. It will show unity, of course," Lisa said, refusing to let Maria win easily. "We've noticed the turnout for ABC's elections has always been poor. With both sororities having a membership at close to fifty a piece, we can easily control the voting. I'm counting on the pledgees as well. Make sure the Kappas are financially active in two weeks. We are. I suggest you all don't rush to sign up. You don't want anyone to become suspicious," Lisa said.

The Alphas had done their homework and Lisa had to let Maria understand her competition. The Alphas were planning to gain power. No longer did they support the soft side of sorority life.

Maria could see that Lisa was shrewd. Angel was right again. "Are you speaking on behalf of the sorority?" Maria asked, testing Lisa's ego.

"I didn't think you wanted this to be a sorority issue. Rita would be discussing this with you." Lisa stood up to leave. "I guess our little talk is over."

Maria did not want Lisa to leave angry. She really liked her. After their little discussion, she became more intrigued with the person Angel told her to do battle with. "All I'm asking for is restoration," Maria said softly.

"You got it," Lisa responded, looking at Maria with a grin.

"She was supposed to become President next year. You know how the Kappas are," Maria said with sincerity. "Do you think Rita will go for this?" Maria asked.

"Can we say things just happened to turn out this way?"

"Can I offer a little small advice?" Maria asked pleasantly.

"Sure," Lisa responded.

"You have a lot of power in your head so use it wisely. Never get mad, get even because some things aren't worth it."

Chapter 16

Lisa sat quietly observing the Alphas prepare for the Ceremony of Wisdom. It was obvious that there was a division in the sorority. The Neophytes unintentionally separated themselves from the Prophytes. The Alphas who had graduated were talking amongst themselves. Carla, Gina and Jessica were talking together. They seemed to be having a good time. Gina looked very relaxed and extremely happy. She and Carlos had begun dating after graduation. Jessica was relaxed too. She was a probation officer with the State of Missouri. The incident with Kenneth was behind the two women. They socialized as if nothing had happened.

The sorority had become concerned about Lisa's very close relationship with Maria. Some Alphas accused Lisa of selling out the sorority because of the deal she made with Maria. Others questioned Maria's sexuality and hoped Lisa wouldn't get the same reputation. Lisa knew that with Jennifer being a strong contender for president of the Association of Black Collegiates, the Alphas wouldn't have a problem with anything they wanted to do. Jennifer trusted Lisa and that was the reason she agreed, but the Alphas were having a difficult time accepting the arrangement. The problems were mainly with the older sorors because the Neophytes trusted Lisa. Some believed a little jealousy was brewing with Rita.

Carla walked to the kitchen. Lisa rushed to her before someone interrupted.

"Congratulations Carla," Lisa said happily.

"Thanks, Lisa. I've got so much to do. I never imagined planning a wedding could be such hard work," Carla said with a bit of exhaustion.

"I hear Gina might marry Carlos," Lisa said.

"I wouldn't be surprised if she did. He had always liked her. I think she secretly liked him too," Carla said in a whisper.

"It must be nice," Lisa said to give a hint of her problem.

"What happened to the cute little Beta that was so daring? Are you still seeing him?" Carla asked. Lisa shook her head and looked off. "You'll find someone else. At least girls today have more options," Carla said, trying to be consoling.

"How long does it take to get over someone?" Lisa asked.

"The key is to never sit around moping. There are a lot of nice boys on campus who would love to date you. You need to give some of them a chance. They won't be the same as the cute Beta, but they will be special in other ways," Carla said in her counselor's voice. She paused, "I hear there is a little tension in the sorority. What's going on?" she asked.

"Everybody is trippin'. Well not everybody, but Rita and some of the others are trippin'," Lisa said.

"Lisa, it's time that you stop using slang. It's acceptable when you're a teenager. How are you going to communicate when you are looking for a job?" Carla said gently.

Lisa let out a deep breath. "People are accusing me of selling out the sorority. I'm just trying to move us to bigger and better things. Everybody wants to sit around and worry about whether or not the Betas like us or if the Lambdas want to do functions with us. I want us to stand alone."

"Um hum," Carla said. She heard how Lisa gained a lot of power and control of the organization. She had chaired several committees and got a lot of recognition for the sorority. It didn't set well with the Prophytes.

"I wanted the sorority to do all sorts of things when I was president but the sisters were afraid to let go of the security blanket. We will bestow upon you the power of Alpha Wisdom. What you feel in the ceremony will determine how you will perform your responsibilities. Do what needs to be done to bring Alpha to the forefront. Those who want the sorority to be the best will work with you and those who don't care won't be around. Just be ready when they come starting trouble," Carla concluded.

Lisa looked lonely. Carla put her arm around Lisa's shoulders.

"You need to get ready for the ceremony," Carla said and walked Lisa out of the kitchen.

The auditorium was filled with students, waiting for the speeches to begin. It was mostly Greek members in attendance. Lisa tried making eye contact with Maria, who was sitting with a select few. They were a little nervous because Jennifer hardly got a word in at the debate. The two boys strategically ignored and omitted her from voicing an opinion. Sean emphasized his strengths and academic achievements. Titus stressed the division among black students created by the Greek organizations.

Some students, mainly Kappas and Alphas, were angry at the male moderator, who allowed it to happen. It was the first time a female student was a serious contender for the president.

Lisa rehearsed Jennifer all week long on the speech. It was important because several Alphas weren't convinced after the debate. Although there were problems in the sorority, the older Alphas were still supportive of the sisterhood because Iris, Lisa's and Rita's pledge daughter, was running on the same ticket with Jennifer. The Alphas were primarily forced to vote for Jennifer if their soror was going to be a candidate for president next year.

There was no doubt that Jennifer would win but Lisa and Maria wanted the Alphas to vote for her because she would do a good job, not out of obligation. Lisa had it all planned. If Jennifer won with Iris as her Vice

President, the Alphas would be on an even keel in popularity. Iris would be voted president of the sorority and president of ABC the next year. It was an excellent long-term plan, therefore, Jennifer's presidency was nothing to fear. Maria knew it too but it was the only way the Alphas would support Jennifer. Maria hoped that Alexis would allow Candice and Jennifer to negotiate with the Alphas. It was the only way the sorority would keep from suffering further loss.

Sean began his speech. He tried a different approach. He skewed off the achievement route and bashed his opponents by using words such as emotional, weak and timid, referring to Jennifer. He used words like, poor planner, lack of vision, and inability to communicate well to describe Titus, last year's president. Titus' reputation for not being articulate was exploited heavily in Sean's speech.

It was Jennifer's turn. Lisa knew Jennifer was ready because she rehearsed the speech over and over with confidence. Lisa searched the room to see how the audience responded as Jennifer came to the microphone. They were at attention. The gentle voice, which was quiet for so long, spoke:

"I want to welcome my brothers and sisters to this very important program. Tonight, you are going to witness the famous Divide and Conquer routine, mainly by individuals who will do anything to get a vote. I hope that I won't get too emotional as I inform you of your hidden strengths to get things happening for us on campus.

"This microphone is a very useful tool. It helps project my voice to get my message across. Alone, I cannot be half as effective and that is my message: 'A united black student body.' As one, we are weak, but as many, we can get things accomplished.

"I was never so insulted to hear my fellow opponents bash each other just to get a title but I tell you, we can't get anything done with a leadership that embraces hate.

"One talked about being strong and unemotional. It takes a strong person to apologize for causing his sister pain and embarrassment. And we can't afford an 'unemotional' machine who cares nothing about anyone but himself.

"One talked of how much he disliked the black Greeks on campus. Remember brothers and sisters, we are one, all for one and one for all. How you choose to spend the rest of your time at school is your business. If you want to join the Klan, it's all right with me, just as long as you stay out of the way of those in motion trying to do something positive.

"I went to a Rape Awareness Seminar which was sponsored by the women of Alpha Theta Lambda Sorority. I saw Kappas assisting with the programs, Betas helping with the audio, Gammas performing as ushers and Upsilons working on the committee. Let's not talk about the support we got from the white sororities. It was a successful event because we pulled forces.

"The white students got REO Speedwagon to perform this year. I say we can get Earth, Wind & Fire. The white students got a poet that I've never heard of, and a white dance company that no one had ever seen before. If

we work together, we can get the school to pay for Maya Angelou or Alvin Ailey to entertain us. We can't do it if we continue to support separation. Too long we, as black students, have sat apathetically.

"Something horrible happened to me this winter but you didn't hear me bad mouthing my black brother who caused the pain. I embraced him and prayed that he would get better. If I can turn the other cheek, I'm certain that you as intelligent black students can rid yourselves of differences. I'm not asking for you to vote for me. I'm asking for you to vote for unity. I say united we stand, divided we fall and I'm not lying down for anybody."

Jennifer walked away from the microphone. The students clapping sounded like thunder. Lisa sat very still. It wasn't the speech they had rehearsed. They discussed a united front theme, but Jennifer came out fighting. The entire speech didn't sound like Jennifer. Lisa let the part on the rape incident sift through her brain. Jennifer had to have known it would make many students angry. Lisa did not expect Jennifer to use that weapon. The issue that Titus supported separation wasn't discussed either. They agreed there would be no bashing, only uplifting her as the perfect candidate.

Jennifer sounded sincere and honest in her delivery. Her voice was gentle and her body language was excellent as she looked at Sean and Titus while talking about them. She extended her hand gently to the two young men as she spoke of their character, forcing Sean to see the injury and the spirit he tried to destroy. Lisa believed there would be no mercy voting. She saw a side of Jennifer she never knew existed. It was revenge.

Titus walked to the microphone slowly. The audience was quiet. Lisa and Maria made eye contact. Titus had to be embarrassed about how Jennifer exposed him on bashing the black Greeks. Seventy-seven percent of the voting population was Greek and he was unaware. He was washed up.

Kyle promised Jennifer and Lisa that he would let them practice driving his car so they could get their driver's licenses. The two had practiced driving on the Wal-Mart lot when it was empty but now it was time to hit the streets. Kyle realized earlier it would be one of the biggest challenges he would face. Jennifer was tense and gripped the steering wheel tightly. She drove very slow. Lisa, on the other hand, drove fast, hardly paying attention to the road and talking constantly.

Jennifer was first. She crept the car onto the streets in the early Sunday morning traffic. She drove 20 mph the entire time, braking constantly. She slowed down to the point of inching the car to the stop signs. Kyle encouraged her to drive the speed limit, 35 mph. She got the car up to the speed limit and slammed on the brakes causing the car behind them to screech to a stop.

"What's the matter?" Kyle asked loudly. Jennifer narrowed her eyes and let out a deep breath.

"There was a squirrel trying to get across the street," Jennifer said with tensed lips.

"You are going to wreck my car trying to keep from hitting a squirrel? It knows how to get out the way. The car in the back almost hit us," Kyle said trying to remain under control.

"Well, he shouldn't have been riding my tail," Jennifer said angrily. Kyle shook his head.

Jennifer slowly brought the car back to the lot. It was Lisa's turn. The girls laughed and talked while they changed places. Lisa whispered compliments to Jennifer on her driving, telling her she did a good job despite what Kyle said.

Lisa yanked the gears into drive and sped off, not watching for the oncoming traffic. Kyle yelled for her to slow down. As she drove she talked until Jennifer told her the rumor about Rosalyn being pregnant. Lisa took her hands off the steering wheel to turn around. Kyle's heart almost dropped in his pants. He grabbed the steering wheel and pulled the car over and got out. He paced back and forth, leaving the girls in the car. He got back and turned to Lisa.

"*Don't ever let go of the steering wheel again!*" he shouted. "And another thing, *shut up!*" he yelled.

Lisa looked at the outraged person and said, "I'm sorry." She drove the car back to the lot. Kyle made them get out. He pounded them with criticism He had them practice parallel parking on the street behind Wal-Mart. Jennifer was two feet away from the curb and Lisa drove up on the curb. Kyle made them practice until they became tired.

A week later, he took them to the Department of Motor Vehicles to get their licenses. Jennifer passed with an eighty-five and Lisa passed with an eighty. The two beamed taking their pictures. When it was over, Jennifer kissed Kyle on the cheek, which caused him to blush. When Lisa asked to drive back to the dorm, the excitement from Jennifer's kiss quickly went away.

It was graduation day for the Prophytes. Lisa was hoping to talk to Maria after the ceremony. She wanted badly to exchange telephone numbers and addresses. She stood off to the side and watched the graduates disperse with their families. She was able to talk to some of the Alphas who were still friendly with her. Rita primarily cut ties with her, only showing public displays of sisterhood to keep down rumors. Some of the Alpha seniors said they refused to come back to next year's Ceremony of Wisdom. Lisa's spirits were low again.

Lisa saw Jennifer talking to Maria and an older woman in the hall. Lisa decided to approach the group. The older woman was medium height and a little stout with a very short hair cut. When Maria saw Lisa, her face lit up and so did Jennifer's.

"Hello Lisa. I want you to meet my mother. Momma, this is Lisa Arvell," Maria said with pride.

The woman looked at Lisa with the biggest surprise. All of the features were a match. The almond-shaped, hazel eyes and the beauty mark over the upper lip. The small nose and the petite frame were a match too. She even had the dark brown hair, the woman said to herself.

"Hello Lisa. How are you?" the woman said in a sultry voice, extending her hand.

Lisa smiled back at the genuine welcome and shook the woman's hand. It was firm. "I'm fine, Mrs. Jefferson. Nice to meet you," Lisa said. It wasn't like last year when people frowned upon her presence.

"Excuse me, but who is your mother?" the woman asked.

The smile slowly left Lisa's face. Everyone wanted to know who was her mother. Lisa wanted to tell the woman it was none of her business, but she was very pleasant.

"Debra Arvell," Lisa said slowly.

The woman's face lit up. It was like she had found her long lost daughter. "Your mother and I go way back to Lincoln University. She was my pledge daughter."

Lisa looked surprised. Finally a link to the past. "I didn't know my mother was an Alpha," Lisa said hungrily.

"No, she is a Kappa. How is your mother? I heard she is doing quite well," the woman said. Lisa was shocked. First, her mother was a Kappa and now this woman claims she heard her mother was doing well.

"My mother's dead," Lisa said solemnly. The woman gasped. She shook her head in confusion.

"I'm sorry to hear that. I can't believe Debra is dead. What did she die of?"

"I don't know," Lisa said honestly. It was at this point she could no longer accept her mother's death the way it was explained.

"Your mother was one of the smartest people I knew. It was her idea to start the chapter of Phi Kappa Psi at Missouri State. She was quite crafty and ahead of her time."

Lisa wanted to ask the question that haunted her so long. Who was her father? She decided not to embarrass herself. The woman probably wouldn't know. "I met some other people last year who knew my mother too. There was a Barbara Stevens, Marilyn Smith, Bill Smith and Charles Johnson," Lisa said, fishing for a response.

The woman's eyebrows raised. She looked at Maria. "Is there a Kappa by the last name of Johnson, Catherine's daughter? Is Marilyn Smith's daughter a Kappa too?" the woman inquired, looking confused.

Maria hunched her shoulders. "Melanie Smith is that Catherine woman's daughter. I don't know who is Marilyn Smith's daughter," Maria said.

"That's Gina's mother. Charles Johnson is Lionel's father. He doesn't have a daughter," Lisa said, relying hard on memory.

"I thought Charles had a daughter, too. Oh well, I'm wrong again. It has been a long time since I've talked to anyone from Lincoln University. Did you pledge?" the woman asked.

"No ma'am. I am the president of Alpha Theta Lambda," Lisa said proudly.

"I know your mother would be proud to hear that. If you have an ounce of ambition like her, I know you will do well. Maybe I will get a another chance to see you again," the woman said.

"I would love it," Lisa said quickly.

The woman pulled out a gold Cross pen and a small note pad. She wrote her telephone number down and handed the valuable piece of paper to Lisa. Maria and her mother left.

Pride entered Lisa's heart because someone admired her mother and that someone was the mother of one of the people she admired. Lisa forgot about Jennifer. She walked away smiling.

"Where are you going?"

"I'm sorry Jenny, I forgot you were here," Lisa said happily.

"Jenny? Where did that come from?" Jennifer asked. Both girls laughed. "Kyle said he is going to take us home after final exams. He is staying a week with Malcolm."

"Do you think he will let us drive?" Lisa asked. The two looked at each other and burst into laughter.

"Your mother sounds like a super bad momma. How come you never told me?"

"I didn't know."

Jennifer was driving very carefully on Highway 70 East. Kyle was in the front seat, pressing his foot to the floor like an accelerator, hoping Jennifer would drive at least 60 mph. She was more relaxed as she drove on the highway. Lisa sat in the back seat remembering a conversation:

"Boys don't like smart girls so you are going to have to play it cool. Women are smart by nature. Remember my little diamond, while men are sleeping, women are thinking." The woman bent over and kissed the child goodnight.

"Momma, are you going to kiss Angel?"

The woman stared at the other child who always smiled and hardly said anything. The woman forced herself to kiss the little girl on the forehead. She was an angel, the woman thought. She had no reason to hate her.

They were in Columbia, Missouri, when Kyle asked Jennifer to pull into a gas station. He filled up the tank and handed the keys to Lisa. The girls tried paying for the gas but Kyle wouldn't take the money. Lisa pulled off and onto the highway. She sped around slow moving cars and jumped in front quickly. Kyle had his foot pressed to the floor as if brakes were underneath. Lisa drove 70 to 80 mph, ducking and dodging cars. They were in Wentzeville, Missouri, in record time. Kyle had Lisa drive to a gas station, claiming he had to use the restroom. After Kyle emerged, he asked Lisa for the keys.

He drove in the city of St. Louis, trying to find Lisa's house. He pulled up to an old, well-kept, brick house that had a new blue Ford Escort in the driveway. Lisa looked at the car, wondering who was visiting. Kyle removed Lisa's brown suitcase, bookbag and a small box from the trunk of his Impala. Jennifer got out of the car and walked toward the steps. Lisa told them to leave, convincing them she didn't need any help. Jennifer thought she would get a chance to finally see the grandmother that Lisa talked about for three years but was denied the opportunity again.

Once the Impala left, Lisa opened the door. Miss Mattie stood strong, holding out a set of car keys. Lisa looked at them as if they were taboo.

"For me?" she asked.

The woman nodded with a smile.

"Who gave it to me?"

"The Angels."

Lisa nodded and took off to her room.

"Are you ashamed to bring your friends in?" Miss Mattie asked softly.

Yes, Lisa thought, but to tell it to the old woman would break her heart. Talks about spirits and angels were a little too deep for her friends. When she was growing up, kids always thought she was weird. She did not want anyone else to think the same. She was the sorority's president and she could not afford anything to tarnish her future. Miss Mattie knew how she felt. Miss Mattie knew everything.

"No ma'am. I'm not ashamed. I'll bring my friends to visit. It's just not time," Lisa decided.

The old woman nodded in agreement. The young woman used her own words against her. But it was true. It wasn't time. Until the young woman put aside the shame and pain, she would receive the answers from the angels.

Chapter 17
March 1982

It was their senior year. Jennifer sat impatiently waiting on Alexis. Since the combination of Iris and Jennifer as the leadership team of the Association of Black Collegiates, relations between the two sororities had been strained. Iris was very aggressive and overpowered Jennifer in many of the meetings. Because Jennifer didn't want any open conflict, she allowed Iris to get away with most of her activities. But something was very wrong. Iris was using the Association to boost the membership of Alpha Theta Lambda. It was causing other black Greeks to become concerned because the Association was the only neutral territory. The Alphas had already taken large strides in the Black Greek Council with Crystal as President/Chairman.

Jennifer wanted Iris to resign. Jennifer also wanted to approach Lisa concerning Iris. Lisa was so powerful in the Alphas and had so many tight relationships in the Black Greek Council, Jennifer thought to complain would put the Kappas in a bad position.

Members of the Upsilon sorority were supporting Jennifer, but it wasn't enough. The Sigmas were trying to build a name for themselves, therefore, they supported no one. Since the Alphas gave the first all Greek Marchdown in the history of the school and had participation from Greek organizations throughout the Midwest, they had become a powerhouse. They donated ten percent of the profits to help fund projects of the Association and the Black Greek Council.

Jennifer looked at the clock. It was ten minutes after seven. Alexis was never on time. Candice, the Dean of Pledges, was accompanying Alexis to the meeting. Both Jennifer and Candice maintained sorority business. It was known that without those two, the Kappas would be in a heap of trouble. Alexis had the sociable, friendly personality that got along well with people, whereas Candice was very quiet and only socialized when it was necessary. She maintained the attitude from the old regime. She only hung around her sorority sisters.

Jennifer finally heard the knock that she had been waiting for. Alexis came in smiling with Candice looking slightly irritated, walking behind her. "Hi Sweetie, I'm sorry I'm late. I had so many things to do before I left…"

Jennifer interrupted Alexis, "Alexis, I am going to ask Iris to resign and recommend Tarin from Upsilon to take her place."

Alexis gasped. She knew there was conflict between Jennifer and Iris but she thought with Lisa being Jennifer's friend, it would smooth out before it became war. "Can you work it out with Iris? We can't afford to make enemies with the Alphas," Alexis said, almost to the point of fainting.

"I don't want to work it out. She has embarrassed me for the last time. If Lisa wants to support someone like Iris, then we don't need to work in conjunction with them for any event. I'm tired of hearing about how powerful the Alphas are and so is everyone else," Jennifer said as she walked back and forth in the room.

"Who has to vote her out? Or can you do it yourself?" Candice asked.

"It has to be approved by the executive committee," Jennifer responded.

"Isn't Lisa on the executive committee?" Candice continued.

"Yes, but I don't care. I'm just letting you two know what my plans are in case there is retaliation," Jennifer said and sat down. She had become forceful since reigning over ABC but Iris was more forceful.

"I don't think Lisa will allow the organization to become involved. It doesn't seem like her personality to take sorority business to the level of the Association," Candice said softly.

To Jennifer, Lisa seemed to side with Iris at the executive council meetings and not notice any of Iris' behavior. They were both alike and they seemed to get along well. Jennifer had enough of Iris' outspoken, overbearing behavior. She had decided that if she were going to continue as president, she had to do something about Iris.

"We are expecting Ruby Dee and Ossie Davis in two weeks and I don't want Iris to turn it into an Alpha affair," Jennifer said conclusively.

"Let me talk to Lisa and see what can be done before you jump to conclusions. Maybe she can tone Iris down," Alexis said nervously.

"Do what you want, Lex, my mind is made up. I just want the sorority to support my decision," Jennifer said and crossed her arms.

"We will, Jennifer," Candice said as if to give the final word. Alexis was angry. She could not afford the sorority to be in conflict. Some of the girls that were going to pledge Kappa were on line for Alpha.

Alexis smiled as usual. "Of course we will support you. I will still talk to Lisa," she said.

Alexis and Candice hugged Jennifer, who continued to jump every time someone touched her, but they understood. Jennifer chuckled a little. If Alexis talked to Lisa, the conversation would be ten minutes long because Lisa would leave before she waited on Alexis to arrive late.

"You need to put her in check, Lisa. She's causing problems and the sorority can't afford to have her creating a conflict."

"She's testing you in meetings. She's out of control. This can be dangerous."

"I don't care if she is expected to succeed you. This is one person we can afford to step outside the vows."

"If Jennifer can get the executive committee to vote her out, then the sorority is going to look bad. We need for her to resign from both positions."

"I know you like her, Lisa, but the Kappas are gaining territory with the fraternities by playing victims. We need to get off our high horse and get real like the older sorors were."

"Yeah Lisa, pretty soon, no one will like us. People are jealous of our success, even if we did work hard for it. We need to rethink our aggressive position."

After hearing the last one speak, Lisa made up her mind. She had to figure out how she was going to pull it off without causing more problems. She looked at the four young women in the Chapter room. They were serious and supporting whatever she decided. Iris had gone beyond embarrassing Jennifer to the point where it silently angered Lisa. Some of the other Neophytes had become too aggressive as well. A giant monster was created. Lisa had to terminate the creature.

It was true. Iris was testing her, trying to neutralize her power. Lisa wondered if Rita felt the same way. Although she never tried overtalking Rita in meetings or openly challenged her decisions, she still wondered. Sorors gravitated towards Lisa because she could persuade them that her ideas were better by showing how everyone could benefit. Lisa smiled a little. "I'll see everyone at the ABC meeting next Thursday. Don't worry, everything is going to be okay," Lisa said reassuringly. The young women looked unsure.

As Jennifer rushed to the Student Union, she saw Kyle leaving Tilly Hall. He rushed to her. He was in a good mood. She knew he had been seeing a girl at Tilly. His last girlfriend, so he called her, didn't know that he liked her. He had taken her out to eat several times. In his mind, she was his girlfriend but she never responded in kind. He was hurt when she decided to stop going out with him because she did not want to take advantage of him.

"Hey Jen, what's up?" he asked happily.

"What are you doing at Tilly?" Jennifer asked without looking at him.

"I stopped by to visit Vanessa, but she hasn't made it back. Where are you going?" he asked.

"I have a meeting with the executive committee. We have to take care of some serious business," she said.

"What can be so serious with a bunch of idiots?" he asked.

Jennifer stopped quickly in her tracks and looked at Kyle hard. "Everyone is an idiot to you. Where do you get off calling someone an idiot, anyway?" she snapped.

Kyle stepped back. He knew comments like those made her irritated but she was beyond irritated. At these times, he remained silent until she calmed down. She took off walking again. He walked in silence beside her.

They finally made it to the Student Union. Jennifer rushed through the doors and saw Kyle's so-called girlfriend, Vanessa, grinning in the face of a Lambda. Jennifer looked at Kyle who tried to walk away.

"You need a nice girl, Kyle. You need someone who will like you for who you are," Jennifer said angrily and walked away, leaving Kyle bearing the disappointment of another mistake.

Jennifer rushed upstairs to the meeting. She was almost a minute late but she made it on time. When she walked in, Lisa was the only one there. Jennifer felt awkward. She put her note pad down and took a seat opposite and far away. The two quickly spoke. Jennifer fumbled in her purse, searching for an important imaginary item.

Lisa sat poised in a red skirt with legs crossed, showing off long, shapely legs. Since she was voted "sexiest legs" during last year's Greek Week, she wore skirts often. Lisa just looked at Jennifer, wondering what to say. The two had not talked in awhile. It was like making an appointment to see Lisa. She had made friends with other girls from different organizations.

Jennifer let out a deep sigh. "I hope everyone doesn't come late. I want to get this meeting over and done with," she finally said.

"No one is coming. I cancelled the meeting," Lisa said casually.

"Who gave you the right to cancel my meeting?"

"I thought we could settle the issue with Iris without an audience."

"I am sick and tired of people telling me what's best for me. This was *my* meeting and you had the nerve to cancel it? Who do you think you are?"

"I'm your friend. There is always a better way of settling issues before jumping up and doing something drastic."

Lisa was too calm for Jennifer. Lisa's demeanor took on authority. It made Jennifer furious. "If I want to do something drastic, it's my business. I won this presidency on my own merits and I would like to settle problems my own way. I don't need you or anybody else telling me how to run this organization."

"There used to be a time my opinion mattered. And you're right, I didn't have the right to cancel the meeting but if we work together and…"

"I don't want to work with you or anybody else. I'm sick of you acting as if you know everything. If the Alphas want this organization, then they can have it because I quit. I will not be a puppet on somebody's string." Jennifer gathered her things and took off for the door.

Their last little encounter from the year before was nothing like what Lisa was seeing now. Jennifer was hateful. Lisa broke her composure and rushed to the door.

"Move out my way," Jennifer yelled. Lisa stood still, looking at the angry woman. "MOVE OUT OF MY WAY!" Jennifer screamed and walked away backwards. Lisa stood still breathing heavily. Jennifer was beyond angry. Lisa was a little nervous but held her ground.

"What's the matter with you?" Lisa asked. Jennifer threw a note pad at Lisa who ducked when it came flying her way. Jennifer hated Lisa but didn't know why. She was her best friend but yet her enemy.

"Jennifer, wwwhat's the mmmmatter," Lisa stammered.

Jennifer allowed the anger to become tears. They came slow and then faster. She could not control herself. She swung wildly in the air. Jennifer was at war with herself.

"I hate him. He walks around as if nothing happened. That bastard had no right. I hate Michael too," Jennifer cried.

As Jennifer screamed and cried, Lisa closed her eyes quoting Psalms 27, the scripture her grandmother said to use in times of fear. As she recited the passage, no longer did she hear Jennifer yell or cry. The room was peaceful. It was the same comforting feeling that told her, when she was a little girl, that it was going to be okay. She was at peace.

Jennifer felt herself calm down. She felt the strength that helped her escape from that horrible Thursday night. It gave her enough strength to stop Sean from further abusing her. It was now giving her the feeling that she was at the darkest point and dawn would come soon.

The two looked at each other and peace came between the them. Lisa walked to Jennifer and hugged her, there was a connection with this person. She was more than a friend.

"Jennifer, you must put Iris in her place. Tell her to shut up when she interrupts. Don't include her in important activities, give her the mediocre ones. If she doesn't cooperate, then have the executive committee vote her out. It will be easier for them to vote her out because she's not cooperating. You can't keep avoiding conflicts. They just don't go away," Lisa said quickly.

"I feel weak around her," Jennifer confessed, wiping her eyes.

"People like her can sense a coward. I'm not saying that you're one but they can sense cowardly behavior. Iris isn't a bad person, she's a hungry one," Lisa said.

Jennifer didn't look convinced. "You promised we would always be friends. We don't talk anymore. You're different now," Jennifer sniffed. She missed sleeping at the foot of Lisa's bed, asking questions. Alpha Theta Lambda had stolen her friend and it wasn't fair.

"We're still friends. I'm the same person. You don't come around anymore. It's always you and Margo," Lisa said. This was the same conversation she had with Rochelle, but it was a little different. Rochelle practically cursed her out for not going to a card party. Lisa did not want to drink wine coolers or go to card parties anymore. Those things were not interesting anymore. The sorority was not filling the void either.

"You want to go to Kansas City with me this weekend? I'm going to visit Dee Dee and Gina. I can take you by Angel's."

"How much will it cost in gas?"

"Don't worry. My grandmother has increased my allowance to twenty-five dollars a week. I'm rich now."

"I guess I could visit Rosalyn too. I heard she had a little boy, Michael Jr."

"Michael is saying she lied on him."

"Don't they all say that!"

Lisa was quiet on her way back from Kansas City. Her meeting with Gina did not go as planned. The issue with Iris was still unsettled. The only pleasant thing about the trip was seeing Dee Dee's little boy, Cory.

The meeting with Gina was difficult. She did not understand why Lisa was having problems. Her lack of empathy made Lisa wished she had never come. Gina chastised her for allowing the sorority to get into the same situation she fought to eliminate two years ago. Gina could not understand why Iris was vice president. Gina ended the meeting by telling Lisa to discuss her decision with her before taking action. The only thing she was going to do was support Lisa's decision and make sure it was within the steps of sisterhood.

Before Lisa left, they talked about men. It became clear that Gina and Carlos were not on speaking terms. Gina was surprised to find out that Lisa and Cameron were not friends anymore. They talked the two men badly, calling them everything from momma's boys to no good two-timers. It made them feel better.

Lisa thought about the brief visit she had with Linda and Angel. They shared a large, two-bedroom apartment in Grandview. Lisa quickly had an attachment for Linda. She found her personality direct and honest. She asked Linda if her mother knew Debra Arvell. Linda told Lisa that Debra Arvell was one of the Missouri State founders of Phi Kappa Psi. Linda recited the founders names: Debra Arvell, JoAnn Anderson Lewis, Marilyn Jenkins Smith, Catherine Peterson Smith, Susan Richardson Caldwell, and Barbara Wright Stevens.

Angel added to Linda's comments about the founders. The six women were all good friends. Her mother, Catherine, was the president of the sorority during their senior year and led the charge to start the Missouri State Chapter of Phi Kappa Psi. Angel knew that Gina's mother didn't like Debra Arvell and kept silent on the issue.

Lisa was a little confused. She remembered Maria's mother telling her that starting the chapter at Missouri State was Debra Arvell's idea. How could it have been Angel's mother's idea?

Jennifer half smiled the entire time back to Harrisburg. Overall, she enjoyed her trip. She thought about how good it was seeing Angel and Linda. Angel asked Rosalyn to bring over Michael Jr. Angel maintained a mentoring role with Rosalyn, encouraging her to finish school at the University of Missouri at Kansas City.

Lisa, Jennifer and several others were waiting impatiently for the Beta's court to arrive. Lisa thought back to last year when Cameron made a surprise visit. She remembered how angry she was after their conversation. He had written her a letter, apologizing for his behavior and described in detail his feelings. It did not matter. The relationship was over.

It was cold outside and the students were getting anxious to see the arrival of the court. The first car finally pulled up which was last year's queen and her escort. Maria appeared in a long, white, form-fitting dress. When Tina appeared, a hush went over the crowd. People talked about how dainty and cute she was. Lisa thought Tina looked like a little brown China doll. She was so shy that she began to cry. The students clapped louder as she walked by. When Alexis appeared in a red, off-the-shoulders ball gown with a mink jacket, boys whistled. She grinned ear to ear, waving as she walked.

"That heffa is so fake," Alicia said.

"At least she's consistent," Crystal responded.

"I bet she will win. The Betas got a thing for those Kappas," Vicki said.

"Anne took the crown over Candice on the Gamma's court. Tina has a chance to win," Crystal said.

After everyone witnessed the entrance of the court, they rushed inside to get warm. Lisa took her time going inside the Ballroom. She wanted time alone so she went to the sitting room and looked outside the window at the remaining students outside. She felt someone watching her.

He stared at the long, beautiful, shapely legs. He noticed she had not gained back the weight that she lost two years ago. He decided to leave before she turned around, but it was too late. All he could do was look and wait for her to speak first.

"Hello Cameron."

"You look great!"

"How is school?"

"I'll be able to finish in December...if I go to summer school."

Cameron looked mature. His eyes were not glowing like last year. He looked as if he had been up several nights studying. He did not smile.

"So what's new?" Lisa asked.

"I was hoping we could talk after the Ball if you're not busy."

Before Lisa could respond to the request, J.D. walked in. "Hello Lisa. Hey Cameron, man, what brings you back to the Burg? How is school?" asked a happy J.D., shaking Cameron's hand.

"Hey J.D.! What's going on? Man, school is kicking ass," Cameron said happily.

"Everything is going well. I came to see if Lisa was ready to go in for dinner. I have our tickets," J.D. said.

Cameron's face dropped. Lisa felt as if she had been caught cheating. J.D. searched her face for an answer.

"Yeah man, I need to get going. It was nice seeing you again and you too Lisa," Cameron said with a smile and left.

J.D. looked at Lisa to see if anything was wrong. She turned her head. "Are you ready to go in?" she asked.

"Uh, sure. We have seats at the table with Calvin, Alicia, Kung Fu and Crystal," J.D. said softly, trying to understand. They walked out of the room in silence.

Everyone's attention was on the court, waiting to hear the winners. Lisa searched the crowd for Cameron. She heard Sheila's name announced. A lot of girls screamed. She heard the announcer mention Alexis' name. The crowd cheered. There was a long pause and Lisa saw Cameron walk to the door. In a split second, she turned to J.D. and excused herself.

Just as she reached Cameron, the crowd let out the biggest cheers and screams. Lisa turned around to see the little China doll crowned Miss

Beta. When she turned back around, Cameron was gone. Her heart was beating fast. She rushed through the doors and bumped into the back of him, almost falling. He looked at her with sad eyes.

"You said you wanted to talk," Lisa said.

"I couldn't expect you to sit around and wait," Cameron answered.

"What's the matter?"

"My parents have legally separated. Did I say you looked nice tonight?"

"Yes you did. When are you going back to Rolla?"

"Is it serious between you and J.D.?"

Lisa knew he wanted to know if she was sexually involved. She was taking Gina's advice, and pleading the fifth; What they don't know won't hurt.

"We've been dating since last May. We have our ups and downs but things are going fairly well."

"I couldn't expect for you to wait forever. Let me get to the frat house. I'm leaving early in the morning. It was good seeing you," Cameron said. He gave her a long look. They stared in silence for a few seconds before he walked away.

She wanted to follow him and drive to his favorite spot to see the airplanes. She wanted it to be like it was two years ago, before Rolla. She watched Cameron walk away, not looking back.

Lisa walked slowly to the Ballroom. She was able to corner Maria before she left. Lisa told Maria about the problem with Iris. Telling Maria wasn't a threat to Lisa because they enjoyed problem solving.

"I have an idea but you need your own. It's best that you maintain a level of secrecy in your decision. Soror means sister and sisters tell. Sometimes, you have to sacrifice in order to correct mistakes," Maria said.

"How is your mother?"

Maria told Lisa how her mother asked several questions about their relationship. She wanted to know more about Lisa.

"Did your mother know my father?" Lisa asked.

"She didn't say anything about him or maybe she did. What's his name?" Maria asked.

Lisa was embarrassed, but she had to know. "I received four names but they didn't amount to anything," Lisa said.

Maria talked casually to ease the discomfort. "I'm quite sure if you call her, she would tell you. She really likes you," Maria said.

"It looks like she was the only one who liked my mother. When I met Gina's mother, she couldn't stand the sight of me and neither could Angel's father. Lionel's father was pleasant and so was Linda's mother but she plays games. Gina's stepfather ignored me, refusing to look at me," Lisa said.

"I only know that they were friends at one time. My mother was president of the sorority two years before Angel's mother. My mother hardly gets involved in a lot of gossip, so I really don't know very much. Give her a call. She hardly ever gives out her phone number," Maria said.

"Don't be a stranger. I've written you five letters and you've only written me twice," Lisa complained.

"Once you graduate, you have so many things to do. I just don't have time to write. You can call me collect. I will refuse the charges and call you back. It's cheaper that way. My mother insisted that I get my own telephone. She complained all the time about me using hers," Maria said. They talked a little more before Lisa left to congratulate Tina.

"Sorors, we have two more candidates to vote on so please, please be patient and let us keep our tempers under control. Next is Lyndsi Ross. Okay, I see three hands. The floor is open for discussion."

"She dresses sloppy and her hair is a mess all the time."

"The only thing I have against her is that press and curl hairdo. She must do something about it. My flesh crawls every time I look at her head."

"Her clothes need ironing. She looks like a bum."

"Sorors, we can give her an iron and help her style her hair. There is nothing wrong with Lyndsi, after all, her father has a car dealership."

"Maybe I can get a discount on a car when I graduate." The group chuckled.

"Let's come off this crazy shit, y'all, and vote her in."

"Soror, please refrain from cursing. Let's vote on Miss Ross. Is there anyone who does not want Miss Ross to become a candidate for membership into Phi Kappa Psi Sorority?... Good. The last one is Sabrina Chess.... What's the matter, soror?"

"The girl is a thief!"

Everyone gasped in disbelief.

"I have always thought Sabrina was a very noble person!"

"Well, she stole my boyfriend!" The girls laughed loudly.

"What are you talking about, Patrice? Roger and Sabrina having been dating for years. I didn't think you were interested in nerds, only Jennifer."

The girls laughed again.

"She goes with Roger? With her attitude, I thought she was dating Michael Jackson. She thinks she has a prize catch!"

"Come on y'all. I am sick of this sh...I am trying not to cuss. Let's vote on this heffa."

"Soror, please control yourself. Patrice are you really voting against Miss Chess?"

"No, I just wanted to have fun."

"Before we start voting on the Pledge Class of 1982, I need to make an announcement. Effective today, I resign as President of Alpha Theta Lambda Sorority, Zeta Psi Chapter. Due to circumstances that I cannot discuss at this time, it is necessary for me to give up the office. Crystal Brown will be installed as President. Since this is effective immediately, we must select a new First Vice President and a Dean of Pledges because Crystal will not be able to carry out her duties as Dean of Pledges. The floor is open for nominations for Dean of Pledges."

The girls were shocked, especially the Genie line of 1980. It was hard for anyone to say anything.

"Wait a minute Lisa. You have handled a great deal since I have known you. What's up? This is a shock more than a surprise."

"I cannot discuss it now, Soror, but I will later. Please, let's elect new officers so we can vote on the new Pledge Class."

"I nominate Arlene Todd for Dean of Pledges."

"Lisa, we need to talk before you resign. Maybe we can help alleviate some of the stress. We can't afford for you to step down now."

"Soror President, are you accepting my nomination for Dean of Pledges?"

There was a long pause before Alicia spoke, "Who in the hell do you think you are? Our president has just resigned and you don't want to hear why?"

"You have really been obnoxious since you've become a member. You have embarrassed the sorority in the Association of Black Collegiates. Jennifer had to tell you to cool it; now that's not good."

"Let's calm down, sorors. I will discuss it later, but we need to vote on a Dean of Pledges," Lisa said.

"As long as I have been knowing you, Soror President, you have never waited for later to discuss anything. I am only accepting your resignation as President if you act as Dean of Pledges," Crystal said.

"Soror, it must be a nomination," Lisa said, making a concentrated eye contact with Tina, who proudly nominated her.

When the voting took place, everyone except four Neophytes voted for Lisa. She opened the floor for nominations for First Vice President. Three Neophytes were nominated, including Iris. The room was tense until the Sergeant of Arms called the votes. Iris was leading until the last six votes. Ashley Walker tied with her and pulled away, taking the last three votes. Iris sat quietly, looking around the room. She knew the presidency wasn't hers next year.

"Let us vote on our Pledge Class, sorors. The girls will be called in alphabetical order. All nay votes must be discussed in detail. Please leave personal feelings out the way as we discuss each girl. Let us begin with Deidra Brown."

"I want to see someone vote against the new president's sister," one said. Some laughed.

"You pulled it off, Lisa. I was sweating bullets. You know Iris is challenging the voting, saying that she was pledge daughter to the president."

"And so is Ashley. Crystal was installed as President. She wasn't acting president and that made the difference. What Iris should have done was control the position of Dean of Pledges. With me being around the Genies so much, I was able to build Ashley as a strong leader. It wasn't difficult because she is a strong leader. I tried to convince Rita that Iris was bad news but she wouldn't listen."

"The Ceremony of Wisdom went on without Rita. What she doesn't realize is you took her place by being a past president. I have to give it to you; you are one smart sister."

"Thanks Gina. I've always admired you. I hope we can keep in touch. After all, I do consider you my sister," Lisa said with humility. "Iris has shunned away from everyone. She believes we concocted that scheme because we didn't like her," Lisa said.

Although Iris was a handful, Lisa liked her. They came from similar backgrounds, neglecting mothers. Iris practically raised herself because her mother was an alcoholic. She didn't trust anyone but Lisa. "I guess if she wants to stay away, well let her," Lisa said, unbelieving of every word.

"That's not the right attitude. Donna wasn't a good Dean of Pledges. Your line complained about Marsha because she was tough on you ladies. We had three very strong personalities to control: yours, Alicia's and Evelyn's. Give Iris your telephone number. Extend the invitation for her to keep in touch."

Lisa was unsure if Iris would accept the invitation. Lisa decided to drop the subject. She stood back and looked around the busy hall at all the graduates and their parents. Miss Mattie couldn't make the trip because she was ill. Lisa had no other family to see her graduate summa cum laude. Maria couldn't come because she was traveling with her job, and Carla said she may not be able to make it either.

Gina looked at Lisa as she fought to maintain strength. She was a very brave and shrewd person. It was a shame that no one could be there to see her walk with honors.

"Summa cum laude! Congratulations!"

Lisa spun around quickly and rushed to Carla. She gave her a big hug. Lisa couldn't speak. All she knew was her pledge mothers had come to see her graduate. "I thought we could go to the Steak House to eat. We all have something to celebrate," Carla said. Lisa wiped her eyes without anyone noticing.

Jennifer walked up jovially with Angel and Linda. They congratulated Carla on her marriage to Dennis.

"Where is he?" Gina asked.

"He went to the bathroom. I hope he hasn't gotten lost," Carla said in response to Gina's question.

"Sweetie, Linda and I must get going. I would love to see your father but I'm afraid we have to go. When I come to St. Louis, I will see him then," Angel apologized. Jennifer tried not to look disappointed.

"I would stay dearie but I'm riding with Miss I'm Every Woman. Maybe when she slows down, we can all spend time together," Linda said.

"Linda, you can ride back with me and Carlos," Gina offered.

"That's okay. I don't want to ride in that tin can you call a car," Linda said.

"Carlos drove."

"Me, ride in that big, monster, ghetto, tractor-trailer he calls a vehicle? No thanks. Jennifer, make sure you visit me, hun. Now you know I don't like writing, so don't get mad if you don't receive a letter. I hate it when you whine," Linda preached.

Jennifer continued to embrace the ambience of hearing Linda and Gina fighting again. It felt like home. Angel hugged Jennifer and Linda waved her famous "ta-ta". Jennifer watched the two people who had helped shape her life leave the auditorium. She left to have lunch with Kyle and his parents.

A happy Dennis approached the group with Carlos walking at his side. Dennis put his arm around Carla's waist. "We thought you were over there," Dennis said and pointed at the door.

"Yeah, I swore up and down this woman was Lisa. We were too embarrassed when she smiled and kept walking while I was talking to her," Carlos said with a wide grin.

"So sweetheart, where do we go from here?" Dennis asked, nibbling on Carla's ear. It didn't seem to bother her. They were openly affectionate, which made the rest of the group a little uneasy. Gina cleared her throat and Dennis stopped.

"What's the matter?" he asked innocently.

"Nothing man, I need to get on my job," Carlos said and pulled Gina to him. He kissed her softly on the cheek. She flushed with embarrassment. Lisa cleared her throat. The couples looked at her.

"Are we still going to lunch?" Lisa asked. They all agreed and walked out the auditorium to the cars. Lisa spotted Iris walking away alone. Lisa called her. Iris turned around but kept walking.

"Is that the one who was starting trouble in the sorority?" Carla asked.

Iris confided in her, trusted her, and she took away the only opportunity for her to feel important. Iris would probably never trust her again. Lisa took up the defense.

"She didn't start any trouble. She has a strong will. Many sorors were not accustomed to her personality. There's nothing wrong with her," Lisa rushed to say.

Carla looked at Gina for an answer.

"Donna wasn't a good Dean of Pledges. She allowed selfishness to rule the line," Gina whispered to Carla.

The two women sent the men ahead. Lisa quickly explained the entire story to Carla, starting from the pledge program to the election. Carla did a quick analysis. They all got in Dennis' car. Lisa spotted Iris. Carla parked the car and the three got out quickly.

Lisa called Iris again. She turned around. This time she stopped. As the three approached her, she looked like a deer caught in headlights. Lisa introduced Carla to Iris. She said nothing.

"Lisa told me of your many positive attributes," Carla said. Iris remained silent. "I was president..."

"You are Carla Merriweather Williams, chapter president 1978-1979. You crossed May 5, 1976. You are my grand pledge mother, if that means anything," Iris said without losing focus. She was medium height with shoulder length hair that was always curled. She wore glasses which gave her an astute appearance. She hardly ever smiled.

"I'm impressed. I am glad that we have finally got a chance to meet,"

Carla said, not weakening to the young woman's anger.

"I hear you are pretty aggressive. Blacks have never taken an interest in the Student Government Association. You should consider running for an office. A personality like yours does very well in politics. You have to be tough and strong. You will probably meet your match, that's if you're not afraid," Gina said, challenging Iris.

"I'm not afraid. I wouldn't have any support, especially not from the sorority," Iris said, giving Lisa an unwelcomed look.

"An Alpha never walks alone. She has the support of her sisters and you will get that support. I will make sure of it," Carla said and turned to Lisa. "Give Miss Clark your telephone number before you leave Harrisburg. I want the sorors to support her in any campaign she chooses, but Miss Clark, you must do it in the name of sisterhood which is unselfish," Carla said.

It was the first time Iris ever witnessed anyone taking authority over Lisa. She still did not want to trust the women. "Here is my work and home telephone number," Gina said, handing Iris a card.

"Here is my home and work number too. If you need me, call. My mother was an alcoholic. I know what it's like to raise yourself. I expect to hear from you and so does Miss Smith and Miss Arvell," Carla said.

Iris was confused with the emotions stirring within. The women seemed genuine.

"Would you like to have lunch with us?" Carla asked pleasantly.

"No thank you," Iris said firmly. It was Carla's expression that made her soften. "I have to study for my Advanced Accounting test. Thanks for the offer," Iris said compassionately.

"I expect to hear from you," Carla stressed.

"I also expect to hear updates on your efforts with SGA," Gina said, looking at Iris with an intense glare.

"You will," Iris said. She felt better. The women seemed to care about her. Iris didn't understand but chose to let it drop. She turned to Lisa to forgive.

"Congratulations, Lisa. You won't be the only one graduating summa cum laude."

Chapter 18
August 1985

It was three years after their graduation. Jennifer worked as a staff accountant with a mid-size advertising firm. Lisa was hired as a monetary analyst at the Federal Reserve.

"I know it's hot but you can't sit around the house on your birthday. I'll pick you up around eight, okay?"

Jennifer sighed. The last thing she wanted to do was to see male strippers. "Okay, I'll be ready. Who's all going?" she asked.

"Me, you, Roach and maybe Alicia."

Jennifer let out another sigh. "Can Margo go?"

"I don't care."

"We can trail you to East St. Louis."

"Everyone should ride together. It's safer that way. I'll see you later."

Jennifer hung up the phone and continued working. The department made a big deal of her twenty-fifth birthday. She had received gag gifts and prank calls all day, mourning her youth. With all the excitement surrounding her birthday, she was feeling depressed. The situation at home with her stepmother had become intolerable.

When the phone rang again, Jennifer debated whether to answer it. She snatched the handle and spoke.

"Miss Peterson, you have a package at the front desk."

"I'll be down in a few minutes," Jennifer said and hung up. She wondered if it was another gag gift. She decided to go along with the joke. She liked her co-workers. She was the only black professional employee. Only one person bothered her. The woman would always tell Jennifer that she was different from other black people as if it were a compliment.

When Jennifer arrived downstairs, a tall big black box standing on the receptionist counter greeted her. She wondered if it was a real gift and who sent it. The receptionist looked nosy. "You must be a very special person to someone," she said and handed Jennifer the large box.

Jennifer stared, amazed at the large, black box with a silver tuxedo on the front. She walked up the stairs slowly. She passed by a few co-workers who followed her to the cubicle.

A girl screamed, "Look everyone! Jennifer has received Black Tie Roses."

A small crowd rushed to Jennifer's cubicle. Jennifer looked puzzled at the excitement on her co-workers' faces. Everyone knew what was inside the box except her. She opened the box and pulled back the pink tissue. She gasped at the sight of the dozen long-stem, pink roses. She removed the card and read:

"HAPPY BIRTHDAY, JEN"
LOVE, KYLE

"You never told us you had a boyfriend! Who is Kyle, Jen?" one asked.

"He's a friend from college," Jennifer responded, trying not become annoyed with the innocent person.

"A friend? Friends don't send Black Tie Roses. Are you sure he's not more than a friend? Maybe he's trying to tell you something," another said.

"Do you have a vase for your roses?" one asked.

"No," Jennifer answered.

The girl took off. Jennifer looked curiously at the beautiful roses. They had to be special because everyone was making a big deal about them. The girl came back with the vase and instructed Jennifer on snipping the stems so they could bloom properly.

Jennifer took her time with the precious gems. She displayed them proudly on her desk with the tuxedo box standing behind them. She quickly flipped through her rolodex. She punched in a 1-800 number and waited impatiently.

"Good afternoon, Linda Stevens."

"Hello Miss Stevens, this is Jennifer."

"Hello sweetness, how are you? I see you've finally got the hint and stopped writing."

Jennifer chuckled. "Have you heard of Black Tie Roses?" she asked.

"Of course! Why are you asking?"

"I received some from a friend."

"A friend? My. My. If it's a man then marry him but if it's a woman, quickly get the hell away from her."

"Are they expensive?"

Linda found the question humorous. "Yes they are! Who gave them to you?"

"Kyle."

"Who is Kyle?"

"He went to Missouri State. You remember him don't you? You once called him a re-tard."

"Sweetness, there were a lot of men I called a re-tard. Kyle doesn't see your relationship as a friendship. If he's not so bad looking, I say snatch him up. A man that sends Black Tie Roses just to say 'hi' is someone you want around for a very long time."

"He sent them as a birthday present."

"Oh my goodness! It's your birthday? I am going to send you something because you have always sent very thoughtful presents on my birthday. Tell Margo I said 'hello.' By the way, I want you to be a bridesmaid. I'm getting married April 30 of next year."

Jennifer tried to control herself. Keith had proposed several times before Linda said yes. "Congratulations!" Jennifer said, trying not to burst at the seams.

"I hope he doesn't have any lawsuits from now until April. He will be standing at the altar alone. I'll talk to you later."

Jennifer hung up the phone. The idea of Kyle wanting more than a friendship made her mind go blank. She looked at the card again: *"LOVE KYLE."* He had never made advances toward her since she had known him. She had to thank him for the roses. She flipped through the rolodex and found his number. She punched the numbers slowly and prayed he was gone for the day.

"Hello, this is Kyle Thomas."

"Uh, hi...Kyle?"

"Yes?"

"Kyle, this is Jennifer. How are you?"

"Hi Jen! Happy birthday!"

"I received the roses. They are very pretty and I want to say thank you." There was a moment of silence. "The roses made my day." Kyle still didn't respond. Jennifer didn't know what to think of his silence. His behavior was weird.

"Like I said before, they are beautiful and I want to thank you for being so nice."

"I'm glad you like them," Kyle said bashfully.

"I won't hold you. Thanks for the gift," Jennifer said.

"Happy Birthday Jen," he said.

They both hung up. Jennifer thought Kyle's reaction was unusual. If he was trying to tell her something, he didn't do a very good job. She decided to finish her reports so she could leave on time.

Lisa and Rochelle talked simultaneously in the front seat. Jennifer was crunched between Alicia and Margo in the back seat. Alicia asked Lisa to turn up the radio. The noise level was driving Jennifer crazy. Margo silently enjoyed herself. She had never gone out with Lisa, Rochelle or Alicia.

"I can't believe you're coming with us, Alicia. Aren't teachers supposed to set an example for their students?" Rochelle taunted.

"If I see any of my students tonight, it's time for me to quit," Alicia said.

"What grade do you teach?" Margo asked politely.

"Third. I'm having second thoughts about it. When you're new, the St. Louis Public School District shifts you around too much. You don't have flexibility to be creative either," Alicia complained. She had become much more quiet since becoming a teacher. She let her hair grow out longer. She wore less casual clothes.

"Remember when we did those Christmas carol skits? That was fun!" Lisa said.

"I got an 'A' on that project. My pledge mother Cheryl gave me that idea. She turned out to be nice after all," Alicia commented.

"All of them were. When you are pledging, they try to kill you but after it's over, they're all smiles," Lisa added.

"Don't think they didn't say the same thing about you Big Sister Ask Not What Your Sorority Can Do For You!" Alicia said with a laugh. Lisa laughed too.

"Let's not get on this sorority shit. Every time I think about how those women used me as a personal slave, I get mad," Rochelle said with lips poked out.

"Oh, I'm quite sure you didn't do any of that, Big Sister Atomic Roach," Jennifer said.

"They had the nerve to get mad when I had the Cherubs call me that," Rochelle fussed. Alicia shook her head sadly.

"The Kappas were used to eating steak and potatoes for dinner. Your loud butt brought in the ham hocks and greens for supper," Alicia said. Margo burst into laughter.

Alicia looked at Margo and asked calmly, "When are you and Peter getting married, Margo?"

Jennifer elbowed Margo in the side but she didn't catch the signal.

"We are planning a June wedding next year. Are you getting married soon?" Margo asked.

"Hell no! These men don't want to act right. I don't have time for their mess. I heard Alexis is marrying a judge. I heard he's fifteen years older than her. I guess it ain't bad if he's kickin' it in bed. I also heard Monica Watts is unmarried with two kids. She used to think she was so much in school," Alicia said. Jennifer knew she was in for an earful of gossip but Margo was intrigued.

"Monica was all right. Girlfriend just got caught. You can't hold that against her. Did you say kickin'? I can't believe you're talking slang. When will you finish your Master's?" Rochelle asked.

"In December," Alicia answered.

"I heard Melvin Hill is gay. Can you believe that?" Rochelle asked.

"You are lying! That man has seen more sheets than a Chinese laundry. How can he be gay? Give me a break."

"So Lisa, what's up with you and J.D.? You've been keeping quiet about homeboy," Alicia asked bravely. Lisa was quiet for a few seconds.

"What's the matter girlfriend, cat's got your tongue?" Rochelle asked.

"We haven't been on speaking terms for three months. He seems to be threatened by my job. We talk every now and then but nothing has been happening with us for over three months. I have to move on. I need someone who doesn't care about the money I make. He makes jokes about me dating white men. Ain't nothing funny about dating a white man," Lisa said seriously.

"Where does he work?" Margo asked.

"He's a substitute teacher during the school year. He's having a difficult time finding a job in Mass Communications. I've tried to give him leads to network with people but he gets touchy. He has a difficult time meeting new people."

"Now that's funny. A person who majored in Mass Communications is having a difficult time networking? Men are sickening. If you don't make enough money, they act crazy. If you make too much money, they act crazy. I'm tired of dealing," Alicia fussed.

"Alicia, weren't you seeing somebody not too long ago?" Lisa asked.

"Um, hum. Now *he* was crazy. He was talking marriage two months after we started dating. I should have known something was wrong when he gave me four telephone numbers to reach him," Alicia complained.

"Oh, so he was looking for a place to stay," Lisa said.

"You know it. When he found out I had my own apartment, he was in love. I should have given him four telephone numbers too," Alicia said.

Margo was curious. "How did you know he was looking for a place to stay?" she asked.

Alicia looked surprised. "Why do I need four telephone numbers to get in touch with someone? If I ask you for your telephone number, you will give me two at the most. One to your job and the other to where you live," she said.

"Um," Margo said to herself. She was still surprised that Alicia knew the man was close to homeless.

"I've got one to top that. I exchanged numbers with this one nut. He called me all the time, all day long. I didn't have to call him because he called me constantly. When I finally used the number, it was to his job," Rochelle complained.

"Oh, so he was married," Lisa said.

"Damn right! He had the gall to tell me he wasn't happy and that he and his wife weren't sleeping together. What man do you know will turn down a piece of ass if it's looking at him every day?" Rochelle said.

Margo was amazed. "A man is married if he calls you all the time?"

"A man is married if you don't have his home number," Rochelle corrected.

"This one old teacher at school is trying to talk to me. This dude looks close to forty years old. He told me he served in Vietnam," Alicia said.

"Oh, now he's *crazy!*" Lisa commented.

"For sure you're right. I don't wanting him having an Agent Orange episode on me. Where do these old men get off in trying to talk to somebody young?" Alicia complained. Margo continued to be amazed at the women's analysis.

"So Lisa, I guess you're ready to get back into the scene. I thought you and J.D. had broken up before?" Alicia inquired.

"It stopped for awhile when I got my own place, then it started again, and now it stopped. It's time to let him go especially since you know who called today," Lisa said grinning.

Jennifer perked up. She knew who the person was because she and Lisa discussed him the other day. She remembered Lisa telling her to stop conjuring up old problems.

"Who is, you know who?" Alicia asked.

"Cameron."

Rochelle and Alicia screamed, "What?"

"Now I thought you two made a very nice couple. Both of you were quiet and studious," Margo said innocently.

Alicia looked at Margo as if she had lost her mind. "You mean Cameron was quiet," Alicia corrected.

"Lisa was quiet too. She wasn't as gregarious as you and Rochelle," Margo said politely. Alicia and Rochelle laughed hard.

"So Lisa, why did my man call? Don't tell me he's getting married and wants you to be a bridesmaid," Rochelle joked.

"He's coming to St. Louis for a conference and wants to see me," Lisa blushed.

"What does he do?" Margo asked.

"He's an engineer with the public transit system in Atlanta," Lisa said blushing.

"You know, I've always thought he looked better than Lionel. Lionel looked too sweet to me. I wouldn't be surprised if he turned out to be gay. Weren't you seeing him in school, Jennifer?" Alicia asked daringly.

Before Jennifer could respond, Lisa jumped in, "That was Angel's man."

"Excuse me, but I was talking to Jennifer. And he wasn't Angel's man more like Denise's. Besides, I thought I heard that you and Angel had a little spat over him," Alicia said to Jennifer.

Jennifer could feel her anger rise slightly. "That's not true," she said.

Lisa drove up on a gravel parking lot. The girls looked at the strange surroundings. It looked abandoned.

"Are you sure this is the right place?" Margo asked hesitantly.

"Hell yeah! Let's go and see some butts," said a happy Rochelle, climbing out the car. Jennifer and Margo moved slowly. They looked up mortified at the large neon pink and green sign "Flashes." Lisa and the other two walked swiftly into the club while Jennifer and Margo trudged behind.

Inside was dark. The decor was fairly nice. There was a stage off to the right side of the room. They all agreed they didn't want anyone to see them so they found seats near the back. They continued talking until and someone handed them a flyer with photos of all the male strippers. Rochelle noticed first. "Isn't this Michael Shannon?"

Lisa looked at her flyer and her mouth flew opened. She looked at Jennifer who looked as if she were going to pass out.

"It is Michael! Brother is calling himself the Cherry Popper," Alicia said.

"The man's got a baby in Kansas City, and he's taking off his clothes in front of strange women. I can't stand him," Rochelle said.

"I heard he did Rosalyn wrong. I heard she came to him for money to get an abortion and he basically ignored her. If you're not going to take care of the baby, then pay for the abortion, that's my philosophy," Alicia said.

"Let's leave," Lisa said.

"Naw, we paid our money. I want to see his sorry ass show. That punk screwed over Jennifer too," Rochelle said.

"What did he do to you, Jennifer?" Alicia asked.

"Nothing! He didn't do a thing," Lisa answered with a huff.

Alicia looked at Lisa again. "Is your name Jennifer? Why are you answering for her?" Alicia asked agitated.

Before they could bash Michael some more, the house lights went down and the first stripper began dancing. The group looked unimpressed. Rochelle commented about the dancer needing socks in his G-string. Margo laughed so loud that several people turned around.

Four strippers danced before Michael. He was the main attraction. Women in the audience were going inside their purses when he was announced. He came out in a police uniform. As he removed an article of clothing, the women beckoned for him with money. He moved his hips and touched his body slowly and the women screamed.

Rochelle went in her purse and pulled out several one dollar bills. "I want him to earn this. He's got the audacity to come out in a police get-up. Somebody needs to lock his ass up for paternity." Rochelle waved several dollars out in the aisle. She was able to get Michael's attention. He danced back to their table.

The spotlight didn't follow Michael to the back so Rochelle was ready. She danced up to Michael waving the money. He smiled as he danced provocatively with her. Alicia danced up to Michael too

"Remember us, Mr. Popper? We're from your past," Alicia said happily.

"See this money? We're giving it to the baby you left behind in Kansas City, and the woman who has to raise it alone, you cheap ass bastard. Take your butt back to the front and earn a living," Rochelle said and put the money back in her pocket and danced away. Alicia laughed, pointing at him. Michael frowned hard. He left their table and the women in the audience continued to beckon for him.

Lisa became jumpy. "Let's leave before trouble starts. Jennifer take my car keys and leave quietly. Alicia you follow her. The rest of us will be right behind you," Lisa said and handed Jennifer the keys. They slipped out quietly before Michael was finished.

Lisa trembled as she started the car. When she pulled off the lot, three men rushed outside the club. Lisa took her time making it to the highway to head back to St. Louis. She knew that was her last time in East St. Louis. "What's wrong with you two? Don't you know gangsters own places like that? Are you trying to get us killed?" Lisa shouted. Everyone was quiet.

"I'm sorry Lisa. I just get mad every time I think about how he has treated so many girls at school," Rochelle confessed.

"We embarrassed him by showing up to see him strip. We didn't need to go that far," Jennifer said. She knew in Lisa's spirit something was wrong and she couldn't relax until she felt the "sign."

They were quiet, looking for an excuse to talk. Usually, Lisa got mad and brushed it off, but she still looked nervous. Margo broke the ice, "Let's go to Culpeppers for hot wings and a salad."

"That sounds good. The night is still young and Jennifer hasn't had her birthday drink. What are you drinking, Jennifer?" Rochelle asked. Jennifer hunched her shoulders.

"How about it, Lisa? Are you up for Culpeppers?" Alicia asked.

Lisa drove to Culpeppers and squeezed her car in between two cars. All were tense until she finished parking. She managed to squeeze into a space the size for a Volkswagen Beetle.

"Where in the hell did you learn to park?" Alicia finally yelled.

"At school. Kyle taught me and Jennifer," Lisa said and grabbed her purse.

"I remember him. He was that goofy brother that wore short-sleeve shirts. I bet homeboy is making long money now," Alicia said.

"Of course he is. He bought Jennifer Black Tie Roses for her birthday," Lisa said by accident. All eyes were on Jennifer. She gave Lisa a very dirty look.

"Jennifer, you didn't tell me you got Black Tie Roses for your birthday!" Margo said happily.

"Is Kyle your man, Jennifer?" Alicia asked.

"No, he's just a friend," she answered.

"Friends don't buy Black Tie Roses for nothing. He might be your friend but you are definitely not his," Alicia said.

"What are Black Tie Roses?" Rochelle asked. The group stared at Rochelle unbelieving.

"You are so uncouth," Alicia said.

"Go to hell," Rochelle said angrily.

"Look, Jennifer doesn't like him so let's drop it. I'm hungry. Let's hurry before we have to wait thirty minutes," Lisa said.

They were fortunate that the wait was only fifteen minutes. They continued to talk to Jennifer about Kyle. They were surprised that she kept in touch with everyone from the nerd herd. The more Jennifer talked, the more Alicia asked questions and the more Lisa tried to respond to the questions. Eventually, Alicia told Lisa to be quiet and let Jennifer talk.

They were learning more about each other. Margo found out that Rochelle liked talking slang just to see how people reacted. She had spoken it for so long that it had pretty much become a part of her vocabulary. She claimed her father, the superintendent, almost died when he overheard her talking on the telephone.

They talked about their jobs. Margo was surprised to learn that Rochelle wanted to open a nail shop. Alicia confessed to wanting a daycare center. Rochelle began to tease. "You a daycare provider? I can see if you looked pleasant like Jennifer or Margo. You look too mean. I can see you now, cursing out a bunch of little kids," Rochelle said.

"Oh, listen to the homegirl manicurist. What are you going to name your shop: For Color Girls Only?" Alicia cracked and Margo rolled with laughter.

"Well, I won't be sending my child to Grits de la Grits," Rochelle said.

"What child? You mean monster don't you. You won't have to worry about me coming into a nail shop with a fan in the window for air conditioning," Alicia said.

The waitress brought out the salads. They ate heartily. In between forkfuls, Alicia asked Margo about her background. Margo talked and it became evident that she came from the other side of the tracks. She attended private schools and grew up primarily around white children. Alicia became very interested in Margo's family, especially her parents. Alicia complimented Margo and it made Lisa mad.

"There is nothing wrong with growing up poor in the hood. You turned out fine, Alicia. There is nothing wrong with welfare or a one-parent family or slang for that matter," Lisa said defensively.

Alicia didn't ask any more questions. The waitress brought out the rest of the food. They ate in silence.

"I hope I didn't offend anyone," Margo said softly.

"You didn't offend anyone, Margo," Alicia said.

"You didn't offend *me*!" Lisa stressed.

"I used to receive that same attitude from some of the girls in the dorms in my first year at Missouri State. I never understood. I too was angry. Women who are lighter than me were not necessarily prettier than me. People who graduate summa cum laude are not necessarily smarter than those who graduate with a 2.85 GPA. It might mean they stole the test or study harder *or* gave it up to the professors," Margo said softly and continued to eat without looking at anyone. Rochelle chuckled and looked at Lisa.

"I guess we all have our little insecurities," Margo threw in and kept eating. Alicia smiled and looked at Lisa who looked confounded. She looked around the table and everyone waited for her to apologize.

Lisa let out a sigh. "I apologize."

"I accept."

Chapter 19
October 1985

Lisa took one last look in the bathroom mirror. She freshened her lipstick and fluffed out her hair. She wanted to look perfect when Cameron laid eyes on her for the first time in over three years. She was meeting him at the hotel where the conference was being held. He bragged about the lunch buffet and said she had to try it.

She knew he loved her legs, so she decided on a grey suit with a straight skirt at the knees and a double-breasted jacket that hung an inch below her hips.

She took off down the street to the Hilton. As she crossed the street, butterflies came. She wondered what she would say after three years. She didn't know if he were dating anyone, or if he were married for that matter. They chatted briefly on the phone because he had a dinner meeting with his supervisor and some vendors. *He had better not be married*, she said to herself.

She rushed through the revolving doors, looking for the hotel's dining room. She found it and searched the area for Cameron. She walked up and down the hallway, looking at her watch the entire time. It wasn't like him to be late. He said he would be waiting in the hall. On her way back to the door, broad shoulders in a crisp, white, starched shirt and a dark, multi-color tie stood in her path. She looked in the familiar eyes that sparkled. He had a light beard and mustache with a box haircut. He wore the famous Johnson smile.

He felt a little guilty allowing her to walk back and forth so he could look at the gorgeous legs. The coral lipstick emphasized the beauty mark above the upper lip. Her hair was fuller and thicker than he had ever remembered. Her eyes were mysterious. Who would speak first?

"I didn't know if this was a stand up or a new pattern of being late."

"With legs like those, I had to watch you strut a few times."

"You were out here the entire time?"

Cameron gave an impish nod. She elbowed him. "Stop, you're hurting me," he whined and then laughed. He didn't realize how much he missed the playful times in school when she used to punch him out of habit.

"You have filled out. Now you have what women call a chest," she teased, keeping her focus away.

"Looks like you are trying to get back your black girl's butt and…" before he finished, she elbowed him again and narrowed her eyes.

She pointed her finger playfully. "You leave my butt alone," she said.

"I only got one shot and blew it," he said daringly.

She turned red. "Let's go inside," she said.

Cameron enjoyed listening as Lisa talked about her job and the headaches involved in doing statistical work. He asked more questions about the Federal Reserve Bank. Lisa was surprised to see he was interested in her career. Before she could ask about his job, she realized it was getting late and she had to get back to the office.

"What are you doing this evening?" he asked.

"Nothing."

"How about going on a dinner riverboat cruise with me? We can finish our conversation."

"What time? I have to go home and change."

"You look fine unless your skirt is too tight and you need more belly room for dinner." The two laughed again.

Lisa rushed back to work and called Jennifer. Lisa waited impatiently to hear her voice. "Jennifer, he is fine. Too fine. He was pleasant as always. I'm just surprised he decided to call after all these years."

"He asked me if I thought you would mind him calling and I said no."

There was a moment of silence. "Cameron called you?"

"He has called a few times asking about you. He finally got the courage to call. He asked if you were still seeing J.D. I told him the truth. He knew he had hurt you. He wanted to be careful approaching you. He loves you, Lisa."

"At least you could have told me! I don't appreciate you…"

"Cut it, Lisa! Remember when I wanted to get rid of Iris and you cancelled my meeting? I understood."

"That was different. You were getting ready to make a mistake."

"And so are you. You have always liked Cameron and he likes you. Don't let him slip through your fingers because of a little pride. Call me tonight and give me the lowdown on the cruise. I hope you are not jealous because Cameron called me?"

"What?"

"Good. I'll wait up for your call. Talk to you later."

Lisa drove to the riverfront. She took her time as she parked her brand new 1985 Mazda 626 between a BMW and a Grand Am. She figured Cameron was already on the boat. She had to take her time walking on the cobble stones in pumps. Sure enough, he was standing in the doorway in khaki baggy pants and a navy sports jacket. He smiled as she approached the door. She managed to smile back.

She smelled his cologne as she got closer. His body chemistry mixed well with whatever he was wearing. He extended his hand to help her on board. He pulled her close to his side. She almost stumbled.

Cameron could smell her perfume. He liked her selection. It was something spicy. Her hair smelled nice as always. He thought about the women he dated with curls and the oily mess it left on his clothing. He thought about how he spent lots of money on some of the women in Atlanta, only to find that was all they wanted.

He wondered if she still liked the outdoors. He remembered when they found bikes and went bike riding in Harrisburg. She talked the entire time, not getting tired and not allowing him to say a word because he was out of breath. Tonight was their first real date and he wanted to give her everything he thought about in the past.

"You care for a drink?"

"I really don't drink. I don't want to start any bad habits."

"You were always a good girl in bad clothes."

"You don't drink either!"

"You're right, I don't."

They sat on cushion-covered chairs in the lounge. Cameron crossed his legs and crossed his fingers, placing his hands in his lap. *Damn, he's fine*, Lisa thought as she crossed her legs, slanting them at an angle. *Wow, those legs are sexy*, Cameron said to himself.

"You've heard about my job, so there's not much else to tell," Lisa said blushing.

"You are going to be the youngest executive at the Federal Reserve. I believe that in my heart," Cameron said smiling.

"What about you? There are other things in life, correct?"

"What are those other things?"

Lisa stopped blushing. "Hobbies, relationships and other things."

"Hobbies, well, I like playing tennis. As far as relationships, I would like to have a sincere and meaningful one. What about you? Are you still seeing J.D.?"

She was perplexed. Jennifer had already told him about J.D. Maybe he was testing her. She didn't want any games. "I'm not seeing J.D. anymore," she said, trying to take control of the conversation. "I'm quite sure the women in Atlanta are not letting you sit at home on Friday nights. It would seem as if there would be a large pool of sincere women to pick from."

"I'm not seeing anyone. I dated one person who I thought was really nice but I had to pay to have her hair done, nails done and whatever else she wanted. It would be nice not to pay for what I want."

"It depends on what kind of woman you're looking for."

"My father told me quality is everything. I'm hoping quality is still interested."

"Jennifer told me that you called," Lisa said, moving slightly in her chair.

"I like talking to Jennifer. Every once in awhile, I would call her and get updates on you. Finally she told me to stop calling her and to call you, so I did. I was a little nervous at first, but when you answered the phone and said my name, it went away."

Lisa looked away, blushing again. She couldn't keep from blushing. Everything was going so well. She felt the boat leave the dock.

"I've never known Lisa Arvell to keep quiet. A penny for your thoughts?"

"That sounds so white!"

"I know, but this is who I am," he said unthreatened. "Would you care to dance to the white music?" He extended his hand and escorted her to the dance floor.

He wondered if he was too direct. Maybe he scared her or maybe he sounded desperate. He figured however the evening turned out would decide their future.

She wondered if she was playing it too shy. She had always enjoyed his company, especially when he was a bookworm. She didn't know how to recover from the embarrassing comment about him being white. It was her only protection from having her feelings hurt again. She could feel his hand on her back, stroking the way he did so well. It felt more experienced this time. She didn't want him to go back to Atlanta thinking she didn't want him.

"You know, they say long distance relationships don't work," she said, waiting for his response. This was the only way she knew how to keep her foot in the door.

He stopped dancing and held her hand tight. "I want to see you again," he said.

She didn't want to tell him she was afraid. She remembered what Jennifer said; don't let him slip away. "You have my phone number and address," Lisa said.

He continued to stare into her eyes. He knew she didn't trust him so he figured he would have to try harder. They danced a few minutes more and then walked to the dining room, which was very cozy. Candles were on the tables. He walked ahead and beckoned her to follow.

When she arrived at the table, her eyes were fixed on the dozen roses and a card with *Lisa* on the front. Her heart beat fast as she picked up the card and read the back:

With All Of My Love,
Cameron

She looked at him, not knowing whether or not to kiss him, at least on the cheek. He made the decision easier by pulling out her chair. She sat down, holding the card tight. J.D. had given her flowers on Valentines' Day, but never a dozen long-stem roses. She wanted to smell them so that she could understand the excitement behind receiving roses. Such behavior would immediately show him that she was not used to the finer things, so she decided not to.

She sat smiling, trying not to make eye contact. His expression was serious. He was on a mission. He ordered Perrier for them. He suggested that she try the grilled salmon. He chose lobster. He was in full control of the evening. She really didn't mind because she hated being in charge all of the time.

When she and J.D. dated, she chose the restaurants or the movies. At first, she thought he was being thoughtful, allowing her to make decisions, but then she realized he really had no idea about what to do. Even if Lisa insisted he make the decisions, he still put the choice in her corner. She really liked J.D., but they had definitely grown in different directions.

It was May when they decided it was time to give each other space. Lisa felt bad because J.D. struggled to keep his head high during their discussion. He had so much pride, but the idea of her having a successful career was a little too much for him. She called a few times to give him job tips. He was always polite and kept the conversation brief. She still considered him a friend.

Lisa looked at the silently aggressive man sitting across from her. He sat with back straight and shoulders relaxed. Cameron was never weak. She knew that from pledging, doing daring things, getting everyone in trouble. She liked him because he wasn't afraid to take chances.

"I don't mean to bring up any bad topics, but how are your parents'"

"Divorced. It became final two years ago. My father wanted out and he got it."

"What is your mother doing now?"

"She's trying to keep busy."

"How did Lionel take it?"

"Lionel is a quiet person when it comes to showing pain. He's fairly close to my father."

"They are probably just alike."

"People tell me that I'm like my father, a young Charles Johnson. I refuse to follow in his footsteps."

Lisa looked at Cameron oddly. The waiter came with the dinners. "I don't mean to bring up any more bad memories but when you were seeing someone in college, you ignored me, hoping I would go away. I know you said that you are not seeing anyone now but I need to hear it again. I don't appreciate anyone lying to me," Lisa said, looking directly into his eyes. Miss Mattie always said the eyes don't lie.

"I dated someone for a year, but I called it quits three months ago. She calls but I haven't gone out with her since the middle of July. If I have to date you long distance, then I will," Cameron said without blinking.

Lisa saw the truth. He wanted her. She let out a shrewd smile. "Where do we go from here?" she asked.

"Well, a cruise to the Bahamas sounds good. Or did you say the next time should be Egypt?" said a shrewder Cameron.

The response caught her off guard. It was difficult to continue with the dialogue. "This looks good. Last one finished is an old rotten egg," Lisa said playfully and picked up her fork.

Jennifer was doing spring cleaning on her car. Kyle and his two friends were coming to town and she was taking them around. Jennifer went inside the house to take a shower. Her stepmother, Nadine, was feeding Mitchell, Jennifer's three-year-old stepbrother. Since the baby, Jennifer's stepmother hardly anything to say. They basically greeted one another, and that was the extent of their conversation.

Jennifer hurried to dress. The last thing she wanted to do was babysit. She planned to take Kyle to the riverfront where they could see the Arch and had a choice of night clubs. She rushed to the front door with her purse under her arm.

"Jennifer, where are you going? I need you to watch Mitchell this evening," Nadine said without turning around.

"Some friends are in town and I'm showing them around," Jennifer said, gripping the doorknob. Something told her this would happen. Nadine always waited until the last minute for everything. This was a bad sign for the evening.

"Why didn't you say something about going out? I need you to watch Mitchell," said the irritated woman.

All Jennifer could think about was having her own apartment. She would not have to worry about babysitting or anything else. "I'm sorry Nadine, but I made plans this evening. Why do you wait to the last minute to ask me to babysit?" Jennifer asked loudly.

Nadine looked at her with a scowl. "Don't talk to me in that tone of voice. Furthermore, I'm not asking you to babysit, I'm telling you. As long as you live in this house, you will follow rules," Nadine said sternly.

Jennifer gripped the door knob tighter. "I have plans this evening," she said and rushed out of the house. Nadine called her, but Jennifer kept going. She jumped into her car and drove off mumbling to herself.

She arrived at the Radisson Hotel sooner than expected. She was so angry that she had forgotten Kyle's room number. Kyle was standing in the lobby with two other nerdy looking guys. They had on slacks and a shirt. Kyle had on a sports jacket. She approached them smiling, but Kyle frowned.

"What do you have on?" he asked, almost disgusted.

Jennifer looked down at her slacks. "Clothes. Why are you so dressed up? We're going on the riverfront, to the Arch. You didn't have to dress up," she said, slightly annoyed.

"We tried telling him, but he insisted," one of the nerds said. Kyle looked disgusted which had Jennifer baffled. He never dressed nicely in school. Now, he exhibited an attitude of fashion consciousness. As they walked to Jennifer's car the two nerds became more excited but Kyle dragged along.

They went to the Arch first and rode to the top. Jennifer gave them the history behind the Arch. The two nerds listened attentively but Kyle's attention seemed to be elsewhere.

They went inside a few night clubs. The two friends were enjoying themselves while Kyle walked around the bar searching for women. He stopped to talk to a white girl. He was laughing, having a good time. Jennifer became a little jealous. She tried to ignore his behavior, but it was difficult. In college, he practically worshipped her. But now, he did not want to be around her. She continued to talk to the two friends.

The nerds wanted to check out another club. They searched for Kyle. He was talking to a blonde. "Hey Kyle, we are getting ready to check out another club," Jennifer said, trying to talk over the music. Kyle looked irritated. He said something to the blonde and left.

When they got outside, one of the nerds pointed to a club across the street. As they approached the club Kyle asked, "Do you know of any upscale places?" The question threw Jennifer for a loop.

"There's nothing wrong with these places," one of the friends said.

"Do you want me to take you back to the hotel?" she asked angrily. She was insulted. Kyle kept walking.

The group went to two more clubs and decided to call it quits. The two friends were bubbling. Jennifer suggested they grab a bite to eat at Calico's restaurant. It was one of the few restaurants still open. When they walked inside Calico's, Kyle let out a sigh.

"What's the matter now?" Jennifer asked, losing patience.

Kyle shook his head. "Nothing. Nothing at all."

They sat down and ordered. Jennifer ordered an ice cream drink and the two nerds ordered Margueritas. Kyle tried impressing the waitress with his knowledge of wines. He embarrassed her by asking for wines which were obviously not on the list. She knew nothing about any of the wines he asked about. Kyle flirted with the redheaded waitress. She tried being polite. The group watched as Kyle made a fool of himself.

The two friends talked lively about the Arch and the clubs. "Had I known, I would have suggested something more suitable," Kyle said sarcastically.

"What are you implying? You used to like those kind of places. You have been very critical this evening," Jennifer said. She had taken enough of his gratuitous comments.

The group ate and talked until closing. They all piled into Jennifer's car. One of the friends asked Jennifer to stop at a gas station. He filled her tank and paid for it. When they arrived at the hotel, the nerds said, "Good night," leaving Jennifer in the lobby with Kyle. She wanted him to go also.

Kyle was arrogant now. The only physical change in him was his clothing. He had nothing positive to say the entire evening. His comments dripped with sarcasm. He talked formally about all the trips he had taken over the past year. He talked of his new friend William Smith who had been a big influence on him. The two met at a networking function two years ago. Kyle was impressed with this man for some reason.

Jennifer was bored listening to him. "What's up with the slacks and jacket? Was that William's idea too?" she asked to keep her interest alive.

"If you want success, Jennifer, you must dress and think it at all times. Those two guys are still learning. I still have a little more grooming to do with them," Kyle said as he rubbed his hands together. Jennifer wanted to burst into laughter. They talked another thirty minutes before Jennifer left.

Jennifer knew it wasn't going to be pleasant when she got home. She had never yelled at either parent before nor had she ever walked out. She wondered what her father would say. She even thought he might hit her. She received her last spanking when she was ten.

She was nervous as she turned the key in the lock because the lights were on in the living room. She took a deep breath and entered. Her father looked at his watch. It was 3:30 a.m. He looked at her with big, brown eyes. "Where have you been? Your mother asked you to babysit and you walked out," he said.

"Some friends from college are in town. Besides, she didn't ask me to babysit. She told me at the last minute. I had made other plans."

"Your mother is upset. You need to apologize. Don't ever raise your voice at her again. What's so important that kept you out this late?"

"Why should I apologize? She yelled at me first. I stay in every weekend babysitting. As soon as Kyle comes to town, I can't entertain my friends."

"Who is Kyle? Is he the reason you've come in so late? What are you doing now, sleeping around with boys?"

"I'm not sleeping around with anybody. I'm tired of babysitting, daddy. I can't ever do anything."

"When your mother tells you to do something, you do it without any questions. If she needs you to stay and watch your brother, that's what you do as long as you are living here."

Jennifer was steaming. It was always going to be "as long as she was living under their roof." She felt like a slave.

"Nadine is my stepmother. She has never talked or listened to me. That's what real mothers do. Why do you defend everything she does? I want to know why I am stuck with a woman like Nadine? She's not doing me a favor. Nobody wants a fat, sloppy woman like her, not even you!" Jennifer yelled.

Her father stepped in front of her and slapped her across the face. It was the first slap across the face ever. The night with Sean flashed back. Jennifer shook. She had to get away before he beat her up. She had to leave. She ran to the door and opened it wide.

"Jennifer, where are you going?" her father asked, coming closer to her.

Jennifer ran out of the house and jumped into her car. She drove off quickly. She had a full tank of gas, thanks to the nerd, but nowhere to go. She decided to go to the hotel where Kyle was staying. She figured she would be safe there.

Jennifer walked to Kyle's room and knocked on the door hard. One of the friends opened the door.

"Hey Jen, what's the matter?"

"Where is Kyle?" she mumbled. She walked into the room. Kyle was in bed in pajamas. "He hit me," she said to him before the tears fell.

Kyle jumped up and put his arms around her. "It's okay. You can stay here Jen, you're always safe with me," he said and fixed the bed for her. He made himself a pallet on the floor. The three men sat quietly on the floor as Jennifer cried herself to sleep. The two friends looked at Kyle, for an answer. "She's going to be okay," Kyle whispered.

It had been two months since the fight. Jennifer took the day off work to move. She had packed the last of her things in her car. She wanted to be gone by the time her father came home. She only had clothes, a stereo and records, a television and a trunk. She refused to take the bed or dresser. Her father paid for it so he could keep it.

Jennifer heard the sound of her father's voice. She looked at her watch. He had come home early. She heard his footsteps coming toward her room. She began to shake. He walked into her room. She turned her head, pretending to search the dresser drawers for an imaginary item.

"The last thing I want is to lose you, Angel. I gave your mother my word to make sure you would grow up safe. Although Nadine is your stepmother, she is still your mother. She helped me a great deal when I was struggling, trying to raise you alone. You gave me your word that you would not give her any trouble."

"I have never given you or Nadine any trouble. I want to live my life without people constantly telling me what to do. I can't continue to live like a live-in maid."

"I know you haven't given us any trouble, Angel, but I can't afford to lose you. You are all I've got left now. I can't bear the idea that I failed your mother."

"Who is my mother? What kind of person was she? How did you two meet? How did she die? Why won't you tell me?"

"I'm sorry, Angel, but some things are too painful. She was a very pretty woman who was very smart. You have her nose and mouth. When you were born, she swore that nothing was going to stop her precious Angel. I'm sorry if I have failed you, but I did my best. You don't have to move. We can work it out. I'm sorry for hitting you."

"You didn't fail me. I'm a woman, daddy. I don't know the first thing about my role as one. Mothers discuss those things with their daughters. Nadine has never been a mother to me. I can't ask you about how to be a woman, daddy."

"No one told your stepmother, either. Always remember, you can come back home." Carleton left the room with his head low.

Jennifer felt her father's pain too. She knew he did his best but it wasn't enough. It was time to go and experience life the only way she knew how and that was by her instincts. She had always felt as if she were on her own. Lisa had helped her to listen to the inner voice and it was telling her it was time to go. To stay would mean to live with Nadine's misery. Whatever pain her father experienced, Jennifer decided to let it go.

Chapter 20
March 1987

Jennifer looked at the figure lying on the floor. He smiled as he rubbed his eyes. When he looked up, she saw something she had never seen before: beautiful brown eyes and a wide bright smile. As she looked at the figure she had ignored for so long, she felt the urge to touch him.

He was content lying on the floor. Occaisionally, he sat up and looked at her. He played with her by tickling her on the stomach. He enjoyed hearing the laughter that rang at the top of her lungs. He sat up quickly to play with her again and she rolled over the top of the bed to play with him. Their heads collided. Her lips brushed the side of his face.

Her body shuddered. She moved her head slowly against the side of his face. His beard was rough, but his eyes were gorgeous, like a four year old receiving an afternoon snack.

He quivered when he felt her lips touch the side of his face. He had to kiss her. The time was now. He had waited nine years. She was still beautiful. The smooth brown skin and the dark eyes were still beautiful. He saw the thickness from the stitches and it was beautiful too.

Her hair had fallen from the barrette. Large curls fell into her face. He touched them, allowing his fingers to twist the curls like he had always imagined. He put a handful to his lips and kissed them. He kissed her forehead and watched how her eyes closed under his touch. He kissed her cheek and then her lips. He kissed the stitches. He kissed her lips again. She opened her eyes and her head dropped a little.

His heart pounded. He was nervous. He wondered if he had rushed it. It had been nine years. He couldn't have possibly rushed it? He wondered if she liked it. She hadn't said anything. She couldn't have possibly liked it. None of them seemed to like it. He was too ugly. He was ready to apologize. He stretched out on the floor with his hands over his face.

"You don't have to sleep on the floor. Why don't you sleep with me?" the kind voice said.

He slowly stood and climbed onto the bed. She flipped her hair as he slid under the covers. He felt one of her legs. It was protected by pajamas. So was his. The quivers continued as he felt her scoot closer to him. Finally, the locks of hair fell on his chest. He couldn't believe it. She liked it. She liked his touch. She liked the way he looked. She liked him. He only hoped she didn't feel his embarrassment. He was too nervous, too shy, too ugly. He wasn't ready.

"Now tell me again. The man's got a baby and didn't tell you?"

"No. I said he doesn't know whether it's his."

"Okay, he doesn't know whether the baby is his. Doesn't sound like Cameron. Hold your hand still," Rochelle said as she polished Lisa's nails.

Lisa reminisced over the visit to Atlanta in November, the year after Cameron's visit to St. Louis. He had fixed her breakfast in bed.

They sat relaxed in bed talking until the doorbell rang. Cameron frowned slightly and left to open the door. Lisa heard a woman yelling and Cameron asking her to leave. The woman got louder, accusing Cameron of dodging his responsibilities. She walked by the master bedroom and caught a glimpse of Lisa sitting relaxed in bed. "Who is this bitch?" the woman yelled.

Lisa remembered looking at the outraged woman out of pity. Cameron rushed to the bedroom and yelled at the woman to leave. She cried, telling him he had a daughter named Celeste and he had not given her a dime in child support. Lisa was surprised at Cameron's cold attitude as he told the woman to leave for the last time. She stormed out of the apartment in tears, calling Lisa a bitch and Cameron a no good son-of-a-bitch.

Lisa tried discussing the incident, but Cameron shut down. He remained silent on the subject for the duration of the trip. She called him a few days later to discuss the baby. He denied paternity and didn't want to discuss it any further. She had decided that she could not continue seeing him, knowing that he had a child that he refused to support.

"Whether it sounds like him or not, the woman said he has a baby girl. That was November. I'm quite sure he's seeing somebody by," Lisa said as she watched Rochelle polish her nails.

"It must have hurt you since this is your first time talking about it. You know, I saw something like this on Oprah. A woman falsely accused a man of fathering her child. His fiancée got pissed and dumped him. He was on Oprah trying to get the heffa back. My girl, Oprah, arranged to have the pale-looking white girl come on the show. They kissed and you know the rest. Maybe this sister is falsely accusing Cameron. Somebody needs to tell Oprah to go easy on the scarves. Some of them are pretty but I get tired of seeing them every day. Sit at the dryer for fifteen minutes," Rochelle demanded.

Lisa sat at one of the dryers by the window. She took a good look at Rochelle's dream. She had the shop decorated in pink and grey with a beautiful pink, grey and dark green border trimming the walls. A nineteen inch color television occupied a corner in front of Rochelle's nail table. It was her connection to the outside world, Oprah Winfrey. Because Rochelle worked long hours, she hardly socialized anymore.

Rochelle was good at nails. She was the best in the city at airbrushing. Although Lisa never liked decorated nails, it seemed a lot of women did. Rochelle practiced until she became the best.

Rochelle increased her clientele by three hundred percent over last year, her first year in business. Lisa remembered how she had long talks with Rochelle because her parents were not supportive when she quit her job at the bank and opened the shop. They couldn't believe she threw away a college education to do nails. Now she had Nails Expressions, a two-room suite. Rochelle turned the next room into a boutique. During the slow months, the sales from the boutique kept her afloat.

Alicia came through the doors smiling. "I'm glad you're not running behind. I was going to leave if you were," Alicia said loudly.

"Sit down! You run over to the Asians to get your nails done and now I have to correct their mistakes," Rochelle fussed.

"You're always booked so I had to go somewhere else," Alicia said and turned to Lisa. "Guess what? Me and a friend are going into the daycare business together. We should start operation next spring," Alicia said joyfully.

Rochelle gasped, "Don't tell me that you are going through with Bay-Bay Kids Baby Sitting Services," she said. Alicia rolled her eyes.

"Congratulations Alicia. Who is your partner?" Lisa asked.

"A friend I met in one of my child psychology courses at UMSL. She's really cool. We're looking for a location now," Alicia said.

Immediately, Lisa felt uneasy. Deep down, Alicia was a nice person and could easily be taken advantage of. "Let me know if you need anything Alicia," Lisa said. She paused for a second. "Mother, my nails are dry. Can I go home and pack?" she asked teasingly of Rochelle.

Rochelle laughed.

"Where are you going?" Alicia asked.

"To Atlanta."

"Well alright! Tell Cameron I said, hi."

"This is for business," Lisa said.

"Yeah we know. Oprah did a show on mixing business with pleasure. It doesn't hurt, as long as it stays in focus. Somebody needs to talk to girlfriend about wearing brown. It makes her look ashy," Rochelle frowned as she complained.

"What's up with you and Oprah? You need to stop watching those talk shows," Alicia complained. Lisa left the two women fussing.

Lisa was talking to an ecstatic Jennifer. She had recently come back from Kansas City. She was going on about her visit and decided to share the news about being attracted to Kyle. Lisa almost stopped breathing as Jennifer described someone who looked like Denzel Washington in a Jimmie Walker body. Lisa joked until she realized Jennifer was serious. The Kyle Jennifer described died in 1983. He was no longer infatuated with Jennifer. The last time Lisa saw him, he was very arrogant. What really made Lisa angry was Kyle's comment about only liking successful business women and that Jennifer had a long ways to go.

"I think you two will make a good couple," Lisa finally managed to get out.

"We're not really a couple. We're not sure about our feelings for each other," Jennifer confessed.

Lisa knew it was Kyle. "How is your new job? You said they gave you trouble about getting sick this winter. It sounds like harassment to me. Maybe you should talk to Maria. You know she's a lawyer now," Lisa said.

"I'm sure it will get better," Jennifer said optimistically.

"Have you heard from Cameron?" Lisa asked in passing.

Jennifer was silent for a moment. "I talked to him three weeks ago. I take it he hasn't called."

"I need to finish packing."

"When you get to Atlanta, call him. He will be happy to hear from you."

Lisa strolled around the perfume counter at Rich's. She picked up a bottle of Samsara and sprayed some on her wrist. She asked the sales clerk the price. Eighty dollars. Lisa decided on the lotion instead. She asked the clerk to hold the lotion as she walked around the counter.

She took several minutes looking at all of the pretty bottles in the showcase. She walked back to pay for the lotion. As she pulled out her wallet, the clerk smiled and handed her a bag with perfume and lotion.

"Wait a minute, I didn't want the perfume," Lisa said.

"The gentleman paid for it," the clerk said cheerfully, looking over Lisa's shoulders. Lisa turned quickly to see a slimmer Cameron standing with an older gentleman. The two men approached her. She didn't know what to do.

"Hello, Lisa."

Lisa said nothing.

"What brings you to Atlanta?"

"Training," Lisa answered.

"Dad, this is Lisa Arvell."

The older gentleman narrowed his eyes slightly. He remembered the young woman from Lionel's graduation, Debra Arvell's daughter. "Hello Lisa. Nice to meet you," he said in a smooth, baritone voice.

"Hello, Mr. Johnson," Lisa said looking at him and then away.

"How long are you going to be in Atlanta?" Cameron asked.

"I need to go. Thanks for the perfume. You didn't have to."

"Where are you staying?"

"Cameron, I gotta go, okay? Nice meeting you, Mr. Johnson," Lisa said and walked off. Her heart was beating fast and her legs felt weak. *No more*, she said to herself.

"She hates me," Cameron told his father.

"She's just angry. It will be alright."

"How do you know?"

"Women like her have a lot of pride. If she hated you, she would not have taken the perfume."

"You said I would know my wife. That's her."

"I should have known."

"Why do you say that?"

"I went to school with her mother."

"Did you like her mother?"

"She was like one of the fellas. She was a very pretty woman, quite cunning. She typed my papers and tutored me. At one time I liked her but she liked my friend better."

"She sounds intriguing. Why didn't you date her? It seems like you would like someone challenging."

"She wasn't challenging. She was a little dangerous. Besides, I liked her friend better."

"Mom was Debra Arvell's friend?"

"No, it was someone else."

"When did mom come into the picture?"

"When she told me that she was pregnant."

Lisa decided to take a long bath. She wanted to retire early, to be fresh for the next day's training. Before she stepped in the tub, someone knocked on the door. She cursed to herself and grabbed the short robe.

"Who is it?" she yelled.

"Cameron."

She let out a deep breath and opened the door.

Déjà vu, he said to himself. Her legs were toned, especially the thighs, for what he could see. Her hair was pulled back with a head band. It was like the first time but they were both experienced. "Can I come in?" he asked.

Lisa stepped behind the door as Cameron walked inside the room. He sat down. Lisa remained standing. "I asked Jennifer for your room number. I hope you don't mind. I couldn't let you leave Atlanta without talking to you," Cameron said. Lisa remained silent.

"I didn't know what to say when Vivian came by my apartment last year. She is a very pretty woman, as you saw. As I paid to have her hair and nails done, she was out dating other men. I saw her out with them and she doesn't know it. I used a condom with her every time, that's why I'm questioning whether the child is mine. I know she needs money so I started paying child support until the test results come back," Cameron said, trying to search for a clue in Lisa's face. She remained silent.

"All I have been thinking about was marrying someone I didn't love. I can't let you get away. I need to hear you tell me to go away," Cameron persisted and walked to Lisa. She stepped back, not able to say either.

She and Cameron had the best times together last year. He taught her how to play tennis. They went swimming and biking together. They played scrabble together. Although he was better in vocabulary, she was a strategist. They could talk about anything: politics; business; and relationships, always in a non-threatening way. It was so difficult to love him.

"I don't hate you," she cleared her throat. "I...can't...stand the hurt. Every time something goes wrong, you shut down. I'm tired of trying to make you communicate when there's a problem. What if the baby is yours?"

"I have to take care of her. I can't pretend she doesn't exist. I made a mistake."

"And that baby has to pay for your mistake!" Lisa yelled.

"If she's mine, I'll take care of her. I won't abandon her like your father did you," Cameron said reaching for Lisa. She pushed him away.

"He didn't abandon me! He just doesn't know who I am. No one told him!" she yelled in anger.

She had to gather her senses. She told herself she would be in full control the next time she saw him. She knew he loved her. She wasn't letting him get away. He just had to work harder for her love. His sincere eyes and naivety told her to play her cards right. She needed someone to love and to love her.

He walked to her. She pushed him away. He wrapped her in his arms. He could feel and hear her breath unwieldy, refusing to cry. He wondered what kind of man would leave a smart, beautiful child to raise herself. He hated Lisa's father, whoever he was.

"I called my father and told him about this situation which has been going on for a year. He made a personal trip to Atlanta to talk to me. We had our first man to man conversation. I wanted to know why I never got his attention. He told me he felt I didn't need it. I was the strong side of his personality, whereas Lionel is his weak side. He said I did things he always wanted to do and Lionel does things that he did." Cameron lifted Lisa onto his lap. She rested in his arms.

"What is Lionel doing now?" Lisa asked.

"He's married with a son."

June 1988

"Y'all should have seen Oprah today. She had these pitiful women talking about being battered. You know they were white, don't you? Keep these claws still," Rochelle complained as she polished the woman's nails.

"I'm getting tired of hearing about pitiful women. Oprah needs a show on women who have kicked their husband's ass," one said.

"Since she gained that weight back, she looks depressed," one said.

"She is depressed! Pick out a color," Rochelle said to the woman in the chair. She grabbed a bottle off the counter.

"They said she lost that weight for Stedman. I don't care how fine a nigga is, I ain't losing weight for nobody," said a very large one.

"She didn't lose weight for a man," another one added.

"Oh yes she did! Women do crazy shit like starving themselves because of a man. One thing I can say about my girl, she has claimed that man on national television. Everybody knows that Stedman belongs to Ms. Winfrey. This color is too light for you. Get a bottle of red," Rochelle said. The woman got up and grabbed a bottle of red polish.

Lisa walked through the door. She had come directly from work. She caught a few jealous eyes from Rochelle's clients whom she called "the welfare queens."

"Hey girl, what's up? I haven't seen you in over two months. How was the trip to the Bahamas?" asked a happy Rochelle.

"We had a ball. We ate all day and partied all night. We stopped in St. Thomas and St. Martinique. I brought you something back," Lisa said and gave Rochelle a bag.

"I bet you did eat all day. You look a little top heavy. I'm glad you got my message and came thirty minutes later. I know Miss Thang is going to be upset. I tried calling her, but I couldn't reach her. You know her so called partner pulled out of the daycare deal," Rochelle whispered to Lisa. It didn't surprise Lisa. Every time she talked to Alicia, nothing had developed.

Jennifer walked in with a blank expression on her face. Lisa was glad to see her but immediately knew something was wrong.

"Hi Jennifer, how are you?" Rochelle asked inquisitively. Jennifer had only come by the shop a few times since it had opened.

"Hi Rochelle. Hi Lisa," Jennifer said with a smile. She sat down beside Lisa.

"I want you to be the first to know," Lisa whispered to Jennifer and extended her hands. Jennifer put her hands over her mouth as she gazed at the sparkling diamond ring.

"Have you set a date?" Jennifer whispered.

"June sixth of next year. I want you to be my Maid of Honor," Lisa whispered.

Jennifer hugged Lisa and whispered into her ear, "I quit my job today."

Lisa refused to believe what she had heard. Something drastic had to have happened to make Jennifer quit. "What happened?" Lisa asked, trying not to talk out loud.

Jennifer shook her head. "I don't want to talk about it." She quickly wiped the tears away. Alicia walked into the room and immediately frowned.

"I tried calling you, but you were not at work or at home," Rochelle said apologetically. Alicia spoke and sat down next to Jennifer. Lisa knew when Alicia was in one of her moods, it was best to leave her alone. Alicia mumbled to herself.

"Hi Alicia. How are you doing?" asked a friendly Jennifer.

"I wished I would have known she was running behind schedule," Alicia continued mumbling.

"How are your plans for the daycare center?" Jennifer asked innocently. Lisa took a deep breath and hoped she wouldn't have to jump into a verbal battle with Alicia.

Alicia turned sharply and looked at Jennifer. Something about Jennifer's eyes calmed her down. "It's not going to happen. My partner pulled out," Alicia said.

"It sounded like a good plan. You shouldn't let one person stop you from reaching your dream. You have always reminded me of Lisa. You two are hard workers and fighters to the end. Lisa worked long and hard to get in the Economics division at the Federal Reserve. You just have to work harder, by yourself, to get your daycare center," Jennifer said and got up and walked proudly out the door.

Alicia knew in her heart Jennifer was right but she was afraid of failing. Her mother had always told her that she would never amount to anything and it was becoming true.

"Your pledge mother, Cheryl, is in the daycare business. Give her a call," Lisa said.

Alicia refused to look at Lisa. She was a failure as captain and a failure as an entrepreneur. Lisa put her arms around Alicia.

"It's going to be alright," Lisa said soothingly.

Alicia shook her head. "She's right. I'm never going to amount to anything," she said in a whisper and wiped her eyes.

"Don't say that!" Lisa said.

"My family is constantly asking for money as if I'm rich. I'm tired of this shit."

Rochelle got out of her chair and sat next to Alicia. "Don't let anyone tell you what you can or can't do. My parents said the same thing. I needed to be my own boss and this shop let's me do it. You got to take a chance. If you don't open that daycare center, somebody else will," Rochelle said and gave Alicia a tissue.

"I can call Cheryl for you if you like?" Lisa said.

Alicia shook her head and cleared her throat, "I'll call Big Sister Most High and Noble Greek," Alicia said and laughed. Lisa walked to the chair to have her nails done.

"Looks like I won't get serviced until midnight," Alicia said and walked to the door.

"I can't wait until you open that juvenile detention center. Wait until those mommas pick up their children late, then you'll understand," Rochelle said as she filed Lisa's nails. She saw the ring and smiled.

"If they come late, I'm charging them extra," Alicia said and opened the door.

"Alicia, come look at this rock on this girl's hand. Why didn't you say something?" Rochelle shouted.

Alicia rushed to the table. Her expression softened when she saw the ring sparkle under the light. "So when is the big showdown?" Alicia asked.

"June sixth of next year. I want you two to be bridesmaids." Both women nodded and screamed with delight.

"I'll talk to you later, Lisa, that's if you ever leave this joint," Alicia said sarcastically.

"When I bring my child up in that daycare center, I'm going to pick him up late every day. I dare you charge me extra," Rochelle said out loud.

"What child? You mean monster don't you," Alicia responded.

Lisa was in a lot of pain. She had been bleeding heavily for two days. As she sat at her desk, she felt faint. She had felt nausea the last three weeks. But when her period finally started, she ruled out pregnancy. She and Cameron were not careful on their last encounter, so she figured the worst but her cycle started. She decided to call Jennifer to see how she was doing since she quit her job. She was working temporary at a finance company.

"Jennifer Peterson speaking."

"Hey Jennifer, how's it going?"

"It's not bad. These people are okay but they are a little mad because I'm taking an extra day for the Fourth of July. I decided to go to Chicago to meet Kyle's friend William. I can't wait to see Professor Higgins. Are you feeling better?"

"Not really."

"You need to see a doctor. You can't afford to keep going at that pace."

"You're right. You want me to come along? I can tell Cameron to stay in Atlanta. He'll understand."

"That's okay. Margo has relatives in Chicago. She needs to get away for awhile. Since the breakup with Peter, she really doesn't do much of anything but eat. She's trying to lose weight but that has become depressing since she hasn't lost any."

"You have lost a lot of weight. What's your secret?" Lisa inquired.

"I'm back to the Miss Stevens' style of eating."

"How is Linda?"

"She's having a baby in August. She's upset because she won't look cute this summer." They both laughed.

"Have you heard from Angel? I know you've been trying to get in touch with her for over two years."

"She has disappeared. Linda said she hasn't heard from her either. Supposedly, Linda's mother and Angel had a big disagreement after Linda's wedding. Angel designed all the gowns for the wedding. Linda's mother had a problem with Angel's commission. The whole thing put a bad taste in Linda's mouth. She talked badly about her mother. Linda didn't think Angel would take it out on her as well. I never imagined those two ever not speaking. Something must be wrong."

"Who knows. Maybe Angel wants to be alone now. Maybe it's time to let go of college friends. Don't you have her father's phone number?"

"That number has been out of service for awhile. She will appear one day, I just know it. I'll call you when I get back in town."

"Drive safely."

Jennifer drove to the west suburbs of Chicago. She looked at the beautiful homes and the well-manicured lawns. Jennifer constantly looked at her directions, driving slowly. She was already late. She didn't want to miss her turn for fear of being later. Kyle had already warned her about being on time.

Jennifer pulled the Corolla into the driveway of a two story frame house with a beautiful lawn. She took her luggage out of the car and walked to the door and rang the doorbell. A tall elegant man opened the door and looked at her gawking. He tried not to show disappointment or disapproval but it was difficult.

"Hi, I'm Jennifer Peterson."

"Hello Jennifer, come in. I finally get a chance to meet you. Kyle has told me a great deal about you. Did you get lost?"

"No, a friend came along. I had to drop her off a few miles away."

Jennifer looked at the beautiful home. Everything coordinated well. The living room was white with a beautiful painting occupying the space on the wall behind the sofa. The furniture looked expensive. Kyle told her that William had a daughter, but she saw no evidence of a family. She walked into the black and white kitchen and saw Kyle.

"Let me show you to the room," Kyle said. He put down a knife and walked Jennifer up the stairs. Everything in the house seemed new. According to Kyle, William and Jean had been married four years. They moved to Chicago after William landed the job with International Foods.

Jennifer set her luggage on the floor. There was only one bed in the room, she assumed it was for her. She saw Kyle's clothes hanging in the closet. They began with small talk. He pulled her to him and kissed her. He was a gentle kisser. She broke away out of embarrassment. It wasn't the first time they had kissed but she felt uneasy being in a stranger's house kissing him.

"What's the matter?"

"Suppose somebody comes into the room?"

"Let them," Kyle said and kissed her again. She enjoyed his touch. Had she known it would feel so wonderful being with him, she would have dated him in college. "Let's go downstairs and join the others. Jean's two kids are here for the weekend. You're going to like them. They are really cute," Kyle said.

Jennifer followed Kyle downstairs into the basement. She saw a tall white woman with a boy and a girl standing over her shoulders as she typed on the computer.

"I didn't know Jean was white," Jennifer whispered.

"What difference does it makes?" said an agitated Kyle. He introduced Jennifer to Jean.

Jennifer thought Jean was much younger than William. She wasn't pretty nor did she have an attractive figure. She was very articulate and pleasant. Jennifer talked with Jean briefly and then she followed Kyle around. She didn't feel comfortable in the house.

After a tasteless dinner, William invited Jennifer down to the basement to talk. She had no idea what he wanted to talk about. He asked her questions about her career and background. The discussion lead to questions about her family.

As Jennifer tried to give a very brief summary of her family history, William interrupted and commented on the ignorance of black people. He talked about blacks having "ghetto mentalities." Jennifer became quiet and let William talk. He was angry for some reason. He told Jennifer that she had no ambition or goals and Kyle was moving ahead and needed a person who was the same.

Jennifer tried to excuse herself, but it seemed as if William didn't want her to go. He told her that Kyle wanted him to help her find a job and as a favor to Kyle, he would do so. After talking with William, Jennifer decided she didn't want anything from him. She was ready to go home. Tears came down her cheeks as he told her that she was just like all hot-tempered black people who think they are showing the man something by giving up. He called her decision to quit her job immature and typical. Her feelings were hurt to the point that she wasn't listening anymore.

William became angry with himself, primarily for upsetting Kyle's friend. "Are you alright?" he asked.

"I'm going upstairs," Jennifer said and ran up the steps to join Kyle. He was outside playing with the two children. He sensed immediately that she was upset.

"What's the matter?" Kyle asked.

"Nothing," Jennifer said with a very big smile. The little girl approached Jennifer, asking about styling hair. Jennifer didn't know how to respond because she had a different hair texture. She took the little girl into the bathroom. They began a girl to girl conversation.

The little girl's name was Wendy. She was twelve. She didn't have many friends. Her real father was an executive with the telephone company in Texas. As the little girl talked, Jennifer realized that Wendy was extremely lonely. Her mother didn't talk to her and her father was angry over the marriage. Jennifer did her best to play dress up with the little girl who was just as lonely as she was. They played very well together like two children. Jennifer began counting the days until it was time to go.

William and Jean took Kyle, Jennifer and the children to A Taste of Chicago. As Jennifer and Kyle walked around the fair, they held hands. She was able to take her mind off William by absorbing the attention Kyle gave her. He tickled her waist until she hit him. When he kissed her hand, William walked up and separated their hands.

"Jennifer, this is a business trip. It's time for you to get serious about your job search. You can do this after you are employed," William said.

The statements floored Jennifer. The real problem came when Kyle immediately put space between them and began talking to William for the duration of the trip. As Jennifer packed her things in the car, William invited her to come back to work on networking and interviewing. He told her he had a few contacts, and it might prove helpful in finding a job especially if she were willing to relocate. He also made her promise whatever happened and whatever that was said was a secret. Everything must be a secret. It didn't seem quite right to Jennifer, but she decided to go back.

Jennifer picked up Margo who was in a very happy mood. Peter had tracked her down and wanted to talk things over. They were talking marriage again. As Jennifer drove home, she thought hard about the things William said. It was true. She gave up too easily but there was still an issue William wanted to resolve with her, and she didn't know what it was.

Jennifer let the phone ring six times. Finally, Kyle answered. He was busy again, just like the last few times. She could hear a voice calling him. A woman's voice. Everything in Jennifer's throat dropped to her stomach. He rushed her off the phone and wasn't polite about it. Jennifer decided not to be rude. "When you are free, give me a call," she said.

"Talk to you later," Kyle responded.

"Good-bye Kyle."

He just hung up. No good-bye Jen. William had to have said something. This was the fourth encounter of being busy, not being able to talk. He didn't want her anymore. She decided to finalize her plans to move to Atlanta. She needed to call Allyn to make arrangements. In her soul, Kyle was her last mistake. She had to prepare for something better and it wasn't in St. Louis.

When Lisa woke up, she gripped the side of the hospital bed. Pain torture her body. All she could remember was grabbing the kitchen table before falling to the floor. Had it not been for Cameron visiting her, she didn't know what would have happened to her. He was looking over her bed with red eyes. She knew she wasn't dead so what was the problem? He rubbed her forehead while she moved in bed, trying to escape the pain.

"Where am I?" Lisa asked.

"You're in the hospital."

"What happened?"

"You had a miscarriage. They had to perform a D&C."

"A miscarriage? I was pregnant? What day is it?"

"Try to relax."

"Something's wrong Cameron. Where's the doctor?"

"You lost a lot of blood, Lisa. It was hard trying to match your blood type. I want you to relax."

Lisa didn't follow Cameron's statement about her blood type. She turned her head and closed her eyes. She heard him whisper, "We will have other children. It's going to be okay."

Chapter 21
October 1988

Gina drove in silence, catching a glimpse of Angel as they got closer to St. Louis. It was evident her cousin was not the same person she remembered in college. Angel was fifteen pounds heavier but not fat. She normally wore a size six but now she fit a size ten nicely. Her face was fuller. A barrette took the place of curls. Something had taken a bite out of her spirit.

The idea that Angel called Gina in Chicago was a big surprise. Gina had not heard from her in over two years. Gina had asked Angel to be godmother to her son Avery but Angel told her to ask Marsha. Angel had never turned down a request for help.

"I can't believe we have traveled almost two hundred miles without talking," Gina said.

Angel looked at her cousin with a soft smile. "I don't have much to say these days. I really appreciate you making this effort. I am going to give you some money when we get back to Chicago," she said.

"You don't have to pay me. This has worked out for the best. I need to see Lisa. You won't believe this but she told me that Paul was her father. I called Paul and told him everything Lisa told me. He almost hung up on me. The poor girl needs a blood donor. She's trying to have fibroids removed. She's afraid that she won't be able to have children, or at least the doctor told her she won't be able to carry full term until they are removed," Gina said.

"How did she come to the conclusion that Uncle Paul is her father?" Angel asked.

"Maria's mother told Lisa something about her mother's ex-boyfriends. Paul's name was mentioned. Lisa believes her father has to be someone from her mother's past because the boyfriends that were after college came after Lisa was born."

"Debra Arvell was her mother, wasn't she?" Angel asked with a frown.

"You should hear my mother offer her opinion about Miss Arvell. She has called her everything from a slut to a traitor. Whatever she did, pissed off momma."

"Aunt Barbara said that a Debra Arvell tried coming between my father and mother. She was the one that caused a lot of problems when they were starting the chapter at Missouri State. Why is Lisa calling you?"

"The Genies from 1980 use the pledge mother creed to the hilt. The one who screwed up the entire pledge period, recently called Cheryl for advice. There was another one who hardly spoke the entire pledge period. She visits Marie, mind you, long distance at least once a year and talks continuously. Marsha tells me a few called her, asking for advice. Lisa has always maintained contact with me, so it's not a surprise. She and Cameron Johnson are getting married in June. I guess she wants to have children, hell I don't know."

"I didn't know Lisa and Cameron were getting married. What a surprise!"

"When was the last time you talked to Lionel? I thought you two were buddies."

"It's been about two years. He's married with a son. He found the prettiest girl to marry and the last time I saw him, he was unhappy. I guess he'd rather have brains over beauty now," Angel said brashly.

Angel's last comment caught Gina by surprise. Angel had never shown an ounce of jealousy. It was written all over her face now. She had come to Chicago with very little money, which was not like her either. She seemed apologetic and embarrassed when Gina came to her father's house to pick her up. Something had definitely gone wrong in Angel's life.

"So Lionel lives in Kansas City? What is he doing now?" Gina asked.

"He lives in Minneapolis. He was managing one of Favor's department stores. The last time I saw him, he was doing fairly well in his career but poorly in his marriage."

"He should do well at Favors. Their stock is on the increase," Gina said. She thought for a moment. "It's hard seeing Lionel settling for someone who doesn't fit the bill. He seemed so ambitious in college."

"Thomas was the ambitious one. Lionel does well with someone telling him what to do. To my understanding, his wife is co-dependent. He has to tell her what to do and that's not good for him."

Gina was curious as Angel unfolded a few secrets of her past. "I see things were a little more than friends after college. What have you been doing for two years? You are not the kind of person who would disappear. Will this be our last encounter or will we still be cousins?"

"I don't want to talk about what I have been doing in last two years."

"Why? Not only are we cousins, but friends too. Why have you turned your back on everyone? Have you gotten so high and mighty that you can't be around anybody anymore?"

"I am so sick of your guilt-trip attitude. You are married with a loving husband and you still feel inferior," Angel snapped.

Gina gulped. Angel had always been her cheerleader, convincing her that she was pretty and smart although the boys preferred Angel and Linda. There were times when Angel refused to go out on a date unless the boy found someone for Gina. It wasn't that she was unattractive, she was shy when it came to dating.

Gina got off at the next exit and drove to a gas station. She got out of the car and stood with her arms crossed. She looked up at the sunny October sky. The light breeze tapping her face brought her back to reality. She had put Angel on a pedestal and now had insulted her without knowing.

Angel got out of the car and walked to Gina. They avoided eye contact which was unusual. "I didn't mean to get angry. A lot has happened and I just want to see my grandmother. I'm a little anxious. If you don't mind, I rather not discuss me," Angel said. The two women got back into the car. Gina drove in silence.

"I want to hear about Avery. Tell me what he's like?" Angel asked, hoping to ease the tension.

"He's a handful. He's working on sentences. It's kind of funny hearing him talk. Linda just had a baby girl, Camille Ali. The baby spends more time with Aunt Barbara than Linda. She and Aunt Barbara are finally on speaking terms since the wedding. What made you decide to visit Uncle Bill?"

"When I received the letter from my grandmother. I wanted him to answer some questions. He said he was happy to hear from me but it was a lie."

"You know he doesn't hold his tongue when it comes to telling how he feels. Linda said she tried calling you at the Youth Center but you had quit. You were doing so well with those kids."

"It was time to leave. Please call me Melanie and no more questions, okay?"

"Yes, right. No more questions. Let's get to your grandmother's," Gina said, blowing out air. She was within the city limits of St. Louis before Angel said anything.

"If you don't mind, I would like to visit Jennifer before we head back to Chicago. I need to see her," Angel said.

"Why don't I just drive you back to Kansas City? I can take Monday off."

"That sounds like a good idea but let's see how the trip turns out. I may want to go back to Chicago for a little while."

"How is Uncle Bill's wife? I can't believe he married a white woman."

"I guess she's okay. She didn't want to be bothered, so I gave her enough space. As far as I'm concern that's my father's house. She came into the marriage with nothing but the color of her skin. They said that dad always wanted a white woman. Mom was rather fair. Dad tried his best to make her into a Suzy white girl."

"Momma says, your mother was the one who helped Uncle Bill become president of Beta Gamma Delta. He wanted someone elegant and sophisticated and he worked like hell to get her. Uncle Bill is a good looking man anyway but momma said that your mother only wanted the best. She had several offers. Uncle Bill had to prove himself worthy."

"According to Aunt Barbara, mom was in love with someone else but dad was a good catch. The reason she married him was the other man married someone else. Aunt Barbara said mom was a lot to digest. She only wanted to be around powerful men. It helped balanced her ego. Aunt Barbara said that dad worked very hard for the prize but didn't know how to keep it."

Gina drove slowly as she approached the address of a well-kept brick house with bushes landscaping the yard near the steps. It had a fresh coat of white paint on the railings around the porch. A white swing occupied the right side of the porch. As Angel walked to the front door, she smelled something fresh, like roses. She looked for flowers, but there were none.

Gina extended her arms. The two embraced. Angel took a deep breath and rang the door bell. She saw the front door curtains pull back and a head peep out. Within seconds, the door opened.

Angel looked at a thin older woman in her seventies. Her posture was fairly decent for someone her age. Her grey hair was neatly pulled back into a bun. She had few wrinkles, a small nose and thin lips. Her eyes glimmered behind glasses. She wore pearl earrings and necklace.

"Are you Matilda Clairmont?" Angel asked, ready to weep.

The woman smiled. Her child had come home at last. When she spoke, her voice was meek. It cracked a little. "You have her eyes and nose but one thing you don't have is her spirit," she said softly with a smile.

Angel walked inside and looked around the house. The paint on the walls was fresh and the aroma in the air was still of roses. The furniture was fairly new considering Matilda was an elderly woman.

"Have a seat. Would you two girls care for something to eat?"

Gina and Angel shook their heads.

"It's been a long time. I'd never thought this day would come. When I'd didn't hear anything after the letter, I'd just thought it was another wrong address. How is your father?"

Angel cleared her throat. "Fine."

"Old Bill Smith always wanted to be high and mighty. I'd guess he got what he's been looking for. I'd got some pictures of your mother. Would you like to see them?"

"Yes," Angel said with joy.

The old woman disappeared for a few minutes and came back with a worn photo album. She gave it to Angel. There were a few old photos in the front. Angel took her time turning the pages. She looked at one old picture. There was something about the woman's presence that made her beautiful. She was smiling with two children. One child sat on her lap and the other stood beside her. The one standing looked like the woman. The one perched on her lap was smiling from ear to ear.

"Is this me?" Angel asked, pointing to the child who was standing. The old woman nodded. Angel looked at the very brown child on her mother's lap. "Is this my sister?" Angel asked out of curiosity. The old woman nodded again. Why was she dark, Angel asked herself. She looked at the picture closely. The child reminded her of Lauren. "This is the one that died in the car accident with mom?"

Miss Mattie smiled at Angel. "No sweetie. She's not dead. She lives with my son. I'd hadn't seen her since she was six or seven. Me and my son haven't spoken in years. This reunion is going to be good for all of us."

"What is her name?"

"Jennifer Michelle Peterson. She lives in this city. I'll call my son to let him know you are here."

Angel continued to looked at the very brown child and let the name Jennifer Michelle Peterson roll over in her mind, over and over. The name connected. Angel looked at Gina who continued through the album. "Gina, this is Jennifer. Jennifer is my little sister," Angel said with watered eyes.

Gina looked at the picture in shock. The child in the picture favored Jennifer strongly but something looked different. The child in the picture had a very innocent glow, not being aware of her surroundings. Gina flipped a page near the rear. There was a high school picture of Lisa. Both turned to face the woman.

"I'd call her my granddaughter. She lived with me for many years after her mother died. She spoils me. She's given me everything in this house," the woman said proudly, pointing to the furniture and some fixtures.

Angel wanted to speak but didn't know what to call the woman. "Ma'am. I need to know. I need to know everything. I know Jennifer. Does she know about me?"

The woman shook her head and walked to a back room. Angel and Gina followed. Candles were lit. The woman sat in an old rocker and closed her eyes.

"I don't know what to call you," Angel said.

"I'm your grandmother."

"I know but I don't know you."

"I'd understand. Everyone calls me Miss Mattie. I'd changed my name because the law was after me years ago. My real name is Matilda June Peterson Mitchell. You have an uncle named Carleton Peterson, your mother's brother, my first born. My first husband, Joseph Mitchell, did quite well for himself. He worked hard to buy land, something colored folks didn't have much of in Georgia.

"I'd was born June 6, 1908 in a small town near New Orleans. My mother was Creole. I'd met your grandfather when I'd traveled up north, to Cleveland, to visit my sister Louise. Joe swore he'd marry me but I'd paid him no mind because I'd had plenty of suitors. We met in 1928 and married 1930. Your mother was born August 17, 1934. My life changed May 5, 1938. It's when some white men came by the house me and Joe had near Covington, Georgia. Those men were drunk. They drove their car in a ditch and wanted Joe to help 'em. I'd knew to expect trouble that day." Miss Mattie paused and took a deep breath before she went on.

"Two were outside with Joe and one came inside the house where me and the children were sitting down to lunch. That man looked at me strange, the way some men in New Orleans looked at women. I offered him some food but he wanted more." The woman paused again and continued.

"Joe came inside the house to get something. He saw the man on top of me. Joe wasn't much for words so he got the shotgun and hit the man in the face with the butt end and then shot that man. The other two came in after hearing the shot. They came after Joe. He was able to get one before the other attacked him with a knife, cutting him in the belly. The gun was pushed to the side. So I'd picked it up and pulled the trigger. Joe was bleeding badly. He told me to get all the money and pack as much as I'd could carry and take the children to Pine Bluff, Arkansas to stay with his sister. He was bleeding badly. My husband died May 5, 1938." Miss Mattie paused some more.

"I'd put on my fancy clothes because I'd look like a white lady when I'd dressed up," Miss Mattie said smiling. "I'd packed my pretty things and put the children on as many clothes as they could stand. When I'd had all my valuables, I'd had Catherine to get in those white men car and keep her head down. Me and Carleton pour gasoline around the house and set in on fire because I'd was scared. I'd didn't want the law to find those white men dead. Good thing it was day light cause nobody saw the fire until the house burned down to the ground. I'd made the children sit on the floor as I'd drove the car like a white woman. If I'd pass a car, I'd smile and wave praying that nobody would recognize me being colored. I'd parked the car two miles from the bus station and me and my children were guided to Arkansas. I'd stayed with Joe's sister, Pearl, until I'd afford me a place to stay." Miss Mattie paused and looked into Angel's fixed stare. She was so much like Catherine but something was missing; she never had Catherine's love like the other one.

"I'd wrote a nice lady back in Georgia to help me sell the land. I'd got it sold and got a little money for it. Of course, the woman and her husband kept a lot of the money. That same lady wrote me, saying the law was looking for me, asking questions about the fire. Me and the children took off for St. Louis. I'd stayed with a nice colored woman who I'd met at the bus station. I'd took Mitchell off my name and started a new life in St. Louis. It's almost time to leave this earth."

Miss Mattie closed her eyes as if she were resting. Angel was overwhelmed by the story of this woman's character and strength. She had been raped; she had murdered someone; she watched her husband die; and she kept going. She did not appear to have any regrets or self-pity.

Angel's head bobbed up and down. Tears finally fell. She thought about how she gave up because of a pregnancy and this woman had experienced much greater tragedies at an earlier age and kept going.

Miss Mattie opened her eyes to see her granddaughter drowning in self-pity. She had hoped the story would stir her granddaughter into doing something. Maybe she should have told them what really happened. She would understand. One of her grandbabies had to have experienced the treatment she received from cruel men. She didn't need to tell everything. It wasn't necessary as long as she didn't lie.

Joe deserved to die. He accused her of making him kill those white men. He blamed her for everything, mainly her beauty. He beat her constantly. She couldn't go anywhere or speak to anyone. Men like him wanted Creole women but feared them.

The story she told was believable because it wasn't a lie. She just didn't tell the whole story. She saw how the two girls were taken by the part when the drunk white man was on top of her. Well, he was. He was trying to kiss her. He was so drunk that she was able to push him away, but Joe saw it. He was so angry when he came in that his rage got the best of him.

He could have easily beat all three because they were all very drunk. Instead, he shot that man. When the other two drunkards heard Joe hollering and slapping her, they came stumbling into the house. One saw his dead friend and began cursing. Joe was so mad that he shot him too. The other man had a knife. It caught Joe in the belly before he shot the other man.

Joe turned on her again. He was scared but she understood. He began beating her again. He told her to pack the children and they were going to live with Pearl. The more he looked at the white men, the angrier he became. He hit her for not moving fast enough. When he pushed her down, she was next to the shotgun. She pulled the trigger, taking a portion of his leg. He was paralyzed, screaming at the top of his lungs.

The rest of the story she told the two girls was the full truth, except telling Pearl a lie. Maybe if she hadn't burned Joe alive, his spirit would be at rest. She wanted him to suffer like she did for so long. He was still beating her from the grave. He took her daughter by appearing to Carleton.

Her son hated women. She couldn't tell if he desired women or not. A lot of women wanted him, but he chose one that wouldn't be much of a problem, an overweight woman who didn't like herself very much. She didn't like the child either. Carleton did all of that to make his mother suffer, but he ended up suffering himself.

Those three white men were angels. They helped her get away but she made a mistake. She should have left Joe to bleed to death. He was killed by his own uncontrollable rage. She had every right to protect herself but her rage went too far. She had been punished and had to learn a lesson. She had done other things that she wouldn't mention but it was only to protect herself.

"Grandmother," Angel whispered.

Miss Mattie's eyes opened slowly. She smiled gracefully. "You don't know how long I'd waited to hear that. Yes, Sweetie."

"I have a little girl named Lauren. I don't know what to do or how to do it." Angel broke down in tears.

The new information made Gina weep too. Miss Mattie knew it all too well. She beckoned for Angel to come to her. Angel knelt down in front of Miss Mattie and buried her head in the woman's lap. Miss Mattie stroked the young woman's hair. It was Catherine. This time she had to do it right.

"You feel alone because you'd given up. Your mother never gave up and her mother never gave up. And Miss Catherine, your great-grandmother, never gave up. Life is funny. Everything happens for a reason. Nobody's here because they just showed up. I'd learned from the mistakes of my mother and Catherine, God bless her soul. If we don't learn sweetie, we make them over again, causing our daughters to pay for them. If you love your daughter, you'd make it right."

"How? I don't know how," said a tearful Angel.

"You're a smart girl because I'd know my Catherine. In your own way, you will make it right. I'd work hard for my children. Catherine appreciated it but Carleton never forgave me for burning his father inside the house. He never understood. His son will learn the lesson."

"You said my sister is living with him?"

Miss Mattie nodded.

"Do you remember her when she was little?"

Miss Mattie grinned. "She was such a precious child, never causing any problems. Your mother called her Angel. She would sit and hum to herself, just as happy. She called you Mamie because she couldn't say Melanie. When she and Debra's child played together she called her Meese. She didn't catch on things too fast. After your mother died, your father took you away and Carleton took Angel, saying Catherine wanted him to raise her. He never trusted me. He thought I'd blamed him for the car accident. Sometimes, guilt is tricky."

"Did he cause the accident?"

"His drinking caused the accident. Drinking ain't nothin' but the devil's spirit."

"Would you like to see my daughter? I could bring her here to see you. She's my angel," Angel said proudly.

"I bet she is an angel. There are angels all around, just like yourself."

Angel shook her head. "I'm not an angel. I have made a lot of mistakes."

"Mistakes don't make you bad, they just slow you down. We all make them. I'm quite sure your friend can tell you," Miss Mattie said pointing to Gina.

"Your grandmother is right, Angel. You can't give up over one mistake," Gina said.

Miss Mattie got up. "Baby, I'd need to get some rest. Stop by tomorrow. I'll cook a nice dinner. I'm gonna fix a pound cake. We can talk some more."

Gina and Angel walked to the door. Angel turned around and hugged Miss Mattie. When Angel let go, she felt the embrace of invisible arms.

Angel was thinking, something she hadn't done in a long time. She remembered telling herself that her mind was going to putty because she wasn't using it. She thought back to Linda's wedding and the big argument over the commission on the gowns. Aunt Barbara bickered about paying the balance of thirtyfive hundred dollars. The two seamstresses who had sewn the gowns needed to be paid. They were hassling her about payment. Barbara used a flimsy excuse, saying it wasn't what they agreed too. Angel was too embarrassed to approach Linda because she carried an air of wealth for years. Linda offered to pay the balance but Angel refused.

Angel reminisced on the visit from Lionel that started the problem. He came to town to console her but she found herself consoling him. He complained about his marriage, blaming his wife for his lack of success. Angel got so tired of hearing him complaine that she told him to shut up. Her reaction startled him. He couldn't figure out what was wrong. She told him how she was out of hundreds of dollars from Linda's wedding. He offered to give her the money but she declined.

As she cried, he held her tight. The comfort of his arms made her vulnerable again. It had been awhile since his last visit and his touch was more inviting than ever before. He kissed her body from head to toe, playfully but gently biting her in spots that no one else had. He spent a long time touching and caressing her which made it more special.

When they finished, he talked about divorcing his wife. Angel didn't want to hear it. She had already broken the vows that she and her friends made in the dorms never to become involved with a married man. She made him leave, angry at herself for allowing it to happen again. He didn't understand. She told him not to visit or call anymore. He was thrown off guard because he knew she loved him. He could not imagine what went wrong. He would simply divorce his wife and start a new life with her.

Angel remembered how she interrupted him as he laid out the plans for their future. She told him that he didn't have the courage to divorce his wife because it would have happened long before. When he left, a part of him stayed behind. She quit her job the third month of pregnancy and stayed out of sight until the baby was born. Every time he called, she could feel the baby move and kick. She decided to change her telephone number.

She remembered the humiliation, asking her father for money so that she could get an abortion. He reminded her about the thousand dollar loan for the seamstresses that she never paid back. That was when she decided that she and the baby would suffer alone. The sound of Gina's voice brought her back.

"Excuse me, but are you going to help me get to Jennifer's apartment? It's getting dark and I don't know where I'm going."

Angel called out directions. Soon, Gina turned into a very quiet apartment community of brick buildings. Angel searched her purse and pulled out a comb. She removed the barrette and fluffed out her hair. "I'm in desperate need of a relaxer," she complained. She pulled down the vanity mirror and rubbed her eyes and cheeks. She fumbled around her purse again but she couldn't find it. She forgot, she had not worn any for so long.

"I can't believe I left…" Before she could complain more, Gina had rubbed the top of a tube of red lipstick with a tissue and gave it to her. Angel looked slightly embarrassed. She had made herself up as quickly and as best as possible.

"I am so damn fat. I have got to lose this weight. It doesn't make sense."

"You look fine. Now you look like you're not starving."

"I liked the starving look. This weight is coming off. You can bet on that," Angel said in her soft low voice, the one that was better known for scheming.

"Let's say hi to your little sister."

Chapter 22

Jennifer watched Lisa hold on to Gina. Angel tried to read Jennifer's expression before speaking. She could not determine if Jennifer was ready to receive the news.

"Lisa, what's the matter?" Jennifer asked softly. Lisa released herself from Gina's embrace and looked at Jennifer ready to share the secret.

"I don't know if I will ever be able to have children. I need to have fibroid tumors removed and it's tough finding a donor with my blood type."

Jennifer was astonished. Lisa never discussed wanting children. Jennifer figured the miscarriage must have deeply affected Lisa. "You're going to have children. What's the big rush? Cameron has waited this long to ask you to marry him, he can wait another year or two for children," Jennifer said trying to comfort Lisa's anxiety. It wasn't working. "What's your blood type? Maybe I have the same as you," Jennifer said.

"O negative," Lisa said.

"Maybe one of us is 'O' negative. If we get tested, maybe we can give a pint of blood towards your surgery. Can we?" Jennifer asked, easing around speaking too soon. Angel and Gina agreed to give blood.

"It doesn't matter, everything is going wrong. The dress I ordered has been discontinued. The Bridal Room doesn't have many nice dresses for the bridesmaids. I can't get a place for the reception because everything downtown is booked," Lisa complained.

"Who is your wedding coordinator?" Gina asked.

"I don't have one and Jennifer is moving to Atlanta," Lisa said with a huff.

"Maybe Angel can help. She has coordinated weddings," Jennifer said without thinking.

Angel's mind flashed back to Linda's wedding. The horror was still clear. Lisa, of all people, never seemed to care for her so why should she take on a job to coordinate her wedding? Lisa was uncomfortable with the suggestion as well.

"If you want me to help you Lisa, I can," Angel finally said, which seemed like eternity.

Lisa knew that Angel was good at fashion designs and arrangements.

The wedding was too important to allow personal feelings to stand in the way. Cameron's family was traveling across the country for the wedding. She believed his middle class background would bring scrutiny on the wedding. All eyes would be on the bride for one day. She couldn't let them know he was marrying someone from a poor background. Lisa thanked Angel. "I came to help you pack so let's get started," Lisa said trying to move the subject. She would figure out later how to approach Angel to begin the wedding plans.

"Jennifer, can I use your phone? I need to check on my son. I love my husband but I know him too well," Gina said. Jennifer pointed to the bedroom and continued to pack.

Angel knew Jennifer was angry with her but she seemed forgiving. "Sweetie, let's go in your kitchen," Angel said maternally.

Jennifer looked at Lisa who ignored her and continued to carefully wrap Jennifer's things. Jennifer followed Angel into the kitchen. They sat at the little breakfast set that resided next to a window.

"I know I have the audacity to ask, but I am concerned about you moving to Atlanta. Who are you going to stay with?"

"I'm staying with Allyn for four months. It should give me enough time to get on my feet."

"I know it's been tough on you but are you okay?"

Jennifer needed to tell somebody what was keeping her up at night. "I couldn't take the politics at the Association. They specifically targeted a minority to hire and they treated me like dirt. I couldn't stay there, Angel," Jennifer said in a rush.

"I understand. You will get another job. I hear that blacks have a better opportunity in Atlanta. With your background in finance, you will do well."

Jennifer decided to talk about Kyle. "I don't know if you remember Kyle Thomas from Missouri State?"

Angel frowned a little and shook her head. The name was familiar but she couldn't put a face to it. Jennifer told Angel the story about a budding relationship that had turned into unreturned calls and then to rudeness. She left out the part about William. It was a secret.

"Have you asked him how he felt about the relationship?"

"He said he wasn't sure. I know he likes me, but I don't know what I did wrong."

"You did nothing wrong. He said he wasn't sure about the relationship. Maybe his feelings have changed. I know it's difficult, but we have to accept when someone doesn't want the same thing we want. If Kyle isn't strong enough to discuss his feelings, leave him alone. He will come around one day. But when he does, you might not feel the same way. You are a very beautiful woman and a lot of men would love to date you."

"Where? I haven't been asked out since Kyle asked me to go to Chicago for the Fourth of July weekend."

"Just be patient and don't start settling. It is when you make mistakes."

It felt like old times, Jennifer and Angel talking again. Now the signs were looking good again. Angel came back into her life. Everything was going to be fine.

Angel wondered if it would be wise to tell Jennifer the news now. She took her best shot. "I'm sorry for ignoring you Jennifer but a lot has gone on in my life," Angel started. Jennifer looked at Angel strangely and went to the refrigerator for some cheese. "I have a daughter now and things have been pretty rough for us."

Jennifer let out a little gasp. "You mean to tell me that you got married and didn't invite anyone to your wedding?" she asked firmly.

"No, I'm not married nor am I working either," Angel said delicately. "I have been hurting badly over the last two years. It was difficult seeing anyone. I know you have tried to reach me and I'm sorry. I promise that I'll never leave you again." They both cried.

Lisa came into the kitchen first to witness the scene. Gina came out of the bedroom and saw Angel and Jennifer hugging in tears. Gina felt a little misty herself. "I say we all go out and celebrate the two sisters finding each other. It's been a long search and now it's over," Gina said joyfully.

"Angel and Jennifer are sisters?" Lisa asked.

Jennifer quickly broke Angel's embrace. Angel looked uncomfortable and did not know why. "What are you talking about, Gina?" Jennifer asked. Her body shook.

Gina looked at Angel's embarrassing look. "I'm sorry Angel, I thought you told her," Gina said apologetically. She felt like killing herself.

Jennifer looked at Angel for an answer. "I found my grandmother or shall I say our grandmother. Her name is Matilda June Clairmont. She sent a letter to my old address. I spoke to her briefly and she told me to visit," Angel said quickly.

Jennifer shook her head upon hearing the news. There was no way she was Angel's sister. "We don't look alike," Jennifer said, feeling the anxiety about to take over.

"We must have different fathers. We can visit Miss Mattie tomorrow, she can tell us. She also said that Lisa was her granddaughter," Angel said looking at Lisa who was mute, not believing a word. She left the room.

"The picture of your mother on the Chapter room wall doesn't look like me. I'm too dark to be your sister. My father..."

"Your father is your uncle. His name is Carleton Peterson. Your real mother's name is Catherine Michelle Peterson Smith. She was married to my father, William Smith," Angel said in a hurry.

The name William Smith sounded familiar to Jennifer, but she could not concentrate on it. Her father lying to her all these years was impossible. Some kind of way, the truth would have come out before now. She thought back to the time when she got her driver's permit and how her father insisted on taking her, giving the lady at the window all of the information. She had never seen her birth certificate because she never needed it, only for the driver's permit.

"Who is my real father?" asked a numbed Jennifer.

"I don't know. Maybe our Uncle Carleton can tell us."

"He's not Uncle Carleton!" Jennifer said louder.

"You need to talk to him about your real father. I'm quite sure he knows who he is," Angel said, trying to calm Jennifer.

"If he did know, he would have told me by now. He wouldn't lie to me," Jennifer said, still in shock from the news.

"Let's go, Gina, I have made things worst," Angel said and walked to the door. Her feelings were hurt. Her idea of being united with her sister was hugs and tears. Jennifer was so angry that it took away the joy of the long awaited dream.

Gina wanted to say something to Jennifer but decided to leave. She saw Lisa standing in exile in the living room. "We can talk later, Lisa. I made reservations at Stouffer's," Gina said and caught up with Angel.

"I'm sorry Angel. You two were hugging each other, I thought you had told her," Gina said.

"I don't care anymore. I think about how my father purposefully kept this information from me. He said he was trying to protect me. My own flesh and blood grandmother has been in St. Louis all of these years and he discarded her existence. Did you notice dad doesn't have any pictures of me displayed in his home? I don't exist either." Angel paused before beginning again. "I asked where my pictures were. He basically told me it didn't go with the decor, the bastard."

"Uncle Bill gets mad but he would never intentionally do anything to hurt you, especially disown you. He's always bragging about you."

"That was high school and college. The competition was to make Uncle Paul feel bad. The two have never been on good terms since dad borrowed a great deal of money and never paid it back."

Gina pulled onto the lot at Stouffer's. Angel let out a deep breath, "I don't have money for a hotel," Angel said.

"I'm tired and you're tired. I don't want to hear you talk about money again. You never used to."

"That was before everything slipped through the cracks."

"You are too smart to let everything slip through the cracks," Gina said and paused for a moment. "I called Linda. She is trying to get a flight out of Kansas City on standby."

"I don't need to see anybody else," Angel said, shaking her head. Her eyes rolled to the ceiling. "This is bullshit."

"No, this is love."

Jennifer stared straight ahead. She was fighting with reality. It reminded Lisa of the night the rape took place. Lisa was stunned too. She was standing with one of Miss Mattie's grandchildren who had been taken away. She talked about them as two girls who were stolen from her. The two girls never had names, only her daughter Catherine.

Lisa remembered having an imaginary friend who was dark like Jennifer. She always thought it was an angel. That is what Miss Mattie called her friend. All those years in college, Jennifer asked about the grandmother she never knew. Lisa was the one who connected the two in conversation. She wondered what she could tell Jennifer that would ease the discomfort.

But Lisa thought about her own troubles, trying to find a father who didn't want to be found.

"Maybe it's time to have a heart to heart talk with your father. You need to know the truth," Lisa said, standing behind Jennifer.

"He's my uncle."

"He should have the answers you need right now. After you talk to him, you need to talk to Angel. She needs you too. When you're ready to meet Miss Mattie, I'll take you," Lisa said. She walked to the door.

"Why should I meeet Miss Mattie? I don't know her."

"You know Miss Mattie, Jennifer. You know her through all the questions in that twin bed at school. She knows you through all my conversations about my best friend Jennifer. Why people lie, I'll never know. Give me a call tomorrow or tonight.?" Lisa said and slowly opened the door. She left a distraught Jennifer.

Jennifer was speeding on Interstate 70. All she could think about was a man that she had never met. She almost slammed her car into the wall by trying not to miss her exit on to Interstate 170. She couldn't believe she had lived twenty-eight years without laying eyes on her real father. She remembered the times trying to convince Lisa that her grandmother was all the mother and father she would ever need but now the shoe was on the other foot.

When she thought about the times she had asked her father about the mystery mother, he never once called her his wife. He made reference to Michelle Peterson as her mother.

Jennifer exited onto Olive Street road. She made the familiar turns to the street that was her playground twenty years ago. She pulled into the driveway, only to see the porch light on. Her father's car was there so she knew he was there too. She sat in the car taking deep breaths until her nerves summoned her out of the car. She walked slowly to the door and rang the doorbell, something she had not done since she had gotten her key. It was still in her pocket, but tonight she did not think to use it.

Nadine answered the door in a nightgown. Jennifer looked at the person who played the role of mother for eighteen years. She weighed close to three hundred pounds, most of it came after the baby. It had been years since she took the effort to comb her hair on the weekends. What Jennifer remembered of Nadine in the earlier years were the heated arguments that sent her father out of the house in a rage. Nadine accused him of cheating. Jennifer never understood the accusations because he never was one to stay out all night. She never remembered other women calling the house asking for him either. Nothing pointed to infidelity.

Jennifer walked inside the house without speaking. She was still paralyzed from the news. Nadine looked at her with a scowl. Jennifer didn't care. She walked to the back, her father's favorite place, the den. There was a beer bottle on the end table next to him. It had been years since Jennifer had seen beer in the house. Nadine would not allow it.

Jennifer looked at a once attractive man who now looked older than his years. He was fifty-six years old but life had taken its toll on Carleton Peterson. He moved slowly. His once large brown eyes drooped. His hair was grey and there were deep creases in his forehead. He was sixteen years older than Nadine, and he seemed like her father as well.

Carleton sat slumped in his favorite chair drinking a beer. He looked out of the corner of his eye to see his precious angel looking into the room. He looked at her then turned his head. "Your sister Melanie is in town," he said.

His cavalier attitude in telling her she had a sister added to the anxiety. All of these years and still, no explanation of her past. Jennifer decided he would have to talk whether it hurt or not. "Who is my real father?" she asked strongly.

"A man by the name of Charlie Johnson."

The name rang a bell but she could not place it with a face. "Where is he? Is he alive, married with children? Does he know about me?" she continued.

"The last I know is he's alive and married with children. He lived in Minnesota. I don't know anything of his whereabouts now."

"What about my mother? I want to know about her. I don't want to hear how pretty she was or how painful the memory is, I want to know about Michelle Peterson. I want you to tell me how she died," Jennifer said angrily. All the secrets from her past were about to unfold. She only hoped she could stomach what her father was about to tell.

Carleton took a gulp from the bottle. His mother told him the day would come when Jennifer would know about her mother and father but he called her a liar.

"She was born Catherine Michelle Mitchell after my grandmother. Catherine was very pretty. Men would whistle at her when she was only thirteen. I promised my daddy that I would take care of her and make sure nothing happened to her." Carleton took another drink.

"Your mother went to Lincoln University. She was very popular, a sorority girl. I don't remember which one but she ran with a group of uppity women. I think it was the same one you belong to. There was one man who was deeply in love with her who she married but the one she loved was your father."

Carleton took another drink. He remained still. Jennifer remembered that Angel's mother was one of the founders of the Kappa chapter at Missouri State. She felt proud. She sat in a chair next to her father. She saw an additional four empty bottles on the floor. "How did she die?" Jennifer asked softly. Carleton shook his head. "Please daddy, I need to know. People are appearing in my life. You have to tell me."

Carleton let out a deep breath. "She called and asked me to take you and her to see Charlie. He was in town that weekend. I had picked her up at momma's. As I was driving, she was complaining about running late. It was raining and I wanted to take my time. She complained so much, telling me to drive faster, so I did.

"A figure from nowhere darted in front of me. It did it a few times. Then it stood in front of me and then the fire came. I swerved to keep from hitting him. The car slammed into a tree on Catherine's side. I swear my daddy was in front of me.

"Catherine was crushed but you were untouched like a protected shield was around you. I wanted to run for help but I couldn't leave Catherine. She was gasping, fighting death. Before she shut her eyes for the last time, she told me to take care of you and not to let anything happen to you. She said the same thing my daddy said. Momma tried to tell me that daddy was dead but he wasn't. He told me the same thing Catherine told me but nobody believes me. I killed her just like I killed daddy," Carleton moaned.

Jennifer now knew the real story of her mother's death. It fascinated her more than saddened her. She was curious to see this Charlie Johnson person.

Carleton continued to sob, talking aloud, "She made me pour that gasoline. I didn't want to do it. She didn't give him a decent burial, that's why he still comes around."

Jennifer didn't know what he was talking about. It was a car accident to her and he whined as if it were murder.

Carleton wiped the tears with the back of his hand. Jennifer got a box of Kleenexes. When she made it back, Carleton had his head in his hand. Jennifer knelt beside him and handed him the tissues.

"Daddy, you didn't kill anybody. It was an accident," Jennifer said low.

Carleton dried his eyes. He could not look at Jennifer. "I understand if you don't want to come by the house anymore."

"Don't talk like that! As far as I'm concern, you are still my father. I don't know Charlie Johnson and he doesn't want to know me. He never came around to see about me. As far as I'm concerned, he is not my father," Jennifer said.

Carleton shook his head. "He doesn't know about you. Your mother kept your birth a secret from him. She didn't want to break up his marriage."

Jennifer pulled back. Her skin itched. "My father was a married man?"

Carleton nodded and took a drink from a fresh bottle of beer. The news was more disappointing. Jennifer felt a rush go up her spine. The signs of the past weren't good.

"When you were born, Bill left after seeing a brown baby. He knew it wasn't his."

Jennifer's chest tighten with each breath she took. It was bad enough she had been without parents all of her life but to find out she was the product of a love affair was outrageous. Pride left. Shame and embarrassment surfaced. She had to go. She had to find Angel. There was no one to turn to.

"I'm to blame for Catherine's death," Carleton said and drank from the bottle.

"No one is blaming you for anything."

"Momma blames me."

"It was an accident. It couldn't have been helped. It's going to be okay," Jennifer said and started out of the room.

"I love you, Angel."

"I love you too, daddy."

Jennifer rushed to her car and took off fast. She forgot the name of the hotel that Angel and Gina were staying in. She searched her mind frantically and then it came to her, Stouffer's at the airport. She wasn't that far so she took her time. She took the airport exit off Interstate 70 and followed it to Stouffer's Concourse Hotel. She drove around the lot until she found a parking space. She walked slowly inside the building and called Gina's room.

Gina picked up on the first ring. Jennifer noticed disappointment when Gina spoke. She was expecting someone else. Jennifer got the room number and took the elevator to the third floor. She knocked on the door and Angel answered. The two were motionless for a few seconds.

"I'm sorry Angel," Jennifer said.

"You don't have to be sorry for anything. I've finally found you," said a happy Angel. "Did you talk to Uncle Carleton?" Angel asked.

Jennifer let the words "Uncle Carleton" sift through her brain. They were still foreign. "He explained how our mother died in the car accident. He tried to avoid hitting something in the road. He lost control of the car."

"Miss Mattie said he had been drinking. He probably hallucinated."

Angel's last comment angered Jennifer. "It wasn't murder. He said he saw something in the road and tried to avoid it. Whether he drank that day or not, something obstructed his view. Maybe it was just her time to go," said a defensive Jennifer.

"You were too little to remember mom. She was an intelligent, highly educated woman. I really doubt if it was her time to go. She died at the hands of an alcoholic and I am not going to treat it as an incident of chance," Angel said. She was angry. Her mother died at the hands of a drunk driver.

"He is not an alcoholic! *Look at me!* Why don't I look like you? I am the product of a love affair between our precious, intelligent, highly educated mother and some married son-of-a-bitch. The woman was an adulterer, not an angel, and neither are you!"

Jennifer's last blow caught Angel in the stomach. She never imagined Jennifer making a comment regarding her integrity. Angel was furious. She walked up to Jennifer and pointed her finger in her face. "When I met you, I told you my name was Melanie. It was *your* choice to call me Angel like everyone else. It was also your choice to put me on a goddamn pedestal. As far as I'm concerned, mom died at the hands of a goddamn alcoholic."

Angel's eyes were blazing. Jennifer was afraid. Angel turned away and stormed into the bathroom. Jennifer was able to breathe again but she was mad. How dareAngel get the last word? Jennifer turned around quickly to see Gina shaking her head sadly.

"Did you see that?" Jennifer asked, pointing to the bathroom door. Gina was silent. "She's always making me look like a fool." Gina remained silent. Jennifer yelled at the bathroom door, "You're not queen of the mountain,

Angel!"

Jennifer spun around quickly, only to see Gina fighting to hold back laughter. Jennifer's expression made her explain.

"You two can't afford to fight. Angel has waited years to be reunited with you. She bragged about the little sister who followed her around all the time. Linda and I would listen, just to be polite. She always felt her sister was alive. She loved you without knowing you."

Jennifer looked depressed.

"You too have loved her without knowing her," Gina said and rushed to answer the ringing telephone.

"Hello...okay, I'll be there in five minutes.... Look Linda, can you stop complaining for once?... I figured. See you in five minutes." Gina hung up the phone.

Jennifer's face lit up, "Is that Miss Stevens?"

"You mean Mrs. Reed. You want to ride with me?"

Jennifer nodded.

Lisa stretched out on the floor, feeling the soft plush carpet under her back. She stared at the ceiling. She had found her father, only to have him deny her like the others. She turn to look at the growing stack of mail on her cocktail table. She had read the cards and letters from her line sisters, individually congratulating her on the marriage proposal. The surprise was receiving cards from Rita and Iris.

Lisa sat up and thumbed through the mail. She came across an envelope from the Department of Vital Statistics. She figured it was the requested copy of the birth certificate for the passport. Cameron was surprising her for the honeymoon. He told her that she needed a passport. She left the old birth certificate with Miss Mattie. She figured it was time she had her own.

Lisa contemplated opening the envelope. The emptiness of reading the familiar "unknown" under father's name crept slowly in her mind. She inched open the envelope and unfolded the certificate inside. Her heart took a leap. A name appeared under father, but it wasn't Paul Smith. It took a few minutes to digest the appearance of a name.

Her eyes watered. The search was over. She had a name. She would soon put a face to the name. Now it was a matter of getting in touch with him in time for the surgery.

Maybe he really didn't know she existed and would be happy to have her as a part of his life. Fear crept in. Maybe he would tell her to go away or deny her existence. She became afraid of meeting the unknown person. She picked up the phone to call Jennifer.

Linda walked into the room first followed by Gina and then Jennifer. Angel stood at attention and looked at Linda without losing eye contact. "Well, well, well. I've heard of fat cherubs, but never a fat Angel. What a contradiction," Linda said and put her Dooney & Burke on the dresser. She was extremely thin, a size four.

"Outside of that cheap tan sweater and those two inches of split ends, you are doing well for a homeless person," Linda said and sat in a chair. Gina sat on one of the beds. Jennifer stood next to Angel.

"So Linda, I see that you are still a bitch," Angel said.

Linda crossed her legs, toes pointed and smiled. "Indeed and a thin one too."

The telephone rang and Jennifer rushed to answer. The voice on the other end was taking deep breaths. "What are you doing there? I just called your apartment. Guess what? I know the name of my father," Lisa said choking and shared the secret.

The pitch in Jennifer's voice rose. "Your father's name is William Curtis Smith? That name sounds familiar. Where does he live?" At that moment, Angel looked at Jennifer with a dropped mouth. Linda and Gina looked at each other.

"Lisa, I'm happy for you. How did you find out?... Oh really?... I think I need to get an official copy of my birth certificate. I just found out about my real father too. His name is Charlie Johnson. He lived in Minnesota but who knows where he is now," Jennifer said as her adrenaline flowed. Angel was numb.

Lisa chuckled a little. "Cameron's father name is Charles Johnson," she said.

Jennifer whispered, "This man was an old boyfriend of my mother in college. They attended Lincoln University together." Gina and Linda could hear Jennifer whisper. They looked at Angel who was comatose.

"Cameron's father attended Lincoln, too. Matter of fact, he lives in Minnesota."

Jennifer was quiet for a moment. She turned to look at the three women. Gina was sitting beside Angel who was hyperventilating. Linda looked at Jennifer with a smile.

"I'm coming over, Lisa. I need to talk to you," Jennifer said in a whisper and hung up the phone.

"Dearie, you look good. I'm glad *you* are concerned about your figure," Linda said and began to unpack.

Jennifer looked at Angel who was breathing heavily. Gina was rubbing her back. "What's the matter, Angel?" Jennifer asked very low. Angel kept breathing hard. It was becoming more difficult to breathe.

"Jennifer, why don't you go visit Lisa. Angel needs time to herself. Give us a call in the morning," Gina said.

"I'll see you tomorrow, Angel," Jennifer asked more than said. Angel didn't respond. "What's the matter with her Gina?" asked a worried Jennifer.

"Why don't you go visit Lisa. She found her father right?" Linda inquired.

"Yes, somebody named William Curtis Smith."

Angel breathed louder.

"Well, we know how happy Lisa must be. I'll call you tomorrow, okay?" Linda said, rushing Jennifer through the door. She was reluctant to leave. She took slow steps, eyeing Angel at each step.

"I'll give you a call tomorrow, Angel," Jennifer said. Angel kept breathing hard.

"We'll see you tomorrow," Linda said.

Jennifer left the room. Angel rocked in place. Gina did her best to hold her cousin but she broke free. "Lies! All lies! That bastard has a daughter and didn't tell me, the son-of-a-bitch. I had a grandmother and he didn't tell me. This is not fair. Somebody has to tell me who I am," Angel said in a husky tone.

"Tomorrow, ask Miss Mattie everything. Don't leave anything to chance. All of us are connected and we don't know it because no one is saying anything. People are trying to hide their mistakes," Gina said.

"Look dearie, don't let all of this shit consume you to the point that you break. We all have secrets, so I say work it to your benefit. You need to get back on your feet and get your life in order. You need to start now," Linda said and handed Angel an envelope. Angel looked at the thin package. "What's this?" she asked.

"Something you earned a long time ago."

Angel opened the envelope. She looked at the check and then at Linda. "It's about time someone made good on all of that hard work. That's your pay plus interest," Linda said and continued to unpack. "One of mother's so-called friends, who came to the wedding, has been trying to get in touch with you. I saw her three months ago. She asked about you. I told her you were traveling. Anyway, that old white broad wants you to do a wedding for her sometime next year. She pays good. Here is her card. Give her a call." Linda handed Angel the card.

"Aunt Barbara owes me the money, not you," Angel said and handed the check back to Linda, who was hanging up clothes.

"It's from mother. I told her how ugly she acted and that I was not going to have anything to do with her unless she paid you the money with interest. The old girl is softening up in her old age. She thought that I wasn't going to bring Camille around. Anyway, you have been like family to me. I will never forget the time when you gave me money for the abortion. You remember how ugly mother treated me when she thought I was pregnant? She called me all kinds of whores and sluts. I fooled her," Linda said.

"Thanks...Linda," said a humble Angel.

"I want you to be godmother to Camille. I still haven't gotten her blessed and it shows. The little hussy acts like a devil," Linda said and closed her garment bag.

"Okay. When are you having her blessed?" Angel asked softly.

"When you lose weight! I refuse to have my daughter photographed with a fat godmother and besides, you can make a special dress to show off your new figure. A few of Keith's friends will be there," Linda said.

Chapter 23

"**W**here in the *hell* have you been? I've been trying to reach you all last night," Lisa yelled. The voice on the other end muttered an answer. "Don't try it! I don't want to hear it!" Lisa slammed down the receiver. Jennifer jumped from the noise. Lisa began pacing, mumbling to herself.

She was up most of the night, talking over plans of finding her father, William Curtis Smith. She called Cameron continuously last night to share the news but he didn't answer. When Jennifer saw the frustration after each attempt, she began talking about Charlie Johnson, the father she never knew. Lisa was unconcerned. Her attention was on the unanswered phone calls. She fell asleep around 3:00 a.m. with the birth certificate in her hands.

The telephone rang. Lisa ignored it and walked into the kitchen. It rang several times before Jennifer got the courage to answer it. A very tired Cameron was on the other end. Jennifer talked to him and Lisa started steaming. Jennifer took the telephone into the bedroom after Lisa slammed a cabinet door.

Jennifer asked Cameron questions. He answered, talking slowly. The battle between certainty and uncertainty rumbled in Jennifer's stomach. As Cameron answered questions and asked them, an electric current went up Jennifer's legs to her shoulders. It was the strangest feeling. Cameron asked more questions and Jennifer answered without knowing. A tingling sensation traveled to her head, causing her to become dizzy when Cameron asked if her mother's name was Catherine, the one he remembered in the heated arguments.

Jennifer succumbed to the vibration of energy that had taken over. She stiffened as she felt the energy pulsate her stomach, chest, throat and head. Cameron continued to ask questions but she could not respond.

Lisa walked into the room to find Jennifer shaking with the telephone receiver on her chest. Lisa quickly picked up the telephone and yelled, "What did you say to her?" Cameron was quiet for a couple of seconds. "Dammit, I asked what did you say to her?" Lisa asked out of fear.

"Calm down, Lisa," Cameron said patiently. Now he knew why his mother was angry at his father for so many years. She had every right to be. He had a sister who was four months younger than himself. He became tense. His father had a love affair that his mother accused him over the years, but he denied it. His father also dated the mother of the woman soon to be his bride. It was embarrassing.

Cameron could faintly hear Lisa plead with Jennifer. He yelled through the phone, "Lisa! Lisa!" His loud voice frightened her.

"What...did...you...say...to...her?" Lisa panted.

Cameron groped for an answer. "I just asked if her mother's name was Catherine. Is she okay?"

"I don't know!" said a frantic Lisa. Before she could say anything else, Jennifer's eyes opened. Lisa looked down and saw a familiar sight, a faint beam of light surrounding Jennifer. It went away quickly. She had not seen that light since she was a child. It was the same light that covered her make believe friend when she was little.

Jennifer's focus turned to Lisa. There were patches of color from Lisa's pelvis to the top of her head. Jennifer rubbed her eyes and they went away.

"Are you okay?" Lisa asked.

"Cameron is my brother."

Lisa looked at the telephone receiver in her hand and brought it slowly to her ear. "Hello," she said.

"Is Jennifer okay?" Cameron asked.

"She's your sister."

"I know."

"I have to go. I'll talk to you later."

"Lisa, I love you. You know I do. I was out with some friends last night. I didn't get home until late." There was no response from Lisa. "You said you wanted to talk about something?" Cameron asked nervously.

"Never mind. I'll talk to you later."

"I'm sorry I wasn't home when you called. What did you want to talk about?"

"I need to see about Jennifer."

"Please Lisa, don't do this. I know you're upset with me."

"That should sound familiar to you. Good-bye," Lisa said and hung up. She looked at her friend and the telepathy began like old times.

"He might be telling the truth."

"I know, but he's still weak. Since I have no proof, I can't accuse him of anything."

"He will only deny it like all of them. He loves you dearly."

"I guess I need to be in Atlanta."

"Don't start making excuses for unacceptable behavior. You're human too. You've been faithful."

"I do think about other men. I guess I'm not like you."

They giggled. Lisa massaged her temples. "When do you want to visit Miss Mattie?" Lisa asked.

"I don't know. I want to see Angel before she leaves. She looked terrible last night," Jennifer said.

"I need to talk to her too. I'm glad she's coordinating my wedding."

"I'm Cameron's and Lionel's sister. I don't know what to do."

"Do you want to meet your father?"

"I don't know."

"I feel the same way."

Angel hung up the phone from talking to Miss Mattie. Angel had a restless night. She thought about her father, mother, Jennifer and the new addition, Lisa. The nerve of her father condemning her when he had an illegitimate child. Their conversation still burned her ears:

"Why are you calling me now? We could have done something about it earlier. How much money do you need?"

"It's not a matter of money, dad. I need help!"

"What kind of help Melanie? If you don't need money then what do you need?"

"Uh...I don't know. I just need help."

"Who is the child's father? Can he help you?"

She was quiet.

"I guess it's Charles Johnson's son. I told you to stay away from him but you wouldn't listen. I tried giving you the best but it wasn't enough. I sent you to private schools and bought you everything you wanted. Everything has gone unappreciated. I busted my ass for you. Knowing Charles son, he's probably married. You are just like your mother, a damn whore. How much do you need so we can end this conversation."

Angel took a deep breath and exhaled. Her father had to pay for mistreating her. She didn't know how, but he had to pay.

Gina stepped out of the shower with a big towel wrapped around her. She talked happily as she dried off, keeping the towel close. Angel saw a big bruise on Gina's right rib. It looked fresh as if it happened recently.

"Gina, what happened to your rib?" Angel asked.

Gina quickly covered her entire body with the towel. She continued the task of drying off. "You won't believe it, but I was trying to keep Avery from falling against the cocktail table and end up falling myself," she chuckled but Angel didn't. Gina pulled the towel tighter, trying not to expose anymore secrets.

"Kids are something, aren't they? We end up hurting ourselves by trying to keep them safe," Angel said.

Gina's towel dropped a little in the back exposing more bruises. Linda startled her when she rushed out of the bathroom to get her toothbrush. The towel fumbled from her body, exposing all the secrets.

Linda's head jerked. "What happened to you?" she asked.

"I was telling Angel how I fell trying to catch Avery," Gina said, desperately trying to retrieve the towel.

"Is Carlos hitting you?" Linda asked directly.

Gina stood straight with the towel gripped tightly in her hands. Her eyes were ready for a fight. "I said I fell!" she snapped.

"Okay," Linda said calmly.

"This is ridiculous! Hurry up, Linda, so that we can check out," Angel said as she directed Linda to the bathroom.

Gina rushed to put on her clothes. She snatched the phone. Although she talked low, Angel heard her arguing. Gina slammed the phone down.

"Let's go back to Chicago. I can visit Miss Mattie some other time," Angel said. Gina shook her head stubbornly.

"I don't want to cause any trouble," Angel said, insisting that Gina comply.

"You're not causing any trouble. So you have a daughter named Lauren," Gina said to change the topic.

Angel smiled a little. "I didn't think having a baby would be so tough. She needs a lot of attention. Sometimes I feel I need a vacation from her."

"Avery is busy all the time. If he's quiet, I know he's up to something. All my friends tell me their kids hate being in their room alone. Not Avery. He prefers to be out of my sight."

There was a long period of silence before Linda opened the bathroom door. She removed her shower cap. "If there is going to be a problem with me coming along, tell me now. I can catch a cab to the airport," Linda said frankly. Gina let out a heavy sigh.

"Linda, hurry and get dressed so we can leave. You still have to pack. Why did you bring so many clothes?" Angel asked to diffuse the tension.

"Because I can."

As the three women approached Miss Mattie's front door, Angel smelled the roses again. She felt the embrace as she came closer to the door. She rang the doorbell. Miss Mattie opened the door and invited them inside. They smelled the delicious aroma of baked cornbread. Gina was hungry. She did not eat last night because Angel was not in the mood. It wasn't a good idea for her to skip meals, but she was going to make up for it.

Miss Mattie told Angel that Carleton wasn't coming. Miss Mattie didn't tell her that he was suffering from a hangover. The child didn't need to know everything, especially when it came to alcohol.

Angel began with the questions. She wanted to know about Jennifer's and Lisa's fathers. Miss Mattie began to tell the story of a woman who had an enormous amount of charisma. In college, she fell in love with a man named Charles Johnson.

"During that time, colored girls were crazy about curly haired boys. But Catherine liked Charlie for another reason. He liked Catherine, too, but it was hard for him to concentrate on her because so many girls had their eyes on him. Old Bill tried courting her too. He too was taken by her beauty more than her smarts.

"That fella Charlie up and fathered a child by some girl that he married. It broke Catherine's heart because she was counting on marrying him. He and his wife moved to Memphis. Catherine hurt so bad because she didn't have nobody to marry." Miss Mattie sighed.

"She talked Bill into marrying her. They started having trouble in the marriage. Catherine found out that he was seeing Debra, Lisa's mother. She later found out that Debra was expecting. When Charlie come to visit for the weekends, Catherine started fooling around with him. I'd always told her two wrongs don't make a right but she didn't listen. She became pregnant, hoping to pass the baby off, but it was too dark. Bill took one look at the sweet child and left. Catherine moved in with me until she died."

Miss Mattie seemed finished with the story but Angel wasn't. Her two closest friends knew the family secrets now. It didn't matter because they were like family. Angel asked if her father knew about Lisa. Miss Mattie nodded. Angel asked if her father knew that Jennifer was still alive. Miss Mattie nodded again. Angel asked if Charles Johnson knew about Jennifer. Miss Mattie shook her head.

"Catherine didn't want to break up the marriage. After Catherine died, your father took you away along with the insurance money. He barely waited until Catherine was in the ground good. Angel was still around for awhile. She was a slow child. They said because she was born premature, she wouldn't have all her smarts but being around Lisa, she began to do better. When she gotten a little older, kids made fun of her so she kept quiet. I'd heard she is smart now," Miss Mattie smiled.

"She is smart and beautiful. You are going to be proud when you see her," Angel said trying to ignore the statement about her father taking the insurance money. Angel figured the insurance money helped purchase the house in Kansas City. Her mother's life paid for it.

"Miss Mattie, why haven't you told Lisa about her father?" Gina asked.

"Because the spirit said she would know in time. She has some learning to do. I'd couldn't go against the spirit. I've already been disobedient. I'd believe she knows his name but she doesn't know who he is."

The three women were perplexed about Miss Mattie's spirit. They decided not to ask about it. "Lisa said her mother died from drugs and alcohol, is it true?" Gina continued with the interrogation.

Miss Mattie's eyes became glassy. She was in a trance. "She died the same way Catherine did, in a car accident," she told Angel.

Miss Mattie's trance was broken when Angel sneezed. "I'd couldn't let Lisa see her momma. I'd just couldn't," Miss Mattie said. She didn't want the two women to continue with the questions. It brought back too many bad memories. "Everything has it's time and place. You are concerned about Lisa?" Miss Mattie said.

"Yes I am. We're in the same sorority."

"Her mother and Catherine were in the same sorority. They had a big falling out about some secrets being told to another sorority. Debra didn't mean anything by it. Her friend was having trouble with her sorority. Debra wanted to help."

"Grandmother, you keep talking about spirits. Do you really hear or see them?"

"Yes. I'd sometimes see things as if they're really happening. Some folks call it your 'first mind.' You're suppose to listen or else repeat life's lessons.

Bad things are not really bad. They just help make us strong. When it happens between folks you love, it will either bring you closer together or further apart. It's your choice."

Miss Mattie was finished with the conversation. She got up and went to the bedroom. She returned with a black notebook and handed it to Angel. "It's your mother's diary. It will answer the rest of your questions."

Angel looked at the priceless treasure. She rubbed it gently. She opened the vinyl covered notebook and took a look at her mother's writing. It was neat and small. The first date logged was September 5, 1952 and the last date was March 4, 1964. Angel closed the book.

It was close to noon when Jennifer pulled into Miss Mattie's driveway. Her heart was beating fast and hard. She was about to meet the dead grandmother her father hardly mentioned. She closed her eyes and opened them slowly. She concentrated on the house. There was a gray cast over the house. She let out a deep breath then it disappeared. Since early that morning, she thought her mind was playing tricks on her from all the excitement. Her concentration went to the colors on Lisa's body. They were brighter than before. She could sense Lisa talking to her. She stared at Lisa.

"What do I call her?"

"She is your grandmother."

"I know but what do I call her."

"I call her Miss Mattie or Grandma Mattie."

Jennifer nodded and rubbed her temples. Grandma Mattie sounded good. They got out of the car and walked up the steps. Jennifer remembered the house from the times of going back and forth to school but was never allowed to go inside. Had she met the woman inside earlier, maybe her life would have been different.

Lisa took out a key and opened the door. "Grandma Mattie, it's me. I got a surprise for you," Lisa said loudly as if giving a warning signal.

Jennifer's muscles tightened as if the air pressure was squeezing in. She heard voices in the other room. When Miss Mattie walked in the hallway, the tension eased. Jennifer saw one of the dead grandmothers. She had a gray cast around her body. Jennifer blinked and it went away.

"Lisa, sugah, don't holler. It's not good for girls to holler. Hello sweetie," Miss Mattie said in a gentle voice that cracked. Miss Mattie had to look long at her grandbaby. She was beautiful and the same innocence was still with her.

Jennifer looked closely at the woman who looked nothing like herself. She was strong in a gentle way. "Hello," Jennifer said shyly.

"I'd fried corn and chicken. I'd cooked some sweet potatoes, cabbage and cornbread too," Miss Mattie offered.

Lisa perked up. "Jennifer, you have got to try Grandma Mattie's chicken. It's the best!" Lisa exclaimed.

A smile grew across Jennifer's face. "Sure I'll try Grandma Mattie's fried chicken."

Lisa rushed to the kitchen. She spotted Gina, Angel and Linda sitting in the living room. She spoke quickly and continued her mission. As she removed lids, she yelled out, "Grandma, why didn't you go to church today?"

Miss Mattie cringed as Lisa yelled. "Velma's son got in late last night. He didn't feel like taking us to the early morning service," she said in a voice that was barely audible. She turned to Jennifer. "Your sister is here. Let's go in the living room where everyone is sitting," Miss Mattie said.

When Miss Mattie touched Jennifer to escort her to the living room, Miss Mattie felt vibrations go through her body. She knew then it was her. The time was coming but she wanted to know when. Jennifer felt something leave her body and looked curiously at the old woman.

Jennifer excused herself to the kitchen where Lisa was busy gathering dinner. The two emerged with bowls and trays of food. Lisa took the china out of the cabinet and set the table. Everyone sat to dine. The telephone rang. Lisa jumped up to answer it.

"Sugah, sit down and finish your meal. What have I'd told you about rushing through your meals?" Miss Mattie scolded.

Lisa became annoyed at the ringing telephone. "Grandma, how come the answering machine hasn't picked up. Did you change the settings again?"

"No, I'd turned it off. That thing makes me nervous. It never worked right."

Lisa let out a big sigh. "I had explained how it works. All you have to do is…"

"Honey, I'd rather not fool with that thing. If folks want to talk to me, they'll call back later."

Lisa shook her head and looked at Jennifer who was sitting next to her. "Old people, what can I say."

Jennifer giggled lightly. "This food is good."

"I told you. Look at Gina's plate. Who is she trying to feed?"

They both giggled and Miss Mattie narrowed her eyes at Lisa who dropped her head and continued to eat. Gina was at the other end of the table. She took big bites and refilled her plate. "You like the fried chicken?" Miss Mattie whispered to Gina who had to swallow before speaking. She was a little embarrassed from eating so fast.

"I'm sorry. Yes ma'am," Gina said.

"How many children do you have?"

"One."

"Just one? Oh? We have to be careful not to take our anger out on our children. We have to solve our problems with the people we are angry at. Sometimes, we are angry at ourselves. That's something your husband needs to know," Miss Mattie said. Gina stopped eating. Miss Mattie walked over to Linda who had a small portion of cabbage and sweet potatoes on her plate. "You hardly have anything on your plate," Miss Mattie said.

"I'm not hungry. I usually don't eat a lot," Linda said, trying to be polite.

"No wonder you're as thin as a rail. Do you have children?"

"Yes ma'am, a daughter."

"Make sure you feed her properly. Children get sick when they are not well nourished. It's okay for babies to be fat. She will lose it when she starts walking and playing. Just don't feed her junk food," Miss Mattie said sweetly. Linda's eyebrows creased.

Jennifer stared at Lisa who looked back. "She's starving her daughter like she did me when I was pledging."

"Yes, but Miss Mattie said it's okay for babies to be fat, not Cherubs." They both giggled again. Linda and Angel looked at the two oddly.

Miss Mattie cut the pound cake. She placed a slice in front of each of her guests. Lisa and Gina went to work on their slice. The other three refrained. Miss Mattie pleaded with them but they were on permanent diets. Lisa helped herself to Jennifer's slice and Gina wrapped Angel's and Linda's slices in wax paper.

Gina looked at her watch. It was time to get Linda to the airport. The three said good-bye. Miss Mattie watched the three women hug Jennifer. Miss Mattie knew lessons would be learned before her time would come.

Lisa pulled Gina to the side. She told her about the name on the birth certificate. Gina pretended to be surprised, but guilt took over her conscience. She had to convince Angel to tell Lisa before she found out and became angry at both of them.

"I don't have a telephone but here is my address. As soon as I get my phone turned on, I'll call. When are you planning to move to Atlanta?" Angel asked Jennifer. She was set to go Saturday after Thanksgiving, but after finding a sister, she didn't want to leave.

"Saturday after Thanksgiving," Jennifer answered.

"I would like for you to see Lauren before you go," Angel said.

"Who is Lauren?"

"My daughter."

"Maybe we can spend Thanksgiving together."

"Great, I'll talk to you later," Angel said.

The two embraced again. Angel turned to leave. Gina was talking to an ecstatic Lisa. Angel was not moved by Lisa's excitement. She was not the sister she had been searching for. Angel refused to add her to the family. Lisa was her father's mistake. He had to bear the responsibility alone.

They were near the airport. "I don't want anyone to know about this. I don't want you telling Lisa," Angel said, looking at Gina.

"She has searched long for her father, just like you did for Jennifer. All she wants is blood for the surgery. It doesn't make sense to prolong the inevitable," Gina said. "What makes you think she will never find out? She already thinks Paul is her father. It won't take her long to connect him with his brother. Why don't you talk to her and let the bad dream come to an end," Gina pleaded.

"I'll make that determination," Angel said stubbornly.

"Are you afraid or embarrassed? After all, she is your sister," Linda said while looking out the window.

"She is my father's daughter," Angel corrected. Linda let out a short sigh.

Gina parked the car. The three hurried to the departing gate in silence. They sat in empty chairs, waiting on Linda's flight to depart. Linda leaned toward Angel and whispered, "Miss Melanie, mother wants you to call her later this week. She wants you to help with Big Sister Lori Bass-Collins' campaign. She is running for Vice President of the Alumnae Chapter. Mother wants you to get some exposure too."

"I don't want to get into that scene anymore!" Angel said, almost losing her temper.

"Linda. can't you see she doesn't want to be bothered?" Gina said.

Linda cleared her throat. She leaned closer to Angel's ear and spoke low, "For some strange reason, I feel responsible for your current situation. Now I know you don't want to be bothered with a group of pretentious women but that is what you do well. Just seize the opportunity."

Angel closed her eyes and whispered back, "Nothing was your fault. The check is going to be very helpful and so will the business card."

Linda continued whispering. "Some of the younger members are talking about splitting. The older ones really don't care. Mother says it's about time they separated the mink coats from the rabbit furs. Mother likes Lori and thinks she will do well with a chapter of her own. Mother doesn't want her creating trouble in the chapter by being a little restless. She knows Lori doesn't have a chance in heaven or hell to win but the exposure will spring you and her politically when the chapter splits. Besides, this is a personal request from Ms. Bass-Collins, too. She and mother have talked. They just can't seem to find you."

Angel remained silent for several seconds. "I don't want a lot of questions."

"Don't answer. Smile and change the subject like always."

Gina was antsy. "Do I sense a little sorority business or am I to be kept in the dark as usual?" she asked.

"Sorority business, dear," Linda said and looked at Gina closely. "You have a gut. If I didn't know better, I would say you are pregnant," Linda said.

Gina's face became blank. "I'll be four months at the end of the month." Angel gave a happy gasp. Gina looked worried. She looked around the airport. "Linda, will you be godmother?" she asked without looking at her. Linda tilted her head slightly, "I hope it's a boy. I'm not having a goddaughter pledging Alpha. When are you due?"

"First of April," Gina said. The boarding announcement was made. The three women walked to the line of the eager travelers.

"Thanks for everything," Angel said and hugged Linda.

"Gina, thanks for calling and take no offense, you need to give Carla a call. You don't look happy. One thing I can honestly say about the Alphas, your sisterhood is very tight," Linda said as she approached the gate. She turned to Angel, "I hope you can lose twenty pounds before Christmas. I want Camille christened by then. Oh, by the way, if mother says anything about a lawsuit, just tell her it was my idea. Good-bye ladies." Linda waved and disappeared through the doorway.

Angel stared at the gate. "How dare she tells me I'm twenty pounds overweight!"

The drive to Chicago was tense. Gina hoped that Carlos wouldn't pick a fight. He was angry because she spent the night in St. Louis. He was probably livid from her hanging up on him. Gina felt the knot in her stomach. The pregnancy was more difficult than the first. Her back was uncomfortable and her head hurt too.

"Getting back into the sisterhood can be a boost for you. The Kappas are into big weddings. You could probably clean up as a wedding coordinator."

"I don't want another atrocity. I don't want people asking questions about Lauren. I would rather stay away."

"Hiding won't help. You went too soft on Aunt Barbara. She took advantage of you. Take for instance, Lisa. She's a business woman. Whatever you two agree upon, it won't change. She knows you're good, that is why she swallowed her pride and took your offer."

Angel knew exactly where the conversation was leading. She decided not to participate. The entire weekend had been overwhelming. She didn't want to think about weddings or sewing. She wanted to think about her sister, the one she searched for. The memory of her childhood with Jennifer was vague. She only remembered a little brown girl who followed her around the house. She really didn't remember how Jennifer looked or if the little girl was her sister. Her father helped erase away the memory. He had to pay.

Gina was fidgeting in her seat. Her headache became worse. The knot in her stomach gripped tighter. She made deep sighs and massaged her neck to ease the discomfort. Angel was worried. "Are you okay?" she asked.

"It's the baby. It's really making me...I don't know. It's not like the first pregnancy."

"Do you want me to drive?"

"I can't sleep and my stomach feels like knots all the time."

"Maybe you need to take time off work. I hear you work very long hours. It's important to relax during the first trimester."

Gina let the words leave her mouth before thinking. "I'm considering an abortion. I don't think Carlos and I are going to make it. He doesn't know about the baby and I can probably have an abortion without him knowing."

"Gina, don't get crazy. How can you think about aborting your baby?"

"Easy! We're having too many problems. As you have seen, it has gotten abusive. The first time he hit me, I was more stunned than hurt and so was he. He left the apartment and didn't come back until a couple of days later. Now he drinks and I can't stand it. Avery is afraid of him too. I don't want another child growing up in that kind of environment." Gina was trying to concentrate on the road through the tears. She was breathing hard because the knot was getting tighter.

"Have you two tried counseling?"

"To hell with counseling. I want out!" Gina said. Her breathing became harder. It was less than fifty miles to Chicago. Angel became nervous when Gina jerked in her seat and then she burst into tears.

"How long has this been going on?" Angel asked.

"The arguing started about a year ago and the fighting began six months ago. He blames me for everything. He can't find a good job like the one he had in Kansas City. Chicago is too competitive for him. He's not trying." Gina paused for a second. "They put me on a promotional team to launch a new product. I have my career to consider."

"You are a very intelligent and brave person. Carlos may not be as aggressive as you when it comes to networking. It doesn't mean he's not trying. Maybe dad can help."

"I don't want him wasting Uncle Bill's time."

Angel frowned. "Let dad decide that. You've been driving the entire weekend. Let's change seats."

Angel drove the rest of the distance in silence. She arrived at Gina's apartment. Gina made Angel wait in the car. Gina rushed up the stairs and opened the door to an angry Carlos. He was sitting on the sofa with beer bottles exposing his drinking. She walked swiftly through the living room to Avery's room, passing Carlos. He jumped off the sofa, following her to Avery's room. Her nerves were on edge.

She turned on the light to see a whimpering Avery who had cried himself to sleep. She couldn't think about what might have happened. She rushed to him, looking at his arms and legs. He was freshly bathed and oiled. He continued to whimper as Gina touched his smooth skin.

"Can't you speak?" Carlos grunted.

"Hello, Carlos."

"Did you think I hurt him? He cried himself to sleep waiting for his momma like he always does. Where were you? Off doing some sorority shit or kicking back with your damn networking club!" he shouted.

Avery woke up and saw Gina. He cried and reached for her. Carlos was mad. He walked so close to Gina that he stepped on her foot. She pushed him away. When he grabbed her off the bed, the fear came back.

The familiar warm fluid filled her mouth when his hand landed on the right side of her face. She punched his concrete chest. The act of defending herself added fuel to the rage. Her face burned as his hand landed again. She relented to the pain that went from the right side to the left side of her face. It left for a second when she lost focus of Avery.

She managed to pull away. She looked around wildly for Avery. Her eyes hurt and they were closing quickly. Her reaction to push Carlos away was in determination to find Avery. Carlos thought she was fighting back. His instincts were to push her away. Gina spotted a little foot under the bed. "He's safe," she mumbled to herself. Just as she stooped to reach for him, Carlos pushed her, causing her to go head first, crashing into the nightstand. She felt wood scrape the side of her face, creating a deep gash in her jawline. She gave up after the knot came back.

It was getting colder outside. Angel decided to go upstairs to see about the delay. As she climbed the stairs, she could hear screams of a child.

She rushed up the stairs to the apartment. She stormed through the door. Avery's screams were piercing. She saw Carlos hovering over Gina. Angel was enraged. She ran to Carlos punching, kicking and screaming obscenities. She cursed him with every word she knew.

Blood covered Gina's face. Angel rushed to the telephone and dialed for help. She rushed to check on Gina. Avery sat beside her crying. Gina wouldn't open her eyes. The knot was back. It tormented her, scraping like nails. It raked her stomach down to her pelvis. The scraping became harder.

Angel winced as blood stained Gina's beige pants. It grew larger. Gina mumbled out loud. What she wanted was happening. Carlos left the room. He sat with his head in his hand. He took another drink from the bottle and left the apartment.

The paramedics and police arrived. The neighbors watched quietly as Gina was carried away. Soon, Angel was left alone with the little stranger and he in turn was with a stranger, too. As he cried asking, "Where momma?" Angel thought about Lauren. She picked up the phone and called the elderly couple who was keeping her.

Angel made noises over the phone. Avery cried out. She had to tend to the little boy. She was so overwhelmed by the weekend that she cried too. She didn't know what to do. She picked up the phone again and called her father.

William arrived thirty minutes after Angel called. She gathered Avery and they left for the hospital. The wait was long. Angel was getting restless. Avery had fallen asleep in her arms, sniffing. Finally the doctor appeared to deliver the bad news, a miscarriage. It took a long time to control the bleeding. The gash on the jawline required six stitches. Other than that, Gina was fine.

William followed the doctor to Gina's room. The tubes in Gina's arms made William's flesh crawl. He didn't know if she was sleeping or defeated. He hoped the sight would not frighten her mother who was coming the next day. He remembered Marilyn going through the same abuse with Gina's father.

William liked Gina a lot. She had the same success drive as himself. She was the one who gave him the contacts which got him the job at International Foods. She wasn't afraid of meeting people. Her career was number one in her life. She prepared herself to climb the corporate ladder and she was on the way up. She wasn't like his daughter who had potential but was soft. Gina was tough and hungry.

William had seen enough. He walked to the lobby where Angel was cuddling a grieving Avery who continued sniffing in his sleep. "Gina is resting. Let's go home," William said. He gathered the sleeping child and they left.

"Why didn't you tell me about Miss Mattie and Jennifer?" Angel was calm. Her eyes demanded an answer.

William thought quickly for a response. She was too much like her mother. She probably already had a question to his response. It reminded him of the night Catherine confronted him about Debra.

"Your grandmother sees things that are not there. It would have been dangerous exposing you to an individual like Miss Mattie."

"You are saying Miss Mattie is crazy?"

"In more ways than many."

"What about Jennifer? Why didn't you tell me my sister was alive?"

William found himself reaching for the bottle of Scotch. He was in for a long night. He wondered; what all did she know? "I didn't know what happened to Jennifer. I didn't know she was alive until this summer."

"Oh really?"

"She came to visit with a college friend who I've been mentoring. It took me a little while to know it was her."

"Why didn't you tell me? You knew how important she was to me. You're lying. You kill off everyone who doesn't live up to your standards."

The last statement shook William. He looked at his daughter who was angry but yet calm, just like Catherine. She was supposed to be dead.

"Jennifer is not my daughter. She is not my responsibility and another thing, I didn't turn my back on you. I have given you everything and you are still not satisfied. You are just like your mother."

"What makes you so holy? Have you fulfilled your responsibility to your other daughter?"

William fought hard to remain in control. He didn't want to discuss Lisa. "I didn't turn my back on you."

"Where are my pictures? When you were married to Dora, my pictures were everywhere. Since you have married white, you can't find me anywhere. I guess having black children isn't a good career move. You called me a whore because I was unmarried and pregnant. Who are you to talk when you have a daughter older than Jennifer?"

William sat the glass down and cleared his throat. "I'm not ashamed of you nor am I ashamed of anything you have done. I never wanted you to make the same mistakes your mother and I made. I only wanted the best for you. I worked my ass off trying to give you the best."

"You worked hard for yourself. I didn't want to go to private schools. That was your idea. You wanted me to fit a mold like the rest of your friends' children. You never attended open house nor did you come to any parent-teacher conferences. You were always too busy. I had to beg you to go to my college graduation." Angel looked around the living room. "It hurts when I don't see my pictures on the mantle."

William avoided eye contact. His daughter's pictures were once his proud display. Everyone wanted to know who was the beautiful girl on the mantle. She wasn't any trouble like some of his friends' children. He heard the complaints of drug and alcohol addictions.

He remembered the day he took down the pictures. It was vivid as if it happened yesterday. Everything had to change. He was starting a new life with a new wife. His business clients had to feel comfortable in his home. He was working hard for Vice President of Operations of the Midwest region.

Once he landed the position, he could bring the pictures out again. As Vice President, no one would care if he had a daughter or not. Right now, too much was at stake.

He turned his head from side to side, trying to stretch his muscles. "When I get the position of Vice President, I will buy a larger house. There will be a room, a family room, with all of our pictures including your daughter."

"Her name is Lauren, your granddaughter. You said once you made Regional Director, we were going to take a vacation and it never happened."

William cleared his throat. "If you or your daughter, uh, Lauren, ever need anything, just ask. First you need a telephone. It's dangerous not having a telephone. I need to get some sleep. Unfortunately, I have a meeting in the morning." He tried to read Angel's emotionless expression. He didn't know what to say. He walked to her. "Do you need any money?"

Angel didn't flinch. She was accustomed to the big payoff. It had happened so many times. She needed money but she wanted this time to be different. She knew the game: Refuse and let him ask again. Look disappointed and stare at him for ten seconds. Give a huff of a laugh and let him offer an amount. Shake the head and purse the lips. Watch him shift a little. A higher offer will come and then smile. Give a much greater amount as to say, This is insulting but if you really want to, here is my price. He nods and walks away.

"Melanie, do you need money?"

Angel stared hard and counted to eight. She gave a huff and raised her eyebrows.

"How about a thousand dollars?" he asked. She shook her head and pursed her lips. He shifted slightly. "How about two thousand?" he offered.

"How about five thousand?" she said.

He nodded and left.

"Sorry I'm late, Marilyn."

"When is the doctor releasing Gina?"

"I think she will be able to go home tomorrow. They wanted to make sure the bleeding stopped. The miscarriage was quite violent."

"When you told me she had a miscarriage, I almost hit the floor. I didn't know she was pregnant. So Avery is at your house with Angel? What brought her to Chicago, money?"

William sighed heavily. "She received a letter from Catherine's mother. I felt we needed to talk in person so I sent for her. When she arrived, she took one look around the house and called Gina. She didn't want to talk anymore. She and Gina had made it back from St. Louis." William paused, "Melanie knows about Lisa."

Marilyn was quiet for a few seconds. "Does she knows about..."

"I don't know what she knows but we have all gotten our lives on track. It's all in the past," William said.

They walked quietly to Gina's room. She was sitting up with eyes closed. Marilyn approached the bed slowly. She sensed Gina knew she was there.

The bandages brought back unforgettable memories of her former life. Her daughter was repeating the same mistakes. How could it have happened? She tried to make Gina strong and tough, fearing nothing. She didn't waste time with hugs, kisses and pampering like her friends did their daughters.

"Hi, momma," Gina said low.

"Hello, Gina. The doctor says you will be able to come home tomorrow. Angel and Avery are at Bill's."

"Angel needs to go home to her daughter."

Marilyn's forehead creased. She looked at Bill. He excused himself. "Paul is coming Wednesday. He's staying until Saturday. You should be able to get around by then."

"How long are you staying?"

"I'm leaving Wednesday when Paul arrives."

Gina turned her head. Again, her mother couldn't spend any time. Why did she come? "I'll see if Angel can stay or if Linda can come. I don't want you to give up another day of work because of me."

Marilyn listened to her daughter's sass. At one time, she would have slapped Gina's face. Marilyn felt Gina's anger. She was probably upset over the miscarriage. She had to learn to move on. "You need to leave Carlos. It will only get worse. In time, you will learn to accept the miscarriage."

"I didn't want the baby. It was a mistake."

"I know you're angry now, but you will be able to handle the loss."

"Did you hear me? You never hear me. I said I didn't want the baby. I didn't deserve the baby. It was an accident, a mistake. It wasn't Carlos' baby and he probably knew."

Marilyn was devastated. She could hardly get her thoughts together. This couldn't be happening again. She didn't know what to tell her daughter. She struggled for words. They never had a sensitive mother-daughter talk. She swallowed hard and spoke slowly, "I don't care what you did. You didn't deserve to be beaten or lose your baby."

"Whatever," Gina said and closed her eyes.

Angel drove the car cautiously from the hospital. Gina was in the back seat with Avery who was squabbling over the bandages around her head. Marilyn was in the front seat looking ahead. She spent a restless night at Bill's house. She and Jean talked most of the night. Marilyn wondered how long the marriage would last.

Jean was a career woman who had it easy through her ex-husband's contacts. Marilyn noticed the casual attitude Jean had towards racism. She couldn't see the hard work and extra effort Bill put into his career. Nothing had been easy for him, everything was a fight. Marilyn only hoped Jean was prepared if Bill got passed over for Vice President. Dora wasn't.

Angel parked the car in front of the three story apartment. Gina saw the gray Camry. Carlos was home. She wasn't afraid anymore. She got out of the car. Angel unstrapped Avery out of the carseat. He saw the familiar car and grabbed at Gina who kept walking. Everyone walked up the stairs on guard. Angel opened the door. The apartment was very clean. It smelled of furniture polish and potpourri. Carlos walked into the living room from the kitchen. Marilyn stared angrily and so did Angel. It was awkward for everyone, including Avery.

Carlos faced Gina for the first time since Sunday night. He called the hospital checking on her condition, but refused to see the damage. He tried to keep his voice from shaking, "I cleaned up so your mother can be comfortable. I'm staying at Derrick's. Hiss number is on the clip board in the kitchen."

Gina said nothing and walked passed him into the master bedroom with Avery running at her heels. Carlos watched as his son avoided him as if he were a monster. Carlos concluded he was. The little toddler had seen too much. Carlos decided to leave. He picked up his keys and turned into an angry Marilyn.

"If you ever lay another hand on my daughter, I will kill you, myself."

Carlos hesitated before walking around Marilyn, "Can you tell Gina that Carla and Dennis will be in town next Thursday?" he asked. Marilyn didn't respond. Carlos eased himself around her and walked to the door. He wanted to say good-bye to Avery but decided against it.

Gina heard the door close. Her face and head hurt. Her body still ached from the miscarriage. She wanted to rest but Avery wouldn't let her. He kept touching her and chanting "momma".

"Will you *shut up*! Get out of here!" Gina yelled through the pain. Avery stopped and looked wide-eyed at the angry woman. He walked out of the room pouting. Marilyn decided to say something. She went into the bedroom. Gina was propped up on pillows.

"You want to talk about it?"

"I'm trying to get some sleep. He keeps bothering me."

"He missed you. That's how you can tell when something is wrong with your child, their behavior changes."

"Oh, is that right?" Gina said sarcastically to fuel Marilyn, but she was not biting the bait. Her daughter was in trouble. All Marilyn could see was hurt and pain from being neglected and beaten. Marilyn sat on the bed, Gina shifted away. "I can tell you decorated the bedroom. Flowers are everywhere. Everything is stacked away neatly."

Gina wanted her to leave before Wednesday. Paul always made better company. Her mother was useless, talking about the decor and things stacked away neatly.

"Avery can stay in Kansas City until you get on your feet. Ronnie and Aaron will be happy to see him."

Gina was steaming under the bandages. Now her mother was talking about being a grandmother. "Why do you want Avery in Kansas City? He's not familiar with anyone there. No one has bothered to come visit us. Had it not been for Carlos putting me in the hospital, you wouldn't be here. Avery is fine with me. I'll manage."

"You're right. I haven't done a good job at keeping in touch. That's why

I'm staying as long as you need me."

The statement was confusing. Gina didn't know what to do with the new mother. Gina wasn't ready to accept the new mother because she was still angry. "You haven't done a good job period. Carla will be here next Thursday. You can go back to work Wednesday."

Marilyn had to swallow her pride. It didn't make sense to fight with Gina. Her points were valid. "I remember the fighting between your father and me. It was a very painful and embarrassing time, especially having a daughter watching as I took blows. I couldn't get help from anyone. It was a lonely feeling. You were too young to remember but people didn't help...battered women at that time. It was always your fault. Women provoked a beating."

Gina remembered. She was young but she remembered. She wanted to touch her mother after the fights but was told to go away. Now she was treating Avery the same way. She was being punished. All she wanted was to further her career. The move to Chicago was supposed to be good for all of them. It took a long and difficult time convincing Carlos to leave his accomplishments in Kansas City. He was a black studies professor at one of the junior colleges. He earned extra money from the black newspaper by writing a column called Brothers Speak. He was getting a lot of exposure.

"Momma, you can't be mother now. I am a woman and I don't need your time. You should have done that a long time ago."

"You're right. I should have done things differently a long time ago but I can't change the past. I am going to stay until you're on your feet or until you ask me to leave."

The two looked at each other. Marilyn continued to feel the pain; the swollen jaw; the aching ribs; the busted lips and humiliation of feeling defenseless. All she could offer her daughter was physical help.

Gina couldn't say anything. It was embarrassing for her mother and Angel to see her helpless. They were a tough audience and Carla was coming next week. She had to be strong. She decided to get out of bed and cook.

"Where are you going?" Marilyn asked.

"I need to fix Avery something to eat," Gina said.

"Get back in bed. Your body is still weak. I'll cook Avery something to eat. I'm cooking stew tonight."

The pain left for a few seconds. Marilyn's stew was Gina's favorite dish. She couldn't remember the last time her mother cooked stew. It had been years. She wouldn't cook it even if Gina begged. She was always too busy. Gina got back in bed obediently. She was feeling groggy. The medication was taking effect.

"Thanks momma."

Chapter 24

Keith and Linda were at a pre-holiday Thanksgiving social. Linda talked happily to the group of doctors' wives. She was usually the center of attention. The women were always taken by her charm. She was one of the few young wives that participated in the doctors' wives club.

Keith rushed to the group of women. He looked upset. Linda caught a glimpse of him before he interrupted. "Excuse me ladies. I need to talk to Mrs. Reed," he said, trying to maintain control of his voice.

"Make sure you bring her back. We were just discussing our little Christmas charity project," one said. Keith took Linda by the arm and rushed her to the hallway. His tense grip made her jittery. He took her mink coat out the closet.

"What's the matter Keith?" she finally asked while being helped with her coat. He took breaths for a few seconds before speaking. "Your mother just paged me. She fed Camille and put her to bed. When she checked on her a couple of hours later, she wasn't breathing. She wasn't breathing when the paramedics took her away." Keith took another deep breath. Chills raced through his body.

Dr. Hollis, the party host, came to the hallway. "Are you two leaving already?" the older gentleman asked.

"Our daughter is ill. We have to go," Keith said in a rush.

"I'm sorry. Give me a call if I can do anything."

"Thanks Dr. Hollis. Please tell your wife that..."

The older gentleman raised his hand. "Give me a call tomorrow," he said.

Linda and Keith left the house in panic. Linda couldn't think clearly. Camille was fine when they left her parent's house. She couldn't understand what could have caused her to stop breathing. She didn't have respiratory problems. Linda suddenly felt something warm tingle her stomach and traveled up her chest. She shuttered.

"Where did they take her?" Linda asked.

"Children's Hospital. I know a few doctors on staff. They are the best in pediatric care," Keith said to ease his wife's fears. But she didn't look worried. There was no expression. He never could read her. She didn't want to be a mother but agreed to having a child. She wasn't pleased when the doctor announced it was a girl. He felt she intentionally tried not to bond with their daughter. He wondered how she would be affected if worse came to worse.

"She's going to be alright," he emphasized, but nothing was registering. Linda's focus was ahead. She didn't know what it all meant. She fed her more like Miss Mattie said. Camille even smiled at her when waving "bye-bye."

They finally made it to the hospital. Keith rushed Linda through the emergency entrance. They were directed to the room. Linda was feeling emptier as she approached the room. They rushed in only to see her parents looking distraught. Camille wasn't there.

Linda looked around wildly, "Where is she?" She searched her mother's face for an answer. Barbara opened her mouth but nothing came out. She shook as if being cold.

"They couldn't get her to breath again. They call it Sudden Infant Death Syndrome, honey," her father said. He took Barbara in his arms. Keith left the room quickly, looking for the doctor.

Linda looked at Barbara. "What did you do to her?"

"Your mother didn't do anything. I don't want you blaming her for Camille's death," Edward said as patiently as possible.

"Death?" Linda whispered. It touched her like a feather. Her baby had died like a snap of the fingers. She closed her eyes and didn't wake up. Linda listened when her mother's friends told her that she would know if something was wrong with her child. They called it maternal instincts. That evening, she felt nothing.

Keith came back looking torn. He tried to mumble something but broke down in tears. Linda just stared at him. She had never witnessed a man crying before. Her own mother never cried. Keith sobbed unashamed. Linda was confused. He had delivered stillborn babies and some died due to premature deliveries. He never cried. He was upset the first time a baby died under his care but later it was business as usual.

"Where is she? I want to see her," Linda demanded. Keith escorted her out of the room.

Barbara's hands trembled. "It happened again, Edward."

"Linda is upset. She's in shock. She doesn't know what she's saying."

"She believes I killed Camille. She really hates me."

"She's upset. She loves you. It's hard for her to express it."

Jennifer and Margo were twenty miles outside of Kansas City. Several Kappas were coming from out of town to the funeral. Although it was a sad occasion, Jennifer was happy that she would get chance to see Angel and Lauren. Angel was doing well. She called the Youth Development Center to see if there were any positions available. The director of the Center was so happy that she called. Angel was offered a position as Associate Director.

Jennifer parked her car in front of Angel's building. She and Margo took the luggage up the steps. They could hear Angel softly chastising. Jennifer quickly knocked on the door. Angel opened the door smiling. She looked at least five pounds thinner.

Jennifer laid eyes on Lauren for the first time. She was sitting on the floor with a mischievous grin. The little brown girl had on blue corduroy pants and a red and blue long sleeve shirt with two colorful mushrooms on the front. She had pretty red and blue ribbons on two bushy ponytails. She clapped when she saw Jennifer and Margo.

Jennifer felt an immediate connection with the child. Jennifer picked her up and began baby talking, "Hi Lauren. My name is Jennifer. Can you say Jen?" Lauren clapped as Jennifer cooed. "Say Jen, Lauren."

"She can't hear you. She claps when she's happy. It's her way of communicating," Angel said.

Jennifer was still for a few seconds. The little girl was too pretty to have a disability. It wasn't fair. Lauren clapped again and motioned to get down. Jennifer tried standing Lauren but she stooped.

"She doesn't stand very well. Her equilibrium is off. She suffered a terrible ear infection when she was five months old. It caused serious ear damage. That's why she's deaf. She can hear very loud noises," Angel said.

Angel took her hand and rubbed down the length of her hair and pointed to Jennifer. Angel did it several times until Lauren mimicked. Angel clapped after Lauren did it. Angel gently tapped the top of her head and pointed to Margo. Finally Lauren did it and they both clapped again. Jennifer looked at Angel for an answer. "These are what you call 'sign names.' Since she cannot hear you, you have to do physical movements to communicate."

Angel took Margo and Jennifer into the bedroom. Lauren crawled in behind them, watching Jennifer and Margo busily unpack. Lauren rubbed her hair and Jennifer stared. She felt terrible. Lauren rubbed her hair again. Jennifer jumped when she heard Angel clapping. "If she does your sign name correctly, clap your hands," Angel said and left.

Lauren made sounds but Jennifer couldn't understand them. Lauren crawled out of the room and Jennifer rushed to the kitchen where Angel was preparing spaghetti. Jennifer leaned over to Angel and whispered,"I haven't told anyone we're sisters." Angel smiled and nodded.

"Lauren is very pretty."

"Yes she is, just like you."

"Edward, you have explained this Infant Death over and over. I can't understand how a healthy baby just closed her eyes and died. Something is wrong. Has she been drinking again?" the old woman complained. Her nose was turned up as she sniffed for clean air.

"Mother, lower your voice. I don't want her hearing you."

"Ha! She's probably drunk. I told you not to marry her but you wouldn't listen. I could tell by the cracks in those cheap shoes she was from the other side of the tracks. You have this bleeding heart for uncouth women," the woman continued, trying to get comfortable on the sofa. She surveyed the room of Chippendale furniture and the corners of her mouth turned down. "Two babies dying doesn't make sense. She has a problem. A real problem. Edward, get me some water, dear," she whined.

Edward walked off quickly to the kitchen to face an angry daughter. She overheard the conversation. Generally, she got along fine with her grandmother but something bit her.

"Are you well rested, dear?" Edward asked.

"What is Gran-Mary talking about? Does mother drink?"

"No honey. She did about twenty-eight years ago but it didn't last long."

"I don't remember her drinking. What is this about two babies dying?"

Edward was in conflict. Linda was no longer a child. Her own baby had died and they were still keeping secrets from her. "Let me get your grandmother some water. We'll talk when I come back."

Edward rushed from the kitchen with a glass of water. The old woman began moaning and complaining but he ushered her into the guest room in the far corner of the house. He had to think quickly before approaching the kitchen. Barbara never wanted Linda to know about the twin. Maybe if he told the whole story, Linda would heal a little faster knowing her mother had gone through the same trauma. The only sign of grief Linda displayed over the last few days was staying over at their house. She hadn't talked about Camille's death nor had she cried.

Edward cleared his throat to announce his entrance, "Your grandmother is a handful."

"Yes, I see. I didn't know she hated mother. I thought mother was the bear."

"Your grandmother doesn't hate your mother and your mother is not a bear. She worked hard to get where she is. She has taken a lot of punches trying to make well of her life. Not only do I love her but I respect her too."

"She doesn't strike me as someone who has struggled. She has never talked about it. All she wants is name and prestige. She doesn't have a problem saying she married you for your money," Linda said.

Edward smiled. Barbara's honesty was the one thing that attracted him to her. She wasn't like the other women who played little games for his hand in marriage. The others were either too snooty or too common. Barbara meant what she said. She was looking for a doctor. She told him if it wasn't going to be him, it would be someone else. She even called him Fats Domino because of his stomach. She wasn't too turned on by his appearance but she said he was interesting.

Barbara was very honest. If he asked her how she felt she told him, except for the time he asked about the other man. She lied, the first time ever. He was happy. She loved him enough to lie. He was glad when it was over. He thought she cheated on him because of the loss of the baby. He soon understood he could not satisfy her sexually. She was gentle about it but it was a problem. She even asked him if he was homosexual. Of course he denied it. Sex was something he never openly explored in his earlier years. It had gotten better over the years. She had learned to live with it. Cheating was no longer her interest, the sorority politics was.

"Your mother is the oldest of seven children. She grew up in Titusville, Alabama. She worked very hard to leave. When she did, she never looked back. She sent her mother money until she died two months after you and your twin sister Melissa were born. Your mother always felt she was being punished because of being ashamed of her past."

Linda sat shaking her head, hearing for the first time of a sister named Melissa. "Why hasn't anyone told me about this twin sister?"

"Honey, it happened so long ago. Melissa died when she was a baby. Your mother doesn't like talking about it and I tried to respect her wishes. I don't want you grieving the way your mother did. She drank for awhile but was able to put it away and move on. You have to do the same thing."

Linda could not comprehend everyone's concern over her behavior. Camille was gone, the end. There was nothing she could do. Of course she was going on with her life. "How did Melissa die? Gran-Mary talks as if mother killed her."

"It was respiratory failure. Her lungs were never strong. After she died, your mother threw her attention on you. At first she couldn't sleep, wondering if you were still breathing. She has always been overprotective of you. She took you everywhere with her, not wanting you out of her sight. You thought she was being a bear but she was being a worried mother. When Camille stopped breathing that night, the nightmare came back. I don't want anyone blaming her for the deaths of those babies. She has suffered enough. We both suffered."

Linda never heard so much information about her mother. It had become interesting. Linda wanted to know more about Barbara Ann. Because they argued constantly, Linda never asked questions nor did Barbara volunteer any information.

"Why have I not seen mother's brothers and sisters?"

"I made sure you knew your aunts and uncles on my side. It's up to her to personally introduce you to her past." Edward stood and stretched. "It's time for you to go home to your husband. He has called several times. Don't think this doesn't affect him too. Goodnight, honey. We'll see you at the chapel tomorrow."

Edward kissed Linda on the forehead and walked up the winding staircase near the front door. Linda decided to go home.

Everyone walked by and looked at the little body in the casket. Some sniffed as they viewed the body and others shook their heads. Linda watched as Angel and Gina wiped tears from their eyes. She saw Jennifer bawling, Margo whimpering and Rosalyn sniffing. The big ordeal over the death of a baby wasn't understandable. The ushers escorted the family to the front. Linda watched her grandmother cry as she looked at Camille. Her uncle had to escort her away.

Barbara took short steps to the casket. She looked down at the peaceful child. Camille was wearing the pearl earrings and white christening gown Barbara had bought. She removed the white cap and rubbed the wisp of soft hair scattered over the smooth head. She rubbed the cold golden brown cheeks with her pointer finger. All she could see was Melissa. Barbara held the side of the casket and the tears came. They kept coming. They had been held back for forty years. Strong people did not cry. That's what her momma said but she felt weak now. Helpless. Her daughter would never trust her again.

Edward took Barbara in his arms and kissed her forehead. He held her tight. It was a struggle to walk her away from the casket. As they walked, he prayed the drinking wouldn't start. He would lose her for sure.

Linda and Keith were the last to see Camille. Keith touched his daughter's face and rubbed her little fingers. He bent down and kissed her forehead. He put his arm around Linda's waist. She looked at the little cap that had been removed. She took the time to put it on Camille's head. Linda reached up and lowered the top of the casket.

Linda watched as Angel fought to comb Lauren's hair. The little girl tossed and muffled sounds. She would occasionally hit at Angel's hand. Finally, Lauren took both little hands and held the hand with the comb and shook her head. "Yes," Angel said and nodded. Lauren shook her header harder. She mumbled crying sounds. Angel stopped for a moment and gave Lauren a bottle. Lauren sat quietly and sucked the bottle.

Lauren had a temper. She wore Angel down. It was humorous to Linda because Lauren won the fight. No one had ever won coming up against Angel. Soon Lauren fell asleep. Angel eased the little sleeping giant over her lap and finished combing. Angel won, Linda thought but Lauren was defenseless so it wasn't a real victory. Linda chuckled and Angel looked at her.

"What's so funny?" Angel asked as she put Lauren to bed.

"You and Lauren."

"Isn't it terrible. I'm being paid back. I was the same way, according to my mother's diary. I've read some interesting things about mom and her friends. She talked about how the Kappas didn't want them because they didn't have the money to pledge. They didn't want Aunt Marilyn, period."

"How were they able to pledge?"

"They made a big impression on the Kappas. Aunt Barbara stayed up all night for weeks, sewing six cocktail gowns for the Lambda's Cotillion. According to mom's diary, the dresses were gorgeous. Debra Arvell got all of them dates. She was the pretty one. Guess who were their dates? Dad, Uncle Paul, Lionel's father and three Lambdas. Aunt Barbara had a date with the Kappa president's ex-boyfriend who was a Lambda. Back then, dating a fraternity man was a big deal."

Angel went into the kitchen to get something to drink. "The Kappas decided to accept them on line to get back at them. They thought mom and her friends would drop line. The philosophy: Don't get mad, get even came into full swing."

Linda was amazed at the story. More about Barbara Ann. "I want to read your mother's diary."

Angel waited a few seconds before asking about Keith. Linda had stayed over a week. Angel figured it was time for her to go home. "Jennifer called. She's not moving to Atlanta. Allyn has gotten a job offer in Texas so Jennifer moved in with Lisa."

"Who is Allyn?" Linda asked.

"She pledged with Jennifer," Angel replied.

Linda had a questionable look but dismissed it quickly. "How is the sister thing working out?"

"There is no difference in our relationship."

"What about Lisa?"

"What about her? I don't care anymore. After reading mom's diary, I feel kind of sorry for her." Angel paused for a few seconds. "Linda, you need to go home to be with Keith. He calls constantly."

"He's at the hospital all the time. He only misses me at night. I'm not up to having sex these days. By the way, Keith's friend John asked about you. Shall I give him your phone number?"

"John the doctor?"

"Well, he's not a real doctor. He's a podiatrist, but he might have a few dollars tucked away. Have you heard from Gina? I hear she's having a few problems on the job." Angel shook her head.

"I'm glad you lost weight. I couldn't bear the idea of shopping in the double digit sizes for your Christmas present. I didn't shop there when I was pregnant." Linda got up and started packing her garment bag. "What time are you coming for dinner?" she asked Angel.

"What time is it? Aunt Marilyn wants me and Lauren to stop by too?"

"At five. Keith's friend, David, will be there. He's a dentist."

"Jennifer might come to Kansas City for Christmas. Is it okay for her to come?"

"Of course," Linda said and started packing the overnight bag. Her attitude was business as usual.

"How is Aunt Barbara?" Angel asked.

"We haven't talked since Camille's death. She avoids me. When I come in the room, she leaves," Linda said putting the last item in the large bag.

"She's probably feeling guilty. She really loved Camille. I don't know what I would do if something happens to Lauren."

"Mother will be fine when she finds another playmate. She has never let anything get her down."

"I don't know Linda. I have never seen her upset until the day of the funeral. She was torn apart."

"When I die, she will probably clap."

"That's not fair! Don't ever say that!"

"Oh, I keep forgetting. You are the daughter she never had. Thanks for the hospitality," Linda said and took her bags to the door.

Angel rushed in front of her. She was agitated by Linda's attitude. "You never gave her a chance to be your mother," Angel said.

"You're right, I didn't. She was the one that screwed you out of three thousand dollars. Good-bye, dear." Linda walked around Angel and left the apartment.

Linda heard screams. She sat up quickly in bed when she heard a loud crash. She got up and walked down the hall towards her parents room. She could hear her mother calling for her. Linda opened the door, there was Barbara staggering with a glass in her hand.

"There she is, Barbara. I told you she was alive," Edward said.

Barbara faced Linda. She watched her mother's smile turn into a scowl. "You lied to me. Marilyn told me you had an abortion, you little bitch! Come here!"

Linda walked away backwards. Barbara staggered forward but Edward caught her before she fell. Linda rushed back to her room. She picked up the phone in a hurry and called Keith. He sounded as if he had been waiting for her call. Linda sat in bed with her arms around her legs breathing hard. She wanted to leave but she didn't want to go home. Her door opened and she jumped. Her father walked into the room and sat on the bed.

"Your mother doesn't mean to hurt you."

"Yes she does. Stop making excuses for her."

Edward gathered Linda in his arms like old times. She wasn't frowning as usual this time. She cried a little. "She and I had hoped you would have come to us about the abortion. Your mother and I know too many people She kept quiet, hoping you would say something but you continued to lie."

Linda concluded she was being punished for the abortion. God took Camille away because of the abortion nine years ago, Keith's baby. Why did God have to punish both of them?

Linda wondered what was taking Keith so long. They only lived fifteen minutes away. The doorbell finally rang. It was Keith. Her father went downstairs to let him in. Keith rushed up the steps to her bedroom. It was almost the same since the first time he had seen it. It was the first time they had sex. He never saw it again.

Keith hugged Linda, but she didn't respond. She continued to sit with her arms wrapped around her legs. Edward left the room. "You want to go home?" Keith asked softly. Linda shook her head. He rubbed his face with his hands. He hadn't slept well since Camille's death. It was time to give Linda space. He fluffed the pillows behind her. "If you need anything, I'll be in one of the guest rooms," he said and left the room slowly. It was his toughest challenge: losing his child and possibly his wife. He closed the door quietly.

Angel was a little nervous. It was the first time Barbara and Edward had seen Lauren. She was crawling around the unfamiliar territory with ease. Angel had dressed her in a maroon, velvet dress with a white, lace collar, white tights and black, patent-leather shoes. Angel took the time to comb Lauren's hair into a curly ball on top with lacy, white and maroon ribbons.

Jennifer was upstairs with Linda. David was enjoying a friendly conversation with Angel until Lauren pulled up next to them. David tried talking and playing with her but it was difficult. Lauren muffled sounds. Angel became embarrassed and David politely excused himself to talk to Keith. Angel was insulted.

The food was ready and everyone was waiting on the hostess. Edward was a little nervous, not knowing how Barbara would perform. She finally made her entrance in a dark red mid-calf dress that was cut low to the waist in the back. She wore diamond and ruby earrings and necklace. She smiled upon entering. She spoke to everyone but when she saw Angel, the smile became calculating. Angel had some explaining to do. "Hello dear. How are you?"

Angel stood and gave Barbara a hug. Lauren crawled under the Christmas tree. Angel rushed to get her. Lauren muffled complaints. "I'm sorry, Aunt Barbara. This is Lauren."

Barbara looked curiously at the mischievous child. Lauren reached for the sparkling necklace. Barbara picked up Lauren who came willingly. She muffled sounds as she rubbed the necklace. Barbara sensed immediately that something was wrong with Lauren but something about her personality Barbara liked.

"You like Aunt Barbara's necklace?" Barbara cooed. "I know Catherine's bloodline when I see it, always wanting the best." Barbara faced Angel, "Where is your sister? I want to see her."

Angel was a little troubled with the question. She asked her friends to keep a secret and it was no longer. She had nothing to be ashamed of but soon Lisa would find out. "Linda told you about Jennifer?"

"Malinda tells me nothing. I had a feeling when I first saw her that one night at Missouri State. She's my godchild," Barbara said with attention focused on Lauren. Barbara rubbed the little girl's smooth face and smelled her hands. She looked at the little white nails. Lauren smiled and clapped. She reached to get down. Barbara gently stood her on the floor but Lauren sat.

"Shouldn't she be walking now? I thought you said she was fourteen months."

"She is but her equilibrium is off. A terrible ear infection caused her deafness."

"I see you bought your dress and the baby's too. You've stopped sewing?"

Angel didn't want to discuss sewing or weddings either. She couldn't imagine ever working for Barbara again. She didn't want to disrespect her by saying so. "I still sew," Angel responded.

Edward entered the room with his mother. He overheard Angel talking about Lauren. He approached Barbara and kissed her on the cheek. His mother turned up her nose at the sight of it and sat on the sofa.

"Hello dear. Hello Melanie. I see we have a new edition," Edward said, watching Lauren take off for the Christmas presents. Angel spoke and quickly chased Lauren.

"Oh let her go. She's just enjoying herself. Make sure she doesn't pull up on the tree," Barbara said.

"The young woman is trying to be a responsible mother, Barbara. I suggest you let her have that opportunity," the old woman gruffed. Barbara left the room.

"You said she wasn't born deaf? Maybe it can be corrected. Have you taken her to an ENT specialist? I know someone who is excellent. Before you leave, remind me to give you Clyde's number. He's a good friend of mine," Edward suggested. Linda and Jennifer entered the room.

Barbara announced dinner was ready. Everyone followed her to the dining room. Edward put the wooden high chair they bought for Camille at the other end of the table. He took the seat at the head of the table with Barbara to his right and his mother at his left. Keith was at the other end with Linda at his right with Lauren and Angel at his left. Jennifer sat between Angel and Barbara. David sat between Linda and Edward's mother. David stared intensely at Jennifer who wasn't paying attention.

Edward said the blessing and the group began eating. David continued to stare at Jennifer. Finally, he struck up a friendly conversation. The two talked back and forth. Jennifer politely laughed at his jokes and he chuckled at hers. It was obvious to Angel he was interested in Jennifer. Angel turned her focus to Lauren who was making a mess of her food.

Linda watched as Angel fed Lauren who wasn't interested in eating. Angel wiped Lauren's mouth when she spit out food. Angel tried baby talking the deaf child into eating but Lauren banged on the high chair with a spoon. She dropped the spoon and banged with her hands. It became louder. Linda's tension mounted.

"My God! Put her down. Can't you see she doesn't want to eat," Linda snapped.

Angel was embarrassed. She removed Lauren from the high chair. "Leave her alone, Melanie. She's just a baby. I'm quite sure a little noise won't hurt anyone," Barbara said.

"We're trying to eat, Barbara. That child is boisterous," the old woman rumbled.

Before Barbara could respond, Angel had Lauren out of the high chair and walked into the family room. Angel removed a toy from the diaper bag. Lauren wasn't the least bit interested. She cried to go back to the table.

The noise made Angel tense. When Lauren cried, it was dull, monotone. She continued to cry and hit Angel. The more Angel said, "Stop" the more Lauren hit. Angel had never disciplined Lauren. She didn't know how.

Lauren hit Angel again. Finally, Angel became so angry that she hit Lauren hard on the legs and yelled, "*Stop!*" Lauren stretched out on the floor and screamed. Angel yelled, "*Shut up!*" She reached down, grabbed Lauren by the front of her dress and snatched her up. Angel swung her hand back but Barbara caught it before it landed.

"I see she's spoiled," Barbara said.

Angel continued to look at Lauren with spite. She wouldn't release her grip of the crying child. Barbara slowly released Angel's hand and picked up Lauren who was crying and rubbing the sides of her face.

"Just because she's deaf doesn't exempt her from discipline. Make sure you talk to Edward before you leave." Barbara rubbed Lauren's back. The gentle touch made the child a little more quiet.

"I can't stand it!" Angel snarled. "She's always crying. I'm tired of her embarrassing me. I can't go anywhere with her. No one wants to date me because of her. I'm sick of her. She's embarrassing."

"She's not embarrassing. It takes special attention for children with special needs. You have to find a person who is going to love you and your child. He might be older or look less handsome. You don't have to lower your standards, just change them a little. Whoever you choose must accept your child as his own. Who is her pediatrician?"

"I don't have one."

Barbara gasped. "Why not?"

Angel was fed up with all the questions. Because of Barbara, she was in her present condition, struggling. The reaction made Angel feel as if she wasn't a good mother. "How dare you ask why? You took over two years to pay me. Now you pretend nothing happened. I busted my butt for you. You made money off of me, lot's of money. No, she doesn't have a pediatrician because I can't afford one." Angel caught her breath. She was having a difficult time breathing. She had to control her emotions. She couldn't afford to get excited.

Angel's statements stunned Barbara. She never believed she took advantage of anyone. It was business. "Do you need money?" Barbara asked.

Angel was ready to scream. She was tired of people buying her off. She loved Aunt Barbara. She wasn't like her father. "I don't want money. An apology would do," Angel said without losing eye contact with Barbara. Asking Barbara to apologize was asking a lot. She apologized to no one, even when she was wrong. Angel moved the pawn in for check.

"I am a business woman. You had a contract with me, not Malinda. I asked for specifics. You decided to add the extras because Malinda wanted it. Besides, it wasn't a lot of money," Barbara said firmly.

"Okay, Aunt Barbara, since you are a business woman, I'm looking for the rest of my money. You contracted with me as wedding coordinator and seamstress at a cost of six thousand dollars. You contracted the two dresses to the boutique as original designs. My fee is two hundred dollars for every design and twenty dollars an hour on labor. The additional dresses came up to four hundred for designs and five hundred dollars for labor. Do you need to see copies of my time tickets to refresh your memory?"

Barbara smiled as Angel yelled checkmate. Barbara thought back to the time she borrowed a hundred dollars from Catherine. Barbara needed to buy fabric and patterns for a white client, her first job. At that time, a hundred dollars was a lot of money. Edward's business wasn't strong then. His clientele was mainly poor black women and banks were not lending to black businesses.

After making all the dresses for the white client, Barbara only made twenty dollars from the job. She didn't have the money to pay Catherine who gently reminded her of the debt. Barbara knew Catherine needed the money especially when Bill's support had stopped. Barbara used every excuse. She convinced Catherine that she had twenty-five percent ownership in her business. Barbara wondered if Angel had the letter that created a binding contract with Catherine.

Barbara decided not to worry about it. It was time to make amends with Catherine and Angel. The thought of both sorority sisters struggling because of her made her uneasy. It didn't matter. It was cheaper to pay Angel the balance than to pay her twenty-five percent of all profits that went unshared.

"I don't need copies of your job tickets. I will pay you."

"I don't want the money. If I did, I would have sued you."

"Why did you threaten me with a lawsuit?"

Angel was puzzled. It came to her, the conversation with Linda in the airport. "I didn't threaten you, that was Linda's idea."

Barbara nodded. "I need to get back to my guests. After you freshen up, bring Lauren back to the table. She needs to learn how to behave at a formal sitting."

Barbara tried to give Lauren back to Angel. The little girl refused to go. "Now listen, young lady, Aunt Barbara has entertaining to do. I want you to allow your mother to freshen you up, okay? You understand me?" Lauren clapped. "That's better." Barbara gave Lauren to Angel.

Angel did not want to go back to dinner. She wanted to talk. "You said Jennifer is your godchild? Did you know she was alive?"

"Bill told me she died in the car accident. I didn't know your mother was dead until after Bill moved to Kansas City. He buried her before any of us knew. Debra tried calling some of us but it was after the fact."

"I have mom's diary. She wrote some interesting things about you two."

"If you think your mother's diary is interesting, you should read mine. Will I see you two at the table?"

"Yes ma'am."

Gina nervously dialed Lisa's number. Carla's long talk made her realize she had an obligation to Lisa. It wasn't going to be easy because Angel expected her to keep it a secret. The whole scheme was foolish because it was only a matter of time before Lisa found out. It was Christmas and what better present to give her pledge daughter, information about her father.

Lisa picked up on the third ring. Gina talked slow. Lisa listened carefully. Gina unfolded the secret. The news was so awesome that Lisa remained silent until she hung up. Cameron searched her face for an answer. She walked to the sofa and sat.

"What's the matter? Gina didn't upset you, did she?"

Lisa shook her head. Cameron played with her hair. She pulled away. He decided not to press the issue. He put her legs across his laps.

"I know who my father is. I have a sister too," Lisa said.

"Great. Maybe you can have the surgery soon," Cameron said softly.

Lisa became defensive, "What's the big rush for children?"

Cameron twitched. "I haven't rushed you. It was your idea. What's going on? What did Gina say to you?" Cameron snapped.

"Don't you talk to me like that!"

"Like what? You're always accusing me of shutting down, now look at you!"

Lisa got off the sofa. "Don't you walk away from me little woman," Cameron said and pulled her back. She swung at him wildly. He ducked. "Lisa, stop it! You stop it now," he said and picked her up in a bear hug. He was squeezing her so tight that she couldn't breath.

"Let me go, Cameron, I can't breath," she managed to say.

He released his hold. His face was flushed. "I don't want you ever hitting me again. Now what's the matter?"

"My sister doesn't want me to know who she is or my father either. She doesn't like me," Lisa said between gasps. Cameron turned around angrily, "How do you know she doesn't like you? You don't know who she is. I'm tired of you thinking everyone hates you."

Lisa was fuming. She stormed into the bedroom and slammed the door. Cameron gave a sigh and knocked on the door. "Get the fuck out of my house!" Lisa yelled. Cameron opened the door and sat on the bed next to her. Lisa tried yelling again but Cameron put his hand over her mouth.

"Stop swearing. And I'm not leaving either," Cameron said. Lisa turned her head. She was frowning. "You have found your father and you are still unhappy," Cameron said in distress.

"You don't understand," Lisa whimpered.

Cameron rubbed his neck and look at the ceiling. He looked helpless at his bride-to-be. "Baby, help me understand. I won't know unless you tell me. I've opened up when I didn't want to. Now it's your turn, Lisa Willet."

The tears fell. She was named after him, William-Willet. Cameron became upset. "Where does this man live? We are going to see him together. You won't have to worry because I will be with you," he said, on a rampage.

"She doesn't want me to see him. He probably doesn't want to see me either," Lisa sniffed.

"You're wrong, Lisa. My father wants to see Jennifer. I know your father wants to see you. If your sister stands in the way, we'll deal with it when it happens. Besides, you have to concentrate on the wedding. When are you meeting with Angel?"

Lisa cried harder.

Chapter 25

Jennifer went back and forth asking and answering questions. Angel made her put Lisa on the telephone.

"When are you coming to Kansas City for the first fitting?" Angel asked.

"When do you want me to come?" Lisa answered.

"It doesn't matter. I need to know so I can reserve a fitting room. I'm glad you are considering rose for your color scheme. I have finished a sample bridesmaid dress. If you bring Jennifer, you can see how it looks on."

"Okay."

Angel paused. Their conversations were getting more difficult. Lisa was losing interest. The first time they talked, Lisa was excited and full of ideas. Now, Angel was ready to throw in the towel. It wasn't as if she was making a lot of money from the wedding. "When are you coming Lisa?"

"How about next weekend?"

"Sounds good."

Lisa gave the phone to Jennifer. She and Angel talked briefly before hanging up.

Jennifer watched as Lisa suddenly became busy. She hadn't been the same since Christmas. Jennifer decided to go to bed.

"You want to go to Kansas City next weekend?" Lisa asked before Jennifer retired.

"I can't. David is coming to St. Louis. We're going to Wash U's Alumni Valentines Day Social. Let's go week after next."

"No, I told Angel I was coming next weekend."

"You can change it."

Lisa shook her head and went into her room.

Barbara listened as Lori rambled. The young woman was definitely power hungry. She was impatient too. Barbara looked closely at the three women who asked to meet with her. All three were working women with small children. Their husbands were about the same age. One's husband was a stockbroker and business was bad. The other's husband was a cartographer with the federal government. Lori's husband was an internist who was just beginning to make a name for himself. Angel walked into the room and Barbara smiled. She motioned Angel to sit next to her.

"Ladies, I hear your concerns. There are reasons why most National Officials and sorority officers are older women. Our children are adults and most of our husbands have been at their craft for years. When you are given the responsibility of sorority business, there can be no excuses such as: My child was sick or I can't take off work or heaven forbid; I can't afford it. The women in control can afford to be there financially as well as socially, not saying you ladies can't," Barbara said.

Two of the three looked around in embarrassment. Lori kept her focus on Barbara. Lori's mother told her that Barbara Stevens fought like a tiger but Lori admired the tigress. "What do you think we should do? Shall we split?" Lori asked.

"Let's not use the word split, expand is better. Besides, I won't take it personal and neither will the others."

"Will you support us?" Lori continued.

"I stopped supporting children when Malinda got married."

The small group chuckled.

"How is Malinda? I haven't seen her at the last two teas," Lori said.

Barbara had to choose her words carefully. These women respected her honesty and she didn't want to tarnish her reputation. "It's been tough coping with the loss of Camille, but she's fine. She'll probably be a strong supporter of you girls."

"So Melanie, tell us about your daughter," Lori said with a small drip of sarcasm.

Angel knew it was bound to happen. The questions. "She's just a regular little toddler with beautiful, brown eyes. Oh, Aunt Barbara, Jennifer won't be coming to visit next weekend. It seems as if Dr. Howard is making house calls these days."

Barbara smiled, picking up on Angel's hint. "Ladies, Jennifer is Melanie's sister, my godchild. She's dating Dr. David Howard. The dentist?"

The group raised their eyebrows and said, "Oh."

Linda walked in the room. She wasn't smiling. "Hello ladies. Hello mother."

"Hello Malinda dear, how are you?"

"Fine mother. Are you ladies discussing the new chapter?"

Lori smiled. "Why yes! Care to join us?"

Carlos sat relaxed. It had been a long time since he talked to Ray. They reminisced over the days Carlos worked for the newspaper. Carlos hoped that Ray could help him get started again. Ray asked about Gina and Avery. Carlos gave positive responses. His mind went back to the conversation with Gina. He called on Avery's birthday. Carlos heard Gina fussing and begging Avery to come to the telephone. Carlos heard Avery shout, "No!" Gina complained about Avery's behavior. She found herself spanking him often. The exhaustion in Gina's voice concerned Carlos, but he had to go on with his plan.

The two separated right after the fight. Carlos decided to move out. He quit his job at the start of the new year and moved back to Kansas City. He felt comfortable at home. He knew he could get a good job in Kansas City. If Gina wanted to stay in Chicago, it was fine with him. He had to start his life again.

Ray asked Carlos when he wanted to get started. "Right away," Carlos said eagerly.

"Cool brother. Why don't you bring Gina and Li'l Man by the house. We can sit down and rap some more."

Carlos scratched his head. He couldn't lie to Ray. He, like Dennis, had been like big brothers to him. "Gina is in Chicago. We're separated."

Ray's eyes widen. He couldn't imagine the two ever splitting. Gina supported everything Carlos wanted to do and he in turn allowed her to be a corporate star. Ray had known Carlos for five years. Ray was impressed with Carlos after reading a letter Carlos sent the newspaper, complaining about the exploitation of violence. The anger and fire in the letter reminded Ray of himself during his tenure with the Black Panther Party. The older man searched Carlos' face for a reason.

"Hey, that's deep. Chicago is a rough place to leave a young brother to raise himself."

"I'm taking care of my son. Gina has her own agenda. She's taking care of business at International Foods. I'm happy for her. I don't want to stand in her way."

"The white man has helped run us out of our own homes with welfare and giving black women jobs quicker than black men."

"I know. I can't get a break in Chicago. You have to know somebody to get somewhere. Gina is off into this networking club. I'm not into that bougie shit. It's just ain't me."

Ray nodded. Another black man feeling castrated by his woman. "You should have said something earlier. I have plenty of contacts in Chicago. I could have hooked you up with my buddy at *Chicago Voices*."

Carlos expression changed. He read *Chicago Voices* often. He thought the paper was too soft. They didn't challenge issues the way he thought they should. Carlos already had ideas for the paper.

"If you're interested in radio, I have a couple of contacts there too. You have good ideas and I would like to see them put into action. KC is too small for brothers like you. Chicago has a larger audience. Don't get too comfortable in KC. When you put your guard down it makes you soft."

Carlos liked Kansas City. It was big enough for him. He didn't want to go back to Chicago. He didn't want to see the scar. "KC is cool. There's a lot of work that needs to be done here."

"Young brothers are carrying guns at age fourteen now. In Chicago, I hear some are as young as ten. I'd hate to hear about Li'l Man robbing somebody at gunpoint before he's old enough to drink. If you love your woman, you can make it work. Gina is a hustler. She works hard and her man has to as well. Whatever you decide, come by the house tomorrow and we'll talk some more."

The comment about Gina's man had to work hard, nagged Carlos. It wrestled with him for a few seconds. As far as he was concerned, there was nothing to discuss. He was staying in Kansas City to continue where he left off.

Lisa took her time trying to find the boutique. She was in rush hour traffic but it subsided as she drove west of the city. The roads began to wind with deep curves. She took her time after approaching the first landmark, a four story glass office building on the corner. One more mile, she made a left and then a right at the first traffic light.

The area's population was mainly businesses. Land was probably selling at a premium, Lisa figured. Butterflies swarmed her stomach when she arrived at the first traffic light. She saw the boutique. Lisa thought the name Influential Originals was cute. The awnings were white and a large mahogany door greeted the customers. It really looked nice, something she expected from a rich woman. She parked beside a white Honda Civic. She figured it was Angel's car.

Lisa waited a few seconds before getting out. She didn't have the faintest idea of what to say to Angel. Gina's comment "Please don't tell Angel. She doesn't want anyone to know" bothered Lisa. She was an embarrassment to Angel.

Lisa thought about Miss Mattie. She held the secret so long because the spirits told her to keep still. Lisa was tired of hearing about the mysterious spirits. They had kept her whole life a mystery. What kind of help were they anyway? It was time to let go of the old beliefs. She was ready to go at it alone without the guidance of forces she could not see.

Lisa got out of the car and knocked on the door. Angel came to the door in a light blue smock. Lisa sensed Angel was just as uncomfortable about the meeting but it was business. They greeted each other politely and Lisa walked inside. She strolled the boutique, surveying the long shimmering gowns on one side of the room. Black gowns rested in the back. There was a spiral rack of glittering, short dresses. On the other side of the shop was a group of very trendy gowns. They looked like prom dresses for teenagers. The array of bright colors and various lengths looked out of place.

Angel walked Lisa to one of the fitting rooms. She saw it for the first time. It sparkled under the lights. The bodice was shear with delicate lace covering the front and sleeves. It dropped in a "V" at the hips. Small beads trimmed the seam where the top met the bottom, which was made of chiffon. Beads trimmed the high neckline and wrists. It looked nothing like the sketches.

Lisa walked around the back of the dress. It was open, exposing the entire back. It was trimmed with beads too. Angel watched Lisa's expression closely. She hoped Linda's old wedding dress would pass Lisa's inspection.

"You like it?" Angel asked.

Lisa couldn't say anything. She just nodded. Angel went quickly to get the sample bridesmaid's dress. She hoped Lisa liked the fabric and design. One of Barbara's friends ordered the fabric by accident. Instead of red, the woman ordered rose. The manufacturer dyed the fabric to the shop's specifications. Angel was able to purchase thirty yards of silk polyester blend fabric for almost nothing.

Angel took her time carrying the mannequin. She opened the door and watched Lisa smile at herself in the wedding gown. Angel had to admit, Lisa looked very pretty and dainty in the delicate dress. Lisa was caught off guard when Angel began the fitting. She put a few pins in the shoulders and sides. Now she had to sell Lisa on the bridesmaid dress.

Angel helped Lisa out of the gown and hung the dress up. As Lisa dressed, Angel walked the mannequin around to catch Lisa's first reaction. Lisa was determined to have blue but getting the fabric so cheap, Angel convinced her to at least consider rose. The cost of the dresses would help Angel make more money on the wedding.

Lisa looked at the dress curiously. She gave Angel no indication as to whether it was acceptable.

Angel started her pitch. "I call it my June Cleaver cocktail gown. The diamond back will give sex appeal to a simple sleeveless dress whose unique feature lies in the lowered back hemline. The skirt is not too full therefore it can camouflage the uniqueness in figures. It also allows everyone a choice of a bra."

Lisa continued to stare at the dress. "I don't know about pink," she said.

"Rose. It's rose. It's darker than pink. You have a few dark girls in your wedding party. This color will allow them to photograph well. I'll try it on so that you can get a good idea as to how it looks."

Angel took her time with the dress. She hoped she would see a difference in Lisa's eyes. Angel zipped the dress at the side. It was slightly big. She quickly grabbed a large black piece of fabric and wrapped it around her shoulders. Lisa's expression changed. She smiled at Angel. She really looked pretty in the dress. Lisa wanted to say something about their father. She felt that they were sharing a special moment. At least that is what her gut feeling was telling her. She decided to ignore it and remain quiet.

"I like it with the black shawl," Lisa said.

"Wrap. It's a wrap," Angel corrected.

Lisa turned her head. Angel realized she insulted her. "A shawl is a wrap. Shawl sounds like an old lady unless you all are going to hobble down the aisle," Angel said wobbling as she talked.

Lisa laughed a little. She went to her briefcase and pulled out a notebook. "Are you ready to go over the checklist?" she asked.

"Sure," Angel said. To her surprise, Lisa had done almost everything. The meeting went smoothly. Lisa took notes under Angel's instructions.

"How much do I owe you?" Lisa asked and brought out her calculator.

Angel was amazed. Normally, she had to broach the subject of payment. "Your dress, with alterations, is going to be six fifty. You can pay me half now and the other half when you pick it up."

"What about the bridesmaids dresses?"

"It will be one fifty, which also includes the wrap and alterations."

Lisa punched in some numbers on the calculator and wrote a check.

She handed it to Angel who was even more surprised. Lisa paid half for all the dresses. "I forgot to ask how much are you charging for coordinating? We never discussed it," Lisa asked.

Angel shook her head. "Nothing. You have done most of the work. I'll come to St. Louis on Thursday before the wedding."

"Are you sure?"

"I will need a place to stay and a plane ticket. I can get a discount from Linda."

"Okay, it's a deal."

Angel heard a knock on the door. She wasn't expecting anyone. She and Lisa walked to the door. Angel saw Lauren with her new friend. She quickly opened the door. Her smile faded when she saw the frown on her friend's face. Lauren had been crying.

Leonard spoke roughly and came into the shop. He put Lauren on the floor. He made eyes at Lisa who was looking at Lauren. He turned around to Angel. "I thought you said you were coming over after you closed the shop? I got things to do tonight. I can't babysit," he said.

"I told you I had a client this evening and that I was going to be late," Angel said, trying to control her temper. She looked offended at the slightly older gentleman with a receding hairline. The gaps in his teeth didn't help his looks nor did the stomach that challenged the size of his pants. His attitude had changed drastically from the earlier dates. He had become rude and impatient. He was equally obsessive too.

"Thanks for picking her up," Angel said and opened the door to show him out. Leonard walked out and leaned close to her. "When are you coming over?" he asked.

Her flesh crawled. "I will give you a call," she said abruptly and closed the door. She felt like throwing up. The idea of him touching her again made her ill. Once was enough. She didn't care what Aunt Barbara said. The next man would have to be attractive.

Angel took off Lauren's coat and unsnapped her bibs. She was soaking wet. Angel removed the dripping wet diaper. Lauren clapped. Angel had to take a deep breath and count to ten when she saw the red spots between Lauren's legs. Angel quickly finished drying Lauren.

"You said you and Crystal are coming tomorrow at nine?" Angel asked Lisa.

"Yes," Lisa answered.

"I'll see you tomorrow. I have to get her home," Angel said.

"Mrs. Stevens, is Linda there?"

"She hasn't made it home?"

"No ma'am. I'm getting worried. She's not.... Could you hold please?"

Barbara waited until Keith took the other call. She was feeling worried too. For the last two months, Linda didn't go home. She was either at their house or at Angel's. It wasn't like her to stay out late.

Keith came back on the line. "That was your husband. He's bringing her to your house. It's where she wants to be." Keith sounded disappointed.

"Honey, don't worry. We'll bring her home."

"No Mrs. Stevens, let her stay as long as she wants. Good-bye." Keith hung up. Barbara was frustrated. She went back to the family room. Angel had finally gotten Lauren asleep.

"What's the matter?" Angel asked.

"It's Malinda. She'll be here soon with Edward," Barbara answered. She began shaking. She needed a drink. The bottle was upstairs on her vanity table. As she watched Angel gently rub Lauren, the idea of a drink became paramount. Barbara took off toward the winding staircase. Edward opened the door with Linda in his arms. She had a vacant look, a look of detachment. Barbara knew it all too well.

Before Edward walked Linda to the stairs, Angel came into the room. Linda frowned. "What are you doing here?" Linda growled.

Angel jumped. "I'm Visiting."

"Why?" Linda demanded.

"Malinda stop it!" Barbara snapped.

"Why?" Linda insisted. "I keep forgetting, she's the daughter you never had. Does she remind you of Melissa, the sister you never told me about? What else have you kept from me mother?" Linda asked, approaching Barbara up the stairs.

"I want you to apologize to Melanie!" Barbara said between clenched teeth.

Linda's anger continued to challenge her mother. "Why should I apologize, you never do. And what's so special about her anyway? Melanie, Malinda and Melissa. We sound like triplets."

"Malinda, stop it now!"

"Why? Because you love her more than me?"

"That's not true and you know it."

"I do? Why did you give her my Barbie dolls. You gave her my Skipper Dream House too."

"You weren't playing with them and besides I bought you new ones."

"I didn't want new ones. I wanted my old ones. You took them without my permission!" Linda yelled. Barbara shook more. She needed that drink.

"You gave her everything. My clothes. My dolls and even you. I'm your damn daughter," Linda continued as she followed Barbara up the stairs.

Angel's head throbbed from the commotion. She rushed to the family room to get Lauren. Angel gathered the sleeping child in a hurry.

"She doesn't mean to hurt you. She has nothing but love and respect for you. It's the pain from Camille," Edward said. "She was at the cemetery looking for her twin sister's grave."

Angel had Lauren in her arms, struggling with the diaper bag. Edward took the bag from her. "Have you called Clyde?" he asked. Angel looked confused. "My friend who is the ear, nose and throat specialist," Edward said.

"Not yet. I've been busy with..."

"Don't put it off, honey. The longer you wait, the less chances for corrective action. Call him Monday."

Angel nodded.

William drove to the hotel in silence. Two young men opened the car doors. William got and escorted Jean through the front doors. They walked to the ballroom. People were outside sipping drinks. Women were in formal dresses and men were in tuxedos.

Todd Meyers from the search committee approached William and Jean. "Walter Evans would like to meet you and Mrs. Smith."

William took Jean by the hand and approached the small group. He saw Walter Evans for the first time, the man behind the bio. He was rather short and thin. His hair was almost gray. He looked very neat in his tuxedo. When he smiled, creases formed deep around his mouth. He had three deep wrinkles in his forehead. When he spoke, he used hand gestures smoothly.

William made eye contact with Phil from the search committee. "Excuse me, gentlemen. William, have you met Walter Evans?" Phil asked happily.

"No I have not. Mr. Evans, I'm William Smith and this is my wife Jean."

Walter extended his hand and gave William a firm handshake. Walter shook hands with Jean too. He was quite pleasant with ferocious eyes. "William, I have heard a great deal about you. I hope we can talk soon," he said.

"It would be my pleasure. Congratulations!"

"Thank you." Walter turned around to a short brown woman. "Honey, I want you to meet William Smith and his wife Jean. This is my wife Christine."

"Hello," said a very clear and heavy voice.

William looked pleased at the woman. She was pleasant, not overly nice. Her hair was very short, salt and pepper. She had few wrinkles. She was poised. It was her personality that reminded him of Marilyn. They all walked inside the room for dinner.

As William drove home, Jean looked at him out of the corner of her eye. She had to say something. He had been quiet since the appointment of Walter Evans two weeks ago. "Walter's biography sounds impressive but his wife seems stiff," Jean said.

"She's not stiff. Her husband is in a position where she does not have to be overly gregarious," William said sarcastically.

Jean knew he was in a bad mood. The promotion was his life. He felt it was over. "William, there will be other promotions. Other Vice Presidents will retire or leave."

"My career at International is over."

"What are you talking about? You've only been a Regional Director for five years. Just because you didn't get the promotion doesn't mean you have to leave."

"I have been grooming myself for that position. If I can't make Vice President of the smallest region in the country, that's my signal to go. Harold was in that position for ten years. It was time for him to go."

"Walter has a very impressive background. He has accomplished..."

"My background is more impressive. I've taken risks that no one thought would work. I have proven myself. It's not like it's a big region. They are intimidated by me. They bring in another black man who worked at a company as large as one of my divisions and make him Vice President. What do you think they are trying to tell me, Jean?"

"Don't tell me this is racism? Walter is black like yourself. He has an impressive background like yourself. As far as I can see, you two are equal."

"You don't see very far. They dressed up his biography. They only need one of us. I have to leave. This is not by choice, it's by design," William said. He drove the car into the garage. He got out of the car and stormed into the house. He went to the basement and played old albums. Billy Holiday soon flooded the basement. Jean went to the bedroom.

The telephone rang. William ignored it. It rang again and again. Then it stopped. He continued to let Billy soothe his soul.

Jean ran down the basement steps. She swallowed before speaking. "William, Gina wants to talk to you. It's about Melanie."

William took a couple of seconds to discern Jean's expression. He rushed to the telephone on the desk. He snatched up the receiver.

"Yes Gina," William said roughly.

"Uncle Bill, Angel is in the hospital. She's been shot."

David insisted on coming to Jennifer's apartment. She was too afraid to tell him no. He surprised her with roses and a beautiful silk scarf. They had a good time at the dance but she knew he wanted the evening to go further. She wasn't ready for anything intimate. When Kyle came to town, he never imposed.

They walked up the stairs slowly. David tickled her occaisionally. Jennifer took her time to take out the key to open the door. The lamp in the corner was on. "How romantic! The mood is set," David said and kissed her on the lips. His touch was gentle but it wasn't Kyle's. He pulled her close and kissed her on the ear. She wanted it to stop.

The telephone rang. Jennifer tried pulling away but David held on tight. "Let it ring. You have an answering machine," he whispered in her ear.

"No! Something must be wrong. No one calls here at two in the morning," Jennifer said and rushed to the telephone before the answering machine picked up.

Lisa was on the other end. She told the terrible story about how Angel was almost carjacked and was shot in the process. Jennifer started panting. Lisa tried to calm her down but was unsuccessful. Jennifer dropped the phone. David rushed to pick it up. He talked to Lisa and then hung up.

"I have to go to Kansas City. My sister needs me."

"Why don't you lie down. I'll take you in the morning."

"I don't want to lie down. I want to go now!" Jennifer protested.

David held her as she cried. "If you don't get some rest, Jennifer, I won't take you so lie down," David insisted. He walked her to Lisa's bedroom.

"This is my roommate's bedroom. You can sleep in here," Jennifer said and pulled away from him. She walked away backwards to her bedroom and closed the door. She had no intentions of lying down. She was too upset.

So many thoughts consumed her like the conversation she had with Miss Mattie. It was strange, as if receiving a message. Miss Mattie told her privately that she had to stay strong. She had to finish the course of her mother's work. Miss Mattie told her about patches of lights and beams of lights.

According to Miss Mattie, if she saw patches of colors, it told what part of a person's spirit is ailing. If she saw a beam of light, angels were at work. Either they were helping or transforming. Before Angel left, Jennifer saw a faint beam of light around her and a dull green light at her chest. Jennifer couldn't determine what it meant.

Fatigue took over unexpectedly. Jennifer was forced to lie down. The picture of her mother, the one Miss Mattie had shown her, was in her mind. The woman's face was very clear. When Jennifer first saw the picture, she couldn't see the resemblance but now she did. The woman in the picture was dead but now alive and so was she.

Chapter 26

Lauren sat on the kitchen floor looking around curiously. She put her thumb on her chin. Barbara looked compassionately at the little girl who had been crying for an hour. Barbara thought Lauren was hungry so she picked her up and put her in the high chair.

Barbara soft fried an egg. She put it on a small plate and put it in front of Lauren. She put her thumb on her chin. Barbara began feeding her. Lauren turned her head, refusing to eat. She put her thumb on her chin again and Barbara offered the eggs again. Lauren cried. Barbara figured the child didn't like eggs, so she picked her up and rocked her, trying to think of what to cook.

Edward came in the room seeing Barbara comforting Lauren. It brought back memories of Camille. Lauren continued to rub the sides of her face. "I wonder if she has an earache," Edward said. Barbara felt Lauren's forehead. It was very warm.

"I'll check her temperature. I'm taking her to Clyde on Monday. Something can probably be done to correct her hearing," Edward said. They left the room and went into the study with a fretful Lauren. Edward removed an otoscope from his medical bag to check Lauren's ears. She moved frantically.

"She has an infection. I'll go to the drug store to get something for it. By the way, Keith called World Airlines. He got a four months leave of absence for Malinda. He wants her to start therapy immediately."

"I doubt if she goes," Barbara said, rocking Lauren, who put her thumb on her chin.

"She might if we encourage her and go along with her," Edward said, closing his bag. He refused to look at Barbara's expression. He knew he was asking a lot.

"Hurry and get something for this child," Barbara said.

The next day, Lauren pulled up along side Linda's bed. As soon as she got her balance, she threw the bottle, hitting Linda on the head. Linda opened her eyes slowly to see the little houseguest point to the bottle. When Linda saw Lauren, she saw Jennifer.

Lauren pounded on the bed, pointing at the bottle. Linda chuckled and sat up. Jennifer was never demanding.

"There is a better way of asking for what you want," Linda said. She took the bottle and got out of bed. Lauren raced on her hands and knees to the top of the steps.

Barbara came out the bedroom just in time to see Lauren rush to the steps. Barbara dropped the glass in her hand and broke into a run. "Lauren don't!" Barbara shouted. Lauren stopped immediately. Linda appeared around the corner, almost colliding with Barbara. Linda could smell alcohol on her mother's breath. Barbara turned her head. She picked up Lauren and started down the steps.

"What is Lauren doing here?" Linda asked.

"Melanie is in the hospital. She was shot by a teenager trying to steal her car."

Linda leaned against the wall. She put her arms around her stomach and rocked. Barbara felt woozy as she walked slowly down the steps. Her legs were giving out. She held onto Lauren for dear life and screamed for Linda to get Lauren. Linda rushed to Barbara and took Lauren quickly. Barbara stumbled down a couple of steps. Linda called for her father who was already at the top of the stairs. He kicked the glass coming down the steps.

Linda rushed through the story about Lauren crawling in her room with the bottle. Linda went on to describe how she and Barbara almost collided trying to keep Lauren from falling down the stairs.

Edward looked at his wife without sympathy. Too much was coming back. Barbara was drunk at the time thirteen-month-old Linda was left roaming around the house. She tumbled down six steps, hitting her face on the last one. When he came home from the office, he was enraged when he saw his daughter's puffy face. He decided to hire a nanny. Barbara stopped drinking when Edward stopped talking to her.

Edward grabbed Barbara by the arm and dragged her up the steps. He had always been calm but the fury inside exploded. "I am not going through this with you again. Do you understand me?" he yelled, jerking Barbara on every other word. She tried to stand but was unsuccessful. Her knees buckled. He forced her against the wall. He had to catch himself. She was defenseless. He let her go slowly and apologized.

"She stopped breathing, Edward. I didn't know what to do," Barbara explained.

He held Barbara tight. He never blamed her for Melissa's death. His mother did. Before he walked Barbara into the bedroom, he looked at Linda. "You need to go home. Your husband needs you. But as long as you are here, I want you to take care of your mother. She's not feeling well."

Linda watched her mother struggle to stand. Nothing was ever a struggle for her. She was a tiger with deep claws. She didn't need her help. Lauren looked at Linda and put her thumb on her chin. Linda returned the little girl's look.

"She's hungry, fix her something to eat," Barbara said.

William sat still as Walter talked. He praised William on his accomplishments. He small talked for twenty more minutes. William was ready to cut to the chase. Walter had bad news to deliver and he wanted to hear it. "Walter. I'm sorry. Do you mind if I call you Walter?"

"Not at all."

"Is there something you're trying to tell me? I would prefer if you were direct."

Walter liked William's frankness. He had heard about the hot tempered William Smith, a person one needed to tiptoe around, but he wasn't like that at all. He was like himself, a person who didn't like wasting time. It intimidated white men.

"The company is going to do some shifting. Your position is being phased out. After reading about you and meeting you, I will make the process extend over nine months. It should give you time to find another a job. It is the least the company can do for all of your hard work."

William knew the company wasn't doing anything. It was Walter who was trying to help.

William thought about taking a vacation. Then he thought for a minute. Melanie was getting out the hospital tomorrow. After the hard work and sacrifices, it came down to nine months. He refused to sacrifice anymore.

"I need to see my daughter in Kansas City. She is being released from the hospital tomorrow. She was a victim of a carjacking,"William said.

"I'm sorry to hear that. We can get you on a flight to Kansas City immediately. I want you to do an assessment of the Kansas City distribution center. Take all the time you need to complete the project. I will need updates weekly."

William smiled to himself. Walter was not going to be the pushover the old boy network thought he was. "Thank you Walter."

"After you finish the project, I have a few people I would like for you to meet. I also would like to have you and Jean over for dinner when you get back."

"Sounds good."

"Do you play golf?"

"A little."

The attendants helped Angel in the back seat. She was hurting all over. She didn't think a gunshot wound to the stomach would be so painful. She was swollen and depressed.

William drove slowly, watching her from the rearview mirror. She had not said much. Just hello. He did not know if she was angry or in pain. It was the first time in a long time he wanted to hold her. It didn't dawn on him until he was in flight that his daughter could have been killed.

He stole a peek at her again. Her eyes were closed. She was so much like Catherine, full of happiness and disappointments.

He parked the car in front of her building and opened the door to let Angel out. She had a tough time getting out. He extended his arm for her to use as support. She finally got out and tried to stand. It was painful. She tried walking and it was equally painful. She winced after each step.

William stooped and gently swooped Angel into his arms. He could not remember the last time he held her. It was like the first time he brought her home from the hospital. She rested peacefully in the blankets, only moving when he nibbled little kisses on her hands and face. He gently kissed Angel on the cheek. She opened her eyes and then closed them.

William opened the door for Edward and Linda. Edward was carrying Lauren. William saw her for the first time. She was the little brown girl that broke up the marriage. He said nothing.

"Lauren, you want to go to your grandfather?" Edward cooed. Lauren held his neck tight. Edward tried to pry the little arms loose but she started to cry.

"It's okay, Ed. I'll hold her later. Where's Barbara?"

Edward cleared his throat and explained how Barbara had not been feeling well lately. He removed his and Lauren's jackets. William started a conversation with Linda, first giving condolences. She excused herself and slowly approached Angel's room. Angel was propped up on pillows.

Linda remembered how ugly she behaved a week ago. She felt so ashamed. They had never had an argument, even when Barbara gave away the Barbies and Skipper Dream House.

Lauren crawled quickly passed Linda and pulled up on to Angel's bed. Angel opened her eyes and smiled at the precocious child. Lauren smiled and bounced with delight. Angel tried clapping and so did Lauren. She fell down in the process. Linda rushed to pick her up. She and Angel made eye contact. Lauren put her thumb to her chin.

"I hate to say it but she's greedy," Linda said and stood Lauren by the bed. Angel frowned after the comment. She never knew Lauren to eat a lot.

"She's never had a big appetite. Maybe she missed me," said a groggy Angel.

"We fed her every time she put her thumb to her mouth, begging for food," Linda said proudly. Angel's mouth opened and then she laughed but stopped because of the pain.

"What's the matter?" Linda asked.

Angel shook her head slowly. She put her thumb on her chin. "This means mother in sign language."

Linda hesitated and then laughed. "We've been stuffing her for a week. She would turn her head at times but we thought she was being picky," Linda said with a laugh. Angel laughed lightly.

"I want to thank you and Aunt Barbara for taking care of her. She can be a handful."

"She's okay. She gave mother a fit about combing her hair."

"Aunt Barbara is such a fanatic about hair. Remember how she had you teaching me how to hot curl my hair? She's a mess," Angel struggled to say.

"I can stay over to help you get back on your feet," Linda said quickly.

"Dad is going to be here for awhile. He's going to help me. I'm afraid Lauren is going to drive him crazy," Angel whispered

"I'll keep her. I'm out on a four month leave of absence. I'll be at mother's." Linda hesitated but decided to ask. "Angel, who is Lauren's father?"

Angel ignored the question. "How is Keith?"

"He's fine."

Edward walked into the room jovial. "I hear you have strong stomach muscles." Angel blushed. He continued, "I have good news. Clyde says he can probably restore eighty percent of Lauren's hearing. They have a laser procedure that has been proven excellent. The problem is a build up in the inner ear due to prior ear infections. We can get her in for surgery as soon as you say go."

"That's great Uncle Edward but I have to consider cost and time off work too."

"She rubs her face constantly. Did you know she was having earaches?"

Angel shook her head. She was hurting and exhausted. She did not want to discuss Lauren. Angel sighed, "I'll talk to your friend as soon as I get stronger. Thanks Uncle Edward."

Edward decided to back off. It wasn't the time nor place to discuss Lauren. "Sure honey. Get plenty of rest," he said.

"What's wrong with Lauren?" William asked, leaning against the door post.

"She's deaf," Angel said.

Another imperfect child, he said to himself. She was just like Jennifer, a slow learner. He could not imagine how she graduated from college. It had to have been the help of God. William left the room.

Lauren pulled up on the cabinets and walked around the kitchen. She took her hands off a cabinet handle and was standing by herself. She tried easing to the floor but became scared. She made noises to get Linda's attention. Linda turned around and saw Lauren standing by herself.

"Oh Lauren! What a good girl! Come to Linda." Linda stretched her arms but Lauren stood and rocked. She started fussing. She took a step and wobbled. She fussed again but Linda coaxed her into taking another step. Lauren took another step and fell down. She crawled to Linda who picked her up and kissed her.

Barbara walked into the kitchen in a robe. She walked to the stove and saw breakfast in the skillet. She turned her head. Linda tried cooking eggs, sunny side up. The yoke had spilled.

"Where is Mina?" Barbara asked dryly.

"She's coming in at eleven. She had to take her sister to the social security office," Linda said nonchalantly. Barbara took a tea bag from the pantry. "The water in the kettle is hot," Linda said.

"Lori called. She has questions about the forms you sent her," Linda said.

"My God! Can't she read? If you girls want your own chapter, you need to know how the system works."

Linda ignored the obviously vexed woman. Linda gave Lauren a piece of bacon and sat her on the floor. As Lauren chewed the meat, she kicked her legs and hummed.

"Put her in the high chair. She's a person, not a puppy," Barbara snapped.

Linda put Lauren in the high chair. She began protesting. Linda walked away to avoid the cries of injustice. Barbara walked over to Lauren and shook her finger at her. "Look little lady, I'm not having this out of you so early in the morning. You sit and eat like a human being."

Lauren cried and Linda was perturbed. "Call me if you need me," she said and walked to the doorway.

"I need you to clean up the mess you made. You know how I feel about my kitchen."

Linda swung around. "What? I cooked you breakfast!"

"Correction. You cooked yourself breakfast. I don't eat eggs."

Linda marched to the sink and began flinging bowls and cooking utensils. Barbara sipped her tea, turning deaf ears to the noise. "I have a taste for a southern breakfast. I would like fried tomatoes, fried potatoes, sausage, grits and toast, please," she said with a catty grin.

Linda was ballistic. Her mother hardly ever ate a big breakfast. "I don't know how to make fried tomatoes," Linda said, fighting to hold her temper.

"I'll show you," Barbara said, turning around smiling. Linda narrowed her eyes. Her lips became tight. Barbara stood. "I'm not feeling well and you are supposed to take care of me. Remember? Now let's see, fried tomatoes. You need cornmeal, green tomatoes.... Oh my! You have to go to the store or go home," Barbara said, eyeing her daughter. Linda continued to wash dishes. Barbara took a sip of tea.

Angel shuffled around her apartment. Linda was in the kitchen cooking. Lauren was sitting on the kitchen floor with one of the many black Cabbage Patch dolls Linda bought. "Where is Uncle Bill?" Linda asked.

Angel shuffled to a chair at the kitchenette set. "He went to get my computer at the Youth Center. He is driving me crazy. He has nothing to do. He hasn't called the office once since he's been here."

"Mother is driving me crazy too. She's playing games with me. Everything I cook, she doesn't like so I have to cook specifically under her instructions. One day, she accused me of poisoning her. Can you believe that? I told her if I wanted her dead, I would just shoot her. Why let her live longer so she can harass me. I'm going home."

"I'll be okay with Lauren, especially since she's walking." Angel turned to Lauren and cooed, "My baby's walking." Lauren giggled.

"I can keep her until you're well. We've become friends since she's stopped throwing her bottle. She stopped when mother threw it in the trash can. Lauren managed to knock over the trash can and handed it to mother with the sweetest eyes," Linda said, smiling at Lauren.

Angel was a little nervous at Linda's attachment because she didn't like sharing.

"Lauren doesn't have godparents. Would you and Keith do the honors?"

"Of course! I'll tell him tonight." Linda's face lit up but then it went sour. "I was telling mother about Keith. He is so boring. She told me I might be the boring partner. I need to do something interesting to spice up the marriage like going to his office in a teddy underneath my mink coat. She says when it comes to sex, women are responsible for teaching men because they don't know. Can you believe she would tell me something like that?"

"How would you feel if I told you that Aunt Barbara did the same thing," Angel said with a devilish grin.

Linda shoulders jerked back. She put her hands on her hips and said, "Oh no she didn't!"

"Oh yes she did. It's in mom's diary. It wasn't a teddy. I think it was a baby doll night gown."

"A baby doll night gown? I cannot believe mother could be so sleazy. I need to read your mother's diary. It sounds juicy."

"Do you think Aunt Barbara would mind finishing the dresses for Lisa's wedding? I won't be able to start on them until the end of April. I have so much to catch up on at The Youth Center. Lisa's dress is done except for the alterations."

"She won't mind." Linda hesitated. "Have you two discussed the sister issue?"

Angel shook her head. Lisa had called several times checking on her. She felt responsible for the accident. Had it not been for Lisa pushing the teenager away from the car, Angel probably would have gotten hurt worse.

Angel escorted Lisa to Crystal's apartment. Lisa decided to stop at a gas station in a rough part of the city. Angel turned back to warn her because she knew Lisa was unaware of the neighborhood. Angel got out of her car to tell Lisa who had walked towards the pump. No sooner had she stepped out, a teenage boy quickly approached her with a gun pointed low.

He tried forcing her into the car but Angel pleaded for him to take the car and leave. He looked around nervously and brought the gun up to her chest. He cursed her, threatening to shoot if she didn't get in. Angel refused, knowing of the bizarre gang initiations. She begged louder. All Angel remembered was seeing Lisa push the boy's arm away and feeling her stomach burn. The boy took off on foot and a green Thunderbird picked him up.

"Lisa is smart enough to find out about dad. It is not my problem, that's between him and her. Is Aunt Barbara going to the sorority's convention?"

"She hasn't said anything about it. She's getting bored with the sorority. I don't know what's wrong with her. She asked me what would I do if I found out I wasn't in her will. I told her I would contest it and tell people she was crazy like Joan Crawford. She just laughed."

William came through the door carrying a computer monitor. He looked happy. He spoke to Linda and went to work setting up the computer in the living room. Angel closed her eyes and turned her head. She wanted it in her bedroom.

"The people at The Youth Center are very nice. I told the executive director how I can install a LAN in the building to make information sharing easier. She was pleased with my ideas. She's a smart woman. She told me you wrote a grant for a quarter of a million dollars."

"I told you about the grant," said an aggravated Angel. "Jean called. She wants to know when are you coming home," Angel said.

William stopped for a moment but ignored the question. "Malinda, is Bart Shanks still at World Airlines?"

"Who is Bart Shanks?"

Gina stepped over blocks to get to the ringing telephone. She cursed silently when she stubbed her toe on the cocktail table. It was her mother on the other end. They discussed Avery for awhile. "I have to go out of town for four weeks. I don't have anyone to keep him," Gina complained.

"What about Carlos?"

"I would have to take Avery to Kansas City. I can't afford it. Carlos may not be able to keep him."

"Why not? He is his father. I'm sure he can pay for Avery's ticket. Can Linda get a discount?"

"I don't know and besides, Carlos may not want to babysit."

"Gina, men don't babysit their children and besides you have to keep your job. They are becoming impatient with you. Face it. You have to travel at times. Don't let Carlos off the hook. Women constantly allow men to dodge child rearing."

Gina rubbed her eyes. She wasn't in the mood for a speech but her mother made good points. "I don't know if he can find a reasonable daycare," Gina added.

"He'll find one. It's about time he pays for something. It's cheaper for you to send him money to keep Avery than to risk another write up. I'll check on him. Sweetheart, call Carlos and tell him that he needs to keep Avery for a month."

Gina never remembered her mother calling her sweetheart. She swallowed. "Okay. I'll call you back after I talk to him. How's Angel?"

"She's fine. Bill is staying with her for awhile."

"Oh really? That's good. They hardly spent time together when she was in Chicago."

"Give me a call after you talk to Carlos," Marilyn said in a hurry. They hung up.

Gina watched Avery play with his blocks. "Guess what, Avery? Momma's taking you to Kansas City. Don't you want to see daddy?"

"No," Avery said and threw a block.

Carlos tried to concentrate on the morning show. The news of Angel being shot consumed his thoughts. The gunman was only sixteen. The police finally caught him from the license plate number Lisa reported. Another incident that nagged him was a thirteen-year-old robbing an elderly woman at gunpoint. Carlos put on the headphones and waited for his cue.

He began his usual opening phrase. The morning's topic was Violent Crimes by Youths. He had invited a representative from the police department, a youth detention center and child psychologist, Carla Williams.

The telephone lines were flooded with calls from victims of youth crimes and youths as well. Carlos listened intensely, hearing fear in the voices of people who have become prisoners in their homes.

One caller, who pleaded for advice, stayed with Carlos throughout the entire show. She was recently divorced with a seven-year-old son whose behavior had changed since the divorce. She complained about having to discipline her son more often than usual. Something about the woman reminded him of Gina.

Carlos was happy when the show was over. It was one of the most depressing shows. People called after the show was over. He personally thanked Carla. She was professional, but cool with him. She had shut down since the fight. Dennis had extended an invitation to their home but Carlos decided to stay away. He didn't want to create problems between Dennis and Carla.

Carlos spent the rest of the morning calling daycare centers. The search was more difficult than he expected. If they weren't expensive, they couldn't take another child. His frustration was growing. He hadn't slept well for almost a week. Avery was stubborn. He refused to go to bed early. His bed wetting wasn't helping much. Carlos was happy that his mother was on vacation for the week. She kept Avery for two days. Carlos refused to take Avery back to the first daycare center when he heard a teacher tell a child, "Sit down fool."

Carlos was at the ninth daycare center on the list. He asked numerous questions. The woman was very polite. She encouraged Carlos to visit before bringing Avery but Carlos felt comfortable talking to the woman. He didn't need to visit. He signed Avery up immediately for the next week. A surge of energy went through him. He was singing when one of his co-workers came in the room. He had been dating her since he began working at the station.

"Hi Carlos. Are we still on for tonight?"

"Yeah. Let me call my mother to let her know I'll be home late," he said with a grin. She waved to him and left. He hummed as he dialed. His mother sounded sour. He told her he was coming home late. She asked if he had to work late. He said, "No."

"Are you crazy? You have a child. You don't have time to go out with your friends. This boy is driving me to nut city. Me and Shirley are playing bingo this evening."

Carlos got off the telephone and broke the date. He drove home annoyed. Avery was playing with his blocks when Carlos came into the house. His mother was leaving as he entered. "I didn't have time to fix him something to eat," she said and left.

"I gotta pee," Avery yelled.

Carlos took him to the bathroom. He thought back to the first time he took Avery to the bathroom. He tried hopping on the seat. Carlos had to teach him to stand and use the toilet.

Carlos wasn't paying attention to Avery. He was thinking about the broken date with Sherri. The wet liquid on his hands brought his concentration back. He started cursing. The telephone rang. He tried rushing Avery but he wasn't moving fast enough so Carlos left him in the bathroom. He was out of breath when he answered the phone. It was Gina.

"Where's Avery?"

"In the bathroom."

"By himself? Don't you know he can get into any and everything?"

Carlos tightened, "I thought you said he was potty trained."

"He is."

"He doesn't know how to use the bathroom. He tried sitting on the seat."

"That's how he uses the bathroom."

"Boys don't sit dammit, they stand!"

"Put Avery on the phone. I'm paying for this call. I'm not going to let you holler at me on my money."

Carlos stormed away and got Avery. He was playing in the toilet stool. Carlos washed Avery's hands. He mumbled and cursed. Avery took the phone and said a few words to Gina. He happily handed the phone back to Carlos and disappeared.

"So what kind of daycare is he in?" Gina asked.

Carlos' hands were sweaty. He rubbed them on his pants. "We're getting ready to eat."

"Y'all haven't eaten yet? It's almost eight o'clock. What time do you feed him?"

"Like you said, this is your money so bye." Carlos hung up the phone. He looked around for Avery. He was in the kitchen removing pots out of the cabinets. One pot hit his little foot. "Dammit!" Avery shouted. Carlos' mouth flew open. The telephone ringing made him forget about Avery again. Carlos rushed to answer.

"Nigga, don't you ever hang up on me again!" Gina yelled and slammed down the phone in a huff. Carlos closed his eyes and went back in the kitchen. He put the pots back into the cabinet and put a coat on Avery.

Avery was moving around. He wanted to play with the menu. Carlos tried to keep him still. The waitress brought a large sausage pizza, a soda and a mug of beer. Avery reached for the pizza. Carlos broke off a slice and put it on a plate. Avery played with it. He pushed it across the table. In the process, he knocked over the soda. Carlos was angry. He wiped it up and fussed at Avery.

As Carlos drank his beer, Avery eased down off the chair and took off running around the restaurant. Carlos called him but Avery was having fun. He looked back at Carlos and laugh. The restaurant was half filled with families, mainly white ones. Carlos was embarrassed. Avery knocked down a chair in his path of play. Carlos ran and grabbed him. He shook him and yelled out loud, "Boy when I say come here, that's what you do!"

The guests became quiet. Avery trembled with fear. Carlos looked around at the startled faces. Slowly, the eyes turned away except one white boy who was sitting beside someone who appeared to be his father. A woman sat across from him, patiently holding a very small child. The boy looked at Avery and then at Carlos. The man rubbed his head and asked him to finish eating. Carlos looked at his son who was crying. He left the pizza and beer on the table and went home.

Carlos ran a red light trying to get to the daycare center. He had been late twice that week. The daycare charged a dollar a minute after six o'clock. He drove so fast that he had five minutes to spare. He was discontent with his present situation. He was broke. The daycare was taking his spending money. He canceled another date with Sherri. She was getting aggravated with him. He couldn't wait until Gina came for Avery. At least he would get a breather.

It was the usual scene when Carlos walked through the doors. Kids were running around. He felt a little uncomfortable about the daycare center. Avery never wanted him to leave in the mornings and was anxious to go in the evening. It was becoming increasingly difficult leaving him. Carlos had to bribe him to stay.

Carlos searched the area for Avery. He wasn't waiting near the door as usual. Carlos went to the back room and saw Avery sitting on an aide's lap. She was holding an ice pack on Avery's forehead. Avery whined and reached for Carlos. He picked him up and saw the large protruding inflammation on his forehead. Carlos frowned hard at the aide. "What happened to him?" he growled.

"Tabia hit me," Avery whimpered.

"Who is Tabia?" Carlos demanded of the aide.

The fairly young woman tried to be careful as she selected her words. "One of Avery's playmates, Dontavius, hit him by accident."

"Accident? I want to speak to Dontavius' father."

"His mother should be here any minute. Mr. Simmons, sometimes accidents happens."

"I can see if he had a scratch but this big ass knot on his forehead ain't a accident. What the hell did he hit him with and where were you when it happened?"

"Mr. Simmons, we have lots of children. We can't prevent every accident from happening. Why don't you talk to Ms. Cherry, the director."

"Oh no! Since you can't prevent a child from being hit with large objects, he won't be back. This shit is crazy!" Carlos walked out of the room with Avery in his arms. He pointed to a little stout kid in a down coat. The little boy was much larger than Avery. His mother frowned as she gathered him to leave.

"He hit me," Avery said, pointing to the little stout boy.

Carlos approached to the woman. "Excuse me, but can I talk to you for a minute?" Carlos asked, semi-politely. The woman's lips were stuck out. It was apparent she had an attitude. She just frowned at Carlos. "Your son struck my son with a large object," Carlos said trying to be polite. The woman looked as to say "so." Carlos released a heavy sigh. He thought the woman would at least looked surprised.

"What the hell do you want me to do about it? How do you know Donté hit him?" she asked roughly. She even handled the little boy roughly.

Carlos was losing patience. "Because my son said so," he said smartly.

"Well, you need to teach your son to hit back," the woman said and yelled at the little boy to come along.

Carlos thought about how Gina would have handled the woman. She would not have walked away without an apology. The woman was right. Avery needed to learn how to defend himself. Carlos cringed at the notion of Avery being a punk. He also cringed at how Gina had taken care of their son without his help.

He was fuming as he drove home. Now he had to find another daycare. Avery was crying in the back seat, asking for Gina. He also complained about his stomach hurting. Carlos drove to McDonald's. Avery did not want his usual fries and coke. Carlos continued to drive. He decided to stop by Dennis' house.

Carla answered the door. She saw that Carlos was upset, so she invited him in. She saw the bruise on Avery's forehead and began asking questions. Carlos was irritated by the implications. Carla all but accused him of the bruise.

Avery cried and complained again about his stomach. Carla asked Carlos about Avery's last bowel movement. Carlos didn't know. Carla took Avery to the bathroom and removed his pants. She had Carlos hold Avery down while she inserted a suppository. Avery put up a fight but Carla held firmly. Carlos weakened as Avery cried for him. Carlos tried to get Carla to stop but she made him leave the bathroom.

Minutes later, Carla appeared with a tear-faced Avery. He reached for Carlos. "Children, just like adults, should have a bowel movement every day. You need to cook healthy meals for him. Fast food will only make him sick. Is he taking vitamins?" Carla asked, trying to keep her temper under control.

Carlos shook his head and Carla shut her eyes hard.

Carlos lost his temper. "Look, I'm doing my best!"

"Your best needs to be better!" said an angrier Carla.

Carlos was ready to go. Dennis walked through the front door with his four-year-old son Eric. Dennis was happy to see Carlos. "What's up, frat? It's about time you came to visit," Dennis said happily.

"Dennis, lower your voice, Tyler is sleeping," Carla shushed.

"Thank God," Dennis said low. "Eric, take Avery to your room and play with him." The two boys walked away. Dennis took Carlos to the basement. It was a half-finished basement. There was a leather sofa, reclining chair, cocktail table and bar in one large room. A laundry room was to the left and a door leading to another room to the right. Carlos plumped himself on the sofa.

"You have a nice house," Carlos said.

"It will do for now. So tell me, what's going on."

"Man, I don't know if I can take it. I have to find another daycare center. It will be the third one. It's eating up my cash. I can't go anywhere because I don't have money for a sitter. Gina hasn't sent a dime."

"Carla tells me Gina is flipping all the bills since you left."

"That's a lie! I've given her money!"

"You're only giving her a portion of your salary. At one time she had your entire check. You need to make a decision on whether or not you and Gina will divorce. You better prepare yourself for a larger payout for child support. This little money you're paying now ain't nothing. You've heard the song It's Cheaper to Keep Her?"

"Man, she was fuckin' around on me!"

Dennis was silent for a few seconds. It was the first he heard about Gina cheating.

"Did you catch her with somebody?" Dennis asked.

"I just know."

Dennis had to be careful. He knew Carlos wasn't happy about the separation, but he wasn't happy in the marriage either. "And now you're fuckin' around on her so there, you're even. What you've been doing with Avery these few weeks is what Gina has been doing for a few months. It hasn't been easy for her either."

"I need to get things happening for me. I'm not going back to Chicago."

"I'm not saying you should but you need to make some decisions about your son. If it's over between you two, then it's over."

"I'm not saying it's over," Carlos said surprisingly. Dennis kept quiet. "I can't trust her anymore. I know she was screwing somebody. She had a miscarriage and I know that baby wasn't mine," Carlos said. He finally got it off his chest.

Carlos suspected Gina's infidelity nine months ago. He wasn't sure because he couldn't remember the last time they had sex together. He was drunk many times and Gina would push him away. He only had hunches and it was good enough for him.

"Have you confronted her about it?" Dennis asked.

Of course not, Carlos thought. If she would have confirmed his suspicions, he probably would have killed her. "There's nothing to talk about," he said. The hurt and pain was forming on Carlos' face. Dennis allowed him to seethe in his anger.

The two boys were at the top of the stairs. Eric yelled down that Avery wanted his daddy. Carlos went to get him. He sat on the sofa with Avery in his arms. Dennis could see the frustration on Carlos' face and the bruise on Avery's forehead.

"What happened to him?" Dennis asked.

Carlos let out a huff. "Some kid at the daycare hit him with something."

"Tabia hit me," Avery said sadly, pointing to his forehead.

"Check it out, nobody saw a damn thing. The boy's momma copped an attitude with me. That shit really pissed me off. Now I have to find another daycare," Carlos complained.

"Our children go to Kinder World. Carla really likes it. She knows the director. Matter of fact, she graduated with you, Cheryl Moore."

"I know Cheryl. Another Alpha. They're all tight with Gina. Carla already accused me of hitting Avery."

"Avery is only going to be here for two more weeks. At least it's quality care."

The two began discussing the cost. Carlos looked sadder when Dennis told him he was paying one hundred a week, a discount for two children. Dennis looked at the father and son resemblance. Avery no longer looked like Gina. He was favoring Carlos strongly.

"Does he have your personality?" Dennis asked, pointing to Avery.

Carlos looked down at Avery, "Naw, he's stubborn like Gina." When Carlos said Gina's name, Avery looked up.

"My daughter Tyler is just like Carla. It means that she and Avery will get along well. We're taking the kids to Magic Land tomorrow. Why don't you bring Avery?"

"I have to work."

"We'll take him with us. He can spend a night too. Maybe you can spend some time with that new sweet thang I saw you with," Dennis said. Carlos laughed. "Thanks man. I got tickets to the Royals' game next Sunday. You want to go?"

"Sure. You want to shoot some pool? I bought a table for my birthday. Carla's been complaining ever since. I deserve something nice to entertain my friends."

Carlos was excited but then looked down at Avery, "I better get him home."

"He'll be okay," Dennis said. He called Eric downstairs to play with Avery. The two men walked into the other room. Dennis racked the balls and began chalking his cue stick. He handed the cube of chalk to Carlos.

"You need to watch your mouth around your son. You don't want him cursing," Dennis said.

Carlos said nothing. He remembered how he reacted hearing Avery say "dammit" when the pot hit his foot.

"So are things serious between you and the new honey?" Dennis asked, bending over, trying to size up his shot.

"Naw, man, she's helping to pass the time."

"Good," Dennis said and shot the ball.

Chapter 27

Barbara took her time putting on her smock. It was 9:30 a.m. Her clients expected her at 9:00 a.m. She entered from the rear of the boutique. She didn't want any customers to see her because they would talk, making her later. She had to freshen her face. She took deep breaths and walked into the fitting room. Six young women stared at her. Only one smiled. A tiny twinge of embarrassment pecked Barbara but she dismissed it immediately.

"Hello ladies. I'm Barbara Stevens. Miss Arvell, Miss Smith asked me to complete the contract. Is it okay with you?"

Lisa looked at Barbara for a few seconds. "My work is excellent. I taught Miss Smith," Barbara said sarcastically.

"It's okay," Lisa answered.

"Good. I want to start by taking measurements." Barbara pulled out a measuring tape but no one moved. They continued to stare. Barbara wondered if they were angry because she was late.

"Ladies, I only have eight weeks to complete the dresses. Can we get moving? I'll start with you, Miss Peterson."

Jennifer rushed to Barbara and whispered hello. She lifted her arms like a child reaching for a balloon. Barbara lokked strangely at Jennifer, but continued with taking measurements. She commented on each girl. She told Jennifer to do sit ups to firm her stomach. She complimented Alicia on her figure and told her to stay away from junk food to clear her skin. Rochelle was told to leave the decorations on the nails to the streetwalkers. Crystal had poor posture and breast reduction was recommended to Lisa's co-worker, Sonya. Barbara just smiled at Tina and told her to get a professional hair cut.

Lisa tried on the wedding gown. Barbara got busy with the pins. She looked at Lisa's back. It was smooth and spotless. It curved a gracefully from the neck to the waist. Barbara stepped back to get a better look at Lisa.

Barbara saw the strong resemblance the young woman had to her mother. The almond shaped eyes and the small round nose were the same but the big difference was the lips. Debra had full sensuous lips. She smiled constantly. After Bill called it off and decided to marry Catherine, she didn't smile anymore.

Barbara believed Bill really loved Debra at the time but was too taken by glamour. He belonged to Debra. She was his match. She forced him to stand his ground, something he was weak in. She was smarter than Catherine but not the elegant, sophisticated type. Most thought Debra looked better than Catherine too. The two were similar. Both were power seekers. Catherine was a manipulator and Debra was a negotiator. With Bill, they both ended up losers.

Barbara decided to make Lisa's wedding the one that belonged to Debra. It was the least she could do. They were sisters. It was going to be beautiful and elegant, the way Debra always wanted to be. It was going to be flawless, typical of the straight "A" Debra.

Barbara inventoried Lisa's friends. There was nothing she could do about the selection of bridesmaids but camouflage as much as possible. "Okay Miss Arvell. You're set to go. I'll have it finished two weeks before the wedding. At that time, you can come back for the final fitting. I will bring it with me Thursday before the wedding."

"You're, you're coming to the wedding?" Lisa stammered.

"Why yes! Miss Smith said you contracted with her for wedding coordinator too. Maybe you need to tell me exactly what you and Miss Smith discussed because I don't have a copy of the contract."

"Well we talked about…"

"Please dear, later. Business should be discussed in the appropriate setting, between you and me. You never want your friends to know everything about you. Isn't that right Miss Sims?" Alicia jumped, then nodded.

Barbara looked around. "Now where is the bridesmaid's dress? Miss Arvell, do you remember how it looked?"

Lisa went quickly to the corner and brought over the mannequin. Lisa draped the black fabric around the mannequin. Barbara frowned when she saw the dress.

"Oh no, that will not do! A full skirt on some of you girls will make you look heavy. Besides, black and rose is for the bedroom."

Barbara walked around the dress. She liked the diamond cut back. She liked the idea of the wrap too. She swung around and glared at Lisa, "Miss Arvell, I'm going to do something special for you. I will remove the skirt and make it straight with a twelve inch open vent in the back. The wrap can stay but it must be rose. I'm also suggesting gloves, elbow length, rose of course. How does it sound?"

Lisa didn't think it was negotiable. It sounded expensive. "It sounds nice."

"Nice? Oh honey, it will be the most elegant wedding you will ever attend. I hope you are not having a Tupperware bowl reception," Barbara said, slightly frowning.

Rochelle laughed out loud. A few snickers went among the rest.

"It's going to be at the Radisson Hotel near the airport," Lisa said.

"Oh, the new one. Good. Now what time will the wedding start?"

"Four o'clock."

"Change it to five."

"I told the church it would start at four. The pastor is going to be angry if it starts late."

"Are your invitations printed?"

"No."

"Then five it is. You're Baptist aren't you?"

Lisa nodded. "They always start late. This will give the minister time to arrive," Barbara said and the group's eyes got big.

"Mrs. Stevens, I've already decided on most everything."

"It's okay, dear. All you have to do is relax. Some things need a little fine tuning. Why don't you ladies step out for about three hours. I want to complete a sample dress," Barbara said. She smiled at the group. They all looked at Lisa as she gathered her things and left quietly.

Everyone went to Houlihans to eat except Lisa and Jennifer. They drove to Angel's apartment. Jennifer was excited. She talked about David the entire time. He was taking her out that evening. She was going to meet his parents.

They arrived at Angel's apartment. Lisa got out and opened the trunk. Lisa took Jennifer's garment bag out of the trunk. Jennifer stopped her.

"I'm staying at Rosalyn's," Jennifer said.

"Why? Angel probably needs help."

"Her father is staying with her until she gets on her feet."

Lisa stopped cold. She didn't want to go upstairs. It was the moment she had waited for but was afraid of. Usually, her gut feelings would give her indications of uncomfortable situations but she felt nothing now. The angels had left her. She was alone.

"I can't go up there," Lisa said. Her face was flushed.

Jennifer saw colors on Lisa's body again. A big pale green circle took over her chest. Lisa paced the parking lot, holding her stomach. Jennifer put her arms around her. Chills rushed up Lisa's back. She looked at Jennifer and the fear went away.

"Angel's father is my father," Lisa said with a cracking voice.

"You and Angel are sisters?"

Lisa nodded. "Gina told me who William Curtis Smith was. Miss Mattie confirmed it. All these years, I had a sister. Angel told Gina not to tell me. She hates me." Lisa's voice had all but faded.

"It's time to meet him. He probably doesn't know about you."

"He knows. He just doesn't want me. I can't..."

"Yes you can. Don't let this opportunity go by. He owes you. He abandoned you. You have to tell him something."

The two were facing the building, contemplating on whether to go in. Lisa was shaking. The door opened and a tall figure walked out. He came face to face with Jennifer and Lisa. Jennifer was surprised to see William. Finally it clicked. He was William Curtis Smith.

William looked at the anger in Lisa's eyes. The secret was no longer. She knew. Miss Mattie promised not to tell. He should have known better. How could he believe someone who blackmailed him for fifteen years? Although Miss Mattie didn't call it blackmail, it was. She always needed something for Lisa, constantly reminding him of the insurance money. He had to say something but was clueless. Debra's spirit had come to haunt him.

"Hello, Jennifer. How are you?" William said.

Jennifer remained silent. William was jittery. "Hello, Lisa. Finally I get a chance to meet you," he said and extended his hand.

Lisa looked at William's hand. "I met you eight years ago at Angel's graduation, remember?" she said low.

"Yes, I remember. So what are you doing now?"

"What do you care? You weren't nice to me eight years ago, so why are you being nice now? Jennifer I'm leaving," Lisa said hoarsely.

"Lisa wait! I want to see Angel."

"Either you come or get left behind. I'm not staying," Lisa said frowning. Her face was firing sparks. Jennifer backed away and walked inside the building. Lisa jumped in the car and sped off. William decided to go back into the building.

"Lisa was here," William told Angel. She said nothing. "She was a mistake," he said calmly.

"A mistake? She graduated summa cum laude with a double major in economics and finance. She is one of the few black junior economists at the Federal Reserve. I don't call that a mistake," Jennifer snapped. Hearing Lisa's credentials impressed William.

"Angel, why didn't you tell her? Gina said you didn't want her to know," Jennifer continued. The mentioning of Gina's name sent sparks of fire through Angel. Gina betrayed her. She told. Angel could hear Jennifer ranting in a distance. Hearing about her obligation to Lisa angered her more.

"I don't owe anybody anything and stop telling me she's my sister," Angel said sharply. She struggled to stand. She walked to William with arms folded. "She's your responsibility. Mom did what she did because you had an affair with Debra Arvell. Mom was beginning to love you and you wanted more. You pushed her away and me too."

Angel tried catching her breath. It was difficult. She put her hands to her chest. She was wheezing. The last time William witnessed his daughter's asthma attack was fifteen years ago. It frightened him then and it did now. He outgrew asthma and thought Angel had too. He picked her up and ordered Jennifer to find the spray pump.

Angel felt her chest tighten. It was becoming painful. "Dad help me," she managed to say. Her large, brown eyes pleaded with him. William yelled at Jennifer to hurry. Jennifer looked around frantically. She went to Angel's bedroom. Something prompted her to look behind the dresser. The pump was lodged between the dresser and the wall. Jennifer pried it loose and rushed to the living room.

William put the pump to Angel's mouth and compressed quickly. He did it again. Angel could feel relief coming. She was less tense. William held his daughter tight and rubbed her hair. She tried to relax but it was difficult to breath. She took the pump and inhaled again. She began breathing slowly. It was becoming stronger. She rested in William's arms.

"She was beginning to love you. You accused her of manipulating you into marriage. You never gave her a chance. It didn't stop with Debra. What about Aunt Marilyn? How could you?"

Angel cried. "You took down my pictures. You erased me out of your life like you did mom. We were suffering and you didn't care," Angel said.

As she laid in William's arms, he weakened. He had heard enough. His life was caving in fast. It was time to go. He carried Angel to the bedroom. He fluffed the pillows behind her. She was still crying. William turned around to face a distressed Jennifer. She eased herself around him and pulled up a chair next to Angel's bed. He walked out of the bedroom.

Lauren wobbled into William and handed him her bottle. He took it to the kitchen. Lauren followed, rubbing the nap from her face. He filled it with milk and gave it back to her. She put her little hand to her mouth and extended it. William didn't know what she wanted. She walked away and so did he.

Lauren walked in Angel's room sucking the bottle. Jennifer picked her up. She dropped the bottle in the process. Jennifer picked it up and gave it to her. Lauren put her hand to her mouth and extended it. Jennifer smiled.

"She said thank you," Angel said weakly.

Jennifer gave Lauren a kiss. "Lionel called. He heard about the shooting. He wants your phone number," Jennifer said and eased Lauren to the floor.

"I don't want him to have it."

"He's divorced."

"I don't care."

"Angel, our mother was a good person wasn't she?"

Angel couldn't lie. To tell Jennifer about the early years of deceit and betrayal would destroy everything their mother tried to overcome in the later years. What was the best answer?

"She worked hard to make sure we didn't starve. She went without before we did. She was a smart woman. Very smart."

"Angel, are you alright?"

"Yes."

"David wants me to meet his parents tonight."

"It means he's getting serious. Don't fall for any foolish lines. Make him prove everything he tells you and make sure you take money with you."

"He says he's never met anyone like me before."

"They all say that. If you are special, put it to the test. Buy a wig and see if he goes berserk over you cutting your hair."

"He says he wants me to move to Kansas City so that we can be together more often."

"Wait until he marries you. Don't give up everything over a cheap promise."

"He says he's falling in love with me."

"He wants to have sex. Make him wait."

"But I'm ready."

"Not yet, Jennifer. It's not time."

"Okay."

Lisa sat quietly in the back while Barbara sewed. Barbara removed her glasses and gave a sigh of relief. She completed the dress. She was pleased with herself as usual. It had been years since she designed anything. She was the one who critiqued, giving life or death to all garments made in her boutique. "Would you mind trying this on?" Barbara asked Lisa.

Lisa stood mechanically and removed her clothes. Barbara slipped the dress over her head and stood back. She put pins in the back and sides for a fit. "This straight skirt looks so much better than that hoola hoop Melanie created."

Lisa closed her eyes and then asked, "Mrs. Stevens, you knew my mother didn't you?"

Barbara showed no reaction, "Yes I did. Debra Jean Arvell, Miss Beta Gamma Delta of 1954. I made her gown." Barbara removed pins from the cushion and continued to fit the dress.

"Were you two friends?"

"She was my sorority sister. We met the first month of our freshman year. We had a lot in common," Barbara said, avoiding the question.

Debra wasn't friends with anyone. She trusted no one. Most everyone was treated the same unless you crossed her. Barbara chuckled thinking back to the time Debra wrote a plagiarized paper for Charles. Debra found out that he was seeing Catherine. Although Charles treated Debra as if she were somewhat special, he really never dated her.

Debra never said a word. She smiled and gave Charles the paper in class the day it was due. He turned it in without reading it. The paper came back with an "F" and a threat to kick Charles out of school. He knew Debra was nothing to play with. The games with her were over.

"What kind of person was she?" Lisa asked with a smile. Barbara nodded pleasantly. They both were similar, runaways from incest.

"Very smart describes your mother perfectly. She was two years younger than the rest of us and twice as smart. She gave several of us the incentive to do well in school. She knew how to do things no one else did."

Lisa was delighted. "Like what?"

Barbara felt the young woman was pushing it. Out of the five, Barbara was the only one who liked Debra. Catherine did until it came down to the voting for president. Both met their match.

"Your mother encouraged several young women to pledge Phi Kappa Psi. At that time, the sorority was extremely strict with whom they selected."

"What did she do?"

"She got us to believe in ourselves and gathered the courage to become something we never were," Barbara said smiling. They all became thieves.

Barbara hoped that was the last question about Debra the thief. The Kappas only wanted Debra and Catherine. Had it not been for Catherine's "don't get mad get even" attitude, the rest would have pledged Alpha, except for Catherine. She really wanted to be a Kappa.

Catherine gave birth to the idea of becoming well-to-do women and Debra created the scheme to do it. All were partners in crime, literally. Since Barbara could sew, Debra stole the fabric that would turn all eyes on six unknown freshmen. Debra had Catherine dress up, passing for white. Catherine went inside the fabric store to buy fabric, and Barbara went in to buy zippers. They hope that the poor white woman would ignore Barbara and not pay attention to Debra.

Catherine had the woman place a bolt of fabric on the cutting table and then changed her mind. She had the woman assisting her in selecting another bolt. Debra swiftly removed yards of fabric off the bolt and stuffed it in a burlap sack. She removed yards of fabric off other bolts while Catherine had the woman's attention at the cutting table. Debra slipped out the door unnoticed. Catherine would buy at least a yard of fabric and Barbara bought zippers and thread. Had it not been for Debra, Barbara's creative mind wouldn't have gotten six dresses from the stolen fabric.

Debra and Barbara took jobs cooking and cleaning at rich white women's homes. Debra stole an item of clothing or jewelry every day, simply by wearing it under her own clothes. She never got caught. Barbara picked up tips on fine dining by being around the white women. Her acting skills came in handy especially by being on her own for so long. The white women thought she was such a humble and sweet colored girl that they gave her clothes, shoes and jewelry. She and Debra never discussed the money they had stolen or the things they did to get money. The two shared everything with the other four. Debra taught Barbara to never sweat, stutter or stammer. It was their secret.

After the Lambda's Cotillion, the six freshmen were among the best dressed girls on campus. They became closer during the pledge period. Barbara encouraged Marilyn to wear makeup and Catherine encouraged all of them to keep their weight down. It gave them an opportunity to share clothing and choices of men to date. According to Catherine, men didn't like fat women. Lisa's next question slightly startled Barbara.

"Do you know my father?"

"Who is your father, dear?"

"William Curtis Smith."

"I know him as Bill," Barbara said, trying to keep comfortable.

"Did he and my mother date in school?"

What could she say about Debra the whore? That's what some called her. Debra was accused never caught. What Debra did never bothered Barbara. It started in the middle of freshmen year. First it was Bill. At the beginning of her sophomore year, it was Paul. After Paul left, she hung around Charles. Then it was Bill again in her senior year. Bill really liked her because he was very shy and she did things other girls wouldn't do with him. He was willing to take the risk with her until Catherine showed an interest after graduation.

Barbara thought back to the Lambda's Cotillion. Catherine sent Debra to convince six boys to be their escorts. Catherine selected Charles and Bill because of their looks. Debra promised four Lambdas, which included Paul, a good time after the dance. Debra only knew to promise the men a good time with six gorgeous women. The six men arrived at the girl's dorm to find six beautiful well dressed women waiting patiently.

Catherine took over. She introduced Barbara to the ex-boyfriend of the Kappa's president, Marilyn to Paul, Susan to the short Lambda, JoAnn to the heavy Lambda, and Debra knew Bill from one of her classes. Catherine took ownership of Charles by simply standing next to him.

After the dance, Barbara and Catherine asked their dates to take them home. Debra disappeared with Bill. Marilyn found out that Paul expected her to perform favors for him but was happy to know she was a nice girl. JoAnn and Susan had a tough time getting away and became extremely angry with Debra. Barbara and Catherine stayed up the entire night laughing and talking about the Kappas' reaction. That night the plotting began when Debra snuck in late with a grin on her face.

"Your father and mother did date in college but he married someone else," Barbara answered.

Lisa became quiet and Barbara smiled. She figured it would shut the young woman up for awhile. "So Miss Arvell, who is your husband to be?"

"Cameron Johnson. His father attended school with you too."

Barbara began removing pins from the dress. "Charles Johnson's son?"

"Yes ma'am."

"How nice. What does he do?"

"He's an electrical engineer with the public transit system in Atlanta."

"Oh. And what do you do?"

"I'm a junior economist with the Federal Reserve in St. Louis."

Although Cameron wasn't a doctor, he did have a respectable job, Barbara thought. Lisa was the surprise. Barbara could not previously tell that the young woman had such an impressive job. She wasn't refined but Barbara was impressed. It was something about Lisa she liked.

"What swept you off your feet?" Barbara asked smiling.

Lisa blushed. She never discussed with Jennifer why she liked or loved Cameron. She really didn't know. "He has always made me feel special. He works very hard. He wants a lot out of life."

"Sounds like a good catch. And what do you want?" Barbara asked as she removed the dress over Lisa's head.

Lisa turned around to Barbara. "I don't want anyone to ever look down on me again."

"Then never look back," Barbara said. "You can't move forward if you're always looking back. Your mother felt the same way. She made sure if people didn't respect her, then they got out the way."

"People respected my mother?"

"If they didn't, they got out of the way," Barbara repeated.

The whole sorority got out the way when Debra the traitor told the sorority secrets about starting a chapter at Missouri State to Ruby Lane the Alpha. According to Debra, if two black sororities attempted to start chapters at predominantly white universities, then at least one would be accepted. May the best group win. She and Ruby were rivals but also friends to some degree. It was the beginning of the end.

Debra was next in line for president but the sorority was split. Carol Bradley was her pledge mother. Debra was expected to become president. Catherine wanted to be president too, trying to find a way to pull away from the old regime. It was a new breed of women in the organization. The sorority was ready for a change.

Once Marilyn started with the rumors of Debra's reputation, it ruined her chances of keeping the old protocol alive. Almost everyone separated from Debra. It hurt her deeply. She and Ruby became closer. No one really knew what Debra told but the pledge mother/daughter program was the Kappas' tradition. Debra even told Ruby about the Partners-in-Crime theme "All for one and one for all."

"Did you know Carol Jefferson?" Lisa asked.

"I think I know who you're talking about."

Carol Jefferson was Carol Bradley, the one some Kappas accused of being a lesbian. They questioned the very close relationship between her and Debra. Barbara remembered boldly asking Debra if Carol was a bulldagger. Debra's only response was a laugh.

All the bridesmaids came in talking loud. They told Lisa about seeing some Upsilons from school and how fat they were. Barbara motioned for them to quiet down as she dialed Linda's number.

"Hello, Malinda. The tea is at our house next Saturday and I'm doing brunch. I need you to make a crab quiche."

Linda complained about not wanting to cook and how Barbara criticized her cooking weeks earlier. "Look dear, I need you to make enough for fifteen and also make some potato cakes too."

Linda sighed and agreed. Barbara hung up. She was glad that Linda agreed to make the quiche. Barbara had bragged to the doctor's wives about Linda's quiche. It was excellent. Linda was a natural at gourmet cooking and presentation as well. Barbara gave her a few instructions and Linda went with it. Barbara had Linda at the house at least twice a week. All Barbara did was lecture and complain, but Linda's company had become interesting to her.

"Lisa, who are our escorts?"

"I don't want anybody ugly."

Barbara looked at Alicia in disbelief. "Who cares about how he looks? If he has money and you can stand to look at him, then he's a good catch. You can always have apple pie for desert," Barbara said with a cunning smile. The group grinned and looked at Lisa.

"I have a good catch and apple pie," Lisa bragged.

"*You* are one of the very few. Okay ladies, let's see how the dress looks on. By the way, where is Miss Peterson?"

The group looked at Lisa. "I left her at Angel's," she responded.

"The name is Melanie. Why must you ladies address someone by a nickname? Please go and get her. I need to see how this dress looks on her because I have some alterations to do. Isn't she the maid-of-honor?"

"Yes," Lisa said and left the shop listlessly.

Lisa prayed on her way to Angel's apartment. She had no idea if she would be embarrassed. She felt no gut instincts. Within minutes, she was outside Angel's apartment building. She sat in the car for a few minutes before going inside. She took her time going up the steps. Before she knocked on the door, she heard his voice. She let out a deep breath and then knocked. Jennifer opened the door. The two stared for a moment.

"It's time to make peace with yourself," Jennifer said and stepped to the side. Lisa walked around her slowly and saw William. He sat stiff on the sofa. He had no remorse from ignoring her all those years. He almost looked pleased.

"I hear you are a junior economist. I'm happy to know that Hillside Preparatory paid off," he said, taking full control of the conversation. Lisa looked at Jennifer for an answer.

"I thought you would have chosen Harvard. Your grades were quite impressive."

"Why did Miss Mattie send you my grades?"

"Since I paid for your education, she thought I should know my money was well spent. I paid for your pledge period, your allowance and your car, the Escort."

"Why didn't you call?"

"I wanted to make sure you were taken care of and you were."

Lisa felt insulted. He chose his words carefully. She had to leave. She turned to Jennifer and said, "Mrs. Stevens wants you back at the boutique." The anger that had been buried for so long exploded. She turned to William and shot fire. "One thing, Mr. Smith, I didn't need you to take care of me. I've been taking care of myself for a long time."

"What happened between me and your mother was an accident. It should have never happened. Miss Mattie told me what you needed and I took care of it," William said calmly. He didn't want to mislead her nor did he want to hurt her feelings.

"In other words, you didn't want to be bothered."

"Developing a relationship with you was not possible at that time. I was married with a family."

"What about the other times? The times when you were not married. I guess you were always a loving husband and father. The tone of this conversation concludes your innocence."

"I'm not innocent."

"Hell no, you ain't! Why don't you come out and say you didn't want to be bothered. You never wanted to meet me and when you did, you frowned so hard that your face cracked. What makes you think I sat around waiting, hoping you would come and take me to a fuckin' carnival or a got-damn park? Well, I didn't. I don't want to hear another thing from your cowardly ass. You got your nerves saying you were married with a family. Look at Jennifer…"

Lisa stopped suddenly. Her friend's somber expression made her forget the anger. "I'm sorry Jennifer. I didn't mean anything by it." Lisa walked toward Jennifer but she took off running to Angel's bedroom. Lisa watched the door slam, shutting her out. William stood.

"You have every right to be angry. Jennifer tells me you need blood for surgery," William said.

Lisa gave no thought to William's words. She had to apologize to her friend. "I don't need anything from you," Lisa said between clenched teeth. She went inside Angel's bedroom. Jennifer was on the floor playing with Lauren. Angel's eyes were closed.

"Jennifer, I'm sorry. I didn't mean anything by it," Lisa said low. She sat on the floor. Jennifer refused to look at her. She focused her attention on the busy child whose world was surrounded by silence. Lisa placed her hand on Jennifer's shoulder but she shook it off.

"Why must you be so difficult? You even give Cameron a hard time and he loves you. Everyone who loves you gets hurt," Jennifer said.

"He doesn't love me," Lisa said. Her voice was shaking.

"He's willing to give you blood for the surgery but you're throwing it away."

"He doesn't care about me."

"What do you care? All you want is blood, be it from him or a stranger which he is. Why are you so angry? You've been defensive as long as I've known you."

"That son-of-a bitch left me. He left me alone with her. She didn't care about me either. She left me alone too. She left me with that man who was always trying to touch me. I hate him and I hate her too," Lisa screamed. Her body jerked fiercely. Her hands trembled.

Angel opened her eyes. She looked at Lisa. Jennifer saw a bluish color patch near Angel's throat. "The only difference between you and me is I saw him more. He didn't spend time with me either. Your problem is you have a quick temper, always trying to make a point. You will never accomplish anything by flying off the handle or getting people told," Angel said and sat up slowly. She cleared her throat. "Why should you pay for your wedding? Make him pay for it," she said in a burly tone.

"I don't want anything from him," Lisa mumbled.

"Yes, you do, but you can't have it and neither can I. Get what you can. If you want to hurt him, then hit him where it matters the most, in his wallet."

The bluish patch on Angel's throat became darker. Jennifer noticed it didn't go away. Thinking about what Miss Mattie said, Angel's spirit wasn't ailing, it was getting stronger.

"Miss Mattie knew how to get to him. Swallow your pride and tell him you need money for your wedding and blood for the surgery. What do you care about pride anyway? All it has done is made you angry," Angel continued. She knew she had Lisa's attention.

"He won't give me money for the wedding," Lisa said shyly.

"When you ask, stare him down. He has a conscience. It just doesn't show. Now if you really want to sock it to him for all the years of neglect, tell him, don't ask but tell him to walk you down the aisle. Believe me, all the pain you have ever felt will go away when he publicly acknowledges you as his daughter," Angel said without smiling but Lisa smiled.

Jennifer saw a violet patch on the top of Lisa's head. Then it began to darken. Something about her was getting stronger. Lisa laughed and looked at Angel who smiled maliciously. The whole world would soon know that William Smith was a bastard when he escorts his illegitimate daughter down the aisle. Public recognition of his wrongdoings would bring honor to her mother's grave.

"How do you like Aunt Barbara?" Angel asked pleasantly. Lisa put her hands to her mouth and laughed. "She told us in so many words or less, when it comes to men, we can have our cake and eat it too."

"Believe me, she means it," Angel said. She looked at Jennifer who occasionally look over at them. "Where is David taking you tonight?" Angel inquired.

"We're meeting his parents at a place called Harry Starker's"

Angel's eyebrows raised. "Well, I'll say. Harry Starker's is very expensive. What are you wearing?"

"I brought a skirt and blouse."

Angel shook her head. "Lisa, look in my closet and see if you can find a red dress with spaghetti straps," Angel ordered the new edition.

Lisa rushed obediently to the closet. She flipped through the dresses. She came to a red dress that was knee length with spaghetti straps. It was simple but the back was cut rather deep. She came out holding the dress to her body, walking seductively to Jennifer. "You better be careful in this hot thang!" she teased, hoping Jennifer had forgiven her.

Lisa's mouth flew open. "OHMYGOD! I'm suppose to bring Jennifer back to the boutique. Mrs. Stevens is going to have a fit!" Lisa shouted.

"There is a telephone by my bed. Just tell her Jennifer has a date with Dr. Howard. She won't mind," Angel said. Lisa rushed to the telephone. Jennifer saw the patches disappear slowly.

Angel and Jennifer heard Lisa on the phone apologizing to Barbara. They heard Lisa chuckle. Jennifer looked at Angel and did the hand sign for "thank you" and Angel signed back "you're welcome."

Chapter 28

Carlos found himself breaking another date. He wasn't interested anymore. The women he met were either boring or begging. They were the only ones who did not mind him being married. The ones he really liked shunned away but still, something was missing with them too.

Sherri was perfect, he thought. A very beautiful brown sister with gorgeous legs. She was smart and articulate, just like Gina but a little bossier. He didn't mind because he liked strong women, ones who knew what they wanted. The first time they made love, it was too mechanical, no passion. He tried it again with her and tried making suggestions. She got offended and his interest died fast. She told him he had a problem with passion. He wanted to be served.

Gina had passion. She never got offended. She was aggressive in bed. When she pushed him away, he knew things had changed. She said it was the beer but he knew it was another man.

Carlos shook his head to clear his mind. He had the afternoon to himself. Avery was spending the weekend with Gina's mother. Some Lambdas were meeting at Dennis' house to watch the fights. Carlos decided to bring beer. He had stopped drinking it for a short while after Avery had drunk some from an unattended bottle. It was time to keep it out of his son's sight.

It only took ten minutes to get to the store. Carlos browsed the aisle and picked up two six packs of Lowenbräu. He stood in line and waited patiently. He handed the cashier a fifty dollar bill. He shoved the change into his pocket and took off.

Before he could make it to his car, three young teenagers approached him. One had a board in his hand and another had a knife at his side. Carlos knew he was in trouble. The one with the knife looked the youngest. Carlos eyed the knife close. He watch it come up. One asked for his wallet but Carlos' attention was on the knife.

"Mothafucka, I said give up the wallet," one yelled.

Carlos turned around and met the board in the face. He was stunned. He stumbled back and a chain caught him several times on the head. He tried to look for the knife. He saw it coming. He swung one of the six packs hard, catching the attacker at the side of the face. It knocked him out. Carlos swung at the one holding the board. He ducked. The two assailants looked at their friend stretched out cold and took off running.

Carlos looked around wildly. His chest expanded rapidly. Onlookers in the parking lot looked at him strangely. He looked down at the body that did not move. He asked someone to call an ambulance. People continued to look and move sluggishly. Carlos was afraid. He bent down slowly to check the boy's pulse. His hand shook as he reached for the boy's neck. He closed his eyes and touched the motionless victim. He felt a pulse. He dropped his head in his hands. His face hurt and blood covered his hands.

The store's overweight security guard came out huffing and puffing. The sirens of the ambulance sang loudly onto the parking lot. Carlos saw the boy's bottom lip tremble but his eyes didn't open. Carlos turned his back. He forgot about the beer on the ground. The paramedics took over.

"Let me take a look at your face," a paramedic said. Carlos didn't move until the young man touched his nose. He jumped from the excruciating pain. "You need to go to the hospital. I think your nose is broken," the paramedic said.

Carlos didn't respond. He watched them carry the boy away on a stretcher. Before they put him inside the wagon, Carlos asked them what hospital they were taking the boy. They told him and left.

The crowd looked at Carlos strangely. A woman handed him a facial tissue. "Thank you," Carlos said and patted his face. He decided to take the paramedic's advice and go to the hospital. He wanted to see the boy.

"I can't believe you are leaving Avery with Carlos for another week. Cheryl says he cries a lot. You better get him soon."

"My mother told me to let Avery stay another week. She says Carlos needs to get a full dose of his own medicine. I really needed the time alone to concentrate on my presentation. Give me Cheryl's number. I need to know what's going on with my child. The last time I talked to Avery, he was whining and Carlos was talking about reconciling."

Marsha was quiet for a few seconds. "He wants to reconcile? I hope he doesn't think you're going back to him. He must be crazy."

"Of course he's crazy!" Gina lied. All she could think about was reconciling. She had hoped Marsha would say something supportive. The brief weeks with Leon were a mistake. He lied. He wasn't serious about a relationship with her. He used her for the contacts she had. He had been unavailabe since the miscarriage. She concluded he was dating someone else. She didn't miss him or the sex. She had to work too hard in bed.

Maybe it was time to manicure her own lawn. Carlos wasn't a bad person. Times were good until he started drinking. It was too hard trying to do everything alone. She didn't feel strong. She needed help. She wanted him back but everyone expected her not to go back. She missed him.

"Here's Cheryl's number. She told me Carlos has been extremely polite. She only gave him a discount because of you." Marsha called out seven numbers.

"Did Cheryl say how Avery looked?"

"Don't worry girlfriend, Carlos hasn't embarrassed you. Avery's clothes match and he's clean. His hair is always cut and brushed. Cheryl says he's one of the neatest kids there. He gets happy when Carlos comes to get him. Cheryl also said she once saw Carlos kiss Avery. Can you believe that!"

Yes, Gina thought. She could believe it. She wanted to believe it. She had to get her son and husband back. "I'll talk to you later,Marsha, and thanks for the number."

Gina removed a comb from her purse and began blending the layers of the new cut in place. She dug deeper in the crowded leather sack and pulled out a tube of lipstick. She dug deeper and found the compact. It became customary to focus only on the lips. To look further was painful.

She rubbed her lips together and put everything away. She waited anxiously for the plane to land. It had been six weeks since she had left a clinging Avery. She wondered if he was mad at her. She also wondered if he had grown taller or lost weight. Cheryl said he looked fine but she still wondered. Her mother told her not to call Avery so much. Carlos needed time to experience parenting alone. He needed to stop rescuing.

Gina jumped when the plane landed. It was a little bumpy but that was usual. Her hands trembled and that was unusual. She wondered what would she say or should she say anything? She was there to pick up Avery. Nothing else.

Passengers rushed to be the first to leave. Gina sat by the window, allowing everyone to leave first. The rush of people stopped. A man, around her age, smiled at her. He extended the invitation for her to go in front of him. She wasn't ready. She needed more time. His smile was too pleasant to decline. She eased out into the aisle, holding up the line of irritated passengers by trying to get her overnight bag out of the overhead compartment. The man helped release the American Tourist from captivity. Gina blushed, keeping her head turned slightly. When he handed her the bag, the blush went away immediately. She saw the ring. She said a quick, "thank you" and hurried down the aisle.

Gina walked to the doorway of the gate, taking control of her breathing with each step. She emerged through the doorway and laid eyes on her son. He looked like a shiny penny. He bounced in Carlos' arms. Avery yelled for her. She allowed the chants of "momma, momma" to lift her spirits. She missed him, even if he was getting difficult to handle. Then she saw the white bandage on Carlos' nose. She could not discern if he were smiling or frowning. It didn't matter anymore. The fear was gone.

Carlos put Avery down. He ran to Gina grinning. She picked him up and hugged him tight. She kissed him and he giggled. Carlos walked to Gina. He smiled as best he could.

"What happened to you?" Gina asked keeping her head turned slightly.

Carlos felt guilty, watching her hide in public. It was his fault. He cleared his throat. "Three teenagers tried to rob me. One broke my nose with a board," he said sounding nasal.

They took off toward the baggage claim. "You really look nice. Did you get your hair cut?" he asked. She nodded, avoiding eye contact. Avery began talking to her. She answered his questions with exhaustion. She had been up three nights straight preparing for a presentation that was almost a disaster because one of the group members forgot to get slides made.

"So how was your trip?" Carlos asked.

Avery interrupted again, trying to get Gina's attention. She was trying to tell him to let momma talk but he kept talking. Carlos took him from her. Avery began to whine.

"Hey! What did I tell you about that?" Carlos said firmly.

Avery stopped and put his head on Carlos' shoulders. "I want momma," Avery whimpered.

Carlos looked at him and said gently, "Momma is talking to daddy right now. When she's finished, she'll talk to you, okay?" Avery nodded reluctantly. "What does that mean, Avery?" Carlos asked, still being gentle.

"Yes," Avery said barely. Gina let out a sigh of relief.

"So how was your trip?" Carlos asked again.

"Fine," Gina said, looking straight ahead.

They made it to the baggage claim. Luggage was coming up on the carousel. "Do you have a good product?" Carlos continued.

It had been months, almost a year since they discussed her job. He used to be interested but the beer put an end to it. "It will probably do well for awhile. I just don't think pasta is the way to increase revenues," she said and paused. She didn't want to do all of the talking. She stopped showing an interest in Carlos' career once they moved to Chicago. He wasn't doing much so there was nothing to talk about.

"Cheryl and Carla told me that your talk show is gaining popularity. Carla really liked the one on the black male's role in the community. She said you brought out some powerful points on the extended family."

"Since I've been back, I realized the black family is in more trouble than my original analysis. Just like the teenager I hit with the beer bottles..."

Gina frowned. "You hit a teenager with a beer bottle?"

Carlos nodded. His face throbbed. He didn't know if it was his nose or the question. "He and his friends tried to rob me. One hit me in the face with a board and the other hit me upside the head with a chain. The one I hit tried to stick me with a knife. I had to protect myself."

"It's really getting bad. They could have killed you!" Gina exclaimed.

Carlos felt pampered from Gina's excitement. "Yeah baby, you're right. They could have killed me and Angel too. But there is hope. Like I was saying about the young brother who tried to stick me, he's only thirteen. His mother is a hardworking sister like yourself. She was surprised when I didn't want to press charges and offered to help. I hooked her up with the Boys' Club. I don't know if it will do any good but I believe there is hope."

Avery looked at Carlos and pointed to Gina. "Momma?" he asked sweetly. Carlos smiled and handed him to Gina. She really didn't want to hold him. She was tired.

They waited in silence for her luggage. Carlos thought, within two days, his son will be leaving and he and Gina had not talked. He saw the familiar American Tourist and rushed to retrieve it. He took her overnight bag and they walked to the car in silence.

Gina didn't want to break the silence. She was always the one who spoke first. He started the fighting. He walked out on their son. How dare he feel sorry for a juvenile delinquent? She was firm about letting him be the one to do the talking, especially if they were to reconcile.

"Do you want to stay over my mother's? I haven't finished packing Avery's clothes."

"I'll finish packing them. I need to see Angel. She hasn't been talkative these days."

"What happened to her was traumatic. She may never get over it. She's not like you. She's pretty soft."

Gina thought how wrong he was. Angel was one of the strongest people she knew. She was a survivor. She didn't break under pressure. "Something else is bothering her," Gina said, thinking whether Lisa told Angel the truth.

"We're near Dennis and Carla's. You want to stop by?"

"Don't you think we need to call first?"

"They don't mind. I do it all the time."

"They were probably being polite. We are going to call."

"I left it in Chicago."

Carlos pulled the car into a telephone booth at a gas station. He got out and walked to a pay phone. Gina looked back at Avery thinking he was asleep. He saw her face and began asking questions. She closed her eyes and tried to be polite with her answers.

Carlos got back into the car. "They said it's okay," he said, mocking Gina's voice.

"I wasn't going to drop by, just because we're friends," Gina chastised.

"Yes, dear," Carlos said teasingly. Gina frowned and turned her head.

Carla opened the door. She and Gina hugged. They talked loudly. Dennis motioned Carlos down to the basement. Tyler walked into the room and immediately pushed Avery. He pushed her back.

Gina was surprised. "Avery! I don't want you hitting her again," she scolded.

"She hit me," Avery said, pointing to Tyler, who looked innocent.

"It's okay Gina. She's a ball of fire," Carla said.

Avery pouted and went to the basement steps. He yelled down, "Daddy, Ty-ur hit me."

Gina got mad. She beckoned for him to come. He remained at the steps. Gina threatened to spank him but he kept saying, "Ty-ur hit me."

"Gina, it's okay. She gets into fights with boys all the time. She's always starting them. She and Avery play well together. They will be fine," Carla said, trying to ease the tension. She could hear footsteps from the basement.

"I don't care, Carla. I don't want him hitting girls," Gina said.

Carlos appeared. "What's going on?" he asked.

"Avery is hitting girls. I told him to come to me and he won't," Gina complained.

Avery started crying, "She hit me."

Carlos picked him up. "I'll take him to the basement. We are going to have a talk about hitting girls," Carlos said to Avery and took him away.

Tyler rushed to the basement steps and yelled, "A-V".

Carla shook her head. "Dennis, come and get Tyler so that she can play with Avery."

Carlos appeared again. "Now, if I bring you down the steps, I don't want you fighting Avery, okay?" The little mischievous child nodded.

Gina sat with arms folded. Carla listened as Gina expressed her desire to reconcile. "Whether or not you reconcile is your decision. What I think should not matter. Stop looking for approval from other people."

"I don't want to make a mistake."

"None of us do. It may or may not work. Either way, you're taking a chance. What has he said?"

"Nothing yet. I'm waiting for him to open up."

"Gina, don't get your hopes up. Maybe he really wants a relationship with Avery. Carlos is really beginning to enjoy Kansas City. Are you willing to move back? If you are seriously thinking about getting back together, you two need counseling."

Gina hadn't given any thought to moving back to Kansas City. She didn't want to step backwards in her career. This was tough. Carla was probably right. He may not want to move back home. He may only want a relationship with Avery. She felt stupid, opening her heart and expressing her feelings to Carla. She really felt stupid. She wanted to go to her mother's house and go to bed.

Dennis popped in a compact disc. Soon the melancholy sounds of Sade filled the room. He offered Carlos a drink. He took a soda. He didn't want to spoil the evening with Gina with the smell of beer on his breath.

"What did Gina say?" Dennis asked. He relaxed in the reclining chair.

"We haven't talked," Carlos answered. He was embarrassed. Dennis told him to talk to Gina before she came to Kansas City. Dennis told him it might be awkward when Avery left.

"What's the hold up? Are you scared?" Dennis teased.

"Yeah man, I am. This is going to be tougher than I thought. She doesn't want to talk," Carlos said sincerely.

"Women are like that. When you want to talk about a problem, they're not ready, but they will wake you up in the middle of the night if they're mad," Dennis said.

Carlos watched how Tyler and Avery played. They were running, shrieking with excitement. One minute they were fighting and the next minute, they were friends. "I thought if I brought her over here, Carla could convince her to talk to me," Carlos said.

"By the time you leave, she'll be relaxed to talk. Carla has a special magic. By the way, you did cool things with Sherri, didn't you? Gina won't run into any surprises, will she?"

"It's been over between me and Sherri for over a month."

Tyler ran in the room chanting, "A-V, A-V." She giggled as she climbed onto Dennis' lap. He narrowed his eyes at his daughter and looked at Avery. He had an impish grin.

Dennis looked at Carlos. "Man, I like you but I don't want your son touching my daughter. I might have to shoot him."

There was silence as they rode to Carlos' mother's house. Carlos decided to break the silence. "We need to feed Avery," he said and drove to Houlihans.

The restaurant was crowded with couples. Gina took her time going over the menu. "I think I'll have the turkey sandwich and the chicken fingers for Avery," she said.

"Believe it or not, he likes salads and rice. I don't think he cares much for meat," Carlos said.

"Hum, I'll let you order his meal," Gina said.

Carlos couldn't determine if she was angry or agreeable. "He might eat the chicken fingers. I had noticed he eats salads and rice very well," Carlos said.

"It doesn't matter. Every time I've ordered him something to eat, he's always messing over my money. I'm assuming it's your treat since you suggested that we eat out," Gina said in a joking way. Carlos knew she was joking but it always bothered him when she said, "my money."

"Daddy, I gotta pee," Avery said out loud. Gina tried to hold in the laughter because Carlos looked embarrassed. Small things embarrassed him. He always wanted things to run smoothly. He got flustered when they didn't. But, to Gina's surprise, he smiled at his son and said, "Come on man, let's go." He picked up Avery and walked away.

Gina watched how he maneuvered around the tables and chairs. Since he had stopped drinking beer, his stomach had trimmed down and he had lost a noticeable amount of weight. She could still smell the cologne he was wearing, something he had not done in a long time.

She watched his butt. She was a butt person. Angel liked a tight stomach; Linda liked a big chest, next to a big wallet; Carla liked strong arms; and Marsha like thighs and legs. To Gina, the butt was the sexiest part on a man's body and Carlos had a nice one. She felt herself itch at the chest. She had to remind herself that it wasn't going to be that kind of party.

They arrived at Carlos' mother's house. She was home and Gina didn't like it. Gina tried not to make an issue over Mrs. Simmons' behavior but it was tough being around her. Carlos' mother always accused Gina and Marilyn of being high and mighty. Mrs. Simmons refused every invitation Marilyn extended. Carlos knew his mother was being unfair but there was nothing he could do.

When Gina walked through the door, Dorothy Simmons turned her head. Gina spoke but Carlos' mother didn't. Gina stayed near the door while Carlos walked to his bedroom. He turned around and motioned

Gina to follow.

"I don't won't no shit going on in that room," Dorothy Simmons said.

Carlos was angry. "Momma, don't curse around Avery," he said trying to hold his temper.

"Nigga, this is my house. I do whatever the hell I want to do. If you don't like it, you can move your black ass out," she said. "And let me repeat myself, I don't won't no shit going on in that room," she threatened.

They walked into the bedroom. Carlos began throwing Avery's clothes into the suitcase. Gina stood in front of him. Her forehead touched his bottom lip. She removed a pair of Avery's pants from his hands. She folded it neatly and placed it in the suitcase. She removed the tumbled clothes from the suitcase and began folding.

"These clothes belong to your son. If you are mad at her, then throw her clothes," Gina said softly and continued to fold. When she finished, Carlos picked up the suitcase and they walked out of the room. Gina kept her focus on the front door.

Dorothy Simmons was resting in her favorite chair. "I guess I don't have to cook for him anymore. Come give your Grandma Dorothy a hug," she said with outstretched arms. Avery walked obediently to her and hugged her. "Make sure you visit me again. You hear?" Avery nodded. She kissed him on the cheek and picked up the remote control. The three left.

As Carlos drove to Gina's mother's house, he pulled at a way to get Gina to talk. She was never short for words. She had to know he wanted to discuss reconciliation. He would look at her out of the corner of his eyes. Her focus was straight ahead. He assumed she didn't care about their son's future or their's either.

He drove the car up the long driveway of the beautiful large home Paul had built. It would probably be awhile before he saw Avery again. He slowly put the car in park. Gina opened the door. When she moved her legs, her skirt inched well over the knees. It made him feel warm.

"Can you get the suitcases?" she asked.

"Sure," he said and opened the trunk and got the suitcases out. He watched as she carried a sleeping Avery. It had been a long time since he had seen that sight. She struggled to push the doorbell. He rushed and did it for her. Marilyn opened the door.

Carlos set the suitcases inside the door and took Avery out of Gina's arms. He had to hold him one more time before he left. Carlos held Avery tight and listened to the light breathing. He remembered how he thought he had rolled on top of Avery because he didn't hear him. He was a light sleeper like Gina. Carlos placed a gentle kiss on Avery's forehead.

"Put him in Gina's room," Marilyn said.

Carlos took off down the hall. He passed Paul on his way to the living room. They spoke and Carlos kept going. He laid Avery on one of the girly beds dressed in flowers. Carlos carefully removed Avery's clothes, trying not to wake him. The little boy continued to sleep soundly. In less than forty-eight hours, the words, "Daddy I gotta pee," would not wake him in the mornings.

Carlos listened to the very low chatter from the living room. He liked being at Gina's parents home. It was peaceful. No cursing. No arguing. No fighting. Always pleasant. He got off the bed and took one last look at Avery. Carlos removed the stuffed poodle from the bed and put it on the dresser.

Carlos walked to the doorway. Gina came to the room. She tried getting around him but he pinned her in between the doorway. She was wearing the Channel perfume he bought for Mother's Day last year. She said it was her favorite. Her hair bushed his top lip. It tickled the bottom of his nose.

"Gina, we need to talk," he said trying to breath through the cast. How could he think about making love to her when he looked hideous with the bandage on his nose? He knew how she felt with the bandage around her head. Ugly.

It had been a long time since she felt his chest. It had been a long time since the reeking of beer didn't cover his breath. It had been a long time. Her chest itched and so did the back of her ears. She didn't look at him. She just said okay and allowed herself to feel him close for a few more seconds.

Angel was washing dishes. Linda put the last of the leftovers in a Tupperware bowl. Lauren was concentrating on removing the tape from her fingers that Linda cleverly thought of to keep her busy until she and Angel finished.

"Is Uncle Bill okay? Aunt Marilyn told mother that he's been down lately."

Angel didn't know whether to tell. She had never seen her father so vulnerable. He agreed to give Lisa three thousand dollars for the wedding. When she left, he complained terribly. He finally told his daughter that he would be out of a job in November. He was also depressed because he couldn't get the director of the Youth Center to give him a contract to install the LAN system they previously discussed. She didn't want to talk to him about it either. He decided to let it go because he didn't want to jeopardize his daughter's job.

"He's okay. He met with Lisa awhile back. He handled it fairly well. Thanks for dinner. I didn't know you could cook so well."

"You can thank mother. When I had to take care of her those horrible weeks, she complained constantly. I had to cook this way or that way. Now, she wants me to cook every time she has a club tea or a sorority meeting. I told her I'm not cooking for her anymore."

"You must be good if she wants you to cook for her friends. You know how particular she is."

"Yes, but I'm not cooking for her or the mink coat mommas. She's having the National Conference committee meeting at her house next Saturday. Some big shots are coming to town. She wants me to all but cater it. I told her no!"

"Linda! Do you know how important it is to have any National committee to entertain?"

"I don't care! She should have never invited them. She's really making a big deal out of this meeting. Maybe it's time she's brought down to earth. She's always trying to show off. I'm sick of her trying to be 'Miss It.' Mina has cooked for her all these years. Now she wants me to be her slave. I'm not doing it."

Linda went into the living room and sat on the sofa. Lauren walked to her and extended the fingers with the tape on it. Linda unraveled a little and put one of Lauren's fingers on the loose portion to finish the rest. Lauren sat down and quietly continued her task.

Angel came into the living room. She moved fairly well. She was released to go back to work. She still felt pain but it was tolerable. "Linda, the sorority is very important to Aunt Barbara. She went through a great deal to become a member. She is the only one who took the sorority seriously."

"Why does she do all of this pretentious bullshit? Why does she take it so seriously? She can do other things with her life. Did you know she's selling the boutique?"

Angel almost leaped off the sofa, "No!"

"She says it's losing money. Her taste in fashion isn't selling well. She says the women who have good taste aren't buying originals anymore. It's not important to be different. Other words, they're getting old."

Angel had to talk to Barbara. She could not sell the boutique without her knowledge. It was time to bring some things to light. "Linda, mom's diary talked about how mom and the rest pledged. The Kappas really laid it on Aunt Barbara. They teased her constantly about being from Alabama. They called her Cherub Country Bumpkin."

Hearing that made Linda indignant. "What did they call your mother?"

Angel didn't want to answer but decided to tell the truth. "Mom was Cherub Cinderella."

Linda was annoyed. "Cinderella? How nice!"

Angel ignored the comment and continued the story. "One day it was raining. A couple of big sisters were sharing an umbrella. They saw Aunt Barbara walking from class. They made her give up her umbrella. One made her walk barefoot since she was from the country and probably not used to wearing shoes. One time she had to use the bathroom. One Kappa made her leave the dorm and piss behind the building since she was probably used to an outhouse." Angel stopped. Linda's eyes were angry.

"She swore that one day she would see eye to eye with those girls and no one would ever do that to another Cherub. The sorority is important to Aunt Barbara because it gave her something to work towards. She had to show everyone that Barbara Wright Stevens is classy, beautiful, elegant, graceful and charming. She was never accused of being those things."

Linda stood. "May I use your phone?"

"Sure."

Linda's hand shook as she pressed the numbers. She cleared her throat when her mother answered. "Hello mother. What did you want me to prepare for Saturday.... No, I'm not going to be busy.... Do you need my help, um assistance?... I think broiled salmon and filet mignon is better unless you can't afford both dishes.... No, let's go with potatoes. I've been working on a New Potatoes recipe that is great!... I'm sure it will turn out fine.... I'm suggesting wok stir fried vegetables unless you girls have to be careful with your dentures. I can boil them until they're soggy.... Pie is fine if you don't have to watch your weight. I'm thinking more on the line of a strawberry whip cream mousse. It will be in individual glasses and the presentation will be fabulous.... Of course it will be low cal.... PUNCH? I thought these were the mink coats. Do you think dad will increase your allowance so that you can buy a blush wine?... Yes, I know it's a luncheon.... Well those are my suggestions.... Good. We'll talk on Wednesday. Good-bye."

Linda hung up the phone. Angel was standing beside her smiling. She had a bag in her hand. "I found some of the Barbies Aunt Barbara gave me. The Skipper Dream House was given to the Goodwill by good ole dad." Angel gave Linda the bag.

Linda looked inside the bag to see three of the five Barbies that were given away. She looked at Lauren who finally managed to remove the tape. She walked proudly to Linda and stuck the tape on her pants leg. Lauren rubbed her hands together and walked away.

"Give these to Lauren. Apologize for me. I would have never given her a white doll. Tell her they're from Aunt Barbara. I need to go."

"Don't forget to come to the Blessing on time."

"I take it that her father won't be there?"

Angel shook her head.

"Mother and dad will be there. Dad keeps asking about the surgery?"

"I am considering the surgery but I am considering the cost, too."

"Don't you have insurance?"

"Yes, but it doesn't cover one hundred percent. I will still have to pay something. I don't know how much it will cost."

"That is why you have godparents," Linda said smiling.

The telephone rang. Angel took her time to answer. She knew Linda was going to be an excellent godmother for Lauren. Angel picked up the phone. The color left her face. Linda was worried and decided to hang around. Angel motioned for her to leave but she wouldn't. Angel spoke in code. She was discreet until she said the name.

"Okay Lionel, thanks for calling. Good-bye." She didn't catch it until she looked at Linda.

"That was Lionel Johnson? What did he want?"

Lauren came out of her bedroom making humming noises. Linda looked at the little girl closely and saw the connection for the first time. She had Angel's eyes but they were dark like Lionel's. The nose and mouth belonged to him too. Even the shape of her face.

Linda took the the bag of Barbies from Angel and handed them to Lauren. "These are from Aunt Barbara," Linda said, wildly waving the palm of her hand with the thumb tucked in.

The little girl took the bag roughly, spilling the dolls on the floor. She looked at the foreign objects. They looked nothing like the brown babies that covered her bed. She left them lying on the floor.

"I'll see you tomorrow. Ta-ta!"

Barbara made sure the dining table was set properly for eight. Mina spent two nights making sure everything was spotless. Linda had been there since Wednesday, taking her time on the meal. She barred Barbara from the kitchen because she made her nervous.

Barbara took another look at herself. She was dressed in a simple black dress with the traditional pearl earrings and necklace. The dress was fairly loose. She had lost weight, at least ten pounds. She wasn't worried because she would rather be too small than too large. She was so exhausted that she didn't find time to eat. The sound of the doorbell cued her to begin the script she had rehearsed all week long. She waited to start her lines.

Mina invited four women inside. Barbara could hear the low ooos and ahs. She would wait until the doorbell rang again before appearing. She took another look at the table. Malinda did a fantastic job with the centerpiece. She took fresh flowers and arranged them with maroon and gold ribbons. She made fans in the wine glasses with maroon napkins. Each guest name appeared on a card in script writing. It leaned against the water-glass.

The second doorbell sounded twenty minutes later. Barbara went in the kitchen to get Linda. She looked oddly, at her mother, who was nervous for the first time ever.

"Malinda, I want you to meet the sorority's National President," Barbara said smiling.

So this was the important lifetime event, Linda thought. The head mink coat-in-charge was coming to lunch. Linda put down the large serving spoon and walked to her mother. Barbara put her arm around Linda's shoulders and walked her to the living room. Linda felt awkward because her mother never really hugged her as long as she could remember.

They walked into the room that was overpowered by perfumes ranging from flowers to spices. Linda saw a room filled with black dresses and pearls. Everyone must have had a hair appointment that morning because every hair was in place. The surprise was the National President. She looked different than the pictures Linda had seen in the quarterly mailing. She had to have been ten years older than the photograph. Her makeup was too heavy. It enhanced the wrinkles. She was much shorter and heavier in person. She didn't exemplify the physical evidence that everyone on the local level tried to maintain.

What Linda noticed about the head mink coat was the clothing and jewelry. The fabric of her dress was wrinkle-free. It was well constructed, no seams pulling or loose threads. It didn't pucker either. The diamond earrings sparkled. They must have been freshly cleaned.

"Madame President, I would like you to meet my daughter, Malinda," Barbara said proudly, articulating each syllable.

The woman's smile was very warm. She spoke softly with head held high. "Hello, Malinda. I finally get a chance to meet you. Your mother has spoken highly of you. We can't wait to taste the salmon that she has bragged about for three weeks."

Linda almost frowned. She had just agreed a week ago to do the luncheon. Her mother and Angel played against her. Angel probably told her mother she would convince her to cook. It was okay. They won fair and square. Angel caught her on a weakness.

"Madame President, it is an honor to meet you. Believe me, you will not be disappointed in the salmon," said a confident Linda.

The President nodded and sat down. Barbara introduced Linda to the others. When Linda met one of the women who pledged her mother, she turned a sour face. She made sure Barbara wasn't looking. Linda had to let the woman know she didn't like her and it didn't matter what title she was packing.

The women ate and talked. They stayed four hours. Linda was tired of waiting for them to leave so that she could clean the kitchen. She decided to step out for awhile. She thought about going to Keith's office and strip, a little advice her mother gave her to bring excitement into the marriage.

Linda went to the sitting room where everyone was having coffee and cake. "Excuse me, mother. Do you need anything before I step out? I'll be back in an hour."

"No honey. Thanks for everything," Barbara said, glowing.

One of the mink coats surprised Linda and said, "Barbara, you're so lucky to have a daughter like Malinda. My daughter would have left a long time ago without saying a word."

Another one said, "Mine is so lazy. The idea of her preparing such a spread is unheard of. Malinda hun, thanks for everything. We see why your mother brags about you. We just thought she was just being, um, pretentious." The group laughed.

Linda heard comments about ungrateful children. She was so surprised. These were National figureheads complaining about their children like regular women. The Kappas on the local level only said good things, bragging like her mother. The real mink coats didn't care.

Linda drove to Keith's office. It didn't look anything like her father's. It was small and cramped because the furniture Linda picked out was too big for the room. When she walked through the door, his eyes got big. He stammered a greeting. His wife never paid him a visit. He couldn't imagine what she wanted. He knocked over some papers when he stood.

"Where is everyone?"

"My last patient left thirty minutes ago. I told Shanora, she could leave."

"Who is Shanora?"

"She's my weekend office manager. Beverly only works during the week."

Keith remained standing as Linda walked around the office. She looked out the window. It was a very bright and pleasant April day. People were out and about. Linda closed the blinds. She left the office and came back. Keith was still standing.

She continued to probe, taking inventory, not saying a word. It always made him feel uneasy. She liked seeing him fumble. It felt good being in control. She looked at the husband whom she compared to Mickey Mouse for years. He wasn't bad looking. His ears were just big. She was glad when he took her advice and stop wearing his hair very low. The box haircut sized down his ears. He wasn't bad looking after all, matter of fact, he was cute. Mice were cute. He gave a schoolboy grin as he sat down to gather his papers from the floor.

She got the nerve to try it. She walked around his desk and sat on his lap. His eyes became big. They were big pretty eyes but they looked tired, like he had been up for nights. She kissed him gently on the lips. He pulled her close and gave her a long kiss. She pulled back, not breaking her stare and began unbuttoning her jacket.

She took a deep breath, allowing her chest to expand and then exhale slowly, allowing her lips to part. She performed a strip routine to music in her head. She was down to her skimpy underwear when Keith stood up and removed his lab coat. She could see an erection through his pants. She got excited seeing him aroused so she slowly removed her underwear.

He rushed to remove his pants. He was down to boxers and T-shirt. She walked over to him and began rubbing his chest with red nails. Her hands traveled down to the boxers. He pulled her close but stopped quickly.

"What's the matter?" she whispered.

"The door. I must lock the door," he panted.

She laughed and stepped back and stretched out on his desk. "Don't go anywhere," she said seductively.

Keith kept looking at the door. He didn't want anyone to walk in on them. But she told him not to go anywhere. He always did what she said. This was the first time ever she was the aggressor. If he didn't ask for sex, he never got it.

He took one more look at the door and then leaned forward quickly. He kissed her breast and stomach in a hurry. He rushed through the foreplay. She brought her knee up and extended her leg, forcing him away with her foot. It rested on his shoulder. She let toes caress his chest.

"The door is locked," she said low.

She put her toes on his chin and laughed. He looked at the cute little hinges that were painted red. He kissed them quickly, one by one. He saw how she reacted. He kissed her leg until she wrapped them around him and pulled him close. She did inventory. Gina was right. Keith had a nice body, especially a cute butt.

"Let's go slow. That's the way I like it," she whispered.

He leaned forward again. He had to concentrate on going slow. He kissed her slowly on the lips. Her reaction stimulated him to touch her slowly again. He took his time to make love to her. It was easier because she wanted to.

Linda drove to her parents' house with a big smile. The smile faded quickly when she saw the ambulance at the front door. She drove up the driveway fast, almost forgetting to put the car in park before getting out.

The white coats had Barbara on a stretcher. Linda rushed to them. She saw one holding a bag of fluid and two carrying the stretcher. "What happened to her?" Linda asked before they put Barbara in the wagon. "Where are you taking her?" Linda demanded.

"Your mother suffered a diabetic reaction. She called us, saying she felt strange. She's one of the smart ones. She was able to leave the door open. We found her on the kitchen floor. I think she was washing dishes."

Linda looked at her watch. She had been gone for two and a half hours. She was due back well over an hour ago. "She's a diabetic? Is she going to die?"

"Oh, hell no, Malinda. Could you please clean up my kitchen? I probably *will* die if I see it looking like that again," Barbara said weakly.

"Well, Evilene, you might as well take your last breath because I'm not cleaning up that kitchen. I'm going to call dad and then go to the hospital," Linda said, looking down at the frightened woman.

"She is so stubborn. Take me to the hospital," Barbara demanded.

The paramedics looked at one another, daring not to become involved in the family feud. One raised his eyebrow and the other gave Linda directions to the hospital.

Angel sat patiently, at Barbara's bedside, listening to the story of the historical event, the visit of the National President. Angel let Barbara finish the story. Angel gripped the envelope until it was time. She calmly asked, "Aunt Barbara, were you and mom ever in business together?"

Barbara's face almost turned sour. She knew that Angel had found the letter. "Yes we were. She had a twenty-five percent ownership in the boutique."

"I hear you are selling the boutique. When were you planning on telling me?"

"Are you interested in buying or do you want to know when you will receive your share?" Barbara said to the point of being insulted. She didn't owe the girl anything. Maybe her mother, but not her. The nerve of her.

Angel tried to look humble. The last thing she wanted to do was offend Aunt Barbara. "I don't want you to sell the boutique. I have some good ideas on promoting the designs," Angel lied.

"It cost too much to make our own garments. People aren't spending money on originals, anymore. I was fortunate to buy that piece of land for almost nothing. Now it's worth almost one hundred thousand dollars to a developer. The question is when will we collect," said the business woman. Barbara sat upright and extended her claws. "When we settle, I take it that Lauren will have the surgery because you will be able to afford to pay for it. My daughter is weak when it comes to friends. She never had that many," Barbara said without taking a breath.

"I never expected Linda to pay for Lauren's surgery. I'm sorry if I offended you," Angel said meekly. She stood up and kissed Barbara on the forehead. Angel eased the letter into her pocket. "I never imagined us not working together," Angel lied. She gathered her purse and walked to the door. "Take care of yourself and make sure you eat properly," she said with a smile.

"Come here, sweetie," Barbara said. She couldn't tell whether or not to believe the young Catherine. Both were survivors. They made an art out of making people feel guilty. Angel walked back to the bed.

"It was tough for me to accept my dream coming to an end. Now it's time to dream a new one. You have to develop your own dream. Do whatever it takes to make it a reality," Barbara said sincerely. She retracted the claws and embraced Angel.

"We had so many good times there," Angel said honestly. She released the embrace and saw Barbara's bland expression. The boutique was her lifeline. Angel thought about Lisa's wedding. She wasn't sure if Barbara would be able to honor the agreement.

"Will you be able to complete Lisa's dresses?" Angel asked.

"I'm not dying, Melanie, of course I'll be able to. Have you seen the bridesmaid's dress? I had to change the skirt. You have a bad habit of creating garments only for thin people," Barbara fussed.

"I was just worried about you. I really like the dress, but Jennifer's dress is a little too revealing. She may not feel comfortable wearing it."

"Tsk. I want David to think marriage when she walks down the aisle. Have you seen Malinda? I'm glad *you're* thinking about me."

"She told me she spent the night at the hospital. She hasn't come by the room?"

Barbara waved her hand. "I don't know."

Angel kissed Barbara again and left. Barbara frowned at the idea of being insulin dependent. She fought for years to maintain her weight. She even put Linda on the same regiment. It all seemed to be in vain. As Barbara finished her pity party, Marilyn walked in. They chatted for a moment about the luncheon. It lifted Barbara's spirits. Marilyn told her about Jean filing for a legal separation.

"It doesn't surprise me. I don't understand why Bill keeps getting married. It won't help his career," said a disgusted Barbara. She closed her eyes.

"Maybe he will stay single for awhile. I think Jean is going to clean him out," Marilyn said with sympathy. "No better for him. It was horrible how he ended it with Dora." Barbara gave Marilyn a sneaky look. "Guess what? He's escorting Debra's daughter down the aisle. Unbelievable, isn't it?"

"Why?" Marilyn gasped.

"She's his daughter! Don't you remember the big fight between Debra and Catherine? Didn't she tell you?"

Marilyn shook her head. Catherine didn't trust her and neither did Debra.

"Oh Marilyn! Debra became pregnant by Bill during their little brief encounter. Debra thought Bill was leaving Catherine but he told her that he was staying. Well, Debra went to Catherine and toyed with the notion of knowing Bill's whereabouts on several occasions. Then she lowered the bomb and told her she was pregnant."

"Did Debra ever tell Catherine that she had an affair with Bill and the baby was his?"

"She didn't have to. You know Debra, she liked playing the guessing games. It was no secret. I heard about it in Kansas City. I'm surprised you didn't."

"Debra was sick, unstable. She was down right dangerous. She said and did all that to get back at Catherine."

"She never had a grievance with Catherine. They basically played the same games. Debra worshipped Catherine. Debra had a bone to pick with Bill. He was the one who dumped her at the last minute, getting her hopes up."

"The woman was dangerous and crazy. She went to extremes for revenge," Marilyn said. She took a few seconds to gather herself. The horrible night flashed back. The night she met Debra. Twelve-year-old Gina received two letters from Debra, telling of a love affair between Marilyn and another man whose name wasn't mentioned. Marilyn drove to St. Louis to meet Debra, hoping to put an end to the madness. Her daughter was too young to be put in the middle of a dispute.

Marilyn met Debra at the Gold Coast Lounge on Natural Bridge Road. Debra came to the table wearing a very tight red dress showing off shapely legs. She sat down smiling as if to say "long time no see." She quickly lit a cigarette, ordered a drink and commented on Marilyn's Afro. Marilyn stared at the gaiety of the sick person. They said nothing until the drink came. Debra asked Marilyn to pay for it. She did. Debra giggled. Marilyn assumed she was high. It was time to break the ice.

"If you have a problem with me, then deal with me. I don't want you sending my daughter another letter."

Debra laughed. She took a sip from the drink and a long drag from the cigarette. "How is Bill?" she asked casually and blew the smoke in Marilyn's face. She closed her eyes, allowing the smoke to take residence in her hair.

Debra put her chin in the hand that held the cigarette. "I used to think ministers' daughters were so innocent but I was wrong. It seems like Barbara was the only one of us who didn't fuck Bill. That's some kind of loyalty isn't it? But of course you would have to know about loyalty to understand what I'm talking about." Debra tapped the cigarette and the ashes fell on the ash tray. She took a gulp from the drink and kept revealing the secrets.

"I was surprised when I found out about you. You seemed so...clean. You're the type that make men feel safe but I can make them talk. You were married and so was Bill. No strings attached. When I heard about the miscarriage, I felt so, so bad," Debra said looking sympathetic and then burst into laughter. Marilyn became angry.

"Looks like you want to kick my ass," Debra said out loud and laughed again. She motioned the waiter to bring another drink. "Bill took advantage of you just like he did me. And now he's trying to be Mr. Big Time Businessman but I will put an end that shit. You can bet that nappy-ass Afro on your head, he will pay," she said with confidence.

The waiter came with the drink. Debra looked at Marilyn. She paid again. She couldn't believe what she was hearing. "What do you want from me,

Debra? I'm not going to let you blackmail me."

"You're not that strong. You never were. Paul has a daughter and he doesn't want to believe it. Her name is Lisa. Are you following me?"

Marilyn didn't respond. "I hear you two have been real cozy these days. All I need is a few dollars so I can buy Lisa some milk. She's only ten-years-old," Debra joked and laughed hoarsely. She finished her drink.

Marilyn stared at the duplicate standing behind Debra's chair. The big difference was the missing beauty mark over the upper lip. Debra noticed that Marilyn was preoccupied. Debra turned around to face her twin. Emotionless, she turned back around.

"Paul will be served a subpoena for a blood test in a few days," Debra said and took a sip from the drink.

"Hello Della. I guess you don't see me standing here," the duplicate said. Debra lit another cigarette. The duplicate sat down. She wasn't smiling. "You left me in Georgia, trying to answer questions to a crime I didn't commit," said the angry duplicate.

"Remember Marilyn, just a few dollars. I want people to pay for shitting on me."

"Della I'm talking to you," the duplicate interrupted.

"What do you want from me? I told you to leave with me but you wanted to stay, thinking somebody was going to believe he raped you. Nobody cared about us. Nobody. He deserved to die," Debra said angrily.

The duplicate continued arguing with Debra. Marilyn was puzzled about the duplicate calling Debra, Della. Marilyn wanted to leave quickly. She knew it was time to go. "Debra, I have to leave," she said and the duplicate looked at her.

"Soror, can I borrow twenty dollars. My daughter needs milk," Debra said coolly, as she continued to smoke. Marilyn opened her purse and pulled twenty dollars from her wallet. She threw it on the table. Debra picked it up and put it into her purse.

"Remember, all for one and one for all," Debra said and took a long drag from the cigarette.

Marilyn rushed to her car and drove all night to Kansas City. When Paul heard the story, he became upset. He couldn't deny being with Debra but he denied paternity.

Marilyn focus came back to Barbara, who looked on in mystery. Marilyn found it difficult to smile. She allowed herself to become a prisoner of her own secrets by trying to be self-righteous. Debra was right. Bill took advantage of her. He told her she was beautiful. He sounded sincere. It was special since he belonged to Catherine. The secret went on for a year until it manifested.

She could still feel the blows to the face from her ex-husband. She could feel the baby making it's way out. She could see Gina hiding behind the sofa crying, too little to do anything. The sounds of her oldest son screaming at the top of his lungs were ringing in her ears.

It all started when they turned their backs on Debra. The minister's daughter, the one whom everyone respected, tarnished Debra's reputation because of Paul. It wasn't necessary because the sorority was ready to break tradition and vote for Catherine. But she wanted to feel like she belonged to the group. At first Debra thought it was Catherine but found out a few years later that it was her.

Marilyn cleared her throat. She felt her forehead. It was warm. She had to get something to drink. She looked around the room wildly.

"Marilyn, what's the matter?" Barbara asked delicately.

Marilyn saw a pitcher by Barbara's bed. She stood to pour a drink of water but her legs felt weak. She held onto the chair to keep her balance.

"Barbara, I have something to tell you. I wasn't a good friend to Debra or Catherine. Me and..."

Barbara put her hand over Marilyn's mouth. "If you killed someone then tell a priest. I do believe a fifty-five-year old woman can take the rest of her secrets to the grave," Barbara said, slowly removing her hand.

"I feel like I'm being punished," Marilyn said gasping.

"We all are," Barbara responded. "You're right. Debra was dangerous. She met her end violently. They said the cute beauty mark that all the men loved was cut from her face."

Before Marilyn could say anything, Linda entered the room carrying a plant. She spoke to Marilyn who spoke back.

"Aren't you going to speak?" Barbara snapped.

"You didn't give me a chance. Hello, mother. I hope that you do a better job with your diet when they release you. You might have to take insulin. You know how I feel about needles. Uck!" Linda said and stuck out her tongue. She looked at Marilyn recuperating. "What's the matter, Aunt Marilyn? You look as if your best friend died. Don't worry, she will probably outlive both of us," Linda said. She sat in a chair and filed her nails.

Lisa finished addressing an invitation for the last name on Gina's guest list. They were all Alphas, the old heads from 1980. At first Lisa wasn't going to invite them but after news got out about Lionel, Thomas, Steve and a few others being there, they were treating her wedding as if it were a step-show at the House.

Lisa gathered her box of invitations and decided to check on Miss Mattie before leaving. She was still fighting a cold. Her cough was raspy. It shook her fragile body every time. Lisa peeked into the room. Miss Mattie was sitting in bed with her hair tied down under a net. She was reading the bible.

"What are you reading, Grandma?"

"Acts of the Apostles. How'd the wedding plans?"

"They're coming along fine. You need anything before I leave?"

Miss Mattie beckoned Lisa to come closer. She sat on the side of the bed. "You have always been a good girl. Stay that way. Don't let anything or anyone make you act different. You hear?"

"Yes ma'am," Lisa said. She frowned when Miss Mattie coughed up phlegm. Lisa handed her a tissue.

"Remember what I told you. Always let the spirit guide you. You'd never go wrong. Every day may not go well with Carl."

"His name is Cameron, Grandma Mattie."

"He's such a nice young man. Kind of firey but nice. Make sure you get a cast iron skillet just in case his head gets too hard." They both laughed. The doorbell rang. Lisa looked at Miss Mattie.

"Are you expecting anyone?" Lisa asked.

Miss Mattie shook her head. Lisa tiptoed to the front door and turned on the porch light. She pulled back the curtains like she had seen Miss Mattie do for years. The man looked familiar, but she refused to open the door. She remembered opening the door for a man and her mother beat her good. "Who is it?" Lisa yelled.

"Carleton. Carleton Peterson," he said.

Lisa ran to Miss Mattie's room and told her Carleton was outside the door. It was time to make peace with her son. It was time to put the secrets to rest. "Let him in," the old woman said.

Carleton walked back to the old familiar room that lived the spirits of the past. It had been twenty-one years since he had seen the powerful little figure. She was so frail that it hurt to see her again.

"It's good to see you, Carleton."

He remained quiet.

"Children aren't responsible for the acts of their parents. I killed Joe, not you. It's time you stop blaming yourself," Miss Mattie said.

"What about Catherine?"

Miss Mattie paused a little. "You'd weren't responsible for her either."

Carleton wasn't convinced that his mother believed what she had just said but she was calling a truce.

"You did a good job with Jennifer but it's time to let her go. She doesn't belong to you. She never did," Miss Mattie said. She sat up in bed.

"What happened to those babies? The twins that were born almost two years after Catherine. They didn't die. You gave them away. Why?" Carleton asked.

"Your father made me give them away. He claimed they weren't his."

"Were they his?"

"We were married weren't we?" Miss Mattie said and relaxed in bed. It was over. Her son would no longer be haunted by his father or the guilt behind Catherine's death. Both tragedies would be released from his thoughts. Miss Mattie closed her eyes to sleep.

Lisa dropped the invitations in the mailbox and ran upstairs to the apartment. Jennifer was in one of her "leave me alone" moods, which seemed to be frequent. She was playing Phyllis Hyman.

"Hello!" Lisa yelled before going to her room.

Jennifer came into Lisa's room with a note. It was an address from Ruby Lane, an Alpha chapter founder. Lisa was bubbling. She interrogated Jennifer for a telephone number. Ruby Lane didn't leave one. Miss Lane knew Lisa was a grand line pledge daughter and wanted to meet her. Lisa sat down and immediately addressed an invitation to Miss Lane.

Lisa began taking off her clothes. Jennifer watched. Lisa became uncomfortable. She quickly put on a large shirt. It was something about Jennifer's personality that was changing. She seemed childlike. She was curious about everything now. Her voice sounded babyish at times and her questions bordered on infantile.

"Lisa, how does it feel when a man makes love to you?"

Without thinking, Lisa pulled out another large shirt and tossed it to Jennifer. Lisa turned on the light beside the bed and turned off the overhead light. She tossed a pillow down at the other end of the bed. Jennifer jumped under the comforter. Lisa turned on her side and snuggled under the covers. "It's different for everyone. The first time is going to hurt like hell but the right person will make it special."

"What's special about it?"

"The sensations that go through your mind. Having your skin tingle, being held after it's over and being told that you are loved."

"That is special. So Cameron is good, huh?"

"I can't discuss that with you Jennifer. And besides, he's your brother. Has Kyle called? Cameron told me he was trying to work up the courage to call you."

"I don't want him to call. I don't think I feel the same."

"David looks soooo much better but he seems arrogant. He's not rushing you into having sex is he?"

"Na. I'm taking my time with him. I'm not in a hurry."

"Do you love him?"

"I don't know. Sometimes I think I do but I'm not sure. When did you know you loved Cameron?"

"When I was willing to accept his daughter. Did I tell you the test came back positive?"

"No! He lied to you!"

"He said he used a condom every time. There was at least one time he didn't. Men tend to forget those times. Make sure David uses a condom when you're ready."

"I'm going to miss you, Lisa."

"Don't start with that mushy stuff. Cameron says his father wants to meet you."

"I've already have a father."

"I saw him tonight. He came by to see Miss Mattie."

"We talked last week. It's time he forgave her."

"You have a cool grandmother. Make sure you take care of her."

"I will. She's your grandmother too."

"Good night, Jennifer."

"Good night, Lisa."

Chapter 29
June 6, 1989

Jennifer looked at her alarm clock. It was 1:00 a.m. She could still hear them talk about Missouri State and men. She decided to get up and join the group. She figured they were probably helping Lisa pack. Boxes crowded their living room. Cameron and his friend were coming up after the honeymoon to move Lisa to Atlanta. Jennifer decided to move in with Miss Mattie for awhile. Her large things were already in storage so there wasn't much to move.

She walked into the living room. The group was wide eyed. Tina and Crystal had pallets on the floor. Rochelle was sitting on the sofa talking a mile a minute. Lisa was sitting at the dinette writing out bills. Alicia had left.

"Hey girl. I see you can't sleep either," said a lively Rochelle.

It was true, she couldn't sleep. The dream came back. The woman in the photo, her mother, was able to catch her. She held her, gently tugging her to come along. It wasn't as frightening as the first time but it caused her to awaken each time.

"I can't relax," Jennifer said.

"Are we making too much noise?" Rochelle asked. Jennifer shook her head. "We were commenting on how good Kyle looked. I didn't know contacts and a haircut could make a man fine. I thought he would need plastic surgery," Rochelle said.

It was nothing new to Jennifer. She knew Kyle was attractive. The contacts showed off his pretty eyes. His features were not hidden behind the glasses. He was dressed nicely and his hair was cut very low. He didn't have much to say to her at rehearsal. He was polite and kept his conversation minimal.

She thought if she pretended that nothing happened, then they could continue where things left off. She was wrong. He was almost pompous. It hurt her. He was the one who cut off communications. The few significant moments they had shared proved valueless to him. She decided it was time to move on. Her only relief was knowing David was coming to town to be with her. He had a room at the Radisson. He wanted her to spend the evening with him. She knew what that meant. Maybe it was time. Kyle's attitude was a sign to let go.

She decided to do something she never did before, talk the "hey girl" talk. It was always fun listening. It was time to participate. "Yeah girl, I hear you. Kyle did look good. What about Brad? Brother is FI-EENE!" Jennifer said. Rochelle raised her hand for a high five and Lisa stopped writing.

"What about Lionel?" Tina asked. "He really looked handsome in those small round glasses."

"Yeah, but I think black women are still into the curly hair syndrome," Rochelle said.

"Thomas and Steve Rowe are coming," Jennifer said. Rochelle stood and did a dance. "Thank you, Jesus!" she shouted.

"You know who I would like to see? Craig the Lambda. I heard that Phil the Gamma is fine too," Jennifer added.

"Whatever happened to those ugly mothafuckas you used to hang with Jennifer?" Rochelle asked. At one time, Jennifer would have been insulted but she wasn't anymore.

"Malcolm moved to California. Tommy works for Fastrak Rails. Gerald lives in Phillie. He's a financial advisor or something," she answered.

"Hum, they're probably making good money. I asked Kyle what he was doing now. That bastard tried to act uppity. He turned up his nose when I told him I had a nail shop. What he doesn't know is I can run circles around his income," Rochelle said and rolled her eyes.

Jennifer knew it to be true. Lisa did Rochelle's taxes. Although Lisa didn't tell Jennifer how much Rochelle earned, Lisa commented that it was more than twice her salary. Now Rochelle wanted to do something different. She wanted to be a nurse.

"I can't wait to start nursing school," Rochelle said and stretched. Lisa kept writing and Tina laughed. "Are you laughing about me going to nursing school?" Rochelle asked politely. Tina stopped laughing.

"I didn't know you wanted to be a nurse," Crystal said.

"I've always wanted to be a nurse," Rochelle said low.

"You are going to make an excellent nurse," Jennifer said. "Alicia is starting the Psychology Ph.D. program at UMSL in August."

Everyone seemed surprised. Comments circulated through the women, especially Rochelle. "You laughed at her when she talked about her dream, Rochelle. You are getting a little payback. You are going to be good at nursing but first you must remove those streetwalker hooker nails," Jennifer teased.

Rochelle laughed out loud. "You're right. I do." She looked at Lisa who had removed herself from the conversation an hour ago. "So what's up with you? You're having second thoughts?"

"I'm trying to settle up some things before I move. I had hoped we could go on our honeymoon after the wedding but we won't be leaving until next Sunday. It's a surprise," Lisa said.

"I hear you. So your father is walking you down the aisle? Why didn't he come to rehearsal?" Rochelle asked.

Lisa hunched her shoulders. She hoped that he wasn't trying to back out. Mrs. Stevens told her not to worry. She had more faith in his commitment than Lisa did.

"Are you getting nervous?" Tina asked.

Lisa tried to keep from snapping at Tina who looked very sophisticated in her new haircut. She had practically gotten all of her hair cut off. "I'm fine. I just need to take care of some things," Lisa repeated.

"Your mother-in-law to be didn't look too happy. What's her problem? Is she stuck up?" Rochelle asked.

"No, she's not stuck up. She and Mr. Johnson are divorced. It's probably tough being around him," Lisa answered.

"Um, I bet it is because that brother was probably kickin' it in his day. I bet he was a 'ho' in college like Lionel. He looks good for his age but still, that curly hair don't mean shit. He's too dark to have hair like that anyway," Rochelle said.

Lisa continued writing, allowing Rochelle to insult Jennifer's father and brother. Lisa knew Mrs. Johnson's problem, Jennifer, the product of a love affair. Out of loyalty to Jennifer, Lisa promised not to tell anyone. Jennifer stayed away from Charles Johnson during rehearsal. When Cameron introduced him to her, she kindly extended her hand. It made Cameron happy to see Jennifer snub their father.

Rochelle stood and stretched. She yawned too. "I need to get going. I'll see y'all in the shop at eight. Please do *not* be late because you will *not* get your nails done. Somebody please call Alicia to remind her. She's probably cursing out her houseguests by now." Rochelle gathered her keys. Lisa walked her to the door.

"Well my sistah, this is your last night of freedom. You want to go see some male strippers in East St. Louis?" Rochelle teased.

Lisa rolled her eyes. "Honey please!"

Lisa opened the door and Rochelle left. Crystal and Tina looked tired too. Jennifer was wide awake. "I guess I'll get to bed. Jennifer, if it's alright with you, why don't you sleep with me and let Crystal and Tina have your bed?" Lisa asked. Jennifer agreed quickly. The two house guests removed themselves from the floor and rushed to Jennifer's bedroom.

Lisa opened her dresser drawer. She removed a large T-shirt and put it on. Jennifer was already in a gown. She laid at the foot of the bed. Lisa turned off the lights. Jennifer could see a faint beam around Lisa for the first time ever. At first, it was patches of colors but now it was a beam. Jennifer assumed the angels were interacting with Lisa, at least Miss Mattie would assume it.

"You are going to have to *up* the T-shirts when you're with Cameron," Jennifer said playfully.

"Some of that sleazy stuff I got from the bachelorette party is going to get me pregnant," Lisa said.

"I can see you with three hardheaded boys."

"They can go visit their Aunt Jennifer for the summer. I want you to be godmother to at least one of them."

"It will be my pleasure. Isn't it great that we are going to be relatives? It's going to be our secret."

Lisa was a little disturbed by Jennifer's statement. She behaved as if they were children playing a game. "It's not a secret anymore, Jennifer. Although I haven't told anybody, people will find out eventually. Mr. Johnson wants to talk with you. I think you hurt his feelings by ignoring him."

"I don't need a relationship with him. It's different with me. It has always been different with me. It's important that you talk to William Smith tomorrow about the blood. It's real important."

"Good night, Jennifer."

"Good night, Lisa. Now don't be afraid. Everything is going to turn out perfect."

"I'm not afraid. I'm a little concerned about the threat of rain in the forecast. They say if it rains on your wedding day, it means bad luck."

"Only if it rains during the ceremony."

She read the invitation again. It was so easy. Lisa still hadn't learned, "Never open the door to strangers". She was invited so there was nothing Miss Mattie could do. The idea of Bill escorting Lisa down the aisle made her laugh again. She had waited a very long time.

It had been years since she had been in St. Louis. She wondered if the Gold Coast Lounge was still on Natural Bridge Road. It didn't matter. It wasn't her type of crowd anymore. All she wanted to do was go to the wedding to say "hello" to Bill. It would be nice to see Charles too. The idea of his son marrying Lisa was unbelievable. Charles often said she wasn't his type but neither was Catherine. She had ulterior motives like all of them. Maybe Marilyn and Paul would be there. She laughed again. Although it was Lisa's wedding, it had to be done. She would forgive her. The young woman was just like her.

"Mrs. Farrow, your car is ready," the young man said.

She took her time getting in the front seat and drove off to the hotel, the RitzCarleton. "Ume," she said out loud. She loved the name Carleton. He told her the whole story about the famous fire in Covington, Georgia, her home town too. Everyone knew about the fire but no one knew the whereabouts of Matilda Mitchell. Carleton told her everything. He was so vulnerable. Had it not been for him, she wouldn't have had Miss Mattie by the neck for so many years, babysitting and giving her money. It didn't bother Carleton. He didn't mind; he hated Miss Mattie.

She thought back to the last time in St. Louis. It was midnight when she went to see Miss Mattie. She told her everything. Miss Mattie just stared at her and became angry for some obscure reason. She was telling the truth this time but the old woman did not believe her, Miss Mattie said if she didn't leave, she would call the law.

All she wanted to do was see Lisa and explain. She never intended to abandon her but it was necessary. She could not have her daughter on the run. She really didn't want children but she learned to love the little bundle that gave her no trouble during delivery. It was rough for the two because she could not take care of her baby. Miss Mattie was a blessing.

She remembered the time she had to cut Henry for touching Lisa. He was nice to her but she didn't respect any man that tampered with children. It brought back too many bad memories.

She wanted to stop by Miss Mattie. It would probably give the old woman a heart attack. She didn't want to be charged with another murder. She didn't consider her sister's death murder. She had to protect herself. Her sister was stark crazy that night, cutting the side of her face. She tried to stop her by pushing her away. She fell into the window, causing her to fall to her death. She felt badly about her sister's death, but she didn't want to die either. Both Della and Debra had to die. She made sure Georgia and Missouri knew Della was dead but Missouri buried Debra too.

She remembered how Miss Mattie told her to go away and never come back. It was mean. Miss Mattie was mean. She was old and dangerous. Any woman who could shoot her husband and burn him alive was nothing to play with. Miss Mattie also threatened to shoot another man for patting Catherine on the behind. Carleton said Miss Mattie took her pistol and walked up to the man. She told him if he ever messed with her or her children again, he was going to meet his maker sooner than he wanted too. She liked Miss Mattie. They were just alike because they came from the same breed. Miss Mattie had some explaining to do.

She was at the Ritz-Carleton. She kept the sunglasses on for protection. After she checked in, She saw one of the partners in crime leaving with a veil in her hand. Barbara looked fantastic. She was glamorous, elegant, charming and beautiful. She always said she would make a liar out of everyone. She laughed again.

Lisa sat quietly in a robe while the bridesmaids were getting dressed. She noticed their attitudes changed when they put on the gowns and gloves. Crystal's posture was much better. Rochelle hardly said a word. Alicia kept her head high. The makeup looked very nice since her skin was clear. Sonya didn't use her hands when she talked. Tina smiled constantly and Jennifer looked like an Egyptian queen.

Lisa's hands felt clammy. She wasn't nervous until now. Angel and Mrs. Stevens had finished with everyone. They approached her. She looked around for Miss Mattie. She wondered where Carla and Gina were too. They promised to talk to her before the ceremony began. She didn't want Angel or Mrs. Stevens to touch her before she saw those three.

"Where is my grandmother, Carla and Gina?" Lisa asked in a rush. Angel looked at Barbara and left to get them. Barbara decided to ease away. She began complimenting the bridesmaids again.

The three appeared with Angel. Miss Mattie approached Lisa and Angel pulled up a chair for Miss Mattie, She took Lisa's hands. They were a little damp. She tightened her grip around them. They began to feel warm. "You've stopped listening haven't you?" she asked calmly. She coughed, still trembling. "Everything is going to be fine with you and Carl."

"It's Cameron, Grandma."

"That boy has such a strange name," Miss Mattie said. "They are here right now. They are protecting you. Do you believe?"

There goes that foolish talk again. The spirits. Miss Mattie meant did she have confidence. The warmth of Miss Mattie's hands brought back the feeling of love. They were the hands that held her when kids teased her. They cooked the meals she loved. They sacrificed by cleaning houses, just to take care of the two. Yes, she believed. She could feel them too. The spirits. If they were Miss Mattie's spirits, then they were hers too.

Lisa nodded, looking into Miss Mattie's eyes. They were tired but loving. Jennifer and Angel were the luckiest people to have someone like her.

Miss Mattie closed her eyes when she removed her hands. "Now, you let Melanie and Miss Barbara help you get ready. Pastor said the wedding is running almost an hour late. Are you feeling better?" she asked pleasantly. Lisa nodded and stood. Miss Mattie hugged her and left.

Carla and Gina stood beside Lisa. Carla put her arms around her and asked if she would be fine. Lisa nodded. Carla kissed her on the cheeks. Gina told her the butterflies would leave once the ceremony began. Gina and Carla left Lisa with Angel.

"Dad is here," Angel said low.

Lisa wet her lips. The stage was set. It was time to start. The bridesmaids were ready to do their part. Mrs. Stevens beckoned Lisa. "Melanie, freshen her makeup and help her into the dress. I'm going to start the program. Everyone but the maid-of-honor come with me. As soon as you finish with her, Melanie, send Jennifer upstairs," Barbara commanded and disappeared with the five bridesmaids. They all gave a final wave to Lisa.

Angel opened a large case filled with make-up and began working. She started with the press powder. Lisa heard the organ play. The mothers were being seated. Next Anita sang softly *The Lord's Prayer*. The candles were being lit. Angel removed the rollers and combed the curly locks to the top. Lisa heard readings from the Old and New Testaments. Angel had finished the hair. Anita was on again singing *Evergreen*, one of Mrs. Stevens' suggestions. It was getting time for the bridesmaids.

Jennifer helped Angel remove the dress from under the plastic. To Lisa, it beamed. She slipped the garter on and walked to the dress. Jennifer and Angel lowered the dress over her head. Dee Dee read a poem "Love, the Unconditional Verb." Jennifer zipped the bottom part of the opening and took her time buttoning the high collar. It was almost time.

Lisa looked at Jennifer for dear life. This would be the second time they separated but it would be for life. Jennifer gracefully approached Lisa and hugged her tight. Electric currents flowed between the two. It was time to go.

Angel removed the veil carefully, slowly assembling the beaded band into place. Lisa heard Anita sing her favorite song, *You Bring Me Joy*. A string of beads fell to the right side of Lisa's face. Angel gently painted on coral lipstick. As the veil came over the face, *Avé Maria* played softly, the bridesmaids were going down the aisle, one by one.

"Are you ready to go up?" Angel asked.

Lisa began walking without saying a word. The organ sounded louder as she approached the door that led to the vestibule. She walked through the door and Jennifer caught a glance of her before she took a step onto the carpet.

Eyes complimented Jennifer as she walked. Smiles warmed her shivering self-esteem. She gracefully carried the strapless gown to the altar. It was cut so low in the back, it exposed her birth mark that was two inches above the tail bone. The only cover her back received was the long flowing fabric that went across her chest, around the shoulders and attached at the lower part of the cut in the back.

Cameron smiled broadly as Jennifer came closer. Lionel smiled too. Brad and Tony looked hungrily. Kyle stared in amazement. She looked different to him. The dress took her beyond beautiful. But he had to stand firm. Yes, she was beautiful but like William said, he needed someone who could help his career. Besides, Sally was waiting for him to get back, at least that is what he hoped.

Lisa could feel William standing beside her. Her chest tightened. She shook when he extended his elbow. She wasn't sure if it was a mistake to have him escorting her down the aisle. "You are very, very beautiful," he said.

She didn't look up nor did she say thank you. All fathers had a parental responsibility to tell their daughters they were beautiful on their wedding day. Lisa replied by taking his elbow.

The organ played another round of *Avé Maria* before Barbara handed Lisa the bouquet. She almost dropped it.

"Honey, this is not the time to get nervous. Everything is going well. Bill, you know what to do, don't you?" Barbara asked slightly jittery.

"Yes Barbara," he replied exasperated.

"You should. You've been here enough times," Barbara mumbled under her breath. She was still a little angry at him for not showing up for rehearsal. She motioned the hostesses to open the doors. The *Wedding March* sprang from the organist's fingertips. Lisa walked slowly, shaking the entire time. Cameras flashed in her face. She had practiced smiling but forgot at various times. She wanted it to be over so that she and Cameron could live happily ever after, whatever that was.

She saw Miss Mattie smiling. She was going to miss her. The bridesmaids smiled. She was going to miss them too. Jennifer looked serious. Something had happened. She didn't know what was wrong with her friend but she would be missed the most.

Cameron's smile faded as he looked at the most beautiful woman on earth. He couldn't understand his father. He *was* marrying his mother. She and Lisa were just alike, gentle and loving. His father had the boldness to tell him he would not respect someone like his mother, someone co-dependent, always needing, never acting on her own. His mother wasn't any of those things his father alleged. She was smart and independent. "Lionel married your mother, you're marrying your equal. Let's hope it turns out well for you," his father said. The conversation did not go well. He practically uninvited his father to the wedding.

Stacy, Lionel's wife, was nothing like his mother. She never wanted

Lionel out of her sight. She could not make a decision unless he made it for her. Cameron remembered when he and his brother, Jason, went shopping with Lionel and Stacy. She wanted Lionel to approve everything she bought. Afterwards, they decided to go to the gym to shoot some ball. Stacy wanted Lionel to stay. He offered to take their son Damon but she wanted him home. They all knew it was coming to an end. Lionel didn't need to feel guilty. He tried hard. Their mother wasn't like Stacy. Even when their mother wanted their father around, he hardly was.

Cameron's concentration came back when William gave him Lisa's hand. He looked down at the freshly manicured nails. She once told him it was the French look. Whatever look it was, they were beautiful. He could not wait to slip the ring on her finger. They turned and faced the minister.

Everyone talked and laughed at the reception. Lionel stood and proposed a toast to the bride and groom. Everyone cheered. Thirty minutes later, the disc jockey began the music. People danced. Cameron weaved through the crowd with Lisa beside him. He introduced her to his aunts, uncles, cousins and grandparents. They complimented her on the wedding. The women of the group raved about the dresses. Everyone seemed happy, except Mrs. Johnson. She continued to stay at armslength.

Lisa looked for Miss Mattie. She was at the table with Angel and Mrs. Stevens. Lisa pulled Cameron. They walked over quickly to Miss Mattie's table. "Miss Mattie, I want you to meet Cameron's family," Lisa said radiantly.

Miss Mattie held up her hand. "I will later on. I'm a little tire right now," she said, trying to keep smiling.

Lisa became worried. "Miss Mattie, is something wrong?"

"No sugah. Go on and enjoy yourself. I'll meet Carl's family later."

Lisa decided not to correct her and tapped Cameron on the shoulder. She whispered in his ear. He nodded and smiled. "Mrs. Stevens, I know this may not be the best time to pay you but we really want to show our appreciation for the hard work. My aunts and cousins are crazy about the dresses," Cameron said.

He took out his checkbook and presented Barbara with a check. She smiled and looked down at the amount. Her mouth opened. She quickly recovered and thanked them. Lisa personally thanked Angel too. The couple walked feeling good.

Barbara sucked in her jaws and looked at Angel. "Why didn't you tell me you were doing this wedding for free?"

Angel's eyebrows went in. "Did they pay you the balance of seven hundred and seventy-five dollars?"

Barbara eyed Angel closely and realized the wedding was a favor. For all of the designing, sewing and organizing she had done, the young couple's check for nine hundred dollars was barely a tenth of what she would normally charge for a wedding like Lisa's. Barbara was settled on selling the boutique. She smiled at Angel and said, "Never mind dear. Never mind."

"Aunt Barbara, they don't have a lot of money. A large portion of their savings paid for this wedding," Angel said, defending the pair.

"Barbara, I see you are still greedy. Can't you ever do something nice for people?" Miss Mattie asked congenially.

Barbara looked at Miss Mattie oddly. Now wasn't the pot calling the kettle black.

Barbara remembered Catherine telling her about Miss Mattie's second husband. That is what he was, a second husband. Miss Mattie had taken care of an old white man for many years, cooking and cleaning. He had a lot of money and property. His family had primarily abandoned him because he was so sickly.

The old man was knocking hard at death's door. It was only a matter of time before he passed away. He became delirious, telling Miss Mattie he loved her and wanted to marry her. She knew he was talking out of his head. Miss Mattie felt she deserved something for taking care of him for years. She called a preacher friend of hers to perform the ceremony. They were married and the old man died a month later. Before the old man died, Miss Mattie had the will changed by a black lawyer.

The white family contested the will and agreed to give Miss Mattie ten thousand dollars, which helped Catherine get into school. They gave her one of the man's houses that he owned. Miss Mattie never had to pay rent again. She never did for anybody unless they did for her and her children.

Barbara chuckled at Miss Mattie. She liked her. "Yes Miss Mattie, I can be nice to people."

Lisa and Cameron went to the large group of friends who had taken up a huge section of the Ballroom. Lisa's line sisters immediately surrounded her, quickly separating her from Cameron. They walked her to the tables occupied by the old heads: Carla, Gina, Marsha, Jessica, Cheryl, Donna, Marie, Rita, Gail and some others. Lisa stood, facing the women that had helped mold her. She was a little nervous because they sat smiling, not saying a word.

"Congratulations, Soror! We are very proud of you. The hard work and accomplishments made during your tenure as president of Alpha Theta Lambda has gone unmatched. Remember, we are your sisters and we love you, even the ones who could not attend. Let the spirit of Alpha be with you always," Carla said and extended her arms. The group clapped.

Lisa took small steps to Carla. She hugged her. Lisa was so nervous that she finally cried. She wouldn't let Carla go. So much was happening in her life like the wedding and moving, leaving her friends. Now the person she considered a mother figure told her she did a good job for the sorority.

"What's the matter?" Carla whispered.

"I don't know. I'm...scared."

"You have my telephone number, don't you?"

"Yes...ma'am."

"Call me anytime. I don't want you taking this walk alone, making unnecessary mistakes like some of us. You hear?"

Lisa nodded. Carla motioned for Cheryl. She came looking a little worried. "Take her to the back and talk to her," Carla said low.

Lisa shook her head. "I'm fine," she said and wiped her eyes with her hands. She turned to the group and told them Ruby Lane, one of the chapter founders, called and left her address. Lisa went on to tell how she sent Ms. Lane an invitation to the wedding. Carla looked disturbed because she heard Ruby Lane who later became Ruby Cornell died three years ago from cancer. Carla sat quietly.

Lisa looked over the group of Alphas. Six from the ones she pledged were there including Iris. All but three Genies from the line of 1980 were in attendance. No knew where Janet was. Evelyn had a crack addiction. Paula was unemployed and couldn't make it. Everyone else was doing well.

"I'm thirsty. Tina, get me some punch, please?" Donna asked. Tina took off.

"Phyllis, could you please ask my husband what time he's leaving?" Jessica asked with an attitude. Phyllis kept her temper under control and left to deliver the message.

"Alicia, could you get me some punch, too?" Cheryl asked.

Alicia turned to one of the younger Alphas and asked her to get Cheryl some punch. The young woman took off. Lisa noticed it was like the first night of pledging because Gina and Carla asked her and Crystal to get them some punch too.

Several Betas talked and teased Cameron. They had bought drinks at the cash bar and were looking quite jubilant. Tony was trying desperately to get information on Alicia. Brad gave up on Jennifer since he found out about David. He, too, was a Beta. Brad turned his eyes to Tina. Thomas, Steve, David and Carlos talked to Lionel. They were comparing notes on their lives.

Carlos listened closely to how Lionel talked, with compassion, about his ordeal at Favor's department store. Without anger, he discussed the divorce between him and his wife. He expressed his feelings on not seeing his son and how the lawyers were responsible for driving a stake between him and his ex-wife. He tried desperately to become friends with her so that he could get visitation rights but it was moving very slowly.

Thomas, a divorcee, commented favorably on the lawyers' actions, calling it necessary. Steve, a Major in the Air Force, disagreed strongly. He got into a heated debate with Thomas. It was something about Thomas' attitude that rubbed Steve the wrong way. David stood back to be entertained by the two.

Carlos caught Lionel's attention. The two turned away from the argument. They started with small talk, catching up on each other. Carlos listened as Lionel talked about how he started his computer consulting firm. He started with nothing, working long hours. Carlos nodded as Lionel talked.

"I hear you and Gina have a son," Lionel said.

Carlos smiled broadly. "He's a handful."

"I know what you mean. My son Damon is busy too. So what's been happening? I hear you are tearing up the air waves in KC?"

Carlos took a deep breath. He didn't want to talk about the radio show. He wanted to talk about what was bothering him. He didn't have any fear talking to Lionel. Carlos trusted him. "Gina and I are separated. Uh, um.... How can I start?" Carlos said, pausing for a few seconds.

"You don't have to talk about it," Lionel rushed to say.

Carlos waved his hand. He had to get it off of his chest. He told Lionel about how the match made in heaven has just about ended with four fights. Lionel looked stunned. He could not imagine Carlos, the militant, the advocate of respect, hitting a woman. Carlos openly opposed brothers on campus who cheated on their girlfriends. He even sat Lionel down a few times to discuss his behavior.

"I'm having a hard time digesting what I'm hearing. I can't imagine you hitting Gina or any woman for that matter. It seems like you got it together. You have always had it together," Lionel said.

Carlos was at a loss for words. He couldn't discuss the suspected infidelity, an indication of him failing as a husband. The only thing he could express was Gina's success and his lack thereof. As he talked, Lionel put his hands in his pants pockets and stared at the floor. He looked up at Carlos' face which reflected the same frustration he had two years ago.

"I remember feeling guilty when you called me a 'daddy's boy' because I depended on my father for everything. At first I thought you were jealous because my parents could afford to send me to school and you had to hustle. I later realized you were right. I allowed my father to run my life, making all of my decisions. The only time I went against him is when I pledged Beta. I've always admired and respected you for being a hustler," Lionel said.

Carlos turned his head away and looked at Gina. She sat quietly with her hand at the side of her face. Her behavior was unusual, especially around the women who respected her. It was his fault. He turned to face Lionel again.

"To tell you the truth, I was jealous. You didn't know how good you had it. You had parents that cared about your education. I never had that. But, I can say you are a hustler now," Carlos said and extended his hand. Lionel shook it.

"I went to counseling with my ex-wife before we split for good. I had to accept that I was unhappy with myself and her expectations. It wasn't her fault, it was mine. It hurt when Stacy and I decided to divorce. I had a hard time signing the papers. My father is not my hero but he said something that made a lot of sense. Sometimes, we get married for the wrong reasons," Lionel said.

Carlos absorbed everything Lionel said but disagreed about marrying for the wrong reasons. He and Gina loved each other, he believed. She had mentioned counseling but they had not discussed it. He shared his feelings about counseling to Lionel.

"I didn't want to go to counseling either. They say men have a tough time accepting counseling and it's the truth. Counseling puts everything in perspective. The only thing I'm grieving is not seeing my son. It hurt the last time I dropped him off. I can still hear him cry," Lionel said.

Carlos remembered how Avery waved happily, saying, "Bye daddy." It hurt too.

A group of women screamed when the number one song *Super Woman* began playing. The men laughed. Some gathered women to slow dance. "I guess this is the black woman's theme this year," Lionel joked. Carlos ignored him and watched Gina sing to herself. He excused himself and walked over to the table of judgmental women. They looked at him with contempt. He gathered the courage to ask Gina to dance. She took his hand and they walked to the dance floor.

Carlos didn't know how to start the conversation. He just listened as Karyn White sang of a love gone bad. "How is Avery?"

"He talks about you constantly. He's still a little rebellious at times. I guess he got that from you."

"From me? Oh woman, you are so wrong. You are so bullheaded, stubborn..."

"And you are so bullheaded and stubborn. I guess he didn't have a chance."

Carlos laughed. He hesitated but said it, "Every time I see the scar, I hate myself. I thought for so long you were cheating on me. I thought you lost respect for me because I didn't have a good job. I'm sorry for making you lose the baby. I can't imagine hitting you again because I know if your mother doesn't kill me first, your sorors will do the honors," he said jokingly but Gina wasn't laughing. He was giving her a way out.

"Seriously Gina, whatever you decide, I will respect your decision. I have always listened to you, that's why I agreed to move to Chicago. All I want is to be a part of Avery's life," Carlos concluded.

The song was over and Gina had said nothing. He placed a gentle kiss on her forehead and escorted her back to the table. He walked away without looking at the jury. He and Cameron almost bumped into each other on their way to Lionel.

"So little brother, how does it feel being married?" Lionel asked.

Cameron looked bashfully at Carlos. "Great, I guess. I'm glad the ceremony is over. It was making me nervous. Thanks for coming, Carlos. Jennifer made sure Lisa invited you," Cameron said.

Lionel's attention turned to the youngest brother Jason who was talking to some Betas.

"I see Jason is talking to the frat brothers. Is he having a good time?" Lionel asked.

"Yeah! I introduced him to Jennifer too. He likes her," Cameron said, looking at Lionel for approval. Lionel smiled at Cameron.

"That's great Ron! Now why don't you introduce her to the rest of the family," Lionel said sarcastically.

Cameron's jaws tightened. He turned to walk away. Lionel pulled him back. "I'm sorry. I didn't mean it. She's a great person. You know how I feel about what has happened. I'm angry with dad. It has nothing to do with you or Jennifer," Lionel said, trying to comfort Cameron.

Lisa rushed over happily to the small group. Her request was playing. "Come on Cameron, let's dance," she said. She searched his face. "What's the matter?" she asked.

"Nothing," Cameron said and took his bride away.

Carlos looked at Lionel and asked, "What was that about?"

"Just a little family business. So what's happening with Angel these days. I heard she keeps a low profile. I also heard she has a baby and it's retarded or deformed."

"I didn't know her little girl was retarded," Carlos responded.

"Oh, a little girl," Lionel said, searching the crowd for Angel. He spotted her at the other side of the room.

The lean figure made it's way to their table. There was no where to hide. She had avoided him the entire evening. He greeted everyone at the table. Barbara reacted as if he were looking for her.

"This used to be our favorite song. You care to dance?" he asked.

Angel didn't respond. She looked at Barbara and then at Miss Mattie. "Honey, go on and dance. I'll sit with your grandmother," Barbara said. Angel got up slowly and took his hand.

They danced without saying a word. She looked the same, he thought. He asked small questions about the shooting and her new-found grandmother. She was brief with her responses. He wanted to ask about the baby but decided not to. He wanted to tell her about his computer business, but she probably wasn't interested or was bored with him. She probably didn't care anymore.

The song was over. He walked her back to the table. She remained quiet. She was no longer the center of attention. Thomas was barely polite to her. Steve was very cordial but he wasn't under her like he was at school. Both men were trying to get Jennifer's attention. Even David was supposed to be for her but turned his attention to Jennifer.

Angel saw how the others were enjoying themselves. They were probably laughing at her. Everyone had to know that both Jennifer and Lisa were her sisters and that her mother had a love affair with Lionel's father. It was too much. It was time to go.

She looked at him. He frowned slightly. The five o'clock shadow made him look sexy. His hair was faded on the sides and in the back. She heard he wore glasses but he had to be wearing contacts now. Maybe if she told him about Lauren, he would probably want her. No chance, she thought. He was already paying child support. He would probably think she, too, was trying to hook him. She had to say something, "Thanks Lionel. I'll talk to you before you leave."

"I'm leaving in the morning. How about tonight?" he asked quickly.

No way! she thought. She wasn't about to jump in bed with him again. He was still weak. "What about the group?" she asked, pointing to the lively side of the room. She was weak too.

"I'll see them later. I think they are going to be here for the long haul."

The D.J. called all single women to the floor for the bouquet toss. When Lisa threw it, Alicia's arms stretched up and Rochelle bumped her, causing the bouquet to fall into her arms instead. Alicia popped the bouquet out of Rochelle's hands and it landed in Margo's arms. She screamed loudly. Rochelle turned a dirty, playful look to Alicia. "Yeah heffa. If I can't have it, you can't either," Alicia said and walked away.

Jennifer saw Kyle talking to William when the garter was being tossed. She wanted to try again, to assure herself he wanted nothing to do with her. Their friendship was on the line. She had made up her mind that it could be nothing more than friendship between them. She walked gracefully over to the two men and spoke. William complimented her but Kyle said nothing.

"So Kyle, how have you been? I haven't heard from you in awhile," Jennifer said. She tried to rekindle the friendship. But to her chagrin, he appeared uninterested. He was very bland when he said, "Things are fine." She took a long look at him. She didn't know what created the silence in the first place. ·He was the one who was always busy. He also made the promises to call back and didn't. If he had a girlfriend, that's all he had to say.

She concluded, whatever he had to prove, it wasn't going to be at her expense. She saw David standing at the cake table. He had waited patiently all evening long. He allowed her to visit and talk to her friends without being an imposition. It was time to enjoy the company that enjoyed her.

"It was good seeing you again, William. Take care, Kyle," Jennifer said and tossed her hair. She walked away without looking back.

Something was playing tricks on him. He didn't want to insult her. He had lapped behind her for so many years. At one time, she wasn't interested but now she was. It didn't feel the same to have her wanting him. It was awkward. It wasn't the same.

Something churned in Kyle's stomach when he saw them kiss. She looked happy as he beamed at the sight of her. He was attractive. He looked like a professional, a business man. His suit looked expensive, even his tie. She fed him cake as if he were a baby. He licked her fingers playfully. It was enough. Kyle couldn't watch anymore. He had to leave.

Lisa saw Miss Mattie sitting alone. She coughed and her body shook, trying to recover. It was time for her to go home. Lisa approached Jennifer, who was talking to a small group from Missouri State. Lisa tapped her on the shoulder. "Do you mind taking Miss Mattie home?" Lisa asked.

Jennifer wasn't ready to go but if Miss Mattie wanted to go home, then she would take her. Jennifer agreed and walked over to the lonely table. "Grandma Mattie, are you ready to go home?" she asked.

The old woman eyes pleaded with Jennifer. The young woman wasn't ready to take her home and she didn't want to go just yet. "Oh no! I'd like to stay for a little longer, if that's okay with you."

"Just let me know when you're ready. Why are you sitting by yourself? Why don't you come up front?"

"I'm fine right here," Miss Mattie said with a smile.

Jennifer smiled and walked back to Lisa. "She's not ready to go," Jennifer said.

Lisa went back to sit with Miss Mattie. They talked some more about cast iron skillets. Then Miss Mattie told Lisa about the real Debra Arvell, a loving person. It didn't make sense to tell the child everything. Even her mother didn't want her to know everything. It was all over. It had to be a happy ending for everyone.

Charles Johnson finally made his way to William. It was uncomfortable for both men. "I didn't know Catherine was pregnant," Charles said. Bill remained quiet. "It didn't last long. She wanted to make it work with you. And I agreed. I couldn't leave my wife either. It should not have happened," Charles said.

Bill wasn't ready to forgive. Regardless of his own infidelity, Charles was his friend. His wife should have been off limits. He had an opportunity to marry her, if he wanted too. She loved him anyway.

"She doesn't want to have anything to do with me," Charles said, looking at Jennifer as she enjoyed her friends.

"I guess we're in the same boat. I was used as an escort. She's just like her mother," Bill said, looking at Lisa.

"I find it hard to believe that we are in-laws in a roundabout way," Charles said with a chuckle, but Bill didn't laugh.

"Jennifer is a good girl. She's tough. It will take some time to get comfortable with her," Bill said.

"I guess you're right. I'm used to boys," Charles said. He saw Lionel talking happily with Angel. "I see my son still has an interest in your daughter."

Bill turned his attention to the couple. They smiled as they talked. "He should. They have a daughter," Bill said and turned away.

"What? Lionel hasn't said anything about a daughter. How old is she?" Charles asked. He was shocked.

Bill concluded his daughter was like her mother. She made a mistake and would suffer with it. Catherine made a mistake with him and was willing to suffer until she found out about Debra. She still suffered because he left her penniless. "She will be two in August. Her name is Lauren. Look Charles, don't say anything. Maybe this is her way of telling him," Bill said unsure.

To Charles, Lionel didn't look as if someone told him that he had an illegitimate child. Charles was disappointed in his son. He tried to shake it off. "How are things at International Foods. My friend Walter Evans was recently given the Midwest region," Charles said.

Bill froze. He didn't want to talk about work. It opened the pain. "We're going through reorganization. I won't know how things will settle until November," Bill said, trying not to give anything away.

"International has been doing a lot of shifting lately. Walter told me they are preparing to downsize," Charles said carefully. He and Bill were eye to eye.

"When was the last time you talked to Walter?" Bill asked. Enough beating around the bush. His business was already known. Either Charles would help him or kick dirt in his face.

"Last Thursday," Charles said and cleared his throat. "A friend of mine at Allstar informed me that they are moving one of its breweries to Colorado. I'm not interested in beer but if you are, I know the person you need to talk to." Charles saw how Bill's eyes lit up. He hoped they had reconciled.

"Sounds good, Charles. Thank you," Bill said and extended his hand. Charles shook it. It was over.

It was almost nine o'clock. It was time to make her entrance. Most of the guests would probably be gone by the time she arrived. She knew he would still be there. Knowing he walked Lisa down the aisle made her laugh again. She put on a black dress and black hat. She made sure the pearl earrings and necklace were in place. She looked in the mirror and ignored the ugly scar at the side of her face. She still looked good for an old broad of fifty-three. She grabbed her black purse off the dresser and left.

Jennifer and David were very cozy on the dance floor. He pulled her close and gave her a long kiss. He rubbed his chin against her forehead. This was the first time dating someone like her. She didn't give two cents whether or not he was a dentist. She never discussed marriage either. He thought back to the time when he brushed her off because she wouldn't spend the night with him. She didn't care. She never bothered to call him back. She had to be the one. Maybe the wedding put him in the mood but he wanted her to be with him tonight. She had turned him down many times but tonight, she had to. He couldn't wait any longer.

"Jennifer," he said softly. She looked at him innocently. He battled with the best way to ask. "I want you to stay with me tonight. I won't rush you into anything. I figure we can watch a movie and eat chocolate covered strawberries. We don't have to do anything. I want you to get comfortable being with me," he said, talking an inch above her lips.

Now would be the perfect time to experience "it." He was nice, gentle and pleasant. He thought everything she did was perfect. She couldn't have asked for a better person. She was ready.

She looked at Lisa and Cameron slow dancing. He would kiss her various times during the song. She didn't look around to see who was watching. She was enjoying the attention. Jennifer's focus went to Miss Mattie. It was time to take her home.

"Yes David. I will spend the night with you. I need to take my grandmother home and then I'll come back. Do you have a condom?" she asked boldly.

He didn't think she would stay but to ask for a condom was absurd. No, he didn't have one nor did he have any intentions of getting one. He didn't want to introduce her to sex tonight. It wasn't time. He felt jittery when he kissed her again. "No, I don't have a condom. Jennifer, we don't have to do anything. I just want you by my side."

"Just in case, David. Just in case. I need to go now," she said sweetly. She smiled when she looked at him.

"I'll go with you. It's too late for you to be out by yourself," he said.

"I'll be fine. You need to get one of our little friends," she teased and aggressively kissed him on the lips. He was stunned.

Cameron was itching to start the pre-honeymoon adventure. They had a suite with a jacuzzi. Lisa was excited, too, but wanted to hang around a little longer. As she enjoyed her friends, she heard Brad tell Tony that Lionel was trying to get "some" from Angel. The two men slapped five and Lisa got mad. She had to control herself. She couldn't afford to get angry. Her attention went to Miss Mattie. She sat like a lonely bump on a log. It was well past her bedtime. She needed to go home. Lisa turned around into a beaming Jennifer. Lisa saw the light around her and it didn't go away. Lisa knew Jennifer was holding onto something.

"I'm getting ready to take Miss Mattie home but I'm coming back," Jennifer said, busting at the seams with a secret. Then she told, "I'm going to spend the night with David."

Lisa closed her eyes. *No*, she said to herself. It wasn't time. "Jennifer, are you sure? Why don't you wait?" Lisa said.

Jennifer looked puzzled. She and Lisa both said their husbands had to be sexually compatible and David was getting serious. He had been talking marriage lately. "What am I waiting on?" Jennifer asked curiously, waiting for Lisa to respond. She didn't know either. It was time to let Jennifer go.

Lisa watched David as he comfortably talked to Thomas. She thought David was arrogant but he was nice to Jennifer. Lisa smiled and nudged Jennifer. "Make sure he wears a condom," Lisa said.

"He will. Let me take Miss Mattie home."

"Is David going with you?"

"He can stay and enjoy the party. I'll be fine."

"No Jen, take him with you."

Hearing Jen didn't bother her anymore. She was moving on. "I'll see if Angel wants to go," Jennifer said, looking around for Angel. She was spotted talking to Lionel in the back of the room. The scene made Jennifer's heart leap with joy. She turned to Lisa quickly. "If I don't see you before the honeymoon starts, have fun," she said.

"You too," Lisa struggled to say. She grabbed Jennifer and hugged her tight.

"Thanks for everything Jennifer. I love you."

"I love you too. Good-bye, Lisa."

"Good-bye, Jennifer."

Jennifer approached Miss Mattie. The old woman was ready now. "Are you ready to go?" Jennifer asked.

Miss Mattie smiled at the angel. Jennifer helped her up. They walked to the back of the room.

Lionel called out to Jennifer. "Where are you going?" he asked brightly.

"I'm taking my grandmother home."

""Lionel, I want you to meet my grandmother Matilda Clairmont," Angel said.

Lionel extended his hand and lightly shook the freezing, fragile hand. Miss Mattie looked at the one whose father brought the pain. The younger version wouldn't do the same to her granddaughter. She was much smarter than her mother.

"If you tell the truth, good spirits will always be around to protect you. But if you lie, you keep bad spirits unrested. Nice meeting you, Larry. Did you know today is my birthday?" Miss Mattie asked pleasantly.

Lionel was thrown off guard. He was still cordial and replied, "No".

Angel was embarrassed. Miss Mattie was born June 6, 1908. "I'm sorry Grandmother. I forgot. Happy Birthday!" Angel said.

"It's okay, sweetie. I'd never told my age until the day you visited. I'd celebrate it on July 4 like Uncle Sam. They say a woman who tells her age will tell anything."

"How about if I take you ladies out for a light celebration," Lionel suggested.

"I need to get her home. Why don't you two finish your conversation," Jennifer said and smiled at Angel. She returned the smile. It was the first time she enjoyed talking to Lionel. She didn't want the conversation to end.

"Are you sure? I'm staying with her," Angel said.

"I'll be back," Jennifer said firmly.

"Take an umbrella. They said it's pouring down outside," Lionel said. Jennifer said good-bye and left with Miss Mattie.

The rain was coming down harder. She had to hurry. Two wrong turns made her thirty minutes later than her expected time of arrival. She hoped he was still there. Once she gave him the papers, she would leave laughing. She didn't want to create a scene at the wedding. Lisa deserved better. She wanted to get him alone. It was perfect. He openly accepted Lisa. The light turned yellow as she approached the intersection speeding. She had time to make the left turn.

Miss Mattie sat quietly. Jennifer was quiet too. Her defroster was taking forever to come on. She wanted to hurry back to David. "It" would soon happen. She was waiting impatiently for the green light. She thought about asking Miss Mattie about sex. After all, she was her grandmother. Lisa said Miss Mattie was direct. If she didn't want to say anything, she wouldn't. Before Jennifer could say anything, Miss Mattie said solemnly, "It's time to go." Then Miss Mattie smiled.

Jennifer pulled off. The beam of light hit her head on. It surrounded her then it went away. Her head slammed against the steering wheel. The impact was so forceful that her chest caved in. The pain was excruciating.

She tried calling for help but nothing came out. She couldn't move.

Jennifer turned to check on Miss Mattie, she wasn't there. The woman from the photo was in front of the car. She had her hand out. Jennifer felt light but managed to scream. It is then she felt the unbearable pain. The longer she fought to move, the more painful it was becoming. She stopped fighting when she saw Miss Mattie standing beside the woman.

"Your work is done. I promise you will return," Catherine said and held out her hand. Jennifer went.

Barbara was ready to call it an evening. She talked to Bill and Charles the entire evening. Everyone was more like their old selves, comfortable. They laughed and shared small secrets. They admitted to the mistakes made out of pride and lust. The mistakes of the past brought humility to both men. They had to face them. No more hiding.

"Gentlemen, I must be going. I have an early flight tomorrow," Barbara said and stood. Both men stood too.

"Thanks for everything Barbara. The wedding was nice," Bill said.

"Nice? Don't you mean fabulous?" Barbara exclaimed. The men laughed.

"I can take you home Barbara," Charles offered. She declined firmly. She bid them farewell and left.

"She was the most loyal out of all of them," Bill said.

"Lord knows I tried many times in school but she flat out told me that she wasn't interested," Charles admitted. "I'm coming to Chicago first part of next month. Do you play golf?" Charles asked.

"A little," Bill said.

The rain was heavier than Barbara thought. Good thing she valet parked. She always did. She put her glasses on before leaving the hotel. A young man ran to the hotel yelling something about an accident at the front entrance. Barbara pulled off.

As she drove closer to the traffic light at the front entrance of the hotel, she saw the collision ahead. She recognized the creme color Corolla. Barbara picked up speed. She stopped her car and grabbed an umbrella. She rushed out of the car without closing the door.

Barbara quickly looked inside the little Corolla and saw Jennifer pinned under the steering wheel not moving. Blood was coming from her head, down the rose color gown. Crumbled glass covered the front seat. Rain made its way in. Barbara saw that Miss Mattie wasn't injured like Jennifer but she didn't move.

"It can't be happening again," Barbara mumbled. She was angry. She stormed to the other car. All the glass in the windshield had crumbled. She got a good view of the murderess, slumped over the steering wheel.

She lifted her head weakly and said, "Barbara Ann, I got a job for you."

Barbara's expression changed when she saw the familiar beauty mark. She took small gasps. Although *she* looked different, *she* was alive.

"Take the papers and hotel key out of my purse. I'm staying at the Ritz-

Carleton, room 1011. You can destroy the papers or do as you will with them. Hurry before someone sees you," *she* said.

Barbara walked quickly over to the passenger side and opened the door. The black handbag was lying on the floor. She quickly removed the papers and key and slid them up her sleeves. She closed the purse and rubbed off all imaginary fingerprints. She tossed the purse on the floor.

Barbara wanted to check on Jennifer but she couldn't leave. Flashing lights of the ambulance and loud sirens of police cars were making its way to the scene. *She* mumbled again, "Remove some keys from my suitcase. One opens my safe deposit box. I don't want him having anything. Make sure she gets everything and whatever else that's left from the insurance money. Tell her I'm sorry and that I didn't mean to leave her behind."

"The wedding was elegant. She looked like a little doll, just like you," Barbara said between tears.

"I know," *she* said weakly.

"Bill escorted her down the aisle," Barbara continued. The paramedics were getting out. The police officers began securing the scene.

"The reception was fantastic. Bill danced with her," Barbara lied.

She opened her eyes and smiled. "Thanks Barbara, I knew I could count on you. Box number 3450. You are my cousin, if they ask. Your name is on all of the documents. Remember, I want roses at the funeral. I've always loved them," *she* said.

She saw glimpse of Catherine but it was in a distance. She couldn't determine if it was because of Catherine or Debra. Catherine could have manipulated Debra into stopping her because she had a score to settle. But they were supposed to be on the same side. She couldn't make out the little girl with Catherine. Then she remembered, it was Lisa's little playmate, Charles and Catherine's daughter. Then she saw Miss Mattie. Ah, yes. Maybe it was Miss Mattie, a woman of revenge. She mumbled as she saw them faintly, "Okay, you've won fair and square."

"We won. We were on the same side, soror. Bill paid for mistreating us."

"Let it go, sweetie. Your sisters are here."

Her breathing became slower. *She* thought, when *she* got the opportunity again, *she* had to try a new strategy. *She* wouldn't be so mean. There may be nothing wrong with being nice. It might produce the same results. It was something to consider. *She* could feel Barbara's warm hand turn cold. *She* closed both eyes.

Barbara had forgotten about Jennifer. Before she could rush to the Corolla, a police officer began asking questions. She had to think quickly as she responded to the man's questions, trying to keep Debra's identity a secret. She had to do one more favor.

Chapter 30

It was after eleven o'clock in the morning. The sun was beaming over the church. The ceremony was over an hour long. The chime sounded. They all stood in black dresses and pearls. Barbara spoke. JoAnn hit the chimes. Barbara spoke. Susan hit the chimes. Barbara spoke again. Marilyn hit the chimes three times.

Barbara stepped down from the pulpit. The other three followed. They stood over the casket and chanted the last passage to the Final Rites. They walked past the casket and stood in a straight line at the head. The room of thirty black dresses was ready to view the body. Everyone, except Angel.

Barbara motioned her friend from the St. Louis Alumnae Chapter to start. Even Rochelle's mother, a long time colleague of Barbara's, was in attendance. The older black dresses walked past the casket first. The body lied peacefully under the Phi Kappa Psi symbols in a black dress, pearl necklace and earrings.

It was time for Angel and her group to continue the procession. Linda motioned the others to go on. Angel stood with tears streaming down her face. She had shed tears earlier but now it was time to put the body to rest. It wasn't fair, she kept telling herself. She had searched a long time. Not only did she find her but a grandmother too. She only got a chance to enjoy them a few months. She didn't need to see Jennifer. She knew how she looked. They did their best to hide the cut across the forehead. Her only comfort was knowing Miss Mattie died of a heart attack before impact.

They all bowed their heads to pray. Barbara removed the sacred cloth that covered Jennifer's body. She fold it and handed it to Angel. Linda made sure she stuffed a small teddy bear in Jennifer's arm.

People anxiously waiting for the Kappas to finish their ceremony. Several Alphas were standing with Lisa. She had barely spoken a word since the accident. She looked at those who had the nerve to come. Michael and his whore were there. Sean and his next victim were there. Kyle continually stared out the window. He hadn't talked to anyone, not even Cameron. And then there was the biggest nerve, William. She wanted them all to leave. Only ten people had the right to be there. They were the only ones who really loved Jennifer.

Lauren patted Keith on the shoulder and put her thumb on her forehead. She pointed to Lionel. Keith didn't have a notion of what she wanted. He rubbed her back. The next time she did it, Lionel saw her. She smiled and clapped. Keith began coaxing her to be still while he held her.

Alicia caught a glimpse of Lauren's actions. She had seen the little girl only once when she traveled to Kansas City. They did a little sign language together. It was mandatory for all the St. Louis Public School teachers to take sign language because they were mainstreaming the hearing impaired with the others. What surprised Alicia is what the little girl signed and how Lionel ignored her.

The doors opened. The ushers asked for the family to come forward. Carleton, Nadine and their son Mitchell walked in first, followed by Lisa, Cameron, Lionel and Charles. David was next and Bill strolled in behind him and sat next to Angel, who was being held by Barbara. Linda sat next to Barbara and Keith brought in Lauren who was humming and clapping.

Everyone's attention turned to the minister in the pulpit. He was accompanied by a large screen and a television set. He started the ceremony. Anita sang *I'm Going to Fly Away*. A few people in the audience became a little misty. The minister read from the New Testament, then he read condolences. Alexis read condolences from sorority members. Alicia sang *Amazing Grace*. Her smooth strong alto voice brought tears to the eyes of many people in the audience. Shouts of praise went through the crowd.

It was time for the eulogy. Lisa didn't move. Cameron walked her to the pulpit. He removed the podium and adjusted the standing microphone to her height. Everything was in place. Lisa was speechless. She stood, looking over the crowd of mourners. The nerve of some who came.

Cameron cleared his throat. He apologized for his wife. It had been tough attending the funeral of her grandmother and now her best friend. He went on to explain how Lisa gathered photos and made a slide show presentation. She also wanted to share Jennifer on tape.

Cameron gave a quick look to Lisa, who continued to condemn the crowd silently. There was the phony Alexis reading condolences. She even tried to go after Cameron, knowing he belonged to her. There was Rosalyn who gave Jennifer her first fistfight. Lisa smiled because Rosalyn lost. Although she turned out fine afterwards, she still caused her friend grief earlier. The one who really pissed her off was the make-believe mother who sent Jennifer out into the world blindfolded.

Cameron became increasingly nervous. He asked someone to turn off the lights. He began the music to the slide show. The first photo made the crowd laugh. It was a picture that appeared in the year-book of their freshman year, Jennifer dancing with Kyle at the freshmen dance. Her arms were up doing the "Gigolo." Kyle was in short-sleeve shirt and tight slacks. He looked as if he was doing the twist. The sight of the picture made him wince. He let the tears fill his eyes. He missed her already, even though they hadn't talked in months. He missed her.

She told him once that he and Lisa were her best friends. He couldn't stand to see it anymore. He had to leave. He rushed from his seat to the back door.

Lisa saw Kyle exit. She smiled. She wanted to make sure he saw himself when he was in his James Brown hey-days. He wasn't always a fashion "do." She wanted to make sure he saw Jennifer and hurt the same as she did when he ignored her. One down and four to go.

There were slides of Jennifer acting silly with Lisa and other friends. In one picture, Jennifer had Noxema on her face. Another one showed her after getting her hair shampooed. There were pictures of her at the Beta's Ball. Lisa saw Lionel wipe his eyes. It was okay because he really liked her.

There was the picture of the four going to Morrison Hall for the induction ceremony. There was the picture of Jennifer dancing with Cameron the night the Genies got in trouble. Lisa remembered because Cameron's lip was busted and his jaw was swollen. She saw her husband put his head in his hand. It was okay. He had always liked Jennifer. She was his sister.

Lisa found pictures of Jennifer posing with Angel, Linda and some of the older Kappas. Then there was a slide of Jennifer with her line sisters. Margo cried loudly. Rochelle put her arms around her. Patrice got up and left and Allyn followed. Alexis sat wiping her eyes. What a phony bitch!

Lisa found herself getting excited. The most important pictures were coming. First was the picture of Jennifer being crowned Miss Lambda. Lisa looked at Sean and rubbed her hands together. The next picture was of Jennifer delivering the speech for the presidential election of ABC. She made history, the first female president. One of Jennifer's eyes was dark in the picture. Lisa looked at Sean again. He had the gall to look upset. The son-of-a-bitch put his head in his hand. What an asshole! Two down.

The slide show was winding down. The picture of David licking her fingers after eating cake was before the last picture. Lisa wanted Michael to see how someone who wasn't a Gigolo thought Jennifer was good enough to be with. Michael looked sad. What a punk! Three down.

The last picture was Jennifer sitting on her mother's lap with Angel standing at her side. Lisa wanted to make sure William and the evil stepmother saw the picture. William looked sad. *Yes,* Lisa said to herself. That is your wife and family you left. It should remind you of the illicit love affair with Debra Arvell and the child you abandoned. What a jerk! Lisa's attention went to Nadine, the stupid woman who told Jennifer nothing. Lisa wanted Nadine to see that Jennifer had a beautiful mother who loved her.

The lights came on. The slide show was over. Lisa continued judging the crowd. The nerds were there. It was okay. They liked Jennifer, even Kyle but he was a butthead. The Forty Thieves were there. Michael, Superfly, was the only real thief. He stole Jennifer's trust. The rest were fine. J.D. and his fiancée along with a few Gammas were there. They were okay as well. Lisa's list went from ten to one hundred. She had gotten back at everyone who didn't deserve to be there. She gave a wicked smile but it went away. Her short lived victory was taken by applause, even from the people who didn't deserve to be there. She became angrier.

Cameron turned on the VCR and began the video. He had bought Lisa a camcorder for her birthday. Jennifer taped Lisa's bridal shower. The part that was playing was Lisa's spiel on friendship. She was thanking everyone for coming. She was giving special thanks to Jennifer who hosted it.

"I remember meeting her for the first time at Morrison Hall. Neither of us had a room. I say destiny brought us together. We would squeeze in the tiny little dorm bed at night, talking until morning. If you only knew how many questions Jennifer has in her head...(laughter and comments were made from the women.)

"When we decided on different sororities, I thought for sure it would be different but it made us even closer. I'm rambunctious and she's calm. I'm ready to fight and she would walk away. It takes a certain personality to deal with me. Jennifer may be shy but by no means is she weak, even though at times she felt that way. Friends like her are not a dime a dozen or one in a million. They are once in a lifetime. Thanks, Jennifer."

Everyone chanted "speech." Jennifer gave Rochelle the camcorder. She was moving it up and down. Finally, she was able to stable it but she was taping Jennifer too closely. Her eyes were wet as she spoke. She didn't cry. Just wet eyes.

"Lisa is right when she said destiny brought us together. My father insisted that I attend Missouri State University. He said it would make me a better person. Lisa's unique personality helped me to become stronger. I remember how she swallowed her pride and helped Angel get me ready for the Beta's Ball. She was the one who told me I could win queen. She has always been my cheerleader. I thought she said things out of friendship but I soon realized, she only says what she means.

"If you know Lisa, you know she's ready to fight. (Comments were made and the women laughed, even Lisa.) But now she fights differently. She has always done her best to protect me because she knew I was naive and probably still am. You're my best friend, Lisa. This bridal shower is a small token to a friendship for life. Although it cost me an arm and a leg (the women laughed again) it was worth it. Congratulations, Lisa and good luck!"

The tape was on pause with the two embracing. Rochelle taped it too closely, Lisa thought. They could see tears on her face. The lights came on and Cameron turned off the television and VCR. Lisa looked at everyone again. Jennifer said on tape that she was her best friend, not Kyle or anyone else. She was the only one who deserved to be there. She walked to the microphone to tell them so.

When Lisa opened her mouth, nothing came out. Cameron walked her back to her seat. The two sat behind Linda. Everyone clapped and stood. Lauren was standing on the pew between Angel and Barbara. The little girl gave a happy wave to Lisa who, was too busy suffering to see.

Lauren's attention was on Lionel. He took off his glasses to wipe his eyes. He put them back on to get a better look. Lauren was pointing, waving at him. He waved back. She tapped Angel on the shoulder and pointed. Angel turned around to face Lionel. Lauren put her thumb on her forehead and pointed to Lionel. Then she clapped.

Lionel's mouth opened. Angel slowly turned around. Lauren patted her on the shoulder again. Angel shook her fist low. "Yes Lauren. Yes," she said in a whisper. Lionel kept looking at the little girl, who was fascinated with him. She looked a lot like Jennifer but she had Angel's eyes. Barbara made Lauren turn around and sit. She began to fuss.

Everyone told him that Angel dropped out of sight after she had a baby. Everyone said the little girl was retarded. She didn't look retarded to him, she looked perfect. She wasn't Angel's baby. She was their baby. Angel never said a word last week. She never mentioned she had a baby.

More than six wanted to carry the casket. It ended up being Carleton, David, Lionel, Cameron, Kyle and Malcolm. Many stood at the grave as the minister said, "Earth to earth. Ashes to ashes and dust to dust." He sprinkled dirt over the casket. Linda came forward and removed the backing of a plate. She brushed some of the grains of dirt off the casket and placed "Queen of the Nile" in Arabic on top. She stood there shaking her head. The minister looked at her, wondering if she would walk back. Keith looked at Barbara. She rushed to Linda and put her arms around Linda's shoulders and whispered, "Honey, let's go."

Tears fell from Linda's eyes. It came from the loss of Camille and now Queenie. Both were innocent creatures of faith. Linda looked at her mother and shook her head and demanded,"Why?"

All Barbara could do was hold her daughter. She couldn't think of anything to say. No scheming. No calculations. No games.

"I'm sorry, honey. I wished I knew," Barbara said softly.

It was the first time Barbara apologized. Linda wept in her mother's arms. Barbara hesitated but then slowly lifted her hand and wiped her daughter's tears. The feeling tickled her stomach like the first time one of the twins kicked. Barbara placed her head on top of Linda's, squeezing her tighter.

The crowd watched the emotional moment shared between the two women. Barbara glanced around and straightened quickly. She walked Linda back to where Keith was standing. He was holding Lauren who was holding a black Preemie Cabbage Patch doll.

Lauren watched Linda cry. Barbara did her best to console her. Lauren muffled sounds and offered the doll. Linda ignored the gesture. "Malinda, take it," Barbara said gently.

Linda took the strange looking doll and extended her hand from her mouth and said, "Thank you." Lauren smiled, as she bouncing in Keith's arms. She was getting restless so Keith took her for a walk while they lowered Jennifer's casket into the grave.

Everyone watched Carleton step to the hole to say good-bye. "I love you, Angel. I did my best. Tell your mother I love her and I did my best. Tell your grandmother I love her and to forgive me." He dropped a rose in the grave. He stared at the hole for a couple of minutes before he, Nadine and

Mitchell walked away. Carleton approached Angel and gave her a hug.

"Don't be a stranger. By the way, this is your cousin Mitchell," Carleton said. Angel bent down and gave Mitchell a kiss on the forehead. He hid behind Nadine.

"Why didn't you say something the first time I met you?" Angel asked.

"I was trying to protect your sister," Carleton answered. He kissed Angel on the forehead and then came face to face with Bill. They hadn't seen each other since Catherine's funeral. Carleton remembered how quickly Bill put his sister in the ground and took the little girl, along with the insurance money. He dreamt of the time he would face Bill again but it was no time to hate. He had to forgive the man who was stupid enough to believe he fathered Debra Arvell's daughter.

Carleton knew the truth and so did the baby's father. Debra wasn't a bad person. She was almost like an angel. She helped him get back at his mother. She helped free Catherine from Bill but she didn't realize it until a month before her death.

Carleton stared at Bill who looked a little bothersome. "Bill," Carleton said with a nod and walked away, not giving Bill time to respond.

David stood at the grave with a rose in his hand. He kissed it long and dropped it into the grave. He could still taste the cake from her fingertips. He stood over the hole thinking about what could have been; the wife he could have had; and the children she could have given him. Knowing she would never laugh at his "dry jokes" as she called them, was too painful to accept. He should have gone with her that night. It was all he thought about. It was time to go home. He quickly walked away, waving to Angel, Linda, Barbara and Edward.

Kyle watched David leave. It was time to be alone with her. It felt like years since they talked. They shared too many good times for her to leave him. He didn't get a chance to explain. He could have been the one licking her fingers at the reception but he chose to follow the advice from others and not from his own heart. Never again, he told himself. He walked to the grave and squatted. It was peaceful as if she were sitting next to him.

"I know you are in heaven, probably teaching some other guy how to dance. I looked like a fool doing those splits, didn't I? I just wanted you to know I love you, even if I didn't behave that way. I've always loved you.

"Remember the time when I taught you and Lisa how to drive? You gave me my first gray hair. Remember when you taught me how to roll your hair because I wanted to see it curled and you said it was too much trouble to roll? No one can ever take those memories from us. I remember when you told me I deserved a nice girl. I was too afraid to see you. I'm sorry if I was an asshole and treated you mean. I didn't mean it. I...well," Kyle couldn't finish. He looked around. Everyone was staring because he talked loudly.

He gathered himself to leave. Cameron walked to the grave quickly. "Hey Kyle, she loved you too. She told me that herself," Cameron said. Kyle nodded. He looked at Lisa, the final judge. She closed her eyes. Kyle left. Cameron walked back to Lisa, who didn't believe what he told Kyle.

"She did love him. She told me that herself," Cameron said. Lisa thought how wrong he was. Jennifer loved Kyle but it wasn't how Cameron said it.

The crowd began to disperse. Angel stood next to Bill and a few Kappas. Cameron held Lisa and Maria was standing next to them. Linda was with Barbara and Edward. Gina stood beside Marilyn and Carlos, who was holding a sleeping Avery. Lionel was standing next to Charles, eyeing Angel. She refused to look at him. They all looked at each other.

Lionel walked over to Angel. Her sorority sisters saw him coming and eased away. "This may not be the right time but I have to know," he said. Angel remained silent. "Is she going to be like Jennifer?" he asked, trying to keep his voice down. Bill was ready to speak but Lionel continued, "I guess this isn't the right time." He walked off angrily. Charles followed behind Lionel. Cameron excused himself and followed them.

"Son, wait a minute," Charles said, rushing to catch Lionel. He stopped abruptly and turned to face his father. The blood in his face was boiling.

"I didn't want to be like you. I did *not* want to be like you!" Lionel yelled. He looked at Cameron and then at their father. "I never wanted to be like you!"

"Lionel, listen," Charles said.

"That's the problem. I've always listened. She told me, for the first time ever, I was interesting. What I had to say was interesting. I was talking about my business, dad. She found it interesting and you don't," Lionel said out loud. He took off his glasses, wiped his eyes and put them back on. His eyes challenged his father.

Cameron looked worried. Lionel was fifteen the last time he yelled at their father. Charles knocked Lionel out, setting an example of what would happen if the others stepped out of line. Thirteen year old Cameron sat up all night putting ice packs on Lionel's face. Their mother did nothing. Lionel was lucky that his jaw wasn't broken. He never talked back again.

Cameron stood in front of Lionel and asked, "Will you help me and Jesse move Lisa, Saturday after next?"

Cameron's question threw Lionel for a loop. It was so off-beat that it made him laugh. Cameron pleaded with his older brother to put down his guard. Lionel looked at his little brother to assure him that their father couldn't hurt him anymore. He was a man now.

Charles watched as Keith chased Lauren near the gate. The only reason Charles attended the funeral was out of respect. "You don't have to be like me. There she is," Charles said, pointing to Lauren as she hobbled trying to run. Charles looked at his son for an answer.

Lionel was confused. His father always told him what to do. Now he had to make a decision in front of him. Lionel put his arm around Cameron's shoulders. "Little brother, I'll help you move Lisa. Would you like to meet my daughter?" Lionel asked playfully.

Cameron looked back at their father. "Sure. A few brothers want to play some ball at the "Y" this afternoon. You gamed?"

"What about Lisa? She has just lost her best friend. Ron, you have a wife now," Lionel scolded.

Cameron had forgotten about Lisa just as quickly as he had forgotten about Jennifer. "I'm sorry. I forgot," said a humble Cameron. He was ashamed of himself.

"It's okay little brother. See, you've never had anyone show or teach you how to be a man. First, tell Lisa that you will be gone for a couple of hours. Then, don't come home until the next day. Right dad?" Lionel asked sarcastically, daring his father to make a move.

"You have the chance to make it right. There she is," Charles said, swallowing hard. He turned to walk away.

"Dad, will you help us move Lisa, Saturday after next?" Cameron asked in a shaky voice.

"If you need me, call," Charles said and walked away. When he made it to his car, he waved. Cameron waved back but Lionel looked at Lauren.

"Let's meet your niece. By the way, basketball is not what's happening. The game is pool," Lionel said, punching Cameron. He tried to dodge the shots.

"Man, you are getting old," Cameron said smiling.

Linda rubbed the doll's clotheless body. Lauren was so rough on things. She had removed the clothes from all of her dolls. "I think I'm having a boy this time," Linda said point blankly.

Barbara shook her head. "What did you say?" she asked.

"I think I'm having a boy this time. I'm pregnant. I'm due in February."

Barbara let out a little huff and crossed her arms. "And when were you planning on telling me?"

"I just found out yesterday morning. You're the first to know. I haven't told Keith yet," Linda said, slightly irritated.

Barbara quickly rethought her attitude. Her daughter never told her anything without her having to ask. When Linda was pregnant with Camille, Barbara had to ask if she was pregnant and Linda was four months at the time. Barbara felt a sense of honor. She called her husband over. He excused himself from talking to Bill.

"Edward, Malinda is having a baby. She's due in February," Barbara said with tears in her eyes. Edward looked at Linda and smiled. Before he could say anything, Barbara took off to Marilyn.

"Now you see why I don't tell her anything? She has a big mouth. Everyone is going to know before Keith," Linda said pouting.

Gina came over first. "Congratulations," she said. Linda sighed and began complaining about her mother's lack of secrecy. Gina chuckled a little but stopped after catching Edward looking at her face.

"What happened?" he asked as he gently rubbed the scar. It wasn't that noticeable but he could see the thickness from the stitches.

Gina closed her eyes. "I hit the side of a dresser," she said.

"I have a friend that is a plastic surgeon. He's good. I want you to talk to him. He can probably help remove or eliminate some of the thickness," Edward said and walked away to join Barbara.

"*The Washington Post* is with Uncle Bill now," Linda said and looked at Gina. "You should let dad's friend check out that scar. You know he knows everybody. I don't know about you but I'm much too vain to walk around with stitches in my face," Linda said with her nose turned up.

"Congratulations," Angel said and gave Linda a hug. She began complaining about Barbara again but stopped. "Gina, are you godmother to anyone?" Linda asked.

"No."

"What's the matter? You give cheap gifts?"

Gina put her hands on her hips and was ready to respond. "Calm down. Will you be godmother to my baby? He's due in February, as you all know. You are a tomboy. You can handle little boys," Linda said. The three laughed. Gina was thrilled. She felt like part of the group again.

"So is the saga going to continue between you and Lionel?" Linda boldly asked Angel.

"I don't know. He's trying to find himself," Angel said.

Lionel made it clear last Saturday, he had no intention of getting married again. He was paying back child support. He was pleased with his small consulting firm. He shared his secrets with her that night. He didn't go to law school with Thomas because he wasn't accepted. He was accepted in graduate school on probation and did well despite. He found out he did poorly because he needed glasses. He was fired from Favor's which was the lowest point in his life. He made his father's friend look like a fool. A few months later, Stacy left because he stopped looking for a job.

He had taken several telecommunications courses in graduate school. He did extremely well. One of his professors contacted him after Stacy had left. He told him about the government hiring minority contractors for a special project. He started there and made contacts across the country.

"So how are things between you and Mike Tyson?" Linda asked Gina.

Gina had learned over the years to ignore Linda's comments but she was too sensitive about her problem with Carlos. "I don't find it funny," Gina said sharply.

Linda paused for a few seconds. "I'm sorry. How are things going between you and Carlos?"

Gina decided to lower her defenses and get her friends' opinion. "He has an interview with the *Chicago Voices*. He wants to come back. He doesn't want Avery to grow up without him."

"It sounds fine but what about you? He has to live with you. It can't be about Avery or whether he gets a job," Linda said directly.

"He apologized about the fighting. He promised it will never happen again. I hear they all say that and the fighting never stops."

"Sometimes it doesn't, Gina. You are taking a chance but it sounds as if you want him back. You can't be ashamed of that but you have to be careful and pay attention to the warning signs. You shouldn't go back unless he agrees to counseling," Angel said.

"We're suppose to discuss it after the funeral. But..." Gina paused. She remembered how apologetic and sincere Carlos was when he admitted he believed she was cheating. The replay of the scene pounded her. She had to tell her friends. She couldn't keep the secret any longer. "It's not all his fault," Gina started bravely. "I wasn't so innocent myself. I had…" she broke into tears.

"Honey, don't! No one needs to know. Tell it to a counselor or a priest. I wouldn't tell either one. And besides, no one deserves to be beaten. One time, my father yelled at my mother. She promised him hot grits. I don't know what it means but I hear southern women are into hot grits. He never yelled at her again," Linda said.

"Marsha says I'm crazy to go back," Gina said.

"And that's why she doesn't have anyone. She is much too brash. No offense but is she a lesbian?" Linda asked.

"No! Matter of fact, she's engaged. She's getting married."

"That's a surprise," Linda mumbled.

"So, how are things with you and Mickey Mouse?" Gina asked.

Linda laughed and wet her lips. "Mickey Mouse and I are fine. He has the cutest butt. You told me that yourself."

"It doesn't look as good as Carlos'."

"No one has a washboard stomach like Lionel's"

Gina and Linda gave Angel a curious look. "Are you talking recent exposure?" Linda asked.

"No. I believe he still has a washboard stomach."

Lionel beckoned for Lauren. She wobbled to him smiling and rubbing her hands together. Keith picked her up and she muffled sounds. She put her thumb on her forehead and pointed to Lionel. He asked what was wrong with her and what did she want from him.

"She's partially deaf but it's correctable. She won't be able to hear as clearly as other children," Keith answered. "My wife and I are her godparents. We will start our sign language class in two weeks. I really don't know what she wants," Keith confessed.

Lionel reached for her. She went willingly. He was so drawn by her eyes. They were Angel's eyes. He asked Cameron to get Angel. He continued to stare at his daughter. She had a very happy and innocent glow about her. She looked so much like Jennifer. The emotions were stirring again.

Angel approached them cautiously. She couldn't determine if Lionel was happy or angry but she soon found out. He glared down into her brown eyes. Anger flared into his eyes. He didn't know why he was mad. He just was.

"I have no intention of getting married again," he snarled. "Nor am I financially secured to pay child support."

Lauren jumped. She looked at Lionel and reached for Angel. She took her from him, not knowing if he had done anything to hurt her. Angel was stunned from the display of rage.

"What makes *you* think I want to marry *you*? I have never asked you for anything nor have I told you she was yours, you son-of-a-bitch!" Angel snapped. Keith excused himself from the pair and walked back to Linda.

Angel took off behind him.

Lionel rushed to catch her. He grabbed her arm. "Let me go, you...bastard!" she yelled. Her face was red. Her breathing was becoming short. She tried desperately to fight for control but it was like breathing through a straw. She almost dropped Lauren whose little arms held tightly around her neck. Angel panicked when she realized she didn't have her pump spray. "Dad, help me," she wheezed.

"Mum...mum," Lauren muffled.

Angel immediately stopped wheezing. She held Lauren tight.

"Mum...mum," Lauren said again.

"She talked. My baby talked," Angel cried, squeezing Lauren tighter. She kept muffling, "Mum...mum."

When Angel's breathing became normal, Lionel put his arms around them. Lauren took her tiny fist and hit him in the chest. She tried pushing him away too. It didn't matter if his daughter retaliated. Angel was right. He was a bastard. It was the second time the scene happened and both times he turned his back on her. He kissed Angel on the top of the head.

"I didn't mean to say those things. As soon as I get back, I'll talk with my lawyer and have Lauren taken care of," Lionel said defeated.

"Don't touch me! I don't want anything from you!"

"I don't know what's happening to me. As soon as I think everything is going fine, something else pops up."

"Well, don't worry about us. We are going to pop right out."

"No. That's not what I meant. Every time I think I'm getting stronger, I fall weak again, doing something stupid. Stacy has taken my son out of my life and I don't want you to take Lauren away, even if you can't stand the sight of me," Lionel pleaded, looking at the pouting little girl. He blew her a kiss and she swung her fist at him. "Let me know if you need anything. I don't want you sitting around suffering," he said.

"I'm not suffering. I need to get back," Angel said stubbornly. Lionel wouldn't let her go. "I want us to be friends again," he said. His attention went back to Lauren.

"Look at her. She looks just like Jennifer," he said.

Angel looked at Lauren who returned the look shyly by putting her head on Angel's shoulder. Angel choked. She began to cry again. She should have been in the car too. Maybe they would nott have had the accident.

"It's my fault. I should have been with her," Angel cried. She realized she was being selfish when Lauren began crying. She had to take care of Lauren. Angel rocked her, asking her not to cry. Lionel reached for Lauren but she turned her head.

"Don't say those things, Melanie. It's not your fault," Lionel said. He reached for Lauren again, but she refused his offer.

"Come to daddy, Lauren," Lionel said softly.

"Go to Lionel," Angel pleaded with Lauren.

"I'm sorry, Lauren. This will never happen again. Come to daddy," Lionel said softly, smiling, extending his arms. Lauren took her time and reached for him. He gave her a big hug. She pointed to the ground and Lionel looked at Angel.

"She wants to get down," Angel answered.

Lionel planted the little feet on the grass. Lauren ran wobbly around in circles. Lionel laughed at her. He turned to Angel. "What does this means?" he asked with his thumb on his forehead.

Angel extended Lionel's fingers to an open palm. "It means father."

Lauren saw Lionel making the sign. She ran to him and did it too. He reached down to pick her up but she hit him and took off running, wanting him to chase her. Instinctively, he did and caught her, tossing her roughly into the air. Angel fleshed crawled.

"Lionel, please be gentle with her. She's a girl," Angel said while cringing.

"I'm sorry. I'm used to boys," he said, still handling Lauren roughly. She didn't seem to mind.

Keith had just received the news about the new addition. He and Carlos were talking. Linda turned her attention to Gina. "Keith tells me that Angel and Lionel were fighting. I guess she probably will take Dennis up on his brother, Arthur."

Gina looked a little surprised. "Angel and Arthur are seeing each other?"

"I said she will probably take Dennis up on his brother, Arthur. Dennis and Angel talked after Lionel left the reception. She said it was a good conversation. She said Arthur sounded boring, but so was Lionel, until recently. Boring men offer a greater challenge to her," Linda said.

"I have always pictured Angel with Lionel. I imagined her married, before me, with a boy and girl. Never could I ever imagine her struggling with a child," Gina confessed.

"Struggling? Oh no! Not Miss Melanie. Mother says Angel has put those awful years behind her and has vowed never to struggle again. She is about to come into some big money. Mother is selling the shop and our dear little pitiful friend will receive twenty-five percent of the take. We're not talking small change either. Angel is strong, just like her mother. She's going to get exactly what she wants, be it Lionel, Arthur, Thomas or Steve," Linda joked.

Gina almost lost control. "Thomas and Steve want Angel?"

"My sources tells me that Steve is coming to town for the Fourth of July and Thomas called this week sending condolences. He will happen to be in Kansas City the week after next and wants to have dinner with her. She's getting back into the swing of things. It just took a little prompting. My sources also told me that little Lauren had a baby sitter but Miss Melanie couldn't possibly think of Lauren not seeing her aunt for the last time. Don't you think it's real cozy to get a final shot at Lionel?"

"Oh," Gina said.

"Everyone thinks the soft innocent approach is weak and the hard tough personality is strong. Keith thinks Angel is weak. I knew then my sources were right, men are sleeping while women are thinking."

Gina chuckled. "May I ask who are your sources?"

"Mother."

"And when have you ever started listening to your mother?"

"My, my. Look who's coming. Isn't this cozy?" Linda said, turning her attention to Angel and Lionel who was holding an energetic Lauren.

Avery's head popped up when he saw Lauren. He pointed to her and demanded, "Name?" Lauren smiled.

Lionel held up his hand. "Excuse me young man. You have to come to my daughter better than that."

Carlos' eyes widen. "What? Daugh..." Gina nudged him hard.

Lauren took her doll from Linda and handed it to Avery. He reached for it. Carlos put up his hand and said, "Un, un. My son doesn't play with dolls." Everyone laughed.

"We need to celebrate," Keith said and kissed Linda long. It surprised her, making her eyes close. "How about if we all go out for dinner tonight? Does anyone play pool?" Keith asked. All the men were in agreement.

Carlos turned to Gina. He took her by the hand and walked her away from the group. Avery's attention was on Lauren. He wanted to go back but Carlos quieted him by tickling him on the stomach.

"I never wanted to end up in jail like my oldest brother. And I never wanted to father a bunch of kids like my other brother. I worked hard to get an education, so I could be good enough to marry someone like you. I realize now that everything is a risk. You get out of life what you are willing to put in. I want us to try it again. I'm willing to go to counseling," Carlos said. Gina remained quiet.

"Dennis and Ray have given me a number of contacts in Chicago. Most are not high paying jobs but I can continue with my research in African American studies. It will help me get to the point where I can make some big money but it's going to take time. I don't want to stand in the way of your career, Gina, but some things are worth letting go of. The pressure at International may not be worth it. Think about it."

Gina eyes were swelling with tears. She was having a harder time at International with the downsizing. It had gotten to the point where she worked between sixty to seventy hours a week. She really wanted to discuss "it." She wanted to clear the air about the affair, but it would ruin everything. She felt like a prisoner. She wanted to cleanse her soul.

"Carlos, I'm sorry," she finally said, trying to maintain control.

He held her in his arms. "It's okay," Carlos said. Avery's eyes got big. Carlos had to convince his son that his mother wasn't hurt so he kissed Gina softly on the scar. Finally, he was able to do it. Gina dropped her head so Carlos began nibbling her ear. She always liked it when he nibbled her ears. He continued until she giggled. Avery saw Gina laughing so he smiled.

Carlos felt good seeing his son smiling and Gina laughing. He felt a connection having Gina in his arms again. It brought back the night when Gina came to pick up Avery. Neither expected to end the evening making love but it happened. Carlos let down his guard and got off his high horse. Sherri told him that he was a lazy lover. She was bold enough to tell him that she understood why his wife cheated on him.

That night, it was unconditional. He had to prove to Gina and to himself that he was not a monster so he unleashed his passion. He did things he dreamt he would never do to satisfy Gina. To his surprise, seeing her react to his touch satisfied him. For the first time, she told him it was wonderful. He did not assume or wonder. He knew. He smiled thinking about that night. Gina broke his concentration.

"Linda isn't the only one having a baby," Gina said, smiling tenderly at Carlos. He grinned and kissed her passionately on the lips. Avery put his hands over his eyes. Carlos grinned and waited until Avery removed his hands. Carlos kissed Gina again and again until Avery stopped hiding from the interaction between his mother and father. Carlos wanted his son to see his mother happy. He wanted his son to see a woman happy from the touch of a man.

Cameron hugged Lisa tight. "What's the matter?" he asked.

"Jennifer has just been buried and everyone is treating it like a party," she complained, pointing to Angel's group. She was angry because Alicia and Rochelle were going out with Brad and Tony.

"For some reason, everyone is feeling good. Some people are getting a second chance," Cameron said, thinking of his brother.

Barbara Stevens came over to Lisa with a cloth in her hand. She was happy too. "I want to personally make sure you received your mother's ceremonial cloth. We bless all of our sorors, who leave this world, with it."

Barbara handed Lisa the cloth. It looked new. Lisa opened it. The Kappa's sorority symbols were embroidered on it and her mother's name was at the bottom with her birth and death dates. It also had "All for one and one for all" scripted at the bottom. Lisa felt a twitch after reading the phrase. Barbara left.

William approached the newlyweds. "Where are you going for your honeymoon?"

Lisa looked at Cameron. "Egypt," he said smiling and Lisa jumped up.

"Sounds like a good trip. So Lisa, do you have any job offers in Atlanta?"

"I can accept a position with the bank examination division at the Federal Reserve but I'm going to graduate school, at Emory University, in the fall. I received a fellowship. I won't be able to do a lot of traveling," she said.

William felt proud. "If ever you need anything, give me a call. Oh, by the way, I will get in contact with the Red Cross about donating blood to your surgery. It surprises me that you are having a difficult time receiving 'O' positive blood."

Lisa was at the point of fainting. He had to have "O" negative blood. He was her father. Maybe her mother was the one with the same blood type but she was dead. "Thank you, William," Lisa said and shook his hand. William shook Cameron's hand and walked to Angel and her group.

"Lisa, aren't you 'O' negative?" Cameron asked.

Lisa didn't want to answer. She wanted to be alone. "I heard the Forty Thieves are playing basketball at the 'Y' this afternoon. Are you going?"

Cameron did his best to hide his interest. "No, I want to be with you."

"We are going to be together all week long. You may not get a chance to see some of them for a long time or ever again," Lisa said in short breaths.

"Are you alright?"

"I'm going back to the apartment to take a nap. I'll see you later," Lisa said and walked to the grave. Cameron walked over to Lionel's group. He decided against basketball. He needed to be with his wife.

Lisa was at the grave. She carefully looked around, making sure no one was looking. She whispered, "I love you, Jennifer. Kyle loved you too but didn't have the heart to say it. Remember, you and Miss Mattie are my guardian angels. Tell her I miss her and Carl does too. She knows who I'm talking about. And do me one *big* favor, if you see my mother, tell her I love her too."

Lisa wiped her eyes with the ceremonial cloth. Two funerals in one week was too much. Miss Mattie's funeral was joyful. The old women sang happily, sending Matilda June Clairmont home to Glory.

Lisa burst into tears. It was her fault from sending them out in the rain. They could have stayed at the hotel. Everything was her fault. Her own mother didn't want her around because it caused her boyfriends to want to touch her. Although her mother never blamed her for the man not coming back, it was still her fault. She cried harder. The more she wiped her eyes, the faster the tears came.

She felt something swish around her. She sniffed loudly and looked around. Angel and Lauren were standing beside her. Lisa brushed her hair from her forehead. She took the last rose and dropped it into the grave.

Lauren reached for Lisa. She picked her up. Lauren smiled, holding the Preemie. She gave the doll to Lisa. She took the doll and smiled.

"What's her name?" Lisa asked in her baby voice. Lauren pointed to Lisa with a smile.

Lisa gave the doll a big kiss. She wondered if the angels were with Lauren. Miss Mattie said it was easier for the spirits to protect children and "folks who don't know no better" because smart people thought they knew everything. Lauren gave Lisa a hug and a kiss. Lisa didn't know if it was the sun but the little girl seemed awfully bright.

Epilogue

It had been two months since she moved to Atlanta. After going over the bills, she realized she had to get a job soon. She didn't know Cameron was in so much debt. The insurance money from Miss Mattie's will caught them up with a little to put into a savings account. Carleton got Miss Mattie's house. She got everything in the house. Angel agreed to sell the remaining items for her. All three split the insurance money. Had it not been for Jennifer's portion being divided among them, she would have received much less.

She was also angry about Cameron agreeing to pay Vivian six hundred dollars a month in child support. They had been arguing recently about going to court to reduce the support payments since Vivian didn't want him seeing the little girl. Cameron left quietly for work that morning after another heated argument.

The telephone rang. The man on the telephone was friendly. He wanted to offer Lisa the position in their mergers and acquisitions department. She gave the usual, *Let me think about it* line and hung up. They were offering her a salary almost comparable to an MBA, mainly because of her economics background.

She couldn't wait to tell Cameron. She decided to surprise him later that evening with his favorite dinner. She made out a grocery list and grabbed her purse. The doorbell rang. She peeped out the little hole and saw the postman. She opened the door. He handed her a certified registered package. She signed for it and shut the door.

The large brown envelop was heavy. She sat down and sifted through the papers. Some were very old. There was no letter enclosed. She looked at the postmark to see where it came from. Texas. She slowly sifted through the papers. There was a court subpoena and medical information on blood analysis. She didn't understand the medical information but she did understand the court papers. It declared Paul Nathan Smith father of Lisa Willet Arvell.

She had to take deep breaths. Maria's mother told her that Paul was her father but he denied it. Maria's mother also told her that Debra Arvell dated him for a very long time. Angel was right, she wasn't her sister. Paul had to have known about her because he took the blood tests. How could he turn his back on her? He was horrible to allow his brother to take the blame. But William's name was on the birth certificate. The situation was becoming uglier as Lisa thought about it. Maybe it was all innocent.

Lisa wondered if Miss Mattie knew. Maybe she allowed William to take responsibility because he left her daughter. Miss Mattie was a resourceful woman.

Lisa rushed to call Cameron. The secretary said he was in the field. Lisa left an urgent message for him to call home.

Over and over, the video of Jennifer saying how she learned to fight differently consumed her. She was fighting with how to fight. It had become a battle. She didn't know how to fight the right way. Paul had to pay for denying her. She didn't care if he was Gina's stepfather.

The telephone rang again. It was Angel on the line. She sold the furniture in the house and was sending a check for twenty-three hundred dollars. Good, Lisa thought. More money to help. Angel continued about the new house she was going to buy. She invited Lisa up for the house warmer which was in October. Angel told her that Lauren was having surgery in two weeks. Then she asked how everything was going.

"Everything is great. Thanks for selling the furniture," Lisa said.

"If you need anything, give me a call. Has dad called you? He's moving to Colorado. He got a job with Allstar."

"Uh, no he hasn't but tell him I said congratulations when you talk to him." He wasn't her father so why should he call her?

"Here is his number in case he forgets." Angel ran off the seven digits. Lisa forced herself to write them down.

"By the way, I got an offer from American Petroleum."

"Oh Lisa, congratulations. I knew it wouldn't take you long to find a job. Tell Cameron I said hello."

They hung up. Lisa didn't know why she couldn't tell Angel the truth. It felt good having a sister or at least a partial one. They were developing something of a relationship. Angel had called weekly, checking up on her since she moved to Atlanta. Lisa assumed Angel missed Jennifer. Angel freely discussed her feelings about Lionel. They were friends and Lauren got along well with him. Angel was moving on with her life and wanted to be called Melanie.

The telephone rang again. It was Cameron. He sounded worried. He thought she was still angry from last night. "I'm sorry about the bills, Lisa. When I get home tonight, let's talk about a budget. You're good at that kind of thing. I'm just frustrated. I pay six hundred dollars a month and can't see Celeste. I want Celeste to know who I am. I hope you can understand," Cameron said.

"What time are you coming home? We can start the weekend early," Lisa said seductively.

"I should be home by seven. Was there anything wrong? Your message said urgent."

"Oh, yes. Angel sold the furniture and is sending us a check for about two thousand dollars."

"That's your money, Lisa. Buy whatever you want. You took the insurance settlement and paid my bills."

"Cameron, we are not going to have your money and my money. This belongs to both of us."

Cameron was silent for a few seconds. "I want you to buy something nice with it. Something you have always wanted."

"I will. I'll see you later," Lisa said and hung up the phone. She couldn't tell the truth about the news. She quickly gathered the papers. She wanted to put them in her personal safe deposit box. A white envelope fell from the stack. She picked it up and opened it. There was a letter addressed to her from a law firm in Texas. It said she had a settlement from her mother's will. There were papers for her to complete. Her heart pounded fast. There was a number for her to call. She quickly called.

She almost stopped breathing after she talked to one of the lawyers. Her mother gave her one of the biggest financial gifts she could ever imagine, an insurance settlement close to forty thousand dollars. The lawyers wanted her to get the papers notarized and fax them so they could at least start the process. They promised she would get the money immediately upon receipt of the actual documents.

Lisa got off the phone, asking herself questions. Her mother hardly worked so how could she have insurance to pay such a large amount? Lisa figured maybe interest had caused a potential insurance settlement to accumulate so large. She immediately dismissed the questions by remembering something Miss Mattie told her, "Never look a gift horse in the mouth." She stopped thinking and rushed to complete the forms.

She got down to the line that asked for a bank account number. She wrote down her account number at Boatman's Bank in St. Louis. She had a little over one hundred dollars left in the account. Miss Mattie told her a woman needs her own money. Although she was talking about a job, Lisa took it to mean everything. She would tell Cameron later, she told herself. Much later. He didn't need to know everything. Not right now. Some things a woman needs to take to her grave.

Lisa hurried to have the papers notarized. She rushed to Office Depot to fax them. She made copies of the documents and sent the originals by Federal Express. She hurried to her safe deposit box and locked the papers away. No one needed to know. Not right now.

She drove happily to the mall in Buckhead. She walked around until she came to a lingerie shop. Cameron liked her in teddies and skimpy lingerie. She felt more comfortable in oversized shirts and flannel gowns. She figured if she were going to surprise him tonight, go all the way.

She walked inside and looked around. Everything looked skimpy. She saw something she liked, a fire engine red teddy with a G-string back. She picked up an extra small and sized it to her body. She saw something else she liked, a pink teddy with black lace down the front exposing the crotch. She remembered Angel saying the color was rose, not pink.

She giggled. Her taste in lingerie had changed quickly. As she turned around, enjoying the adventure, she saw a familiar face. She had gained at least fifteen pounds since their last encounter. She had to be at least a size twelve. She was with a friend. Lisa wanted to leave, but they were standing near the door.

Lisa kept her back turned. The voices came closer. They were standing beside her. She turned to leave and Vivian saw her and frowned. Vivian cleared her throat and said out loud to her friend, "Looks like I need to take Cameron back to court. I need more money. He must think I'm a fool."

Lisa was angry. Cameron was paying the greedy woman six hundred dollars for nothing. She wouldn't let him see Celeste. Something took over Lisa. Her thoughts became calculating. She smiled brightly when Vivian looked at her again. All Vivian could see was the beauty mark over the top lip.

Lisa walked boldly to the rack where Vivian was standing. "I wouldn't say you are a fool. I would personally pay you to keep that monster away. Cameron and I need time to ourselves. Mater of fact, I like you. Let's do lunch sometimes," Lisa said. She held up a teddy like the one Vivian had in her hand and called out to the sales clerk. "Excuse me, Miss. Do you have this in an extra small?"

The sales clerk rushed to Lisa. Vivian looked at the audacious woman as she sashayed to the dressing room. Vivian decided she wasn't going to let her get away with it.

Lisa came out to find Vivian and her friend at the counter checking out. They were buying underwear. The sales clerk said, "I'm sorry but we don't have this particular one in an extra small."

"That's okay. I'll take these two," Lisa said and reached over Vivian, handing the sales clerk an American Express Gold. *She* felt alive.

Cameron came through the door excited. He saw a cozy setting for two. He called for Lisa, but she didn't answer. His skin tingled. He rushed to the bedroom, not knowing what to expect. He smiled as he saw her lying nude covered with rose petals. She removed more petals from the stems.

She smiled at him. "Which one should I wear for dinner?" she asked seductively, pointing her toes to the teddies on the dresser. The tone of her voice sounded different.

"Neither one," he said smiling.

"When do you want to work on the budget? We can start now," she said teasingly. She tossed the petals from the bed, laughing.

"How about after dinner?" he said seriously, unbuttoning his shirt. She was never like this before, teasing, talking seductively. He liked it. He found it sexy. He had always enjoyed the chase.

"I've got good news. I got the job at American Petroleum," she said, turning on her stomach, exposing the rear. He removed his pants and sat on the bed. He stroked her body, kissing her back gently. She purred.

"I knew you wouldn't have a problem finding a job," he said moaning. She was relaxed with him. It was different. "I got good news too," he said, easing onto the bed. He kissed her shoulders. "Vivian wants me to start keeping Celeste on the weekends, starting tomorrow."

Lisa could not help but laugh at Cameron's naivete. She never understood women like Vivian until today. "Um, that is good news but not this weekend. We have plans. You call her and tell her that we will love to keep the little darling next weekend but we have plans for that weekend too," she said and turned around.

She hissed when he caressed the length of her body again. The sound of her voice made his body shiver with excitement. He flashed the famous Johnson smile. "Whatever you say," he said and kissed the beauty mark that he had always loved.

She had to stop and think for a moment. She was being mean. "I got a great idea. Let's take Celeste to Six Flags next month. She is going to love it. Then we can take her to Stone Mountain Park the following month..."

He listened to her in a distance. He continued to kiss her. He had nothing to fear. His father was wrong. Very wrong.